Contents

Holly and Ivy

by Mary Davis

Dedication

Dedicated to Hollie, my good friend for over forty years.

Thanks be unto God for his unspeakable gift.
2 CORINTHIANS 9:15

Chapter 1

Maryland
November 1890

You did what!" Holly Harrison scurried down the servants' hall after her sister. "You're going where?"

"I already told you. Washington Territory." Ivy slowed, and her voice chirped out like a little bird's, happy yet small. "I'm getting married." Not quite convincing.

Yes, yes, Holly knew that. She'd asked the wrong question. "*Why?*"

Ivy stopped and spun around. "*Why?* Why does anyone get married?"

Holly could think of many reasons. But instead of answering, she planted her hands on her hips, waiting for her sister to give *her* reason.

The sigh Ivy released spoke volumes about her exasperation. "So they don't have to grow old alone. So they always have someone. So they can be happy."

Marriage held no guarantees.

"You're not alone. You have me, and I have you. We are all each other has."

"It's not the same. I want more. Your logic renders us both old maids. I'm nineteen already. I have two, maybe three, years before I'm completely overlooked and am written off as unmarriageable."

What did that make Holly, four years her senior? She had felt her own hope waning and accepted that service might be her lot in life. "But you have a good job here."

"Good?" Ivy held out her red, cracked hands. "Washing other people's clothes all day every day is not *good*. I want a home and a family of my own. Don't you?"

Of course Holly did. But for now that wasn't possible. "Why not find a husband here? Why go clear across the country?" She didn't want her only relative to be so far away. "Why marry a man you don't know?"

Her sister threw her hands up. "If you haven't noticed, young men are scarce around here. Most of them have gone west. The ones left are either married, too young, or too old."

"But you know nothing about this man."

Ivy pulled three letters from her apron pocket and waved them in the air. "We've been corresponding. He's told me everything about himself."

Holly doubted that. "How do you know it's all true? How do you know he didn't leave important things out? Did you tell him *everything* about yourself?"

Her sister worked her mouth back and forth before answering. "What purpose could he have in lying?"

"Oh, I don't know, maybe to get a naive young lady to travel all that way. By the time she realizes what she's gotten herself into, it would be too late."

Ivy jammed her fists onto her hips. "I am *not* naive. I have put a lot of thought into this. And I *am* going."

Yet she had kept her plans and correspondence a secret for quite some time.

Why did the callow young never acknowledge their lack of experience?

"I leave the day after tomorrow. I will miss you, Sister." Ivy spun with a flourish and stormed back to the servants' bedroom they shared in the large mansion.

Holly couldn't believe her sister. How could she convince Ivy to reconsider? When her sister set her mind on something she wanted, she wasn't easily dissuaded. Holly would need to come up with something else to distract Ivy. And fast.

Two days later, at wits' end, Holly sat opposite Ivy on the westbound Union Pacific train. Having been unable to persuade her sister out of her foolish impetuousness, Holly had needed to resort to drastic measures. She'd taken a leave of absence from her job as a cook in the same well-to-do household as her sister—with the promise she *and Ivy* would return soon, before Christmas—and booked passage west. The week-long trip would give her ample time to coax Ivy into rethinking her folly and to make her see reason. Hopefully, success would come in not more than a day or two, then she could return with her job and sister intact.

As the Maryland countryside rolled by, Holly worked her crochet hook in and out of her half-completed doily. Complete a stitch then glance at the countryside, another stitch, a glance. She had never seen anything beyond Bethesda, other than traveling into the District of Columbia and Alexandria, Virginia, once each.

Holly was grateful for the cast-off clothes of their employer that she and Ivy had remade for themselves. One would hardly know them from the originals. She and her sister appeared quite respectable. Neither did they look as though they were putting on airs. Except they *were* servants, and one of them *was* running away.

"Good afternoon, ladies." A man in a smart blue suit stood in the aisle at the end of their seats. With one hand on the back of Holly's bench, he tipped his derby hat with the other. "I couldn't help but notice you lovely ladies are traveling without an escort." He had the gall to slip onto the seat next to her.

Holly clutched her crochet work and scooted as close to the window as possible.

Ivy glanced up from her novel, eyes wide, and stared hard at Holly.

Good. Maybe this intrusion would make her sister reconsider her rash decision and realize she could end up with an ill-mannered man such as this one.

Holly tilted her chin up. "Sir, you have sat down uninvited."

He gave her a sly smile. "You don't mind, do you, darling? My name is Jonas Miller."

The audacity of this man. She would not give him her name as he obviously wished. "I am *not* your darling! Please withdraw yourself."

He leaned toward her. "And if I don't?"

There wasn't much Holly could do. Gathering up her crocheting and handbag, she stood. She would sit next to Ivy. But when she tried to move to the facing bench, the interloper put his foot up on it, trapping her and Ivy next to the windows.

Ivy pulled at her skirt fabric caught beneath the man's shoe.

"*Sir*, remove your foot and yourself." Not that Holly expected this insolent man to comply. Still standing, she gripped the handle of her crochet hook, determined to jab this man if necessary.

But suddenly, he stumbled to his feet and backward.

A tall, rugged man dressed in denims with a black canvas duster, black leather vest, and black hat held the other by his coat collar. "I think your seat is up there." He shoved the intruder, who staggered forward and tumbled into a seat in the first row.

The cowboy took off his hat, revealing dark wavy hair, and pointed with it to the seat Holly had vacated. "Do you mind?"

She did. Why would she want to replace one pest with another? And this one prone to violence. But he had just run off the annoyer. Would he be just as tiresome? Did he think that by rescuing her and Ivy, they now owed him something? His deep blue eyes held no emotion—no lingering vexation he'd had for the interloper, no lechery, no impatience for her to answer quickly—but still said so much. *Say yes. Trust me. I'll wait you out.* Nodding her consent, she slipped onto the seat next to Ivy. She would keep an eye on this man. And keep her crochet hook handy.

The cowboy stretched his long legs across the facing seat with his feet and ankles hanging off the end of the red velvet bench into the aisle. He leaned his head back against the window and covered his face with his hat.

Holly stared at him. That was it? No explanation of his actions? No forced conversation? No words of warning?

Apparently, he didn't plan to be obnoxious after all. But what were his intentions?

Nick Andrews's Stetson hung low enough over his eyes so people couldn't see them but high enough to track those around him. He kept one eye on the women and one on the other passengers. Especially the men.

With him there, the other men on the train wouldn't bother these foolish women traveling alone. Were they going to Columbus, Ohio, or all the way to Chicago? Genteel ladies dressed as they were wouldn't likely be going any farther west than that.

Women! Why did they think they could take a trip without an escort and not be hassled by ne'er-do-wells? He would see to it they weren't preyed upon again until they reached their destination. Then he could enjoy the remainder of his trip in peace.

The women whispered in tones just loud enough he could listen to what they were saying but low enough he could ignore them. And *that* was what he chose to do. Ignore them.

"This trip is all your fault," the lady in the deep green traveling suit said.

Don't listen, Nick.

"You didn't have to come," the other in dark blue replied.

So the older sister was the levelheaded one. At least, he assumed they were sisters by their resemblance. And the older one had obviously tried to talk the younger out of this trip. But then the younger would have been *completely* alone. Not good. Even worse

11

than the pair of them traveling without a male escort.

But he wasn't going to listen.

"If we go back now, we can return to our jobs."

Yes, go back where the pair of you belong.

The younger's voice squeaked as she spoke. "I don't want mine back."

Don't listen.

"I can't believe you think this is a good idea," the sensible one said.

"You're just jealous because you're older," the other replied.

"You don't even know this man."

"His letters were quite comprehensive. I know him as well as anyone."

"Don't be naive."

And just like that, Nick had gotten sucked into their conversation. He wasn't quite sure what they were talking about. Amazing how little others thought you could hear with your face covered.

"Let me see the letters." The sensible one's black leather boots shifted as though she had turned to face her sister.

The brown boots remained firm. "Those are my private correspondence from my *fiancé*."

"If this man is so wonderful, then you have nothing to hide or worry about."

The younger sister harrumphed.

Then a rustling of paper.

Silence.

Paper rustling again.

More silence.

He wished she'd read them aloud.

Paper rustling a third time.

Then the infernal silence.

Paper again!

The black boots crossed at the ankles and tilted to one side. "These tell you nothing about this man. Anyone could have written them."

"He's a cattle rancher."

So am I.

"Does that make him a decent person?"

No. I know ranchers and farmers and other scoundrels I wouldn't give a mule to. Not even one I didn't like.

"He can obviously provide well."

Nick furrowed his eyebrows under his hat. Were these women talking about what he thought they were talking about? The younger sister had a fiancé, but all she knew of him were some letters? These silly females were mail-order brides. They had no clue what they were getting themselves into.

He squirmed inside. *Stay out of it.*

"I've heard that one hard winter can do a cattleman in. The more important question is, will he treat you well?"

12

She was right. If a rancher didn't plan ahead for bad weather, it could be all over. So why was black-boots a mail-order bride if she was so against her sister being one? Obviously, her intended wasn't a rancher. And likely not a farmer either for the same reason. Precarious at best. But that left a lot of possibilities.

"Why do you always assume the worst in people?"

"I don't. But you could be heading straight into trouble. I'm concerned for your well-being."

"Well, you needn't be. I can take care of myself. If you can't support me in this, I don't want to discuss it any further *with you*. Why don't you head back on the next train and not give me another thought?"

Heading back was fine advice for *both* of them.

Chapter 2

Holly and Ivy had transferred to a second train bound for Chicago and now boarded their third and final train for the longest leg of their journey into the wilderness. Holly had been unsuccessful in swaying her sister to return home.

Her insides tightened as the wheels churned into motion and pulled the train out of the station. She'd been grateful that the cowboy had changed trains in Columbus and had sat silently with them again. No one had bothered them. He'd bidden them farewell with a tip of his hat.

Now she and her sister were on their own. She wished she'd had the funds to afford a private compartment. Hopefully, no other passengers would disturb them.

The door at the end of the carriage opened, and the cowboy swaggered in.

What was he doing here? He wasn't following them, was he? Even with that thought, relief swept through her.

He scanned the interior and stopped short when his blue gaze locked with hers. He seemed upset and looked toward the windows. He took off his hat and ran a hand through his dark hair. He settled his hat firmly back on his head and continued up the aisle. He stopped next to the benches Holly and her sister occupied.

If he asked, would she allow him to sit with them? There were other seats available.

He indicated the vacancy across the aisle and addressed the elderly couple there. "May I?"

The man nodded, and the woman spoke. "Of course, young man."

He sat, not even glancing in Holly and Ivy's direction as though he'd never seen them before.

A scruffily dressed man stopped in the aisle and removed his hat. "Good afternoon. May I have the honor of keeping company with you two ladies?"

Before Holly could answer, the cowboy did. "Take one of the seats back there." He jabbed a finger in that direction.

The man eyed the cowboy and complied without another word.

Holly let her breath escape. She hadn't looked forward to a confrontation with the man and now addressed the cowboy. "You didn't have to do that, but thank you."

Without so much as a *you're welcome*, he leaned back and tilted his hat over his face.

How rude! But better he ignore her than become a pest himself. And it was nice of him to look out for her and Ivy. She studied him with his long, denim-clad legs stretched out into the aisle. Something inside her yearned to have a conversation with her guardian. But what could she say? They hadn't been properly introduced.

They hadn't been introduced at all.

"Sir?" she ventured. When he didn't stir, she repeated herself. "Sir?"

"Mister?" The old man tipped his head to peer under the cowboy's brim. "I think he's asleep."

Already?

"Do you know him?"

She shook her head. "I just wanted to thank him properly. We've been on the same trains since Maryland. I don't think he realizes that his mere presence has kept undesirable types away from us."

The old man nodded. "I'm Hank Carter, and this is my wife, Thelma."

The diminutive woman gave Holly a nod in greeting. "What are you making?"

"Doilies. I like to keep my hands busy. I'm Holly Harrison, and this is my sister, Ivy." The cowboy gave a soft grunt.

The old man grimaced. "I think we're disturbing his sleep."

She supposed they were. But if a man could fall asleep so quickly, would whispering wake him? "Where are you headed?"

"Minneapolis," the man said.

His wife shifted to look around him at Holly. "We're going to visit our daughter. She has three children. Where are you girls headed?"

She didn't want to admit to Ivy's folly, but what could she say?

Unfortunately, Ivy decided to speak up. "Washington Territory. I'm getting married."

All at once, the cowboy's outstretched legs raked the floor toward him, and he removed his hat, leaning forward. "Don't be foolish. Traveling across the country to marry a man you have three letters from is—is—daft! Go home where you belong."

Three letters? Those were only mentioned two trains ago while she'd thought he was sleeping. Evidently not. "What right have you to speak to my sister that way?"

The cowboy swung his gaze to Holly. "None. None whatsoever. But your feeble attempts have fallen on deaf ears. She needs a good spanking."

Holly gasped. "Sir!"

"And I do know that my presence is keeping ne'er-do-wells away. That's why I've stayed close. I thought the pair of you would have enough sense to stay in Chicago. But apparently not."

He had been awake the whole time? "It's considered ill-mannered to eavesdrop on other people's conversations."

"Kind of hard not to hear the conversations around you in such small quarters. And it's *not* Washington Territory. We have been a state for a year now." He stretched back out and replaced his hat.

How uncivil. But Holly couldn't stop staring at him. Why had he taken it upon himself to be their protector? But more than that, he agreed with her on Ivy's foolishness. Even with his rude outburst, she held a fondness for this man who had elected to see to their well-being. He'd identified himself with Washington Terr—State. So he would be near almost the entire trip, if not all. Comforting. He could be her ally in her quest to change her sister's mind. "Sir?"

He didn't move or make a sound.

"Sir? I know you can hear me."

His voice came from under the brim of his hat. "Then just speak your mind."

"It's hard to hold a conversation with your face covered."

"I don't plan to be part of any conversation."

"Well, I find it difficult to speak to someone when I can't see their face."

"That suits me. Although, you seem to be doing just fine."

She looked to the older couple for help.

They shrugged.

What should she do? Why wouldn't he remove his hat? What was his reluctance? Could she knock it off and feign innocence? But knock it off with what? And if she did manage to displace it, he would just replace it. Oh, bother. Maybe she would just have to speak to his talking hat.

Blessed peace. Nick sank deeper into the plush seat. Now maybe he could rest.

Washington! Why did they have to be going all the way to Washington? At least he would be able to watch over them. He smiled at that. Holly certainly had spunk. She might do all right in the rugged—but beautiful—Pacific Northwest.

Maybe his feigned anger and outburst would send the pair of them scurrying home to their family. How ludicrous to marry men they hadn't even met. He would never marry a woman he hadn't met. But then, he never planned to marry at all. Women couldn't be trusted. Not one of them. These two were proof that the whole lot of them had bad judgment.

Suddenly, his hat was gone.

He jerked his eyes open and grappled the air for his Stetson to no avail.

It sat on Holly's lap, her hands folded primly atop it. "That's better."

She took his hat? He stared at it nestled atop her green skirt. She *took* his *Stetson*. The bold minx. "May I have my hat back?"

"Not if you're going to put it on your face again."

She wore an impish smile that should irritate him more than he already was but didn't.

The old man chuckled.

What should he do now? Grab it from her? Like a schoolboy locked in the outhouse, he waited to be rescued. "Please give me back my Stetson."

"Answer my questions first."

Plucky little nymph. But he would best her. He folded his arms, leaned his head back, and closed his eyes. He could ignore her just as well without his hat. She would soon grow tired of holding it and return it without a fuss.

"What is your name, sir?"

Ignore her.

His thigh was tapped by something. "Your name?"

He cracked one eye open a slit.

His Stetson hung from her gloved hand, close to the aisle.

He had a mind to reach out and snatch it away from her.

The old man spoke. "If I were you, mister, I'd tell her. She doesn't seem to have a mind to give up. You won't get no peace until you do."

Nick forced his eyes open. "Nick Andrews. Happy?"

"Mr. Andrews, I'm very pleased to meet you."

He could not reciprocate the sentiment. But, surprisingly, he *was* pleased to meet her and to finally know her name.

"My name—"

"I know who you are, Miss Harrison. And you are traveling to Washington *State* with your sister, Ivy. You've asked your question, and I've answered. Now will you return my Stetson and leave me be?"

"I said 'questions.' What did you mean when you called my sister foolish?"

Ivy jerked her attention from her novel. "Holly!"

Holly swung her gaze to her sister. "Don't you want to know as well?"

"Not from a rude, overbearing brute."

Holly shrugged and turned back to him with determination in her eyes. "Why did you call my sister foolish? You know nothing about her."

She wasn't going to give up. He should have held his tongue. He stared into her hazel eyes. Eyes that held intelligence. Eyes that captivated him. He sat up straight. "Return my hat, and I'll tell you."

"Holly, stop." Ivy reached for his hat, presumably to give it back. "I don't care about a ruffian's opinion."

Ruffian! Humph. Little she knew.

Holly moved his hat from her sister's reach but within his. With a pout, Ivy turned her face to the window, apparently wanting nothing to do with her sister's question.

He sat forward and latched on to the brim but didn't yank it from the older sister's grasp. Instead, he waited for her to release it.

Without looking, she tugged on the hat, but he held fast. She shifted her gaze from her sister to his Stetson and glared at his hand. Her glare slid up to his face.

When her expression changed to defeat, his mouth twitched up on one corner. "We both know I can simply take it."

"Then why don't you?"

It would be rude. She might be discouraged from interacting. He didn't want to lose their tenuous connection. *Connection?* They had no connection. He released his Stetson. Women were trouble. Nothing but trouble.

Her eyes widened, changing her defeated expression to surprise.

He'd surprised himself as well.

"Why—why—why did you let go?"

The old man chuckled. "He's being a gentleman."

That was the last thing Nick wanted Holly to believe. It was better these two ladies caught a glimpse of the rougher side of life before they reached the untamed West. He shrugged. "It's not like you're going anywhere." He pointed to the window with the countryside speeding by. "I can retrieve my Stetson at any time."

"I could open the window and toss it out."

She wouldn't dare.

"Then I would spend the remainder of the trip in the stock car with the horses where the company would be more agreeable. That would leave you ladies to fend for yourselves."

She straightened her shoulders. "Sir, I know a bluff when I hear one."

"As do I." He settled back into his seat and folded his arms. "I'll answer one more question."

"Tell my sister why being a mail-order bride is foolish and. . .and. . .daft."

"That is not a question but a request."

"Very well. What did you mean when you called my sister foolish?"

"It's none of my concern what the pair of you do."

"It seems to me you have made it *your concern* by following us around and deterring unwelcomed attention."

He should have stayed out of it. Trouble.

The old man spoke up. "He's right, you know. Those letters mean nothing. For all you know, an old man like me wrote them. Or a bank robber in a gang."

Nick nodded to the elderly gentleman. "Thank you. Why are women always so foolhardy?"

Holly stamped her booted foot. "I am *not* foolhardy."

He swung his gaze back to her. "What do you call traveling across the country without a chaperone to marry a man you don't know? How many letters do you have from your intended?"

"My what? I'm not a mail-order bride. How preposterous."

That pleased him. "Then why are you on this train heading west?"

"To convince my sister to reconsider and return with me. That is why I'm soliciting your help."

She didn't plan to stay in Washington?

He leaned forward, resting his forearms on his thighs. "Maybe *foolish* was too strong of a word. *Ill-advised.*"

Holly pointed to her sister, who continued to feign interest out the window. "Tell her."

He shifted his gaze to the younger sister. "Miss Harrison. If you had taken along a chaperone who could determine the character of this man—"

Ivy turned on him. "My sister came along as an *uninvited* chaperone."

"I meant a *male* chaperone. Like a father or brother or uncle. Someone who would be able to determine the integrity of the man you intend to marry."

Holly bristled but didn't interfere.

Ivy straightened her shoulders. "We have no male relations."

"Ivy! Shush."

With no one to advise her, no wonder she had made an unwise decision. Nick knew women were scarce out West, but a man who sent away for a bride like he would order a plow or suit was suspect. "This man expected you—his bride—to travel all the way across the country by yourself. He didn't even have the decency to go and escort you. Is that the kind of man you want to marry and spend the rest of your life with?"

"He is a busy man. He has all that. . ." Ivy flipped her gloved hand in the air. ". . .that ranching stuff to do. He can't be expected to just leave all that."

Nick had. "He's not much of a businessman if he can't leave his ranch in his foreman's capable hands for a couple of weeks for something as important as his future wife."

Ivy's determination seemed to falter. "I've made up my mind. I can't exactly change it now that I've used his train ticket." The girl almost looked scared. She'd gotten in over her head and didn't know how to free herself.

"Where in Washington is this man?"

"*Yaykeyma.*"

There was no such town. Then he realized. "Yakima." That was just a spur line south from his stop. "I'll go to Yakima with you and meet this man."

"He's meeting me in Ellensburg."

Nick's stop. "Even better. If he seems to be upstanding and respectable, I'll let you know. But regardless, if you decide you don't want to marry him for any reason, I'll take care of it."

Ivy's face brightened. "Thank you. But I don't think that will be necessary. I'm sure he'll be a fine gentleman." She opened her novel.

"You would do that for us?"

Nick turned back to Holly, who had an appreciative expression. He thought he'd do a great many things to receive a look like that. He had to stop allowing such thoughts into his head. Trouble. "It's not a problem. My stop's Ellensburg." He folded his arms, reclined back into the seat, and closed his eyes.

"Don't you want your hat back?"

He shrugged. He liked that she held it. And he liked that she wasn't a mail-order bride as well. He shook off that thought. It shouldn't matter to him if she was a mail-order bride or not. It *didn't* matter. She was a woman, after all. And women were nothing but trouble.

Chapter 3

Holly stared out the window as the barren landscape sped past mile after mile. The dry air sucked the moisture right out of her skin. She could literally feel her face shriveling. This Washington was so different from the lush one back East. Not that nothing grew here, but what seemed to have grown in the spring and summer stood sparse and stunted like malnourished children. Was the whole state like this?

"Next stop Ellensburg," the conductor called as he strolled through the carriage.

Fortunately, the vegetation had thickened some in the distance, and she saw evidence of more plant life going up the mountain range. But still, nothing like her Maryland.

The town up ahead was larger than Holly had expected. There was more than a single clapboard main street. Along with the wooden structures, there were larger buildings of brick or stone. Beyond the town, mountains jutted into the air.

Ivy clamped a gloved hand around Holly's. "I'm so glad you're with me." Her tone hinted at uncertainty.

Dare Holly hope her sister had changed her mind? "If you've reconsidered, we don't have to get off the train."

Ivy gave a weak smile. "It's not that. I suddenly find myself giddy with excitement. I'm going to be a married woman soon, with a house of my own. You'll stay for the wedding, won't you? It may not be for a week or two. I'm so glad you're here to share my special day."

Holly couldn't afford to stay. But neither could she abandon her sister.

Mr. Andrews huffed out a breath and leaned forward, resting his forearms on his thighs. "Miss Harrison, a man who sends for a mail-order bride expects to marry her right off—the same day they meet."

"But we hardly know each other."

What happened to the letters from him telling her *everything* she needed to know? But voicing her frustration wouldn't help her sister.

Ivy twisted her hands together. "Don't you think he would be willing to wait if I explain it to him? I mean, it's only a couple of weeks."

Mr. Andrews scrubbed his hand over his mouth. "And where do you expect to stay during these two weeks?"

Her sister's gaze darted from the cowboy to Holly.

Holly shrugged, glad Mr. Andrews had taken up the argument.

Ivy turned back to Mr. Andrews and finally offered, "A hotel?"

Mr. Andrews took a slow breath. "And who will pay for this hotel room for two weeks?"

"My husband-to-be, of course. He can't expect me to pay."

"He won't be expecting to pay either. He's *expecting* a bride to step off the train. He's *expecting* to head home tonight with his new wife. He likely won't have the money to frivolously spend on a hotel room. And if he does, there are a dozen other things on his ranch the money would be better spent on."

The train chugged to a stop with a screech of the brakes.

With large round eyes, Ivy straightened herself. "I'll just have to make him see the benefits of waiting."

Mr. Andrews shook his head as he stood. He removed Holly's and Ivy's carpetbags from the overhead rack, tucking one under his arm and gripping the handle of the other. Then he took down his saddlebags and flung them over his shoulder. "Let's go see who this lucky gentleman is."

Once outside, Holly stood on the Ellensburg train platform with Ivy. The cold fall air felt fresh on her face. She shivered.

Mr. Andrews helped collect Ivy's luggage. Ivy had a lot more than Holly. She had packed everything she owned, planning to stay. Not having planned to travel even this far, Holly had packed only the bare essentials.

Mr. Andrews set Ivy's two large traveling cases next to their carpetbags and his saddlebags. "Stay here."

Holly's insides twisted in panic. "Where are you going?" She'd come to rely on him.

"I have to see to my own cargo in the stock car. I'll be right back." He walked off.

Ivy looked to and fro. "I wonder where Mr. Bosco could be."

Holly prayed the man wouldn't show up at all, and make everything easier.

When the crowd thinned, Ivy pointed to a gentleman talking to the conductor. "I think that's him. He just asked the conductor about a female passenger. He's quite tall. And handsome."

Holly studied the handsome man. He was dressed decently, not unkempt. His appearance suggested respectability. Maybe all her worry was for naught. Maybe Mr. Bosco would make her sister very happy. Maybe this was all in God's plan.

But he wasn't as handsome as Mr. Andrews. She found too many of her thoughts were of the cowboy lately, but that was just because he'd been so kind and helpful to them.

Ivy nudged her. "Go tell him I'm here."

"Me?" Holly stared at Mr. Bosco. "I'll tell him to leave without you."

Throwing her shoulders back, Ivy lifted her chin. "I shall tell him myself." She strode up to him and the conductor. "Mr. Bosco?"

Holly scurried to catch up.

The tall gentleman turned with an annoyed expression. Then his face twisted into a grin. "Miss Harrison, I presume."

"You presume correctly."

His appreciative gaze traveled down the length of Ivy then shifted to Holly. "Who might you be?"

"Her sister."

With narrowing eyes, he shifted his attention back to Ivy. "You didn't mention I'd be taking on the responsibility of your sister."

Ivy tilted her head. "You're not. She simply escorted me out."

He smiled and tipped his hat at Holly. "Well, then. Welcome."

"All aboard!" the conductor called.

Mr. Bosco turned back to Ivy and tucked her hand around his arm. "It's not far to the preacher's."

Having taken only one step, Ivy stopped. "We're getting married right now?"

"Of course. We can return here in time to catch the train south to Yakima."

Ivy stiffened. "I thought we'd get to know each other first."

"There's no time for that. The preacher's waiting."

The metal wheels slipped on the rails as the train chugged into motion. The grinding echoed Holly's heartache for her sister.

"I think I'd like to wait a few days." Ivy formally withdrew her hand from his arm.

He latched on to her wrist, and his expression hardened. "I paid your passage, and you agreed to marry me. We are getting married *now*, and you *will* be my wife."

Dropping her mask of dignity, Ivy gasped and pulled back. "Let me go."

Holly stepped closer and clutched her sister's arm. "Unhand my sister."

He pointed a finger in her face. "Stay out of this. You weren't invited."

A large, muscular hand clamped on to Mr. Bosco's forearm. "Release her."

Holly drew in a relieved breath. Thank goodness Mr. Andrews had returned.

"She's my bride, Andrews."

They knew each other?

"Not yet, she isn't. And it doesn't sound like she wants to be. Release her before I make you."

Mr. Bosco let go of Ivy's arm and jerked free of Mr. Andrews's grip in one move. "You can't take my wife from me. I paid for her."

Holly couldn't believe this man. Thankfully, Mr. Andrews was standing up for Ivy.

"You didn't pay for *her*. You bought a train ticket." Mr. Andrews called over his shoulder, "Holly. Ivy. Go wait inside."

Holly didn't have to be told twice and guided her sister swiftly inside the station building.

Ivy drew in a ragged breath. "What was I *thinking*? I changed my mind. I'm so sorry. I can't marry that man. What do I do?"

Finally, Ivy had come to her senses. Too bad it took a week-long trip across the country. Holly wrapped her arm around her sister. "No. You don't have to. Mr. Andrews will take care of it just as he promised." At least she hoped so. She had no idea what the laws in the Wild West were. Maybe Ivy's agreement in her letters to marry this man and her acceptance of his train ticket were binding.

Lord, please get Ivy out of this. And please don't let Mr. Andrews get hurt in the process.

Nick studied Bosco. What would the man do? Cause trouble? Or realize he was bested and back down?

Why hadn't he asked the name of the man Ivy Harrison intended to marry? He could have saved the young woman the whole trip. If he had known her intended was Bosco, he could have talked her out of this back on the first train. Saved them all a lot of heartache. But. . .

But what? But then Holly wouldn't be here now.

He mentally shook himself. No. It would have been better if Holly weren't here and he hadn't gotten to know her. She would be better off. He would be better off. Or would he?

"May I have a word with you?" Nick stood between Bosco and the door the women had entered through.

Bosco narrowed his eyes. "This is none of your business. Don't think you can take my bride from me."

Nick had made it his business back in Maryland. "The girl is obviously scared and has changed her mind. You'll only be bringing trouble on yourself." Women and trouble went hand in hand.

"What about the money I paid for her train fare?"

The man could have afforded a private compartment.

"I'll reimburse you." Nick removed money from his pocket and held some out to Bosco.

Bosco stared at it. "You want the girl for yourself."

"That's not it at all." Nick didn't need to explain his actions. "You won't be able to force her into marrying you, so why don't you cut your losses."

Bosco snatched the money and stormed off.

Nick hoped the ladies had seen the last of that scoundrel. He watched the man for a moment longer, glad Bosco had left without a fuss, before he went inside.

The ladies sat on a wooden bench, huddled together. Holly stood. "What happened?"

What happened? The animosity between him and Bosco had dug deeper. "He won't be bothering either of you anymore."

Ivy stood. "I don't have to marry him?"

Nick shook his head. But now what?

"Thank you." Holly's shoulders visibly relaxed. Her whole demeanor relaxed. "Thank you so much. We need to book passage on the next train heading east."

The station manager replied from where he stoked the potbelly stove. "Next eastbound train will be coming through in three days."

Holly drew in a quick breath. "*Three* days?"

"We've had a couple of engines break down. Messed up the entire schedule."

Ivy gripped her sister's arm. "What will we do?"

"I don't know. I can purchase our tickets back home but not a hotel room for three nights."

Nick could put them up in the hotel, but he wasn't sure Bosco wouldn't return and

23

cause trouble. "You'll both stay at the ranch."

Holly swiveled her gaze slowly toward him. "What? We can't do that."

"I wouldn't feel comfortable leaving the pair of you in town with Bosco here."

"You think he might come back for Ivy?"

"I don't know. Do you want to risk it? I'd stay in town to make sure he didn't, but I've already been gone too long. I need to get back to work."

Holly knit her eyebrows together. "Wouldn't the ranch owner mind?"

Nick stared at her a moment. Evidently, she didn't realize it was *his* ranch and he would make the decision. Just as well. The last thing he needed was some sense of overwhelming gratitude making her set her sights on him. "It's only three nights. He won't mind." He would give them the house, and he'd sleep in the bunkhouse with the hands. "I'll rent a buggy." He escorted them outside but didn't want to leave the women unattended in case Bosco returned even for the short time it would take.

A young boy in a brown coat sat on the end of the platform with his legs dangling over the edge and fiddled with a stick.

Nick walked over to the lad, who looked to be about eight. "What's your name?"

The boy glanced up and brushed aside the sandy-brown hair on his forehead. "Sonny."

"Are you trustworthy, Sonny?"

"I don't know. What is trust. . .a. . .thy?"

"If I gave you a job to do, would you do it without dawdling?"

The lad tipped his head and squinted up at him with one eye. "My auntie says if there was a straight path to perdition I'd wander off it. But I wouldn't. I can stay on a trail if I have a mind to."

Obviously, the boy hadn't caught his aunt's exasperation. "Could you stay on a task for a nickel?"

Sonny dropped his stick and jumped to his feet. "All day, mister."

"You know Mr. Tremble at the livery?"

"Sure do. He's sweet on my auntie."

Nick smiled at that and took out four bits. "You give this money to Mr. Tremble. Tell him Mr. Andrews needs to rent his buggy. Then lead the horse and rig back here."

"I can drive it easy."

Nick hadn't wanted to assume. "Can you remember all that?"

"You want me to rent a buggy and bring it back here."

"What do you do with the money?"

"Give it to Mr. Tremble."

"And what is my name?"

Sonny straightened. "An. . .An. . .Anderson?"

"Andrews."

"Andrews." The lad cocked his head. "Where's my nickel?"

"You'll get it when you return with the buggy." But what if the boy took off with his four bits? "Do you know what will happen if you run off with my money and don't get the buggy?"

The boy heaved a sigh. "You'll tell my auntie, and she won't let me have dessert for a week."

Not exactly what Nick was thinking. But at Sonny's age, no dessert was probably a bigger threat than telling the sheriff. "Right. Be quick. And no wandering."

"I won't." The lad jumped the four feet from the platform to the ground then turned. "Mister?"

"Yes?"

"What's perdition?"

"That's one path you *want* to wander off of and never go back to."

"Really?"

"Perdition is where bad people go."

The lad's eyes widened. "Oh. I'm not going there. It's good that I wander off." And with that, he ran around the station building.

After the buggy rolled up and Nick paid the boy, Sonny ran off toward the mercantile. Probably to buy a nickel's worth of candy that he'd eat all at once then be too sick for supper.

Nick loaded Holly's and Ivy's luggage onto the back of the buggy and drove to the livery to tell Tremble he'd send the buggy back with one of his men.

"Oh." Holly straightened. "Before we leave town, I need to send a telegram." She turned to Ivy. "To let the Wadsworths know when to expect us back."

Something shifted inside Nick at the mention of Holly leaving. He pushed the feeling aside and drove the buggy back toward the train station, where a smaller building sat beside it—the post office and telegram station. He dropped the ladies off and strode over to the stock corral on the other side of the building.

His men had taken the horses he'd brought from back East and left his mount as he'd instructed them. Had he known he'd be driving the ladies to his ranch in a buggy, he wouldn't have needed Ranger. He led the horse to the buggy and tied the reins to the back.

When Holly stepped out of the telegram building, his heart galloped in his chest. *Easy, boy.* "Did you get it sent?"

Holly nodded as she took his hand to climb up into the buggy.

Her satisfied expression irritated him.

Remember, women are trouble even if she's nice. . .and sensible. . .and pretty. . .and smelled like a spring meadow. Trouble.

She would leave in three days.

Then everything would be as it should be.

Chapter 4

In front of his house, Nick hauled back on the reins, bringing the buggy to a stop.

His foreman approached from the corral that held the new mounts.

"Wait in the buggy." Nick jumped down and met his foreman. He kept his voice low so the ladies couldn't hear. "I need a favor."

Gil eyed the contents of the buggy. "I was going to compliment you on the fine horseflesh you brought back. But I see you have something more. You pick those up back East as well?"

"No—yes—no." Holly and Ivy were too difficult to explain in the few seconds he had.

"One of those lovely ladies special to you?" Gil winked.

"No!" Nick glanced back at Holly and her sister to see if they had heard. They didn't appear to have. Gil knew him better than to think he would fall for a woman. He didn't need *that* kind of trouble. "They're stranded and need a place to stay for a few nights until they can catch the next train heading east. Let them think you're the ranch owner."

One of Gil's eyebrows kicked up.

"Just do it." Nick didn't need his foreman judging him, even if he was his best friend. And Gil had once been part owner.

"No good can come of this." Gil rounded the buggy to the ladies. "Welcome to the Rocking A Ranch." He helped them down. "I'm Gil Coons." He bent at the waist, sweeping his hat in front of him. "At your service."

"I'm Holly Harrison, and this is my sister, Ivy. Mr. Andrews said it would be all right if we stayed here until we could catch the next train east. But we don't want to impose."

"No imposition. *Mr. Andrews* did not step over the line in offering you a place. Rocking A is plenty big enough. Let me show you where you can bunk down." Gil glanced over his shoulder. "Nick, would you bring up the ladies' luggage?" He winked and guided Holly and Ivy inside.

Apparently, Nick's oldest friend was going to enjoy his short stint as ranch owner. Nick didn't mind carrying the bags. He gathered them up, tucking the smaller carpetbags under his arms and grasping the handles of the two larger cases.

He would trust Gil with his own sister—if he had one. But still, he hurried inside for propriety's sake. The ladies didn't know Gil the way they knew Nick. Not that they really knew him, but they knew he'd looked out for them. And they trusted him enough to come out to the ranch on his recommendation. So they knew him well enough.

He caught up to the trio at the doorway to a spare room with two narrow beds on opposite walls. "Which bags go in here?"

Leaning against the hall wall opposite the doorway, Gil inclined his head. "The ladies would like to share the same room. I told them they would have the house to themselves. The owner will sleep in the bunkhouse with the men."

Nick smiled to himself. His foreman thought a lot like him. He set the bags on one of the beds. "We'll leave you to get settled."

Gil pushed away from the wall. "I promised to show the ladies around the ranch."

Nick wanted to fill Gil in on all that had transpired. "What about the buggy? It's rented from Tremble."

The foreman's mouth curved up. "You should return that right away."

Nick gritted his teeth. Gil was enjoying this a little too much. "I'll send Jesse."

His foreman nodded. "Ladies, why don't we start the tour outside since you still have on your coats?"

Holly nodded and glanced to Nick. "You're coming, aren't you?"

She *wanted* him along? That warmed his heart. "Certainly."

At the corral, Gil introduced the ladies to the ranch hands with more formality than was needed. "Jesse, Frank, Montana, these fine ladies are Miss Holly Harrison and her sister, Miss Ivy Harrison. They'll be staying for a few days. Remember how ladies are to be treated. I don't want any of you pestering them. Or you'll have me to answer to." He jammed a thumb toward Nick. "And him."

Nice of Gil to include me.

All three hands wore sloppy smiles and managed to greet the ladies with a tip of their hats and either a *good day* or a nod.

Nick addressed Jesse. "Return the buggy to Tremble. Take my horse."

Jesse trotted off.

After Gil had shown them the barn and pointed out the Black Angus cattle spread out on the grazing land, the tour concluded back inside the house.

Holly scanned the kitchen. "We want to be of service while we're here, Mr. Coons. Do you think your cook would mind if we helped in the kitchen?"

"Sadly, we don't have a cook. We do the best we can preparing meals for ourselves."

"No cook?"

"No, ma'am."

Holly took an apron off a peg in the kitchen. "I feel badly that we have been foisted upon you and that you have given up your home for our benefit. We'll cook all the meals for you and your men while we're here."

Nick spoke up. "You don't—"

Gil held up his hand and stepped forward. "That would be much appreciated. We could use a good meal. The men would be mighty grateful."

Nick narrowed his gaze at his foreman. "Let me tell you about those horses I brought back."

"Good idea. I'm interested in your whole trip and *everything* you brought back." He tipped his hat to Holly and Ivy. "We'll leave you to it."

Outside, on the way back to the corral, Nick elbowed Gil. "Why are you taking advantage of them and making them work?"

"I'm not taking advantage or making them do anything. They offered. It'll allow them to feel as though they're earning their room and board."

Nick grunted. He hadn't brought Holly here to work. He'd brought her here to protect her sister from Bosco. Nothing more.

"Do you really want to subject those fine ladies to our cooking?"

That was a dreadful thought.

"It's only three days. If it bothers you so much, tell them you own this ranch so you can forbid them to cook." Gil clamped a hand on Nick's shoulder. "But admit that you would like to taste a woman's cooking again."

Nick's mouth watered. He pushed thoughts of delectable food aside. No women on his ranch since Gil's wife ran off suited Nick just fine. . .until now.

After Nick relayed the events of the trip, Gil leaned his forearms on the corral fence. "So why has their presence promoted me to owner?"

"I don't want either of them to set their cap for me because of my position."

Gil nodded. "I understand." His tone teasing, "You want one of them to set their cap for you because of your charm."

"No."

"What does it matter if either or both of them fancy you? They *are* leaving in three days. Aren't they? Hardly enough time for even the most romantically minded female to fall in love. And certainly not with your prickly exterior."

Gil's jab should irritate him, but he found it comforting. No chance that either would fancy him. He pictured the appreciative gaze Holly had gifted him with on more than one occasion during the journey west. He wouldn't mind if she fancied him just a little bit.

Three days later, Holly woke in the early morning hours. Wind howled in the eaves of the house. She crawled out of bed and padded in stocking feet to the window. Pitch black. The full moon from the night before didn't illuminate anything. The clouds must be thick. Mr. Andrews and Mr. Coons had said yesterday that it felt like snow. She squinted into the darkness but couldn't see any in the air. Good thing, because she and Ivy were to leave today.

She lit the bedside lamp, keeping it low, and tilted her pendant watch to the light. Four in the morning. Not much point in going back to bed. It was seven back in Maryland. She would have been up for nearly two hours already. And in a week, she would need to adjust back to the East Coast time, so she might as well start now.

Instead, with a shiver, she dashed back under the warm covers. Mayhap a little more rest wouldn't hurt. She could adjust her sleeping habits on the train. Her stomach tightened at the thought of leaving and of taking another week-long trip, this time with no one to protect her and Ivy from unwanted attention.

She pictured Mr. Andrews reclined on the bench opposite them with his hat over his face. How silly of her to think he'd been sleeping. Every time a man stopped near them, without hesitation, he'd immediately encouraged him to move on. When a lady and her two children had sat across the aisle from them, he kept them from being disturbed as well.

Even though he'd tried to appear gruff, she could tell he had a kind and chivalrous heart. But she doubted he would admit to it. He helped others without expecting anything in return.

Muted light grayed the curtains when Holly opened her eyes again. She threw back the covers and flew out of bed. How could she have overslept? Though Ivy was already up and gone from the room, her two large traveling cases lay open on the floor with her clothes still strewn about.

Holly struggled to cinch her corset and then dressed quickly. She stuffed her belongings into her carpetbag and carried it downstairs. After setting it at the foot of the stairs, she headed to the kitchen.

Ivy sat at the table with Mr. Andrews and Mr. Coons, each with a cup of coffee in front of them.

As Holly entered, the men stood. She gazed at Mr. Andrews a moment, already missing him. "When do we leave for the train station?"

"We don't." He pulled out a straight-backed chair for her.

Ivy stood and crossed to the stove. "Coffee?"

Holly shook her head and addressed Mr. Andrews's comment. "Why not?"

He went through the kitchen doorway to the front room and drew back the curtain.

Holly followed and stared out the window. Snow blew sideways. "We can still leave, can't we?"

He shook his head. "It's a bit early for this kind of snow, but there'll be no going to town today."

"But we have to catch the train." How could he be so casual about this? Holly had sent a telegram to their employer that they would both be on that train. They were expected. They had jobs to return to. She couldn't lose her job. What would she do? She'd already been gone too long.

He dropped the curtain. "I don't know what this storm is going to do. If it gets any worse, we could be stranded between here and town. You'll have to take the next train."

That was not good. But what else could she do? "When will that be?"

"A week, maybe. Not sure. When it's safe to travel, I'll send someone into town to find out."

She was trapped. Oddly, a calm washed over her. She was staying. At least for the time being.

Then she replayed his words. *He* would send someone to town? Why not Mr. Coons? Mr. Coons probably relied heavily on him. One of his many duties.

As days slipped by, she quickly fell into the rhythm of the ranch. Breakfast, dinner, and supper. Evenings spent in the front room with Mr. Andrews and Mr. Coons discussing the ranch while she and Ivy worked on the mending the hands had hired them to do. The extra money would come in handy.

At the end of the evenings, Mr. Andrews would stock the fire in the hearth while Mr. Coons banked the coals in the kitchen stove. By the time she and Ivy came down in the mornings, a fire blazed in the hearth, warming the room, and the stove had been heated and was ready to start cooking on, and a pail of fresh milk sat on the table.

She saw the other ranch hands, Jesse, Frank, and Montana, only at mealtimes. All of them behaved cordially, obviously heeding Mr. Coons's instructions to behave themselves. And to Holly's delight, they were never short on compliments about the food.

A week later, with a reluctant spirit, Holly rode on the wagon seat between Mr. Andrews and her sister. She had counseled herself to look forward to heading back to Maryland. But now that the day had come, it had come too soon.

Cooking for a handful of cowboys had been a refreshing change. No preconceived ideas of how the food should be arranged on the plates for the best visual appeal. Just gratitude to have food in front of them. She could prepare anything she liked, and they were thrilled. So easy to please. Which made her want to prepare the finest and most tasty foods she could. She and Ivy had baked a cake, two pies, and several dozen cookies for the men as a parting thank-you.

No evidence remained of the storm that had blown in with such fury the week before. Not a lot of snow had actually fallen but had mostly blown around in the air, making it impossible to see. If the tempest had come twelve hours on either side of that day, she would be back in Maryland by now. Back to working in the sweltering kitchen for people who *were* hard to please. It was as though the Lord had given her a small respite from the job that was wearing her down. Now that she'd had a break, she understood better why Ivy had been so desperate to escape.

Today the sun shone, making the late-November day almost balmy. She shivered. *Almost*, but not quite. She still needed her coat, gloves, scarf, and hat.

She drank in the beauty of the landscape, which had a calming effect on her and fed her weary soul. She wished she could stay. What had seemed like a semibarren countryside held promises of an abundance of foliage. Too bad she wouldn't be around to see it burst forth with life. Leaving hurt more than she imagined it could.

Dread coiled in her chest as the train station came into view and the wagon pulled alongside the platform.

Mr. Andrews helped them down.

"I want to check for a return telegram." Holly entered the smaller telegraph and post office building. "Did a telegram arrive for Holly Harrison?"

"Yes, ma'am." The telegraph operator dug through a pile of papers on his desk. He slid one from the others and handed it to her. "Vance has something for you at the station as well."

She tilted her head. "Who?"

"The train station manager."

She couldn't imagine what it could be. No one knew she was here. She left one building and entered the other.

"The gentleman next door said you had something for me, Holly Harrison." If she'd known the station manager's surname, she would have addressed him by it. How different life was here. So casual. Though it made her a little uncomfortable, it also made her feel free and. . .a little bit wild.

"Yes. Came two days ago on the train." He unlocked a door to a storage room.

Holly tugged off her gloves one finger at a time as she peered around the doorframe to see what he would bring back, but he disappeared behind a mountain of crates and barrels.

Ivy sidled up next to her. "Did you receive a telegram from Mr. and Mrs. Wadsworth?"

"Yes." Holly had almost forgotten in her curiosity to find out what had been sent to her. She unfolded the telegram. No NEED TO RETURN. HIRED NEW HELP. SENDING REST OF BELONGINGS ON NEXT TRAIN.

She blinked in disbelief. She couldn't have read it correctly, so she reread the cutting words.

Ivy snatched it from her feeble grasp. "We have no jobs to return to?"

Vance dragged a trunk out from the storage room.

Holly stared at it. The rest of her belongings. She waited for her heart to sink. But it didn't. It sat in her chest, waiting. But for what?

"What will we do?" Ivy asked.

Holly had no idea. She read the letter accompanying the trunk, an expanded version of the telegram that also wished her and Ivy well.

Nick came inside, bringing a rush of cold air with him. "I left your luggage on the platform."

Ivy held out the telegram. "We have no jobs."

He took the paper and perused it.

Ivy grabbed the letter from Holly and handed that to him as well. "We've been sacked."

"Ivy! Don't tell everyone our business." With dread hanging over her, Holly stared at the two pieces of paper.

"I'm not telling everyone. Just Mr. Andrews." Ivy waved her hand at the station manager. "And I'm sure he overheard. Hardly *everyone*."

Vance spoke up. "You still want those two tickets to Maryland?"

It would take the last of her money. "Yes." With a heavy heart Holly turned to her sister. "We can seek out new employment once we get home." How long would that take? And where would they live?

Mr. Andrews cleared his throat.

Holly swung her gaze to him.

He hesitated for only a moment. "You can continue to work at the ranch. Both of you. The men love your cooking."

Stay? Her heart danced. Though kind of him to offer, she couldn't. Could she? "Mr. Andrews, I appreciate all your help, truly I do. But we can't continue to take advantage of Mr. Coons's generosity."

"I wouldn't exactly call it generosity. He took advantage of your circumstances. Besides, he'll be fine with you two being hired on."

She had grown comfortable there and wanted to stay. They needed the work and the place to live. Working and living at the ranch solved their problems. And then there was Mr. Andrews. If they left, she would miss him. Just why, she didn't know. But it wouldn't be right to force themselves on poor Mr. Coons without permission first.

"I don't feel right about abusing his kindness." Holly wanted to say that she and Ivy would be fine and he shouldn't bother himself with them any longer, but she couldn't. Instead, she gazed into his blue eyes and wanted him to insist she—they stay.

"I can guarantee you'll be hired. Gil said he wished you would be cooking *all* the meals from now on."

She wanted to say yes for purely selfish reasons. She wished Mr. Coons were here to tell her so himself. It wasn't right imposing. Mr. Coons would likely say it was fine. But would it really be? She turned to Ivy to see what she wanted to do.

Ivy nodded. "I want to. I prefer working at the ranch rather than the big house back East."

Warmth swirled inside Holly at her sister's perfect answer. She took a deep breath and shifted her gaze back to tall, dark, and blue-eyes. "Very well. We accept." Lest she seem too eager, she hurried on. "But if I suspect for one moment that Mr. Coons has any doubts about our presence, we will take the next train east. And only until we secure other employment." But if they were truly welcome, she knew she wouldn't be looking.

The smile that broke on Mr. Andrews's face reminded her of Sonny's when the cowboy had given him a whole nickel.

She had hardly ever seen him smile. He didn't do it often, but when he did, it softened the hard lines of his face and made him appear younger. And happier.

Made her happy, too.

Chapter 5

Holly dipped her head in appreciation to Mr. Andrews, who held the train station door open for her and Ivy.

As though Holly's prior thought had conjured the boy, Sonny, bundled in a brown coat, sat perched on one of Ivy's large hard cases. His sandy-brown hair stuck up on his crown. He jumped down when Mr. Andrews backed out the doorway dragging the first of two trunks. "I kept both my eyes on your stuff, Mr. An. . .And. . ."

Mr. Andrews straightened. ". . .drews."

"Mr. Andrews. I knew it weren't Anderson. I seen you put them here and made sure no one taked them."

Holly suppressed a smile. The boy certainly was adorable, but his grammar could use a little attention.

He crossed to Sonny and stared down at him. "I'm sure you saw me drive into town and followed us over."

Oh dear. Holly hoped the tall cowboy wasn't purposely intimidating the boy for taking advantage of his previous generosity.

But Sonny held his ground and tipped his head way back. "Yes, sir. I figured you mighta needed help again."

"I bet you did." Mr. Andrews cocked a half smile at the industrious boy. "As circumstances would have it, I could use a little help. My rig's out front. You said you could drive a wagon."

"Yes, sir."

"Then bring it around to that end of the platform." Mr. Andrews pointed. "So I can load the trunks."

Sonny ran along the platform, jumped to the ground, then swung around. "Yes, sir." He ran off.

Had Mr. Andrews asked too much of the boy? Holly approached the cowboy. "Do you truly think the boy will be able to get the wagon where you want it?" To drive a conveyance was one thing. To position it in a precise place was quite another.

He shrugged. "Doesn't really matter. It'll be close enough."

That made Holly feel better. Mr. Andrews seemed to be an even-tempered man.

"Since you'll be staying on at the ranch, you must call me Nick."

"I prefer to stick with Mr. Andrews."

He thinned his lips. "I insist you call me Nick. Everyone on the ranch does. It will only confuse the men if you don't."

She didn't want to cross that line of informality. At least not yet. If she stuck with the formal, she could keep her feelings in check. Using Nick felt too familiar. "And *I* must insist that I use your proper name."

His lips pressed harder together then turned up into a playful smile.

A smile that sent her senses dancing.

He took a step closer to her. Too close for propriety. "The next time you call me *Mr. Andrews*, I think you'll wish you hadn't."

Was that a threat? But his droll smile said otherwise. "I can't imagine what you mean."

He took another step toward her. "Then let me make it perfectly clear. Each time you call me *Mr. Andrews*, I'll kiss you."

Her stomach flipped at his declaration. Stretching her eyes open wide, Holly stepped back. "You wouldn't dare. I—I know a bluff when I hear one."

He took another long stride toward her, catching the hem of her dress under his boot. "It's no bluff."

She pulled her skirt free and stumbled back against the side of the building. "Yes, it is." Her voice shook.

He planted a hand on the wall on either side of her head and leaned in. "It's a promise. Test me."

His warm breath fanned her face. He wouldn't dare. They were at the train station, for goodness' sake. Not that there was anyone about except Ivy, who apparently saw no need to offer her any assistance whatsoever. But Holly didn't have the confidence to *test* him. Mayhap he wasn't as even-tempered as she'd originally surmised. "Sonny's brought the wagon."

His smile widened. "Don't forget, it's *Nick*." He swaggered to the edge of the platform and jumped to the ground.

Ivy sidled up to Holly. "What was that about?"

"Nothing."

"It didn't look like nothing."

She would not embarrass herself further by explaining the incident to her sister.

Sonny had difficulty getting the vehicle close enough. Mr. An—Nick. . .*Andrews* patiently instructed the boy until he had the wagon backed up into place. *Mr. Andrews* put his palms on the floorboards and swung himself back up onto the platform. Sonny set the brake and clambered over the seat and across the wagon bed. With a big grin, he stood next to the cowboy and held out his hand.

Mr. Andrews dug into his pocket and dropped a coin into the boy's palm.

The boy's enthusiasm failed. "This ain't a nickel." He squinted at the coin. "Ain't even a penny. Just a ha'penny. Where's my nickel?"

"Did I say I'd pay you a nickel? Or anything at all?"

Holly couldn't believe this. He had to know the boy expected the same pay.

"But you gave me a nickel before."

The cowboy crouched. "Before you accept any job, make sure you settle on your wages first."

Sonny hung his head. "All right."

Holly was impressed that Mr. Andrews was teaching the boy good business sense. Sonny lifted one foot and swung it to turn himself around.

"Sonny?" Mr. Andrews said.

The boy's voice came out small as he glanced over his shoulder. "What?"

"I need help loading the ladies' luggage into the wagon."

Holly knew better. Mr. Andrews was more than capable of managing on his own.

"Yes, sir!" The lad hoisted one of the carpetbags with both hands.

Mr. Andrews folded his arms. "Sonny?"

"What?"

"Did you forget something?"

The boy thought a moment then shook his head.

"So, you're working for free?"

His little brown eyes widened to show the whites all the way around the irises. "How much you gonna pay me?"

"How much do you think this job is worth?"

Sonny eyed the luggage. "At least a nickel. Maybe even a whole dime."

Mr. Andrews chuckled. "I'll pay you a nickel." He held out his hand.

Shifting the carpetbag, the boy took one of his own off the handle and shook on the deal. Though the trunks were a bit of a struggle, he didn't complain. When finished, he accepted his wages and ran off.

Mr. Andrews turned to Holly and Ivy. "Let me reposition the rig so you can step directly to the seat."

That was thoughtful of him, even if his threat—promise—wasn't. She just wouldn't refer to him by any name at all. Then they'd both get what they wanted.

When the wagon was in place, he stood and stepped onto the platform. Ivy climbed aboard first, then Holly. "Thank you, M—" She'd almost used his name. His *proper* name.

Mr. Andrews gave her a wink and positioned himself back on the seat beside her. He snapped the reins, putting the wagon into motion.

Why hadn't she gone first so Ivy sat next to him?

A better question was, why had she refused so hardily to use his first name? Because, in the two and a half weeks she had known him, she had already developed feelings for the cowboy. He was charming when he wasn't trying to be obnoxious. He'd been respectful to her and Ivy. He'd been chivalrous. And he'd been protective. Not to mention his alluring smile, when he chose to show it, and his ravishingly handsome looks.

She surveyed him out of the corner of her eye. If she was too difficult, he might not find her appealing. And she decided she would very much like for him to find her appealing. Mayhap this was the Lord's plan all along. Who would have thought that Ivy's absurd notion to marry a stranger would turn into something Holly welcomed?

Three weeks ago she had no fanciful notions of romance, and now she could think of little else. She was making huge decisions based on it. Logic said to head back East.

But her heart said stay. It couldn't hurt to use his first name.

It was settled. She would call him Nick as he'd requested and see what became of it.

Ivy leaned forward to peer around Holly at him. "Mr. Andrews?"

"I insist you call me Nick."

Ivy tilted her head. "But we hardly know you. Are all people out West so informal?"

"If you mean do we call each other by our first names, then I suppose so."

"Very well then. Nick it is."

He cocked his head toward Holly. "See how easy that was."

She did and looked forward to picking the right opportunity.

"You had a question, *Ivy?*"

"Yes. Since we'll be staying on at the ranch indefinitely, will Mr. Coons continue to sleep in the bunkhouse? It was generous of him to give us the house, but I doubt he's comfortable out there. And certainly not for the long term."

Her sister had a good point. Holly added her opinion. "With both of us in the house, it wouldn't be improper for him to sleep under his own roof."

Mr. And—*Nick* gave them a sidelong glance. "About that. As you said, since you'll be at the ranch permanently—"

"Only if Mr. Coons agrees." Holly didn't want to be presumptuous.

"I feel as though I need to clear up a little misunderstanding. The ranch doesn't belong to Mr. Coons. It belongs to me."

Holly stilled her breath, not daring to breathe in or out. The ranch belonged to him? No. That couldn't be. "But you. . . ? You lied to us!"

"Technically, I only failed to correct your misconception. I never said he was the owner. You assumed that."

This was bad. Very bad. This would not do at all. Not if he was a ranch owner. "I can't believe you misled us that way."

Ivy spoke up. "What does it matter who owns the ranch? We have good work and a place to live."

It mattered a great deal. If she started calling him Nick now, he would think she was after him because he was a wealthy ranch owner. "That's why you offered us jobs. And why you kept guaranteeing we'd be hired and everything would be fine with the owner. Because *you* are the owner."

She should have known her romantic musings would be dashed. This hurt more than the thought of leaving had. It wasn't as though she were in love with the cowboy, but she did care for him far more than she'd realized.

If she had known he was the owner, she never would have let her emotions dally and go unchecked. She knew better than to think romantically about someone above her station. Just like with George Wadsworth, her previous employers' handsome and charming son. She knew nothing could come of fancying him, so she never allowed her heart to stray in that direction.

She would have to rein in her foolishness and put romantic notions of Nick—*Mr. Andrews* out of her head. Now and for good.

Nick couldn't figure Holly out. "I'm sorry. I was wrong to mislead you."

Holly nodded but didn't say anything.

Why did it upset her so that he owned the ranch? As Ivy had said, what did it matter who owns the ranch? But it *had* mattered to him. Wasn't that why he'd let them believe what wasn't true? He hadn't wanted either of the ladies to turn their affection toward him. He'd made a terrible mistake. Gil had said that no good would come of it.

"To answer your original question, I'll continue to sleep in the bunkhouse."

Holly straightened. "You can't do that. It's your home."

It wasn't really a *home*, just a house. A place to lay his head at night.

She went on. "Do you have a second bunkhouse or other outbuilding? Like an unused smokehouse or summer kitchen?"

What a ridiculous notion. "Even if I had such a place—which I don't—I'd never put you in it. I'll be fine out with the men."

"It's not proper. Turn the wagon around."

Nick knew why. "If you're thinking to catch that train, I'm afraid you'll miss it. Besides, I'm not about to take you back to the station. If my men knew I could have brought you back to cook for them and didn't, they would rebel."

"It's not right." Holly shifted on the seat. "Stop the wagon. I'll walk back to town."

"No, *you* won't. And no, *I* won't."

"What if I jump to the ground?"

She wouldn't dare. He couldn't let her go. He needed her to stay. No. The *ranch* needed her. He never should have threatened to kiss her. He didn't know why that notion had popped into his head or why he'd said it. But by the look on her face, it was drastic enough to get her to comply. So fortunately, he would never need to act on it.

He eyed her fancy dress. Well, at least fancy for these parts. "You are no more going to jump than my granny's going to rise from her grave."

Holly made sputtering sounds then fell silent. And stilled.

Good. She must realize she wasn't going to get her way.

Ivy spoke up. "Holly's right. It's not fair to you."

Not her, too.

Holly folded her arms. "It's just not right."

"We'll keep the arrangements as they are until I can figure something else out. Does that suit the two of you?"

Ivy nodded right away, but it took longer for Holly to agree. When he pulled to a stop at the ranch, Holly scrambled past her sister, leapt to the ground, and dashed inside the house.

Something inside him twisted at her ire toward him. She hadn't even waited for him to set the brake, which he did now. He wished he'd been up front from the beginning. But he'd had his reasons. Hopefully, she wouldn't insist on leaving. If she brought it up again, he would need to have a compelling argument prepared to convince her to stay. He needed her to stay.

For the ranch's sake. That was all.

Gil met the wagon and made it around the conveyance in time to help Ivy down.

Ivy left her hands on Gil's shoulders for a moment longer than necessary. "Thank you."

Was something brewing there? That could be to his advantage.

Nick wound the reins around the handle of the brake and jumped down. He spoke to Ivy. "Why don't you go on inside? We'll get the luggage."

After a lingering look at his foreman, she sashayed inside.

Gil cocked his thumb toward the house. "Did you forget why you went into town?"

"Nope. They received a telegram saying they no longer had employment back East. So I hired them permanently."

Gil's mouth kicked up into a crooked grin. "The men are going to like that."

The men? Gil liked that. And likely for more than just the prospect of good cooking.

"I can't figure Holly out." Nick circled to the tail end of the rig and lowered the hinged rear gate. "I told them the ranch was mine—I figured I should if they were going to be staying—and that seemed to upset her more than not having jobs to return to."

"Trying to figure out a woman is like trying to get an egg back into its shell. Just give up and make scrambled eggs." He pointed. "A trunk first?"

Nick nodded and grabbed the handle at one end. "That's no help."

This was proof that women were trouble. There was no pleasing them and no figuring out what went on in their pretty little heads.

But he'd like to know what Holly was thinking. Then he could fix whatever it was he'd done wrong. It had to be more than just not correcting her misunderstanding of his position at the ranch. Ivy accepted it readily enough. Why couldn't Holly?

Chapter 6

Holly stood in front of the two trunks Mr. Andrews and Mr. Coons deposited in her and Ivy's room.

When the last of their luggage had been brought in, Mr. Andrews said, "You both don't need to share this one room. You could each have your own."

"That's all right. We prefer to share." Holly smiled to assure him.

A deep V appeared between his eyebrows. He glanced at Ivy, who shrugged.

Good. Ivy hadn't contradicted her. She'd had Ivy as a roommate for as long as she could remember. Ivy, being four years younger, had always clung to Holly. So Ivy plotting to hop a train and head west without consulting Holly had been a shock. She would guess that it had been a bit of a surprise to Ivy as well. But her sister had been increasingly discontented with her life.

"Very well then. If the two of you want to share, far be it from me to separate you." Mr. Andrews gave her a nod and left.

Mr. Coons smiled at Ivy before he followed his boss.

Holly exhaled her half-held breath, glad she hadn't made a fool of herself by using Mr. Andrews's Christian name.

She couldn't imagine what Mrs. Wadsworth had found of Holly's to fill *two* trunks. Certainly all her belongings would have fit into one. It wasn't like there would be anything of Ivy's. She'd brought almost all her things with them on the train trip out, not having planned to return. Holly, on the other hand, *had* planned to return and brought very little. And look at her now. She'd agreed to stay in the home of a man she was growing increasingly fond of but could never have a future with.

But maybe she didn't have to stay. Ivy was a good enough cook to satisfy the men on the ranch. She didn't need Holly. Holly could look for work elsewhere, away from the likable, attractive ranch owner.

No. That would never do. She couldn't leave her sister on a ranch full of men without a chaperone.

Holly was stuck. Couldn't leave and couldn't take Ivy with her, because she'd promised to return and cook. She'd made a verbal agreement. Besides, she doubted her sister would ever agree to leave. Ivy loved it here already. It *was* beautiful country, and the work easier. Why would anyone want to leave? She certainly didn't. She should but was stuck here. At least for the time being.

She turned to Ivy. "You want to help me unpack?"

Her sister stood, staring at the doorway. "Um. . .I need to use the necessary. I'll be

39

right back. You start without me." She hurried from the room.

Holly shrugged. No reason to wait. They were her things, after all. So she unbuckled the first trunk and lifted the lid. Clothes. It was full of her clothes. She took out her dresses. They were fine dresses, castoffs from Mrs. Wadsworth. With alterations that Holly and her sister had done themselves, they fit beautifully and were finer than anything they could have afforded. Nothing in here she hadn't expected, and everything she had expected. What could possibly be in the other?

Unbuckling the straps, she opened the second trunk. Atop the fabric of unmentionables was a folded sheet of fine linen paper. Picking it up, she unfolded it. *A few things I don't have need of any longer to help you and Ivy start your new lives.*

Holly removed the items and laid them out on the beds. Four petticoats, two cotton and two wool. Two pairs of pantaloons. Two chemises. Two corsets. Two pairs of stockings. She divided the underclothes between the beds. Mrs. Wadsworth had made sure she and Ivy had equal shares. She'd always tried not to show favoritism with her staff. Tried a little too hard.

Nonetheless, this had been thoughtful of their former employer. Likely more of a guilt offering for dismissing them so readily than true selflessness or kindness. Though their employers were always considerate. And generous in their own sort of way. Not as equals, but as benevolent benefactors. They liked to give to the less fortunate as a show of how good they were.

Holly never minded receiving Mrs. Wadsworth's castoffs. They were always in like-new condition and of finer fabric than Holly or Ivy could ever afford.

She stared back into the trunk. A royal blue walking suit with a light blue blouse. This would look lovely on Ivy. She laid it out on her sister's bed. Next, a violet walking suit with a lilac blouse. She draped this one on her bed. Mrs. Wadsworth hadn't worn either of these suits in a couple of years. Holly and Ivy would put them to good use.

Gazing into the trunk again, she froze at the sight of the emerald-green taffeta gown. Ivy had cooed over this dress, vowing to one day have a gown such as this. Now she did. Holly lifted it by the shoulders and draped it across Ivy's bed. Her sister would be so pleased.

Turning back to the trunk for the final article of clothing, she caught her breath. The deep red velvet gown Holly had admired. She lifted it gingerly then held it up to herself and spun around. Then she studied herself in the small mirror above the washbasin.

Definitely guilt offerings. Mrs. Wadsworth apparently felt bad about dismissing them. More than likely, it had been *Mr.* Wadsworth who had insisted on their dismissal. He never liked to have his household disrupted, and Holly and Ivy leaving on a moment's notice would have been tantamount to chaos.

She and Ivy wouldn't have much opportunity to wear such fine clothes on a cattle ranch, but she appreciated them anyway and loved owning them. Ivy would, too.

Where *was* Ivy? A trip to the necessary shouldn't take this long.

Holly tucked the red velvet gown back into the bottom of the trunk and laid the green taffeta one on top of it to surprise Ivy. She closed the lid and trotted downstairs. When she didn't find her sister in the kitchen, she peered out the window.

Ivy stood by the corral snug in her coat, talking to Mr. Coons. The smiling man gazed at Ivy in a similar manner to the way George Wadsworth had looked at Holly. Only, less entitled, more captivated. This could not be good. She couldn't allow a romance to bud between her sister and the foreman. Her sister had shown that she wasn't in a state of mind to make good decisions. Wasn't her trip across the country proof enough of that?

Holly snagged a black canvas duster from the peg by the door and swung it on, holding the front closed, and stepped outside. "Ivy!" She waved her arm.

Her sister turned and gave her a brief scowl.

Holly motioned her to come to the house.

Ivy turned back to the foreman and smiled broadly then dipped her head in a coquettish manner before heading toward the house.

Not good at all.

Holly ducked back inside to wait. As she turned to remove the borrowed coat, she stopped short at Mr. Andrews standing in front of her. "I—uh—I'm sorry. I was just borrowing this."

"No need to apologize." He gave her a disarming smile that caused the air to catch in her lungs. "Glad to see you're making yourself at home."

She shucked off the duster and returned it to the peg. "I hope you don't think me too presumptuous." Though she didn't see a future in her staying, she also didn't want to be fired.

"Not at all."

How could this man stand there doing relatively *nothing* and cause her insides to twist and turn?

"I have to ask about the ride back here to the ranch. You seemed upset. I'm sorry I didn't tell you from the start that I owned the ranch."

She didn't know what to say. She didn't want to talk about why she'd been upset. And it wasn't because he owned the ranch. Well, in a way it was. It was because his station in life was now too far above hers for her to have any hope.

What could she say so he'd drop this conversation? For good. "Apology accepted."

"Then you're not mad at me?"

How could she be? "Certainly not."

His smile broadened as he ducked out the doorway a moment before Ivy stepped inside.

What had that look been for?

Ivy took off her coat. "Nick seems pleased. What did you say to him?"

Holly drew in a calming breath. "Nothing. You shouldn't be calling Mr. Andrews by his first name. He's our employer. It's not proper." And Holly couldn't call him by his last name without dire consequences.

"But he invited us to use his given name."

"It's still not proper. It confuses the lines between our stations."

"I suppose. Why'd you call me in?"

Because her sister had no business flirting with Mr. Coons. No. That hadn't been her original reason. What was it? Mr. Andrews had flustered her. The clothes. That was it. "I have something to show you." She led Ivy upstairs and, when they entered their room, made a flourish with her hand toward Ivy's bed. "Mrs. Wadsworth sent us some of her castoffs."

Ivy darted to her bed. "This is wonderful! It almost makes being dismissed from our jobs worth it."

Almost, but not quite. They wouldn't have been dismissed if not for her sister's ill-thought-out trip. But that didn't matter now. What was done was done. Holly opened the trunk. "One more thing." She lifted the emerald gown. This *would* make it worth it to her sister.

Ivy gasped, caught the gown up in her arms, and twirled around. "I can't believe she gave this to us."

"That one's for you. I have the red one." Holly held the other up to herself.

"We'll look so beautiful in these. Wherever will we wear them?"

Out here? No place. But the gesture was nice. "We'll have to alter everything." Mrs. Wadsworth had been a bigger woman than either of them.

Holly gazed at herself in the small mirror. What would Nick—Mr. Andrews think of her in this? Would she ever have an opportunity to find out?

Holly looked up from sewing a patch on a pair of trousers for one of the men. "Where are you going?"

Ivy swung on her coat. "Gil is going to show me how he ropes a cow."

"Gil?"

"Mr. Coons."

"I know who Gil is. You shouldn't be using his first name. It might give him ideas."

Ivy's mouth twitched up on the corners. "I hope so." She sashayed off.

"You did not just say that," Holly muttered to her sister who was no longer there. How unseemly for Ivy to be chasing after a man. Holly set the mending aside, donned her coat, and went outside.

Her sister was nowhere to be seen, so she approached the corral where Mr. Andrews and his other ranch hands stood with a horse. They all seemed interested in the horse's back hoof and leg.

Holly cleared her throat with an "Uh-hum. Excuse me."

The men turned at the same time.

Mr. Andrews said something to the others and broke away, then came outside the corral to where she stood. "What can I do for you?"

"I'm looking for my sister. She said she was going to watch your foreman rope a cow."

"He's one of the best. She won't be disappointed."

"That's not what I mean. Where are they? I don't see them."

"Off to find some cattle."

Infuriating. "My sister should not be traipsing around with him."

"She's perfectly safe. If any harm comes to her, he'll have me to answer to."

He had no sense of decorum. A lady alone with a man to who knew where? Just being alone with him could ruin her reputation.

"Tell me where they've gone, and I'll go get her."

He dipped his head to one side. "I don't think so." He walked back to the gate.

Even more infuriating. She stomped her foot. "Mr. Andrews!"

He spun back around.

"I'm not finished speaking with you."

His mouth twisted up into a knowing smile, and he closed the gap between them, standing far too close. "Yes?"

What had she said to put that mischievous grin on his face? She'd only called him by his— *Oh dear.* "I—I mean. . ."

He wouldn't dare. But he looked as though he would. In front of his men?

She turned to flee.

Before she could escape, he placed his hands on the corral railing on either side of her, preventing her departure.

She tried to duck under his arm.

He moved his hand down. "I told you to call me Nick."

Trapped. Until now, she'd been avoiding calling him anything at all. But he'd been so vexing she'd forgotten. "I'm sorry. I didn't mean it."

He stared at her for a long moment. "I'll let it pass this time. But next time? I'll have that kiss." He left with a satisfied grin.

She hurried to the house before he could change his mind. Once inside the kitchen, she leaned against the closed door. She'd escaped. He hadn't kissed her. She thought about that a moment. Why not?

Disappointment settled inside her.

She pictured him hovering over her, poised to make good on his promise.

What would it have been like to be kissed by the cowboy?

Chapter 7

Holly watched time march by, as November ended in another flurry of snow. Was that a precursor of things to come, both with the weather and turmoil in her life? But December dawned sunny though chilly. By mid-December, Holly wondered if any snow would return in time for Christmas.

Ivy smiled often these days. Mostly at Mr. Coons. Holly wanted to intervene, but her sister was so happy. Happier than she'd been since before their parents had died seven years ago. She would hate to spoil Ivy's pleasure. Maybe Ivy could get a happy ending. If so, then maybe Holly could go someplace else and find one of her own. With someone who wasn't out of her reach.

She stared out the kitchen window at Ivy standing with Mr. Coons. He held a saddled horse by the reins. Her sister was smiling at him. She *was* happy. Truly happy. Not the fake smile all the servants would put on for their employers.

Holly wasn't sure how she felt about whatever was developing between her sister and the foreman that caused Ivy to smile so. Would Holly get a chance to smile like that?

She watched Mr. Andrews every chance she got. Out the kitchen window. Across the supper table. From the front porch. Anytime she could go undetected.

Stop looking for him.

Stop thinking about him.

Stop dreaming of a life with him.

He's out of reach. Why couldn't she convince her heart of that? Her feelings, of their own accord, kept growing for him. But nothing could ever come of them.

She shifted her gaze to Nick—or rather, Mr. Andrews—as he worked with one of his new horses. He trotted the horse around the corral in a circle.

This was where Holly found herself most days, in the kitchen, alone and separated, staring out at everyone else living life while she waited for some point in the future to start her own.

But just because she needed Ivy to be settled first didn't mean she had to be alone. Pretending to be busy. Oh, she could come up with enough to keep herself busy in the kitchen, but a lot of it wasn't necessary. Back East, she spent all her time in a hot, gloomy basement kitchen. She didn't need to here. So she wrapped a shawl over her head and swung on her coat. Then she stepped outside.

Disappointingly, Mr. Andrews no longer worked a horse in the corral. Ivy and Mr. Coons stood there instead with the saddled horse. The three ranch hands sat on top of the corral railing, watching. Ivy stroked the horse's neck.

Holly approached the enclosure. What were her sister and the foreman up to? "What are you doing?"

Ivy turned with a beaming smile. "Gil's going to teach me to ride a horse."

"You're kidding, right?"

Mr. Coons looked Holly straight in the eyes. "I'll make sure she's safe. Cookie's a real gentle horse."

"But that's not a sidesaddle. How is she supposed to sit on it?"

"Astride." He said it so calmly, like the fact was a given.

"I don't think so. Ladies do *not* sit astride."

From behind Holly came Nick's voice. "On a ranch they do. We'll have to get the pair of you riding skirts."

Holly spun around to counter his declarations, but the words caught in her throat at the sight of him and a second saddled horse. She had a sinking feeling, and her stomach twisted. "Wh–what's that for?" She pointed at the horse.

"You."

She shook her head too vehemently in short jerking motions. "I'm not learning to ride a horse."

He gave her a disarming smile. "You don't know when you might need to ride. I hope you never need to, but I want you prepared just in case."

Holly shook her head again. "No, thank you."

Nick opened the corral gate and walked the horse in. "You don't have to be afraid. Ranger is very cooperative."

"I'm not afraid." But she was, a little. "I just don't see the need. I have things to do in the kitchen."

Nick held out his hand palm up. "Do you trust me?"

Trust him? It scared her how much she *did* trust him. She didn't know if that was the wisest thing. Of its own volition, her gloved hand lifted and rested in his. She followed him into the corral.

He closed the gate behind her.

She would *not* be riding a horse. Ranger, Cookie, or any other one.

She shifted her gaze to her sister and Mr. Coons, who bent down, locking his fingers together. Ivy placed her foot into his cupped hands.

Holly took a step forward. "Ivy."

Nick spoke softly near her ear. "She'll be fine." His warm breath fanned Holly's cheek.

She hadn't realized he was so close and shivered at his nearness, but at the same time she felt comforted. If he was near, she was safe. And Ivy was safe.

Ivy put her free foot into the stirrup. Mr. Coons steadied her and helped her swing up into the saddle. Her skirt hem rode up to her calf, showing her boot and black stocking.

How unseemly.

Holly started toward her sister to see what she could do to rectify the situation. But she stopped at the gentle grip on her arm. Not strong enough to hold her back if she wanted to pull free. But she stayed put.

Mr. Coons gave Ivy the reins, and then he took hold of the bridle and walked the horse around the edge of the corral.

"Look, Holly. I'm riding a horse."

Her sister's eagerness encouraged Holly.

Nick pulled the other horse in front of Holly. "Now it's your turn."

She stared straight at the horse's mouth and tipped her head back a little. "I—I. . ."

"You'll be fine." Nick stroked the horse's nose. "This is Ranger. Ranger, this pretty lady is Holly."

The horse bobbed his head and made a sputtering noise.

Holly stepped back. She didn't mind horses in front of a wagon or carriage, but not up this close. And certainly not to ride upon.

Ranger stretched out his neck toward her.

Holly went rigid, squeezing her eyes shut.

Something soft and warm tapped her shoulder and then rested there.

She pried one eye open and looked sideways into the horse's jaw. "What is he doing?"

Nick gave a slight, muffled chuckle. "He likes you."

She didn't think so. "But why does he have to be so close and touching me?"

"To show you that he means you no harm."

A hand wrapped around hers and then raised it to pet the horse on the opposite side of his face. "Tell him, 'Good boy.'"

"Good boy." Surprisingly, her voice *didn't* shake.

Ranger removed his chin from her shoulder and turned sideways as though inviting her to climb up.

Nick laced his fingers together as Mr. Coons had done.

Seeing no way out of this, Holly took a deep breath. She put her boot on the offered step, gripped the front and back of the saddle, and straightened to a stand.

"Wait. Come back down."

She did. Was she going to be spared this embarrassment? "What's wrong?"

He shucked out of his black canvas duster. "Give me your coat. The back split isn't long enough to hang on both sides of the saddle. Use mine."

"I can't take your coat. You'll get cold."

"I'm fine."

She removed her coat, and he held his out to her. She slipped her arms into the sleeves, and his warmth enveloped her.

As she buttoned it up, he draped her coat over the corral fence. Then he returned and held his hands together.

She took a deep breath. She could do this. She stepped up and swung her leg over as instructed. Once seated, she leaned forward to pull the hem of her skirt down but couldn't reach far enough. *Ignore the impropriety.*

Nick handed her the reins. "Ranger has a bit more spirit than Cookie does. Cookie wouldn't run if her tail were on fire."

"What? Is this horse going to run off with me on him?"

"No. He won't run unless you tell him to."

"What if I accidentally tell him to?" She had no idea how to direct a horse.

"You won't. Relax."

"I can't relax way up here. What if I fall off?"

"You won't. You're doing fine." He guided Ranger around the ring the way Mr. Coons was doing with Cookie.

This wasn't so bad. It was good to know Ivy had the safer horse.

Mr. Andrews gave her some instructions on steering the horse on her own and let go of the halter.

She sucked in a breath, waiting for the horse to bolt or rear. But Ranger just plodded along the perimeter of the ring.

"You're doing well. Keep directing him along the fence."

Doing well? She hadn't tugged either direction on the reins. Afraid to. Ranger was walking on his own. She suspected he would keep on this way without any guidance from her. But she decided to test her theory. She was up here to learn to ride a horse, after all. So she jerked the reins toward the middle of the ring.

Ranger turned and cut across the enclosure toward the gate.

Without the fence right next to her, she felt off balance, like being on a cliff's edge with nothing to hold on to. "What's he doing?"

"What you told him to do. Turn."

"I didn't want him to turn that much. How do I stop him?"

"Ease back on the reins and say whoa."

She did as instructed, but Ranger moseyed over to the closed gate before obeying and stretched his neck over the top of it. He stopped then only because he couldn't go any farther. "I think he wants to go back to the barn."

"Well, he can't."

"I don't mind stopping. This was actually kind of fun."

"If he goes to the barn now, he'll know he doesn't have to obey you. He needs to know you're in charge. Move the reins to one side, put pressure on his sides with your legs, and click your tongue like this." He made a clicking sound out of the side of his mouth.

That made sense, and she did as he directed.

The horse didn't move.

"Do the same thing but give him a gentle kick with your heels. Not hard, more of a tap."

She did.

Ranger bobbed his head but stayed rooted in place.

"Again."

On the third try, Ranger blew out hard from his nostrils and reluctantly lumbered around the ring. She could swear the horse gave Nick a dirty look.

There was something empowering about controlling an animal so much larger than herself.

After she'd gone three more times around the ring, Nick told her to stop Ranger on the far side of the corral.

She did. "Why over here and not by the gate?"

"So he knows you're getting off by choice and not because he wants you to." Nick clasped her waist and lowered her slowly, as though she weighed no more than a down pillow. Once she was on the ground, he didn't remove his hands for a moment.

If not for her corset—and his duster—she might be able to feel the warmth from his hands. As it was, heat rose up her body and set her face afire. She stepped back, out of his hold. "Is Mr. Coons your partner?" Why had she asked that? Because this man in front of her flustered her.

Nick chuckled, low and warm. "Unfortunately not."

"I don't understand. You treat him more like your partner than a simple ranch hand like the others—I'm sorry. You don't have to answer that. It's none of my business."

"It's not mine to say why he's not my partner. You'll have to ask him if you want an answer to that question."

She couldn't do that. The fact Nick wouldn't tell her told her it was a personal matter. So therefore, none of her business.

Mr. Coons helped Ivy down and led her horse out of the corral with Ivy by his side.

Nick spoke as Mr. Coons walked by. "Gil. Holly wants to know why you aren't my partner."

Holly widened her eyes. "No. I don't. It's none of my business."

Mr. Coons gave Nick a black look and kept walking.

When he and Ivy were well into the barn, Holly turned on Nick. "Why did you do that? You said yourself it wasn't yours to tell. Did you think forcing him would make it all right?"

She had overstepped the boundaries as the hired help but didn't care. She wouldn't have thought him the kind of person to do something like that. She shook her head and walked away.

He caught her arm and stepped around in front of her. "I'm sorry. You're right. I was out of line. I just get fed up with him punishing himself for something that wasn't his fault. Forgive me?"

He seemed genuinely contrite.

She nodded. "But I'm not the one who deserves an apology."

"I'll speak to him as soon as I'm sure you're not mad at me."

She gave him a half smile. "Go." She wasn't sure if she could ever be truly mad at him. He smiled back and headed into the barn.

Now she was more curious than ever about what had transpired between these two friends to cause one to feel so inferior to the other. She had seen nothing on Nick's part that hinted he treated Mr. Coons as an inferior. Quite the opposite.

And that Nick wouldn't tell his friend's secret told her a lot about his character. Character that would make a good husband.

She stomped her foot in the hard dirt and spoke under her breath. "Oh, stop thinking of him that way."

"What did you say?" Ivy came up beside her.

"Nothing."

Ivy pursed her lips. "Before you ask. . .no, he didn't tell me. He offered to, but I turned him down."

"I wasn't going to. I only asked Mr. Andrews in confidence, not expecting an answer. I would never embarrass Mr. Coons by posing a question like that in front of others." But that Ivy had refused the information told Holly how much her sister trusted the man. Was that good or not?

Chapter 8

On the day before Christmas Eve, Holly found herself in the kitchen with no one but Nick. She liked thinking of him by his Christian name. But she used Mr. Andrews when she spoke to Ivy, Mr. Coons, and any of the ranch hands. She was playing a dangerous game with herself. But no one would be the wiser.

In the two weeks since the near kiss, Holly had thought of little else. She couldn't stand not knowing any longer. She'd finally accepted the fact that she *wanted* to be kissed by Nick. She couldn't believe it herself. Ivy was out getting another riding lesson from Mr. Coons, and Nick was sitting at the table with his third cup of coffee.

Why hadn't he left already? It didn't matter. It was fortuitous that he still sat here and no one else.

Now what could she say so it sounded natural for her to use his name?

He stood and took his empty cup to the sink then headed for the door.

In truth, she didn't need to have anything real to say, just get his attention. "Mr. Andrews? No, I mean Nick."

He turned slowly with a smug expression. "What did you call me?"

"Nothing. I didn't call you anything." But she knew he'd heard her. "Never mind. Go on."

"You called me Mr. Andrews. You know what that means."

She did. And she wanted to stand there and wait for him to kiss her, but she needed him to believe that her calling him Mr. Andrews was a mistake, so she backed up. "I—I—I—"

He closed the gap between them in two strides.

"You don't have to do this." But her plea sounded weak even to herself.

"I'm a man of my word. I *always* keep my promises."

Suddenly wishing to change her mind, she squeaked out, "Always?"

Now just inches from her. "Always." He cupped her face and lowered his lips to hers. Not as she'd imagined. Instead of hard and demanding, his lips were warm and soft. But he didn't stop at a quick peck. The kiss lingered.

She should push him away. A good girl *would* push him away. But a *good girl* also wouldn't be rude, so she leaned into him. This was better than she ever could have imagined.

At last he drew back and stared at her a long moment. His breathing ragged. His words came out low and husky. "Let that be a lesson to you."

She nodded mutely. *Much* better than she'd imagined.

He didn't turn to leave. He just stared at her and looked as though he might kiss her again. He cleared his throat. "A lesson."

It had been a lesson all right, but not the one he'd thought he was giving. What she learned wasn't to call him Nick but to eagerly anticipate his next kiss.

"A lesson," he said with less confidence than the last time.

He leaned toward her then straightened abruptly and headed for the door. His shoulder banged against the frame.

"Oh!" she exclaimed.

But he didn't turn and staggered a bit as he pushed his way outside.

Disappointment settled upon her. Disappointed he'd left. Disappointed he hadn't kissed her again.

And disappointed she wouldn't be able to call him Mr. Andrews again without him knowing it was on purpose.

Nick gripped the corral railing to pull himself together. What was he thinking? He kicked the post. He'd kissed Holly. He never should have threatened to kiss her. What would happen now? He should have known she would test him. He wouldn't have kissed her if not for the threat. He'd *had* to make good on it, or else she'd never believe anything he said. She'd take all his words as a pack of lies. If one thing could be said about him, it was that he was a man of his word.

"What has your chaps in a wad?" Gil said.

"What? Nothing. I'm fine."

Gil shook his head. "You look like an old cowhide left out in the rain and trampled by a herd of your own cattle. Only one thing can put a look like that on a man's face."

Nick narrowed his eyes, ordering his foreman not to finish the thought.

"A woman. You got it bad for Holly, don't you?"

"No. I don't." Nick knew better than to fall for a woman. He never should have invited her to stay. She was too dangerous to him. Trouble. She was a woman and nothing but trouble. He needed to stay clear of her from now on, or he'd be a goner. She was too tempting. And now that he'd tasted her sweet lips, the temptation would be all the greater.

Gil clamped a hand on his shoulder. "Not every woman is like Petunia."

Why'd he have to bring *her* up? Nick's fiancée had left him for another man. And then there was his mother who had run out on him and his father when he was just a lad. But he wasn't the only one to experience hurt from a woman.

Nick gave his friend a straight look. "I wouldn't expect you, of all people, to think highly of women. What about your Nelly?" Gil's wife had left him and then died of consumption.

His foreman's eyes narrowed at the subject they both avoided. "Nelly had her faults, but I still loved her. I'd take the heartache again to have all the good we had before she got restless. She just couldn't cope after losing all those babies before they were born."

Nick didn't understand how Gil could accept the betrayal. It hadn't been easy at first, but he'd seemed to have settled the issue within himself. Still, Nick didn't anticipate Gil ever marrying again even though he was still young.

"Just the same," Nick said, "I think I'll spare myself the heartache."

Gil guffawed. "I think you missed that train."

Nick ached for Holly to be different from the other women who'd ever entered his life. And left. But how would he know until. . .she betrayed him? "Women can't be trusted. Not one of them."

"Not true."

He'd never thought Gil to be delusional. "Then how can you tell which women can be trusted and which can't?"

Gil shook his head. "Can't know who can and who can't. Women *or* men."

"Not true. I can trust you. I trust you with my life."

Gil smiled. "It's much easier to trust someone with your life than with your heart. If you put your life in someone else's hands and they let you down, you go home to be with the Lord. But if you give someone your heart and they let you down, the pain lives inside you the rest of your days."

The truth of that settled firmly inside Nick. "So how do you reconcile a heart betrayal? You've obviously come to terms with all Nelly put you through."

"How? God."

"So you've forgiven her?"

"Had to. If you forgive those who sin against you, your heavenly Father will forgive you."

"But how?" His mother abandoned him. So did Petunia.

"With God's strength. We as human beings are incapable of true forgiveness. It's only with God's grace we can forgive. 'Forgive us our debts as we forgive our debtors.'"

Nick always skimmed over the second part. Not wanting to give it much thought. "But they don't deserve forgiveness." Not Nelly. Not his mother. And not Petunia.

"None of us do. It's not about the person receiving the forgiveness, but the person giving forgiveness. It's not about the other person's worthiness of being forgiven. It's about the one who forgives letting go of the bitterness, resentment, spite, hostility, anger. All those things poison the soul and make you miserable. God loves Nelly the same as He loves me. And He loves Petunia as much as you."

"If I forgive her, won't that be the same as condoning her actions?"

"Jesus died on the cross for our sins and forgave the very men who drove nails into His flesh. Do you think He condoned their actions?"

"Of course not."

"Put your trust in God, not people. Trust He will turn everything for His good."

"How did you get so smart?"

Gil took a deep breath. "Spent many sleepless nights after Nelly left wrestling with God. When I finally let her go and gave her over to Him, He freed me. I certainly do appreciate you not firing me when you should have for my poor behavior and irresponsibility."

Nick had seen the change in his friend. He'd been angry and hostile after Nelly left.

Then one day, he had a peace about him. Nick had understood the pain inside Gil that fueled his actions. Gil's pain had come out with loud words and broken chairs. Nick kept his tucked inside to fester.

He longed for the kind of peace Gil had from letting his pain go. "Thanks. You've given me a lot to think about."

After saddling Ranger, Nick rode out across his land.

He stopped by a pond where several dozen of his Black Angus drank and grazed. He had so much. But what was the good in having an abundance with no one to share it with? Did he truly want to arrive at the end of his life alone? That was part of what Petunia and his mother had taken from him. They'd sentenced him to be alone. Taken his trust.

But God was trustworthy.

Still in the saddle, he tipped his head back and gazed into the blue sky. "Lord, I think I'm finally ready to forgive them, but I don't know how. I feel as though I can never truly love others while I still hate *them*." And he wanted to have the capacity to love Holly.

"Cast thy burden upon the LORD, *and he shall sustain thee."*

Psalm 55:22—Nick hadn't recalled that verse in years. His father had muttered it over and over to himself after Mother had left.

With the reins laced through the fingers of one hand, he opened them both, palms up. "Take them. I give You my mother and Petunia. I give you my hurt and my bitterness and my anger."

Like a festering wound being lanced and drained, first came a sharp pain, then relief. His whole body relaxed in the saddle.

But now that the tremendous weight had been lifted, he didn't know where to focus his attention. There was an emptiness inside him where all that hate had been.

"Let Me fill it with love."

"Yes, Lord."

Warmth and peace and happiness flooded him.

He rode back to the barn to stable his horse.

Nick put a hand on his friend's shoulder and gave him a nod.

Gil nodded back. "The storm's past?"

"I'd say so." Nick felt free from chains he'd shackled himself with.

"Glad to hear. I meant to ask you something earlier. Are they going?"

"Who? Where?" His friend had obviously jumped a fence into a different field.

"The ladies. To the Christmas Eve service and social."

"I assume so. We all go. It's part of being on my ranch."

"Do they know that?"

Again, he had assumed but hadn't said anything to them. "I'll go let them know right now." It gave him an excuse to see Holly. He strode into the house through the kitchen door.

Both women sat at the table peeling apples. And when he entered, both went silent and gave each other strange looks.

"Am I interrupting something?"

Holly shook her head, her cheeks red. "No. We were just peeling apples for pies."

She remembered their kiss. "Mmm. The men will like that." He would like that.

Her face pinched into a sour expression. "The men?"

"Of course." He suspected he might have been given a hint of some sort but evidently hadn't caught it. If women wanted men to know something, they should just come right out and say what they mean. He wouldn't worry about that now. "I came in to tell you that we all go to church on Christmas Eve for the service and social. I expect the two of you to go as well."

"Social?" Ivy's eyebrows rose.

"Yes, ma'am. It's all in the afternoon so as folks can get home before dark."

Holly and Ivy exchanged looks again, and Holly said, "Dresses?"

Ivy echoed. "Dresses."

They both stood and dashed out of the kitchen.

He glanced at the half-peeled fruit. "What about the pies?"

Holly called back to him. "No time right now. They can wait."

What had he said to make them run off like that? Did that mean they agreed to go or not? There was no figuring out women. He'd told them they were expected to go, so he would assume they understood and were going.

Chapter 9

B etween the rest of that day and the following morning, Holly made a chocolate cake with frosting while Ivy made two extra pies to take to the social. And they altered their gowns.

Holly dressed and helped her sister fasten up the back then turned to have Ivy do the same for her. Then she faced her sister to ask if she looked all right. But instead, she sucked in a breath at the sight of her sister. "You look beautiful."

"So do you. And just so you know, I'm glad I accepted Mr. Bosco's proposal so that we could be here on this one day."

Holly was glad as well.

Nick called up the stairs. "You ladies ready?"

She could hear the impatience in his voice. He evidently wasn't used to waiting for ladies to get ready. "We're coming down now." She let Ivy lead the way.

Nick and Gil stood at the bottom of the rugged stairs.

Gil smiled broadly. "Now, you were well worth waiting for." He stepped forward and took Ivy's hand. "You look beautiful."

"You think so? You really think so?"

"Most definitely." He held out her coat for her.

Holly had waited at the top for her sister to descend and now went down herself.

Nick stared up at her with an unpleasant expression as though she were wearing rags.

She couldn't look that bad. "Well? Aren't you going to say something?" At this point, any words would be good. Even *nice*.

"I—I. . .don't know what to say."

Gil jabbed him with his elbow. "Tell her how pretty she looks."

Nick cleared his throat. "You look pretty."

Though he was just echoing what Gil told him to say, it was better than his silence.

He held her coat open for her. "Very, *very* pretty." Now that had come from him, from his heart, and calmed her fluttering insides.

She released her captive breath and slipped her arms into the sleeves.

Outside on the porch, Holly stopped short next to her sister. She stared at the muddy ground and sighed. They had been plagued with rain this morning.

Nick cupped her elbow. "What's wrong?"

"I'd hoped for snow rather than mud."

"My shoes will get ruined." Ivy poked the toe of her slipper out from under her hem.

A moment later, Mr. Coons scooped Ivy up into his arms. "I'd never let that happen."

Ivy gave a small squeal of delight and then giggled as he carried her to the waiting buggy and set her safely inside.

Nick approached Holly.

She stepped back. "You don't have to—I don't expect—the mud's not that bad."

He leaned in close and whispered, "I can't let my foreman show me up." Then without hesitation, he hooked one arm behind her knees and lifted her into his arms.

She should protest, even though it wouldn't do any good. Instead, she rested her arms on his shoulders. Strong, broad shoulders. "This wasn't necessary."

"I disagree. My honor was at stake."

Hmm. Honor? Maybe that meant he wanted to carry her as Mr. Coons had wanted to carry Ivy and needed an excuse. He placed her gently in the back of the buggy. Ivy already occupied the front seat with Mr. Coons at the reins.

She turned to Nick. "Aren't you going to drive?"

He shook his head. "Gil's got it." He settled in next to her and covered their laps with a blanket.

Holly had assumed she and Ivy would occupy the back while the men sat up front. "What about the other men on the ranch?"

"They went on ahead in the wagon."

On the journey into town, Holly felt emboldened. "What's your favorite part of Christmas?"

Nick was silent for a while. Would he answer her question? She knew he heard her. Maybe she shouldn't have asked. She would be content with the silence. "You don't have to answer. I was just curious."

"I'll answer. I was just thinking. When I was young, my favorite holiday was Christmas. Everyone was happy. Jesus came as a baby to take away the sins of man and, in doing so, gave us the greatest gift of all. A place with Him in heaven."

His answer touched her heart.

He went on, quoting 2 Corinthians chapter 9: " 'Thanks be unto God for his unspeakable gift' " (v. 15).

God had bestowed on her this gift of a different life from the drudgery she'd been living so short a time ago.

"And what about you? What's your favorite part of Christmas?"

Before his answer, she would have said an occasion to wear this fine dress. "I used to think it was all the festivities. But none of this would be possible without an occasion to celebrate. I agree with you. 'Thanks be unto God for his unspeakable gift.' " And what a gift she'd been given in a life now filled with hope instead of grimness. She hadn't even realized she'd been yearning for something different. She'd thought she was content in her circumstances. But she hadn't been. Her heart had been calling out, and God answered.

Awhile later, Mr. Coons pulled up to the front of the church and set the brake. "I'll let the three of you out here, and I'll go park the buggy and unhitch the horse."

Ivy leaned a little closer to him. "I'll keep you company."

The smile he bestowed on her sister warmed Holly's heart. But at the same time unsettled her. Had whatever was going on between Ivy and Mr. Coons become serious? Maybe she should put an end to it. How had she not realized? Because she spent too much time watching Nick and being careful not to use either of his names. She would need to think on just what to do, both about Nick and about Ivy's budding romance with the foreman. Was there something to stop? She didn't want her sister rushing into something again like with Mr. Bosco and his three letters.

She took Nick's offered assistance out of the buggy. "Thank you."

Boards had been laid out so no one had to walk in the mud.

Instead of releasing her hand, he tucked it into the crook of his elbow to guide her inside.

Dare she allow herself to enjoy his nearness? Hope for more than the Lord had already given her? It was Christmas Eve after all. A time of possibilities. "What about the desserts?"

He hesitated before releasing her. He carried a pie in each hand while she carried the cake.

Once inside, a pair of ladies took the pies and cake.

Nick hung Holly's coat with his own on a wooden peg.

A silver-haired lady, who looked to be in her eighties, approached. "Howdy-do, Nicolas. Who's your lady friend?"

"Mrs. Ivan Deny, this is Holly Harrison, new cook at my ranch."

Mrs. Deny openly sized up Holly. "Cook, huh?"

Being in service, Holly was used to being assessed by others. "Yes, ma'am."

"Keep a man's belly fed and you keep him happy." Mrs. Deny winked. "You must call me Pru. Ivan's been gone for twenty-five years." She patted Nick's chest. "That goes for you, too. Now I need the two of you to step to the left. Good, good. Now a step back." Her wrinkled face glowed with a smile, and she looked twenty years younger. "Perfect." She pointed above them. "Mistletoe."

Crafty old woman.

Nick gazed down at Holly. "She went to an awful lot of trouble to get us to stand in just the right place."

It wasn't that much trouble. "I suppose she did." Again she could protest but didn't. People expected couples to kiss in public. It was acceptable. Not that she and Nick were a couple. But she could pretend—just for today.

Nick leaned down and pressed his lips to hers. He lingered a little longer than necessary but not so long as to be indecent. As enjoyable as his other kiss.

Next, the old woman maneuvered Ivy and Mr. Coons under the mistletoe. Apparently, Pru had taken it upon herself to see to it that the mistletoe didn't go to waste.

The lovely service in this quaint little church refreshed Holly. So different from the huge East Coast church she went to. And now, all the food that people had brought was laid out on the tables at the edges of the room.

Three men moved to the front of the space, one with a violin, one a mouth harp, and the third a guitar. They played tunes and couples danced.

Gil bowed in front of Ivy. "May I?"

Ivy giggled and took his offered hand. She giggled a lot lately in Mr. Coons's presence.

Eight-year-old little Sonny swaggered up to Holly. His normally disheveled hair was combed down in place with bear grease keeping it tamed, and he wore a nice pair of brown trousers with a clean white shirt and a tan vest. "May I have this dance?" He spoke with all the decorum of any East Coast gentleman. His aunt must have coached him.

"Hey," Nick said.

Sonny put his fists on his hips. "I asked first." Before Nick could protest further, Sonny latched on to Holly's hand and dragged her after him to the middle of the room. He held her hand with one of his and put the other on her waist. He didn't so much *dance* as totter back and forth.

Holly did her duty and followed his lead. "So which one of the young ladies are you trying to impress?" Several girls the boy's age and a little older stood in various places around the room.

Sonny tilted his head back to look up at her and squished up his face. "Girls? Blech. I'd rather eat a whole bar of Auntie Irene's lye soap before I'd touch a girl. And Auntie Irene's soap tastes really bad."

Didn't he realize Holly *was* a girl? Best not to make mention of it. "I thought perhaps you asked me to dance because you were trying to get a special young lady's attention and make her jealous."

Though he shook his head vigorously, not a greased hair on his head moved. "No way. Not me. I'm no fool. I want Mr. Andrews to know I'm a man, and iffin he's got more work, I can handle it."

Oh my. There was quite an industrious young man in this little boy.

When the dance was over, Sonny escorted her back to Nick, gave him a nod, then strutted off with his hands in his pockets.

Nick tilted his head toward her. "I think someone's sweet on you. Should I be jealous?"

Jealous? She knew Nick would never be jealous of a boy. And Sonny was harmless. But what if it had been a man who'd asked her to dance? Would he be jealous then? She could hope. But that would mean he cared for her. "He's not sweet on *me*. He was trying to impress *you*."

"Me? How could dancing with you impress me?"

"He thinks it will make you look at him as a man and you'll give him more work."

"Crafty little rascal. Have I created a cheeky little imp who's not going to leave me alone?"

"I don't think so. His aunt likely won't let him come all the way out to the ranch on his own. And when you're in town the next few times, you can let him know you don't have any work for him but you'll keep him in mind. That should satisfy him."

A man with a mustache so long it hung an inch below his chin stepped up to her. "May—"

"Sorry." Nick hooked Holly's arm. "I have the next dance." He walked her among the other couples. "You don't mind, do you?"

Well, that answered the jealous question, but that didn't mean he cared. But it gave her hope, even if he was above her station. "Not at all." She thrilled to dance with him.

He could be quite abrupt with other men but never with her. Well, except in the beginning when he thought she was a mail-order bride. For a cowboy, he could dance. And she liked being in his arms. She resisted the urge to lean into his chest and let his strong arms completely engulf her.

At the beginning of the next dance, Mr. Coons tapped Nick on the shoulder.

Not seeing who it was, Nick's face twisted into a scowl before he turned to face the intruder. But his face relaxed immediately upon seeing his foreman and Ivy.

Mr. Coons chuckled, presumably at his boss's sudden change in expression. "Shall we change partners for a dance?"

Nick didn't look as though he wanted to but nodded and took Ivy in the waltz pose.

Holly didn't like seeing him dancing with another woman. Even if that woman was her sister and he kept more distance between them than he had with her.

Mr. Coons clasped her hand in one of his and put his other on her waist. He, too, stood away from her as he moved her around the room. Another cowboy who could dance. "Don't worry. He has no interest in your sister."

"I know." How rude of her. She shifted her gaze to her now partner.

He smiled. "I'll get right to it, because I don't know how long he'll allow me to dance with you."

Get to it?

"Unless you have a male relative I can contact, I'd like to ask your permission to marry Ivy."

Her mouth dropped open. Definitely serious. Before she could order her thoughts and figure out actual words to say, he continued.

"I know I haven't known Ivy long, and you may not consider me worthy of your sister, but I love her. And if you won't give me permission now, I won't give up and will prove to you I'm worthy."

In half a minute, this man *had* convinced her with his earnest words. Not so much the words, but the conviction, respect, and love they were spoken with. But she did have one small niggling doubt. "I think you will make my sister very happy. . ."

He raised an eyebrow. "But?"

"But there's one thing. I can't figure out why a smart young man wouldn't become his best friend's partner when both men clearly want that."

He stiffened.

She hurriedly went on. "I'm not asking you to divulge your reason to me, I just want your assurance that whatever it is won't adversely affect my sister in any way. And your word will be good enough."

He stared down at her for a long moment.

If he wanted her permission, giving his word wasn't too much to ask. If he couldn't do that, how could she entrust her sister to this man? She realized they had stopped moving and stood at the edge of the dancing couples.

"I was married before. Nelly ran off and took a lot of money that belonged to the ranch and Nick. I turned over my share of the ranch to him to pay her—my debt. I don't have the money yet to buy back into the ranch."

"You're married?" How could he ask to marry her sister if he already had a wife?

"I searched and searched for her. By the time I found her, she was near death with consumption. She died in my arms."

"I'm so sorry for your loss." She wanted to ask why his wife had run off. If it was something he'd done. But she didn't need to. He'd paid his wife's debt and told Holly his very personal story.

"I didn't do anything to make Nelly leave, if that's what you're thinking."

"I know." Some people just weren't the settling-down type. Was Nick? He didn't seem to be.

"Nelly left because she couldn't carry a baby. She'd no sooner find out she was expecting than she'd lose it. Seven that I knew of before she took off. I told her it didn't matter. But each loss killed something inside her."

"The poor woman." How heartbreaking. After this woman left him and broke his heart, he still comforted her in death. "You have my permission."

A wide smile broke across his face, and he expelled a breath.

She hoped her sister hadn't been stringing Mr. Coons along. "But you shouldn't go into a marriage with a secret like this between you."

"I've told her. Later that day Nick brought it up. When he apologized, he suggested I should tell Ivy if I cared for her. So I did."

Holly was glad to hear that. Her sister hadn't given any hint that he'd told her something so personal. She hoped it hadn't silently soured Ivy toward him.

"So you can be assured I'll treat your sister well."

She spoke in a teasing tone. "If you don't, I'll send Mr. Andrews after you."

And as though speaking his name caused him to materialize, Nick was at her side. But it was Ivy who spoke. "What are you two talking about?"

Before Holly could give a noncommittal answer, Mr. Coons caught Ivy up in his arms and waltzed her away.

Her sister dancing with Mr. Coons warmed Holly's heart.

The big cowboy standing next to her warmed her all over.

Chapter 10

Nick watched Gil waltz Ivy away then turned his attention to the alluring woman standing next to him. He tried to mind his own business, but where Holly was concerned, she felt like *his* business. First she and Gil were dancing, then they stopped and appeared to be engaged in a serious discussion, then they were smiling, and then he heard his name, his formal name. Would the woman never capitulate? "What *were* the two of you talking about?"

"Oh no." Holly stared off toward the couples dancing. "No, no, no. He can't do this." She turned to Nick. "Stop him. This could turn out very bad."

"What are you talking about?"

She pointed to Gil and Ivy standing alone in the middle of the dance floor. No one danced. No music played. And all eyes were on the pair. "Not in public."

Gil lowered to one knee. The man with the violin pulled his bow across the strings and softly played a romantic tune.

Oh. Too late now to stop him. "Isn't this the kind of romantic thing pretty young ladies like?" Nick asked.

"What if she's not sure? What if she says no? Or worse, what if she says yes because of all the onlookers then tells him no later? To have one's heart lifted up on love's wings only to be dashed to the ground. . ."

He hadn't thought of that. "You don't think she'll say yes?"

"My sister can be fickle. She did travel across the country to marry a man she didn't know only to change her mind."

His friend had already been hurt badly by one woman. Nick prayed that wouldn't happen again.

As Gil retrieved a ring from his vest pocket, Holly sucked in a breath. And didn't release it.

Nick couldn't read Ivy's surprised expression. Happiness? Or dread? She appeared to know what Gil was doing but kept her answer hidden.

"Ivy Harrison, will you marry—"

"Yes." Ivy bounced up on her toes and held out her left hand, obviously excited about the proposal.

Holly expelled her breath.

"Is this what you and Gil were talking about?" Nick asked.

"He requested my permission, but I never thought he'd ask her here and now."

"It seems to have worked out."

She nodded, rushed forward, and hugged Ivy. "I can't believe my little sister is getting married."

Ivy appeared on the verge of tears and held out her ring hand. "Me either."

Why did women cry when they were happy? It only served to confuse men. *Are you happy? Or sad?* How was a man to tell?

As others in the room took their turns to congratulate the newly engaged couple, Nick maneuvered Holly off to the side away from the crowd. "So do you think it was a little fast? You've been here for only two months."

"I would think so, but their courtship wasn't like a normal one. They were around each other every day. So it's almost as though they were courting for three or four times as long."

He liked the sound of that. Gave him hope. "I know I'm a bit gruff, but I can be less ornery if I put my mind to it."

She faced him fully and stared up at him with a sweet expression. "Why is that? You seem to want to keep people away."

He did. . .until now. Now he regretted every cross word and surly look he'd ever thrown at her. "I was engaged once."

Her sweet expression fell. "Oh."

"She left me for another man. I've had a hard time trusting again."

"Both you and Mr. Coons had women walk out on you? How terrible."

So Gil had told her about Nelly. He could tell her about his mother, too, but that might be too much for one day. "I didn't tell you to get your sympathy. I told you so you might understand my behavior and know I'm working on changing. Being a better man with God's help. A man you might see in. . .well, a not too negative way."

"I've always looked upon you favorably."

He couldn't believe that. "Not on the train ride."

"Well, not at first. But when you were sitting with that nice elderly couple and explained the reason you sat near us was to keep disagreeable men away."

That was a polite way of describing it. "As I recall, I half yelled that in an irate tone."

"Exactly. You saw we needed a little help and offered it even when you didn't have to. And probably didn't want to. Then you said something to get Mr. Bosco to release Ivy from her matrimonial agreement." Her voice shook, and she sniffled. "That meant a lot to me."

Oh no. He didn't need her crying. But at least he thought they were happy tears. Women were trouble, but maybe this one was worth whatever trouble came with her. Or maybe it was that wrong women were trouble. A good one was a blessing. He pulled his kerchief from his back pocket and handed it to her. "Please don't cry. I don't know what to do when a lady cries. I may end up yelling at you to make you angry so you don't cry."

A laugh sputtered out from between her lips. Tempting lips.

"That wasn't a joke."

She dabbed the edge of the blue cloth to the inner corner of each eye. "I know. That's what makes it funny."

There was no figuring out a woman. "I'm not prepared like Gil, but. . ."

As she stiffened, her expression turned serious.

He wouldn't get on one knee like Gil because this was likely still too public and she might want to think on getting tangled up with an ornery man like him. If she was smart, she'd think on it.

Why had he started this line of conversation? Should have waited until they were back on the ranch and in private. He understood now why she thought Gil should wait. "I know I'm not the easiest man to get along with. In spite of you seeing me favorably on the train, you must still think me a cad, at the very least obnoxious. But I'm working on changing."

She put her hand on his wrist. Her cool touch soothed him. "I don't think those things of you. You have never acted anything but honorable."

He was glad he didn't have so much to make up for in her eyes, and it gave him hope that one day she could think of him as someone more than her employer. "I don't expect you to say anything right now, but I want you to know how I feel."

Her serious and concerned expression changed again, this time to something akin to hope.

"I trust I'm not presumptuous in telling you. . . I don't expect you to feel the same way."

She heaved a sigh and planted her hands on her hips. "You know, Mr. Coons was wise to use so few words. A girl could grow old waiting for you to say something."

"I'm not good with words."

"I've never known you to be at a loss for them, and you certainly have plenty of them now. I think it best if you say what you want to say as plainly as possible and in as few words as possible."

"Maybe this isn't the right place. I mean, with all these people around."

"Everyone is on the other side of the room. This is precisely the right place. Now *please* say what's on your mind."

This was harder than he imagined. How had Gil done it so swiftly? Nick took a deep breath. "I've come to care a great deal for you."

"And I, you."

"You do? But how? Why? When?"

"On the train when you helped us. When you said you'd been sitting near us to protect us." She took a slow breath and continued. "*That's* when I started. . .falling in love with you." She gifted him with her sweet smile.

"You did? You do?" For him it was when he realized she wasn't a mail-order bride.

Holly nodded. "Do you have something to ask me?" She felt like stomping on his foot to make him say what she hoped he was trying to say.

His words rushed out. "I love you, too. Will you be my wife?"

Though she'd wanted him to ask, dare she agree to marry so soon after meeting this man? As she contemplated saying yes, a sense of peace joined her inner dance. "I would be honored to."

His grin warmed her all over. "You've made me the happiest man in town."

When she had escorted her sister two months ago to keep Ivy from marrying in haste, she never would have imagined all that had happened and falling in love with a handsome cowboy. She couldn't imagine going back to her lonely life. Not now that she knew what it felt like to be in love. But there was one more thing this special moment needed. "*Mr. Andrews?*"

"You need to stop calling me that."

Her mouth pulled up on one side. "Or what, *Mr. Andrews?*"

A smile tugged at his mouth as understanding spread across his face. "Or this." He leaned forward and pressed his lips to hers.

Warm and gentle.

A squeal came from off to the side, and he jerked back.

Ivy beamed. "Does this mean we can have a double wedding?"

Holly feared her face quickly matched the color of her dress. "A what?"

Ivy hooked her arm around Mr. Coons's and drew close. "We are getting married right now. The place is decorated, and everyone's here. It's perfect." She pressed her palms together. "Please tell me the two of you are getting married, too. That would make this perfect."

Holly turned to Mr. Coons.

The foreman held up his hands. "It wasn't my idea."

Nick spoke up. "Gil, if you and Ivy want to marry now, that's fine. But I'm not going to rush my bride."

Holly doubted he'd planned to propose, and clearly he hadn't imagined her accepting.

He looked her straight in the eyes. "I know how ladies like to take months to plan these things. I don't want you pressured."

He was right. She had always thought she would plan something special with all her family and friends around. But all the people she cared about were right here. And the place was decorated, complete with guests. And she wore the nicest dress she would ever own. She wanted to marry him more than she wanted to plan a wedding that wouldn't be half as nice as this. And to share this day with her sister was a bonus. "I don't mind. I don't think I could plan anything better than this. Do *you* want to?"

"Of course. But. . .I don't have a ring."

"That's all right." As long as she had him. "But I don't want to pressure you. I can be patient."

"I'm game. I'll get you a ring right after Christmas."

At that moment, a wrinkled hand holding a diamond ring poked in between her and Nick.

Holly gazed at the old woman who had coerced them under the mistletoe when they'd arrived.

Mrs. Deny grasped Nick's hand and pressed the ring into it. "Take it." She curled his fingers around it. "My wedding present. My Ivan would want it put to good use."

"Thank you."

The old woman winked at Holly. "You're getting a fine man in this one."

"I know."

Soon, the foursome stood before the preacher and repeated their vows in turn. When he said that the grooms could kiss their brides, Holly didn't wait and met Nick halfway.

This was where she belonged. In his arms.

He pulled back.

"Merry Christmas, Holly."

She gazed into his loving blue eyes. "Merry Christmas, *Mr. Andrews.*"

He took her hint and kissed her again.

She would never grow tired of his kisses.

Mary Davis is an award-winning author of over a dozen novels in both historical and contemporary themes, seven novellas, two compilations, three short stories, and has been included in seven collections. She has two brand-new novels releasing later this year. She is a member of American Christian Fiction Writers and is active in two critique groups.

Mary lives in the Pacific Northwest with her husband of over thirty-three years and two cats. She has three adult children and one grandchild. She enjoys board and card games, rain, and cats. She would enjoy gardening if she didn't have a black thumb. Her hobbies include quilting, porcelain doll making, sewing, crafting, crocheting, and knitting. Visit her website at http://marydavisbooks.com, or visit her Facebook at https://www.facebook.com/mary.davis.73932 and join her FB readers group, Mary Davis READERS Group at https://www.facebook.com/groups/132969074007619/?source=create_flow.

Periwinkle in the Park

by Kathleen E. Kovach

Dedication

To Jim, my advocate. And a special thanks to my grandparents,
Milo and Gwen Wiles, who lived in Estes Park during my childhood and provided
the opportunities to grow hopelessly in love with Rocky Mountain National Park.

Chapter 1

Estes Park, Colorado
June 1910

Periwinkle Winfield cringed at the sound of Margaret Stallworth's shrill voice. "Peri! Oh, Peri, it is you!"

Peri turned to her sister, Sunnie, whose eyes took on the look of a frightened rabbit before she disappeared down the notions aisle of the mercantile. She didn't even know how to sew!

"It's so good to see you." Margaret, the only daughter of a wealthy millinery supply mogul based in Denver, grasped Peri's shoulders and kissed her on both cheeks, a lingering habit from her brief time in Paris several years ago. Peri fought the fashionable wide-brimmed hat Margaret wore to avoid getting smacked in the eyes. "I just arrived with Mother in our new Stanley Steamer automobile. Such a lark! You really should get one."

"I couldn't afford one, but even if I could, I'd rather ride my mule." Peri glanced out the open door at Daisy tied to the hitching post.

"If we found you a rich man, you wouldn't have to ride a dusty creature." Margaret placed her finger under her nose, as if she could smell Daisy from inside the building.

Peri had learned a couple of years ago not to engage in Margaret's passive degradations. What she was really saying was that she found *Peri* dusty and smelly and that Peri needed a man with money just to survive.

"How was your winter in Denver?" Peri determined to change the subject.

"Capitol Hill is fine, and the ladies in the neighborhood keep me busy hosting teas, but it's nice to have a change of pace. I love it here." Margaret spread her arms wide, nearly knocking a stack of canned goods off the counter.

"I do too," Peri said. She helped the clerk right the toppling merchandise, then handed him her supplies list. "The Rocky Mountains is where I belong. You can have the big city. Has your husband decided to stay there again this summer?"

Margaret's face clouded. "The big baby is afraid of the drive up, even though the road is so much safer now than it used to be. He says he needs to stay there to run the business, but honestly, he has employees, doesn't he?"

Peri refused to provide fuel for the subject. Even if Hector wasn't afraid of the drive, she suspected he encouraged his bride to take summer-long vacations just to give himself a break. Although Margaret was a full decade younger than Peri, who was beginning to see the backside of thirty-nine, she still appeared to cling to her youth, and to her mother.

"What are you doing this summer?" Margaret asked. "Are you still traipsing into the wilds?" She frowned her disapproval. They'd had many conversations about women taking jobs meant for men.

"I'm still a nature trail guide, yes."

"You really should settle down, Peri. Estes Park is teeming with eligible men now that it's become so popular." With excitement lighting her eyes, she glanced out the window. "I think there are twice as many businesses as when I was here last summer."

Peri merely nodded. As much as she loved the new growth, she missed the smattering of homesteaders in the early days. Papa had semiretired from preaching when they came here for Mama's health.

Margaret fingered a nearby ribbon, then pointedly looked at Peri's hair. "Honestly, how can you expect to attract a man when you keep your hair so short?"

"Thank you for your concern, Margaret, but any man who can't take me the way I am isn't worth my time." While Margaret huffed her indignation, Peri paid for her supplies and made a hasty exit. She glanced around for Sunnie, who seemed to have fallen into a hole somewhere.

Margaret followed her out.

"It was great to see you again, Margaret. I'm sure our paths will cross again soon. I'm teaching a nature class in the lobby of your hotel this week." She set down the crate of supplies and motioned up the hill. "You're staying at the Stanley again this year, I presume."

Margaret nodded.

"Pop in if you'd like to learn about the marmot."

Margaret shuddered. "No thank you. Marmots are nothing but large rats." With her jaw set at a stubborn angle and her Cupid's bow mouth puckered into a tight little prune, she marched off.

That should keep the socialite at bay for a while. Peri chuckled. She had also planned to talk about mountain birds and other small creatures to be found along the nature trail, a subject her young friend would probably find less distasteful.

Peri searched the area. Where was Sunnie? Daisy stood patiently at the rail where Peri had tied her. Peri patted the heart-shaped white spot in the middle of Daisy's forehead. "That's my good girl," she cooed as she removed the items from the crate and stuffed them into her saddlebag.

"Is she gone?" Sunnie poked her head around the corner of the building.

"You're a traitor. No, worse. A deserter." Peri couldn't even look at her sister as she placed the now empty crate near the door.

"I'm sorry, but I know she's going to ask me to be in her little club again this summer."

A grin tugged at Peri's lips. "The Ladies of Good Society?"

"Yes. And I can't do it again. I just can't." Sunnie clenched the railing. "I was never so bored in my entire life. She wants to get away from the city, but then she tries to make our little town conform to her ostentatious ideals."

"I know. She's chosen me as her pet project again this year. She won't be happy until she's made me into a proper woman."

"You?" Sunnie snorted and placed her hand over her mouth. However, her eyes continued to dance in mischief. "You only wear a dress once a week, on Sundays. And I'm sure it's because Mama still has influence over you."

Peri untied Daisy and led her toward the street. "I know many women have hiked into the mountains with their heavy dresses and their high-falutin' hats. But give me breeches any day. Margaret and her society friends may look down their noses at what I do and how I live, but they are of no concern to me."

In fact, Peri had little patience for people with too much money and too few brains. Even though she often guided wealthy clients on nature walks now that Estes Park had begun to boom, she felt it her duty to educate them about nature and try to give them a new appreciation for God's creation. Perhaps, by doing so, she could erase the bloody memory of her first encounter with people of privilege.

And this was why, after her nature talk, she would be attending the contentious meeting between the Protective League and the Association of Settlers. One fought to establish a federal game preserve and the other felt that too stifling to their livelihoods. She, of course, sided with the League.

"Let's get an ice cream." Sunnie broke into her thoughts. "Then I have to get back to the husband. Our lodge doesn't seem to run itself when I'm gone."

Peri pulled out her father's pocket watch and clicked it open. A picture of Mama and Papa nestled inside the watch cover smiled tentatively at her. "Okay, I have some time before the meeting."

"The one where they'll be fighting over protected versus open land? You're not going, are you?"

"Of course I am. Why not?"

Sunnie counted on her fingers. "One, you're a woman."

Peri huffed.

"Two, there will be smoking of smelly cigars and. . .and belching. . .and. . .three, you're a woman."

"You said that. I'm a business owner. And even more to the point, I have a vested interest in the outcome. You know my entire life's work is to preserve life, be it flora or fauna."

"I know."

"Then surely you can see why I must be vocal for the establishment of a national park here."

"I do, and I support you all the way. Frederick does too. He's going to argue on the side of the Protective League."

"That pleases me." Peri and her brother-in-law may not see eye-to-eye a lot of times, but she knew he loved her. He even built her a cabin on his property just outside of town, near the river, a prime spot. It didn't escape her that he was taking sides on her behalf.

They strode down Main Street, coughing occasionally at the smoke coming from automobiles and the dust they kicked up. Peri reached back to pet Daisy on the nose. Give her a loyal steed any day.

When they reached the Confectionary and Ice Cream Parlor, Peri pulled her mule's

71

reins to the rail, but before she could tie them, a noisy jalopy passed by, coughing and sputtering from beneath its metal frame. Daisy raised her head and brayed. No amount of soothing words would calm the normally gentle beast and she broke free, turned away from Peri, and began running with a kick of her back legs.

Not the first time.

"Should we run after her?" Sunnie's eyes had gone wide, as if she'd never seen Daisy in a panic.

"No. She's heading home. Once I get there, she'll be relaxed and feasting on feed."

They entered the establishment, which had a smattering of round tables and a long counter where a mother and child sat sharing a custard.

A table near the window appealed to Peri. As they enjoyed their sweet treats, she took note of the gathering automobiles and horses at the courthouse. The meeting would soon be under way, and she would be in the middle of it.

Clayton McCarrick pulled his Stetson low over his eyes as his horse clip-clopped into town. Behind him, the latest hunting party followed. A buckboard loaded with deer and other game trailed behind, driven by the closest thing he had to a best friend, George Lilley. George was also the best field cook and game dresser he'd ever known. No one would starve on his watch.

"Hey, McCarrick!" Clay swiveled in the saddle to find the voice. His cousin casually gripped a broom in midsweep as he stood on the porch of his self-named restaurant, Harper's Eatery. "Howd'ya do?"

Clay reined to a stop and thumbed over his shoulder toward the buckboard. "See for yourself. You'll have venison on the guest tables within the week."

Tom set the broom aside and limped down the stairs. A bear had busted his kneecap a year ago, effectively halting his own hunting excursions. He leaned over the wagon and patted the top carcass. "Good man."

"And woman," Beatrice Grover corrected in her warbly, high-pitched voice. The wife of Chester Grover, a British nobleman, Beatrice had held her own with the seven men who had paid for the privilege of hunting in the Rocky Mountains.

"Mrs. Grover brought down that ten-point buck."

Mr. Grover harrumphed.

"Now, dear." Beatrice offered a compassionate smile. "You would have gotten your beast if you had not sneezed."

"Yes, dear. But I would not have sneezed if someone had not pushed me out of my warm bed and onto the damp ground."

The two continued to spar, and Tom raised his eyebrow.

Clay removed his hat and smoothed his hair. "They've been doing that for a week."

Tom chuckled. "Better you than me. Hey, you got a minute?"

"Sure. George, go on ahead to the ranch. I'll be there shortly to help unload the game. Folks, you all are released to head to your hotel. Anyone who wants to help skin and dress the meat is welcome to show up at dawn tomorrow."

Beatrice shuddered. "No, thank you! And Chester, you will soak your feet as soon as we get to the hotel. I will not be taking you back to Manchester with a cold."

"Yes, dear."

The party moseyed on while Clay dismounted. "What's on your mind, Tom?"

"You hear what's going on at the town hall?"

"More talk about land use in the mountains?"

"Yep. You going?"

"I hadn't planned on it. We came back a few hours sooner than I expected. Even so, I don't want anything to do with the government."

Tom lowered himself to the porch steps and rubbed his knee. "It's up to you, but talk is they're beginning to seriously debate the purpose of the land." He held out one hand, palm up. "Should it be a nature preserve, or"—he held out the other—"a national park? If it's the latter, that may concern you."

"As far as I know, my land isn't a part of it." Clay sat on the step just below Tom.

"Your land butts up to the initial proposed boundary, though. You might want to make a little noise to let them know that your border can't be moved—like last time, if you know what I mean."

Clay tugged on his hat so that he could see very little of the town. "I know. And thanks for remembering. God wouldn't do that to me twice, would he?"

Tom gingerly stood and looked down at Clay. "If it was God that did it to you the first time, I hear He's powerful enough to do it again."

Clay fingered the rough step.

God or no God, they'd have to pry his land out of his cold, dead hands.

The small room lay shrouded in cigar smoke, creating an ethereal scene as Peri entered. Already some thirty men had squashed into the small space, and they all turned toward her. She lifted her chin, squelched a cough, and pushed into a corner where she would apparently stand throughout the meeting, as no one offered her a seat.

One notable absence was Enos Mills, a resident of Estes Park and a naturalist. He'd been Peri's mentor in her early years and was directly responsible for her chosen profession. Enos was off on a speaking tour, rallying support for the cause for which half the people in the room were fighting.

A rotund man with a gavel sat at a table toward the front. He smacked the gavel and called the meeting to order. "Thank you, gentlemen—"

"Ahem." Peri cleared her throat.

"—and lady," he continued, "welcome to our first meeting to determine the use of open land in our majestic mountains."

Several men began their arguments all at once and the gavel came down hard.

"Order! Please. We all have opinions, and there will be time to get to everyone."

The room settled down, but Peri visualized a pot on the stove, the fire turned back but the pot still simmering.

"My name is Howard Trench, and I represent the U. S. Division of Forestry. I've been asked to mediate a series of meetings to determine the best use of the proposed land that comprises several hundreds of thousands of acres in the Rocky Mountains just west of here."

A map had been affixed to the wall to show the area in question.

As he talked, the door opened and a man entered, his clothing full of dust. Peri had seen him around town, but they hadn't officially met. He removed his hat, revealing a full head of matted-down hair, and pressed himself against the wall next to the door.

"Excuse me." He managed to break into Mr. Trench's introduction.

"I'm not ready to take questions from the floor as of yet, sir."

"Oh, I'm sorry, but I just want to clarify something, then I'll leave."

"Go ahead." Mr. Trench picked up his gavel, as if he suspected he'd have to use it shortly. "What is your name and occupation?"

"I'm Clayton McCarrick, rancher up at the Lazy M and hunting guide."

Peri bristled. She knew he made a living as a hunter. She'd seen his buckboard filled with carcasses on occasion.

"What's your question, Mr. McCarrick?"

"I heard you say hundreds of thousands of acres were being considered for whatever reason it is you're setting the land aside. What about the people who live there?"

Sure enough, half the room stood in agreement and began barking similar questions to poor Mr. Trench. Down came the gavel and the din subsided.

"We will certainly take everything into consideration. No one will be taking anyone's land away from them. On the contrary, it's possible that if anyone is willing to sell, they will get top dollar for their property."

The rancher's face turned to hard granite as the others in the room refused to be silenced any longer. A heated debate ensued about the various opinions of land use. Some favored setting the land aside for state use to curtail the mining operations and other activities that destroyed the natural beauty. Others preferred turning it over to the federal government for a national park. Peri was all for that, as it would preserve the natural beauty and protect the animals within the park as well.

Mr. McCarrick spoke up once again. "I make my living not only as a rancher, but also as a hunter. How am I going to do that if most of my hunting area is off limits?"

Peri couldn't be silent any longer. "Are you aware, Mr. McCarrick, that thanks to the European influx of tourists several years ago, there are less than a dozen elk currently roaming our mountains?"

"I'm very aware, Miss—"

"Then surely you must see the need for a wildlife refuge, a place to build up the populace. It's thanks to irresponsible hunters like you—"

"Who are you calling irresponsible? You don't even know me. I haven't shot an elk in years, knowing there are so few of them."

"Then you are the exception to the rule. But if we don't do something soon, we will lose our elk, and many more magnificent animals, to thoughtless tourists. Estes Park is inundated with more and more people streaming up here for recreation. We may not be able to control them, but we can regulate where they go. And a national park is the perfect solution."

Half the room stood and applauded. The other half looked like a bushel of tomatoes about ready to burst, so red and stressed were their faces.

The gavel sounded once again, and Mr. Trench called everyone to order. "What did you say your name was, miss, and your occupation?"

"I am Periwinkle Winfield, nature guide for six years now."

"And a mighty fine one, too." Mr. Hollingsworth, who ran the Summit Hotel, winked under his furry, white eyebrow. "I've sent many a guest her way and they always come back with rave reviews."

Mr. Trench tilted his head in acknowledgment of this revelation and tented his fingers. "Are you willing, Miss Winfield, to take a party into the proposed area? Perhaps several times in the course of this proposal? We have maps, of course, but it would behoove us to have a personal, firsthand account of what we're trying to protect."

"I would be honored."

"Very good."

True to his word, Mr. Trench heard everyone in the room in an orderly manner. When the hour was up, he rapped his gavel. "Our time is up gentlemen. . .and lady. . .I thank you all for coming and expressing your concerns. Watch for postings about future meetings. We want only the best for this area, and we appreciate your feedback."

Of the two factions represented, it was those favoring a national park who smiled at Peri as they spilled out of the building. The others—the miners, ranchers, loggers—left with scowls on their faces. She felt for them, but her priority was preserving life, all life, plant and animal.

The hunter stomped by her on his way to his horse. She couldn't feel sorry for Clayton McCarrick. If his main concern was to placate the spoiled elite who only wanted to kill animals, then Peri would fight him with all her breath.

Chapter 2

Daisy's mule ears flicked about while taking in the sounds of the forest. Peri patted her front flank as she walked beside her. "Easy, girl. We've been here before." She pointed to her left. "See that woodpecker nest up there in the aspen? We watched it being built last year. Remember how the wood chips flew as the little fellow got deeper into the trunk? Looks like the babies are all gone, though, off to find families of their own."

"Who is she talking to?" Peri heard behind her. She had almost forgotten about the half-dozen people trailing behind her.

"I can't be sure, but I think she's talking to her mule." This came from one of the members of her nature hike. Several miles from home, the party worked their way up a narrow trail deeper into the Rocky Mountains. They weren't typical tourists, however. They were members of the scouting party Howard Trench had set up to determine if the land would work best as a national park. Peri planned to take them to a vista where they could see the area in all of its glory. It was up ahead, about half a day's hike.

Lodgepole pine surrounded them like mountain sentinels, their fragrance dancing on the breeze. The clicks and trills of the Brewer blackbirds played a symphony of notes while a blue jay squawked in the distance as if giving a negative commentary. And a curious hummingbird whipped laps around the nature party, apparently fascinated by the fake flower on Mrs. Kealey's sun hat.

Russel Patterson, one of the forestry agents, caught up to Peri. "We sure are grateful for the tour. A few more of these over the course of the year and we should know more about how to proceed. After seeing the vast beauty, the miles and miles of mountain peaks, the verdant valleys, the wildlife, and the untouched meadows, I can't see any reason why we can't push for a national park. I'd sure hate to see any of this ruined by civilization."

"I agree, Russ." Peri shielded her eyes as her gaze perused Longs Peak off in the distance. "It would be crazy not to protect this land."

As she spoke, a sound to her right caught their attention. They had been following a mountain brook for about three miles, and it pooled in this one spot. There was the sound again, as if someone were taking a rug beater to a pool of water. Peri put her finger to her lips and motioned for them to follow her. They moved off the trail a few yards, moving brush out of the way as they forged their own trail. Soon, a beaver pond came into view. Another slap churned the water as the creature dove below the surface, indicating an anxious beaver warning the intruders away. Peri giggled. The smacking of a tail on water wasn't very intimidating.

The party knelt down to enjoy the show. Philomena Cooper, a nature photographer, chose to forgo her bulky camera and pulled out a small Kodak Brownie from her pack. She began to capture images with a gentle *snick*, *snick*. Peri pulled out her sketchbook and a pencil. However, Philomena's process fascinated her.

"I enjoy drawing," Peri said, "but to be able to capture the true beauty of God's creation would also help to bring this blessed land to the people who can't enjoy what we have."

"You have an art studio in town, don't you?"

"Yes. It's attached to my brother-in-law's hotel. My sister sells my sketches and paintings."

"Much of what I do is for postcards. You could also take pictures and provide postcards for the tourists."

"But I don't have a camera."

Philomena smiled and held out the Brownie. "Now you do."

"Oh, I couldn't take your camera!"

"I insist. You have access to this beautiful place that few others do. I believe in the national park. Take pictures and show others why we need one."

Peri held out her hands and the camera was passed to her as if it were a mantle of great importance.

After several minutes—or was it an hour? Time always stood still for Peri when she viewed the tiny mountain folk—they left the beaver pond and continued on.

When the sun hovered just above the nearest mountain peak, Peri called over her shoulder, "We're almost there."

The trail cut to the left and they all began an ascent that lasted about a hundred yards. This led up to a grassy knoll with a dizzying drop-off. As they crested the hill, the world opened up before them and Peri heard gasps all around.

She, of course, had seen this view many times, and it still took her breath away as it had her companions. But she had the added joy of watching the unfettered emotions play out on the faces of those who weren't privileged to be able to hike to this spot on a whim.

The scene before them took on a fairy-tale-like beauty, where green meadows hugged boulder outcroppings and a herd of deer grazed, blissfully ignorant of their audience. Across the natural amphitheater rose mountain peaks with snowy caps, standing stalwart, a perfect granite backdrop. This was her Colorado, and she would fight with her dying breath to maintain its beauty.

For a full five minutes, no one dared speak, as if they stood before the very throne of God. Then Philomena gave words to what the others were no doubt feeling. "Isabella Bird, who wrote *A Lady's Life in the Rocky Mountains,* said it best. 'Nature, rioting in her grandest mood, exclaimed in voices of grandeur, solitude, sublimity, beauty, and infinity, "Lord, what is man that Thou are mindful of him? or the son of man, that Thou visitist him?"'"

They stood in this spot for an eternity, but as night's shadows began to overtake the valley, Peri called them all out of their stupor and prompted them to make camp. She found a spot away from any winds that might spirit themselves from the icy glaciers above and broke out the provisions she had brought. Soon, a hearty stew simmered on the fire.

The next morning they broke camp and headed back. It had taken three days to hike to the Glory Bowl, as Peri had named it. She took them a different way home and showed them many spectacular sites, although none as glorious as the one they had seen at the crest of their journey. She did manage to bring them to a meadow known for its draw of mountain sheep. A narrow creek ran through the meadow and then bloated into a pond, only to continue on again as a creek. Peri compared the sight to a snake that had eaten a mouse, and there it lay in its middle, waiting to be digested.

Five mountain sheep had come down from their craggy homes several miles straight up in the hills above the meadow. Nature could be unpredictable, and she took this opportunity to show off for her guests, knowing that her very future rode on pleasing the dignitaries.

"There was a time when the *wapiti*, the elk, roamed free here," she said. "Please, Lord! Please protect the few left until we can get the government to comply."

"So they are nearly extinct up here?" Russell pulled out field glasses to get a better view.

"Yes, thanks to over-eager tourists who left the meat to rot but took the antlers. Such a waste. The antlers fall off naturally. All they had to do was find where they normally graze and search the ground. Of course, there were also those who wanted a trophy with the entire head." A wave of nausea hit Peri as she remembered that moment in her past when man's cruelty over a different gentle beast changed her life forever. She shook it off, however, not wanting to ruin what had so far been a pleasant week.

"I can't understand that mentality," Philomena said. "That's why I take pictures for my trophies."

"And why I sketch," Peri agreed.

"And why you now take pictures." Philomena tapped the camera hanging around Peri's neck.

Peri saw the hiking party safely to their hotel. Surely after seeing the beautiful, untouched land, they would come to the decision to protect it all. She knew there would be much deliberating on the governmental level, more hikes such as the one they were just on, and a lot of lobbying. But with the Lord's help—and why wouldn't the Lord be on the side of conserving His creation?—it would get done.

A couple of days later, Peri felt the need to go back up, if only to pray over the land. A trail she hadn't yet taken called to her, and so she set out on her own with fresh supplies.

Clay sat atop his horse and patrolled the perimeter of his property, searching for the lost calf. He knew the little guy would be trouble the moment he ventured away from his mom the first time and ended up in a ravine. It prompted him to name the calf Zebulon after the explorer Zebulon Pike, the namesake of Pike's Peak. He'd never named a cow before, but with this one's adventurous spirit, he deserved it.

"Where are you, Zebulon? You'd better not have gotten yourself into trouble again. If I have to get you out of one more scrape. . ."

A sound reached his ear and he leaned forward in the saddle. It wasn't the distressing call of a young calf. He strained a little farther and kept his horse still so he could hear. It was a. . .woman?

He clicked his tongue to move his horse forward. "C'mon, Angus, let's investigate." The sound seemed to be coming from the lake.

A stand of aspen blocked his view. He dismounted and gingerly led Angus through the trees.

A breeze rustled the dollar-sized leaves. He normally loved this sound, feeling it was God's way of telling him to relax. But he couldn't relax knowing a female had encroached upon his space.

And she was still talking.

"Isn't this a beautiful place, Daisy? We've never seen this lake before. Don't know why we haven't ever hiked this direction, but we'll remember it in the future."

Clay perused the clearing where this female had clearly made herself at home. A lean-to had been set up near an oak tree. A campfire already crackled, and a coffeepot simmered on a rock within the ring.

The woman wandered over to her mule with a fistful of flowers. "Here you go." She slipped them into the mule's bridle. "Mountain daisies for my Daisy."

Clay pushed his hat back and scratched his head. As he walked closer, he recognized the woman. She was the one at the meeting the other day. Weird name. Winkle? Winkie? Periwinkle Winfield. That was it.

Clay ventured forward.

A movement caught his eye several feet above Miss Winfield's camp. A mountain lion sunned itself on a large boulder, but watched the human and animal below with interest. An older lion, gray feathering his muzzle. Probably not a threat, but Clay didn't want to take the chance. He searched the ground for pebbles and began pelting the lion in hopes of driving it off.

It appeared to work, at first. The beast stood and stretched, but then it licked its lips as it focused on the mule blissfully grazing several yards away from the woman.

Clay reached over to his saddle and pulled out his rifle. Hoping beyond hope that the big cat would give up its prey and move on. However, as it crouched, apparently in preparation of springing off the rock toward the hapless animal, Clay brought the rifle up and pulled the trigger. His shot rang true and hit exactly where he aimed, just left of the cat where a pine branch splintered away from the tree. The cat sprang away from the sound and sprinted into the woods in fright.

A commotion below caught his attention.

"Daisy! No!"

Miss Winfield desperately clung to the mule's reins, but to no avail. The mule broke free, kicked up its heels, and made a break for it. Meanwhile, Miss Winfield screamed, and a splash followed.

Clay rushed to the spot where she now sat, waves rolling away from her posterior.

"Are you all right?" He reached out a hand to her, but she recoiled.

"You!"

He stepped into the water, the coldness seeping into his boot. "Take my hand." He emphasized every word as he reached out to her.

"No!" Her chin jutted out and her arms crossed, making her look like a spoiled toddler.

Clay moved out of the water. "Then sit there. Catch your death of cold."

"You nearly killed us!"

"I wasn't aiming at you. A mountain lion was poised to pounce on your mule."

"You tried to kill a defenseless lion?" The look on her face did not telegraph gratitude.

Clay backed up, sat on a fallen log, and pushed his hat back. "I didn't aim at the cat. I shot near it so it would run away. It was never in danger." He sighed. "You just going to sit there in the freezing water? A glacier feeds the lake, you know."

"I know," she spat out then gave a little shudder.

Clay stood and tried once more. "Come on, then." He held out his hand and she took it, but she stumbled a little as she put her weight on her left foot.

"You're hurt!" He splashed into the water and pulled her arm over his shoulders.

She limped out of the water, and he settled her onto the log. With her foot cradled in his hand, he lifted her ankle and began removing her boot, but she jerked it away.

"You scared Daisy!"

"I'm sorry about that. I was just trying to keep her from getting eaten."

He tried once more to remove her boot, and she let him, grimacing at the pain.

After his inspection, he lowered her foot. "It's not broken. I'm guessing a mild sprain. You should be good as new in a day or two. Let me help you to my horse and I'll take you to my ranch. It's not far."

"No thank you. I'm fine here. Unless I'm trespassing."

Clay thumbed his hat to the back of his head. "No, you're not trespassing. But I own a few acres just north of here."

"So this is public land."

"Yes, I told you it was."

She perused the area and smiled. "Very pretty. It's a good place to heal."

"I wish you'd reconsider coming back with me. A woman out here alone with a bum foot would just be bait. Remember our friend on the rock."

Zebulon! He still had to find the adventurous calf before that lion did.

"Mr. . . ."

"McCarrick. Clay McCarrick." He tipped his hat in greeting.

Her eyes flashed fire. "Mr. McCarrick. I have been a nature guide for six years. Before that I attended college, majoring in Biology. Before that, I traveled with my parents as missionaries to Indian reservations where I learned how to handle myself in the outdoors. How to treat illness and injury. I am more than capable of taking care of myself, injured or not."

"Okay then. I'm impressed. I'll just go after your mule and bring her back."

"Don't bother. Daisy is probably halfway home by now. She knows where she's going. Thankfully I'd already unloaded my gear, so I have everything I need until I can pack out of here."

Clay hated to leave her. He walked over to an oak tree and examined the lower branches. When he found one he liked, he broke it off with help from his hunting knife.

"What are you doing?" Miss Winfield shrieked from her seat on the log. "You can't just whack at the tree. You're going to kill it!"

"I'm going to fashion you a crutch. You can't hop around this campsite until you're better."

"Well, I'm not going to use it."

"Then the tree will have died in vain."

He proceeded to chop away at the branch until a crude semblance of a crutch appeared.

"Here." He handed it to her and she grasped it, still glaring at him. "I have a calf to find. I'll be back later to check on you."

As he mounted his horse, he expected her to say, "Don't bother," but she remained silent. Before he left the grove of aspen, he turned in the saddle. She was standing and testing out the crutch.

Clay shook his head and smiled.

Chapter 3

Toward late afternoon, as the sky's light dimmed and the temperature dropped, Peri threw another dead limb onto the fire. Then she settled back against the log and propped her throbbing ankle on a nearby rock. She was grateful for the handmade crutch, despite the fact that it had been ripped from a living thing. She would have used her walking stick, but when Daisy reared up and came back down, she snapped the sturdy piece of oak in two. The crutch had helped her gather leafy yarrow to make a poultice for her ankle. The swelling had already begun to go down.

She was enjoying a cup of coffee when she heard movement near the aspen grove and the nickering of a horse. Mr. McCarrick walked in holding two reins, one for his horse and one connected to her mule.

"Daisy!" She started to get up, but he patted the air in a signal for her to remain seated.

"Stay put. I'll take care of her."

He led both animals to the small lake where they lowered their heads to drink. Daisy must have been parched. She lingered over the cool water a few minutes longer than the horse.

"Thank you so much for finding her. Was she very far away?"

"A few miles from here. She must have stopped to rest."

"Well, thank you again, Mr. McCarr—"

"Please call me Clay. I think I've earned it after fishing you out of the water."

"And I'm Peri." She reached her hand up to the man. "How do you do?"

He shook her hand, and she felt the calluses of his profession, yet his hands were gentle. She imagined him helping to birth a newborn calf and comfort its mother with those hands.

This reminded her of his original mission and why he had stumbled upon her campsite in the first place. "Did you find your errant calf?" she asked.

"Zebulon? I did. The ornery thing had gotten itself boxed in between boulders and couldn't figure its way out."

"Zebulon?" She couldn't suppress her giggle.

He told an engaging story about how the calf wouldn't stay near his mother, so he named him after the explorer. She enjoyed the telling, but she also enjoyed how animated he became, and how his face lit up. It was a nice face.

He excused himself to continue tending to the animals. Once they had been fed grains that seemed to magically appear and had been curry combed and rubbed down, he joined her at the fire.

"Pour yourself some coffee," she offered. "There's a cup for you on that rock."

He tipped his head. "Thank you, kindly, ma'am."

"Are you hungry? I have some dried meat and fruits."

"You eat meat?"

"I'm a naturalist, Mr. McCarrick, not a vegetarian."

"Clay." His green eyes had a certain sparkle that made him seem to be smiling even when he wasn't. Very disconcerting!

"Yes, well, I eat meat. I just object to the manner in which an animal is often killed."

"And you believe I, as a hunter, am insensitive to the prey."

She bristled. She hadn't expected the conversation to turn so abruptly into a debate. But she was up for the challenge. "Yes, I suppose that's what I'm saying."

"Have you ever seen me hunt?"

"No."

"Then how do you know whether the way I kill is humane or not?"

"I suppose I don't."

"Have you witnessed other hunters?"

Her throat constricted. "I wouldn't call them hunters. More like butchers."

"Ah, I am sorry. We're not all like that, you know."

She looked deep into his eyes. Could she tell him why she hated hunters so much? She saw compassion and perhaps a longing to know why she was so vehement. But he was the enemy, after all—the one on the other side of the issue in the meeting the other day. Wouldn't he be the one to oppose every argument she had to proceed with a national park?

No, she couldn't trust him with her memories. He would probably try to justify the actions of the men who had done such a dastardly deed, and then where would she be? She genuinely liked Clay. Perhaps she could swing him over to her side eventually.

"You know," he continued, "what you and I do are not so different."

"How so?" Or, perhaps he would try to persuade her. She remained on her defenses but afforded him the courtesy of an open mind to present his case.

"When I host a hunting party, I focus on giving a sightseeing tour as we head up to our prey's location. Often, even if no one bags anything, they comment on what a wonderful time they had, just enjoying the scenery. I may not know the names of certain flowers or trees, but I can point out where an elk or deer has rubbed his antlers against the bark to mark his territory. Or I can be sure we make the vista point at just the right time to see the sun flood into the valley. I know what beauty is." His pause caught Peri off-guard as his gaze seemed to linger too long on her face. "And I know that whatever God has given us, we need to be sure we take good care of it."

"Then why are you so opposed to protecting what God has given us?"

"I'm not opposed to that, but I don't like the government coming here and telling me where I can or can't hunt. But it's not just about me. You know that if the national park is approved, people will lose their jobs. Lumber camps will close, as will mines. Yes, this land will be protected, but who's going to protect the people living on the land? It's oppression that I'm opposed to."

"People can move on. But once the land is scarred, it's scarred forever."

"Yes, people can move on, but at what cost?" He picked up a stick, stood, and hurled it into the lake.

Peri studied the man who had been so gentle with her the whole day become more agitated the deeper they went into the debate.

"This is personal for you, isn't it, Clay—beyond the obvious." Apparently, they had some things in common.

After a deep sigh, he rubbed his neck. Still standing facing away from her, he slipped his hands into his back pockets, and his shoulders sagged as they seemed to bear a weight she couldn't see. "I'm not going to leave you here defenseless. I'll be proper and make camp just around the bend over there." He pointed to his right. "But I'm leaving a gun—" When she started to protest he held up his hand. "Relax, it's not to kill anything. I just want you to shoot in the air if you need me." He pulled a six-shooter out of his saddle bag. "And do be sure to shoot straight up. I don't want to be the first trophy you bag." He managed a small grin and pointed at his face. "Don't think you want this ugly mug on your wall."

He handed her the gun, but she only took it to give him peace. This wasn't the first time she'd been laid up in the forest alone. As he walked to his horse and patted it gently on the flank, her heart skipped to a tune she'd never heard before. *There is nothing ugly about your mug or any other part of you, Clay McCarrick. You are beautiful inside and out.*

Come morning, Peri awoke to the smell of coffee and bacon.

"Good morning, Glory." Clay snickered as he stood over the fire. "Thought you'd appreciate the flower reference."

"Huh?" She scratched her head and felt the unruly mop of hair. She'd never cared about her appearance while on a hike before, but was quite conscious of it now. "Oh! Morning glory. I get it."

"How'd you sleep?"

"Not very well. I tried to keep my foot elevated, but then I'd get stiff and want to turn over. Every time I did, it would fall off the rock and start to throb again." She sat up and rubbed her ankle. "It does seem much better, though. God must have known I'd be in this predicament, because He planted a patch of yarrow just over there, near the inlet."

Clay pulled the coffee off the fire but set it near enough to stay warm. As he turned the sizzling bacon in the cast-iron pan, he glanced toward the area she had indicated. "Yarrow. Is that the plant with little flower clusters over there near the ferns?"

"Yes. It has anti-inflammatory properties. I made a cold poultice for my swollen ankle after you left last night and it seems to have done the trick."

"Where'd you learn that?" He handed her a cup of the steaming brew.

"I mentioned that my parents were missionaries to the Arapahoe. There was a medicine woman, Malti, whose name means 'small fragrant flower.' I suppose the meaning of her name is why she became so interested in the healing properties of plants. She took to my sister and me and became our unofficial babysitter while our parents ministered to the people." Peri took a tentative sip of the coffee to test its heat. "Yarrow has many health benefits. It also stops bleeding."

"Well, I'm glad you didn't have to use it for that."

"Me too." Her stomach growled as the savory fragrance coming from the campfire swirled about her. "So, when's breakfast? It's taking you forever over there."

Clay chuckled. "Patience. A good meal takes time."

Soon he handed Peri a plate of bacon, scrambled eggs, and biscuits. Grabbing his own plate, he settled himself on a nearby rock.

"You really came prepared."

"I snagged a few things when I took Zebulon back to his mother."

"I'm grateful. Thank you."

They ate in silence for a moment, then Clay shifted on his makeshift seat. "I did some praying last night."

Peri's heart did a little jig at this news. Clay knew the Lord. However, an unwelcome thought invaded her celebration. If she were praying for the national park and he was praying against it, whose prayers would God honor?

"I didn't answer you last night when you asked if my passion concerning this land was personal. It is. Very personal."

Peri waited for Clay to gather his thoughts.

He set his plate aside and leaned his elbows on his knees. After rubbing his hands together, he seemed ready to talk.

Clay hated to draw up the old memory, but if Peri knew the truth, or even a part of it, maybe she would step over to his side and help him fight the battle.

"I hate when the government intrudes on people's lives. It wasn't directly the government that affected mine, but they were the catalyst."

He glanced over to see if Peri was interested. She held her coffee cup in both hands and was leaning toward him in rapt attention.

He ventured on. "My father, my grandfather, and even my great-grandfather, all were ranchers. It was in my blood, all I knew. I eventually inherited the family ranch. Made a tidy profit too.

"I met my bride back East and brought her to the ranch, hoping to build a future and a family. But she was a fancy little thing who hated being isolated several miles from town.

"Talk of a new railroad had been swirling for years among the townsfolk. It had been shot down dozens of times, but it was inevitable. Problem was, my land stood between them and progress. Thanks to government funding, a greedy land baron who owned the railroad, stress from the merchants in town who refused to sell to me, and the pleas of my wife, I let them buy me out. It was a stupid thing to do, but I loved her and would have done anything to make her happy. I had come to believe that the Lord wouldn't want me to hold on to things. People were what mattered most."

"That's very noble, Clay. No one could fault you for that."

Clay knew the wisdom of Peri's words, but his nobleness didn't make him feel better when he moved Anna to town and she began seeing the mayor who had encouraged the town to blackball him. He couldn't bring himself to confess to Peri that his wife had had an affair and was poised to leave him.

"If you don't mind me asking, what happened to your wife? I never see you with her in town." While Clay paused, reliving the painful moment, Peri quickly added, "You don't have to tell me. I'm sorry that I intruded."

"No, it's okay. She died in an accident." A mere five days after she told him she wanted a divorce.

"Oh, Clay. How awful."

At some point, he had poured himself more coffee. The handle of the tin cup cut into his finger, and he realized he'd been squeezing it too hard.

The worst part for Clay was that even though he was considered a widower, he had actually lost Anna twice.

Peri put her hand on his shoulder, but it felt like a branding iron. One more female trying to get close to him. He stood to get away from her and tossed the black liquid into the fire where it sizzled in angry protest.

When Clay was through with his confession, he gathered the dishes and took them to the water to rinse them. Peri considered letting him know why she was so adamant against hunters. His vulnerability touched her heart, even though it was an obvious attempt to sway her vote.

"How's the ankle now?" Clay asked on his way back to the campsite. The skillet still sat on a rock in the campfire where the heat cooked off all the grease and bits of food. He picked it up with a rag and proceeded to scrape at it with the dull side of his knife.

"It feels much better, thank you."

"You want to take a little walk? See how it holds up?"

"That would be lovely."

"If you can't make it back, I'll sling you over my shoulder."

"What?" She had just reached for her primitive crutch.

"Relax." Oh, those twinkling eyes. "I'm just joking. . .maybe."

"Clay McCarrick, if you so much as touch me—" She stood and tested the ankle.

"Come on." He waved for her to follow. "I imagine you're well enough to hike a little ways. And we'll let Angus and your mule trail behind. If you can't make it, I'll just toss you up on her back."

Peri stopped abruptly. "I am more than capable of mounting my mule without you manhandling me."

His shoulders shook with laughter.

A grin stretched her lips as well. Their relationship had moved beyond surface politeness to teasing, and it surprised her that she didn't mind the change.

They walked upriver, the incline stretching the tendons in her ankle, but not to the point of discomfort.

They followed a deer trail through tall grasses and past wildflowers, including her favorite, the blue and purple chiming bell, until she could hear the muffled roar of water.

"I'd like to tell you why I have a problem with hunting." How could she not after he'd bared his soul?

They continued to make their way up the trail as she spoke. "Years ago, I was with my family on a train riding through Wyoming. I was five years old. It was my first train ride, and I was so excited. We had been traveling for quite some time and saw no civilization, but we knew we were in Arapahoe country." Her foot slid on a loose rock, stressing her weak ankle.

He stopped and seemed to assess whether he should help. "There's a good place to sit just up yonder, with a good view of the falls. Can you make it?"

Irritation prickled at her. Not because of him but because of her foot. "I'm fine. Just rolled on a small rock." Which she wouldn't have done had she not been injured.

Spectacular falls came into view. The water had formed a small gorge, and it burst forth over the top and plunged perhaps thirty feet.

"Oh, this is beautiful!" She made her way to a boulder with a flat top and climbed to the nature-made seat.

"I love waterfalls," he said. "Probably because of the power of the water. But I also like the glacier-formed lakes up higher."

"Yes, I've hiked to some of them. They're like mirrors to the mountain's soul. Water so clear you could catch the fish by hand. I've seen the Arapahoe fish that way. It's quite beautiful."

"I can tell that you love the native people very much."

"I do. It's not fair how they've been treated through the years. Which brings me back to what I was saying about the train ride."

They settled in, she on the rock and he stretched out on the mountain grass, his elbows supporting him as he leaned on a fallen log.

"As I was saying," she continued, "I was so excited to be riding a train for the first time. My sister was too little to remember, but that's probably a good thing."

She hadn't recounted the story in a long time, and a wave of nausea squeezed at her throat. She swallowed hard and continued on. "The train started slowing down because we were passing a large herd of bison. Beautiful, majestic creatures. We thought the engineer was simply letting us get a good look at them, or maybe there were some on the tracks. But then some of the men in our car grabbed their guns and rifles. They opened the windows and began firing at the unsuspecting beasts." She pulled her hands over her ears, remembering the horrifying sound of explosion after explosion. "Shots came from other cars too. And from on top of the train. It was as if the entire passenger list consisted of only cold-hearted killers. The bison went down, one after another, and they soon began to stampede, trying to flee. But the men were smart in aiming for the ones farthest away on the prairie. When the others smelled the blood ahead of them, they turned back toward the train. The closer they got, the more likely it was they'd be shot." She closed her eyes, but the image still lingered, forever etched into her memory.

"I'm so sorry, Peri." Clay's voice was close. When had he stood to be by her side during the telling? He touched her hand, still cupped over her ears, but she recoiled from his touch. An apology would not bring back the dead.

"When it was over, there were nearly a hundred bison killed that day, including babies still clinging to their mothers' sides."

"I've heard of the bison killings." Clay now stood near the log where he had been lying, his fists at his side. "It was a government-approved act of cowardice to force the natives into reservations by taking away their food source."

"And it worked."

Clay picked up a fistful of pebbles and began chucking them into the waterfall. "How can you trust the government, then, to decide what's best to do with this land?"

Peri drew in a deep breath and turned her face toward the sky. The warmth of the sun became a healing balm, and she imagined her Father Creator pouring His love and grace over her heart.

"The Arapahoe believe in a god they call *Chebbeniathan*, literally, 'Spider of Heaven.' He's a creator god, also known as 'The Great Spirit' or 'Man Above.' It wasn't hard to transition many of them from the false god they were serving to committing their lives to the One True God, our Lord God Jehovah. The beautiful people who gave their lives to the Father and to His Son, Jesus Christ, forgave those who stole their bison. How could I not, when they had lost so much and I had only lost my innocence that day when I watched so much killing."

"But, you've said you hate hunters."

"I said I hate hunting, and the cruel forms it takes. But I'm still a work in progress. Some days I feel I've forgiven the men on that train, and perhaps the government that gave their permission as well. Other days. . ." She let her thought trail off. Other days turned into havoc-infused nights where the images of that day came back in full color.

"My parents live, breathe, and teach wholeheartedly Colossians 3:13," she continued. "It says, 'Forbearing one another, and forgiving one another, if any man have a quarrel against any: even as Christ forgave you, so also do ye.'"

"Good verse to live by. Maybe I'll get there one day. But it's hard to forgive when your heart gets stomped on." Clay strode off and disappeared among the pine.

Peri knew he wouldn't abandon her there. Perhaps he needed to have a talk with God about that verse. She turned her concentration to the waterfall. So much cleansing as white water spilled over rock made smooth by sheer determination. This was how she often felt God dealt with her. He was resolute in turning her jagged heart of stone into a smooth heart of flesh. She wasn't there yet, she knew it well. And neither, apparently, was Clay.

Lord, please heal us both.

Chapter 4

I think that's the most exciting thing I've ever heard." Sunnie poured Peri a cup of tea.

"That the man nearly killed me? Not to mention poor Daisy." Peri sat at one of ten tables in the dining room of the inn that her sister and husband ran on the outskirts of town. It pleased her that Sunnie had found a good man who shared her gift of hospitality. Both girls had followed their parents to Estes Park when they retired from the mission field. Dad still preached occasionally at the local church. They all lived on Frederick's homestead in separate cabins along Fall River.

"No, it's exciting that he stayed near to protect you that night and then was gentlemanly enough to escort you home."

"I could have made it home by myself. Thankfully, Daisy lent her back so I wouldn't have to walk." Her ankle was still a little sore, but she was hardly an invalid.

"Of course you could. If you're able to walk ten miles while snow-blind in the tundra, you're capable of a tiny thing like walking on a sprained ankle. But that's not the point."

Peri shuddered. "Don't remind me. Those were the most terrifying two days I've ever spent in my life."

"The point is," Sunnie said, undeterred, "you've met a nice man."

Peri knew that full well. And it scared her more than the snow-blindness.

"You've what?" The perky voice came from the door.

Margaret.

Sunnie tossed an apologetic glance toward Peri and mouthed, *I didn't see her.* She started to get up. "I have a roast in the ov—"

Peri grabbed her hand and pulled her back, making her squeak like the little pika above the timber line. Sunnie would not abandon her again.

"So." Margaret pulled out a chair at their table and adjusted her tulle hat. "What's this I hear about a man?"

Thankfully, no one occupied the dining area at midday or Peri would have been even more mortified.

Just when Peri was ready to tell Margaret to mind her own business, Sunnie piped up. "The rancher, Clayton McCarrick."

And now his name was out there.

Margaret's face went through several transformations, ranging from intrigue to disgust. "A rancher? Don't you want to move up in the world?"

"I'd say 7500 feet above sea level was up." Peri swept her hand in front of her to indicate where they were. "And I've hiked as high as 14,000 feet."

"That's not what I mean, and you know it. You'll never meet anyone of substance if you keep sequestering yourself on a mountain."

"And why do you care?"

Margaret stiffened her already straight back and jutted her chin forward. "Because, like it or not, civilization has come to Estes Park. And you will be considered that crazy mountain woman who prefers talking to trees rather than people."

"Again, I ask: Why do you care?"

Margaret *tsked* her tongue as her disapproval turned to pity. "Because I care about the beautification of this region, and I'm starting with the population of Estes Park. There are still some rag-tag people living here," she huffed.

"Those rag-tag people are the founders of Estes Park, and the pioneers, and the hard-working laborers who built this town."

"Yes, about that." Margaret leaned forward and spoke in a conspiratorial tone. "I actually came in here to talk to Sunnie."

"Me?" Sunnie had been conspicuously quiet during Margaret's prattle. *Stand up to her, woman!*

"Have you heard of the Ladies of Fine Society Improvement Association, Estes Park Division?"

"No."

"It's no wonder, with you hiding out all day here in this shack."

"Now wait just a minute—" That got Sunnie riled.

"Oh, I know, some would call it quaint, or. . .charming. I don't mean to offend. All kinds of people are coming to Estes Park, and I'm sure your type of clientele is happy to find something. . .affordable." She swiped her gloved finger across the table and looked at it.

"My type?" Sunnie stood, looking ready to do battle.

Peri hoped some fur would fly. Margaret had it coming. But a customer dressed in fishing gear and carrying a pole walked in on his way to his room. Margaret gave Sunnie a self-satisfied grin, saying *I told you* so with her arched brows.

"Well." Margaret stood and brushed her shirtfront as if to fling off any dust or debris she may have collected while sitting in a substandard establishment. "I thought you'd like to join the association, being a businesswoman and all. We have the ear of influential people in Colorado. It could improve your business." She glanced around the room. "If either of you are interested, we're having our first meeting tomorrow at my hotel. Five o'clock."

She sauntered toward the door, but stopped to look at Peri. "A rancher! We can do much better than that." Then she disappeared out to the dirt road and hopped into her automobile.

Peri stood and kicked the chair, causing her ankle to scream in pain. "The nerve of that woman!"

"I know she's insufferable, but remember what Papa always says."

" 'Forgive the unlovable; love the unforgivable.' I know, but even he walks the other way when he sees her coming." They both giggled as they recalled a time when Papa spun on his heel and ducked inside a saloon to get away from Margaret.

"Should we attend that meeting tomorrow just to be sure they don't turn Estes Park into New York?" Sunnie drummed the table with her fingers.

"You can. I've got my hands full with convincing folks that we need a national park."

"I'm not sure I can brave Margaret's kind alone." Sunnie's forlorn look tugged at Peri's heart.

Peri sat again and pulled her sister's hand into hers. "We've been through a lot in our lives. And you, my dear, have been the most persevering of all. Remember on the reservation when Dancing Lake decided you liked the boy she had her eyes on? You stood up to her well enough."

"Because I didn't like Moon Eagle. Ew. He liked to smell his own armpits. And we were only ten."

"And when we were older, in college. Who defended me when the popular girls spread the rumor that I ate tree bark?"

"It would have helped if you'd gone into accounting, like me, instead of plant and animal biology. But no one talks about my sister like that, even if it is true."

"Hey! I only did it that once because we were studying beavers and I wanted to get inside its head. And it was only a nibble." Peri sighed, hoping Sunnie would see what she was trying to do. "There is spunk inside there." She pointed to Sunnie's heart.

Sunnie stood and gathered the empty teacups. "You know what? I'm going to the meeting of the Ladies of Fine Society Improvement Association, Estes Park Division."

"Why?"

Sunnie held up a finger. "One, to keep an eye on Margaret. She's become quite radical of late. And two. . ." She held up another finger. "She mentioned they have the ear of important people in Colorado. The more who hear about the fight for a national park, the better. Don't you think?"

Peri, who rarely showed spontaneous affection, grabbed her sister and hugged her tight. "Thank you. Welcome to the team."

Sunday morning, Clay cleaned up after chores and headed to town. He'd thought a lot about his conversation with Peri. The scripture verse she'd quoted hit him square in the gut. It had been years since that snake, Walter Kratz, had stolen his wife. He couldn't decide if he was more angry at him or at her. He was mostly frustrated that he never got a chance to talk things out with Anna. Perhaps that was why he felt stuck. No way to resolve the issue.

When he got to the white clapboard church, the last strains of the bell trailed away, and off-tune, but boisterous, voices drifted out the door singing "Amazing Grace." He remembered that hymn from childhood, when he'd sit between Ma and Pa and fidget. There was always something better to do than to listen to adults talk about God. A new calf. A favorite fishing spot. A rumored game of marbles out behind the soda shop. As he got older, he drifted from the church but came to know God more personally later in life. Who else would you turn to when the foal is breech and her mama is on death's door? Or when a freak snowstorm isolates the herd for days. Or lightning strikes the barn and fire takes all the hay?

The early years gave him a foundation, but how easy it became to forget all that in the face of betrayal.

New anger surged and he nearly hopped back on his horse, but the song had finished and he heard someone introducing Reverend Winfield.

Winfield. Peri's father. Was she inside?

He walked lightly up the steps and slipped inside the door. There she was, in the front pew, sitting between two women, one with brown hair in a bun and the other with gray. Peri's short light-brown curls couldn't be missed in a sea of feminine locks. That's one thing he liked about her. She wasn't frilly, like Anna. No, a natural beauty, Peri didn't need powders and jewelry to show off her femininity.

And she'd make a sturdy wife.

He squelched that thought. He didn't need another woman in his life. They only caused grief. Plus, they were on two sides of an issue right now, and he didn't see how they would ever resolve it.

He sat in the back corner and forced himself to listen. Clay could see Peri in her father. The same tender eyes and the same strong, resolute chin.

If he hadn't already surmised that God had prompted him to go to church, he was convinced when he heard the subject of the day. Forgiveness.

Reverend Winfield started out with an anecdote about how he named his two daughters.

"When my wife and I first started in the mission field, the Lord led us to a Cheyenne tribe. My lovely bride"—he pointed to the gray-haired woman sitting next to Peri—"was with child—our first." He then pointed to Peri. "When the time came, our daughter entered the world with quite strong opinions."

A chuckle rippled throughout the room.

"Ah," Reverend Winfield continued. "I see you've met my daughter."

Yes, Clay had not only met the elder daughter, but had come face-to-face with her strong opinions. He joined the gentle laughter as he watched Peri's head drop. He would have felt bad for her, but from his vantage point he could see that she was smiling.

"But there were complications." The pastor's sober tone subdued the crowd. "We nearly lost Mattie. A kind medicine woman who was helping with the birth calmly, and with great authority, made up a concoction that she gave to Mattie to drink. The bleeding stopped forthwith. When I asked her what was in the potion, she said 'šee'eeháséto,' periwinkle."

A collective "Ah!" rose from the group.

"And from that day forward, to honor the woman and the plant that God provided, our little bundle was known as Periwinkle."

Peri, clearly at home among the congregation, stood and faced them, giving an exaggerated bow. When her head swooped back up, she stopped abruptly when her eyes locked on Clay. He touched his right eyebrow in salute. He expected her to crumble into an embarrassed heap, but instead she nodded in acknowledgment, turned, and lowered herself onto the pew.

The reverend went on to tell about how he had named his younger daughter. "Thank the Lord, there was no life-altering circumstance. As we made our way through Colorado and to the Arapaho camps, we were struck by the sight of vast yellow fields of sunflowers. And so we named our second daughter Sunflower, Mattie's favorite. The flower, not necessarily the daughter." More tittering from the congregation. "Although there may be days. . ." He let the sentence trail to gain the full effect of what he'd just implied.

Clay liked Peri's father. Unconventional for a pastor, to be sure, but apparently not afraid to speak his mind. Much like his daughter. He went on to tie in the story of how he and his wife had named their daughters in the same manner as the native people that they loved, by choosing something that was meaningful to them at the time of the birth.

He continued to explain how many of those he'd ministered to had forgiven those who had taken their land. They opted to trust in a peace-loving God rather than to dwell on hatred.

Peri had spoken to him about that the other day.

The pastor concluded with, "Forgive the unlovable; Love the unforgivable." Peri and her sister glanced at each other and seemed to suppress some giggles. Why would they laugh at such a thing?

He dismissed them as he thought about the statement. How could he love or forgive Anna? She had used him from the very beginning of their marriage, and she abandoned him when she was through. His jaw tightened. If he was to forgive the woman, God would have to make a more compelling argument than the sermon he had just heard.

Chapter 5

Peri fidgeted as Papa finished the sermon. Had Clay come as a result of their conversation? If so, then she silently thanked the Lord for putting the right words in her mouth. She longed to turn in her seat to see how he reacted to the sermon but didn't want to convey the wrong message. She went over in her head just what she would say to solidify what he'd just heard. At the last "Amen," she glanced over her shoulder to see Clay duck out the door.

Please, Lord, let me catch up to him.

She swam through the sea of people who wanted to talk about her unusual name now that Papa had spilled the beans. But she made it outside in time to see Clay near his horse, talking to the owner of Harper's Eatery. *Thanks for holding him up, Lord.*

She approached the two men as they seemed to finish their conversation with a handshake and familiar pat on each other's shoulder.

Clay noticed her and introduced her to his cousin, Tom Harper.

"I know Mr. Harper from our congregation. I also know your restaurant very well. You have excellent breakfasts."

"Thank you, Miss Winfield. Your father gave an outstanding sermon today, as always. I look forward to his visits."

"I know what you mean, but then again, I'm partial."

Mr. Harper excused himself, leaving Clay to carry on the conversation.

Peri patted Angus on the neck as she addressed Clay. "It was good to see you in church today."

"I almost didn't come in."

"Why ever not?"

He kicked at the dust with his already dusty boot. "I don't know. It's been a long time."

"Then it was good you joined us. God doesn't care how long it's been. In fact, He doesn't have the same time constraints as we do, so to Him, there may not have even been a gap."

Clay's mouth pulled into a grin. "Always positive, aren't you?"

"Well, not always. You've seen me close to my worst."

"That wasn't your worst? Spitting like a wet wildcat in the middle of the lake?"

She put her finger to her lips, even while a giggle escaped her. "Shh! Not many people know about that."

"My lips are sealed." The mischievous twinkle in his eyes betrayed his words. She knew this wouldn't be the last she heard of the incident.

Just as Peri was about to invite Clay to dinner, Margaret pulled up to them in her Stanley Steamer. A sheer gossamer scarf held her wide-brimmed hat in place.

"Peri, how good to see you again." She spoke to Peri over the *chug-kachug* of her car, but her gaze was turned toward Clay.

"It hasn't been that long, Margaret." *And please go away before you cause me much embarrassment.*

"Would you like to introduce me to your friend?"

No. "Mrs. Margaret Stallworth, meet Mr. Clayton McCarrick."

"The rancher." Margaret nodded as she clearly assessed the man's character with her squinty gaze and tilted lips.

Just as he tipped his hat and said, "Ma'am," she thrust her left hand out—as the other was still curled over the steering wheel—palm side down, as if she expected him to kiss her fingers. He shook it awkwardly.

Margaret turned to Peri, apparently done with Clay. "I have invited your family to Sunday dinner and, of course, you're welcome to come."

"I appreciate your invitation, but—"

"Oh, please don't refuse. It's my treat at the hotel restaurant. How often can you say you've had the best gourmet meal at the finest eating establishment in seventy miles?" One more dig aimed at Sunnie, and she wasn't even there.

"Well, I was about to invite Mr. McCarrick to my home for dinner."

Clay grinned at her. "You were?"

"Yes." She resisted the urge to stomp the ground with her foot to make her point.

"Then bring him along. I'll expect both of you at one o'clock." Margaret turned forward in her seat and drove away, leaving a small dust cloud in her wake.

Peri rubbed her temple. "I'm so sorry about that," she said to Clay. "You don't have to come."

"Now, how can I refuse the best gourmet meal in seventy miles?"

Peri's midsection suddenly felt warm. She placed her palm on her stomach to settle the strange feeling. It didn't seem as if Clay was accepting the invitation because of the food. His warm gaze suggested he had accepted to spend time with Peri.

Oh, what was she getting herself into?

Clay had never been inside the large Stanley Hotel on the hill, built a year prior. He escorted Peri into the fine dining room and immediately felt underdressed in his good dungarees and bolo tie. The men all wore suit coats, vests, and ties. The women wore fancy dresses with lace and ribbons. Peri looked fine. Well, more than fine. Her light-blue church dress, while not as expensive looking as others in the room, still gave her an elegant air. In fact, when he first saw her outside the church in that get up, he had to fight to keep his jaw from dragging the ground. All he'd ever seen her in were trousers and a work shirt. This Peri, the one by his side at this very moment, wore her femininity with grace.

Upon seeing Mrs. Stallworth coming toward them, looking like a cat stalking its prey, he quickly swooped off his dust-free go-to-meeting cowboy hat and smoothed his hair as best he could.

"Peri! Mr. McCarrick! I'm so happy you decided to accept my invitation."

"I'm pleased to have been invited, ma'am." Clay rubbed the top of his boots with the back of his pants to shine them up a little.

"Please, come on in. Our table is over here." She led them to a cozy little corner where a table had been set to accommodate eight places. "Please meet my mother, Mrs. Harriot Sullivan."

Clay did the math in his head. He counted six people, including Peri and himself. Who were the other two?

He pulled a chair out for Peri and started to sit next to her.

"Oh, Mr. McCarrick! Please sit over here." Mrs. Stallworth placed a dainty gloved hand on the back of the seat at the farthest corner of the table.

"Margaret, really!" Peri's protest fell on deaf ears.

As Clay made his way to the chair, another woman joined them. "I'm so sorry I'm late. But the luxurious rooms in this hotel are very hard to leave."

"Nonsense," Mrs. Stallworth said. "You're right on time. Sit here next to Mr. McCarrick." The woman was introduced as Lydia Alexander.

That left one more chair to fill, next to Peri.

Clay didn't know much about protocol, but he did know the upper classes liked their dinner parties even. He had no doubt he'd been paired with Miss Alexander despite coming with Peri. The final chair, by deduction, would be occupied by a male, and obviously one whom Mrs. Stallworth felt better suited for Peri.

He knew her kind. He had married her kind.

"Excuse me, Margaret." Peri caught their host's attention. "Who will be sitting here?" Peri patted the chair with a suspicious look on her face. She knew it too. They had been split up before they could even call themselves a couple.

"For our guest of honor, who should be here shortly. He's a very busy man and has just arrived at the hotel a few moments ago from Denver. I suggested he freshen up before making an appearance."

"Why the secrecy?" Peri pushed back.

"No secret. I just love a good mystery." Mrs. Stallworth shrugged and winked.

They had finally settled down and ordered. Despite the uncomfortable situation and a dinner partner who talked incessantly, Clay was looking forward to the thick porterhouse steak he'd chosen. But before the meal was delivered, Mrs. Stallworth, who had been engaged in conversation with his "companion," looked over their heads, a huge smile blooming on her face.

"There he is. Just in time." She stood and nearly skipped to where the eighth member of their party was apparently approaching from behind Clay. "Ladies and gentlemen, may I introduce to you our state senator, Walter Kratz."

Peri could not believe Margaret's boldness. What was she thinking, pairing her with a senator from Denver?

A chair *skritched* across the floor and toppled over. Clay had stood abruptly, white as a snowcapped mountain peak. Margaret's mouth flew open in surprise, as did everyone's in the room.

"Mr. McCarrick! Explain yourself, please." Margaret's heel stomped the floorboard like the foot of an agitated rabbit.

Clay pointed at the new arrival. "I'm not eating with the likes of him."

Was it his issue with the government that had gotten him so riled up? If so, it seemed a good time for Peri to see this side of him before she got too emotionally involved.

Walter Kratz set his feet apart and balled his fists to his side. Was he bracing for an attack? Peri couldn't blame him the way Clay was acting.

"McCarrick. I didn't expect to see you here."

"Well, you won't see me for long." Clay grabbed his hat from the floor where it had landed when he stood and jammed it on his head. "My apologies, everyone. Mrs. Stallworth, I'm sorry I ruined your party."

He stormed out, nearly upending a waiter with a tray full of fancy desserts.

Peri ran after him. "Clay, please wait." But she was too late. He had already swung himself into the saddle, pulling the reins so tight that Angus fought the bit. Then he galloped down the hill, no doubt toward home.

When she returned to the table, everyone had resumed their conversations, although Margaret sat fanning herself with her napkin, still quite agitated. Walter Kratz stood, as did her father, and pulled her chair out for her. She felt compelled to apologize for Clay's bizarre behavior, but then again, they barely knew each other. She wasn't responsible for Clay. She tried to see his side, but regardless of what he felt about the government, rude was rude, and she couldn't excuse him.

"Thank you, Mr. Kratz," she said as she sat. "Or is it Senator Kratz? I'm afraid I've not been schooled on proper etiquette when it comes to government officials."

"Please, call me Walter." He flashed a politician's smile, but it seemed genuine enough. He was older than she, perhaps late forties or early fifties. A sprinkling of gray in his dark hair had begun at his temples, which only made him seem more distinguished.

"And call me Peri."

"Unusual name."

Peri laughed, remembering her father's sermon earlier that day. "It's short for Periwinkle. Don't get me started."

"I look forward to finding out more about it."

"What brings you up here? The fresh air?"

"That, and I wanted to see firsthand what all the fuss was about regarding the state-funded land versus a national park. I've never visited this area before."

"You just missed a tour I gave about a week and a half ago."

"I heard about that. I would have been with them, but my schedule didn't allow for it. They told me their guide was a very knowledgeable woman, but when Margaret told me you were a naturalist I never made the connection."

"Really? Then she has been paying attention."

"Excuse me?"

"Nothing. Margaret just doesn't seem to take much interest in my work."

"Well, she seemed quite proud of you when I expressed to her that I was sorry I missed the tour."

What could Peri make of that? Unless Margaret had just said anything to make Walter want to come and meet Peri.

"I can take you on a tour while you're here."

"Regrettably, I must leave in the morning. But my schedule is clear at the end of the summer. Might I be able to book a tour then?"

"Absolutely."

"I'd like to bring some of my aides and perhaps their wives, if they're willing."

"Perfect! And I know just where I'll take you. I just recently found a beautiful little lake and a thirty-foot waterfall."

"That sounds wonderful. I'll be back in August."

"That's fine. The temperature will be comfortable as summer winds down."

"I look forward to it, then."

Their conversation flowed easily throughout dinner. Peri hated to give Margaret the satisfaction of knowing her matchmaking had not gone horribly wrong. So she avoided the ridiculous half-moon grin on the other side of the table.

At one point, Walter asked why she had chosen to become a naturalist. As she had with Clay, she related her experience as a missionary's daughter, and Malti, the woman who had taught her about plants.

Walter nodded. "I've always been fascinated with healing herbs. My grandmother believed in natural treatments, so I know a little bit about it."

"The place I want to take you has some yarrow. I was just up there last week, and I needed it to make a poultice for a sprained ankle. There are bushels of the delicate white flowers up there."

"Ah, yes. I remember Grandmother chewing the leaves for all kinds of scrapes we boys got ourselves into. If you thought your mother licking her thumb to get dirt off your face was disgusting, you should have seen us after she put that messy glob on our knees."

Peri laughed. "I carry a mortar and pestle that I use to make a poultice, but chewing works too. That's how Malti did it."

Before they parted, Peri promised Walter she would go to Denver sometime during the summer to present her case for a national park at a meeting he would set up with the governor of the state.

"I've been taking photographs along with my sketches. Should I bring those?"

"Yes, by all means. Some of those people have never traveled higher than a mile above sea level. Your pictures will bring the mountains to them and hopefully convince them of how much we need to protect the land."

That night as she prepared for bed, Peri thought about her day. The surprise of seeing Clay at church, the warm feelings she had toward him when she realized he would brave an afternoon with Margaret just to be with her, his anger toward Walter for no other reason than because he represented the government, and finally, her gaining a toehold in the fight for the national park.

She opened her Bible to where she had left off the night before in 2 Timothy chapter 3 and read verse 13, "But evil men and seducers shall wax worse and worse, deceiving, and being deceived." A cold chill wormed through her. Was this a warning? About Walter? About Clay? Or had she been the one seducing the senator in order to sway him to her beliefs?

"Lord, please give me discernment. I want what is best for Your creation, but I don't want to step outside of Your will. Lead me and guide me as I navigate this next leg of my journey."

Chapter 6

Clay stayed on his ranch for the next couple of weeks, mostly because of the extraordinary amount of calves being born, but also because he was too embarrassed to see Peri again. Was he sorry he had stormed out on the dinner party? No. He'd do it again. But that didn't erase from his mind the look on Peri's face when he'd attacked his nemesis, Walter Kratz.

As the words were coming out of his mouth, Peri's eyes had grown wider and wider. He couldn't take the judgment he'd seen in her face, so he'd hightailed it out of there. He knew she had followed him outside, but he couldn't face her. Couldn't reveal what that man had done to him.

The only thing that could entice him to go to town was the Independence Day celebration and Frontier Days. No self-respecting rancher could miss a good Wild West show, complete with bronco busting and calf roping.

He'd shaved that morning, trying to convince himself that he'd done it for comfort and not because Peri might be there. No, sir. He was through with women.

As he and Angus clip-clopped to the fairgrounds, he nearly turned around at the sight of all the people. They looked like prairie grass blowing in the breeze, with barely a space between them. Surrounding the festivities were horses, buggies, and autos, a testament to the changing times.

He tied Angus to a post where a trough of water had been placed and set out on foot among the throngs of people.

He made his way to where the broncs were corralled. He knew some of the cowboys who had come the last two years, ever since the town had started the celebration. A couple of them were well-known broncobusters in Wyoming at the Cheyenne Frontier Days. When they heard about the Wild West show in Estes Park, they jumped at the chance to perform at seven thousand feet above sea level, just to say they did it.

"Hey, McCarrick! What's a no-good lanky cowboy like you doing in a swanky place like this?"

Clay spun around, knowing who that voice belonged to. "Who you calling lanky, Stick? How're you doing?" Stick Mitchell stood six-feet-six-inches and had the waist of a twelve-year-old boy. Clay shook the slender paw suddenly thrust toward him.

He'd known Stick ever since his days with Anna. Stick and Tom had kept him from falling apart. Stick had been the one to finally convince him to move to Estes Park to be with Tom and to heal.

"How's the ranch?" They walked and talked as they moseyed around the corrals.

"Can't complain. It's turning a profit."

Stick pulled a piece of hay out of a bale and stuck it between his teeth. "I hear tell of some folks making noise to turn your backyard into a national park."

Clay kicked at a dirt clod. "Yeah. It seems to be happening all over again. First the railroad takes my land, and then this."

"You gonna let it?"

"I'm going to fight it."

"Atta boy. At least this time there ain't no filly to muck up your head."

Clay cleared his throat.

"Is there?" Stick pressed.

"No! Of course not." A nervous chuckle escaped Clay's lips, and even he knew he didn't sound convincing.

"That ain't what I heard."

Clay turned to Stick, who had stopped at a corral fence and placed his long leg on the bottom rung while leaning his elbows on the top.

"Is my cousin talking over the back fence again?"

"Hey, he's the only gossip I know here. If it weren't for him, I'd never know what you're up to." Stick flicked the straw to the ground. "I'd warn you off her, but Tom likes her. Says she'd be good for you if you'd only let her rope you."

Clay pulled his hat low to his eyes and leaned on the fence. "I've got a calf at the ranch who seems to think it's better to be off on his own. We're made from the same cloth, he and I."

Stick sighed. "Don't let your bullheaded stubbornness keep you from a good thing." He tapped the top of Clay's hat. "I gotta go. I'm up for calf roping at ten o'clock."

Clay brooded for just a little while longer while he watched the corral full of spirited horses. Anna had been one of them, impossible to bust. But Peri, now she was a feisty filly that would be a shame to break. She was perfect just the way she was. If only she weren't so dead set on the national park.

Peri settled herself on a bleacher next to Sunnie and Frederick. "You know I hate these kinds of exhibitions."

"I know," Sunnie responded. "And yet this is your third year attending."

"Someone needs to watch after the poor animals. Honestly, the rough way they're treated!"

Frederick leaned forward, reached across Sunnie, and offered Peri his popcorn. "That's how they do it on the ranch, you know. Calves need to be branded, so they need to be caught. Horses need to be broken in order to be useful."

"I know all that, but it doesn't make it any less distressing." She allowed her gaze to sweep the fairgrounds from her vantage point on the top bleacher.

"He's here." Sunnie picked through the popcorn in her hand.

"Who?"

"You know who."

"I'm sure I don't know what you're talking about." Peri crossed her trouser-covered legs and placed her elbow on her knee. "And besides, I don't want to be associated with such a rude, stubborn—"

"Oh, there he is." Sunnie pointed to the left of the bleachers.

"Where?" Peri stood before she knew what she was doing. Her movement must have caught Clay's eye as he looked up. Peri pretended she hadn't seen him and stretched nonchalantly.

Clay started to walk away and Peri bristled. She knew he'd seen her, so why didn't he come up to sit with them, or at least wave? "Oh no, you don't Clayton McCarrick." She hopped down off the side of the bleacher, grateful for her mountain climbing skills and strong ankles. Ignoring the disapproving looks from a group of older women, she sprinted to where she'd last seen him. As she rounded a blind corner, she ran into him, literally.

"Whoa! You got a bear chasing you?" He braced her by the elbows, keeping her from toppling back.

"Is that all you have to say to me?"

"Well, no." He released her and pushed back his hat. "But it's all I know to say at the moment."

Peri took a breath to settle the adrenaline coursing through her veins. "Look, I know this is awkward. But can we talk somewhere?"

He glanced around at the crowd, who had just cheered on a calf that escaped the chute. "Come with me."

He gently cupped her elbow and led her to the edge of the throng. They stopped at the corral with wild horses. A dappled Appaloosa trotted up to the fence. Peri reached into a small knapsack she was carrying and whipped out a carrot.

"You came prepared." He laughed.

"If these poor creatures are going to be abused, the least I can do is give them a pleasant moment in their day."

"I was wondering how you felt about the Wild West show. Doesn't seem like your cup of tea."

"It's my third year. I like the clown."

"I'll never tell," he whispered. He was close enough so that Peri felt his breath on her cheek.

Clay leaned on the fence. "So, you want to talk."

"Yes." She stood straight and faced him.

He held up his hand. "Before you start, I want you to know that I'm not ready to talk about what happened at the hotel and the dinner party. It's a personal matter between Kratz and me."

"But, just because he's a government man—"

"I said I don't want to talk about it." He turned to leave, but she stopped him.

"Wait, that's not really what I wanted to discuss."

He stood with his back to her, but glanced at her over his shoulder. "I'm listening."

Now she had to come up with something to discuss because the incident at the hotel was exactly why she had just chased after him. "We talked about my going with you on a hunting trip." She mentally kicked herself. Why, of all things, was that the first thing out of her mouth?

When he turned, his eyes narrowed, and he placed his hands on his hips. "Why?"

Think, Peri. "You said you weren't like other hunters. I'd like to see that for myself."

"Okay." He scratched his jaw. "I'm leaving with a group in a couple of weeks."

"I'll be there."

"Okay."

"Okay."

Peri held her head high and walked past him to go back to her seat, praying the Lord would find all the animals good hiding places that week.

Chapter 7

What was she thinking?

Peri sat on Daisy and trailed behind the hunting party, seriously considering turning tail and running the other way. But if she did, she'd be stopped by George, Clay's partner who brought up the rear in the buckboard. In front of her were three men and two women in single file, atop horses, with their rifles tucked into their gear. Clay led the crew on Angus, both looking as if they were masters of their domain. Which he no doubt was. This was Clay's world. Peri had hiked this land and knew it intimately, and yet she felt like a fallen daffodil petal amongst a grove of pine. She didn't belong in Clay's world. "You doing okay up there, girlie?" George called to her from the buckboard.

Rankled, she called over her shoulder. "I'm fine, George, how are you?"

He snickered. "Oh, I'm good, but you're looking a little stiff up there. Bareback getting to you? Maybe you should get a saddle."

"Daisy and I don't need a saddle." She turned back around and tried to ignore her sore backside. She didn't usually ride Daisy unless she had to. Her mule was more for packing gear. Peri would walk by her side, enjoying the stretch of the legs and the feel of solid earth beneath her feet. But the hunting party went faster than she could walk, bent on reaching the camping spot that would be their headquarters for the next three days. Therefore, she opted to ride. Daisy was up for it, though, her strong back more than capable of carrying Peri.

"I think you're doing splendidly." Mrs. Moore's words became balm to Peri's soul.

If Peri identified with a daffodil petal, Erline Moore was a rose. The older, genteel lady held herself with grace, as if she were at afternoon tea rather than sitting atop a dappled mare. She and her husband had come all the way from Boston to take advantage of the many recreational opportunities they had heard about from their friends.

Mrs. Moore slowed in order to ride next to Peri, her broad-rimmed sunhat flopping. "I'm fascinated by your work, Miss Winfield. May I ask you some questions?"

"Absolutely," Peri said. Anything to get her mind off their agenda, to kill anything that moved.

"I know you're a naturalist. I've seen your flier in various establishments around town."

"I love to share what I know." With tours that didn't involve taking a life.

"Why did you decide to come on a hunting trip? That seems the opposite of what you stand for."

"Mr. McCarrick and I are on two sides of the national park issue. I wanted to be fair and see why he's so adamant that this land should stay with the state forestry service rather than be protected by the federal government."

"Oh, a little reconnaissance. I think that's very smart."

Was it? Peri still doubted her decision to come on this trip. She'd only suggested it because she was flustered that day at the fairgrounds. But when Clay looked at her with such suspicion, she'd accepted it as a challenge.

"I still plan to impart as much of my naturalist education to Mr. McCarrick's group as I can."

"Bravo for you." Mrs. Moore dipped her head. "Don't hide your talent under a bushel. Truth be told, I much prefer your way of thinking. Mr. Moore is the hunter, and I'm only along to share in his passion. But. . ." She lowered her voice. "I'm secretly praying he misses his shots."

"Me too." Peri grinned.

They came to a clearing where Clay announced they'd make camp. "There's a herd of deer that usually graze just over that ridge. We'll have lunch and then head over that way."

Peri had already decided she'd stay behind. It was bad enough she'd have to see the carcasses, she didn't have to watch the murder. Mrs. Moore offered to stay with Peri, with her husband's blessing. Peri enjoyed the couple's interaction, a truly equal relationship with mutual love and support. Just like her own parents.

The weather had been lovely and the day promised to be warm until evening. Peri commented on this and Mrs. Moore said, "I simply love mountain summers. Not too cold, not too hot."

"It does make it more pleasant to hike. But there is something ethereal about the winters. Hiking after a huge snowfall, wearing snowshoes so as not to sink in the deep snow. The pine covered in thick white icing. I'm always sure there's a gingerbread house just around the bend."

"It would seem you've found your own slice of heaven here."

A slice of heaven. Not with the dark cloud hovering over it.

Peri must not have responded with as sincere a smile as she thought. Mrs. Moore tilted her head. "Or maybe not. Is there something wrong?"

"This would be the perfect place to live, but if we don't protect it, not only the land, but the animals, we could lose it all." Peri weighed in her mind whether to confide in this delightful lady. They had been having such a wonderful time, why ruin it by bringing up the killing train? But something, most likely the Lord, prompted her. She went on to relate everything as she had to Clay, leaving no bloody detail out.

"I have heard about the Buffalo Wars. Horrible. And you were a witness? At such a young age, too." Mrs. Moore slowly shook her head.

"My dream for the longest time was to open a bison refuge."

"Have you heard of the island in the Great Salt Lake where an individual took it upon himself to populate it with bison?"

"Yes, Antelope Island. I drew my inspiration from there. Thanks to the efforts of compassionate souls such as these, including President Roosevelt who persuaded Congress to establish several preserves, the healing has already begun."

"I'm so pleased to hear that, but what is the connection with this area?"

Peri stood as she felt the need to pace. "The same thing is happening with elk in this country, although not with the same hostility. The government isn't trying to starve the Native Americans by extirpating their food source. But because of careless killers, elk will soon be extinct. There are less than a dozen in this area, that we know of. It's been a while since anyone has seen any."

"So it makes sense to halt all hunting operations, and the best way to do that is to turn all of this into a national park."

"Exactly." It was refreshing to talk to someone who understood. "We must take care of what God gave us." Peri's heart raced as her passion and adrenaline collided. "No offense to your husband, but there are hunters who come here solely to take home trophies. These mountains used to be teeming with herds of elk, thousands of them, all enjoying the freedom of grazing anywhere they chose. There are now only five hundred to a thousand individual elk in the entire state of Colorado. We need regulation in order to protect these lives."

Mrs. Moore reached out and touched Peri's arm. "I'm sold. My husband owns several newspapers back East. We will do what we can to build awareness and help the cause."

"Oh, thank you!"

"I would like to say, if I'm not overstepping my bounds, I hope you're not including your Mr. McCarrick in with the careless killers you just mentioned."

"No, of course not." Not careless, but she couldn't shake the word *killer.* Even while she had become attracted to Clay—admittedly, she enjoyed the phrase "your Mr. McCarrick"—the biggest stumbling block in their friendship was the fact that she couldn't separate the compassionate man she was coming to know from his chosen profession.

"To tell you the truth," Mrs. Moore continued, "we sought out Mr. McCarrick because of his reputation. Do you know that besides supplying the local restaurants with venison, he also donates smoked meat to the Sunshine Rescue Mission in Denver? We liked that. Now we're a part of something more important than just bagging the big one."

Peri had no idea. She knew Clay supplied the local restaurants, but why hadn't he told her he donated a portion of his profits to charity? It didn't change her mind about the national park, because Clay wasn't the only hunter in the area, but it certainly helped her see him in a different light.

For the next few hours, Peri offered Mrs. Moore her own naturalist tour. They hiked for a little way, Peri offering her expertise on the flora and fauna they found. They especially enjoyed watching a mother bear and her two cubs. From their vantage point, while safely hidden in the brush, they giggled quietly at the twins' antics at the river. Mama seemed to want to teach them how to fish, but they only wanted to frolic in the water. This no doubt sent their dinner swimming away in a frenzy. The trio eventually moved on upstream, thankfully away from the campsite.

Shortly after Peri and Mrs. Moore returned, the hunting party also showed up, morose and disappointed.

"Any luck?" Mrs. Moore asked her husband.

"No, couldn't find a deer anywhere."

Mrs. Moore winked at Peri. "I'm so sorry, darling. I wonder if someone was praying for the poor animals."

"I really wish you'd stop doing that," Mr. Moore groused.

His wife lowered her voice and spoke to Peri. "I may be okay with what happens with the meat from Mr. McCarrick's hunting trips, but I'm still exultant that they came back empty."

"Understood." Peri thanked the Lord for this new like-minded friend.

The next day proved equally disappointing for the hunters, and each time Mrs. Moore and Peri silently celebrated with grins and winks.

Toward the end of the day they decided to let nature win and simply enjoy the campfire for the rest of the evening. Fortunately, George had brought plenty of bread, smoked meat, and beans for a hearty supper.

As dusk was just beginning to soften the mountain edges, Peri suggested to Clay that they take a walk. There was one more trail she hadn't explored this trip, and she was eager to do it with Clay. She had something important to confess to him.

They wandered through the fir trees and over small meadows. Cheery yellow flowers, Golden Banner, brightened their path.

"I want to apologize." That came out easier than she had expected.

Clay's step hesitated for just a second before he continued on. "What for?"

"Mrs. Moore told me about your benevolence in providing smoked meat to the less fortunate. Why didn't you tell me?"

"Would it have made a difference?"

"Of course it would have."

"It's still a dead animal, no matter what is done with the meat."

"I know, and as I've told you before, I'm not a vegetarian, but knowing these lives aren't taken in vain helps me to reconcile it with my cause."

"I'm not heartless when I hunt, you know."

"I knew that the minute you showed up with Daisy when I hurt my ankle. You didn't go after her for me. You were worried yourself that the lion would attack her."

His silence spoke volumes.

"You're a good man, Clay McCarrick. And I'd be blessed beyond measure if I could call you a friend."

He scooted his hat back and scratched an eyebrow with his thumb. "Isn't that what we are?"

"Tenuous friends at best, I'd say. We still have 'The Issue' between us."

"Yes, that we do."

They continued to walk in silence until they came to a small hill. Peri led the way, and as she crested it, her gaze landed on a far mountain peak as the sun began to disappear behind it. They rarely had the colorful sunsets she had seen on the prairies. But watching the mountain slowly become a silhouette as the rock features disappeared into the shadow always fascinated her.

She turned to relate this to Clay when her foot slipped on what she thought was a small stick. She looked down to right herself and realized she was in the middle of numerous sticks, long and short. While puzzling why there were so many sticks in this small circumference where there was no tree, her sight landed on something larger, rounder. . .skull-like.

An elk skull! Her eyes darted all around the ground. She was in the middle of a kill!

Her pounding heart stole her breath. Carnage everywhere she looked. Every step kicked another bone. She tripped over the ribcage trying to get out. Just as spots blurred her vision, strong arms grasped her.

"It's okay, Peri. I'm here."

"Clay. . .bones. . .murderers. . ."

She squeezed her eyes shut to block out the horrific sight. Her feet came off the ground. Clay had swept her into his arms and was hopefully carrying her away from the crime scene.

"No, Peri. It's okay."

"How can it be okay? This was an elk." She murmured into his shirt, her arms clinging to his neck.

He placed her on a boulder and shook her gently. "Peri. A human didn't do this."

She slowly opened her eyes to see Clay only inches from her face, blocking out any unpleasantness.

"What?"

"An animal did this. Probably a mountain lion."

Peri shook her head to clear it. "How do you know?"

"By the way the bones are scattered. Plus, the antlers are still attached."

"It wasn't a hunter?"

His smile held compassion, and he wiped her tears with his thumbs. "Not a human hunter."

Relief swept through her, leaving her nearly as weak as the adrenaline had. "You're sure." It wasn't a question. It was a demand.

"Yes, I'm sure. I would never lie to you."

The tears came freely now. "It was an elk, Clay."

"I know. I'm sorry." He led her off the hill a different way than they had come.

"You don't kill elk, do you, Clay?" Her steps wobbled, but she gained strength the farther they traveled.

"No. And I instruct my tour group to never take a shot at one as well."

"Thank you."

"And thank you for your work. Your passion may be the death of mine, but I want you to know that we need people like you to maintain a civil balance."

She turned to look at this man, this conundrum of a friend. "How are we going to get past this, Clay?"

He stopped and faced her. "Like this."

His arm encircled her waist and drew her to his chest. She gasped as his mouth touched hers with a sweetness she didn't know he possessed. Too quickly it was over, but she still lingered in his arms. "I don't think that helped at all." Then she pulled him into a kiss of her own.

Chapter 8

The next few weeks proved hectic for both Clay and Peri. Tourism peaked and they both stayed busy giving their individual tours. The few times they were able to connect was sweet. Clay especially liked the long walks in the evening and the intimate suppers at each other's cabins.

After one such dinner, hosted by Peri, the topic came up of Peri's trip to Denver the following week.

"I know I'm consorting with the enemy, but I'd love your opinion on these." Peri laid a book on Clay's lap as they cozied on the sofa. Fire crackled in the stone fireplace. A storm had blown through, drenching the valley with rain, lowering the temperatures significantly for August.

"What is this?"

She flipped the cover to reveal photographs inside. "I'm taking these to Denver with me next Monday. I have a meeting with some important people to present my case for the national park."

They had talked at length about the issue between them but Clay wasn't sure what he thought about this next step. So far, it had just been between them, but it looked like Peri would be stepping out and pursuing sympathy for her cause. Perhaps he should show up at that meeting and present his case as well.

But for now, he looked at her pictures with interest. No use hogtieing her ideas before they were even out of the chute. The mumbling he'd heard on both sides of the state versus federal control had been even so far. He was fairly certain the ranchers and loggers would win. They were, after all, contributors to the wealth of the area. However, what few mining interests were nearby didn't sound as if they'd be able to convince anyone to let the land stay with the forestry service. The minerals were proving to be low grade or nonexistent.

The photos he flipped through impressed him. "These are really good."

"They were only taken with my little Brownie camera, but I wanted to include them when I present these." She flipped to the back of the album where several watercolor paintings lay tucked into the pages. "This way, they can see that I haven't made anything up. The paintings serve to enhance the photos."

With each turn of the page he became more and more impressed. She had caught sun-filled valleys and majestic mountain peaks. Bubbling creeks and sparkling lakes. Waterfalls of varying heights. Chipmunks, marmots, and beavers, along with deer, mountain sheep, and yes, even a bull elk with a full rack.

"Where did you see this fellow?"

"Actually, this is several years old. I plan to talk about the dwindling elk population and let them know that this was the last time I'd seen one." She swallowed hard. "Alive."

"Still thinking about the bones we found?"

"All the time." Her pretty mouth curved downward and he placed a kiss at one of the corners.

He looked again at the painting and noticed for the first time the females off in the distance. "I see he has a small herd. And look." He pointed. "A young one."

"Unfortunately, he's not really there. I just added him the other day because I needed hope to hang on to."

"These animals will breed. The herd will grow."

"But how many more hunters will come along and devastate them? Without regulation, anyone with a gun can come in and murder them."

Clay couldn't argue with that. If it weren't for his own livelihood, not only the hunting, but the ranching, he would be excited for Peri. She presented a strong case. But surely there was another way. Why couldn't they both enjoy the things they loved?

He kissed her good-bye that evening with the feeling of dread that she might just make a notch in her case with her visit to Denver.

"Tell me why you're doin' this again?" George began loading the delivery wagon with the smoked venison. "You don't usually take the meat to Denver. I do."

"I told you that I wanted to be sure that the food is meeting the rescue center's needs."

"I ain't convinced. I could ask them for you. Giving to them was, after all, my idea."

"And a noble one at that. How is your aunt and her family?"

"Back on their feet, thanks to you."

The two men worked in a familiar rhythm, a testament to the years they'd been partners. They arranged the wrapped meat in the back of the Mason wagon. Cousin Tom had bought the truck last year for faster travel in and out of the mountains when he needed supplies for his restaurant. Clay hated to admit it, but he was grateful for the speedy transportation. The buckboard would have taken forever.

George continued. "If you hadn't helped my aunt go to nursing school, she'd still be homeless. We're forever in your debt." He scratched his nose and gave Clay a sideways look. "But don't change the subject."

"What subject is that?" Clay refused to make eye contact with the man. George was honing in on the real reason Clay wanted to go to Denver, and he felt guilty enough using the rescue mission as an excuse.

"Don't be coy. It ain't your style."

Clay shut the door and leaned on the vehicle with his arms crossed. "I swear, if it isn't you riding me, it's Tom. Can't you two mind your own business?"

"Not when we see you hurting. Be careful, Clay. I like that pretty filly as much as you do, but she's not very sympathetic to what might happen to you if she's successful."

So, George knew he was going to Denver to...what? Convince Peri not to push her agenda? He knew that would do no good. Break into that meeting to present his side? They'd toss him out on his ear. Truth be told, he wasn't sure why he felt the need to be in Denver with her. If he were a woman, he'd call it intuition. The back of his neck tingled whenever he thought of her in Denver. Something didn't feel right, but he wasn't sure what it was.

After Clay delivered the venison to the appreciative manager of the rescue mission, he drove to the state capitol, where he knew Peri would be going. The sun had begun to dip toward the west. Peri's meeting was at four. Perhaps he could surprise her and take her to an early dinner.

The gilded dome of the building came into view. He'd heard it was pure gold leaf and put there to commemorate the Colorado gold rush. Seemed a waste of a precious metal to him. Just one more opulent reason to distrust the government.

As he turned into the parking area, he saw Peri getting out of a brand-spanking-new Cadillac. And helping her out was Walter Kratz!

Clay's blood boiled as he watched the man pull her hand into the crook of his elbow. She wore a skirt that was so tight at the ankles, it was no wonder she needed help moving. The Peri he knew scaled mountains and hiked bare tundra. This woman could barely make it across the parking lot.

The pair laughed easily together, apparently at some joke they'd just shared. Peri placed her hand on Kratz's shoulder as she attempted to gain control of a giggle. Then they disappeared inside the building, leaving Clay with memories of Anna, laughing and touching a younger Kratz on the shoulder. The only thing missing was the kiss in the middle of the street.

Clay ground the wagon's gears, not able to get out of there fast enough. All the way back up the mountains he tried to reason with himself. This was Peri, not Anna. But what if Kratz had coiled her in his grasp, hypnotizing her with his snake eyes? Kratz encouraged her desire for a national park. He spoke all the right words. He tickled her ear with promises. Why wouldn't she choose him over Clay, who opposed her at every turn?

By the time he pulled up to his ranch, he'd convinced himself he was through with women, for good this time. He'd let down his guard with Peri. He'd let her beautiful brown eyes see into his soul and take root there. Her determined yet gentle way almost had him convinced she may be right about preserving the area. He had nearly set aside his own needs for hers. And for what? The minute someone came to town speaking her language, she jumped into his fancy car and joined his bloated world.

Finally home, he skidded to a stop, surrounding the wagon with a cloud of dust. George must have seen him from his cabin. He walked toward Clay, who was still fuming behind the wheel.

George tapped on the driver's side window. "You okay in there?"

Clay opened his door and stepped out. "I'm going to grab my gear and head up to the hunting cabin for a spell. Come get me if anything's pressing here."

George scratched his head but thankfully kept his mouth shut.

Peri sank into the satin-soft covers, courtesy of her hostess, Margaret Stallworth. When Margaret had learned of Peri's meeting, she had insisted on escorting her back to Denver and putting her up in her home, a ridiculously lavish mansion in the most prestigious neighborhood in town. No wonder Margaret was spoiled.

Before she slipped into blissful slumber, she recalled her day.

It started out stressful, with Margaret bent on buying her that ridiculous outfit. Peri didn't care if the hobble skirt was the latest fashion, she never should have agreed to it. It now lay over a chair where she had haphazardly tossed it, the two-foot tear visible down the side after she'd had enough.

The rest of the day proved pleasant, though. Walter turned out to be a delightful host, escorting her to lunch and then driving her to the meeting. She chuckled as she remembered the conundrum of hopping out of his car in her tight skirt. One would never guess that she could mount and dismount a bareback mule with ease. He thought it funny, as well, as she shuffled along, and even though he tried to be a gentleman, he simply couldn't ignore the ridiculous outfit. What did he say that tickled her so? Oh, yes. *"That skirt would be better suited on my Uncle Henry's horse. She needed to be hobbled too."*

The image of a horse wearing her skirt had been too much and she'd forgotten everything Margaret had told her about being a lady. She had snorted a laugh that only made her giggle harder. Which made him laugh, which made her laugh. And so on. It surprised her how well they got along, but she told herself he was only making sure she was comfortable in the new environment. Big cities and isolated mountains were worlds apart.

Her presentation went swimmingly too. All present seemed impressed with her paintings, but moreover, they expressed interest in her cause. She felt certain that if it came to a vote, they would support the preserving of the land.

She drifted into a relaxed dream, where Clay stood by her side as the verdict came in: "The ayes have it for a new national park."

Chapter 9

Clay had been at the hunting cabin over a week, occasionally checking in with his foreman to see if there were any issues. George filled in as hunting guide.

How many days, or weeks, would it take for him to get the image of Peri cozying up to Kratz out of his mind?

How long had it taken to erase the same image of Anna, touching Kratz's arm, laughing with him, kissing him?

Never. He had never been able to get over her betrayal.

The musing clung to him like thistle on a wool sock.

"Lord, I'm through with this. Help me heal." He rode Angus, moseying along the rocky terrain, wandering down one deer trail after another, not even caring where they were or how far from home they'd gotten. Clay always packed a blanket, jerky, and fishing line in case he couldn't make it back. He glanced at the sky, resisting the urge to shake his fist. "I really need to move on from this. I thought Peri had been sent from You. Yes, she's a thorn in my side, and if she gets her way, I'll be out of a job and regulated out of grazing land. But, Lord, I like her. She's helping me forget about Anna. The two women are so different, and she made me see hope in loving again. But then You allowed Kratz to come back into my life. . .into Peri's life. Why, Lord?"

Even though he didn't shake a fist, he made one so hard he felt his nails sink into his palm. If Kratz had been there, he would have used that fist on the man's face.

But then he saw Peri in his mind, that first time he'd seen her, talking to her mule as if it were a friend.

He chuckled and patted Angus on the neck. "We wouldn't know anything about that, would we, boy?"

Angus nickered and nodded his head as if he knew what Clay was referring to.

Clay recalled Peri toppling into the lake and coming up spitting like an angry wet cat. And her using the crutch he'd made against her will. He'd seen passion and fire in her eyes when she talked about the land she loved. And he saw fear when she'd thought someone had brought down one of her beloved elk. And of course, how could he ever forget the image of her smiling at him, inches away from his face, her arms linked around his neck? How could he forget the warm kisses they had enjoyed?

Once again, he told himself, Peri isn't Anna.

"Lord, please take my anger. Help me face Peri with my fears. Forgive me for keeping this part of my past from her. I just didn't want her to see me as weak, for not being able to fight for my woman."

He finally looked around and realized where Angus was taking them. They were on the same trail leading to where he'd met Peri for the first time.

He could almost hear her laughter drifting on a breeze, mingling with the gentle singing of the aspen leaves.

Wait a minute. That was her!

He got to a place where the trees thinned and he could see her on another trail below. The small group moved past the trees on foot. She had dropped back, letting someone else take the lead, probably after informing them the trail would take them straight to the lake.

She joined up with the last person, whom Clay could only see partially through the filter of the trees. Clay followed them on his own trail above. Finally, he had a clear view of the entire party, and the one she was laughing with. Kratz.

Clay couldn't keep his blood from boiling. His right hand curled around the butt of his rifle as he urged Angus to go a little faster so he could get to the lake before them. He would confront Kratz as he should have at the restaurant during the dinner party. As he should have when he first saw his wife in the weasel's arms.

"Peri," Walter said with a big grin on his face, "I've never seen anything like what you've shown us today. It's one thing to see the mountains from Denver at a distance. Being inside them feels like a different country."

"Now that the West has opened up, people are looking for places like this to live and recreate. Look at Estes Park. With the arrival of the Stanley Hotel last year, we've seen quite the boom, and the more people share their experience, the more they will come. Look around. Can you imagine entire neighborhoods? People stepping on the wildflowers, or going above timberline and trodding all over the delicate tundra?"

Walter laughed and held up his hand in surrender, the other gripping a sturdy walking stick. "I'm convinced! I'll do all in my power to push the bill to protect this place."

Relief rushed through Peri. "Oh, thank you!"

"I haven't seen anyone else, but I've heard people live up here."

Clay.

"Yes, there are ranches, as well as logging operations and miners."

Walter frowned in concentration. "It will be hard with people already established here. I believe when Yellowstone was approved, stipulations had to be formed for the residents. One would think living in a national park would be heaven, but they grumbled that they no longer enjoyed the freedom from before. Grazing was confined and hunting banned, taking away a food source. Are the local residents concerned?"

"Yes." Hesitation halted her next words. "Once such person I believe you know. Clayton McCarrick."

Walter paled at the name.

Peri continued, watching Walter closely. "He attacked you when you were here last, at Margaret's dinner party." She was fishing, and not ashamed at all. If Clay were ever to be a part of her life, she needed to know everything about him.

"Yes, we are slight acquaintances."

"I'm sorry he feels the way he does about you. I'm sure if he knew you better, he'd see how caring you are about all aspects of the national park. I'm afraid he's against the government in general, and you must have gotten caught up in his hatred."

Walter gripped his walking stick. "Is that what he told you?"

"Well, not exactly. All I know is that he lost his land a while back and blames the government. Is that how he knows you?"

Walter had begun walking fast, his breathing becoming labored. Peri grabbed his elbow to slow him down, as she would any in her charge who had trouble with the altitude.

"That is where I know him, but there's more to it. I'm not at liberty to talk about it, though."

While Peri really wanted to know what happened between these two men, she applauded Walter's discretion.

Just as she began pondering the mysterious history between these two men, they came to the lake where she had first met Clay.

A shot rang out, and she fell backward as if punched in the chest.

Clay had just broken through the aspen grove. He'd made it to the clearing near the lake before Peri's party, but as they came closer, he saw the same old mountain lion he'd scared off a couple of months ago. It had crouched and sprung toward the party. Clay had no recourse but to shoot.

But when he turned to join Peri's group, she was on the ground, and Kratz was cradling her in his arms. Had the bullet gone through the lion and ricocheted off the rock?

"Peri!" He ran to her side and gently pulled her from Kratz's arms. "What have I done?"

"Did you shoot her, McCarrick?" He deserved Kratz's condemning tone.

"I don't know. I shot at the lion. I should have killed it the first time. Then Peri would be alive."

"I'm alive, Clay." Her voice was weak, but sounded oh, so good. "Please tell me you didn't kill an animal for me." Was the pain in her voice from the gunshot, or from a felled animal? He remembered how angry she'd gotten when he shot at the lion the first time.

"I had no choice, sweetheart. He must have been hungry. Otherwise your group would have scared him off. I had to get him before he got one of them."

Kratz pulled out his handkerchief and placed it over the wound in her chest. "We need to stop this bleeding." He placed his hand on Peri's cheek and turned her face toward him, apparently so she could focus. "Yarrow," he said.

"Clay knows." She pointed past Clay then passed out.

Clay whipped his head toward the greenery she had pointed out to him before. "Yes! There's yarrow over there, but I don't know how to apply it."

"I do." Kratz left the pair and pulled a knife from his pocket.

Whooping and hollering came from somewhere nearby. "Did you get him?"

"I don't know. I saw him jump from the rock."

Two men with rifles entered the clearing. When they saw the gathering, their eyes drifted to the ground where Clay held Peri.

"What happened to her?"

"She was shot."

Their faces blanched. The taller one said, "I saw the lion from up on that ridge back there. We heard voices, but didn't know you all were that close."

"You mean you knew we were down here and shot anyway? You should always check the area before shooting." Clay went over the horrible moment in his mind. He'd seen the lion spring, probably at the same time these men did. Had there been two shots? He'd heard an echo, but maybe it was the second shot. One of them missed, ricocheted off the boulder and hit Peri. But which one?

"Anyone willing to dig a bullet from an animal?"

One of the women in the party jumped forward. "I can do it. I dress my husband's game." Clay handed his knife to the sophisticated-looking woman, somewhat surprised she'd be willing to do this. He continued to bark orders. "Someone please remove a bullet from both rifles so we can compare them to the one in the lion."

Blood soaked the handkerchief at Peri's wound. Clay pulled out his own bandana and laid it on top, pressing to slow the bleeding. "Hurry up, Kratz!"

"Got it!" Kratz scooted over with the plants. He approached Daisy and dug into Peri's bags until he found her mortar and pestle. Clay watched in fascination as he ground the leaves to paste. Clay remembered Peri saying she'd used a poultice of yarrow on her sprained ankle, but that it was good for bleeding too. Why hadn't he asked her how to do it? He never thought he'd admit it, but he thanked the Lord that Kratz was there and knew what to do.

Kratz knelt by Clay and removed the blood-soaked handkerchiefs. With great care, he spread the poultice over the wound.

Peri moaned.

"Shh, it's okay, sweetheart," Clay whispered to her, and she eventually settled down.

As Kratz worked, one of the two women in the group provided fresh, white cloths. Clay raised a brow, wondering where she'd gotten them.

"My petticoat," she volunteered, reading his expression correctly. "I've heard this is how it's done in wartime."

Clay grinned. This was no doubt the wife of one of the government dignitaries in the tour. Had she ever imagined herself in a situation where she'd have to sacrifice her petticoat for the greater good?

Once the poultice had been applied and the clean dressing was in place, a bullet was thrust into Clay's hand, still wet from the lake water in which it had been rinsed. "From the mountain lion." The woman who'd volunteered to retrieve it stood above him with a triumphant look.

"Thank you." He compared the bullet with the two taken from the rifles, praying they would be different. His was a lighter caliber. Relief poured over him. "The bullet is mine."

The two hunters groaned from where they sat on a log, guarded by two men.

"I'm sorry, so sorry." One of the men folded his arms over his knees and sank his face into them.

Kratz finished dressing Peri's wound and she stirred, but didn't awaken.

"We've got to get her to a doctor." Clay scooped her into his arms and headed for his horse. Kratz took her while Clay mounted, then lifted her gently into Clay's arms.

"Thank you, Walter." Clay looked Kratz in the eye for the first time since the tragedy happened. "For taking good care of her."

"Get her to a doctor. I'll deal with these two."

As Clay galloped away, he couldn't help grinning at the thought of the two careless hunters getting called on the carpet by a state senator.

Chapter 10

I'm so sorry, Clay." Peri lay on her bed, bandaged up and resting. "I'm responsible for that poor animal's death."

Clay couldn't imagine why she would say that. "You didn't do anything wrong." He'd made it back to town quickly, despite double the riders. Angus seemed to sense the urgency and set his own speed. Word spread quickly, and a doctor was summoned. The bullet came out easily enough, with no pulsating blood, indicating the artery was still intact. The doc said she was "mighty lucky," but her parents insisted she was blessed.

"I did do something wrong," she insisted. "Part of my job as tour guide is to keep my eyes open. Had I not been in such deep conversation, I would have been more aware."

"And if you had, how would that change the outcome? It still would have attacked, and I still would have shot it."

"I could have frightened it away."

Clay took her trim hand into his palms. "The old boy was famished. He'd probably missed a few meals because he was too slow to hunt. No matter how much noise you made, he still would have gone after you."

She closed her eyes, no doubt shutting out the truth of his words.

Sleep soon overtook her. Clay prayed she'd see the wisdom of the situation and forgive herself.

He reluctantly moved to the room that served as the living, dining, and kitchen area where Reverend and Mrs. Winfield sat at the table, along with Peri's sister and brother-in-law. The doctor was also there, cleaning up his instruments and preparing to leave.

"I don't know who dressed that wound," Dr. Wallace said, "but it was sheer brilliance. What plant was that?"

"Yarrow. Apparently, a medicine woman taught Peri a few tricks."

Mrs. Winfield nodded, her eyes gleaming with unshed tears. "Dear Malti."

Sunnie poured coffee for everyone except the doctor, who said he had to leave. "Change her dressing once a day," he said to Peri's mother. "I'll be back to check on her tomorrow."

After he left, Clay sank into a chair and warmed his hands around the coffee cup. "If I hadn't been there. . ."

"But you were." Sunnie slipped into the chair next to him. "God made sure of it." Her tender smile was full of assurance.

Clay nodded. "He seems to know what He's doing." A resigned chuckle escaped his lips. He had much to discuss with the Lord.

A knock on the door interrupted his thoughts. Frederick opened it and welcomed in the senator, whose face reflected the worry he must have been feeling. "I've brought the mule. She's tied out there at a hitching post." He thumbed toward the door.

"I'll take care of her," Frederick said.

"I'll help." Sunnie joined him.

After Peri's parents thanked Walter for his swift action, they also excused themselves. "Are you going to be here for a while, Clay?" Mrs. Winfield asked. "We're going to spend a few nights here, so we'd like to get some things from home."

"Certainly."

After they left, Clay stood and shook Kratz's hand. "Thank you, Walter. How did you know what to do out there?"

"Peri and I have something in common—a knowledge of healing herbs. For me, it was my grandmother who taught me some basics."

An awkward silence stretched between the two men. Clay never thought he'd ever be standing in the same room with the man, much less shaking his hand and thanking him. Even though this incident helped heal part of the rift between the two, a tiny flame of jealousy remained lit in the pit of Clay's stomach. Did Kratz have eyes for Peri? Worse yet, did she have eyes for him?

Kratz was the first to break the silence. He rubbed the back of his neck. "Can we talk?"

Given the circumstances of the last few hours, Clay's civility forced him to offer the man a chair at the table and a cup of coffee, but everything inside him prepared to throw him out if he were to indicate an interest in Peri.

Kratz cleared his throat. "I want to apologize."

"Apologize?" Clay scrutinized his nemesis. What was his game?

"Yes. I did a horrible thing to you those years past. I was a different person." He held up his hand. "Oh, but that doesn't excuse anything. There isn't a day goes by where I don't feel guilty."

"Really." Clay rubbed his chin. "Why haven't you apologized sooner then?"

"Once I got to the point of wanting to—oh, let's face it. I was a coward to have waited so long. By the time I'd worked up my courage, you had disappeared. After that, it was easy to set it all on the back burner. But it simmered there, clear up until I saw you again."

"I loved her, you know. Despite all of her faults. Did she ever once indicate feelings for me, her husband? Ever express that what she was doing was wrong?"

Kratz stared into the depths of his coffee, still untouched. "I wish I could say something to make you feel better. I hate to speak ill of the dead, but you deserve to know the truth. She had her own agenda, and we were both just stepping stones to an end."

The flame in Clay's gut began to die out to nothing but an ash-covered ember, then fizzled out completely. "Thank you, Walter. I guess I needed to hear that." Knowing the truth of who Anna was freed Clay to realize that she would never have been content with him, no matter how much he would have set her up financially, or moved her to where she'd have friends and parties. Anna, it seemed, was a sad individual who would never have given of herself to make a marriage work.

"Clay?" The female voice caught their attention. They both turned their heads to the back of the house.

Clay jumped up. "Peri! What are you doing out of bed?"

"Honestly. I was shot in the chest, not the leg." The stubborn, wonderful, maddening, beautiful woman walked gingerly to the sofa. "Hello, Walter. What are you doing here?"

Walter rose, bringing his coffee with him. He hadn't touched it, and now offered it to her. She took it with a smile.

"Returning your mule. You left the poor girl with strangers."

Peri sipped the brew. "I knew she was safe." She reached out to take his hand. "Thank you for taking good care of her. . .and of me."

"Always willing to be there for one of my constituents." He stood and gently squeezed her good shoulder. "I'll be going back to Denver now. We have much to do if we're going to turn this place into a national park."

Clay walked him to the door. Kratz shook his hand as he leaned in and whispered, "Take good care of this one, McCarrick. You both deserve some happiness."

"I will, if I can keep her from getting shot again."

Clay shut the door and returned to stoke the fire and retrieve a blanket. He placed it across Peri's lap then snuggled in close to her, pulling her to his chest.

"I have made a decision," he said.

"Go on."

He picked at an imaginary piece of lint on his dungarees. "I'll comply with whatever the government wants. And if they want my land, they can have it."

She sat up quickly and winced, no doubt regretting her decision. "No, Clay! There's got to be another way. Besides, we don't know if the national park will be approved."

"Now, don't go getting soft on me, Miss Periwinkle Winfield. You've been fighting tooth and nail for this."

"Yes, but I hate how it will affect you. Even while pushing for the park, in the back of my mind I've been trying to figure a way where we could both have what we wanted."

"If we get through this still friends—"

"Friends?" Her eyebrow rose.

"More than friends." He kissed the eyebrow and it gave up its indignation to return to its rightful place. "I just think you're more important than any land I might own."

"I don't think it will come to that, but thank you."

They sat together for a moment, Clay enjoying the feel of her next to him. Finally, he could not be silent about his past any longer. "I want to tell you about Anna."

"There's no need. I heard the two of you talking."

He pulled away to look into her eyes. "Eavesdropping? A fine, upstanding Christian such as yourself?" Relief flooded through him. He really didn't want to relive Anna's betrayal.

"Yes, and alas, a sinner. But confession is good for the soul." She paused, seeming to weigh her next words. "I'm so sorry for pushing you to talk to Walter. I had no idea how much he'd hurt you."

Clay chuckled. "It seems the day for apologies."

"Have you found peace, Clay?"

"I believe I have, thanks to Walter's apology."

Peri shook her head. "No, I don't think that had anything to do with it."

"You don't?"

"Peace is an elusive wisp that can only be achieved through complete trust in God. It helped that Walter apologized, but you didn't have to accept it. And what Anna did will never be corrected. Do you have peace about that? Have you forgiven her?"

Clay searched his heart. Seeing Peri bleeding in Walter's arms helped him to turn a corner. Life was for the living, not the dead. And he had to admit, his relationship with Anna, at least the way he'd seen it, was never alive. "I think I have."

"Then you have learned how to forgive the unlovable, and that, my friend, is a miracle."

"And you, what about the bison hunters?"

"I believe I told you that most days I feel I've forgiven them. My occasional nightmares would suggest otherwise. But I haven't had those dreams for a while now. I think I've finally made peace. It's like your situation. I can't go to those men and confront them, so I've had to come to some balance in my own heart." She paused as if searching within herself before speaking again. "Yes," she finally said. "I have forgiven them."

"Then we're going to be okay, you and me."

"Yes, I do believe we are."

Chapter 11

I never thought it would happen."

"Yes, you did."

Peri turned to Clay, giving him a look she hoped conveyed he didn't know what he was talking about.

They had hiked to where the elk were known to graze. Almost a year ago, in January, all of Peri's efforts came to fruition and Rocky Mountain National Park was established. Two years prior, not long after they had said their wedding vows, Peri and Clay joined the Estes Valley Improvement Association and were instrumental in importing forty-nine elk from Yellowstone National Park.

"You think you know me so well," Peri said, even as she nestled under his arm to use him for a windbreak.

Autumn had come to the park—her national park—and a brisk breeze blew over the meadow, making the golden quaking aspen shudder. But it didn't affect the magnificent creatures, or curtail their mating ritual. The rutting season had begun. One such fellow, probably nearly nine-hundred pounds, lifted his head and bugled a high-pitched scream followed by *chuck-chuck-chuck* coming from the deepest part of him. Another, smaller, bull elk was sneaking up on the group of females that the first had gathered for himself. He'd managed to cut one of them from the herd before the larger one had seen him. But once discovered, the battle was on. Heads clashed together, antlers clacked, echoing through the valley. And finally, the victor returned to his herd with the stolen cow running to join the others. The defeated one returned to his vantage point and waited for the larger elk to turn his back again.

"I do know you so well," Clay said. "Of course you knew there would be success at getting the national park approved. I've never seen such tenacity in a woman."

"And is that a bad thing?"

"No, because you used that tenacity to catch me, didn't you?"

"Oh, you!" She punched him in the side, but then snuggled even deeper into it.

"Are you cold? Ready to go home?"

"No, just a little while longer." She still loved the thought of being home with Clay McCarrick. He'd decided to keep his ranch and comply with the grazing regulations. At one time, he had mentioned this was the price to live in paradise. His hunting days were done, however. He had promised Peri on their wedding day that he wouldn't kill another animal, because it upset her too much.

"But what about the smoked meat for the rescue mission?" she'd asked him, concerned about leaving them out.

"I'll donate beef instead."

She laughed and said, "Well, that should take care of that."

Clay loosened his coat and drew it over her shoulders so the two wore the same garment. "You aren't usually affected like this from the weather. How many years have you basically lived outdoors?"

"More than I care to count."

"Are you getting sick? If so, we probably should—"

Peri put her fingers to his lips. "Shh. You'll wake the baby."

"The what?" She drew from him to watch his face. He didn't disappoint. He'd gone from pure confusion to dawn to elation. He stood and whooped like the elk in the distance, and for once, the mountain creatures went silent and observed the new family.

Kathleen E. Kovach and her husband, Jim, raised two sons while living the nomadic lifestyle for over twenty years in the Air Force. She's a grandmother, though much too young for that. Now firmly planted in Colorado, she's a member of American Christian Fiction Writers and leads a local writers group. Kathleen hopes her readers will giggle through her books while learning the spiritual truths God has placed there.

At Home with Daffodils

by Paula Moldenhauer

Dedication

For Grandpa Curtis,
Whose grave lies just outside Camp Gruber
Near the old general store at Qualls.
You were the master storyteller.
No doubt the hours I spent mesmerized by your stories
Influenced my decision to become a writer.
I look forward to sitting on a front porch swing
(if they have them in heaven)
With you and Jesus.
No doubt He'll chuckle as Grandma whispers,
"I wouldn't tell that one if I was you!"

Chapter 1

Not again!

Dilly hiked her long black skirt and burst down the road. The older boys surrounded Tommy, who hunched forward on the old wagon. Heavens, if they didn't look like vultures circling a kill! Dilly ran harder, scanning the dirt road for rocks that might cause her to twist her ankle. If only she could run faster in this stupid skirt!

An overgrown boy in patched overalls hopped onto the wagon, and Dilly gasped.

"Stop it this instant!" The damp wind carried away her voice, and not one of the hooligans looked her way.

The tormentor leaned down and whispered in Tommy's ear. No doubt something demeaning. When he thumped her nephew on the back of his head, the pest laughed as Tommy slumped farther and began to cry. Her heart broke.

Almost there, Tommy.

Tomorrow she'd get to the job site earlier to walk Tommy home. But that wouldn't protect him from the treatment the unruly young men gave all day.

A little farther and she'd give them what for!

Suddenly a tall, muscled man stepped forward. In one quick movement the stranger lifted the troublemaker off the wagon by his overall straps. The lout landed on the ground feet first but then tripped and fell. The stranger towered above him. He put a heavy work boot on the ruffian's back, not hard, but firmly enough that the rascal didn't move. "From now on, anyone who picks on this young man goes through me first."

Oh the authority in that deep voice! With his broad shoulders and protective stance, the man made an imposing figure. The man stared down the gang clustered around Tommy, and one by one, each of the hooligans looked away. When the boys scattered like crazed cattle, disappearing into the trees lining both sides of the road, Dilly bit her lip to keep from cheering.

"You all right, son?"

Close enough to hear the tenderness in the softly spoken words, Dilly blinked back the surge of tears. Surely the Lord had answered her prayers to help Tommy. Dilly stumbled, and the sound caused the man and Tommy to look her way. There was something familiar in the warm, green-eyed gaze that met hers.

"Well hello, Silly Dilly."

Jace would recognize those intelligent brown eyes and that smattering of freckles any-where, even with the becoming flush climbing up her neck and into her cheeks. His heart skipped a beat, like it had as a smitten sixteen-year-old. But the vision before him was no longer a skinny little thing. Miss Daffodil "Dilly" Douglas, the very reason he had moved back to Rock City, stood there in the flesh, all filled out and very much a woman.

Dilly's brown eyes flashed, and her mouth stiffened into a pout. When Dilly whirled from him and stalked away, he could've kicked himself for using her hated nickname.

"Come, Tommy." The clipped words didn't hide the melody of her voice. It was deeper now, more confident. But even in her huff it sounded as sweet as ever.

He stepped to follow her and apologize for the teasing when it hit him.

The boy.

Same brown eyes and freckles. Same sweet spirit.

Dilly Douglas had a son.

Which meant there was a husband.

Which meant he had no right to follow and charm her out of her snit.

Jace groaned. Why hadn't he considered this possibility when he signed on for a minimum of three months in this job?

More important than that, why hadn't he come home sooner, before someone else captured the heart of his girl?

No. Not his. He hadn't deserved her attention then, and he didn't now. It was right she'd moved on.

Chapter 2

Dilly ignored the temptation to kick at the mud that squished on either side of her sensible black boots. It wouldn't do to act like a child simply because Jace Gruber brought back all those childish feelings. Silly Dilly. For Pete's sake!

"Are you okay, Aunt Dilly?" Tommy's small hand squeezed hers, bringing her back to the present.

"Of course I am."

"You don't seem okay."

"Oh, honey. I should be asking how *you* are." She pulled his coat tighter and buttoned the top button. A blast of wind tousled his hair, and Dilly looked at the dreary sky. Sometimes it seemed here in northeastern Oklahoma that it clouded over on Thanksgiving and stayed gray until Easter.

"I didn't get to thank him."

"Who?" She knew who.

"The man who saved me."

Jace *had* saved him. "Perhaps you'll see him tomorrow. You can thank him then."

"Did you hear what he said?" Tommy's eyes glowed. "He said if anyone wanted to bother me, they had to go through him! And nobody's gonna do that. Did you see those arms of his?"

Oh, yes, she noticed the bulging muscles when Jace lifted the hooligan off the wagon like he was a sack of potatoes being unloaded for Mama's general store.

"That man is strong. And nice. Don't you think he's nice?"

Not when he used that awful nickname! The first time it happened, more years back than she wanted to count, she was daydreaming about *him*.

Silly Dilly her foot! It'd taken hard work to prove herself capable enough to shed the nickname. She wasn't about to let it be resurrected.

"I *said*, 'Don't you think he's *nice*?'"

"You don't even know him, Tommy."

"Yes I do. He's the man who saved me from the mean boys." Tommy put his too-thin arms on his hips. Dilly hid her involuntary smile. She was about to get a tongue-lashing from the nine-year-old, and she didn't mind a bit. It was good to see some life in her young nephew.

"Anyone who tells the mean boys to leave me alone is a good man, and you know it." Tommy's eyes filled with tears. "You didn't even let me say thank you!" The boy turned from her, running right past the general store. Most likely he was headed for the tree house his daddy built before he'd moved their family to the farm.

Before the *accident*.

Best let Tommy work this one out on his own.

Dilly sighed. Truth was she was ashamed of herself. She'd prayed for little Tommy's burdens to be eased, and Jace appeared out of nowhere and rescued her nephew. Instead of offering the gratitude he deserved, she stalked away like a wounded child, ignoring Jace's kindness and the good Lord's provision.

With a sigh she climbed the two short steps and entered her mother's store. The store that would be hers if all went as planned. Mama's voice called from the storage room. "If that's you, Dilly, I need you to finish up the inventory."

"Yes, ma'am." Dilly turned toward the back wall of shelves and cubes, which were filled with everything from sewing needles to soap to children's socks. She picked up where she'd left off earlier, making notes in her little black book. Periodically she righted the merchandise. Customers often moved things when they changed their mind about a purchase or looked for an elusive item. When she came to the nails, screws, bolts, and such, Dilly frowned. Usually she enjoyed making sure everything, big or small, was in its proper place, but the sight of screws all jumbled up with the nails was a sad picture of life. One minute you're living right, thinking you've made sense of the way things are. The next thing you know, your emotions are a jumbled mess. No matter how long it took her to organize this section of the store, it would be less time than it was going to take to get her nerves straightened out now that Jace Gruber was back.

It was nearly closing time when Dilly finished the inventory. She stepped outside to clear her head and watch twilight come to town. It slipped in slow and steady: first a hint of a thin winter glow as the sun disappeared behind the hills, then a silvery gray light that outlined the shadows as they cloaked the few buildings of Rock City.

She chuckled at the exaggeration. Rock City wasn't a city at all. It was more of a hole in the road that boasted Mama's general store, which housed the first official post office in the area. They were lucky to have it, just two years after statehood, and its location helped bring in customers. Across the road stood a small café and a smattering of houses. Most folks lived nestled into nearby hills, where the oak and black walnut trees shielded them from passersby. People in these parts worked odd jobs and cleared the land for cattle and big gardens.

The silvery gray turned deep blue, then black. As night fell, so did Dilly's spirits. Not that they had far to fall. It was the day's end, and even though Jace was right here in Rock City, working outside of town at the rock quarry, he hadn't come. Sure, she'd snubbed him, but the old Jace—the Jace who had promised to marry her once they were old enough—would have come anyway.

How many years had she stood here, watching the night turn black, squinting into the shadows, hoping one of them would take the shape of the boy she once knew? Her best friend swore he'd return. But he hadn't.

Over the years she'd given up watching for him.

Until today.

And here she stood, the old ache reawakened.

Mama had long since headed home, so Dilly heaved a sigh, closed up the store, and trudged to the house on the back side of the property. It once seemed small, when all three of her sisters were home and fighting over space, but only Dilly lived with mama now. Even her baby sister, Anne, found a husband and moved to Tahlequah. But no one ever caught Dilly's eye, and after seeing Jace today, she knew why.

Her heart was waiting.

A drizzle filled the air. Before morning it would crystallize into tiny bits of ice and coat the tall weeds beyond the fence. With a sigh, she pulled open the screen door, holding it with her foot as she fumbled with the knob of the main door. She gave a push. It was prone to sticking.

"Close the door quick!" Mama called from the kitchen. "The damp is still in my bones just from the short walk from the store."

Dilly sniffed as she pulled the door shut. Mama had cornbread finishing up in her cast-iron skillet. Fried potatoes and beans were already on the table. Usually the simple fare was welcome but not tonight.

"Grab plates. Let's eat while it's hot."

"I'm not very hungry."

"You've seemed out of sorts all day. Aren't you feeling well?" Mama pulled the golden brown circle from the heat and cut a generous slice.

"I'm just tired. I'll have a little cornbread and milk and turn in early." She and mama didn't raise a cow or chickens, but people from the surrounding area traded milk and eggs for goods from the store.

Mama shot her a disapproving glance but didn't argue.

Dilly put cornbread in a tin cup and covered it with milk. Grabbing a spoon, she headed toward her room. She could feel Mama's questioning gaze as she closed her bedroom door. Mama surely felt shut out, but Dilly's swirling thoughts begged for space to sort things through. Setting her supper on the little table next to her bed, Dilly built a fire in the small, wood-burning stove in the corner, then quickly changed and crawled beneath the stack of handmade quilts. The fire would go out before morning, but she'd stay mostly warm with enough covers.

Soon enough the heat from the stove took the chill out of the air, and Dilly climbed from beneath the quilts and went to the trunk at the foot of her bed. Carefully laying aside the items on top, she dug until she found her journal. She opened the book and flipped past the childish scrawl that included her name and declared the journal private property. Opening to the first entry, she grinned at the childish fantasies she'd recorded. Mama said she had a rich imagination. She turned a couple of pages, and her gaze went to his name, scrawled right there on the first line. What had she been, twelve? Thirteen? She thumbed through the next many pages. Almost every entry included something about Jace. The longest was written the day he left. For a while the entries were regular, bemoaning his absence. She'd even written poems of angst.

Dilly flipped another page and pulled out the letter pressed there. It was short, but it was from him. Posted six months after he moved.

Dilly shook the journal, allowing the letters to make a pitiful little pile on her bed.

She'd never known if the erratic correspondence was related to the lack of an official post office at the time or to the nomadic lifestyle of Jace's family. She sighed as she opened the first letter, then she re-read them all. They didn't say much, a new letter arriving after months of silence, right when she started to give up hope. She always wrote back, but she suspected he didn't see her responses. When a new letter came, it never referred to anything she said.

His always carried the same message.

Someday he would come back.

Only he never did, and for the last three years there had not been even one letter.

Not even after they became a state and got their own post office.

She flipped to the end of the journal.

The last few entries didn't mention Jace at all. She dropped the journal and turned from it, burrowing into the quilts. When Dilly finally fell asleep, her dreams were restless.

Chapter 3

It was still dark when she heard Mama in the kitchen. Dilly forced herself from bed. Usually she dreaded the cold splash of water she poured from the pretty purple-and-white pitcher into its matching wash basin, but today she needed the invigorating shock.

After she tidied up, she reached for her plain cotton shirtwaist and hesitated. It wouldn't hurt to wear her best one to work this once. Dilly fingered its lace detail. Maybe wearing it would lift her spirits.

Who was she kidding? A certain someone would surely show up today! Why else would she risk wearing her best shirtwaist at work? Shoving down such thoughts she schooled her expression and headed out to breakfast.

"Don't you look nice! What's the special occasion?"

"Oh nothing."

Mama didn't look convinced, and Dilly searched for a new topic of conversation. "You wouldn't believe the mess the nails and screws were in yesterday."

"Good thing you straightened them up. I'd hate to see you do such work in your best shirtwaist."

"Um. . ." Dilly grabbed a biscuit and a cup of coffee. "I'm heading on over to the store." She ignored Mama's comment, allowing the creaking screen door to slap behind her like a happy little clap.

The feel of sun—real sun!—upon her face lifted her hopes further. Surely this was a glorious, new day. She glanced at the field on the other side of the fence. Ice coated the tall weeds, and the sun sparkled upon them, giving the illusion of dancing grasses. Dilly did a bit of a jig herself. Oh yes. She had high hopes for this day.

Jace rested his hammer and rubbed his eyes, hating the groggy feeling that accompanied lack of sleep. Letting go of the dream of reuniting with Dilly felt impossible, but to pursue a married woman was unthinkable. Why had the Lord sent him back if she was married? Was it some kind of cruel joke?

Jace frowned. He should have written. Found out if he was even welcome back in Rock City. But how do you write after years of silence?

Jace swung the hammer. When it connected with the huge metal peg, a dissonant ping echoed through the quarry, matching the turmoil inside. When he'd heard about the job at Rock City Quarry, he'd believed God had prepared the way for him to return.

When the doubts about the decision preyed on him, he'd thought it was God's very Spirit helping him overcome his feelings of unworthiness and fear.

But what if it wasn't God at all? He could be headstrong when he wanted something. Maybe the move back was pigheaded determination, not God's guidance at all.

He gritted his teeth. To believe it wasn't the Lord who sent him to Rock City was easier than dealing with the alternative. Because if God brought him back to all this pain, that was nothing short of mean. If God loved him like Mama said all those years, why would He dangle a carrot, like a man leading a horse, only to snatch it away?

Surely he hadn't heard God at all.

God wouldn't lead him to such pain. Right?

Lord?

Trust never came easy, but to believe God was in this mess of crushed hopes was a far stretch harder than even the usual struggle.

Again he swung the hammer hard.

Hot anger surged.

Swing. Connect. Hear the metal ring. Swing again.

If only hard work could make him forget.

The clang of metal upon metal resounded. He focused his attention on the sound and the rhythm of work, upping his pace without neglecting the strength of his swing.

Didn't scripture say God had good plans for His children?

But how was sending his deepest hope to the grave good? The next three months stuck in Rock City would be the longest of his life.

He glanced up to see her boy atop the wagon. Jace joined the others in filling it. Yesterday there were insults hurled at the lad. But not today. Guarded glances in his direction confirmed that the frisky young men had gotten the message when he intervened the day before. He winked at Tommy. The boy's smile stretched ear to ear.

Maybe *that* was what this was all about. Protecting that lad from senseless abuse. Jace stood taller. Even though Dilly wasn't his to love, he could bless her by loving her son. *Thank You, Father, for a purpose.*

Wagon loaded, the men swung their hammers again. The noise of steel upon steel allowed for little conversation and plenty of time to think. Shouldn't Tommy be in school? Why did his mama allow such a little tyke this hard labor?

The lad returned for several loads. Always the boy had a smile for him, and soon Jace was eager to see the wagon return. But as the day wore on, so did Jace's worries. Dilly obviously married young, and something hadn't gone right. There was only one reason a boy that age worked a job like this.

Because his pa didn't.

Jace knew too well what it was like to grow up too fast to make up for a father's inadequacies.

Pain twisted Jace's stomach. Had sweet Dilly married a no-account? Without a father to guide her, she could have been swayed into an unwise marriage. Maybe he should talk to her. Make sure she was okay.

Jace swung the huge hammer.

Clang!

No.

The torch he carried made any kind of relationship with her like playing with fire. A married woman was a married woman. Jace would not dishonor the Lord by befriending Dilly.

Unable to think of an excuse to skip yet another meal, Dilly sat at the thick wooden table and tried to make normal conversation. Her beautiful new shirtwaist was wasted on a bunch of women and the Prescott twins. They were of marrying age, but who could notice them with Jace Gruber back in town? She picked at her fried chicken. Mama was a wonderful cook, but tonight the chicken might as well be sawdust.

"Are you sure you're not coming down with something?" Mama felt her forehead, making her feel like a child instead of a grown woman.

"I'm fine."

"You don't look fine."

"Please don't meddle, Mama."

"Come on, angel. You're my Daffodil with that sunny yellow disposition! It's not like you to be out of sorts."

Dilly forced down a bite of mashed potatoes smothered in flour gravy. Maybe if she ate, Mama would quit prying.

"Is it Tommy? You've worried about him something fierce."

"Actually Tommy seems better."

"Oh?"

She hadn't told Mama that the older boys picked on Tommy. Mama would tell Jenny, and Jenny wouldn't know what to do. Jenny had four children to feed, and she needed Tommy to work. Knowing her son was unhappy would only add to Jenny's burdens. "Um. . .I think he's adjusting to working. And I'm helping him with his reading and sums on the weekends."

"I'm glad you're doing that. I hate to see him missing school." Mama stared out the kitchen window, her dark braid lying long down her back. "Life isn't fair, is it?"

Dilly stared at her courageous mama. Born and raised in Indian Territory before statehood, she'd fought her share of unfair battles. Dilly compared her skin to the darker, creamy tones of her mother's. "No, but you make the best of it, Mama. You never let life pass you by."

"Is that how you feel? That life moved on without you?"

"I guess."

The probing expression in Mama's dark brown eyes caused Dilly to squirm.

"Are you sure taking over the store is your dream, honey?"

"Of course. I worked all these years to learn the trade so you could pass it on to me."

Mama's gaze softened. "My early bloomer, practically running the store at sixteen! But you can do anything with your life, Dilly. There's not much around here for a young woman. Except maybe the Prescott twins."

Dilly rolled her eyes, and Mama laughed.

"I'm sure they are fine young men. Just not for me—as I've told you and half the ladies at church!"

"Just trying to add a little levity. Heaven knows there's enough trouble in this life without marrying someone you don't love."

But that was the problem. She had loved Jace since she was thirteen years old, but even though he had finally returned, he didn't love her enough to seek her out.

"Maybe you need a new challenge. You've learned everything you need to know at the store."

"It's not the store."

"But you're lonely. And why not? A young woman should have options. Not spend most evenings alone with her mama."

"I guess I am lonely." *Now more than ever.*

"What if you went to Tahlequah and visited Anne? You could leave tomorrow and stay a few weeks. Meet other young people."

"No!"

"Why ever not?"

"I'm just not interested."

"I can manage here just fine."

"Maybe in the summer if I'm still fighting melancholy."

"Honey," Mama's gaze searched hers. "You don't have to take care of me. I've grown to depend on you, but we can change our timeline for you taking over the store. You shouldn't be in Rock City out of obligation."

Dilly grabbed her mama's hand. "I don't feel obligated. Taking over the store *is* my dream, and I want to do it in a year, like we planned. I'm doing exactly what I want to. I just have a few things to work through in my head." She jumped up and gathered the dishes. "Why don't you go on to bed and read awhile? It's my turn to clean up."

Dilly worked hard, finding extra chores. But no matter how she scrubbed or how carefully she swept, the ache didn't go away. No matter how busy she kept her hands she couldn't get her thoughts under control. They kept running off on their own, dreaming up ideas about how she might bump into Jace Gruber.

Chapter 4

Dilly unpacked the shipment of hard candies. After dressing up for Jace three days in a row, she hadn't even bothered to fix her hair. She pulled it quickly into a chignon, no curls or frills, and wore her plain white waist.

She had to find a way to hold on to her joy! Organizing the brightly colored, hard candies typically lifted her spirits. But not this time.

When the new fabric arrived, Dilly imagined a new dress that would catch Jace's eye, and that only devastated her further. Even pretty new clothes couldn't get someone's attention if that someone didn't come around. The latest edition of *McCall's* was in the same shipment as the fabric, and Dilly climbed on the tall stool Mama kept behind the counter, determined to distract herself. But every picture of a man took on one familiar, dear face. Dilly slapped the magazine onto the counter.

No one man should have such an effect!

Hopping off the stool, she stomped to the storeroom and grabbed the broom. She'd swept at closing the day before, but something had to be done! After the floor surely didn't boast a speck of dust, Dilly made a pail of vinegar water and scrubbed down the counter. The pungent smell, at least, was a brief distraction.

"Hey, Aunt Dilly!" Tommy sauntered into the room and plopped on the stool next to her as she rung out the rag.

"Hey yourself, Tommy. You look chipper for a young man who worked all day."

"It's not nearly so hard now. Not since Mr. Jace stood up for me!"

Jace, again! "No more teasing or thumping you on the head?"

"Nope. Sometimes Mr. Jace finds me at noon break and shares his lunch with me. Did you know he's lived all kinds of places? And he has a sister but no brother. Like me. All I got is sisters at home. He said it was just him and his mama and his sister for a long time."

Dilly pretended to rearrange some postcards. "What happened to his daddy?" It was Jace's no-account pa who made them leave Rock City.

"Mr. Jace says he doesn't know where he is. For a long time Mr. Jace worked hard to take care of his mama and his sister, like I do. Then his mama died."

Dilly blinked back the sudden tears. The kind woman was gone? "Does his sister live with him now?"

"She grew up and got married. That's why Mr. Jace moved here. To go somewhere different since he was all alone."

Alone, huh?

The fluttering in her tummy was surely hope. Could it be coincidence that Jace came back to Rock City when he felt lonely?

Surely he needed her.

The girl he promised to marry.

"Anyway, it's not as hard to work with Mr. Jace around. It's like I told you. He's a *nice* man. And I *did* tell him thank you."

Which is exactly what she would do!

Jace was probably waiting on her apology. After all, she *had* snubbed him when he was doing the most wonderful thing in the world, rescuing her nephew. "I'm glad you thanked him."

"Me, too. Better get home. Mama's probably waiting supper."

Dilly glanced around the store for something to send with Tommy. "Hold up there." She filled a pail with milk and packed a bundle with eggs in it. Jenny hated handouts, but she wouldn't reject the extra food if Tommy brought it home. "Tell your mama the hens are laying extra this week, and we don't want the milk to spoil. Mind you don't break an egg in your rush to supper."

"I won't!" Tommy flashed that contagious smile, and she couldn't help grinning as her nephew skipped from the store.

So Jace came back because he was lonely. It was high time she found him and ended this ridiculous distance her hasty temper had caused. If Mama didn't mind her leaving the store for a bit, maybe she could catch Jace as he left work.

A snap startled her, and Dilly looked up to see Old Lady Bishop's fingers in her face.

"Dilly!" The woman practically shouted at her. "If you can get your head out of the clouds for a minute, I'd like my mail!"

"Yes, ma'am." Dilly turned to collect the woman's mail, but not before she heard Old Lady Bishop whisper, "Silly girl."

Dilly's cheeks burned. It was all too familiar. Jace was back, and she was daydreaming. After working hard to prove herself to the community, to hold her imagination mostly in check, the appearance of one green-eyed man whisked it all away. Her sense of duty. Her clear thinking. If she wasn't careful, people would start calling her Silly Dilly again, and she would deserve it.

She couldn't have that.

Not after all she'd done to prove she was reliable. Let Tommy and Jenny thank Jace. Their gratitude would be sufficient.

Besides, if she meant so little to him that one incident would keep him away, who needed it? His long absence only confirmed her fears of the first day.

Jace no longer thought of her like she thought of him.

The lad looked at him like he hung the moon when he pulled the wagon up for the first load of the day. Jace hoped he wouldn't let the kid down. Being on a pedestal was never a comfortable perch—and with Dilly married, he would be out of Rock City as soon as he fulfilled his work contract. Out of respect for Dilly, he tried not to pry into the boy's life. All Jace knew was that Tommy adored his mother and was proud to earn money to help support his sisters. The poor kid never talked about his pa. What kind of monster had Dilly married?

Jace sighed as he carried a load to Tommy's wagon. Being there for the boy gave him purpose, but it didn't heal his heart. The hurt hadn't eased, but logic had stilled his anger. Most likely the Lord had sent him back to Rock City to learn Dilly had married. Lord knows he couldn't have moved on to another relationship as long as there was even the slightest possibility Dilly had waited all these years. In time his heart would heal, and this brief jaunt into the world of his past would help him find the life of his future.

It had to.

Jace worked steadily all morning, the bright spot being the joy Tommy's smile evoked each time the lad pulled the wagon around.

Was it wrong to enjoy Tommy so much? If he were honest, while he liked the boy for himself, being around Tommy also gave Jace a bit of Dilly. He often heard Dilly in a turn of phrase or saw her in the way the boy's intelligent brown eyes lit when he learned something new. Jace would be proud to call such a fine lad his son, but each conversation reminded him that he and Dilly would never have a boy of their own. He slammed the large hammer harder than necessary. Tommy's pa oughta be hog-tied. How could a father take no interest in such a fine boy?

When the noon whistle blew, Jace waited for Tommy. Soon the boy plopped down beside him and opened his typically sparse lunch. They ate in silence. The lad tended to wolf down his meal. Today was no exception.

"I did it again, Tommy." Jace feigned concern. "Packed too much food. If I had a wife, she'd surely think me wasteful. Then again, if I had a wife, maybe she'd pack my lunch and put in the right amount."

The hungry look in Tommy's eyes said what he was always too polite to suggest.

"Are you too full, son? I hate to throw out good food."

"It *would* be a shame, sir."

"Could you help me out? If it wouldn't be too much trouble, I mean."

"Sure!"

If he hadn't already, Tommy would soon catch on that Jace always packed an extra sandwich. But Jace suspected the boy would never let on. He was too hungry.

Tommy flashed a proud smile. "I have something to share with you today."

"You do?"

"Yup. Yesterday Aunt Dilly had too many eggs at the store, so she sent some home with me, and Mama had enough flour and molasses to make cookies!"

Aunt Dilly? Jace's breath sucked right out of him.

Tommy pulled a big blue handkerchief from the bottom of his lunch pail and presented the molasses cookies with that boyish grin.

Jace fought for breath. "Now don't those look good!" He forced a bite, but his mouth was so dry he could hardly swallow.

"You okay?"

"Of course." How could he be such a fool?

"I hate how grown-ups always say they are okay when they aren't. It's not like I'm a little kid and you hafta keep stuff from me. I'm doing a man's work, and I can be a friend, too."

Jace resisted the urge to hug the lad. "Oh, I know you're a good friend to folks. You've been a mighty fine friend to me. The best I've got right now in Rock City."

"You ain't foolin'?"

"Oh, no. But you better not let your A–a–a–unt Dilly"—he stuttered with emotion and slowed his speech—"hear you say *ain't*. She's a stickler for proper grammar."

"Don't I know it! Aunt Dilly graduated top of her class."

Of course she did.

"And she's schoolin' me on the weekends. She don't let me get away with nothin'."

"Don't you mean she doesn't let you get away with anything?"

Tommy sighed. "If I speak too high falutin', the boys might tease me again, even with you here. They used to pick on me about that, too. But I'm real careful around Aunt Dilly." The boy's face brightened. "You should meet her proper. She's really nice. And you already saw her, so you know she's awfully pretty."

"So your Aunt Dilly never married?" He needed to be absolutely sure.

"Oh no, sir!" The boy gave him a sly look. "Folks around here say she'll make some man a mighty fine wife."

Jace almost choked on his cookie.

"Aunt Dilly made me mad that first day we met you. She didn't let me thank you for helpin' a feller out. I don't know what got into her."

He did. "Did I ever tell you I lived here when I was a little older than you are now?"

Tommy's eyes widened, and he shook his head.

"Your aunt and I were friends."

A crease appeared in Tommy's forehead. "You sure didn't act like it." He bit his lip. "Actually, it was Aunt Dilly who acted strange that first day. She wasn't very nice to you, and she's usually very nice."

"I think I hurt her feelings."

"How?"

Jace considered his explanation. "You remember how it feels to be teased about something that embarrasses you, don't you?"

"Oh yes, sir!"

"When your aunt was younger, she was prone to distraction. People said she was a daydreamer, and the kids teased her something fierce. They called her Silly Dilly."

Tommy laughed, and Jace fought his own chuckle. Back in the day, the fastest way to catch pretty little Dilly's attention was to use the dreaded moniker. "Your aunt hated that nickname, and I can understand why. It wasn't nice of us to tease her." He paused, remembering when they were kids and how the tears welled in her young brown eyes the last time he'd called her Silly Dilly. He swore off teasing her like that and never used the nickname again.

Until last week. "That first day we met, I slipped up and called her by that old nickname."

"If it hurt Aunt Dilly, why did you do it?"

"I'm not exactly sure, but I'm sorry I did." Jace sobered. "Now, son, can you promise you'll never hurt your aunt by calling her that old nickname or telling it to anyone else?"

Tommy's eyes narrowed. "*I* would never do that." He shook his head. "No wonder she hates you."

"She said she hated me?"

"Oh, no sir! But it ain't. . .I mean *isn't* like Aunt Dilly to stomp away without even a how-do-you-do. She must've been really mad." The lad glared. "I wish you hadn't done that."

"I'm sorry I did, Tommy. I'm going to try and make it up to her."

Tommy puffed his chest out. "See that you do."

When the whistle sounded, Tommy stomped off. Jace grimaced. Hopefully he hadn't fallen too far off that pedestal. The crew lumbered back to their work positions, and Tommy climbed onto the wagon. He didn't even look Jace's way as he drove off, and Jace sighed.

Well, first things first.

Jace approached the crew boss. "If it wouldn't cause undo trouble, I'll like to take the afternoon off."

The man frowned. "You're a good worker, Gruber. I'm assuming this is important."

"Yes, sir."

"You realize your pay will be docked."

"Of course."

His boss gave a curt nod and walked away. Jace couldn't get out of there fast enough. The only question was whether to take time to go home and clean up before heading to the general store.

If Mama wasn't nearby, Dilly would've slammed the storage-room door. But of course it would do no good. Acting out would not take away the sting of Jace's rejection. She needed to face the facts. Jace was no longer interested.

Oh how silly all those years of secret waiting were!

Mama walked over and put an arm around her. "Guess what I heard from Drew Benningway this morning. You know Drew, the crew boss out at the quarry."

Dilly's heart pounded, but she feigned innocence.

"I heard something I think might explain your mood swings, little miss. It seems an old friend of ours is back in Rock City."

Dilly hung her head.

Mama put a gentle finger beneath Dilly's chin and tipped her head. "I don't blame you for not telling me. A woman has a right to her private thoughts." She sighed. "I take it he hasn't come to see you."

Dilly dropped her head again, fighting the melancholy that escalated from a dull ache to overwhelming emotion. "No." She barely got the word out.

"Jace Gruber." Mama sighed. "You were the best of friends. I can't believe he hasn't stopped by."

That made two of them.

"Is he why neither of the Prescott twins captured your attention?"

Dilly averted her gaze. This conversation needed to end. *Now.*

"All these years. . ."

Mama didn't finish her thought, but she didn't have to. The unthinkable truth was finally in the open. Dilly Douglas had secretly pined for Jace for much longer than made any sense at all.

"Honey—"

"Mama, please." She managed a choked whisper.

"Oh, my sweet girl."

The silence stretching between them was anything but golden.

Mama sighed loudly. "I'm meddling again, aren't I?" She squeezed Dilly's arm and took a step away. "I'm sorry, Daffodil. I'll keep my thoughts between God and me until you are ready to talk about it. But don't try to bear it all by yourself. Remember He who is your refuge and very present help. He's with you right now, Dilly. Cast your burden upon Him for He careth for you."

"I'll try, Mama."

Mama studied her for a moment. "I hate to ask this of you right now, but could you watch the store alone for a while?"

"What kind of question is that?" Dilly forced lightness into her voice. "You know I could manage the store in my sleep."

A quick nod. "Very well. I'm nursing a headache and think a bit of rest might do me some good."

Dilly stood straighter. "Of course you should rest!" She forced a smile. "I'll be fine. As always."

As soon as Mama stepped out the door, Dilly's shoulders slumped. And why not? Her dearest dream was nothing more than a foolish childhood crush. Maybe Mama had a point the other night. She could go to Tahlequah or even back East and search for a new life. Dilly sniffed as she stacked the canned goods neatly on the shelf, wiping the dust off with her apron as she went. Her love of the store, of keeping things neat and organized and providing what folks needed, lived on. But was the store enough without Jace?

Why had she been such a ninny? Hanging on to the thought of him much longer than was sensible!

The ringing of the bell above the door brought her out of her reflections. She glanced up to see the very object of her angst. Her heart beat as he strode toward her, and she fought with all her might to shove the emotions down. After all, the Good Book said to guard one's heart, and hadn't her heart taken more than its share of hurt? "Can I help you?" She hadn't meant for her voice to come out cold and emotionless, but the Good Book also said the mouth spoke out of what was in the heart. And hers was empty and cold.

Jace halted. "I. . .uh. . ."

The silence stretched as he studied her. Dilly fought to keep her expression neutral. If she let him see how deeply she cared, it would destroy her when affection was not returned.

"Um. . .how are you, Dilly?"

"Fine." The word was terse but she couldn't take it back.

He stared, his expression unreadable.

"If you don't need anything,"—she stepped around him—"I'll get out of your way and let you browse." She turned her back on him. It served him right. But it killed her as she walked away. Oh would she ever untangle all the jumbled-up emotions? She strode to the counter and made a show of straightening the jars of hard candy. She wouldn't look at him. His footsteps sounded. Came closer. But she would not turn his way. She felt him draw near. Pause. Stand close. So very close.

"Dilly?" His voice was soft. Tender.

Tears rushed into her eyes.

"Won't you look at me, Dilly?"

Oh how she longed to, but the stupid tears would give her away.

Two halting steps back. Then hard footsteps toward the door. At the last minute she turned, catching a brief glance of his pained expression.

Was there a more foolish notion than a grown man nursing a childhood dream? He couldn't even count the women—good, salt-of-the earth women—who flashed their come-hither smiles over the last many years! He could've had his pick, but he ignored all of them. Why? Because in his irrational heart he was still a ridiculous lad hanging on to a fantasy named Daffodil Grace Douglas.

But why was he surprised?

He'd always known she was too good for the likes of him.

Guess she knew it, too.

He'd fought a hard battle to return to Rock City with the voice whispering he wasn't good enough for her. If only he'd heeded the message instead of fighting it off! Then his heart wouldn't be shattering into a million pieces.

He kicked a stone in his path, and it went sailing down the road.

"Jace! Wait!"

Dilly. He stopped, fighting to compose himself before turning toward her.

"Jace. Please. Please don't go."

He turned, and his breath caught in his throat when she ran right up next to him, tears streaming down her beautiful face.

Oh, Dilly.

Against his better sense, he reached to wipe away the moisture with his thumb. The next thing he knew she was in his arms sobbing, and while her cries cut at his heart, he couldn't help the joyful feeling that she was finally right where she belonged.

"Oh, Jace!"

She stepped back, and he felt the loss of her.

"I'm sorry I wasn't very nice to you just now. Or the first day you came. You've been so good to Tommy. You deserve my thanks, not the cold shoulder."

"Hey, now, no need for tears." Jace glanced around. A couple he didn't recognize stepped out of the café and watched them. He and Dilly didn't need gossip spreading before they even got things sorted out. "Why don't we take a walk?"

He offered his arm, and she took it, glory be! As the road curved away from the prying eyes and became a tree-lined lane, he breathed a prayer for courage. He paused and turned toward her, allowing her hand to slip from his arm. "You want to explain why you've done nothing except snub me since I came to town?" His voice came out gruffer than he meant it to.

Her quick, doe-eye glance was spooked.

He needed to speak more gently. "Are you still sore about the old nickname? I'm sorry about that, Dilly. I meant it affectionately." And suddenly he understood why it had slipped out. He'd fallen for sweet Silly Dilly, the feisty young girl who knew how to dream.

"At first. But I overreacted."

"Then what was that about at the store today? A man returns after years of separation and doesn't even get a how-do-you-do from the girl who used to claim to be his best friend!" He swallowed hard. His heart was on his sleeve already, so he might as well let it all come out. "I promised you I'd come back. I'm here. But don't trifle with me. If you've moved on, tell me outright."

"You're the one acting like he's moved on!"

The rise in her voice gave him hope.

"I'll admit I wasn't very nice when I first saw you, but that wouldn't have mattered to the Jace I knew." Tears welled in her gorgeous eyes. "I waited for days. Wore my best shirtwaist and everything."

He fought the slow grin claiming his face. "You dressed up for me?"

"Not that it did any good." She looked away. "You never came."

Oh. "I thought you were married."

"*Married?* Of all the ridiculous—"

"Sure! Tommy looks like you. Acts like you, too."

"You thought Tommy was my *son?*"

He chafed at her incredulous tone. "A lot of girls marry young. It's perfectly reasonable to think you were married with a batch of young'uns."

She stared, wide-eyed, then her shoulders started shaking. When a giggle slipped out, he stepped back. "I don't see what's funny, Dilly."

Now the giggles flowed freely. "It's not. . .funny." A cute little hiccup exploded into an out-all laugh. "Oh, Jace. I'm incredibly relieved!"

She looked at him again, big eyes sparkling, and pursed her lips, obviously trying to hold in her mirth. But her joyful laughter spun into the air then went way down inside him and untangled the knots that got all twisted when he'd thought she was taken. He was surely grinning like a fool now, but he didn't care. Not one iota.

When his own laughter rose, he let it ring out unbridled. They were both grinning to beat the band when he offered his arm again, and she took it. They meandered down a muddy path. The trees around them raised knobby, bare arms to the sky, but a hint of green hue was barely discernible beneath the brown weeds and grasses that grew in the forest. They walked a while in silence and then he realized where his feet had taken him.

"Look, Dilly." The big old oak still stood next to Greenleaf Creek, its limbs hanging out over the water. Someone had strung a rope onto the biggest branch. Their old fishing hole would likely invite many a young swimmer come summer. An old log lay near the bank, and he gestured toward it.

She smiled at him as she sat. "Remember all the fish we caught?"

"Crappie mostly." He grinned back at her and eyed the log, trying to decide how close he could sit without seeming improper. "Our expeditions rounded out many a sparse meal at my house."

"Mama was always glad to have a mess of crappie. As long as I cleaned and fried them. Said she didn't have the patience for such a small fish."

"They were small. But tasty enough."

The creek gurgled, free to move beyond the sliver of ice lining the calm water at the bank. The happy little sound combined with the damp earthy smell welcomed him home.

Home. Was Rock City home, or was home simply wherever Dilly was?

Dilly shivered, and he realized she'd run after him without a wrap. The February day was warm, but the trees blocked the sun. He took his coat off and snugged it around her. Her smile of gratitude was shy.

A lot of years lay between them.

"Where have you been all this time, Jace?"

Evidently she felt the passage of time, too. But it wasn't only the years that stretched between them. Gazing at her innocent expression, he fought the battle between exposure and vulnerability. She was one of the few he trusted. But it had been a long time, and things had gotten worse in the years they were apart. "Many a small town. Following Pa place to place when the notion hit him to move on." Or when Pa was run out of town after he made a scene. Shame warmed his neck, and he fought the memories. "After Pa disappeared, I did my best to take care of Mama and Ruthie, going wherever the work was. Mostly quarries."

"Your pa disappeared?"

"It was for the best." He rushed on before she asked more questions. "When Mama died, Ruthie and I stayed put for a while. She was sweet on a young man who worked at the livery, so I waited to see how it would play out. Hoped she would have a chance at a normal life." He lifted his gaze to hers. "She did. I was mighty proud when they married. She's a good woman, my sister, and the Lord gave her a good man."

"I'm glad."

"After their wedding, I made plans to come back to Rock City." That was the story. Without the messy details. "And here I am." He looked away from the questions in her eyes and let the silence fall.

Finally she spoke. "All this time I've been here. Same town. Same house. Working at the same store."

Living her stable, wholesome life.

Should she pry? She had an idea about his daddy's part of the story, but to bring it up would be to bring up Jace's shame. Did he still carry it like a gunnysack full of flour, forever burdening his strong back?

And what about his sweet mother? "I always liked your mama. I'm sorry she's gone." She dared place a gentle hand upon his shoulder, but removed it when she felt him tense.

"Died of a broken heart, I reckon." His words were whispered. "Buried her in a pretty little spot out near Guthrie. Ruthie planted a rose bush. Her husband promised to keep up the grave."

"You must miss her something fierce." The raw emotion in his green eyes tore at her. "I do."

He stood abruptly and offered his hand to help her from the log. Even with the tension emanating from him, his hand felt strong and safe. He didn't let go once she stood, and Dilly made no attempt to pull away.

"I wish I could ease your pain." It was his grief, of course, so why did it smart as though it were her own?

The only answer he gave was a gentle squeeze to the hand he held. She didn't have many answers to her unasked questions, but if Jace hadn't changed over the years, he would talk when he was ready. It was better not to push. They walked the path through the woods in silence, hand-in-hand, and she could feel his tension slowly drain away.

"Thank you." His voice was soft, no longer hard and edged with grief.

"For what?"

"Being here. With me."

Her heart leapt, and she wanted to voice its truth. There was no place she'd rather be than wherever he was. She didn't speak but dared give his hand a squeeze. When she did, Jace's grip tightened, and her heart beat faster.

A light breeze teased the short curls at the back of his head. The urge to reach out and finger them surprised her, and she looked away quickly, only to see the huge flat rock. It was still covered in light green lichen and spotted with rich emerald moss. The only discernible change was the brown leaves dotting it this time of year. She stumbled to a stop, and his soft chuckle warmed her. So he remembered too.

"I used to dream about this place." His voice was low and husky. "I believe I sat right there—"

"And I was over there, near that patch of moss."

"I promised I would come back for you."

"And I promised I would wait." She remembered now. It wasn't only that her heart couldn't let go, it was that it needed to keep its promise. "I've avoided this path as much as possible." She pulled her hand from his and hugged herself.

"Why?"

His gentle question held no mocking.

"At first this place made the expectation of your return so strong I couldn't bear it when you didn't come back. Over time. . ." How could she explain it? "Over time, as the hope faded, I didn't want to remember."

"But you do? Remember?"

"Of course I do, Jace."

"I'm sorry it took me this many years to keep my word."

The involuntary little sob surprised her.

"Oh, Dilly." He took a tiny step in her direction.

Was he about to pull her into his arms?

"I never wanted to hurt you."

"You stopped writing even."

He looked down, not meeting her gaze. "Those were hard years, Dilly." His voice was barely a whisper. "Ruthie and Ma needed me, and I battled to step up and become the man who could meet those needs."

"You were right to take care of them."

He lifted his head and stared at her for a moment. "Then"—Jace took her hand and drew her atop the big rock, to the spot she'd pointed out on the dark green moss—"you stand right there." His eyes twinkled as he dropped her hand and stepped back a few paces, to the spot where he'd stood when he was sixteen. "Miss Daffodil Grace, I have returned as I said I would, and now I request permission to officially court you."

Telling her feet to resist the temptation to rush past the space separating them, she raised an eyebrow. "And if I say yes?"

"Then we'll pick up where we left off. We'll get reacquainted and see where we stand."

And there it was again—the joy bubble that danced when she understood why he hadn't come to see her. Only instead of manifesting in giggles, this time it was a current of emotion wetting her eyes. In two steps he was there, wiping the happy tears.

"Are you okay, Dilly?"

She managed a nod. It made no sense, how she could laugh and cry at once!

"So. . .you're happy?"

"Yes, you silly goose. Can't you tell?"

His grin stretched, making him irresistible. Dilly stepped toward the path before she behaved improperly and planted a kiss right on that dear cheek! He stepped behind her, and their banter was natural as they followed the trail, which soon joined the dirt road. The sun shone, and the birds sang, and life was the glorious happy thing she always knew it should be.

"Oh, look!" She rushed to the edge of the road. "The first flowers of spring!" She knelt by the patch of short grass that was attempting to turn green, enraptured as she was every year that the tiny bluets and Virginia spring beauties would dare show their pretty little faces in February.

"Where?" He crouched, and she pointed to them.

"Well ain't that somethin'?"

"Isn't!"

"Hmm?"

Did she really correct his grammar? "Umm. . .nothing." She'd best keep the teacher in her under control.

"*Ain't* it just the amazin'est thing?"

She whipped toward him to see the flicker of humor.

"It is amazing. *Isn't* it?" This time she spoke with her customary spunk.

"Look at you. Miss grammar lady. Graduating top of the class."

"Who told you?"

"Don't matter, do it?"

She swatted his arm. "*Doesn't!*"

He grinned then reached for a tiny purple flower. When he picked it, the little blossom almost disappeared between his huge thumb and forefinger. He bowed. "Peace offering?"

"Oh you!" She took the minuscule flower. Tonight's entry in her journey would be simple. A date and a flower pressed between the pages. There would be three words. "Jace came back."

They walked side by side as they neared town. A cluster of six or eight people stood outside the store, and Dilly rushed forward.

"I tell you I saw that hooligan running with his hands full of who knows what!" Old Lady Bishop's voice rose. "Someone better check the cash register! Oh *there* you are, silly girl!"

Chapter 5

Dilly took an involuntary step back as everyone turned her way. Heat flamed her cheeks.

"I don't know what's gotten into you and your mama, leaving this store unattended."

Breath squeezed in Dilly's lungs as understanding dawned. She'd rushed after Jace when no one else was there to watch the store. She swallowed hard and forced sound out. "What happened?"

Donna, who ran the restaurant, stepped forward. "I was seeing Mrs. Bishop out when a young fella burst out from your store with his hands full. Being as it looked out of the ordinary, we rushed right over to ask you or your mama if everything was all right. Only we couldn't find either of you."

Jeffers, who lived a piece down the road, stepped forward. "Mrs. Douglas went on home earlier this afternoon with a headache. I saw her when I went in for lunch at Donna's. After lunch I wanted to get my mail—but the store was empty! I waited, expecting Dilly would be back right away. But I waited a good long while, mind you. I went over yonder to rest there on the bench in front of Donna's and must've nodded off because I awoke to quite a racket—Mrs. Bishop hollering after that young man to get right back here, and Donna yelling for her husband."

Then everybody started talking at once, and Dilly couldn't make head or tail of the stories. Only one thing was clear. Silly Dilly's head was in the clouds.

And Mama's store was left to suffer.

She pushed past the little crowd and rushed inside, expecting to see everything in a tumble.

But it wasn't.

She hurried to the register and opened it, running her fingers across the coins and riffling through the bills. Her quick assessment deemed everything untouched. She paced the room, looking for anything out of order. She found it in the back corner. The neatly folded men's overalls were strewn across the floor. She grabbed her inventory book. There should be eight pairs, ranging in size. But there were only six.

Outside the voices rose and fell. Old Lady Bishop insisted she and Donna go and get Mama, and a debate ensued about whether she should be bothered if she was feeling poorly. Jeffers bellowed about coming into the store and giving Dilly a piece of his mind, but the accusations dropped off at the low rumble of Jace's voice, and it was Jace's face that peeked through the door. She met his gaze then returned to her perusal of the flannel shirts. She vaguely registered Jace telling the crowd that everything was in order.

But it wasn't.

Three shirts were missing as well as two pairs of socks. She glanced toward the work boots, which were quite expensive to keep on hand. Both pairs were there. Her breath came more evenly.

The voices outside continued to rise and fall. She caught only snippets of the conversation.

"Silly girl."

"Irresponsible."

"And with her mama home sick, too."

Dilly grabbed her tummy, resisting the sudden urge to throw up.

Jace's voice again. Telling everyone they should head on home, except Jeffers, who still needed his mail. She rushed to the back and grabbed it, meeting Jeffers inside the door.

"That there was a foolish thing you did, young lady."

Dilly stood tall and refused to look away from his scathing glare. Jace clamped a firm hand on Jeffers' shoulder. "If you've got everything you need, why don't you head on home now?"

Jeffers shot a quick glance into Jace's steely gaze and nodded. "I reckon I will now that I finally got my mail. Waited pretty nigh all afternoon for it."

"I'm sorry, sir." There was no defense. Only regret.

Jeffers' gaze softened. "Well all righty then. See it don't happen again."

As he left, Dilly studied the room.

Jace's hand upon her shoulder was steady. "Anything missing?"

"Two pairs of overalls, three flannel shirts, and two pairs of socks."

"Shouldn't be too hard to find the culprit. Look for a dandy in new duds." He grinned.

"This is no time for joking."

He spread his arms. "Just trying to ease the tension. Thankfully, no real harm is done."

"Maybe in a big store in Guthrie those items wouldn't make much difference, but with the volume we sell, that much merchandise affects our profit margin."

She sighed. She'd left the store unattended, and she would make it right. But her meager savings would take a significant hit. "It's my fault, and I'll take care of it. The store shouldn't suffer because I was irresponsible. I can't believe I rushed out with no thought to my promise to watch the store!" Head in the clouds. Silly Dilly.

Silly, foolish Dilly.

"I'm kind-a glad you rushed after me, Dilly. My heart was about broke when I left this store earlier today, but now it's put back together."

"But I could have broken the store! What if that thief got to the cash?"

"He didn't."

"But he *could* have!" Couldn't Jace see how awful the situation was? "All our hard-earned money gone. Like that." She snapped her fingers.

"You keep everything in the register?"

"Well, no, but—"

"Let me pay for what was stolen."

Exasperating man! "*I* will pay for what was stolen because *I* left the store unattended. *I* was irresponsible, and *I* will make it right."

"Don't you think you're being a little hard on yourself? You're not the one who broke the law and took something you didn't pay for."

"Am I? If you owned a store and your employee left it unattended and someone stole from you, what would you do?"

He hesitated.

"You'd fire the employee. We can only hope Mama won't fire me."

"Your mama's not going to fire you. And I'm at least half to blame. Let this go, Dilly. I'll pay for half of what was stolen and you can pay half, and we'll let it go."

"Don't you see? It's not that easy. The whole town lost faith in me today."

"You're making too much of this, Dilly."

"Too much? I'm not making *enough* of it!" Oh how could she have been so stupid? "You need to go on home now, Jace Gruber. You don't understand anything."

How in the world could one woman's emotions go that many directions in the course of one afternoon? Jace leaned against the black walnut tree across from the store and weighed his options. He could go on home like she demanded when she practically threw him out, or he could head back in and try to talk some sense into her.

Truth be told, his own emotions were about done for. He was hungry, and the shadows lengthened. Work began sun-up tomorrow.

Better to let her cool off.

Dilly stomped around the store, righting merchandise that, if she were honest, was already in its place—except for the three shirts, two pairs of overalls, and two pairs of socks that would *never* be in their right places again. How could she have been so foolish?

Jace Gruber, that was how.

What was it about the man that made her lose track of her senses? If that's what love did, maybe she should have nothing to do with it.

As if her smitten heart gave her any choice.

She simply *had* to find a way to keep her head on straight. Maybe it would be wise to suggest he didn't come to the store. She should limit her interactions with him to Sundays, when the store was closed.

But then she'd likely daydream through the sermon. She had to face it—nothing would keep her from thinking about Jace whether or not she actually saw him.

Dilly plopped on the stool behind the counter, face burning as she recalled what folks had said about her.

Silly girl.

Irresponsible.

She was old enough to remember how people ridiculed Mama when she first arrived in Rock City with four little girls and a wagon full of merchandise. How tongues wagged when Mama bought the run-down building! Dilly hated the whispers behind Mama's back, but Mama ignored them, pulled a hammer from her wares, and began the repairs on their very first day in Rock City. After a week of Mama's determined efforts, the whispers lessened. In another week, they turned into offers to help.

Everyone respected Mama.

That's how it had to be if a person was going to build a solid business.

Which is why Dilly had worked all these years to gain the same kind of respect Mama had.

Because only then would she be worthy to take over the store.

A tear made a wet track down her cheek. Mama's plans were ruined, all because of Dilly's thoughtless abandonment of responsibility.

Another tear began its descent, and she allowed it free rein. Her imagination had often carried her attention away from the matters right in front of her nose, but she'd been able to keep it mostly in check in recent years.

Until Jace.

Even as a girl she hadn't been able to keep daydreams of Jace in their place.

After he left, she had worked hard to limit her daydreams to the pages of her journal—mostly—and people had started to trust her. They even trusted her when they had special goods to order instead of waiting until Mama was there like they used to.

But would they now?

She had broken their trust. Mama's trust. Her own mantra of responsibility.

Maybe she wasn't cut out to run the store after all. Without the respect of their community, she wouldn't be able to turn a profit. She couldn't bear it if her presence at the store ran Mama's hard work into the ground.

Dilly slowly began closing up. She'd lock the store then head home to tell Mama how she'd failed them both.

Before sunrise, Jace pulled on his work clothes and headed into town. No way could he go to work without knowing Dilly was okay. Their time in the woods finally righted the trajectory of their renewed relationship, but her despair yesterday stole their joy. If it weren't for the robbery, he'd be whistling instead of worrying—and his early morning visit would be about courting.

It was taking a chance to head by her place before normal folks even had their breakfast, but Dilly and her mama always used to get up early to take care of their chores before opening the store. His heart beat faster as he rounded the general store and followed the worn path to the small house behind it.

A dim glow flickered behind the curtains in the front room, and its presence emboldened him. He raised a fist to the door, hesitating only a moment before knocking. When the door opened, it wasn't Dilly.

"Hello, Mrs. Douglas."

Dilly's mama stepped onto the front porch, pulling the door gently behind her. "It's good to see you, Jace."

He took off his hat. "Thank you, ma'am. It's good to be back."

"You came for Dilly."

It wasn't a question. "I wanted to know how she's doing after yesterday's hoopla."

"She's finally sleeping. How about you walk with me to the store?"

"She didn't rest well then." He stepped off the little porch, turning to look again toward the faint light in the house.

"She has it in her head that the good folks of Rock City lost all respect for her yesterday. Said she no longer wants to take over the store."

"Take over?"

"I planned to sign it over to her next spring. She'd run it and give me a small stipend in return."

Dilly wanted to run the store on her own? No wonder she overreacted to yesterday's heist.

Mrs. Douglas sighed. "I'm saving for a trip back East to stay with my sister. I wanted to take next summer to consider my future. I'm not getting any younger. But now. . . ."

"You're not firing her!"

"Of course not. It was a serious oversight, but"—she stopped and offered a knowing grin—"I understand her distraction."

He looked at the hat still in his hands. "I'm sorry for my part, Mrs. Douglas."

"She took full responsibility. Said you didn't realize she was the only one in the store."

"I honestly never gave it a thought."

"Why would you?" Mrs. Douglas started walking again. "It wasn't your responsibility."

"Is the financial loss as significant as Dilly thinks?"

"She already repaid the store for the stolen merchandise. I doubt she has much left in her savings. I wouldn't have required her to do that, but I allowed it in hopes it would ease her mind."

"Do *you* think this incident proves she is not ready for the responsibility of the store?"

She sighed. "It won't matter what I think if Dilly thinks she can't do it."

Chapter 6

Dilly sat up with a start, squinting at the sun streaming through the window. Ugh! Add oversleeping to her list of failures.

The straight line of Sunbonnet Sues on her quilt top mocked her. The faceless girls were created from old dresses. Mama's. Grandma's. Her own. How she'd loved the quilt and its connection to her heritage—Daffodil Grace Douglas, daughter of a strong, respected woman from a line of strong, respected women. Women who overcame odds like prejudice and hardship. Great-grandma survived the Trail of Tears. Grandma stood up to censure when she married a white man. Mama established a general store in Indian Territory without the help of a husband.

Dilly sighed. Was she cut from the same cloth?

Quilt. Cloth. A humorless chuckle escaped.

Even when pondering serious thoughts her imagination distracted her with a pun. What was wrong with her anyway? Dilly shoved the covers back and stepped onto the cold wood floor. No matter how hard she tried she couldn't stay focused. Instead of staying logical and sequential like Mama, like the line of quilt girls in her heritage, her thoughts flitted about untamed.

Splashing water on her face, Dilly pushed through her morning routine and out the door. As she rounded the corner to the store, she groaned and ducked behind the side of the building. Of all people to encounter this morning, Old Lady Bishop was the last she wanted to see. Dilly slipped behind the store, escaping into the trees. She pulled her wrap tighter. It was cool in the shade, though the sun shone today in a rare cloudless sky. Maybe a walk would do her good.

She wandered aimlessly, climbing the long, wooded hill behind her home. The redbud trees showed a hint of green, and she imagined them in a month—a glory of purple peeking between grey limbs. When she reached the top of the hill, she found a sunny spot and sat on a big lichen-covered rock. Thanks to the bluff below her, the view was expansive.

Now what, Lord?

It wasn't like her to duck out of responsibility when she should be helping Mama in the store, but she needed to breathe, and fresh air and sunshine always seemed to help. Dilly could see quite a piece from her perch. Greenleaf Creek, the same creek she and Jace sat next to down the road a ways, rolled through the hills and trees and fields below her. To the right more tree-covered hills rose and fell. To her left cattle grazed where trees were cleared, and she laughed out loud at the antics of the frolicking calves. Then she sobered.

If only her heart were that free.

Maybe she pushed too hard to grow up, with all the talk of being an early bloomer like her namesake. What if she was too young to take over the store?

What if she would *always* be too dreamy to carry that much responsibility?

She sighed and gazed at the old home place in front of her. She didn't know who owned the property or where its previous tenants had gone, but the run-down old shack of a house was in desperate need of repair, and the large barn in just as bad shape. Still, it was one of her favorite places, and she had named the property, "Potential." Not only was it beautifully situated, with a little stream running right through the land to join Greenleaf Creek, but in a month or so the field next to the house would be bright with yellow daffodils.

For years Dilly made a point to come up here in the spring with the sole intent of looking down upon them. When they bloomed it was like gazing on sunshine itself. It was this very vista that caused her to pick the lines from William Wordsworth's poem to memorize one year in school. Well, this view and the fact she was named after the flower.

She whispered the familiar verse, sending it as a hopeful prayer over the barren field below.

> I wandered lonely as a cloud
> That floats on high o'er vales and hills,
> When all at once I saw a crowd,
> A host, of golden daffodils;
> Beside the lake, beneath the trees,
> Fluttering and dancing in the breeze.

Mama often said Dilly was like a daffodil because she was an early bloomer, capable of much. Running the store. Handling inventory and the books, even. Dilly sighed. Truth was she was more like the daffodils in the poem. Fluttery. Dancing. Carried this way and that by the breeze. It was hard to tamp down all that dreaming, dancing energy. What if she hadn't promised Mama she'd take over the store? What if she hadn't worked so hard to stop the fluttering, dancing of her daffodil personality?

What else had Mama said? Something about blessing customers with her sunny disposition. What about that? Her joy often came because of the imagination that lived beneath the surface.

Could it be of some value after all?

"What do You think, Lord?" She flung the prayer into the expanse before her. "What makes me, me? What do I need to change, and what needs to stay? I always wanted to run Mama's store, but is that a childish dream, or a realistic plan? And where does Jace fit into all of this?" What if her determination to take over the store was simply a way to stay put and wait for Jace? But she did love it. Didn't she?

She lingered on the rock, listening. No answer came on the gentle breeze that drew wisps of hair from her chignon, but the sunshine and sweet earth smell lifted her spirits. "I understand if You aren't ready to clear all of this up right this instant, but I ask that in the coming days You help me sort it out. And right now, I need courage to do what I should have already done. Walk into Mama's store and face the public."

Dilly stood and wiped the back of her skirt. It was a bit damp, but nothing of consequence. With determined steps she made her way to Mama and the store they both loved.

If he timed it right, maybe he could peek in on Dilly over the noon hour. He could eat while he walked, and if he walked fast, he would have at least ten minutes with her. When the noon whistle blew, Jace set off for town. The warm day held the golden promise of spring. As he rounded the bend into Rock City, he glimpsed Dilly climbing the steps into the store.

"Wait up a minute, Dilly!"

She paused, but a frown turned the corners of her mouth. He summoned the courage to try anyway. "I dropped in on you this morning, but you weren't awake yet, so I visited with your mama."

Her back stiffened. "I don't usually sleep in."

"I know that, Dilly."

"I need to get to work."

"Can't you spare a minute? I only have about five before I have to get back to work myself."

"What is it that you need, Jace?"

"Don't you know?" He gazed into those brown eyes. "I need to see that you're okay after that mess yesterday."

"I will be." She stared at his boots.

"Your mama says you plan to take over the store when she leaves for a trip next spring."

Her head whipped up, and he ached to touch the wisps of hair that had escaped from her bun and framed her face. He waited but she didn't speak.

"Do you?"

"Do I what?"

"Plan to run the family store?"

Dilly sighed. "Do we have to talk about this now?"

"I wouldn't want a little incident like what happened yesterday to steal your dreams."

"Little?"

"Come on, Dilly. Your mama said you've already paid for the stolen goods." He dared rub his finger along her soft cheek. "Everything has been righted."

Her eyes went from gentle to flashing in an instant. "Don't you understand anything? It's the loss of trust that is the most damaging. A business can't be a success if its customers can't trust the proprietor."

"Folk around here *do* trust you."

"Did. They *did* trust me before I got all silly and ran off with you yesterday."

"I still believe you're making too much—"

"You're not making *enough* of it." At the edge in her voice he stepped back from her. "Dilly—"

"Excuse me, Jace, but I have a responsibility to the store."

When Dilly whirled from him without even a backward glance, he whirled back toward the road. Evidently that was what a feller got when he tried to say a kind word to a stubborn woman. The cold shoulder. He marched a good hundred yards. His Dilly was hurting. His footsteps slowed. He couldn't leave things like this. Not after all he'd been through to reconnect with her. Whether she realized it or not, she needed him right about now.

He took a deep breath and turned back toward the store. He entered and noted Dilly stocking the shelves in the back. He strode toward her. "I know you're busy, Dilly, but I'd like to come back after work and talk this through."

The hard lines on her face softened. "We don't close until seven."

"I'll be here."

If that didn't beat all. Dilly stared at Jace's retreating form. Most folks would be put out with her, but he'd returned even after she snubbed him. This was the Jace she'd fallen in love with all those years ago, the man who did what was right even when he was mistreated. Kind, compassionate Jace.

Lord, forgive me, and—teach me how to treat that man like he deserves.

But. . .what if talking it through didn't mean making their peace? What if he wanted to withdraw his offer to court her?

Oh, she wouldn't blame him a bit! Not after she sent him packing two days in a row!

Please, God. Help him give me another chance.

"Good afternoon, Dilly."

Dilly startled at the salutation, but fought to keep her expression neutral as she greeted Donna. The woman's accusations from yesterday were still ringing in her mind. She bit her lip. "Um. . .how is business at the café?"

"Seems like it picked up a little today." Donna chuckled. "Nothing like a robbery to bring folks out. They're all talking about it—and buying pie while they do!"

Dilly counted to ten, her face on fire.

"None of us recognized the young man who stole from ya'll. Course Rosemary Bishop and I only saw his back."

"I see."

"It was an unfortunate event, my dear, but I reckon it will soon be forgotten. For the time being I'm happy with increased business!"

"Yes, ma'am."

Donna bought a sack of flour, no doubt so she could make more pies. Dilly was glad to see her go, but more customers came in as soon as she left. Every last one of them poked around in the men's section. Evidently word had spread. They obviously came only to sate their curiosity because if they made a purchase, it was something small. A piece of candy. A spool of thread. Oh bother!

Dilly kept a smile plastered on and tried to greet each of them as if nothing were out of the ordinary. When the last patron departed, she sagged against the counter. A mumble of voices floated through the open door. Frowning, she turned her attention to sorting the mail, but Mama stepped outside. Bits of phrases teased her before the door closed. Couldn't everyone drop it and go home? She frowned. What were they saying about her? With a huff she stalked to the window near the door and ever-so-gently opened it a crack, straining to hear.

Jeffers talked loudly, retelling his story from yesterday, obviously enjoying folk's attention. "I reckon that young man oughta be horse-whipped. Stealin' goes 'gainst all the Good Book teaches."

"We certainly appreciate your concern, Jeffers." Mama's voice rang out steady and sweet. "We appreciate all of you. Be assured that the store is all right. My Dilly insisted on repaying the business the monetary equivalent of what was stolen."

"Why, the dear girl!"

Was that Old Lady Bishop?

Approving mumbles drowned out any coherent sentences. There was a clattering near the door, and Dilly rushed away from the window.

Mama.

"You didn't have to tell them."

"It's good for folks to know how responsible you are."

"If I'd been responsible, I would never have left the store unattended, and the town wouldn't be full of unrest today."

Mama put an arm around her. "This sort of thing always blows over."

"It won't blow over in my heart."

"Oh, but it should."

"How can you say that? If I never forget this incident, maybe I'll never mess up like this again!"

"No doubt you've learned from your mistake. I never worry about that with you, but I do worry about something else."

Dilly's stomach clenched.

"My concern, Dilly, is related to trust."

Of course it was. "I'll work hard to help the town trust me again."

"It's not the town's trust I'm concerned about."

"Then I'll do everything in my power to give *you* reason to trust me, again."

Mama chuckled. "Oh my dear Dilly! I never stopped trusting you. Everyone makes mistakes. Yesterday changed nothing in how I perceive you."

"Then whose trust concerns you?"

"Yours."

"I don't understand."

"Before me stands a dependable, capable young woman. The daughter I've entrusted with more responsibility than anyone else."

Dilly hung her head.

Mama put a finger beneath Dilly's chin and lifted it so that their gazes met. "My trust is well-placed, Daffodil Grace. I believe in you."

Mama paused, and Dilly's heart beat hard in her chest.

"Now I want you to believe in yourself."

But how could she when she was hopelessly flawed?

Jace pulled his coat tighter. It was dark this time of year long before seven. The late February day almost felt like spring, but the night was turning cold. March couldn't come soon enough. Spring was the perfect season in northeastern Oklahoma. Warm enough to be comfortable during the long hours at work, but cool enough to keep the sweat from dripping. His was an active, dirty work, even in the cold months. Thankfully, the room he rented up the road came with access to a good well, and he could clean-up of the evening same as of the morning, even though a full bath was allowed only once a week.

Rubbing his hands on his trousers, he fought the self-conscious feeling of being too confined. Overalls were more natural, but he'd traded them in for his church trousers, a clean shirt, and suspenders. It wasn't fancy, but folks 'round these parts didn't much do fancy. Still, his duds were a might too stuffy for a man who spent most days in his overalls. Dilly would think he was trying to impress her.

Which of course he was.

But did that mean he should be so obvious about it?

And what was he going to say to smooth things between them? First off, he'd apologize for his insensitivity. If he'd planned on taking over the business, he'd most likely have felt like she did.

He paused as he passed the store, but it was dark inside, so he rounded the corner toward her house. The small home boasted a full-sized porch, and her familiar silhouette shadowed one of the chairs there, barely visible in the moonlight. A faint creaking signaled she was rocking.

"I'm glad you came." Her sweet voice reached through the darkness.

"I'm glad you let me."

The rocking stopped. "Are you cold? We could go inside, but it's a nice enough night, and I thought it might be easier to talk out here."

Without her Mama listening in.

"I've got my coat." He climbed the single step and plopped down in the chair next to her only to spring up again at the lumpy presence he hadn't noticed. Reaching down he grabbed the quilt lying there and shook it. Once seated, he covered his legs and enjoyed the warmth. He was close enough now to see she was also snugged in.

"Dilly, I—"

"Before you say a word, Jace Gruber, there are a few things I need to say."

Okay. . .

"While I hope it is not truly my nature to be easily ruffled and temperamental,

I must confess I've been just that. Upon reflection I am not pleased with my behavior toward you. You did nothing but offer kindness since the first minute you rescued Tommy from those ruffians. I, on the other hand, have been quick to offense and hopelessly flawed."

"Now Dilly—"

"Please Jace, I'm not finished. I am not asking you to excuse my behavior—"

"There's nothing to—"

"Because I find my behavior inexcusable. I can only tell you that if you give me another chance, I will try very hard to treat you better. That said, I would like an opportunity to explain myself." She paused.

Jace started to reassure her, but she shushed him.

"Do you remember when the kids first started calling me Silly Dilly?"

He shrugged. "Not too long after I moved here."

She cleared her throat. "I've. . .always struggled with a vivid imagination, but once I met. . .you. . .it completely got away from me. It's quite embarrassing to admit. Especially to. . .you. . .but you deserve an explanation. See, the very first time someone called me Silly Dilly, I was daydreaming about you."

"Me?" Now that *was* good news.

"I feel so foolish, even now. I must have been twelve or thirteen, much too young to be so silly, but even then I found you highly. . .distracting—and that was all it took for the teasing to start." Her voice broke on the last word.

Jace resisted the urge to take her hand. "Was the teasing that bad?"

She sighed. "Maybe I was too sensitive, but my family went through a lot of censure over the years. Daddy's parents back East didn't like the fact Mama was half-Cherokee, and they never fully accepted any of us. After Daddy died and Mama moved us to Rock City, people here ridiculed her something fierce. Said no mother with four little girls could set up and run a store. But she did it. By the time you moved here, the teasing had died down. We finally had the respect of folks. I was proud of Mama and wanted to be like her—so determined and capable that I could do whatever I set my mind to and gain people's good favor, even if I didn't have it at first."

"So when the kids called you Silly Dilly—"

"I felt once again the object of ridicule. I feared I brought the shame to my family that my mother worked so hard to overcome."

"I'm sorry I teased you."

She nodded, but tears streamed down her face. This time he dared reach for her hand, and she didn't pull away. "You *do* know why I teased you?"

She shook her head.

"I think it's the same reason the other boys teased you."

"Why?"

"Because saying your dreaded nickname was the quickest way any of us could get your attention. And *all* of us wanted the attention of pretty little Dilly."

"Oh for Pete's sake!"

"I'm not pulling your leg, Dilly. It wasn't lack of respect that made us pick on you."

She looked away, and Jace smiled. Knowing his Dilly, her face was now covered in a pretty pink blush. Not that he could tell in the dim lighting.

"There's more." Dilly sighed.

"If it's about what happened yesterday, I think I understand now."

"You do?"

"Yes. You're afraid our mistake in leaving the store unattended will get tongues wagging and make you lose respect. Without respect you fear you won't be able to successfully run the store."

"I need folks to trust me."

"Sweetheart, folks make mistakes all the time. Not one of us is immune to such things, darlin'. We don't respect people because they are perfect. We respect them because we come to know their character. Even now, only a day after the robbery, folks are talking about your good character, how you wouldn't let your mama or her store suffer, but paid for the merchandise out of your own savings."

Sweetheart? Darlin'? Maybe Jace didn't mean to break up with her at all. And how could the presence of his strong hand wrapped around hers make her flustered and peaceful all at the same time?

"Do you believe me, Dilly?"

"Um..." Believe what? Oh, why had she gotten all caught up in the sweethearts and darlin's and missed the rest? "Did you call me sweetheart?"

His chuckle was low. "Well aren't you?"

"Aren't I what?"

"My sweetheart?"

She swallowed hard, heart pounding. "If you still want me."

He pushed his quilt aside then knelt in front of her, taking both hands in his. "Can you truly doubt my intentions, *darlin'*?"

Oh how his eyes twinkled in the starlight as his deep voice lingered on that last word. *Darlin'*. She was Jace Gruber's darlin'. His gaze dropped to her lips, and the twinkle in his eyes became a smolder. The intensity of his gaze drew her forward. She'd waited for this for a long time.

Jace stood abruptly, shattering the glorious moment into tiny, shimmering pieces. Magic still hovered around him, but its breathless glow became normal moonlight as he stepped away.

"How 'bout I go on inside and have a chat with your mother?"

"What kind of chat?"

He grinned. "I can't officially court you without her permission, now can I?"

Dilly flung herself into his arms and soaked up the low rumble of laughter humming in his chest. Breathing deeply of his scent, she lingered there. "You're giving me another chance."

He stepped back and shook his head. "You don't need another chance because you never lost the first one. Didn't you hear anything I said?"

"I. . .might have been a bit distracted a minute ago."

He laughed. "My point was simply that perfection doesn't exist, and the people of Rock City—including yours truly—know you are a woman of fine character. Nobody is without flaws, not even you, my little Daffodil. Now, with your permission, I'm going right into that house and ask your mama if I can court you before we waste another second."

She couldn't help the grin that stretched across her face.

"I'll take that as a yes." With a wink Jace rapped on the door, disappearing inside at Mama's welcoming call.

Dilly flopped back onto the rocker and hugged herself. How could life go from devastating to glorious all in one day?

Chapter 7

Tommy flashed that impish grin Jace had come to love. Jace grinned back. "Got room for a fella to join you for lunch?"

The boy's eager response felt like a homecoming. Jace plopped down next to him and handed the lad the extra sandwich he'd packed that morning. The boy's quick thank you was almost lost in his eagerness to dig into it. They ate in silence, soaking in the warm noonday sun.

Tommy devoured half of the sandwich. When he slowed to a normal eating pace, it did Jace good to know the boy's hunger had lessened.

Tommy gave him a sly glance, but didn't speak.

"You might as well come out with it."

"Mama says you and Aunt Dilly made up."

"Does she now?"

"She says you asked Grandma if Aunt Dilly could be your girl."

"What do you think about that?"

"It's good."

Jace elbowed the boy. "I'm glad to have your approval."

Tommy snickered and elbowed him back. "Folks 'round here say Aunt Dilly's going to make someone a mighty fine wife."

"You told me."

"Figured you might need a reminder."

Not likely.

When the whistle blew, Tommy gave Jace a little wave. Jace nodded. Thankfully he hadn't fallen too far from the pedestal the day Tommy lectured him about making things up to Dilly. And wasn't it wonderful to be made up with the woman! Jace returned to his post. The hammer wasn't quite so heavy now that all was right in his world. Dilly's mama actually seemed pleased to give her blessing, and the last few days he shared their evening meal. At first Dilly had been shy with him there, but it didn't take long for things to feel natural. There was something special about being comfortable with a woman. It felt like...family. Maybe it was time to get serious about making Rock City a permanent home. No more roaming. No more rented rooms.

As he worked alongside the crew carrying heavy rock, his thoughts went to the old place Dilly was always partial to. If he remembered right, the property had a little stream running across it that joined up with Greenleaf Creek. It would provide water for a garden and, until he saved up for an icebox, a place to keep the milk cool. Didn't

Stanley Burge's son used to live there?

When the workday ended, he took the shortcut through the woods to the Burge's place. The brown-skinned, white-haired man answered his first knock and invited him inside. "Gruber, isn't it?"

"Yes sir, Mr. Burge. Jace Gruber." Jace stuck out his hand.

The man grasped it warmly. "Your mama brought us chicken soup many years back. Whole family laid up sick and hungry. Marched right in here not even taking the germs into account and fed the lot of us."

Tears burned, and Jace blinked them away. "She was a good woman."

"I'm sorry to hear she's gone, son."

"Thank you."

"Why don't you have a sit down and tell me what's on your mind?"

Jace sat, breathing a silent prayer for favor. "I came about the property where your son used to live. Do you still own it?"

"I do." Mr. Burge sighed. "After Jimmy moved the place fell to disrepair. I always meant to keep it up, but my days are long on work—and short on cash."

"I'd like to buy it, sir."

"You don't say. Have you seen it close up since you moved back?"

"Only from a distance."

"The buildings need a lot of work. Land itself is good. But the house and barn won't be usable without a lot of hard work and sweat."

"I understand that."

"So you're thinking of staying, are you?"

"I am."

"Now I'm not one to pry into another man's business, but if I were to consider your offer, I'd want to know that you plan to settle down. Find a good woman and make a home of it. Pearl and I lived there early on, before we bought this property, and I'm sentimental about the old place."

Jace cleared his throat. "That's exactly what I want too."

The elderly man's eyes gleamed. "Heard you're courting Mrs. Douglas's girl. Fine young woman. Going to make somebody a good wife. I hope that somebody is you."

"That makes two of us."

"Well then Mr. Gruber, I think we oughtta talk business."

The deal was sealed on a handshake with a promise of confidentiality. Jace didn't want anyone hearing about his purchase until he had time to fix the old place up and woo the woman he hoped would someday be its mistress.

Dilly frowned at the curling tong heating on the woodstove in her room. Last month her best friend, Lilly Beth, overheated her styling iron and singed a strand of her beautiful black hair off at the scalp. Dilly picked the tong up by its wooden handles and stared in the small vanity mirror. Her carefully constructed pompadour had a nice shape, but with any luck perfect curls would soon frame her face.

When was the last time she took such care dressing for church? Then again, this was the first time she would enter on the arm of a young man. And it wasn't just any young man! Finally, finally, it was Jace.

A rap on the bedroom door interrupted her musing. "He's here, sweetheart. Are you ready?"

Dilly grabbed her wrap, butterflies doing a jig in her tummy. Was it the thrill of her first official outing as Jace's girl, or was it that she wanted his approval? She paused before she opened her door, listening to the strange sound of a deep male voice in their home. What a lot of changes!

When Dilly turned the knob and stepped into the main room, her gaze locked with Jace's. The intensity in his green eyes made her face flame. Was this what it felt like to be truly admired? If so, it was more wonderful—and more exasperating—than she'd conjured in even her most detailed daydreams. "Good morning, Jace." Oh, why did her voice come out all breathy?

He offered his arm. "Shall we go?"

The minute her hand nestled at his elbow, her emotions soared and calmed all at once, like they did when he took her hand a few nights before. What a strange thing it was to embrace romance. She'd heard the giddy talk of schoolgirls before, seen Lilly Beth get excitable when she began courting, but no one told her of the wonder of the calm, at-home feeling that accompanied such soaring joy. Did everyone feel grounded when they found the man of their dreams, or was this different for her and Jace?

Mama followed them onto the front porch and closed the door. Jace offered Dilly his hand and helped her down the steps, then he turned and helped Mama down as well, and Mama smiled broadly. The threesome covered the short distance to the main road, and when the walking space opened up, Jace offered Dilly one arm and Mama the other. He had to be the most thoughtful man in the whole wide world. Dilly lifted her face to the sun and whispered her gratitude to its Maker.

Natural. That's what it was. To walk between his girl and her mama, as he once did between his own sweet ma and Ruthie. It would do Ruthie good to see him this happy, and if the Good Lord allowed the veil to split in this moment, Ma sang praises for sure. She always loved Dilly.

Seemed like creation itself celebrated with him, with the song of birds filling the air and the sky as blue as blue could be. They wound down the road until they came upon the building that served as both a schoolhouse and a church. Situated in the woods, central to the surrounding country folk, it boasted a tall, pointed roof and clapboard walls in need of paint.

His footsteps faltered.

A lot of years lay between him and that church. Ma made sure he and Ruthie attended faithfully with her here in Rock City, but as his pa got worse and moved them so often, even Ma gave up on church attendance. No doubt the truths he learned in that little church carried him through the worst years, even though for a time he told himself he didn't believe anymore. Especially when church folks in town after town shunned their family for his father's behavior.

Maybe without his pa around bringing censure to the family Jace could find his home in church once again.

"You okay?" Dilly's gaze searched his face.

Mrs. Douglas pulled her hand from his elbow. "I think I'll head on in."

It was like her to read his mood and give them privacy.

"Jace?"

He put a hand over Dilly's and squeezed. "Got a lot of good memories here. Some not so good from other churches, though."

"What do you mean?"

"Now's not a good time to get into all that." As if there ever was a good time.

"Surely—"

"Suffice it to say church wasn't my favorite place." Church folks didn't always take kindly to the son of a drunk.

"Ya'll didn't attend anymore after you left Rock City?"

"Ruthie did when I moved her and Mama to Guthrie after. . .my father left us. Mama was sick. Got weaker and weaker. Ruthie cared for her while I worked, so on Sunday I took my turn and let Ruthie go to church."

"But you—"

"It's been a while."

"You're nervous." Her eyes were wide.

"You gotta understand, Dilly. I was mad at God there for a while. He and I got on the same page while Mama was dying. She saw to that." He chuckled. "I may not have been in a church building all those Sundays, but Mama could've been a preacher."

"If you're right with God, then why—"

"It took a while to trust God again after. . .all we went through." How could he help her understand? "I'm not sure I ever made it back around to trusting His people." Hard to trust folks who looked down their noses at a young man—not even fully grown—when he was doing his best. His cold, dark winter lasted years and had nothing to do with the weather. He squared his shoulders. "Let's do this before I lose my nerve."

Maybe this year spring could come fully to his tattered heart.

The grim set of Jace's jaw said more than his sparse explanation. How could she spend all that time in front of her dressing mirror primping and thinking about walking into the church house on Jace's arm and not give one thought to how this day would affect him? Of all the silly, girlish notions!

She squeezed his arm.

"I'm sorry, Jace."

"You've got nothing to be sorry for, sweetheart."

"I didn't know today would be hard for you."

"How could you?"

Yes. How could she if he didn't tell her more about the ten years they were apart? She loved Jace. Always had. Always would. But there was a lot she needed to learn about the man who'd stolen her heart.

He led her forward, the motion breaking into her thoughts. Up ahead Lilly Beth and her husband, Owen, climbed the church steps. Owen held their toddler in his arms. Lilly Beth glanced their way and waved, then headed toward them, pulling Owen along with her. "I heard talk you were back, Jace Gruber!" The look she shot at Dilly said that wasn't all she'd heard.

"Lilly Beth Bushyhead." Jace grinned. "I'd know you anywhere."

"It's Lilly Beth Qualls now. This is my husband, Owen."

Jace shook Owen's free hand.

"And our boy, Stanton."

"He's a handsome young lad." Jace reached for the little boy's hand and gave it a shake. The toddler promptly stuck his thumb in his mouth.

Jace turned back to Owen. "It's nice to meet you. Your wife and my Dilly were thick as thieves back in the old days."

My Dilly. How she loved the sound of that!

Lilly Beth gave her *the look* again.

"Good to meet you too. You and Dilly should come to Sunday dinner next week, don't you think, Lilly Beth?"

"We'd love it!" Her friend actually clapped her hands in excitement, and Dilly grinned.

"We best get inside." Owen led the way.

Dilly sneaked a peek at Jace's expression, pleased to see much of the tension had drained away. Oh the Lord—and the Qualls—were good! *Please, God, help everyone else to be as welcoming, and please help Jace feel right at home.*

Chapter 8

Dilly squeezed Stanton, who sat on her lap contented with a homemade cookie. What a precious child! Lilly Beth bustled around the kitchen, preparing a cup of strong, hot coffee. Mama had insisted Dilly take a morning off from the store for a chat with her good friend, and Dilly jumped at the chance.

Lilly Beth plopped the coffee cup near Dilly, but out of the reach of her toddler, then joined them, nursing her own steaming mug. "Tell me everything!"

Dilly laughed. The last two weeks with Jace were better than she ever dreamed, and that was saying something. "The good news is I'm blushing less, even though he says the sweetest things."

"Do you see him often?"

"Nearly every day. Mama's taken to setting an extra plate out in case he shows up at supper time. Which he usually does."

"It's hard to believe you two are back together after all these years."

"Pinch me. I want to be sure it's real." When Lilly Beth reached with pinching fingers, Dilly pulled back. "Not literally!"

Lilly Beth laughed. "He looks at you like he's a cat and you're the cream."

Maybe she wasn't completely over the tendency to blush.

"I'm glad, my friend. You deserve someone who loves you that much."

"*Deserve.* That's a strong word."

The spot between Lilly Beth's brow creased. "What do you mean?"

"I don't feel like I deserve Jace. He's good and patient. I get testy. Silly. Thoughtless." She hesitated before telling the whole sad story of Jace's first day at church and how she'd been caught up in girlish silliness when the man she loved was carrying a heavy burden.

"Oh, Dilly. Just because you love someone doesn't mean you can read his mind."

"I want to do a better job of loving him."

"Give yourself time. You'll learn his ways."

"I hope so."

Mama set a bowl of buttery stewed potatoes on the table. "Jace better hurry if he's going to catch supper tonight. Probably back at the boardinghouse, getting on his fancy duds for someone special." Mama winked, and Dilly was glad Mama didn't also mention the fact that Dilly had curled her hair after closing the store—and added a new collar and cuffs to her cotton shirtwaist. Her hand flew to her neck.

Mama chuckled. "You look beautiful, honey, and I love what you did with that old handkerchief, turning it into neckwear. But don't be disappointed if Jace doesn't notice. Men don't often notice the details, but it's obvious he appreciates the package."

"He's a good man, Mama."

"I know that."

"He's more patient than I deserve."

"Good men usually are."

Dilly bit her lip. But were most women as hopelessly flawed as she? "I'm not sure I'm worthy of such a good man."

Mama stopped her bustling. "Why ever not?"

"I make so many mistakes. Like with the store. And I can be so caught up in my own thoughts that I don't notice his needs. And I'm easily provoked, usually for no good reason."

Mama stared at her, and Dilly knew the look. It was the one where Mama was silently praying for wisdom while she studied her child. Mama sat across the table. "It's hard to be perfect."

"You don't have to worry about that with me. I'm a far cry from perfect."

"But you try to be."

"Not with any success."

"Oh honey, don't you see? None of us can be perfect. That's why we need a Savior."

Dilly huffed. "I have a Savior!" Was Mama questioning her salvation?

"Yes you do. The question is if you really understand all that means."

"All?"

"Too often we ask Jesus to save us then treat salvation like a ticket to heaven and nothing else."

"What do you mean?"

"Our Savior keeps on saving. Over and over. Every minute. He knows we have flaws we're still working through, but it doesn't worry Him one bit. You know why?"

"Why?"

"Because He sent us His Holy Spirit to change us from the inside out. The Spirit always finishes the good work God starts in us, so when we struggle, our Savior simply covers our faults with His perfection. Then the Spirit moves us forward, helping us become more like Jesus." Mama reached across the table and grabbed Dilly's hand. "Don't take on God's job, Daffodil Grace. Our Savior's burden is easy and His yoke is light. We live in a constant state of forgiveness and walk with a Savior whose job it is to see us become more like Him. If you take that upon yourself, you'll always live from a place of lack. You'll judge yourself and find yourself wanting. That's not how God sees you. He sees you dressed in that robe of righteousness. He knows the finished work you're becoming, and that's what He thinks about. Let go of trying to be perfect, my child. Rest in the plan of the only One who is."

Dilly sniffed. "Thanks." Mama's words settled deep inside, and she felt the knots begin to untwist.

"Give the glory to the Spirit. He had something you needed to hear. He gave those words. They're not mine, child."

A rap on the door interrupted. Dilly wiped at her eyes and rushed to answer. She barely had the door open before Jace grabbed her hand, sending that warm feeling through her whole body. "Hello, beautiful," he whispered.

Dilly glanced toward the kitchen, but Mama's back was turned. She squeezed Jace's hand and drew him to the table. "Mama made your favorite potatoes."

Jace swallowed the lump in his throat. Not only did the Lord answer his prayers of the last ten years when He gave him sweet Dilly, but Mrs. Douglas's attention ministered to the grieving places. He didn't cry much when Ma died. How could he when she was so much better off? How could he when Ruthie needed his strength? But here. Here he could lay it all down and just drink in the caring.

The evening progressed much too quickly, as every moment with Dilly did, and when she walked Jace to the front porch to say goodbye, he wished he could stay.

What was it about the new man he didn't like? Jace stood by the fire at the edge of the work space and poured half a cup of coffee. The day was cooler than most, drizzly and gray, and the bitter liquid felt good going down. He returned the coffee pot to its perch and moved back to his post, watching the man—Jones, was it? He hadn't worked closely enough with him to meet him officially, but the man worked slower than the rest and was often distracted. It wasn't only that, though. What was it?

When Tommy came 'round with the wagon, Jace tugged a heavy load, like everyone else, but he glimpsed Jones meandering around the side of the wagon instead of working. Jace watched, making sure Jones didn't bother Tommy. The man walked past without speaking to the lad, so Jace went back for another load.

A boyish screech, then a rumble. Jace whipped toward the sound. The horses pawed the air and broke into a panicked run. "Hold on!" Jace rushed toward the wagon.

The wagon hit a rock and bounced. Tommy slid.

"Grab hold!"

Jace rounded the first horse. Hooves came at him, and he ducked. "Whoa now!"

Working his way between the horses, he grabbed for the halters, catching one in each hand. "Steady now. Steady."

Bulging, crazed eyes met his gaze.

Huge heads pulled skyward, lifting Jace off the ground.

He jerked hard.

Came back to the earth.

Fought for his footing.

"Hey now. Steady. Steady!"

The big bay pulled to the right.

Jace countered.

"Help him! Somebody!" Tommy's cries pierced the air, rising above the snorting and snapping.

The black came at him, teeth bared.

Dodging the assault, he forced calm words. "Whoa now. Steady."

The horses stopped pawing but continued to shake their heads and snort.

"You're all right. Steady now."

Finally they stood still except for the trembling.

He didn't dare move. "It's all right. You're okay."

Another worker took the halters. "You'd better see to the boy."

Jace nodded and rushed to Tommy. The boy huddled on the wagon, sobbing. Jace grabbed him and held tight. "Steady now. It's over, son. It's over."

He carried Tommy away from the group, which now crowded around the righted wagon. Solemn gazes met his.

"They're gonna make fun." Tommy's choked whisper sounded in Jace's ear.

"Not this time, son," he whispered. "They're all as frightened as you were."

He sat Tommy on a rock. "Somebody bring him some water." If Tommy wasn't too shook up to notice, it would have eased his fears to see how quickly the men jumped to help.

The crew boss came over, face pinched and white. "What happened?"

"Something spooked the horses." Jace shook his head. But what?

"It were him." One of the men pointed toward Jones.

"You. Come." The boss's firm tone left no room for question.

Jones stumbled toward them. "I didn't do nothing." At the man's slurred reply, Jace's stomach roiled.

"Saw you." The first man stepped close and turned to the boss. "He used a stick from the fire to light his cigarette. Then threw the flaming stick at the horses."

"They got too close."

When Jones spoke, Jace smelled it. Hands fisted, he stalked toward the man. "You're drunk." Jones cowered as Jace pulled back, imagining his fist connecting with that weak jaw.

"Don't do it!" Tommy's pleading voice broke through his boiling anger.

The boss grabbed his arm. "Step down, Jace."

"It could've killed Tommy." Jace glared at Jones. "You good-for-nothing drunk could've killed him."

The man sneered. "You think you're so high and mighty. You're nothin'. I know yer daddy." Jones laughed and spoke to the gathered crowd. "He's my best drinkin' partner." Jones shoved a dirty finger in Jace's chest. "You're just the no-account son of a good-for-nothing drunk."

Jace stumbled back. He locked eyes with Tommy. At the confusion in the lad's expression Jace felt himself toppling, toppling, right off the pedestal the boy had built. He glanced around the group, but nobody met his gaze.

He walked away and picked up his hammer.

Three days. Three whole days and not a word from Jace. Was he working late? Or had she done something wrong? Dilly put out the new spring fabrics. Everything had seemed so right. She glanced toward the store window. The sun was sinking. It was almost time to lock up. Usually that excited her, but another night without Jace coming would be hard to bear.

The door opened, and Tommy plopped a handful of change on the counter. "Mama needs sugar and coffee."

Dilly sighed, wishing her sister didn't insist on paying for groceries. She measured out the merchandise, sneaking a little extra in as she always did. "Anything interesting happen over at the quarry?" Maybe Tommy knew why Jace hadn't come.

"If I tell, you have to promise not to tell Mama. She'd worry something fierce."

Dilly's tummy dropped. "What happened?"

"Promise?"

The boy's eyes were wide as he told of his near-death experience.

"Oh, Tommy!" Dilly wrapped him in a hug, and he wiggled out of her embrace.

"I'm fine now."

"But you had to be scared."

Tommy lifted his head. "Mr. Jace said anybody would be scared, and that it was okay."

"Jace was there?"

Tommy didn't meet her gaze.

"You tell me right now Tommy Rutherford Brown!"

"I don't want you to be mad at him."

"Why would I be mad at him?"

As the story spilled out, Dilly felt Jace's emotion as her own.

"And then that mean man told Jace..."

"Yes..."

Tears welled in her nephew's eyes. "He called him a no-account son of a good-for-nothing-drunk."

Everything became clear. "You know that's not true, don't you, Tommy?"

"He's the best man I've known—except for my daddy—but. . .was Jace's daddy a drunk? Is that why Jace had to take care of his family even though he wasn't growed up all the way?"

Dilly nodded. "But I don't think it's right to judge a son by his father's actions, do you?"

Tommy threw his arms around her. "Jace is real sad. I can tell."

"I'll see what I can do."

As soon as Tommy headed home, Dilly asked Mama if she could be excused early.

"Are you going to find Jace?"

"I have to know if he's okay."

"Of course you do. If you hadn't finally decided to go after him, I might have!"

Dilly grabbed her wrap and headed up the road to the farmhouse where Jace rented his room. Widow Carmichael answered her knock. "Hello Mrs. Carmichael. I came to see Jace."

"Don't allow young women in the young men's rooms."

"Of course not! But if you called him, perhaps I could speak with him out here."

"He's not home yet."

Dilly's spirits plummeted. "But he *is* still living here?" She bit her lip.

Widow Carmichael huffed. "Of course he still lives here. Been eating me out of house and home since your little spat. Got used to not cooking for the man when he started courting you."

"We didn't have a spat."

"You better come on inside and wait on him. He's not been himself. Maybe you can cheer him up. Heaven knows I've tried."

The small living area was sparsely decorated, and Dilly chose a hard-backed chair. She barely seated herself when footsteps sounded. She breathed a prayer for wisdom, like Mama did when she faced a trying situation. His eyes widened when he saw her. Widow Carmichael turned from the stove on the other side of the room. "You two can talk right there or take a walk. I don't allow young people to be alone in my house."

"Of course not!" Dilly's cheeks flamed.

Jace nodded to her and backed out the front door. She joined him on the porch.

"I'm dusty from work." He took his hat off and twisted it in his hands.

"It doesn't bother me."

"Let's walk then."

They meandered in silence, the pain evident in Jace's eyes. She prayed again, then the words came. "I told you something when we were kids that you promised never to forget."

He turned, searching her gaze.

"I told you that who you are makes you an honorable person no matter who your daddy is. Remember?"

He nodded and ducked his head.

"And then I said I knew you would grow up into an honorable man."

He didn't look up.

"What I didn't know then is how fine of an honorable man you would become. Jace Gruber, you have exceeded my expectations—and they were already mighty high."

His head jerked up.

"We have a Savior. And He is going to do a good job with the lot of us."

Jace touched her cheek. "He's already done a great job with you."

When he took her hand, she thrilled. Facing him, she reached for his other one. Right there in the middle of the road they stood, simply staring at each other and holding hands. He blinked hard, and she felt moisture in her own eyes.

"Thank you, sweetheart. Today I'll call you Grace and thank the Good Lord for sending you to remind me of it."

Maybe that was why Mama and Daddy had named her Grace. She not only needed it every day, but as she learned to accept it, she learned how to share it.

It was before sunup when Jace carried the last load out of the general store and put it into the wagon he'd purchased from his new landlord. Mrs. Douglas waved, her smile evident in the light of the store. He grinned. It was good of her to meet him before sunrise so they could do their business without Dilly being privy to it. The perfect little ring was on order and the wagon loaded with supplies. He pointed the horses toward his new home—their home, as soon as he could get it ready and she said yes. The birds' twittering began right before the sky was painted pink and orange. He whistled as he drove, his song making good harmony with theirs.

Chapter 9

The picnic basket swung between them, and Jace switched it to his other hand so he could take hers. Dilly claimed she'd made the pie, but Jace trusted Mrs. Douglas prepared the rest, tucking his surprise into the big red kerchief as he'd asked. The March sun rose in the sky, and birdsong floated on the breeze. The words of Psalm 150 from that morning's service rang in his mind.

Praise ye the LORD. *Praise God in his sanctuary: praise him in the firmament of his power. Praise him for his mighty acts: praise him according to his excellent greatness (v. 1-2).*

Yes siree, the hundred and fiftieth psalm just fit this glorious day.

Dilly grinned at him. No doubt his chest puffed right up to have such a beauty holding on to his arm. A little sweat bead formed on his upper lip. Surely she would say yes. He glanced down and locked gazes with those sweet brown eyes, full of trust and promise. Oh yes. It was all going to be okay.

Still, even a confident man had a right to a bit of nerves on the day of his proposal. "Know where I'm taking you?"

"Our fishin' hole?"

"You're close, sweet Daffodil. Very close." She'd soon guess his true destination—the big rock where he'd once promised to marry her when they were both big enough. It took ten years to keep his word, but soon enough they would see its fulfillment. He imagined the tiny gold band on her dainty finger. He didn't have a lot to offer, but all he had was hers.

"I love picnics."

"I love picnics with you."

She giggled, practically skipping down the path. Oh how his heart soared when she was happy and carefree!

At the sound of rustling next to the trail, Jace stepped in front of Dilly and scanned the tree line, glimpsing hunched shoulders and stringy gray hair. *No, God. Please.*

"What is it?"

"Stay there, Dilly."

"Hello, son."

"Don't call me that."

Dilly's gasp cut at his heart. He had to get her out of here. Now. He turned, offering the picnic basket. "I need you to promise me something, Dilly."

"Okay." Her voice was pinched and small.

"Take this basket home to your Mama. Don't open it up or do a thing with it until you're with her. Give it to her, and let her serve the two of you. We'll have our picnic another day."

"But Jace—"

"I need you to do exactly as I'm asking, darlin'."

"I want to stay here with you."

"Please."

She shook her head.

"I need you to go on home now, sweetheart. We'll have our picnic another day. I promise."

Without a word she reached for the basket and headed back down the trail taking his dreams with her.

"Got yerself a woman, huh?"

"What do you want?"

"Can't a man come lookin' fer his own son without an inquest?" Pa stumbled and grabbed for a branch beside the road to steady himself.

"You're drunk."

"Not much."

"How'd you find me?"

"You think I didn't know where you'd go soon as you got the chance? 'Sides, a buddy of mine confirmed your whereabouts. We come out together, and he got a job. Until you took a swing at him and got him fired. Don't know where he is now."

"I never hit him, and he got himself fired."

"Have it your way. I didn't come to fuss."

"Why did you come?"

"What if a man wanted a little help to get his life cleaned up?"

How many times had Pa played that ruse?

"Been a long time since I've had a real meal."

In about an hour Pa would be ravenous for bread and sweets. But maybe he could get something else in him first. "Come on."

He would regret this.

Jace cut through the woods. Maybe he could get to the house without anyone else seeing his pa. The welcher would never make everything up to Jace, but what if this time Pa actually took what was offered and made something of himself?

Pa talked nonsense, and Jace gritted his teeth. The blue tinge on Pa's face indicated that this time he'd had a lot to drink. Jace would need to keep him awake. Try to get some water down him. Then the hard work would begin.

Jace grabbed his pa's arm and led him toward the house. He'd get word to the boss that he needed some time off. Hopefully he'd proven himself, and the decision to try one more time to dry his pa out wouldn't cost him his job.

Mama's sober expression as she unpacked the picnic lunch matched Dilly's.

"Do you think he's okay?"

Mama pulled out the red kerchief and set it aside. "I'm sure he's dealt with this before."

Tears threatened. "Why today? When we were so happy? How could God let this happen?"

"Oh, honey. People make mistakes. It doesn't do any good to start blaming God just when we need Him the most." Mama pulled out a plate and put a pickle and a drumstick on it.

Dilly shook her head. "I'm not hungry. Please excuse me." It was all she could do to make it to her room and pull the door shut before the sobs came.

Pa hung his head over the bucket, retching again. His food lay untouched on the rough table Jace had built when he moved in. It was going to be a long night. The first of many no doubt.

Another long day without Jace. Dilly sent Mama to bed and took her turn cleaning up the supper table. Funny how she thought it was lonely before Jace returned to Rock City. That kind of lonely was nothing compared to the long days without him now that she'd become accustomed to him sitting across the table of the evening. Jace had to figure things out with his pa, but how long would it take?

Jace wiped Pa's sweaty brow with a cool, damp cloth. He was losing touch with how long the two of them had gone without sleep. Sometimes they talked. Most of the time they didn't. The conversation wasn't good. Jace had heard it all before. All Pa needed was a little money to get himself on his feet and start fresh. Jace learned years ago not to give in to the begging. If he did, the money would be spent on another bash.

When the shakes started, Jace tried to steel his heart to Pa's pain, told himself Pa deserved it. But truth was no matter how much hurt his pa had caused, Jace still couldn't stand to see him in such agony. He wrapped him in a blanket. "You're gonna make it. I'm right here."

When Pa finally fell into a deep sleep, Jace got his own blanket. Best get some shut eye before the next round started.

Dilly didn't like the look of the two women huddled together, casting glances at her periodically. Whatever Old Lady Bishop and Donna Smith were gossiping about couldn't be good. Dilly turned her attention to the customer in front of her, concentrating on making correct change.

"I saw it with my own eyes, I tell you!" Donna's voice rose. "It was Tip Gruber, all right. Older and less kempt than I remember, but the man himself."

Oh, no.

The voices fell back to whispering, and Dilly slipped closer.

"Drunker than an old skunk, I tell you. Causing all kinds of ruckus, the likes of which we've not seen in these parts for years."

Jace. She had to find Jace. At the tap on her shoulder, Dilly started. Mama squeezed her arm. "Go on, honey."

So she'd heard too.

Dilly rushed out of the store. Her first stop was Jenny's house, but Tommy said Jace hadn't been to work all week. The boardinghouse was just down the road and Widow Carmichael answered her first knock. "He ain't here."

"When do you expect him back?"

"He moved out. Didn't he tell you?"

Dilly fought to breathe. He wouldn't. Surely he wouldn't. Not after coming back. Not after his promises to her.

But the reality was Jace Gruber was gone.

Jace slammed the door on his little cabin, throwing the empty coffee can that once held his savings. He started down the country road knocking on doors, but didn't get far before the sordid truth came rolling out. Every neighbor had another story of his pa's drunken binge. Jace returned home, unable to face anyone else. Plopping on his bed, he hung his head in his hands. It was happening again. Pa's exploits passed about from mouth to mouth. Like every other time.

Jace grabbed his bag and began stuffing clothing into it. There would be no use staying now. No life available outside of his father's shame. Jace moaned. He was just the no-account son of a good-for-nothing drunk. The church folks would look down their noses. Sweet Dilly would taste of his shame. Best protect her. Folks wouldn't blame her if he left now.

Bile rose in his throat, and he threw the bag against the wall. Pa did it this time. Stole everything. Not only his money. His dearest dream. Oh sweet Dilly.

But who could he blame but himself? He'd fallen for it again. Should've sent Pa packing the moment he saw him. Should've finished that picnic with Dilly. If he'd run Pa off, the disgrace wouldn't have come again.

A sob forced itself out. He knew what to do. That's one thing Pa taught well. Pack up and leave before the townsfolk run you out.

But leaving was harder than ever before.

He flung himself across the bed and let the sobs come. They racked his body, pouring out the anger and grief he'd held inside all the long years since Pa's drinking got bad. He cried for Ma. For Ruthie. For Pa. For himself.

The shadows were long when the grief settled into quiet pain. Reason started to come. He'd see Mr. Burge first thing in the morning. Give him the deed to the place. He'd lose his first few payments, but it was the honorable thing to do. Maybe Burge would buy back the wagon. That would mean some traveling money. Jace looked around at the things he'd purchased to make Dilly a home. He would ask Burge to give it all to her. He dug around for a stub pencil and his paper. How could he pen his last goodbye?

Jace squinted at the light streaming in the window. He must have finally slept. He pushed off his bed and glanced around the cabin. Most everything could be left for Dilly. He'd take the coffee pot and pack enough food for a couple of days. Other than that, he only needed his clothing.

"Mr. Jace."

Not Tommy.

The door opened and in walked the young man he loved like family.

"How'd you find me?"

"I got my ways."

Jace almost smiled at the little boy's attitude. He stood, hands on hips, legs slightly apart and gave Jace a no-nonsense glare. "What's that bag for?"

"Why don't we sit at the table and have a talk?"

"What I got to say comes out better when I'm standing." The proud little chin lifted. "You might want to sit."

Jace sat.

"I know what you're about to do, and it ain't right."

"There are things you don't understand."

"Maybe. I'm only a kid. But sometimes kids see things better than grown-ups."

The kid had a point.

"You're about to run off because your daddy made a fool of himself and folks are talkin'. I never took you for a coward, Mr. Jace. Thought you was the bravest man I ever met."

Jace swallowed hard. "It's not that simple, son. The shame I carry. Let's just say I don't want to share it with Dilly or her mama—or anyone I care about. Like you."

"What shame is that?"

"I think you know."

"I don't think I do. You better explain it to me."

The words. He didn't want to say them. Didn't want to speak out the truth he'd so long fought to deny.

"Well?"

"You heard it already. I'm the no-account son of a good-for-nothing-drunk." His voice broke on the last word. Oh how he wanted to be anything else. He held his head in his hands, trying to avoid a full crying spell in front of Tommy. Trying to hang on to what dignity he had left. The soft touch of the small hand startled him, but it was surprisingly comforting.

"Mr. Jace. I don't think you got that quite right."

Jace looked up into the lad's brown eyes, eyes so like his Dilly's. "You don't?"

"No sir. You are a man of courage and kindness. Your daddy and mine is the same One. He took over since our own papas can't be of much good to us. His name is God the Father. And we are His sons. There ain't no shame in being a child of the Living God."

Jace couldn't help the tears, no matter how much he wanted to save face in front of

Tommy. The little fingers reached out and wiped each one as it fell.

Tommy stepped back and put his hands on his hips again.

"It's time for you to get cleaned up. Church is about to start."

When did Tommy get so sassy?

Jace stared at the boy long and hard, and Tommy didn't flinch. In fact, the longer he gazed into those innocent eyes, the more they morphed into the kind eyes of Someone else.

"Okay, son. I'll be ready in a jiffy, and we'll go together."

Chapter 10

Why wouldn't she go away? Dilly rolled back to the wall.

"Daffodil Grace Douglas, you are too old to be bossed around by your mama, but this situation calls for extreme measures. I'm going to count to five, and by the time I get there you'd better be on your feet reaching for your best dress. No man, no matter how deeply he is loved, is gonna keep my daughter from the Lord's house on Sunday morning. One. . ."

What did mama think she could do if Dilly stayed right where she was?

"Two. . ."

She wasn't a child anymore.

"Three. . ."

Couldn't Mama see how it hurt? How unfit she was to be around people, especially gossips who spread stories nobody needed to hear.

Stories that sent her Jace away.

The bed moved, and Dilly turned toward Mama.

"Honey, I have no right to boss you around. We both know I can't make you go. Truth is my heart is breaking with yours. I need to be in the House of the Lord. I'm not sure I have the strength to go by myself. Not with you here hurting. I need you to help me be strong."

Mama's eyes were red-rimmed and her complexion pale. Mama did need her. Her strong Mama who withstood so much needed *her* today. Dilly reached for Mama's hand. "I'm not used to you needing me."

"I reckon it's harder to handle pain when it's your child's heart breaking than when it's your own."

Yes. The only other time Dilly saw Mama weak was when Jenny grieved the loss of her husband.

"I'll get dressed."

Silence and the crunch of gravel punctuated their walk to the church. When they entered the building every gaze was upon them. Dilly raised her chin and walked to their pew. Second row. Left side. As they walked, she felt it. The gentle squeezes of the church folk as she passed. She lowered her gaze to look, really look into their faces and discovered most reflected her own grief. There was no censure. Only the body weeping with those who wept. She and Mama sat close. They would get through this. One day, somewhere in the distant future, her heart would heal. Until then, they had each other.

A commotion at the back drew her attention.

Jace met her gaze. Did she want him here, or was she embarrassed by his presence? He couldn't look at anyone else, only his dear, precious Dilly. He waited for her signal—anything. A welcoming nod. A dismissing wave. Her desire was his command. He would not hurt her more than she'd already been hurt. If his presence shamed her—well, his bag was packed.

Dilly stood and pushed out of the pew, rushing down the middle aisle, head high, eyes bright, and a loving gaze just for him. His heart beat faster. He took a faltering step.

"Won't you please join Mama and me?" Her voice. Clear. Strong. Unashamed. "We're seated right up near the front."

Her hand stretched toward him. He took one step. Two. Reached for the lifeline she offered. When their hands touched, all sort of hullabaloo broke out.

"Good to see you, Jace."

"Sure glad you could make it today."

Men clasped his shoulder. Shook his hand. Older women patted his arm.

He swallowed hard and dared look into the eyes of the church folk. The gentle, loving eyes.

Pastor met them at Dilly's pew. Grabbed him in a bear hug. "Welcome home, son."

Jace sat between his woman and her mama, grinning when Tommy squeezed in next to Dilly. Mrs. Douglas grasped his hand, dropping the little wedding band there and then closing his fingers over the ring. He slipped it in his pocket and attempted to turn his attention to the preacher while the ring burned a hole.

Chapter 11

Jace leaned against the doorjamb and watched Dilly and her mama scramble to pack a picnic. A week ago the scene was almost the same. Only this time the plan was impromptu. Dilly hadn't baked a pie. Her mama hadn't fried a chicken. But no one cared. Mrs. Douglas placed the red kerchief over the top of the basket and held it out. He reached for it with one hand and for Dilly with the other.

"Hold on a minute." Mrs. Douglas swept up to him and patted his cheek. "I love you like my own, Jace Gruber. You're a son to be proud of." He nodded, unable to speak past the lump in his throat. She grabbed Dilly's free hand. "My sweet Daffodil Grace. You are a wise, dependable woman. I've always called you my early bloomer because you took on so much at a young age. But today I want to say something else. Remember your poem about the daffodils dancing in the breeze? I never want you to lose that joy. That bright, sunny disposition that comes from the delight and imagination the Good Lord placed within you. Today, my dear daughter, may you dream freely."

Jace glanced at Dilly, not surprised to see her eyes bright with emotion. Mrs. Douglas stepped back, setting them free to enter the wide world with her love.

Dilly allowed him to help her down the front steps as he had so many times before. "Where are we heading? To our rock like before?"

So she knew where he planned to take her last time.

"If you don't mind, I think it's time for new dreams and new places."

"Okay."

"Let's go this way." He led her behind the store, down the well-worn cattle trail that traversed the field next to her house. The season's first grasshoppers buzzed in the growth beside them. The air was fragrant with the scent of redbud blossoms, barely visible in the woods next to them, opening their purple glory to the bright sun above. In the distance was a splash of white where a dogwood tried to bloom.

"Has there ever been a better day?"

"Nope." When he started whistling, Dilly grinned.

At the edge of the woods he reached behind the tree to grab his surprise.

"Oh! Daffodils!"

She took the bouquet, inhaling deeply. Then gasped.

How perfect. Dilly fingered the tiny gold band hanging from the blue ribbon that held the daffodils together. "Jace. . ."

He dropped to one knee, and she couldn't help the joy bubble that burst forth in a giggle.

"Your mama told you that you're like the daffodil. An early bloomer. Full of sunshine. But I believe there's more, my sweet Daffodil Grace. A daffodil dares brave the early season, resilient even in the cold. I've seen them blossom in the midst of snow. Daffodils are brave little flowers, pushing through the hard earth after a long, dark winter. My sweet Dilly, you spread your brilliant yellow rays over the winter ground of my heart. Your radiant hope called to me, helping me believe I could leave the harsh, dark places behind and thrive in the spring, planted, right here, with you."

His words, like melody, danced around her, leapt through her, waltzed right deep inside. She and Jace survived their long, lonely, dark winter. And spring had indeed come.

"Daffodil Grace Douglas, would you agree to be my wife?"

Dreamer she was she could never have conjured the way it felt in this moment. The glorious sun streaming, the green breaking out all around them, the pure joy of being loved, truly loved, by the only man who'd ever held her heart.

"Oh yes!" She reached down, pulling him to his feet. To her.

His gaze held hers. The intensity sent his heart to pumping. Her chin lifted, those pink lips parted. Inviting. He took his time. He'd waited so long. The brown wisps the breeze had freed from her fancy bun floated in the air, and he brushed them from her face. Running a finger down the soft cheek, he delighted in the treasure God gave him. She believed in him ten years ago, when he hid his secret pain from the world, telling only her. She saw him then. Told him he would be an honorable man. He believed her, and that belief kept him from crumbling as his world grew darker and darker. Then when he almost gave up, there she was, hand outstretched.

"Oh, Dilly." He cupped her beautiful, precious face in his hands and lowered his mouth to hers. There he tasted the sweetest, softest wonder of his life. Her response, gentle at first, grew strong. He deepened the kiss, a swirl of emotion ringing through his senses.

She broke the kiss and flung herself into his arms. "Oh Jace, I do love you."

He held her for a glorious moment then stepped back and tugged on the ribbon wrapped around the bouquet she still held. Grasping the tiny ring in his thumb and forefinger, he held it to her. "May I?"

Dilly's eyes sparkled like sunshine on water as she stretched her hand and received the token of his love.

"I want to show you something." He tugged on her hand, unable to walk, and jogged forward. She matched his steps, her sweet laughter ringing out.

Huffing their way up the long, steep hill, they giggled and jogged then paused until they caught their breath and jogged some more. Right before they cleared the trees to step onto the bluff, he stopped. "I have an early wedding present. But to fully unwrap it, we'll need to be married. Don't make me wait too long because I'd like to wed you while the daffodils are in bloom."

He pulled her forward then, onto the bluff. Below them, not far from Greenleaf Creek, stood the little cabin surrounded by a sea of yellow. The barn looked proud, boasting its bright, freshly painted red walls beneath its tin roof.

"Oh!" Her gasp tickled his heart, and he chuckled.

"A host of golden daffodils!" She yelled, laughing at the echo. "And now the whole place looks like promise instead of potential!"

"How about we name our little farm, 'Promise' then? We can hang a sign over the gate to the yard."

"*Our* farm?"

"How could I buy any other place when you've always seen the potential in this one, like you saw it in me?"

"Promise!" She yelled, and promise echoed back. She twirled in the sunshine, her hair falling from its bun and flowing free. "Beside the *creek*, beneath the trees, fluttering and dancing in the breeze!"

Jace lifted her into his arms, and they twirled as one.

Author's Note

On a warm summer's day my husband, two youngest sons, my dad, and I drove through Camp Gruber, stopping to swim in the creek where I swam as a child. Afterward we drove on through the camp, coming out the other side to discover a quaint little building. Dad suggested we stop for lunch. Located on Qualls Road in Parkhill, Oklahoma, Jincy's Kitchen is housed in what was once the general store for the old Qualls community. The site was also used for the filming of the movie, *Where the Red Fern Grows*. It still has the wooden cubed walls that once held merchandise. Now it contains memorabilia—antique dishes and newspaper clippings of folks important to the area. We ordered—and enjoyed—our home-cooked meal. Debbie Rucker, the proprietor and cook, left her stove to share the store's history. The store was opened many years before by her grandmother, a single mom. The building was passed down to Debbie, and she opens the restaurant on weekends to keep the spirit of the Qualls community alive for the next generation.

I commented on the french fries. I hadn't had homemade fries like that since my grandmother made them for me many years before. My husband said, "Yes. The fries were just like Grandma Eunice's, weren't they?"

Debbie whipped toward me, "You're Aunt Eunice's granddaughter?" She explained that she had been married to my grandma's nephew. Then the stories began in earnest. She said my grandparents were well-loved in the Qualls community; everyone had a story of a time Grandpa or Grandma had helped them out. Then Debbie began to tell her special story. It was about her daddy and my grandpa. You read a similar version in chapter one of this novella. Only the little boy was her dad, and the man who pulled the big boy off by his overalls was my grandpa. She cried when she told me how hard it had been on her dad to be picked on, such a young child who'd recently lost his father. I cried when I thought of my strong grandpa defending the boy. How I treasure this story! You can learn more about Jincy's Kitchen by visiting: https://www.facebook.com /visitcherokeenation/videos/10153590974318869/.

Of course *At Home with Daffodils* is a work of fiction. Both Dilly and Jace are from my imagination. Their story grew from the historical tidbits gleaned that day in the old general store. Though Rock City is a made-up town, in my mind's eye I saw the rolling hills around Parkhill, Oklahoma as I wrote; the same hills I roamed as a girl. I couldn't resist naming some of my characters and landmarks with the names of real people and places from the area. I hope my friends and family back home will enjoy that.

Down the road from the farmhouse where I lived was an old homeplace. You couldn't see the building anymore, but you could see a field of daffodils (we called them jonquils) that someone planted years before. Every spring I eagerly awaited their arrival, like I did the tiny spring bluets and Virginia spring beauties. After I moved to Colorado, my grandmother sent me the tiny flowers in February. She wrapped them in a damp paper towel, covered with plastic. She also sent bulbs, and so I have cheery yellow faces transplanted from Oklahoma that bloom every spring in my yard.

My best guess about the story Debbie told is that my grandpa and her dad were hired to help build Camp Gruber in the '40s, when most of the people around Qualls were removed to the surrounding area so the government could construct a military base for the purpose of training soldiers.

I hope you enjoyed this fictional account set in the rolling hills of my childhood. The country is beautiful, the culture engaging, and the generous people are salt-of-the-earth. The best thing I received from those years living in the hills of northeastern Oklahoma is a relationship with Jesus. He is indeed the one who removes our shame and finishes the good work He begins in us—no matter how flawed we believe ourselves or our pasts to be.

Author, speaker, and mom of four, **Paula Moldenhauer** encourages others to live free to flourish. She shares this message when speaking at women's events, and it permeates her written work. Paula has been published over 300 times in non-fiction markets and has a devotional book series, *Soul Scents*. Her first published novella, *You're a Charmer Mr. Grinch*, was a finalist in the ACFW Carol Awards. Paula and her husband, Jerry, are adjusting to a sometimes-empty nest in Colorado. They treasure time with their growing family of adult children, spouses, and spouses-to-be. Paula loves peppermint ice cream, going barefoot, and adventuring with friends. Visit her at www.paulamoldenhauer.com.

A Song for Rose

by Suzanne Norquist

Chapter 1

Rockledge, Colorado
1882

C ivilization had come to Rockledge, Colorado, and Rose Miller would be a part of it. When she sang at the new opera house, everyone would remember her name.

Rose clutched her sewing basket and lifted her skirt as she stepped from the dirt street onto the boardwalk in front of the opera house. The intricate carved glass windows on either side of the massive wooden doors reflected the sun.

So much opulence for a small mining town.

She tugged on one of the door handles, but it didn't budge. She tried the other. Locked.

The opera house should be open. Carriages had delivered the New Frontier Opera Company into town yesterday.

Rose followed the boardwalk to the edge of the building and tiptoed through the damp grass to look for another entrance. Had she known she would be tromping through the wilderness, she wouldn't have worn her best dress. No matter. Her singing would impress them. They wouldn't notice her attire.

The side door opened easily.

Rose allowed her eyes to adjust to the dim interior.

The scent of fresh-cut wood and new fabric filled the hallway. Light filtered through small windows along the top of one wall.

The click of her boots echoed on the wooden floor. Otherwise silence.

"Hello? Is anyone here?"

No answer.

A corkboard held a paper sign near the first open door. LADIES' CHORUS had been penned in neat calligraphy.

Should she knock? She had come this far.

When no one answered, she peeked into the room. A long mirror covered one wall and a dressing table ran the length of the mirror. A few chairs sat at the table. A clothing rack filled one end of the room, and several trunks sat near the rack.

So exciting. A shiver danced down her spine.

She walked to the next door.

VIRGINIA ROMINE, SARAH BAKER, NAOMI LOCKHART. Must be the names of the more important singers.

She knocked. Again, no answer.

She cracked the door and took a peek. Although smaller, this room had been arranged like the first.

The sign on the last door before the opening to the stage said, MARIAN CARTER. A dressing room designed for one. Miss Carter must be the female lead.

The men's dressing rooms came next, starting with the male lead.

Rose returned to Miss Carter's door. After knocking, she checked up and down the hall. Seeing no one, she slipped into the star's dressing room. What would it be like to sing in an opera? She touched the vanity and studied herself in the mirror. She moved closer to the colorful wardrobe and stretched a hand toward a red velvet dress.

The sound of footsteps broke the spell.

Rose dropped her hand and returned to the hall.

A tall red-haired man appeared from the stage entrance. Someone from the opera company?

He neared, and his features came into focus. A well-built man in his late twenties, a little older than she. His brown trousers and woven vest made him look important. Handsome. He could be a singer. A lead singer.

She hadn't expected to be alone with a handsome man unchaperoned. No matter. She wouldn't let anyone find out.

"You shouldn't be in here." He spoke to her as if to a child, but his eyes smiled.

Rose lifted her sewing basket. "I came to offer my services as a seamstress. I work at the dress shop across the street. The company must have some sewing needs. Costume design? Mending? Day dresses?"

The man shook his head, amused. "A wardrobe mistress travels with their company. I believe her name is Gertrude."

She lowered her basket, disappointed. "You're not a performer, then?"

"No." He gave a slight bow. "I'm Patrick O'Donnell, the manager of this opera house."

She revised her plan to meet the singers.

"And you are?" His deep-green eyes captivated her.

"Rose Miller. I know everyone in town, and I haven't seen you before. How do I know you're the manager?"

He flashed a grin.

She could imagine Mr. O'Donnell on stage.

"The city council brought me in from Connecticut. I managed an opera house there. Ask around. I'm sure your sources will confirm it." His voice carried a soothing timbre.

She would have noticed him around town if he had been here long. Tonight at supper, she would ask her brothers. But for now, she wouldn't let the handsome Irishman distract her. "Where are the singers?"

He pulled out a gold pocket watch and checked it. "They won't be awake for hours. Musicians don't rise early."

"I can return another time to see if anyone needs my services as a seamstress." Would Sarah allow her to leave the shop in the middle of the day? She would have to come up with an excuse.

"That won't be necessary." He stepped toward her and indicated the exit with his open hand. "Your shop has a sign and dresses in the window. They can find it if the need arises."

She held her position, although he stood near enough for her to smell his musky cologne. "I would like to welcome everyone in person."

His expression hardened. "Miss Miller, the public is not allowed backstage. My job is to ensure that the opera company has the privacy they need to prepare for the upcoming show." Again, he indicated the door.

A distinguished middle-aged gentleman with a moustache appeared behind Mr. O'Donnell.

He must be with the opera company.

This could be Rose's only chance.

"Patrick, my boy—"

She took a deep breath and began to sing "Amazing Grace."

Patrick stared, open mouthed, at the delicate brunette who filled the hallway with her song. He shot a look at James.

The older man shrugged.

Patrick should stop her, but he didn't want to interrupt a hymn. Seemed disrespectful to God. He glanced heavenward.

The girl sang in a beautiful, clear voice. He had heard many sopranos in opera companies back East. Although she sang well, she wouldn't stand out among the competition. He knew the frustration of being good, but not good enough. He would discourage the naive girl.

She wore a green dress, fancier and fuller than most women wore in Rockledge. Must have dressed up for the occasion. Her voice and attitude made it easy to forget her petite size.

When the verse ended, she curtsied. "Rose Miller, soprano. I would love the opportunity to audition to join the New Frontier Opera Company."

James clapped. "Bravo, my dear."

Patrick glared at him. This innocent small-town girl wouldn't survive in the world of traveling entertainment. Women would hate her, and men would try to seduce her. She would lose both her innocence and her enthusiasm. Patrick couldn't let that happen.

The older man bowed to Rose. "Jam—"

"He's not with the opera company either." Patrick turned toward his friend, eyes pleading. "Tom is my assistant. Tom Brown, may I present Rose Miller?"

James looked from Patrick to Rose. "As he said, I'm his assistant, Tom Brown."

She shook his hand. "Mr. Brown. Now I'm embarrassed." Her cheeks colored a pretty pink.

"Don't be." James winked. "I always enjoy a good hymn, especially when sung by a beautiful lady."

Patrick walked to Rose and took her elbow as he moved toward the exit. His fingers warmed at the touch, and his pulse quickened.

She startled, and her eyes opened wide.

Did the contact affect her the way it did him? He held his voice steady. "There will not be an opportunity for you to audition or to harass the members of the company."

She jerked her elbow free and held her ground. "Harass? I would never harass anyone. How dare you suggest such a thing, Mr. O'Donnell?" The color in her cheeks deepened.

"I'm sure you wouldn't, but I don't want to see you around here again." To ensure her cooperation, he added, "I might have to get the sheriff involved."

"Sheriff Bradford? I'm sure he would be reasonable, since he's my brother's best friend. I will get my audition." The petite brunette sashayed out the door.

Patrick smiled. He hadn't enjoyed a woman this much in a long time. He hoped to see her again, even as he turned the lock behind her.

James cocked an eyebrow. "And now I am your assistant, Tom? Couldn't you have given me a name like Reginald or Zeus?"

Patrick stepped around James and headed toward his office near the lobby. "I couldn't tell her you're with the opera. And I especially couldn't tell her you're managing the company. She would pester you night and day."

James kept pace beside him. "Spunky little thing, isn't she? A pleasant distraction."

"What am I going to do with her?"

"Let her hang around. The girls in the chorus could use a little competition. With some training, she could travel back East and audition for a part. She has the looks for it."

The smell of coffee greeted Patrick as he entered his office. He lifted the pot and filled two china cups that sat on the sideboard. "That's what worries me." He offered a cup to James.

James took a seat in one of the cushioned leather chairs. "I could think of worse things."

"I'm sure you could." Patrick stepped behind the oversized mahogany desk and sat in his rolling chair. "But you will leave her alone?" He pictured her jutting her chin in the air as she marched out.

"Why do you care? Young women get into this business all the time." James sat back, waiting for an answer.

Something about Rose touched Patrick's heart, but he wasn't sure why. She reminded him of a time before he lost his passion for music. "She's an innocent."

"She's the first girl to catch your attention since Elizabeth." The older man winked.

"That's not why." Or was it?

"Relax." James sipped his coffee. "I don't have time for another soprano. I don't know why I ever agreed to perform and manage the company at the same time. Too much work."

"Thanks." Patrick relaxed.

James sat back in his chair. "But I'm sure other men in the company will be happy to hear her audition."

"I need to keep her away from here."

The older man nodded. "This life isn't so bad. The music keeps me young, and I've seen more of this country than most men ever will. You wanted it at one time. Can't blame the girl for trying."

"I still love the music." Patrick would always be a vocalist at heart. "I suppose that's why I manage opera houses. But the constant struggle to be good enough. I don't miss that."

James leaned forward in his chair. "Good enough for whom? You could have always had a part." He rose. "Enough of this. We'll see what happens with the girl."

"She could heed my warning and stay away." Patrick didn't believe it even as he spoke.

The older man laughed. "You've been in this business too long to believe that." He handed Patrick a stack of paper he'd carried with him into the office. "I came to bring you the practice schedule. Our days will start after lunch."

"I'll do my work around the stage in the mornings then." Patrick took the papers. "By the way, I appreciate you contracting my opera house to prepare for your run of the mountain circuit. We can use the publicity."

"We both benefit. I need the performers to acclimate to the elevation and dry air. Wouldn't want anyone passing out in the middle of a solo." James chuckled and shook his head. "Several have complained of headaches, but the malady probably has more to do with the saloons than the elevation."

"They'll be ready by the time you perform. Most people acclimate in three to four weeks." Would Patrick be ready? He still needed to prepare some of the canvas backgrounds.

"They'll be itching to move on to the next town by then." James downed the last of his coffee and set the cup on Patrick's desk. "Time to make sure Sleeping Beauty is awake."

After James left, Patrick stared across the street at the seamstress shop.

What would he do about Miss Rose Miller?

Chapter 2

After exiting through the side door, Rose stepped onto the boardwalk in front of the opera house. The building cast a long shadow in the morning sun, and a couple of wagons clattered up the dirt street. How dare that man ask her to leave?

She surveyed the front of the impressive building. Did she need his permission? He probably watched from a window to make sure she returned to her side of the street.

Her face heated, and she straightened her skirt. Under other circumstances, she might find him attractive. His eyes danced, and his smile brightened as he spoke to her. His muscular build reminded her more of a laborer than a man who sat behind a desk.

But he had treated her like a willful child. She spun toward the street, causing her sewing basket to tip. She straightened it. Let him watch if he wished.

Before she could cross to the shop, all nine of the O'Malley children shuffled by. The family lived a few blocks from Rose. The older ones greeted her. "Good morning, Miss Miller."

"Good morning." With four older brothers, an older sister, and a younger sister of her own, Rose understood life in a large family.

Parents paid attention to the older ones and everyone adored the baby. But middle children lived in the shadows, often forgotten.

Amanda, one of the younger girls, lagged. She wore a worn hand-me-down dress. Rose stopped her after the others had passed. "What a pretty yellow dress."

The girl beamed. "Thank you, Miss Miller."

"I have the perfect thing to accent it." Rose pulled a little white lace bow from her basket.

The girl's eyes widened.

Rose held the bow at the girl's neckline below her collar. "Perfect. Can you sew it on?"

Amanda nodded.

Rose placed the lace in her hand. "Stop by the shop if you need help."

The girl stared at her, eyes questioning. "Are you sure?"

Rose nodded. "Yes. Keep it. It is left over from a custom dress I made."

"Thank you." The girl clutched the bow as she hurried to catch up with the others.

Hopefully, Amanda would find a special skill, like Rose's singing, that would keep her from being overlooked.

She glanced back at the opera house. The curtain in one of the front windows moved, as if someone had been watching. Mr. O'Donnell.

Rose hurried across the street, dodging a couple of horses, and slipped into the back of her sister's shop. "Sorry I'm late."

Sarah stood pouring a cup of coffee near the potbelly stove in the back room, which also served as a kitchen. "I was beginning to worry." Her young boys sat at a small table eating eggs and biscuits.

Six-year-old Ted slathered jam on his biscuit. "Uncle David's takin' us fishin' today at Trout Creek."

"Sounds like fun." Rose put her basket on a chair and lifted the teakettle from the stove.

Five-year-old Kenny swallowed a bite of his eggs. "Uncle David said Papa used to be the best fisherman. Do you think I'll catch as many as him?"

"You could. Sometimes David scares the fish away." She poured a little hot water into an empty ceramic teapot to warm it. Painted with pink roses, the pot had been her favorite gift last Christmas. She wouldn't want to ruin her voice with coffee.

"Fishing with Uncle David will keep the boys out from underfoot today." Sarah moved dirty dishes to the washbasin. "I never thought I'd be glad to have so many brothers. . .until I lost Theodore. They all want to act like a father to Ted and Kenny."

Rose couldn't imagine being grateful for so many brothers. "They adore your boys."

Would Mr. O'Donnell enjoy fishing with boys? He appeared athletic, as if he had spent time outdoors. She shook her head to clear out any romantic notions about the handsome Irishman. He stood between her and her singing career.

"Uncle David says Emily has to come with us because they're courtin'." Ted scrunched his nose. "Do ladies like fishin'?"

"Some ladies do." Rose poured out the water she had used to warm the teapot. She filled it with more hot water from the kettle and added tea leaves.

Kenny carried his dirty plate to Sarah. "You don't think they'll kiss, do you?"

"Course they will. That's what courtin' is." Ted headed for the back door. "I need to get my fishin' pole ready."

His little brother trailed behind.

"Why were you late this morning?" Sarah washed the dishes and placed them on the counter to dry. "Tell me you weren't making a nuisance of yourself at the opera house."

Rose had hoped to bring good news about her singing, or at least business for the dress shop. Why must her sister refer to her as a nuisance? "I stopped to inquire if our seamstress skills would be required. I'm finding business for your shop."

"Is that so?" Sarah raised an eyebrow. "And do they need a seamstress?"

"Possibly. Not for costumes, but for their own personal wardrobes." Not a lie. Someone might wish to have a dress made.

"I'll go over with you this afternoon and speak with them." Her sister wiped the table with a damp rag.

"That won't be necessary. I've already met the opera house manager. You'll want to stay at the shop in case you have customers." If her sister met Mr. O'Donnell, they would both watch her every move.

"If it's not busy, I could lock up for a few minutes. Our patrons would understand."

Rose strained her tea into a ceramic cup. She now needed a plan to avoid Mr. O'Donnell, keep her sister away from him, and get an audition.

Challenges on all sides.

Patrick dipped his brush in brown paint and swiped it across the canvas, filling in the body of a wall-sized pirate ship. When he'd accepted the manager's job, he didn't realize he would need painting and carpentry skills. Would he ever get used to working around the theater without performing?

He thought of Rose as he moved the brush. Instead of returning to her shop right away, she had spoken to a group of children. She handed something to a little girl, and from his window, he could see the smile that lit the girl's face. He would enjoy getting acquainted with Rose, if he could do it away from the opera house.

He could see the door to her sister's shop from his office and found himself watching—trying to catch a glimpse of Rose. He wanted to see her again. But if she came to the opera house again, he would have to send her away.

Someone shouting from the dressing room area interrupted his musings. The principal soprano must be on another rampage. "I must have a fresh crystal decanter of water every day. Does this blue urn look like a crystal decanter to you? How am I supposed to drink from an urn? It could hold someone's ashes."

Patrick strained to hear James's reply. "It's a serviceable pitcher."

"How long must I suffer in this barren wilderness?" Patrick imagined Marian draping an arm across her forehead before falling onto her settee.

The clapping that followed must have come from James. "Bravo. Now if you can do that on stage when we need it—"

"The conditions in this opera house are abominable." She must have stood. Her voice carried too well for someone lying down.

"You signed on with the New Frontier Opera Company. This is the New Frontier. You can't expect the same quality service you receive back East. Patrick is doing his best."

Patrick's stomach knotted. He had come to Rockledge to create a top-quality opera house, not a second-rate venue. A failure again. He should ignore Marian's ranting, but her complaint mimicked his father's all-too-familiar voice.

"In San Francisco, I will have a crystal decanter. Why did we stop in this backward town? No one here will appreciate my performance."

James's chuckle echoed in the hall.

"Don't walk out on me."

A door slammed and silence filled the performance hall.

Patrick tried to quiet the condemnation in his mind. Even in Colorado, his father's criticism found him. *"Were you trying to sound like a wounded goat?" "If you'd practiced more you would have won. Pity."*

If he created a premier opera house, his father would have to acknowledge his accomplishment. Instead, with Marian's help, he would earn a reputation for running a sad imitation of a metropolitan venue.

Patrick willed his hand to dip the brush in the paint and fill in the outline of the pirate ship. On the upward brush stroke, he inhaled a long breath. On the downward stroke he exhaled. The memories wouldn't paralyze him. Not today.

Marian's reputation as a prima donna would render her opinion irrelevant. The Rockledge Opera House rivaled its sisters on the East Coast. He had seen to it.

He startled at the sound of the front door. From backstage he couldn't tell who had entered. Would Rose have returned this soon?

A man called out. "Hello. Is anyone here?"

Not Rose. He released a breath. "Backstage." He rested the brush in a pail of water and closed the lid of the paint can. He wiped the paint from his hands with an old rag and glanced at his work clothes. A manager back East would never dress like this.

A young man in clean trousers and suspenders, in his early twenties, climbed the stairs to the stage. He carried paper under one arm. "William Miller. Rockledge Tribune." He approached the work area.

Patrick shook hands with the man. "Patrick O'Donnell, opera house manager." Would he ever get used to the title?

"If you have a few minutes, I'd like to interview you for the paper. I'm working on an article about the upcoming production." William reminded him of someone.

"Are you any relation to Rose Miller?" She had mentioned a brother.

"Rose is my sister." William shook his head. "Don't tell me she's already been around. Let me know if she pesters you too much, and I'll talk to her."

"Would she listen if you discouraged her?"

"Probably not." William laughed. "I see she left quite an impression."

"You could say that." Patrick wouldn't provide details. "Let's sit." He led the way to a couple of wooden chairs on the side of the stage.

The newspaperman propped his paper on the arm of the chair and prepared to write. "You've already provided the basic information about the opera to the newspaper office. But I'm writing an article that gives more of a behind-the-scenes look."

"Excellent. I can arrange meetings with some of the performers." Patrick tried to decide who would give the best interviews. "And you're welcome to watch rehearsals."

"I'd appreciate that. Let's start with you." William's mannerisms and confidence reminded Patrick of Rose. "Our readers want to know the new opera house manager."

Patrick tensed. He had moved west in hopes of leaving his past behind. He took a deep breath and schooled his features. He could act his way through this. "Sure, what would you like to know?"

"I understand you managed opera houses back East. Why come to Colorado?" William wrote something on the page.

Patrick shrugged. "I wanted the challenge of a new opera house rather than an established one. I'd like to turn this one into a top-rate venue."

"The citizens of Rockledge would like that too. Have you ever considered performing yourself?" The man stared at him with intense green eyes. Rose's eyes.

Patrick's heart raced. How should he answer? Say that he trained in opera but never landed a principal role? *Almost good enough.* Sweat beaded on his brow.

He wiped his forehead with a handkerchief. No one cared about his background. "Hasn't everyone dreamed of being on stage?"

"True enough, but some more than others." He jotted a couple more notes. "Like Rose. I'll tell her to leave you alone. Having big brothers has taught her to be headstrong, sometimes a little too much so. We all watch out for her, but she can be a—challenge."

What would it be like to have family who cared? Who wanted the best for you? He would never know. "I'm sure she appreciates it."

William laughed. "I doubt that. She would rather be an only child. Especially when men express interest in her."

Did Rose's brothers intimidate potential suitors? Did she have a suitor now? Not likely. No man would want her to join a traveling company.

Patrick fielded other questions about the production without venturing into his own background. Afterward, he resumed painting as William sketched pictures of the performance hall for his article.

His conversation with Rose's brother had only piqued his interest in her. Could he get to know her without involving her in the opera business?

Chapter 3

Rose had stared at the opera house all day. The performers had to come outside sometime. Without a clear view of the side entrance, she had slipped outside several times to peek around the building. She hadn't seen anyone.

As she sewed the hem of a yellow muslin dress, she shifted her chair closer to the window for a better view. What would she say when she did see them?

Sarah carried a bolt of fabric from the back room. "Why are you pressed against the window?"

"The light's better here." If only her nephews hadn't gone fishing. They could have occupied her sister.

"I know what you're trying to do." Sarah shook her head. "It won't work. I talked to the opera house manager. He'll let us know if they need anything."

Rose accidentally stabbed herself with the needle. "Mr. O'Donnell? When did you see him?" She stuck her finger in her mouth to soothe the sting.

"A couple of minutes ago." Her sister grinned.

"You talked to him without me?" Had he described her audition and his threats?

Sarah stepped toward the window and looked out. "We didn't both need to go."

Rose placed the last stitch in the hem. "Did he say anything about. . .me?"

"No. Why would he?" Sarah returned to her sewing table and folded some scraps of fabric. "Handsome fellow, isn't he? A little young for me, but. . ."

Heat filled Rose's cheeks, but she wouldn't fall into her sister's trap. "I hadn't noticed." Although she'd thought of little else since her encounter with him.

"Is that why you're blushing?"

"I'm warm from working near the window." Rose returned to her sewing table.

"If anyone needs a seamstress, he'll send them over. The wardrobe woman who travels with the company takes care of most of the sewing needs."

"I see." Mr. O'Donnell wouldn't send anyone over. Rose tied off the seam and clipped the thread with a pair of scissors.

"I need to put supper on." Sarah headed toward the back of the shop.

What had Mr. O'Donnell said?

Movement at the opera house caught Rose's attention. She tiptoed to the window.

Three slender young women stood on the boardwalk, fanning themselves. They wore simple calico dresses which appeared newer than those worn by the women in town. These ladies must be cast members.

Rose's opportunity had arrived.

She picked up her sewing basket and slipped out the front door, easing it open to keep the bell from ringing.

Although she wanted to hurry across the street, she slowed her pace in an attempt to appear graceful and professional. She glanced at the opera house windows. The curtains remained in place. Mr. O'Donnell couldn't be watching. Could he?

As she stepped up on the boardwalk, she tripped. She caught herself before anyone noticed. After smoothing her skirt, she sauntered over to the trio of ladies.

"I don't know why he allows her to act that way." A tall blond with a perky nose spoke.

The short brunette spotted Rose and stepped back. "Are we blocking the walkway?"

"Not at all." Rose joined the group. "Are you ladies with the opera?"

"Yes." The shorter woman lowered her fan. "How did you know?"

"You look like performers." Rose shrugged. "And I know everyone in town. What roles do you play?"

The tall blond answered. "We're in the chorus—the unnamed masses."

At least they had some kind of part. Rose shouted over a wagon that passed on the street. "I thought you might be the stars."

The shorter blond with a round face, who hadn't spoken yet, responded. "That would be Marian Carter. You'll know her when you meet her because she'll tell you that she's the lead, whether you want to hear about it or not."

"In that case, I'm glad I met you instead." Rose glanced at the shop. Had Sarah discovered her absence? "I'm Rose, from the seamstress shop across the street."

The tall blond tipped her head. "Anna."

"Grace." The short brunette curtsied.

"And I'm Laura." The shorter blond with the round face smiled.

"I'm glad to meet you." Rose appreciated the easy camaraderie with these women. They could help her find a place in theater. "As I said, I work as a seamstress. Are any of you in need of a new day dress or an evening gown?"

Grace shook her head. "They don't pay me enough to purchase extra gowns."

Rose held her ground. "My prices are quite reasonable, and I can sew any of the latest styles from *Godey's Ladies' Magazine* or the *Ladies' Repository*."

"We can get the latest styles at home, but. . ." Anna bit her bottom lip. "I would love a western-style dress—something like Annie Oakley would wear. Think what the people back home would say."

Laura clapped her hands together. "That would be wonderful. Can you make western dresses?"

Rose prided herself on her fashion sense, but if Wild West costumes would gain her an audition, she could make them. "Of course. I have several ideas for colors and styles that would flatter your features."

Laura seemed more excited than the others. "When should we come by for measurements?"

Rose waved a hand. "Don't trouble yourself. I can come to the opera house tomorrow and measure you when you're on a break."

Anna shook her head. "Hard to tell when we'll have a break. You might have to wait."

Rose needed an excuse to visit the opera house. "I don't mind. I'd enjoy watching you rehearse. I can bring some sewing."

"Perfect." Laura gave her a triumphant grin.

Rose checked the opera house window and dress shop door. No sign of Mr. O'Donnell or her sister. "It must be exciting to sing in the opera."

Grace answered. "On occasion. But it's grown tedious. The western towns all look the same, and constant traveling wears on a body."

"But the adventure of seeing new places…" Rose tried not to show her disappointment.

"Grows tiresome after the first week. I miss my sisters and my little nephew. He'll be grown up by the time I return." Laura lowered her fan as the breeze picked up. "The mail doesn't keep up with us on tour."

Rose welcomed time away from her family. Everywhere she went a brother or sister turned up.

Anna shook her head. "After this tour, I'm staying home where I can meet a nice man and settle down. I'd like to have a family before I grow old."

"But what about the leading man?" Rose tried not to look like an enamored child. "Is he wonderful?"

"George?" Laura laughed. "He's a cad. Seduces a new girl in every town."

"On the road he keeps company with Marian." Anna glanced toward the door, as if someone might overhear. "They deserve each other."

"There must be some nice men with the opera." Rose wouldn't be looking for a man, but both men and women made up the company.

"The director seems respectful, but he's an old man. He was handsome in his prime. I've seen playbills. I've also heard the stories." Anna raised an eyebrow. "His escapades rival those of the young men today."

Grace stepped closer as if telling a secret. "Your opera house manager is quite handsome."

Laura nodded. "Such a nice man. Someone a girl could marry."

Rose stifled a choking cough. "Mr. O'Donnell? Nice? I mean, how so?" She could think of other terms to describe him.

"He treats all us girls as if we're important." Laura stood a little taller. "Even the chorus."

"I heard he used to sing," Anna said.

Mr. O'Donnell? Sing? Rose might need to research this man further. . .after she gained entrance to the building.

The following afternoon, Rose stepped through the front door of the opera house. Mr. O'Donnell wouldn't ask her to leave if the girls had invited her. Would he?

The sun shone through the large front windows, and the ornate chandeliers created tiny rainbows on the wall. Her boots clicked on the polished hardwood floor as she crossed to the performance hall. The room smelled of paint mingled with the scent of fresh-cut wood.

She put a hand on the inner door.

"Rose Miller." Mr. O'Donnell entered the lobby from the side. A smile danced on his lips. "Didn't I tell you to stay away?"

Her heart skipped a beat. "I have an appointment." The girls in the chorus thought him kind?

He cocked an eyebrow. "Do tell. What kind of appointment?"

She stood tall. "I'm to measure Anna, Grace, and Laura for western-style dresses—for their personal wardrobes."

The man kept smiling, like he knew something she didn't. But what a handsome smile. "They're in rehearsal. I'll ask them to meet you at the shop afterward."

Rose had anticipated this roadblock. "We already agreed. It'll be more convenient for them if I come here. I can wait for a break. I'll watch and sew until then." She held up her basket.

He touched her elbow as if to lead her to the exit. . .again. "Theater lighting isn't bright enough for sewing. I'll fetch you when they're ready."

A shiver ran through her, and his pretty green eyes tried to melt her resolve. She shook her arm free. "Why do you insist on sending me away? I have an invitation."

He crossed his arms and studied her.

She tilted her head, studying him, and prepared her next argument.

"Very well. I'll sit with you to keep you out of trouble." He opened the theater door and stepped back.

"I don't know why you believe that I'll cause trouble." She moved into the room ahead of him.

Dark-red fabric covered the walls, and red velvet seats framed with ornate wrought iron filled the space. A handsome tenor sang on stage, and the chorus twirled behind him. Instead of costumes, the performers wore regular clothes. A canvas filled the back of the stage with a half-painted pirate ship.

Rose imagined herself singing on stage.

A full house.

A standing ovation.

Everyone would remember her. Even her family would appreciate her dream.

Mr. O'Donnell led her to a seat toward the back. "We won't disrupt the rehearsal here."

She watched the performers with fascination. Could she sing loud enough to fill this room? She settled into a seat next to him.

The man Mr. O'Donnell had introduced her to the other day stood and stopped the action. "George, you need to move to the left. The girls don't have enough room to dance. Marian, come in a little sooner."

The tenor shifted to the left. "Make up your mind, James. First, you say right, then left."

James? Mr. O'Donnell had called him Tom.

Rose glared at the man next to her. "You lied to me. That man is the director."

He gazed into her eyes, drawing her in. "I wanted to protect you."

"From what?" Her voice echoed through the performance hall, and she lowered it. "I have enough brothers to protect me."

"Professional musicians lead a hard life." He leaned in closer. "You seemed unprepared. I wanted to save you the disappointment. And keep you out of James's way. He has enough to do."

This handsome Irishman thought he knew her after a brief introduction. The girls in the chorus must have interpreted his protective attitude as kindness. "Like my brothers, you're not my keeper. I'll thank you to mind your own business."

The tenor resumed his song, and Mr. O'Donnell spoke a little louder. "I met your brother the other day."

"Which one?" Everyone in town knew one of her brothers. So annoying.

"William, the newspaper man." Mr. O'Donnell sat back in his chair as if he hadn't a care in the world. "How many brothers do you have?"

"Four." Four more than she needed most days.

"Five—no—six children. Where do you fall in the line-up?"

"Seven. Four brothers and two sisters. I'm second to the youngest." Everyone seemed to know her business without ever noticing her. "I'm here to do a job, and I expect you to leave me be."

When the music stopped, James barked out orders. "We'll take a thirty-minute break. Be ready to work on the second act when we return."

Mr. O'Donnell stood. "Stay only as long as you need. Understood?"

Rose picked up her basket. "Understood." She would *need* to stay much longer than he imagined.

"As long as you're going to stick around, you might as well call me Patrick."

One step closer to her goal. "And you may call me Rose."

Chapter 4

O n Sunday morning, Patrick filed into the new brick church with the other worshippers. The architecture imitated the cathedrals back East.

He would have stayed home, but the community expected him to attend. He would never be good enough for God to hear his prayers. Prayers to get the part. Prayers for his father's acceptance. Prayers for a woman's love. All unanswered. Church seemed like a waste of time.

The sun shone through stained-glass windows that depicted the four Gospels. New pews with purple fabric cushions filled the sanctuary. Everything smelled fresh and new—the mark of a boomtown.

He searched the congregation for a familiar face. No one from the New Frontier Opera Company had risen early enough to attend. He hadn't expected them to.

Rose's brother William caught his attention and waved. If Patrick joined him, he wouldn't have to sit among strangers.

And, Rose should be nearby. He welcomed the opportunity to see her away from the opera house, in a setting where he didn't need to push her away.

Patrick watched for her as he made his way to where the newspaper man waited. She stood near the opposite end of William's row, wearing the green dress from their first encounter. As he suspected, she had donned her Sunday best for her "audition." She held a young boy by the hand and spoke with a couple of ladies.

William introduced him to two rows of people, all relatives. Parents, brothers, sisters, sisters-in-law, soon-to-be sisters-in-law, and a passel of children. Rose rewarded him with a smile when her brother pointed her out from the other end of the row.

"Sarah is standing next to Rose. And Rose is with Kenny." William appeared to care about each one of them.

"Is the man with the beard Sarah's husband?" Patrick tried to keep all the relatives straight.

William frowned. "No. Sarah's husband died in an accident a couple years ago. That's when the family pulled together to set her up in the seamstress shop."

"I'm sorry." What would it be like to have a family who cared so much? Patrick had only experienced criticism from his father.

A woman with snow-white hair played the new grand piano and everyone sat. Patrick wedged between Rose's brothers, David and William. He would have preferred a seat next to Rose, but children and sisters surrounded her.

When the music ended, the pastor stepped up front to give a few words of introduction. After the congregation sang a hymn, everyone sat down, and Rose climbed the two steps to stand near the piano.

Patrick should have expected it. She had selected a hymn when she tried to audition. Churches often provided early training for budding vocalists.

"Holy, holy, holy, Lord God Almighty." Her voice rang out clear and beautiful. He closed his eyes and listened. He tried not to judge her singing, but his training kicked in. A little quiet. A few missed notes. Overall, pleasant and genuine.

He leaned closer to David. "Where did she learn to sing?"

Rose's brother cupped his hand near Patrick's ear. "Mama studied singing before she married Papa. She taught all of us, but Rose is the only one who took to it."

Rose might earn a chorus position with her current skills if she were to find a company to audition with. But to move up she would need professional training, and even then she would face disappointment, just like he had. She blessed the people in her church and community with her voice. Why give that up for life on the road?

The New Frontier Opera Company might recognize her talent and ruin her life. He wasn't sure how it had happened, but her innocence and enthusiasm had thawed his disillusioned heart. He cared too much to let an opera company destroy her.

Rose eyed Patrick across the yard behind her family's cabin as she cut a lemon cake on the serving table. Why had William invited him?

True, her entire family gathered for lunch every Sunday, and often someone brought a guest. But why this infuriating man who refused to take her seriously? She had spent most of her week avoiding him, and now he stood in her yard, swapping stories with her brothers. Talking about her, no doubt.

Her younger sister, Elizabeth, nudged her. "Did you see the man William invited? I'm going to talk to him. He's quite handsome."

Rose ventured a glance his direction. The redheaded man stood out among her brothers, dressed in an expensive Sunday suit. Yes, quite handsome.

He caught her stare and winked. Winked? A bold move for someone who wished her out of his hair.

She focused on cutting the cake, but glanced his way when he turned elsewhere. Good thing he voiced his opinions so clearly or he could be a distraction.

Papa announced the meal and everyone stood for a prayer. After filling their plates at the buffet line, the adults sat at three long picnic tables in the shade of several tall pines. Children clustered in groups around the yard with their food. They played more than ate.

She sat near Mama and her sister-in-law at one end of the table. To her chagrin, Patrick seated himself across from her, next to Papa. He could watch her every move. Was that his plan? Did he come here to keep an eye on her? What would he tell her parents?

Throughout the meal, the conversation revolved around happenings in town. Patrick shared stories about construction at the opera house and unusual things that went wrong.

Rose said little but listened intently to his stories. His easy conversation relaxed her. He could be quite pleasant, when not protecting her from herself.

Mama finished her meal but remained at the table. "I'm so happy the opera house is finally ready to open. It will bring some much needed culture."

Patrick cut into his second piece of cake. "William said you studied music, Mrs. Miller."

Papa answered for her. "My Violet won't tell you, but she sings like an angel. Went to a fancy music school."

Mama blushed. "John swept me off my feet. Now I sing for God and family and friends."

Rose needed more. God and family might forget her. But if she were the best, the star. . .

"Did you sing professionally?" Patrick lifted a piece of cake to his mouth.

"I had a few small roles. Nothing big. Too much competition for bigger roles." Mama waved a hand. "How many operas will come to town this year?"

"Two." Patrick settled the fork on his plate. "Travel is difficult in the winter, especially since there is no train to Rockledge. We're lucky to get a few shows on their way to San Francisco."

Two. Rose's pulse quickened. If the New Frontier Opera Company didn't accept her, she would only have one more chance this year.

Papa shook his head. "They built a whole opera house for two shows? Sounds like a waste of money."

"We've booked a Wild West show and a couple of vaudeville acts." Patrick ran his fingers along the edge of his plate. "I also hope to find some local or regional performances to fill the calendar."

Mama stood and stacked the plates. "Rose is working with the children from church on a musical production for Founder's Day. Wouldn't it be fun if they could use the opera house?"

Rose glanced at Patrick and quickly turned her attention to gathering silverware for Mama. Her mind raced. What a grand adventure for the children, but he would never allow it.

"I can arrange that." Patrick handed his fork across the table to Rose, brushing her hand with his. "I know the manager."

Rose dropped the fork. How could he forbid her from entering the opera house one day and invite the children's choir another? She picked up the fork and handed it to Mama in an awkward gesture.

Patrick grinned, watching her every move. "I'd love to help with the production too."

Rose's eyes widened, and she tried not to stare. Why would he volunteer to spend time with her and a group of children?

Papa slapped him on the back. "Excellent. I'm sure Rose could use a hand. Especially with the unruly boys."

Rose found her voice. "Do you have much experience with children, Mr. O'Donnell?"

"I was a child once." Patrick shrugged. "I'll learn from you. What do you say?"

Rose found peace in the thought of spending time with the handsome man across the table—and a little thrill. She nodded. "We practice tomorrow afternoon."

One of Rose's nephews interrupted the conversation by chasing a couple of her nieces with an insect. The girls screamed as they ran by.

Papa stood. "Time for some music. The children have grown restless." He stepped into the house and returned with his fiddle.

He sat on a stool near the head of the picnic tables and played "Clementine." Mama sang and others joined. Everyone knew their part, thanks to Mama's training. The children sat in a semicircle around Papa and chimed in on the chorus.

Rose loved this time with her family. She sang her part, but not too loudly. Her mother had once explained to her that no individual should try to steal the show. Here, no one cared about the music's quality.

When the song had finished, Papa moved straight into "Bound for the Promised Land."

Her brothers' tenor part sounded much better than usual. Clear. Rich. Bold.

She turned.

Her brothers sat silent, staring at Patrick.

His voice filled the void with amazing quality.

In that moment, Rose could picture a future with him. She shook her head to clear it. He stood in her way of that future.

Why had he chosen to hide his talent?

Chapter 5

Patrick blinked as he stepped into the church's dim light. Children's laughter echoed through the sanctuary and someone plunked a poor rendition of "Mary Had a Little Lamb" on the piano.

Rose had said she would hold most of the practices in the church, a familiar place for the children. They would move to the opera house the day before the performance. She expressed concern about boys spending too much time near pirate props.

Understandable. Patrick knew nothing about children, but he'd carried on more than one imaginary sword fight on the empty stage. The thought of half a dozen boys with pirate props brought a smile.

He slipped into a pew near the back to watch Rose. Helping with the choir would allow him to get to know her away from the opera house. Away from the fierce competition.

A dozen kids, including Rose's nephews, chased one another around the pews in the front two rows. A couple of others squatted in a corner studying something on the floor. Most appeared to be primary school aged.

Rose clapped her hands. "Let's get started. Everyone, find your places."

The shouting lowered to a rumble as children lined up in two neat rows on the platform facing the piano. The little piano player jumped from the bench to join the others.

One of the younger girls broke ranks, stepped up to Rose, and tugged on the bottom of her skirt. When Rose leaned down, the girl whispered something in her ear.

Rose nodded and the girl skipped to the back door. An outhouse visit?

When Rose turned her attention to the choir, one of the taller boys let go of the braids of the girl in front of him and looked at the ceiling.

"Let's start with 'Wait for The Wagon.'" Rose sat at the piano bench and opened a music book. "What's keeping Patrick? I thought he could direct while I accompanied."

The tallest girl in the front row stuck her arm out and pointed at Patrick. "You mean that man over there?"

Patrick's face heated. He hadn't intended to lurk in the back. Well, maybe he had. He hadn't intended to get caught doing it.

He stood and moved to the front of the church, portraying a confidence he didn't feel. Why did these children intimidate him? Or was it their beautiful director?

Rose introduced him to the choir, who gave him a schoolhouse welcome.

"Good afternoon, Mr. O'Donnell."

He glanced at Rose, unsure what to do next. If she sensed his anxiety, she didn't show it.

Rose nodded to the music propped on the piano. "We're learning 'Wait for the Wagon.'" She bit her bottom lip. "If you don't mind, could you sing a line and the choir will repeat? The back row sings the verses and everyone sings the chorus."

The children stared at him.

"Of course." Why did his mouth feel like cotton?

Rose played the first line and he sang. "Will you come with me my Phillis, dear, to yon blue mountain free?"

She stopped playing. "All together, now."

She played the line again.

The back row sang with him.

He grew comfortable with the process. He sang a line. They sang a line.

On the last line of the verse, "We'll jump into the wagon, and all take a ride," the children jumped. Patrick flinched, losing his concentration.

He glanced at Rose. Of course she would train them all to jump. He cleared his throat.

"They know the chorus. You can sing it together." Rose played the tune with vigor.

The children hopped around as they sang. Odd.

Rose didn't seem to notice the hopping. Her fingers continued to move on the keyboard.

A boy in the middle of the front row stepped forward. He shouted over the music. "Aren't you going to gallop, mister?"

Gallop? That's what they were doing.

Patrick took a tentative hop. When had he last galloped? His father had discouraged any childlike behavior, even in children. Grandfather had encouraged it on his occasional visits.

The chorus soon ended, and Patrick sang the first line of the second verse. The back row repeated the line.

When Patrick reached the last line, he jumped like the children had before. The action exhilarated him.

Rose beamed and nodded in his direction.

On the chorus, he galloped.

Upon reaching the chorus for the last time, Rose left the piano and galloped next to him.

Patrick had never experienced such freedom in music and play. Although he loved to sing, he had always experienced it as a serious exercise.

No wonder Rose loved singing.

Rose stepped to the piano and riffled through her stack of sheet music. "Next, let's practice 'I've Been Working on the Railroad.'"

Some of the taller boys in the back tooted an imitation of a train whistle. They reached a hand in the air and made a motion of pulling an imaginary rope.

Soon the entire choir imitated a conductor and tooted. Patrick joined them in a lower key.

Rose tried not to stare at him as she searched for the music. The man distracted her. She had flipped through the stack three times and missed the sheet she needed every time.

The train whistles disintegrated into chaos. The smaller children waved their arms in each other's faces, and one of the older boys tugged the braids of the girl in front of him. When the girl turned around, he shoved the boy next to him.

Patrick put two fingers to his lips and silenced the room with a sharp whistle.

Open mouthed, the children gawked at him.

When Patrick glanced in Rose's direction, she focused her attention on the music in her hands.

"Let's do some exercises." Patrick shrugged his shoulders and relaxed them in an exaggerated movement.

The children repeated his actions.

He knew how to hold their attention. . .and hers.

After circling his shoulders, he swung his arms in large circles. Then he rolled his head around as the children followed his movements.

After making large circles with his arms and head, he made sounds.

He stuck his lips out and blew air through them, causing them to vibrate. He sounded like a horse or a baby, she wasn't sure which. The choir imitated the sound with enthusiasm.

"Someone spit on me." One of the girls stopped to wipe her cheek. But she soon rejoined the others in making the sound.

Rose pursed her lips and blew through them. Was he demonstrating a real singers' exercise, or had he made it up to entertain the children?

When he glanced her direction, her cheeks warmed, and she stopped. She turned her back to him and once again focused on the papers in her hands.

Finding the music she needed, she resumed her position at the piano. She played a couple of notes to get everyone's attention.

The sound exercises stopped, except for a few young stragglers in the front row.

Patrick put a finger to his lips, silencing the remaining children. He bowed to Rose. "What now, my lady?"

One of the older girls giggled.

An older boy imitated Patrick. "My lady."

Rose could watch him all day. Children's choir practice had never been so exhilarating. "The choir knows this song. Would you direct them?" She bit her bottom lip.

"I suppose you made up motions for this song too." Patrick flashed a grin in her direction.

Rose's cheeks heated.

The littlest girl in the front row raised her hand. "I know the motions. I'll show you." She started pumping her arms and waving. Then she marched three steps.

Rose laughed at Patrick's bewildered face. "Wait for the music, Esther."

She played the introductory notes and the choir sang.

After learning the motions from the children, Patrick pumped his arms and stomped his feet along with them.

Rose would enjoy spending more time with this Patrick. Too bad he turned into the annoying Patrick when he entered the opera house.

Chapter 6

Later that evening, Rose stood next to Patrick on the boardwalk in front of her sister's shop. The afternoon heat had dissipated, leaving a chill in the air. Although still daylight, the streets had quieted for the evening. The bawdy music from a saloon a couple of blocks away drifted down the street.

A wayward curl blew across Rose's face and she pushed it back. "You didn't have to stay for supper. I could've made your excuses to Sarah and the boys." Patrick had escorted Rose and her nephews to the dress shop after choir practice. The boys had each grabbed an arm and pulled him into the back of the shop, insisting their mother feed him.

"And miss Kenny's fascinating tales of fishing with your brother and his lady friend?" Patrick wrinkled his nose and stretched an arm out in front of his face, pinching his fingers together. "This worm is slimy. Take it. Take it."

Rose shook her head. "That's a pretty good imitation."

Patrick flashed a lopsided grin. "I'll take a home-cooked meal with a family any day. The food at the boardinghouse keeps me alive, but it doesn't tempt my taste buds."

"You exaggerate. I've eaten Mrs. Windsor's cooking."

"She overcooks the stew and burns the edges of the biscuits on purpose to discourage her boarders from eating too much. Keeps the food bill down." Patrick offered his elbow to Rose. "It's getting late. I'll see you home."

Her heart skipped a beat. None of the miners or businessmen in Rockledge had ever offered to escort her home on his arm before. Was Patrick interested in her as a woman? Not likely. He wanted to protect her—like a sister. "No. Thank you. I can make my own way."

"I'm sure you can, but I had hoped to stroll through town with a pretty lady on my arm. Are you sure?" He held her gaze, melting her resolve.

Rose hesitated. He thought her pretty? "Thank you." She placed her hand on his arm, feeling the firm muscle beneath. Walking with her brothers had never warmed her like this.

Patrick led Rose down the boardwalk, past the livery and the general store. "I enjoyed dinner. Your family is the kind I wish I had. They make me feel included, like I'm part of something."

"Mama treats the whole town like family and everyone else follows suit. There are so many of us, a couple more don't make any difference." But, sometimes Rose wished for time alone with her mother or father.

"And the way your brothers help with Ted and Kenny. Those boys won't want for a man in their lives." Patrick scooted closer to Rose as a miner passed on the walk.

Her pulse quickened at his nearness, but she held her voice steady. "When Theodore first asked to court Sarah, Papa sent him away."

Patrick raised an eyebrow as he moved back to his side of the walk. "I find that hard to believe."

"Didn't want his daughter stepping out with a troublemaker. Theodore frequented saloons and card games. Got himself thrown in jail a couple of times." Rose caught her reflection in the post office window with Patrick at her side. A handsome couple.

He glanced her way. "Can't imagine Sarah married to someone like that."

"At first, she liked his roguish nature. Different from our brothers. I can understand that."

Patrick slowed as he neared the end of the boardwalk. He guided Rose down to the dirt street. "Your father allowed him to marry Sarah?"

"Not right away. Papa sent Sarah to live with our aunt in Denver. Didn't want her anywhere near him." Rose brushed her skirt, as if she could keep the dust off. "Theodore missed Sarah so much that he promised to stay away from the saloons and attend church."

"Did he keep his word?" Patrick steered Rose toward her home. "Most men fall back into their old ways."

How much did Patrick know about life in saloons? Rose tried to study his face, but hit a rock with her foot and lurched forward. She held fast to Patrick's arm.

His muscle tensed, and he reached to steady her.

Her face warmed, and she straightened, hoping to hide her embarrassment. "He would act like an upstanding citizen for a couple of weeks and then find his way back into the saloon. But after a while, he spent more time in the church than with the bottle. The change became evident."

"And your father allowed Sarah to return?"

"Yes." Why did Patrick show so much interest? "She had continued to correspond with him through letters while she was away. She begged Papa to let her return. After Theodore mended his ways, Papa relented."

Patrick led her around a rut in the road. "Wasn't your father concerned about his past or that he would return to his old ways?"

"Papa said that if God didn't hold a grudge, he didn't have a right to hold one either."

"Hmmm." Patrick remained silent as he escorted Rose the next couple of blocks.

She resisted the urge to chatter at the handsome man by her side. She glanced at him several times, but his face gave nothing away.

Near her cabin, he led her off the road to a stand of pines. He turned to face her, causing her to let go of his arm.

Rose's stomach fluttered, and her face heated.

Patrick took her hands in his and gazed into her eyes. "I enjoyed working with you and the children. It reminded me that music can be joyful. I've missed that."

Rose spoke in a whisper. "It frees me. . .or brings peace, depending on the song."

Although his words spoke of music, he seemed to be saying something more. His hands warmed hers. Did he want to kiss her? To court her?

"I loved the motions you invented to go with the songs." He let go of one of her hands and moved to caress her neck, teasing a curl that had come loose.

A shiver danced up her spine. "So you do understand why I am desperate to be part of the opera. To make music my life."

Patrick dropped his hands to his sides and stepped back. The cool air replaced his touch. "I'd better get you home." He held out his elbow.

Rose took his arm, but the thrill of his touch had evaporated. She thought he might kiss her, but instead he had withdrawn. Why?

He escorted her to her porch and bid her good night.

Rose entered the house without looking back. She had misread his intentions. She took a deep breath and closed her eyes. How would she tell her heart to forget about him?

After leaving Rose, Patrick returned to the opera house. He slumped in the chair behind his desk. He had almost kissed her. Allowed himself to imagine a future with her. Until she reminded him why he needed to keep his distance. She seemed to interpret any interest from him as encouragement to pursue a career in opera. Darkness settled on the room, reflecting his mood.

Standing, he shook his head and shoulders, as if he could shake away the emotions. He struck a match and lit the kerosene lantern on his desk, creating a shadow along the far wall. When would she give up this fantasy of traveling with the opera?

He lit a candle from the lantern and used it to bring up the lights in his office and the lobby. Silence echoed through the performance hall, bringing with it ghosts from his past. He stared into the dark auditorium as if he could change the memories hidden there.

Long ago, he had given up being good enough. Good enough for his father. Good enough for God. Both demanded a perfection he could never achieve. Both looked down on him, waiting for his next mistake.

He returned to his office, the echo of his footsteps breaking the silence. But it was no use. The empty performance hall called to him. He went back and slipped into a plush velvet seat in the back row.

What had Rose said? Something about God not holding a grudge?

Her father didn't hold a grudge, but his did. Every misstep, every imperfection, forever burned in his father's memory. And God? The ultimate judge.

The lights from the lobby created dancing shadows on the canvas scenes set at the back of the stage. In one moment, a ship stood visible. In the next, the ship had disappeared, revealing a garden. How could a flicker change the impression so much?

God the Father. A father like Patrick's? Or did Mr. Miller represent Him better? God couldn't be like all fathers at once. What if Rose's father spoke the truth? What if God didn't hold a grudge?

Long ago, Patrick had learned to sit through church services without listening. In his mind, he would plan for the week ahead. If he closed his ears and his heart, the words didn't sting so much.

Had something in those messages brought Rose's family joy and peace? He should retrieve the Bible from the bottom of his trunk to see what truth hid within.

Chapter 7

Rose stepped backstage at the opera house carrying a bundle of half-sewn dresses. She had agreed to meet Anna and Grace for a fitting of their western frocks.

So different from her first visit, when Patrick had tried to rid himself of her. He tolerated her presence now, but hovered a bit to keep an eye on her.

Away from the opera house he welcomed her presence. She had even thought he might kiss her. She sighed at the reminder of his gentle touch on her neck.

From the end of the hall, a woman's shrill voice screeched. "Must you do this in every town?"

A man responded in a smooth timbre. "I don't know why you care. She means nothing to me."

Wanting to avoid some kind of lovers' quarrel, Rose slipped around the corner and pressed her back against the wall. They would move on soon enough.

"Don't my feelings matter to you?" The woman grew louder.

"Of course they do." The man lowered his voice. "It's not my fault women seek me out."

Who were they? Rose peeked around the corner, holding her breath. She wasn't spying. Anyone in the corridor could hear the pair.

Marian stood outside her dressing room. Her graceful face contorted into something like a gargoyle. A long curl had fallen loose and bounced as she moved. "You don't have to encourage them. I saw you."

"I was demonstrating proper breathing technique for singing. Nothing more." George, the lead tenor, stood close enough for an intimate conversation and put a hand on the wall next to Marian's head. His wavy brown hair stuck out at an odd angle and his rumpled shirt hung askew.

Rose had heard about men's occasional dalliances in hushed whispers. For some reason, Patrick came to mind. He would never involve himself in such a thing. Her heart ached for the soprano.

"With your arms around her?" Marian waved a hand in a dramatic gesture. "This time we're finished. I deserve better."

Rose should leave the two alone, but she couldn't move without someone seeing her. Her heart pounded.

"You always come back." George stood tall and proud. "You need me. We need each other."

At the far end of the hall, Anna entered through a side door with Grace. "I can't wait to see—"

Rose's friends slowed and moved toward the bickering couple.

Marian straightened her back. "What are you looking at?"

George lowered his gaze and touched Marian's shoulder.

She shook him off.

Anna and Grace slipped into their dressing room and shut the door.

When Marian glanced her direction, Rose shifted farther into her hiding place. Trapped.

"We're finished here!" the soprano screeched.

A door slammed.

Footsteps moved away.

Rose peeked again.

George swaggered down the hall and disappeared.

She released a breath and returned to the hallway. What should she do? Tell someone? Pretend she hadn't seen anything? Anna and Grace had seen the encounter. They would know what to do. She knocked on the chorus dressing room door.

Anna welcomed her into the room. Both girls tried on their dresses, which were still pinned in some places.

Anna stood in front of Rose, holding her arms out. Grace relaxed in a chair, waiting her turn to be fitted.

Rose squatted and pushed a pin into the fabric near Anna's waist. "I saw Marian and George."

Anna shrugged. "They argue every week. I don't know how he puts up with her."

"She seemed upset." Rose stood to check the dress's shoulders. "Something about another woman." She didn't want to carry tales but Anna and Grace already knew.

Grace fingered the fabric of her dress. "He's a cad. They deserve each other."

"Should we talk to her? Try to help?" Rose pushed a couple of pins into the sleeves.

"Won't do any good." Grace stood to check her reflection in the mirror. "I don't want to think about how difficult she'll be at rehearsal."

Anna turned so that Rose could check the back of the dress. "I can hear her now. 'James. You have placed me too close to the edge of the stage. No one can see me when I sing my aria.'"

Grace put a hand on her hip to imitate one of the soprano's tantrums. "'I can't stand next to her. She pulls me off key.'"

Anna pulled the dress over her head. "You sound exactly like her. I'm not looking forward to practice this afternoon." She returned the garment to Rose. "She makes us all miserable."

After Rose finished with Anna and Grace, she stood alone in the hall for a few minutes before moving toward Marian's dressing room. Should she knock? She would want a woman to talk to after the scene she had witnessed. What would she want to hear if she were in Marian's shoes?

She rapped on the door.

"Go away." The soprano's screech carried through the wall.

"You don't even know who it is." Rose should leave, but the woman's pain compelled her.

"I don't care. Go away."

Rose pressed on. "I work across the street at the dress shop and am making Western dresses for some of the other women and thought you might like—"

"Why would you think that?" Marian's tone softened. She would have yelled at George.

"I've brought some sample fabric that would highlight your eyes and complexion." Rose had hoped to talk to the woman today. "I have a style that would complement your delicate features."

"What color?"

Compliments and fashion, the universal language of women. "One is dark red. I thought it would look good with some ivory fringe. The other is pink."

The door opened, and a puffy-eyed Marian tilted her head to motion Rose in.

Fancy dresses and other clothing sprawled across the room, giving it little resemblance to the tidy space Rose had seen on her first visit. She stepped in and shut the door.

Marian reclined on her settee. "Show me."

The room didn't contain another chair, so Rose kneeled nearby. She handed a couple of samples to the woman.

Rubbing the fabric in her fingers, Marian's face softened. "I'll think about it."

Rose took a breath for courage. "Do you mind if I ask you—is it wonderful to sing in front of a full house?"

"Yes. Wonderful." A little smile formed on Marian's face. "I love to watch people's expressions when I touch them with my music."

Rose wanted to reach people with her own song. "When did you start singing?"

"I was ten years old when my mother enrolled me in the conservatory." Marian stared into the distance and smiled as she shared her memories.

Although Marian relaxed, loneliness penetrated her words. The patrons who cheered for her on stage returned to their homes and families at the end of the evening while she faced an empty dressing room.

Rose studied her surroundings. A mirror. A dressing table covered with face paint, a brush, and hairpins. Beautiful gowns on the rack and strewn on the floor.

Marian shared stories of her early days as a vocalist and her first lead role. After a while, she ran out of words. "I'm tired. I'll think about the dresses."

Rose took her leave and walked back to the dress shop, visions of the music world filling her head. She could live like Marian, regardless of what Patrick thought.

Patrick crossed the street to the seamstress shop. Since he had met Rose, he had often found himself staring at the window. Now he stood in front of the door. Would she want to see him?

He needed to know what she had done to soothe Marian's temper. Rumors of the soprano's argument with George had spread through the cast and crew. The entire cast waited on edge for her to arrive for practice. . .late and in a foul mood.

Instead, she appeared more placid than usual. Friendly. Pleasant. Cooperative. Someone said Rose had talked to her. How had she done it?

He reached for the door and pushed it open with a creak.

A bell above the door announced his entrance. Completed dresses, fabric, and sewing things filled the shop. Several work tables lined one wall. The smell of fresh cotton greeted him.

Rose sat at one of the tables, operating a modern sewing machine. With one foot, she rocked a pedal back and forth. She focused on feeding an off-white fabric through the contraption and didn't seem to notice him.

He had almost believed she didn't know how to sew and used dressmaking as an excuse to gain entry to the opera house. But her tiny hands moved the material with grace.

When the machine stopped, he cleared his throat.

She jumped to her feet, bumping the table and knocking a pair of scissors to the floor. "Patrick. What a surprise." She put a hand to her hair and smoothed it.

He picked up the scissors and returned them to the table. "The bell rang, but I guess you didn't hear it. What are you making?"

She glanced at the fabric and blushed. "Pantaloons." She wadded them up and tucked them behind her back.

"I see."

The pink in her cheeks enhanced her beauty. She regained her composure. "Did you want me to sew something?"

"I don't need any women's unmentionables today. Thank you anyway."

She rewarded him with a casual smile. "A suit?"

He would love to flirt with her all day, but he didn't have the time. "I came to find out what you said to Marian."

She stiffened. "I talked to her. That's all."

"Everyone expected her to show up for practice in a foul mood. Instead, she seemed more pleasant than usual."

Her face relaxed. "I'm glad. Poor thing, she seemed so tense after the way George treated her."

He'd never heard anyone refer to Marian Carter as a "poor thing." Many other names, but never that. "What did you say? The cast is calling you a miracle worker."

"We talked about singing and how it feels to have an audience love you." Her voice carried a wistful quality. "She told me about her youth at the conservatory."

Patrick would like to have Rose around all the time. His heart beat faster. "How did you know what to say?"

She straightened the items on her sewing table. "Soothing nerves is a survival strategy in a big family."

"You're the peacemaker." Could her soft words bring peace to his heart? "Why are you so insistent on joining the opera?"

"I'm so ordinary." She glanced at the floor. "Singing sets me apart. Makes me special."

"There's nothing ordinary about you."

"When I was twelve, I sang my first solo in church. Everyone complimented me." She smoothed her skirt. "They noticed me. I wasn't one of the Millers. I became Rose, with the beautiful voice."

"You can be her, 'Rose with the beautiful voice,' without being an opera star. Audiences can be fickle, and good singing is never enough for directors or conductors." Or his father. She had no idea.

"You don't understand what I want. What I need." Her eyes pleaded as if seeking assurance.

How could he convince her that she was already enough? Enough for her family. Enough for. . .him.

Chapter 8

Rose peeled an apple and sliced it into a large bowl. "Are we the only ones baking? I thought Sarah and Elizabeth would be here."

Mama measured flour into another bowl for the crust. "It's the two of us today. Do you mind?"

"I'm glad to have you all to myself." When had she last been alone with Mama?

"I heard you had a male visitor at the shop recently." Her mother cut a scoop of lard into the flour.

"Patrick came by while I was sewing pantaloons for Mrs. Fletcher. A little embarrassing." If she worked for someone besides her sister, she wouldn't be the subject of family gossip.

"Sarah said the two of you seemed quite friendly." Mama shaped the dough into several equal-sized balls.

"She shouldn't have eavesdropped." Rose would like to have known she had an audience. But she wouldn't have said anything different. She enjoyed the easy banter with Patrick.

"Should I ask your father to talk to him?"

Rose's heart beat faster, and she let the knife slip, cutting off the end of the apple slice. "About what?" Had her feelings been so obvious?

Mama raised an eyebrow. "Any young man who's interested in courting you should speak with your father."

"He's not interested in courting. He acts like a brother, trying to protect me from myself."

"A brother doesn't track your every move like he did on Sunday." Mama sprinkled flour on the table. She pressed a ball of dough onto the surface and picked up the rolling pin. "He has eyes for you."

Heat filled Rose's cheeks. She had avoided romantic entanglements. When she encouraged one boy, the others backed away, and she liked attention from all of them.

Patrick interested her like no other, but she didn't understand him. Why did he escort her home like a beau? He had leaned in for a kiss, but then changed his mind.

She didn't understand her mother either. "Why did you give up music after Grandpa paid for the conservatory?"

"I didn't give it up." Mama placed a pie pan over the flat crust to test for size. "You heard me sing last Sunday at church and later at home. I love singing."

Rose shook her head. "You know what I mean."

"There's more to life than standing in front of an audience or becoming famous." Her mother rolled the crust to fit the pan. "I'll admit I enjoyed the attention, but I always wanted to be a mother."

"Don't you sometimes feel like you wasted your training?" Rose tossed a core in a bucket and reached for another apple.

"It wasn't wasted. I taught my children, and I sing in church." Mama folded the dough in quarters and transferred it to the pan. She dusted off the extra flour. "Music isn't wasted if it's used for God."

Rose sliced a long curly peel from the apple. "I can be famous and still sing for God."

Mama shook her head. "One day a man will come along and change your mind."

"I don't want anyone to steal my dreams—especially not a man." Rose wouldn't give up her music for any man. Not even a handsome Irishman. "Without my music, I'm ordinary. I want to be special."

"You'll always be special in the eyes of God and your family."

Rose's family could forget her. At times, they had. And why would God care about her when He had the whole world to manage? But she wouldn't argue with her mother. "Of course."

Mama sprinkled more flour on the table. She set out another ball of dough and started rolling. "When we finish baking the pies, I'll have you take one to Patrick—such a nice young man."

"You don't need to play matchmaker, Mama. Besides, I doubt that even your apple pie could get that man to look at me as more than a sister."

Patrick repaired a broken chair in the balcony. Not exactly the job he had signed on for.

As he worked, he sang at full volume in the empty opera house. The rounded ceiling enhanced his voice, even from the balcony. After hearing so many of the New Frontier Opera Company's practices, he could sing the entire show.

When he came to the tenor's aria near the end, he stood at the balcony railing facing the center of the performance hall. Breath flowed through him, becoming sound, giving him a sense of life, of freedom, of beauty. He held one arm high in a dramatic gesture and hit the final note.

A moment of silence and a deep breath. He couldn't shake the need to express himself through song, no matter how imperfect.

Clapping came from below.

He had locked the door, hadn't he? Who had witnessed his performance?

"That was beautiful." Rose came into his line of sight. "I've never heard anyone sing like you. Not even when Mama took us to Denver to the opera. Why aren't you part of a professional company?"

"Long story." A story he didn't want to share with Rose. . .or anyone. He didn't have to explain his choices. He leaned over the balcony railing. "I'll be right down." He took the stairs two at a time.

Rose had stepped onto the stage, where she studied the large canvas scene. She held a basket, different from her ever-present sewing basket.

The scent of lavender mixed with cinnamon tickled his senses. He wanted to tuck a stray curl behind her ear. To feel her skin beneath his fingers. But he kept his distance. One touch and he might forget why he couldn't encourage her.

"Mama thought you would like some apple pie." She tilted her head toward the basket.

He joined her on stage. "I never turn down baked goods."

She shook her head. "Just like my brothers."

"All of them?" He led her toward the edge of the stage and the lobby.

"Yes." She followed him out of the performance hall. "What about your family? Do you have brothers?"

"No. I only have a sister." He propped the front door of the opera house open. Too much temptation with her alone inside.

"Only two children? That must be wonderful." Her wistful tone told him she imagined something quite different from his experience.

"Not exactly." He carried a small round table from the lobby to the boardwalk and placed it in an alcove by the front window. "With more children, my father may have found one who met his expectations."

"It couldn't have been that bad." She trailed behind and set her basket on the table.

He didn't want to discuss his family. "Are you wearing a new dress? The green ribbon matches your eyes." Talk of clothing should distract her.

Rose glanced down and smoothed her skirt. A pretty pink crept into her cheeks. "You've seen this dress many times before. But the lace is new. I reworked the trimmings."

"That must be it. New lace." He returned to the lobby and lifted two chairs by their backs. One under each arm, he carried them outside to the boardwalk.

Rose stepped aside as he passed. "A table along the boardwalk. What a lovely idea."

He placed a chair on each side of the table.

She removed a pie from the basket and placed it on the table. "Here's your pie. I can come back for the pan."

Did she think he carried the table out for himself? "Will you join me for pie and coffee? It'll be quite proper. Your sister is chaperoning from across the street."

She put a hand on her hip and studied her sister's shop. "She will be watching. But yes, I'd like to share pie with you."

"I'll get some plates from my office. The women on the cultural committee stocked it with a full set of china and silver. An unnecessary luxury." Patrick strode through the lobby and into his office.

Rose followed, but stopped at the threshold. "Mama says you should speak to my father. We spend too much time together." She held his gaze in a challenge.

"Is that so?" Could he court her without encouraging her ambitions? He liked to think she lingered at the opera house to see him. But he suspected her nearness had more to do with the musicians. He would consider pursuing her after the New Frontier Opera Company moved on.

She watched him, unmoving.

He returned and handed her two forks, a pie server, and china plates from the sideboard. "And what do you think?"

She blushed and glanced away. "I'm still deciding. You can be as annoying as my brothers." A shy smile accompanied her gaze.

His heart skipped a beat. She had considered a relationship with him apart from the opera company? "Coffee?" He walked toward the potbelly stove.

"No. I'm protecting my voice." She bit her bottom lip. "Don't all singers avoid coffee?"

Patrick laughed. "Most of them live on it. They keep late nights."

A look of indecision crossed her delicate features. Unusual for the confident woman. "In that case, I'll have a little."

Patrick poured two cups and carried them toward the door.

Rose stepped outside and placed the plates on the table. "You must have enjoyed something about being almost an only child."

He set the coffee cups on the table. Hadn't she dropped the topic of his family? "One time my grandfather on my mother's side came to stay for a couple of months. He took me fishing, played checkers, and told stories." The memories warmed him.

"I like him already." Rose sliced the pie and put a piece on each plate.

Patrick took a long drink from the little china cup. "Your father reminds me of Grandpa—full of life and accepting everyone."

"I suppose so, but I have to share him with so many people." She sipped her coffee and made a sour face.

He laughed. "Coffee's an acquired taste."

"It's bitter." She returned her cup to the table. "I'll stick with my tea."

A group of children ambled past on the boardwalk, talking among themselves. When they spotted Rose, they waved and greeted her.

One of the younger girls stopped at the table as the others moved on. She held her head high and pointed to a white ribbon on her collar. "Thank you for the bow, Miss Miller. I sewed it on."

"Perfect, Amanda." Rose fingered the bow. "Makes you look so grown up."

The girl flashed a contagious grin and ran to catch up with the others.

Every time Patrick encountered Rose, he admired her more. "How is it that you don't already have a suitor or a husband?" The words slipped from his mouth before he considered the implications.

Rose glanced at her uneaten pie. "My brothers frightened away any boys who took an interest."

"I rather like your brothers. They can't be that bad." How would they perceive him as a possible match for their sister?

"I don't mind. Any man who isn't strong enough to stand up to my brothers wouldn't hold my interest for long." She met his gaze. "I suppose that makes me sound fickle."

"Not at all." He reached across the table and covered her hand with his and his heart beat faster. "It makes you Rose. Honest to a fault."

She nibbled her bottom lip and watched him. . .waiting.

Did she expect him to declare his intentions? As much as he wanted to, he wouldn't.

Not while she placed her hope in what she imagined life on the road would be like.

He pulled his hand back, breaking contact. "I'm sorry. I can't speak to your father."

Rose dropped her hands to her lap and dipped her head. "I see."

He wanted to explain, but words wouldn't come. How could he revive the easy banter?

Rose stood, leaving a plate of half-eaten pie. "I should go. You can give the pan to Sarah when you're finished."

Patrick watched her cross the street to the dress shop, head down.

He was a cad.

Chapter 9

A few weeks later, on a sunny Saturday morning, Rose approached the opera house. She hadn't seen Patrick since he had rejected her, and she hoped to avoid him today. When would she learn to keep her mouth shut? She had pushed him into a corner. He saw her as a little sister, not as a woman.

She wouldn't think about Patrick or about the embarrassing incident.

Today, she had come to meet Anna, Grace, and Laura, who had agreed to picnic with her at Barron's Falls. Even though they couldn't help her secure a place with the opera company, the girls in the chorus had become friends.

Rose opened the lobby door and stepped into the dim light. The girls had arranged to meet her here. She wouldn't need to stay long.

Her gaze moved to Patrick's office door.

Closed.

She willed it to stay closed until she had gone.

Anna, Grace, and Laura entered through a side door. They carried on a conversation about something that had happened in rehearsal the day before. Rose longed to be part of their world.

The chorus girls wore the dresses that Rose had sewn for them. Each had added a matching wide-brimmed bonnet. An actress wouldn't want freckles.

When she saw Rose, Grace grinned and twirled in her new Western-style dress. "I love it. Rose, you're a genius."

Rose shrugged off the compliment. The dresses mimicked a modern style, with lines and fringes to give a touch of the Wild West. "I wanted you to be able to wear them as everyday dresses. Costumes would have been fun, but not particularly useful."

Laura ran a hand down her tan skirt. "I can't wait to show my friends back home."

"I'm glad you like them." Rose lifted her basket. "Are you ready for a picnic?"

"A real Western adventure. I can't wait." Anna stepped close and lifted the basket lid. "Smells wonderful."

"I packed bread, cheese, beef, and cinnamon rolls." Rose had included a knife, a canvas tarp to sit on, and other essentials in the basket. The girls trusted her to lead them into the mountains. A serious responsibility. In her family, no one expected her to lead anything.

"Yum. I can't wait." Grace adjusted her bonnet.

Patrick entered from the performance hall, followed by George.

Rose sucked in a breath and turned her attention to the girls. How soon could she leave?

Patrick strode toward his office. "There's nothing wrong with your dressing room. You don't need another buffalo robe." He didn't seem to notice her.

Rose hadn't seen George since eavesdropping on him and Marian near her dressing room. The handsome blond man flashed a roguish grin, dulling her senses. He reminded her of a prince from a storybook.

"Ladies." George gave a little bow. "Are we going on a picnic?" He reached toward Rose's basket as if to take a peek inside.

Flashing him a smile, Laura slapped his hand. "*We* are going on a picnic. No men allowed."

Grace took an exaggerated step toward the tenor. "Unless. . ."

"George. We have business." Patrick glared at the man.

He might as well have said, "Run along now, girls." Rose wanted to pound her fists on his chest, but he wasn't a brother, even if he acted like one.

Still grinning, George put his hands behind his back. "About that buffalo robe."

Rose didn't need to see any more. Patrick treated her like a child, but George could be an ally. His friendly manner relaxed her. He made her feel beautiful and grown up.

Laura opened the door. "See you later, fellas."

Rose followed the chorus girls onto the boardwalk. Then she and Laura took the lead and Anna and Grace followed as they headed up the street.

In a dreamy voice, Grace said, "He's so handsome and protective, the kind of man a girl could marry."

A noisy lumber wagon rattled down the street, making a response impossible.

Rose tapped her foot, waiting for the clattering to subside. "George seems sweet. But didn't you speak ill of him when we first met?"

"Not George." Grace stared at Rose as if she had grown an extra head. "Patrick."

Rose's face warmed. "The way you flirted with George, I thought you had designs on him."

"Oh, honey." Laura patted Rose's arm. "It's a game with George. He charms all the ladies, single or married. But those of us in the company know better than to trust him."

Did Laura see Rose as a naive child too?

"Marian's the only one who gives in to his charms," Anna said. "She thinks she's better than the rest of us."

"Patrick, with his Irish good looks and shining green eyes. He's everything George isn't." Grace stepped off the boardwalk next to Rose. Her tone turned teasing. "I'd like to take him home with me."

She must not have any brothers. Rose pointed toward a side road. "This way."

"Yes, but in a few weeks, we'll be gone and he'll still be here," Laura said.

Grace moved up next to Rose. "I would consider staying back for a good man. No one would notice one voice gone from the chorus."

"Someone said Patrick used to sing in the opera. Word is, he and James are old friends." As the road inclined, Anna began to pant.

The beautiful sound of Patrick's solo from the balcony drifted through Rose's mind. She'd dreamed of blending her voice with one like his. "Why do you suppose he stopped singing?"

"Probably too much backstage drama." Laura shrugged. "I'm supposed to cover Marian's part if she can't sing. But she'll never let me have the chance. If she were coughing up blood, she would sing between coughs. Perhaps he tired of waiting."

"Do you think he wants back in? Wouldn't it be delightful if he could join us on the road?" Halting, Grace put her hands on her hips and gasped for breath.

Rose and the other girls stepped up beside her. "Would they take him partway through the tour?" Was Patrick discouraging her from the very thing he intended to do?

"Not likely." Laura shook her head. "We have plenty of male vocalists. Besides, he seems to like his job at the opera house."

Rose intended to audition and join the opera company, regardless of what Patrick did. He wouldn't see her as a child if they accepted her. Her heart beat a little faster as she imagined life on the road singing with Patrick.

But Laura was right. He wouldn't join the company.

Thunder clapped overhead as Patrick maneuvered the canvas scenes stored backstage. He had built wheeled frames for three of the canvases. Three more to go.

The sight of Rose earlier this morning had brightened his day. The women in the troupe enjoyed her company—even Marian, a minor miracle. The men kept Rose at arm's length, admiring her from afar. The perfect blend of spunk and innocence.

She had encouraged him to speak to her father, and he had rejected her. If only he could convince her she didn't need the opera company. If only he could convince himself of his own worth.

Thunder shook the opera house and rain pelted the roof. Must be heavy. He couldn't usually hear rain from backstage. He'd need to check for leaks after the storm.

In the lobby, a door flew open. A drenched man blew in with the storm, bringing wind and the scent of rain. He slammed the door and relative quiet returned.

Patrick jumped from the stage and strode to greet him.

Rose's brother William dripped in the lobby. He shook his head and arms, spattering Patrick. "Sorry. Didn't mean to shake on you like a dog."

"Come into my office by the stove." Patrick brushed at a droplet that had landed on his face. "What's so important that you would be out in this?"

The drenched man followed Patrick. "Would you believe it wasn't raining when I left the newspaper office?"

Patrick eyed the window. Water fell in sheets, and hail bounced off the roadway. "What a downpour."

"Typical for Colorado in the summer. Should've known better." William held his hands over the stove. "I came to congratulate you. It seems the governor plans to attend your opening night."

"Excellent." A visit from the governor might finally impress Patrick's father. No, it wouldn't. A Western governor didn't carry any weight in the elite circles. His shoulders slumped. Why did he still care so much about pleasing the man?

"The board isn't sure how you did it, but they're mighty proud. I'm supposed to write an article about it for the paper. A follow-up from my earlier piece."

"Patrick?" James's voice called from the performance hall.

Patrick stepped to the office door and called out. "In here."

When James entered, Patrick introduced him to William.

"Have you seen Laura, Grace, and Anna?" James glanced around as if the girls might be hiding in Patrick's office. "They didn't show up for a chorus meeting."

"They left this morning for a picnic with Rose." Patrick gazed at the window where the raging storm took on a new dimension. Was Rose out in this? His heart pounded in his chest and sweat formed on his brow. So much thunder and hail. "Haven't they returned?"

The older man shook his head. "No one has seen them."

Rose's brother appeared unconcerned. "Where did they go?"

Patrick tried to remember the conversation. Images of a drenched and shivering Rose filled his mind. "Something Falls."

"Foxtail Falls?"

"No. It started with a *B*. Boxer Falls?"

"Barron Falls?"

"That's it." Patrick pointed a finger at Rose's brother. "Barron Falls. We have to find her. Do you know the way?"

James quirked an eyebrow. "Her? You mean *them*?"

"Of course. We have to find them." Patrick pulled a long coat from a rack and put it on. He headed toward the door.

William held back. "If we wait half an hour, the storm will subside. They'll return on their own."

Was the man daft? Leave her—them—out in the storm? "How can you say that?"

James looked from one man to the next, as if watching a performance.

"Knowing Rose, she found shelter somewhere—in a cave or under a rock or something." William shrugged. "The storm will have passed by the time we reach them anyway."

The image of Rose in a makeshift shelter didn't bring any comfort. "She's your sister, man. Don't you care?"

"I care, but she's fine. She's always fine." William brushed some of the water from his sleeve.

Patrick grabbed the lapels of the man's shirt. "You don't know that. Someone could be hurt. They should have been back by now." He pulled Rose's brother toward the door.

"Fine. I'll get my brothers and meet you here in ten minutes." William opened the door and stepped out into the storm.

Patrick glanced at James. "You coming?"

"I'll leave it to the young men." James peered out the window. "I imagine the girls are fine. He knows Rose better than you do."

But Patrick couldn't erase the image of Rose, soaked and cold, huddled under a rock. He paced the lobby while he waited for William's return.

Chapter 10

Rose and the girls huddled under a makeshift canvas shelter as the storm raged. She shivered at the roar of rain and hail pelting the covering. Rain misted in from the edge of the shelter, and she huddled closer to Laura. Her damp dress clung to her. How would she get them home?

"Good thing you packed a canvas to sit on." Grace pushed a damp curl from her forehead. "How did you know what to do?"

Rose had leaned several long pine branches against a large boulder and covered them with canvas to form a lean-to. "My brothers taught me. We used to explore the forest as kids." Her brothers had taken the time to teach her survival skills.

Laura shivered against her. "I wish we had a fire."

"As long as we're wishing, I wish I was at the boardinghouse," Grace said.

Rose kept a fire starter in the picnic basket for emergencies. "I would start a fire, but we don't have enough room, and there's no dry wood around." If no one found them, she would have to try to find some farther away.

"Do you think anyone will look for us?" Laura's soaked bonnet drooped around her face.

No one would come for Rose. Her family wouldn't even notice her absence. She should have paid attention to the sky.

Lightning flashed and thunder echoed in the mountains, vibrating Rose's insides.

"That sounded close." Anna peeked out the edge of the lean-to. "How long do you think it'll take for the creek to recede?" Biting her bottom lip, she looked at Rose.

When the rain started, Rose had hurried everyone back toward town. But Trout Creek had already swollen from its normal trickle to a raging river. She knew better than to cross, especially since the girls had no experience outdoors. So she'd built a shelter uphill from the swollen creek.

"Could be sometime tomorrow." Rose remembered stories of people trying to cross creeks during a flash flood. Better to be safe and not get the girls' hopes up.

Anna lifted the edge of the canvas and peeked out. "Is that snow?"

Rose shifted to see the layer of white covering the ground. "It's hail."

"I've never seen hail like that." Anna scooted closer to Rose. "Surely someone will notice us missing and find us."

Someone might come for the chorus girls, but not Rose. She took a deep breath. She wasn't six years old anymore. She wasn't the child who woke up alone behind a hay bale the morning after the square dance. The girl whose family had forgotten her.

A lady had found her and fed her biscuits and eggs. Later that day, her family had come to fetch her.

Rose fought back tears. She hadn't thought about the square dance incident in some time.

She pasted on a smile and shook the past from her mind. "How were all of you selected to join the opera?"

Laura answered first. "I auditioned in Boston after having several chorus roles in smaller productions. The company had placed a call for auditions in the local newspaper."

Rose couldn't imagine an advertisement for auditions in the Rockledge paper. The Denver paper might carry such postings.

Grace nodded. "That's where I auditioned too. The line of potential company members ran out the door."

Rose swallowed hard. "I hadn't realized—" A deafening thunderclap cut her off and the girls huddled closer.

"I had it a little easier. My voice teacher knew someone on the selection committee and arranged for me to join the chorus." Anna turned her attention to the raging storm.

Rose waited for one of the other girls to give a jealous reply, but neither did. Would she need to move back East to find a position in an opera company? "Do you think the company would add someone partway through the tour? If they were really good?"

Anna shook her head. "I've never heard of it. Someone is always prepared to back up the principal roles. And chorus members are expendable."

A wind gust blew rain into the shelter and Rose shivered.

Grace rubbed her hands together. "We're supposed to be at a meeting this afternoon. What time is it now?"

"I don't know." Anna shrugged. "Do you think James would send someone after us?"

Grace perked up. "I hope he sends Patrick. No one from the opera company would venture out in this storm for fear of getting a sore throat."

Patrick. He had seen them leave for the picnic and knew where they had gone. . .if he had paid attention. Rose imagined Patrick rushing to her rescue. Her cheeks warmed. Best keep those thoughts to herself.

Another lightning flash. Another thunderclap.

He had his own work. He wouldn't come for her.

In the pounding rain, Patrick followed the muddy trail behind two of Rose's brothers. Water ran down his face, and he blinked the droplets from his eyes. Pea-sized hail pelted his hat and coat, stinging where they hit. The wind's roar and the sound of hail ripping leaves from the trees assaulted his ears.

Sandwiched between Rose's brothers, two in front and two in back, Patrick longed for a family who would search for him in a storm. Rose's brothers had come, even if he had to convince them of the need.

In places, water filled the trail, turning it into a creek. "Are you sure this is the trail?"

David shouted from in front of him but didn't turn around. "Yes. It's usually dry, but I've seen worse."

Although Rose's brothers were willing to hunt for her, they didn't seem to think she was in any danger.

Patrick had to see for himself that she was all right. She acted tough, but he had seen her vulnerability. Like so many performers, she hid her weakness well. The way she bit her lip when she was uncertain. The way she carried her sewing basket like a security blanket. The way she wanted her singing to validate her.

"The storm might be letting up. At least the hail has stopped." One of Rose's brothers shouted over the wind, but Patrick couldn't tell which one.

His foot slipped on a wet rock, and he caught his balance. What kind of shoes had Rose worn? He hoped she hadn't turned an ankle, or worse.

Patrick slammed into the brother in front of him and stumbled back. The man had stopped in his tracks.

William stared at the raging river that crossed the trail and rubbed his chin.

"Is there a bridge?" Patrick scanned the shoreline.

David dropped the coil of rope he'd been carrying. "This is Trout Creek. Usually you can hop over it without getting your feet wet." He tied the rope to a nearby tree.

Patrick tried to imagine a tiny creek in place of the river. "How did it get like this so quickly?"

"Flash flood."

Patrick's heart slammed in his chest. What if the rush of water had carried Rose away?

"Look. Over there." William pointed across the water.

A large tan canvas was stretched out against a boulder. A shelter? Could that be her?

"Rose." Patrick shouted, but the storm drowned out his words.

David tied the other end of the rope around his middle. He traversed the waist-deep water until he reached the other side. Then he untied the rope and fastened it around a tree.

David climbed toward the shelter while William held the rope and crossed the creek.

Patrick took the rope next. Icy water filled his boots as he crossed through the water. The current tried to pull him downstream, but he held onto the rope.

David reached the canvas as Patrick stepped onto the shore. Rose and the other girls came out from under the shelter. They appeared unharmed.

Patrick sucked a breath. He raced up the slope, slipping on rocks and mud.

He wrapped his arms around Rose.

She held his waist and rested her head on his shoulder. "You came."

"Of course I did." Her response warmed him. The storm and his surroundings fell away. In that moment, only he and Rose existed and he wanted her to be with him forever.

William broke the spell. "I told you she was fine. 'Probably built a shelter,' I said."

Patrick let go of her but stayed close.

Her brothers and the chorus girls stared at him—at the two of them.

Rose straightened her skirt, although it did no good in the rain. "It didn't seem safe to cross the creek. I've heard stories."

David tousled her hair. "You did good, baby sis."

Rose had accused Patrick of acting like a brother. He didn't feel like a brother now.

Chapter 11

Rose took a wool blanket from David and wrapped it around her shoulders. Although damp, it warmed her. She had dressed for sunny weather.

Her brothers handed blankets to Laura, Anna, and Grace and hovered near them. But Patrick never left Rose's side.

The storm subsided, leaving behind hail that looked like snow. Shredded green leaves littered the ground. The wind had let up, allowing Rose to hear the conversations between her brothers and the chorus girls.

William folded the canvas. "Looks like we can head back now." He stuffed it in the pack that he had brought the blankets in. "Nice lean-to, sis."

Her brothers cared, in their own way. "Thanks. Next time I'll put some rope in my basket."

William led the way to the swollen creek.

Rose and the others scrambled down the hill behind him. Her feet slipped on the mud and rocks. She should have worn better boots.

Patrick put out a hand. "Let me help."

His touch caused a shiver, but not from the cold. As he steadied her, his warmth engulfed her. His gaze met hers, showing his desire. Not like a brother. Like a beau.

Rose took a deep breath and pulled her gaze from him. She carefully placed one foot on a mud-covered boulder, but lost her balance.

Patrick's grip tightened. "Are you sure you are all right?"

Rose swallowed. "Yes." She had weathered the storm unscathed. But unfamiliar sensations filled her heart. She cared for Patrick more than she had realized.

Rose's oldest brother, Matthew, lifted Laura when they arrived at the swollen creek. The water had receded some but would cover most of the woman's skirt.

Laura wrapped her arms around Matthew's neck. "Like a play. The handsome prince carries a damsel across the water."

He cringed. "I don't think my wife would appreciate that comparison."

Of course Laura would choose to flirt with Rose's married brother.

"Ahh. Like acting in a play." She flashed a practiced smile. "I appreciate the lift."

He carried her across without holding the rope. But he walked near enough to grab it if necessary.

Next, Timothy carried Anna across. Then William assisted Grace.

David stepped to Rose and put out his arms. "You're next."

Patrick moved between Rose and her brother. "I'll take her."

With a shrug, David retreated.

Patrick lifted her with ease, placing one arm under her legs and the other behind her back.

She hooked her arms around his neck.

His body warmed her.

"Like a prince in a play?" Her soft voice reached his ears only.

"I'm not performing." He put one foot into the water. "I'll speak to your father about courting you."

"I'd like that." Rose leaned her head into his chest as he carried her to dry ground. She could get used to this.

David followed behind. He coiled the rope and looped it on his shoulder. "Everyone ready?"

The chorus girls nodded.

Mud and pools of water filled the path. Rose's brothers aided Laura, Grace, and Anna.

Rose followed with Patrick at a distance that allowed them privacy. She held onto his hand as she traversed the muddy trail. She would have held it even if she didn't need his help. Would he have tried to kiss her if her brothers hadn't been around?

"Why hasn't someone already laid claim to a handsome prince like you?" The way the chorus girls cooed after him, at least one woman must have caught his eye before now.

Patrick stiffened. "I was engaged to a rising soprano. We planned to sing in productions together as a couple."

"So the rumor is true. You used to sing opera." When Rose turned her attention to him, a wet pine branch slapped her in the face, startling her and stinging her cheek.

Patrick lifted the branch. "Careful."

"What happened to your soprano?"

"She landed a principal role in a traveling production and I didn't." He spoke without emotion, as if talking about someone else. "After a year on the road, she told me she had met someone else."

"Oh." Rose froze for a moment before she remembered to move her feet. She stepped over an intermittent stream. She intended to join a traveling production. . .like his ex-fiancée. Would she break his heart too?

"It's for the best." Patrick's grip tightened as he helped her over a slippery rock.

"Could you have gone with her if you wanted to?" Would he go with Rose if she joined a touring company? She didn't want to leave him, but she wouldn't give up a chance if it presented itself.

Patrick took a deep breath. "I suppose I could have joined the chorus, but she wouldn't have respected me for it. And I wouldn't have respected myself."

Would the same thing happen with Rose? "Did you ever get a principal role?"

"No." His sharp tone discouraged further questions.

Rose eyed Patrick as he led her in silence. He intended to court her. He had said as much, and she had agreed. The man had come to her rescue and protected her. He wasn't intimidated by her brothers. In fact, he seemed to want to be part of her big, noisy family.

If she cared about him at all, she wouldn't encourage him. When she joined an opera company, his heart would be broken. . .again.

She and Patrick followed her brothers and the girls to the front of the opera house. Before catching up with everyone, she stopped Patrick. "No need to speak to my father. I can't let you court me."

"But—what—why?" He reached toward her elbow, confusion etched in his face.

She stepped out of reach. "You know why." Her eyes stung. She pressed her hands against the folds of her dress to hide the shaking. He attracted her like no man had before, but she wouldn't give up her dream. Not even for Patrick.

She joined her brothers, who surrounded her, forming a safe cocoon.

She wouldn't lead him on. She was doing the right thing.

Then why did it hurt so much?

Patrick studied the torn curtain from backstage. He should have known better than to construct sets near the red velvet fabric. One week until the opera house's grand opening, and there were several large tears cut through the curtain.

Rose would be able to fix it, but he hadn't seen her since the day of the storm. She had opened his heart to new possibilities and rejected him within a matter of hours.

He missed their verbal sparring, her spunk. The woman had worked her way into his heart. He had watched the street in front of her shop and listened for her voice near the dressing rooms. How could someone who had made herself such a fixture disappear completely?

When he saw the ripped curtain, he went to the seamstress shop in hopes of seeing her. Instead, Sarah promised to come over to help him.

Patrick wasn't sure how he'd offended Rose. He had asked William, who was working on another article about the opera. The man had only mumbled something about women being a mystery.

At the sound of the front door, Patrick hopped from the stage and headed toward the lobby. He hoped Sarah could figure out how to make a repair sturdy enough to hold up through the opera.

Rose entered the performance hall. The sun streamed in the window from behind, giving her an angelic look, like in his daydreams. Sewing basket on her arm, she strode toward the stage.

Patrick caught his breath. He had missed her. "Rose? I was expecting your sister." He closed the distance, meeting her halfway down the aisle. He wanted to take her in his arms but didn't dare.

She stopped and flashed him a wry smile. Her eyes didn't sparkle, and her tone remained subdued. "She decided I needed to talk with you."

Patrick led Rose to the stage and showed her the tattered curtain. He would thank Sarah later.

Rose's eyes widened. "How did you do this?" She fingered the curtain. A dozen rips ran halfway up the middle.

"I'm not quite sure. I was building some trees for the set." He pointed to a trio of wooden and fabric trees in the corner of the stage. "And before I could catch them some of the branches fell against the curtain."

She smiled and shook her head. His Rose had returned, the one who had won his heart. "Why didn't you raise the curtain before you started?"

"I thought I was far enough away." He glanced at the damage.

She ran her fingers along the red velvet. "Are you sure you didn't do this on purpose to lure me over?"

He hadn't, but it would have been a good idea. "It worked, didn't it?" He flashed her a grin.

Rose put a hand on her hip, and her eyes sparkled. "You're incorrigible." She set her basket on the stage and knelt to pull something out.

Patrick brought a chair from the edge of the stage and placed it near her. "Do you have thread strong enough for this? It needs to hold up through the whole performance."

"I brought tapestry thread." Rose stood up then sat on the chair and pushed the end of the thread through a thick needle. She tied a knot at the end.

Patrick moved in to see her work, breathing in the floral scent of her hair. "I didn't appreciate the extent of your resourcefulness until I saw the shelter you built. You amaze me."

"Would you hold these pieces together?" Rose retrieved a pin cushion from the basket.

Patrick held the fabric. When her fingers brushed past his, an electricity passed between them. "Why did you ask me not to talk to your father?"

She poked her needle through the fabric. "You know why."

He let out a breath. What did she think he knew? "No. I don't."

She made quick, tiny stitches, working her way up from the bottom of the curtain. "I plan to join the opera company and leave, like. . .you know."

So naive and innocent. "That isn't going to happen."

She looked up but continued to sew. "Just because you don't want me to have an audition doesn't mean I won't."

He continued to hold the fabric even though she had pinned it. "You don't understand anything about the professional opera business. People train for years. They build all the right relationships. Finally, someone invites you to an audition, only to reject you."

"Is that what happened to you?" She stopped moving the needle and put a hand on his.

He didn't want her pity. But she deserved the truth. "I received a small role with a company. My parents and friends attended opening night. Best night of my life. Performing thrilled me. I loved the music."

Her hands returned to her task. "Afterward, my father met me backstage. Instead of congratulations, he detailed everything that was wrong with my singing. He berated me in front of the entire cast. I never performed again."

She glanced at him. "He had no right to do that. You can't let one man destroy your dreams." She tied off the end of the thread and clipped it with scissors.

He shrugged. "I'm the opera house manager now. It doesn't matter." Even as he said the words, he didn't believe them.

"I'm sorry you gave up your dream, but I won't give up mine." Rose rethreaded the needle and tied a knot. "I've been practicing and building relationships too. I will get my audition, and I will perform. If not with this opera company, then with the next one, or the next."

Patrick's jaw dropped. "You think you're the exception?"

"Yes." She resumed stitching the curtain. "I don't want to hurt you by leaving. So it's best we don't get too close."

She worked in silence as she moved from one rip to the next. The audience wouldn't even be able to see the seams.

As Patrick held the fabric, he relived the moments backstage with his father. He would do anything to protect Rose from that kind of pain.

After a while, she began to sing. Softly. As if she wasn't even aware that she was singing. "Holy, holy, holy. Lord, God Almighty."

The peaceful melody soothed his soul, reminding him that God had a plan.

Patrick sang with her, picking up the tenor part. The words and melody weaved their souls together. He could spend his life making music with this woman.

If he could convince her to let him in.

Chapter 12

After repairing the curtain, Rose slipped backstage toward the dressing rooms. She wanted to speak with Anna about a western-style dress the woman had consigned for her niece. Rose's footsteps echoed in the quiet hall. She knocked on the chorus dressing room door, but no one answered.

She headed toward the side exit. No need to cross the stage and pass Patrick. The man infuriated her. What gave him the right to crush her dreams? If the opera company didn't take her, she could move back East to attend a music school. But what resources did she have to make that kind of a move? Her family would never support her.

"Must be my lucky day. Alone with a beautiful woman." George swaggered out of his dressing room at the other end of the hall, looking as handsome in the dim light as he did on stage. "I don't believe we've ever been formally introduced."

Rose turned her head to see who the tenor had spoken to. No one. He must be speaking to her.

He strode toward her, and when he stood only a few feet away, he gave a little bow. "George Williams, at your service. I'm the star of this little production."

Rose moved aside so he could pass. "I know. I've seen you practice."

"Of course." Instead of passing, he stepped closer, near enough that the musky scent of his cologne assaulted her. "What do you think of the production?"

"I love it. Especially the duet that you and Marian sing near the end." Rose took a step back and bumped into the wall. Must he crowd her?

George nodded, obviously comfortable with such praise. "Our voices blend well."

"Someday I would like to sing in an opera. I'd love to audition for your company, but no one seems interested." She had sung for Patrick in this very hall. Little good it did her.

"Is that so? Could you sing for me now?" He rested a hand on the wall next to her shoulder.

Finally, someone wanted to hear her sing. "Could you back up a little? I don't want to sing in your face."

He grinned. "Of course, my dear." He leaned back a little, without actually moving his feet.

She would make do. She sang "Amazing Grace," like she had for Patrick and James. George's smile encouraged her.

"Wonderful." He resumed his position with his hand on the wall. "Simply wonderful."

Heat crept into Rose's cheeks. "Do you think so?" Someone had finally heard her.

George nodded. "I know of a place for you in the New Frontier Opera Company. You can join us when we leave Rockledge. It's too late for the show here, but you can be in the next one."

Rose's heart raced. "Really?"

"Absolutely. We need talent like yours." George's smile warmed her.

"But Patrick said all the auditions take place back East." Rose didn't want to ruin her chance. How did George know about an opening when no one else did?

"Normally that's true. However, in our last city, one of the girls took ill and had to stay back. Now we're short-staffed." He lowered the hand near her head so that his forearm bumped her shoulder.

"I can't believe it." Despite his reputation with the ladies, he could get her a part. "What do I need to do? I can't wait to tell my family."

George pressed his lips together for an instant. Then his smile returned. "You can't tell anyone. Not yet anyway."

"But my family—"

"You can wire them from the next town." He placed a hand on her shoulder. "If word gets out that we need someone, James might insist on allowing everyone to audition. Or, he could send for someone back East. But if you're already traveling with us—"

"He can't refuse me." Rose understood his reasoning, but could she leave town without telling her family?

He put a finger under her chin and lifted it until her gaze met his. "What's wrong?"

"It doesn't feel right, leaving without telling anyone." Even though she often felt forgotten, she didn't want to hurt her family.

"They'll have the message within a matter of hours. Before they even realize you're gone." He slid his finger to her neck.

A shiver ran down her spine. His nearness unnerved her. "I'm not sure." She stepped around him to the center of the hallway, breaking contact.

He nodded. "It's up to you. But you won't get a chance like this again."

She needed this opportunity. Her family would understand. After all, they wanted her to be happy. "I'll do it."

"Good girl." He leaned against the wall and crossed his arms. "We leave at three o'clock Sunday. Meet us at the boardinghouse next door."

Rose's hands shook and her heart raced. How would she keep her secret until time to leave? She took a deep breath. "I'll be there. I still can't believe it."

George reached for her hand and gave it a squeeze. "Why don't you meet me Saturday night after the opera? I can help you practice before we leave."

"You would do that for me?" Rose sent a silent prayer of thanks for her good fortune. "Where should I meet you?"

"Come to my dressing room." Still holding her hand, he ran a thumb across her fingers, causing her to shudder. "If the performance hall is empty, we can sing there."

"Perhaps. . .but I'll be with my family. I may not be able to get away." Rose wouldn't spend more time alone with George than she needed to.

How would she keep the secret?

The next day, Patrick hummed the hymn he had sung with Rose as he checked the canvas scenes at the back of the stage. He confirmed that they would glide across the stage for the performance tomorrow. Then he inventoried the props.

James slipped in the back door and stepped onto the stage. "Looks like you have everything in order."

"I didn't expect to see you for a couple more hours." Patrick finished his count of wooden swords for the pirates. "What brings you by?"

"The director's work is never done." The older man straddled a chair, propping his forearms on its back. "I won't agree to direct and perform in the same show again."

Patrick pulled a chair near him and sat. "I've seen the rehearsals. The show is ready. Although I wouldn't want to ride herd over all those egos."

"I ignore most of the backstage drama." James shook his head. "I need a favor. Hear me out before you turn me down."

"Anything." Patrick owed James. The man had been more of a father to him than his own.

"George took ill last night. Something he ate or bad moonshine or something. He won't be able to perform." James held Patrick's gaze. "I want you to take the part."

Patrick's heart raced, and he jerked to his feet, knocking the chair over. "No."

"You need to get back in the saddle." James spoke in calming tones. "I heard you singing when you thought no one was around. You've memorized the entire show."

It was true. He had rehearsed the entire score in the empty opera house. He'd done it for himself, not to perform. He couldn't—wouldn't do it. "You have at least three men prepared to cover George's part if he can't sing. They've worked and waited for this opportunity."

"You're better than them and you know it. The governor will be here, and reporters from Denver. I need you." James stood and moved toward the stage and returned his gaze to Patrick. "I'll smooth it over with the others, let them take the role in the next few towns. George needs to come down a peg."

Patrick paced the stage. "I'm not that good. Not according to everyone I've auditioned with. Not according to my father."

James faced Patrick and crossed his arms. "You're twenty-eight years old. How long are you going to let your father run your life? And you know how political those auditions are. Someone's nephew gets a part, and you take it personally."

Patrick stopped pacing and ran a hand through his hair. "I can't—"

"You need this. Music is in your blood." James waved a hand toward the empty seats. "One show. I know you won't go on the road with us, and I'm not asking you to."

Patrick stared into the performance hall, imagining the room full. He wanted to sing for an audience again, to see their faces filled with joy, awe, and even tears.

James must have seen his expression waver. "You could start a local company, nothing as grand as the New Frontier Opera. Enrich the community with music and keep your seats full."

"Maybe." Patrick had considered local performances but hadn't imagined producing or singing in them himself.

"I heard you and Rose singing together the other day." James grinned. "With a few other people, you would have enough for one of the smaller shows."

"Do you always lurk around the opera house, spying on me?" Patrick tried to sound stern, but he liked the idea. He and Rose singing together in Rockledge.

James shrugged. "Better than sitting at the boardinghouse listening to the performers nurse their hangovers and bicker."

"I hadn't thought of that." Patrick no longer dreamed of joining a traveling group or one of the big opera companies. He once did to please his father. But a local group, singing with Rose. His heart beat faster.

"Back to my problem." James returned to the chair. "Will you take George's role tomorrow?"

"You've convinced me." Goose bumps formed on Patrick's arms. He would sing for an audience tomorrow.

James stood and slapped Patrick's shoulder. "Excellent. We rehearse at one o'clock today. Be warmed up."

Patrick nodded. He could do this.

James climbed down the stairs from the stage and exited through the lobby.

That night, after rehearsal, Patrick made plans for local productions. He couldn't wait to talk to Rose again and share his ideas. She could follow her dreams in Rockledge with him.

If she didn't run off first.

Chapter 13

Flanked by her entire family, Rose entered the opera house the night of the performance. Ladies in fine dresses and gentlemen in suits filled the lobby. She recognized most of them as friends and neighbors, but tonight they represented high
society.

Chandeliers and lanterns flickered overhead while excited chatter filled the space.
Music from stringed instruments filtered from the performance hall as the orchestra
warmed up.

Mama adjusted her shawl and surveyed the room. "Beautiful. Reminds me of Whit-
tington Theater. I'm surprised Rockledge could afford something so grand."

Rose shivered with excitement. Soon, she would be part of this. She wanted to tell
someone about her unbelievable opportunity. Anyone. But she held her tongue.

She shuffled into the hall, surrounded by brothers and sisters. Her family filled an
entire row of red velvet chairs.

William glanced over at the box seats. "I see the governor. I'll find him for an interview after the performance."

Soon people would want to interview Rose.

The house lights dimmed, and with the flick of his baton, the conductor directed
each instrumentalist to play a few notes.

Her younger sister leaned across her toward Mama. "What are they doing?"

Mama kept her gaze on the orchestra pit. "Tuning the instruments." Her face
glowed.

The conductor stopped the musicians, and then they played as one. The curtain rose,
revealing a chorus of pirates in front of a ship.

Rose floated away with the music, wondering what her part would be.

One pirate, a tenor dressed in a puffy-sleeved shirt and loose-fitting pants, moved
to center stage.

Patrick? Rose squinted. Dressed as a pirate?

Not George.

The pirate sang out in rich, clear tones, mesmerizing the audience.

Rose's heart raced. Had he joined the New Frontier Opera Company? Why hadn't
he told her?

Mama leaned toward Rose. "Is that your young man?"

Rose could only nod. Her young man. She liked the sound of that.

Curiosity filled Rose's heart as the pirates sang and danced, led by Patrick. Had he been practicing with the company in secret? And where was George? Did he take another role?

A group of women entered stage right, led by James in a general's costume. Marian sang with the women, but soon took her part as the lead, singing with Patrick.

Rose longed to sing with him. Jealousy pricked her heart. She reminded herself that he played a role. A role that would end when the curtain fell.

At intermission the lights came up and Rose stood, but remained near her seat. "It's beautiful."

Mama stood and put a hand on her back to stretch. "Patrick seemed to enjoy singing with us at Sunday dinner, but I had no idea. He must have studied professionally."

He had spoken of his training and disillusionment. Today he must have answered his true calling.

Rose caught snippets of other conversations about Patrick. No one had suspected his talent.

Mama checked her playbill. "Someone named George Williams is listed as the lead tenor. I wonder what happened."

"He must be sick or something." He wouldn't be looking for Rose after the show.

The hum of the orchestra silenced the chatter, and the house lights dimmed. After everyone had settled, the curtain lifted.

Again, the story and music enraptured Rose. She could live in this world forever.

And she would, with Patrick at her side, when they both joined the New Frontier Opera Company.

On Sunday afternoon, Rose slipped away from her house, carpetbag in hand. Some family and friends still lingered in the yard after dinner, but no one noticed her leave. One advantage to being invisible.

She couldn't wait to join Patrick and the company on the stagecoach as they traveled to the next town. She hadn't seen him since his performance. Afterward, a crowd had surrounded him, and her family had whisked her away.

Guilt niggled her as she stole through the side streets toward the boardinghouse. She would wire her family from the next town. They might not even notice her absence before then.

"Hello, Rose." One of the women who frequented the dress shop called from a porch. "Are you going on a trip?"

Rose glanced at the carpetbag and then back at the woman. "Carrying some dresses to the shop." Now she could add lying to her list of sins, but the woman likely didn't care. Her lie hadn't hurt anyone. God would forgive her. Right?

"I'll have to stop in tomorrow to order a new dress. I like to keep up with the latest fashions." The woman waved her on. "See you then."

Rose swallowed hard. "Yes. Tomorrow." She returned the wave and hurried on. If she encountered too many people she might lose her nerve. Patrick's presence would strengthen her.

She tried not to picture the expression on Mama's face when she received the telegram. Mama, of all people, should understand.

Rose rounded the corner to the boardinghouse. The porch stood quiet. No one in sight.

No performers.

No bags.

No stagecoach.

No Patrick.

Her heart raced.

She stepped into the boardinghouse parlor. Again, quiet.

The proprietress, a short, round woman with a kind face, greeted her. "Can I help you?"

Rose's voice came out as a squeak. "Where is the New Frontier Opera Company?"

"Left on the stagecoach a couple of hours ago." The woman wiped a table with a rag.

"A couple hours ago?" Rose's hands shook as she tried to understand. "But it is only two thirty."

"They left at noon." The woman straightened a chair.

"But they were scheduled to leave at three o'clock." Had George forgotten to tell her about the change of plans?

The proprietress cleaned as if she didn't care that Rose's dreams had crashed at her feet. "No, dear, they arranged for a noon stage several weeks ago."

"Several weeks ago?" Had George mistaken the time when he talked to Rose?

"You look pale. Come sit down." The woman patted the back of the gold-colored settee.

Rose shook her head. "No. Thank you." She stumbled to the door.

She sucked in big gulps of air, but it did nothing to soothe her. George and the New Frontier Opera Company had left without her.

Forgotten again.

She should pray, but God didn't care. Otherwise, He wouldn't have allowed this.

Her carpetbag slipped from her hand and landed with a thud.

No one cared.

She dropped to sit against the front of the boardinghouse. Pulling her knees to her chest, she wrapped her arms around them. If she curled into a small enough ball, would she disappear?

How could she be so stupid?

Patrick had warned her.

Patrick.

He was gone. He had joined the opera company and left. After warning her of the dangers and the difficulty in earning a part, he had done exactly what she wanted to do. Had he known even as he told her to give up?

Too numb to cry, she sat until her arms ached and her back tingled against the boardinghouse wall. No one cared about her.

A little sparrow landed on the porch railing. Its clear melody soothed Rose. One of the reasons she loved music.

"You're lucky you don't have to struggle and audition." Wasn't there a verse in the Bible about sparrows not being forgotten? "But God, what about me? What about my dreams?"

The little bird took flight as if startled by the sound of her voice.

Mama often said, "When God doesn't seem to answer prayers, He has something better in mind."

Would God give her something better than singing in an opera? Rose couldn't imagine anything else. Singing had been her dream for so long.

If she stayed in Rockledge, would Patrick court her?

No.

He had gone on the noon stage.

Chapter 14

Sunday afternoon Patrick leaned back in his office chair and stretched his arms over his head. After several hours of entering numbers into the ledger, he had finished the loathsome job. The result would please the members of the opera committee.

He let his mind return to the evening of the opera. He had sung in front of an audience for the first time in five years. Afterward several older women had hugged him and cried. His music had reached the depth of their souls.

The governor shook his hand, but what mattered more were the people he had touched with his song. His community. No one judged him on technical points. They didn't seem to notice the notes he'd missed, and he'd missed a few.

Singing at the Rockledge Opera House had freed him to sing again, imperfect or not. He'd found his voice in a Western mining town.

More than anything, he wanted to sing with Rose. He hadn't seen her since the opera. Had she enjoyed the show? Would she want to sing with him?

The lobby door swung open, and a lad called out, "Telegram for Patrick O'Donnell."

Patrick paid the boy and returned to his office, envelope in hand. He had sent word to his family about his principal role and the governor's congratulations. Now Father would respect him.

He studied the envelope. Did he want to hear his father's thoughts?

Better to know.

He ripped the envelope in one swift movement and pulled out the message.

TOO BAD YOUR FIRST PRINCIPAL ROLE WASN'T IN A REAL THEATER. FATHER.

Patrick stomped into the performance hall and tried to view it through his father's eyes. Was there no pleasing the man?

He crumpled the missive and threw it against the door. "This is a real theater."

His father would never affirm him. He let out a long breath.

He didn't need his father's approval. No one else demanded perfection from him. Not even God.

"If God doesn't hold a grudge..." Rose's father had spoken truth.

Over the past several weeks, he had opened his Bible and re-read the stories of all the Bible heroes. A sorry lot, all of them. Not one lived up to the standard that Patrick had set for himself. God cared about them anyway.

His breathing slowed, and peace filled him.

He would send a telegram of his own. He strolled out of his office and down the street. Nearing the boardinghouse, he mentally reworded his telegram. What should he say to the man who would never accept him?

Activity had died down when the New Frontier Opera Company left on the noon stage. Patrick had seen them off. The man who should have sung in George's place refused to shake his hand but stood tall when James gave him the role in the next performance.

On the now quiet porch a flash of green caught his attention. Had someone forgotten a bag? He stepped toward the item.

A person.

Rose.

She sat huddled against the wall like a child, carpetbag near her feet.

"Rose?" He squatted near her.

She lifted her head, blinked, and stared at him with vacant eyes. "You came back?"

He touched her soft cheek. "Back from where? What are you talking about?"

"You left with the New Frontier Opera Company." She touched his hand as if to make sure he wasn't a mirage. "When you sang—I thought—you didn't go with them?"

He covered her hand with his. "No. James convinced me to sing in one show, to remind me that I still love performing...and that I'm good enough." His words sounded foreign. If he repeated them enough, he might believe it.

Rose unrolled from the ball she had folded herself into. She relaxed her arms and sat taller.

"Why are you here with a carpetbag?" Unusual behavior, even for her.

She whispered a reply. "They forgot me."

"Who?"

"The New Frontier Opera Company." She sniffed. "George said they had a part for me and I could join on the tour. I was to leave with them on the three o'clock stage."

Patrick clenched his fists, and heat rose to his face. He wanted to throttle the man. He knew George played the ladies, but he hadn't imagined this level of duplicity. He would wire James and request disciplinary action.

"Like everyone else, they forgot me." Rose shook her head as if trying to clear it.

"They didn't forget you." He tucked a stray curl behind her ear. "George lied. There was never a part."

"Why?" She questioned him with childlike eyes. "Why would he lie?"

"He was trying to seduce you." Patrick stood. He wanted to punch the wall, to punch something. He squatted back to Rose's level. "He didn't..."

"No." She shook her head. "He invited me to his dressing room after the show to practice. But he wasn't in the show, so I assumed he wouldn't be there."

Patrick tried not to imagine her with George. "What did your parents say when you told them you were leaving?"

"I didn't tell them. George said I could send them a telegram after we left." Rose fidgeted with the carpetbag handle. "My family is so large. They wouldn't have noticed one less person."

Should he strangle the woman who would walk away without a word to anyone? Or hug the broken child who didn't think anyone would miss her? "You don't really believe that." He covered her hand, stilling it.

"I guess not. But sometimes I get lost in the crowd. I feel insignificant." She tipped her head to meet his gaze. "I wanted so badly. . ."

He caressed her soft fingers. "I know. And what of the children's choir and the people at church. They would have missed you."

"I suppose." She gave him a weak smile.

He took a deep breath. "And me. I would have missed you."

"But I thought you had gone with them. I thought I'd never see you again." Rose's face softened. She glanced away. "That's when I realized I was more disappointed to lose you than to lose my chance to sing with the company."

Patrick's heart soared. He stood and pulled her to her feet. "I'm not going anywhere." He pulled her close, hugging her to him, feeling her warmth. He didn't care who saw them.

She wrapped her arms around his waist and rested her head on his chest.

Patrick held her close, caressing her back. "James suggested we start our own local musical theater company."

Rose lifted her head. "You and James? Is he still here?"

"You and me. He said we sound good together." Patrick traced the outline of her chin with his finger as her floral scent drew him in.

Rose bit her bottom lip, drawing his attention to her delicate mouth.

"Let's start a theater company." Patrick bent his head to Rose's and his lips neared hers.

"Okay," she whispered.

He pressed his lips against hers. Gently.

She wrapped her arms around his neck, and his pulse quickened.

He pulled back. "I would love to sing with you all the time."

"Me too." She drew his head to hers for another kiss.

The touch of her soft lips, her floral scent, and her fingers as they moved through his hair warmed him. He broke her hold and stepped out of her embrace while he still had some self-control. "We'll have to continue this later."

She straightened her skirt. "I'll hold you to that."

The following summer on a warm August evening, Rose stood backstage, prepared to sing the role of the general's daughter. She peeked from behind the curtain as the audience shuffled into the performance hall. As usual, her family filled an entire row near the front. She straightened the collar of her costume.

Patrick slipped backstage and stood close behind her, his arms about her, his breath warming her ear. "Our third performance. Are you nervous?"

"Never." She stepped from his arms and faced him. His sailor costume accentuated his muscular build.

"I don't believe you." He took her hands in his. "But your hands are steady, unlike our first performance."

"I'm a little anxious." She pulled her hands away. "How long will you remind me of my jitters that first time?"

He flashed a roguish grin. "Only as long as it bothers you. You sang beautifully in both shows, as you will tonight."

The orchestra played the overture, and the house lights dimmed. Patrick brushed her lips with his. "It's time."

When Rose took the stage, she focused on the show. Nothing else mattered. Her lines. Her cues. The music and words. She thrilled each time she hit a note that had confounded her in practice. Everything else fell away.

As she sang her aria, the audience listened, enthralled. A few of the ladies even cried. This Rockledge audience. Her town. Her friends. She belonged here.

When she and Patrick sang the finale, his voice blended with hers, creating something that neither could attempt alone. Breath moved through her, becoming music. Her clear soprano floated up to meet his rich tenor and filled the room.

The song ended, and the audience cheered. A standing ovation. Through the curtain call, each actor bowed in turn, starting with those who had smaller roles. After everyone else had taken a bow, Patrick took Rose's hand and ran with her to center stage.

Rose thrilled at the applause of her community. She had sung well, with only a few rough spots. And the people of Rockledge honored her.

As the applause died down, Patrick stepped forward and spoke to the audience. "Before you go, I would like to share one more thing with you."

The room quieted, and the people sat back down.

Patrick stood close to Rose and held her hand tight. "For the past year, a beautiful Rose has partnered with me in the Rockledge Theater Company."

She squeezed his hand, energy from the performance still pumping through her. She loved running the theater company with Patrick. She loved him.

"Tonight I would like to make that partnership permanent." Patrick reached into his pocket and pulled out a tiny box. He dropped to one knee. "Rose, will you marry me?"

Her heart raced, and her face heated. If she never sang again, she would be happy to spend a lifetime with this man. She didn't need everyone to notice her. One man would be enough.

Silence filled the performance hall as everyone waited for her answer.

"Yes, Patrick, I'll marry you."

The audience cheered.

Her gaze locked onto his and the audience didn't matter. She would spend the rest of her life making music with Patrick.

He opened the box and removed a ring. Delicate gold petals shaped like a rose surrounded a ruby. "It isn't the traditional engagement ring, but it reminded me of you."

"It's beautiful."

Patrick slipped it on her finger. He stood and wrapped an arm around her waist. Then he gave an exaggerated wave to the audience. "Looks like our next production will be a wedding."

A wedding.

Rose had never pictured her future in Rockledge. But God had something else in mind. Her life with Patrick would be bigger than she'd ever dreamed.

Suzanne Norquist serves as the treasurer to her local ACFW chapter and co-leads the chapter's critique group. She completed the Christian Writers' Guild's Apprentice Class and has attended and helped organize numerous writers' conferences. She holds a doctorate in economics and a bachelor's degree in chemistry. As a result, she has worked at many jobs that sound interesting. Her work frequently involves technical writing, where the attorneys insist on two spaces after every period. Her husband and adult children make sure she doesn't take herself too seriously. In her free time (what little there is), she participates in kickboxing fitness and mountain climbing in Colorado.

The Beauty of Tansy

by Donita Kathleen Paul

Chapter 1

Pierre, South Dakota
1910

Tansy, I've sold the farm."

The paring knife slipped over the potato and nicked Tansy's thumb. Aunt Ophelia's words cut deeper than the blade. Tansy spun away from the rough wood counter to witness her aunt take one more step into the farm kitchen. The tiny woman bounced as she came to a stop, as if halting her progress took unexpected effort.

Aunt Ophelia's personality—enthusiastic, energetic, and sometimes impulsive—shone even in this time of grief. But the stiff smile didn't quite match the cheer in her voice.

"Everything." Aunty O let out a gusty sigh and clasped her hands together. "The land, the buildings, the stock, the feed, everything."

Tansy dropped the potato and knife and popped the wounded finger into her mouth.

Her aunt crossed the room, pulled Tansy's hand down to examine the cut, tutted like an old hen, and wrapped the barely bleeding nick with her handkerchief.

The forced vivacity had fled her expression, and her voice trembled. "I expected you to say something."

Tansy wrapped the little woman in a warm embrace. "Everyone told you to wait six months before making any big decisions. It's only been six days since Uncle Wayne passed."

Her aunt hiccupped on a sob but managed to speak. "I know, dear, but your uncle and I talked about what I should do if he didn't get better. This is what he wanted." She leaned against Tansy and encircled her waist with her arms. "I know he told you to take care of me, but that's not necessary." She gasped in an effort to stay any more tears.

Tansy hurt for her aunt. Hurt for herself, too. Uncle Wayne had been their strength. His strength had been the Lord. They were going to have to be strong without his guidance and his firm belief that God always loved His children.

Aunty O shuddered in her arms. "You're eighteen, old enough to go out on your own. You can follow whatever dream you have. You aren't bound to me in any way."

Tansy swallowed her own tears. Could Aunty O be hinting that she didn't feel able to keep her niece without her husband.

She needed to be strong for this frail, loving woman. Sure, she'd promised Uncle Wayne, but a stronger tie kept her by her aunt's side. The couple had rescued her from the family who'd taken her in after her parents' death. This family had no kindness in their hearts. Their interest was in raising another hand to work the farm.

When Aunty O learned of her younger sister's passing, Uncle Wayne searched until he found Tansy. He brought her to Ophelia and a true home filled with love, laughter, and respect.

For Tansy, their hearts had offered a true refuge, but even as young as she was, she could see having an active youngster in the house put a strain on the older couple. Tansy knew she'd been a burden, even as they called her a blessing. She owed them both. But if Aunty O felt overwhelmed, maybe the time had come to move on.

She loosened her hold. "You don't want me?"

"No! No, that's not what I meant." Aunty O gave her one more tight squeeze before letting go. "I'm parched, Tansy. I talked all morning long. My feet hurt as well. I walked all over Pierre."

"Water or coffee?" Tansy picked up the potato and knife before moving toward the pump, anticipating her aunt's preference.

"Water, please, and a biscuit and jam from this morning's breakfast." She hung her shawl on a peg near the door. After pulling out a long pin, she hung up her hat as well. Then she settled at the kitchen table. A sleek, multicolored cat sauntered into the room and, by way of greeting, circled Tansy's hem with a rub. The calico crossed to the table as the girl delivered a tall glass of water, then launched herself onto Aunty O's lap.

"Now," said her aunt, sipping from the glass in one hand and stroking the pet with the other. "Let's get this straight—"

All movement ceased as the two women locked eyes. The phrase was a standard in Uncle Wayne's conversation. He often started whatever he wanted to say with "Let's get this straight."

Aunty O took a large drink and set the glass on the table. Her voice wobbled. "Oh dear, it almost feels like he's still here."

Tansy quickly stepped to her side and put an arm around her shoulders. "I expect him to come through the door and ask what *that* cat is doing in here. And then chuckle." A family joke—Uncle Wayne usually let the cat in and was always asking what *that* cat had gotten into now.

Aunty O inhaled deeply, then exhaled until nothing could possibly be left in her lungs.

"Well, my point is that you don't have to follow me." Another sigh. "Wayne wanted us to have each other, but it's not written in stone that you must be my sidekick."

The cat butted her head against Aunty O's arm. She responded by stroking her head. "I didn't sell you, C-a-t. You can come with us."

The cat purred, but Tansy felt no comfort in her aunt's words. Their uncertain future loomed over all her thoughts. She sat with a thump in another of the wooden chairs around the table. "Where?"

Her aunt focused her attention on the cat, but answered, "Pierre, of course."

"We're going to live in the city? We don't know how to live in the city."

Aunty O patted Tansy's hand. Rather her fist. She'd clenched the fingers around a small silver medallion hanging from a chain around her neck.

"Now you let go of that piece of jewelry. I've tried to break you of that habit. You must not cling to the past. Cling to the Lord and His Word."

Tansy applied more pressure to the one possession she had from her mother. She forced quiet, calm words from her constricted throat. "How will we live?"

"The same as everybody else, Tansy." Aunty O took a sip from her glass. "Lots of people live in the city. It's a much easier way to live. No eggs to gather. No cows to milk. No butter to churn. No garden to weed. We'll practically be living at ease. When we want eggs, butter, tomatoes, or squash, we'll go to the grocers."

Tansy shook her head. "Aunty O, how will we pay for those things?"

Her aunt pulled Tansy's hand away from the charm and held the cold fist between both of her hands. She rubbed warmth into Tansy's fingers. "That's the best part, girl. I bought a store."

Tansy's voice squeaked. "A store?"

"A storefront. On Elmwood."

A gasp escaped between Tansy's lips. "Elmwood? The part that burned to the ground last winter?"

"Not totally burnt to the ground."

"Gutted."

Aunty O managed a tight smile as she shook her head.

Tansy continued. "Roofs gone. Rain-soaked, charred floors. Broken glass. Those stores aren't fit for the wild animals—rats, raccoons, possums, even snakes—that have probably taken up residence. Aunty O, what are you thinking?"

"I'm thinking hopeful, young lady. And you're to think hopeful, too. We're opening Tansy's Candles, Candy, and Canned Goods."

With chest constricted, mouth gone dry, and tears threatening, Tansy objected. "Why my name?"

"Because the store will belong to you. Wayne wanted you to be set up secure-like in something you are capable of doing."

"But—"

"But nothing, Tansy. You couldn't do all the work needed on this farm. Not even with me helping the little bit I can at my age. We couldn't do it together. Wayne knows best, young lady. We'll do as he counseled."

"But not Tansy, Aunty O. Tansy is a horrible weed. Bitter tasting, used to kill gut parasites, rubbed on raw meat to keep the flies away."

"Don't forget packed in caskets to keep the worms at bay." Her aunt nodded in satisfaction when she saw she'd successfully silenced her niece. Tansy fumed but didn't say another word.

"My sister named you Tansy because of the flower's beauty. At our childhood farm, we always had it planted in the garden with the potatoes and cucumbers. Your great grandmother thought they warded against spirits that caused fevers and sores, but my father said they kept bugs away. We had them on the window sills for flies, in the linen for bedbugs, and in the kitchen for ants. And when Wayne went in the woods to hunt, he stuffed the buds in his pockets and cuffs to keep ticks away."

"Useful." The word Tansy spit out didn't sound like a favorable quality.

"And displaying a delicate beauty." Aunty O relaxed against the back of the chair. Her smile reflected pleasant memories of her sister. "Your mother called the flowers buttons. Yellow buttons, soft and merry. I think she wrote a poem about them. It's a shame none of her treasures came to us when we found you."

Tansy's hand slipped back to the small medallion.

A scraping noise obliterated the peace of the morning. Arthur Blake tilted his head toward the east wall. Someone had definitely taken possession of the storefront next to his. Who?

Amos Downside had been cleaning out the debris and making repairs for two weeks. He must have gotten the burned-out space presentable enough to attract a buyer. That was good. Businesses attracted customers, and all customers liked the convenience of stores lined up for their easy perusal. Only three more storefronts in the row and their block would attract more shoppers.

After the fire, Downside had made it known he wanted to get rid of the property, *all* of the damaged property, as quickly as possible. Instead of selling the block in one piece, he'd had more luck getting rid of one section at a time.

Most of the city of Pierre's new construction was brick. Art had more experience with wood. He'd spent years constructing homes in Nashville, Tennessee. When the pull of the West and a well-placed kick to get moving from his uncle sent him traveling, he'd stopped in Pierre. He'd actually stopped in front of the state capitol.

He found the architecture astonishing. One like it back East would be no sensation, but this neoclassical gem dropped into a prairie city claimed grandeur beyond the surroundings. Perhaps the extensive lawn showcased the structure to advantage. As Art stood admiring the capitol, he decided he'd make Pierre his home.

That was in 1904, and he'd spent several years taking odd jobs building cabinets, staircases, furniture, and sheds until his reputation generated a good income. In the evenings, he applied his skills to a different art form. He made musical instruments— guitars, fiddles, banjos, and cigar-box guitars. Now he had opened his own shop where he made furniture, mostly. He carved in the time to hang a few instruments on the walls.

A crash and a squeal from beyond the wall had him on his feet and running for the back door. He was out behind his place and barging through the opening at his neighbor's while the woman still screeched. He spotted an overturned set of shelves pinning a young woman in tears, sitting on a barrel. Holding an arm tightly against her body, this lady had obviously been the source of the caterwauling a moment before.

Blood streamed between the fingers of the hand clamped on her arm. Art sprang forward and jerked the collapsed shelves off the damsel in distress.

"Let me help you."

She nodded and pulled her hand away from the wound. The five-inch gash showed through the torn fabric of her dress sleeve. Blood oozed but didn't pump out of the gap.

"This is going to need the doctor."

"Uh-huh," she agreed and swayed on her precarious perch.

"Whoa, there." He caught her and scooped her up in his arms. "Lucky you don't weigh more than a minute."

Her pale face, closed eyes, and limp form baffled him for a moment. "What to do first?"

He glanced around the room, looking for some help. A person would be nice. All he saw was a calico cat.

He laid his burden on a long counter. "Now don't you come to and roll around."

Using his knife, he cut off her sleeve. A towel lay across a basket. He grabbed it, folded it and pressed the square against the wound. He snatched the sleeve off her stomach where he'd thrown it down, wrapped it around her arm, and tied it. After wiping the knife on his trouser leg, he shoved it back in its sheath.

"Okay, now we can travel. We'll go the back way. No use exposing you to the gossips in town." He picked her up again, tested the front door and found it locked, then headed out the back. "Just a minute, lady. We've got to make a detour." He hauled her into his shop. With difficulty, he pushed the deadbolt into its backset and turned his out-of-shop sign over. Then he slammed the back door shut using the heel of his boot.

Her prolonged swoon rattled him more than he cared to admit.

The three blocks to the doctor's office didn't even leave him winded, but when he stumbled through the door and found the waiting room lined with patients, his breath totally deserted him. Thank goodness for Emmaline, Doc Ellis' oldest daughter.

"Mr. Blake!" She jumped up from her desk. "This way. I'll get my mother. Dad will be out in a moment."

With force, her little hands guided him into a small room. She no sooner shut the door on them than it opened again and Mrs. Ellis scurried in. "Put her down; put her down. I can't possibly help with her hanging a foot above my head."

Art bent to deposit the young woman on the examining table. "I'm not that tall, Miz Ellis."

The woman bustled around the table and removed the makeshift bandage from the wounded arm. "Yes, you are. You just can't tell from way up there. Who is this?"

"I don't know her name. She was working in the store next to mine. I heard a crash and a scream."

Mrs. Ellis patted away blood with a square of white material. "Jagged tear in her skin. Do you know what made it?"

Art thought for only a second. "Probably a nail from a set of shelves that collapsed on her."

"Oh, that could be bad, real bad. We'll have to be careful of infection."

The girl moaned.

Art backed toward the door. "I'll be going now. You don't need me."

"Afraid of a little blood?"

Art grinned. "No, ma'am. Afraid of a little bit of a gal with honey hair who fits in my arms like a well-made guitar."

"That's almost romantic, Mr. Blake." She flapped her hands toward the door. "Go ahead. Shoo! Truth be told, we really don't need you."

Chapter 2

As soon as she heard the door close, Tansy opened her eyes.

She'd seen Mrs. Ellis at church but had never spoken to the small, round woman. The doctor's wife had a winsome personality and dressed in light, colorful fabrics all summer. Tansy would love to be invited to one of her teas. But she'd noticed that the invitations went to the young married ladies of the town, not single women from the farms.

Mrs. Ellis turned from waving the huge man out of the room. "You're conscious."

Tansy nodded and tried to sit up.

"No, no, no, no." The doctor's wife patted her shoulders, impeding her efforts. "Do you know what happened?"

"Yes. I was moving shelves, and they came apart in my arms."

"Did you hit your head? You were out for a long time."

Tansy grimaced. "No, I wasn't really out for all that time."

Mrs. Ellis' face crinkled with curiosity. "My goodness, sweetie, whatever were you doing?"

"Pretending." The kind woman's confused expression forced Tansy to continue. "I didn't know that man. I woke up, and he was hauling me around from one place to another. It was. . .embarrassing."

Mrs. Ellis chuckled. "That man is Arthur Blake, owner and craftsman of Art's Wood. He's single, though I don't know why. I'd be pleased if our Emmaline attracted his attention. He's been in Pierre for almost a decade. No family. Now, sweetie, what's your name? And who do I call to take care of you?"

"Aunt Ophelia. I'm Tansy Terrell."

Mrs. Ellis rested one soft hand on Tansy's shoulder. "That's all I need, Tansy. Pierre has grown, but it's still a small prairie town at heart. I know about your uncle's death and your aunt's purchase of a storefront. She's very brave."

Tansy's arm ached, reminding her that Aunty O had bravely set her up to handle a lot of unfamiliar work and be bound to a store she didn't want.

"Where is your aunt now?"

"Miss Bea's Boardinghouse."

"I'll send one of my children to get her."

Mrs. Ellis left the room. Tansy berated herself for faking the length of the swoon. Scolding herself out loud made the regrets sound like she really meant them. But she kept her mutterings quiet. She didn't need to embarrass herself more. "You didn't have to be such a ninny. And you didn't have to tell Mrs. Ellis what you'd done. You shouldn't have tried to move that set of shelves on our own. You get stubborn when you get resentful. Aunty O thinks everything she is doing is for my best. I ought to think so, too."

Dr. Ellis came in and introduced himself. He removed the blood-soaked square from her arm. "That's a nasty cut, Tansy."

He must have talked to his wife in the hall. "You're fortunate that you didn't gouge an artery. But we'll have to watch this carefully for infection."

He padded the table under her arm with towels then dribbled a liquid into her wound. She clenched her teeth, hissing as she drew in air. He dabbed the area dry. She thought he was done and gasped in surprise when he doused the wound again.

"Sorry," the doctor said in a robust voice.

Tansy thought he sounded more enthusiastic than sorry.

"One more time."

This time Tansy didn't even flinch. She preferred a warning.

The doctor wiped the moisture from her skin, tossed the cloth aside, then plugged the bottle with a cork. "All the dirt has to be removed. This isn't a dangerous wound unless we let it get infected."

He pottered around the room, poking through the shelves on two walls.

Mrs. Ellis returned. "Charlie's off to fetch the aunt."

Dr. Ellis smiled at his wife. "Set up for stitches, Mae." He peered over the top of his wire-framed glasses at Tansy. "I'll want to examine the gash with a stronger light and my magnifier. We also want the disinfectant to have time to settle in before I apply a soothing salve."

He hurried out, his footsteps indicating he'd entered another room along the hall.

"So busy today." Mrs. Ellis organized needles, thread, a squat blue jar with a tarnished lid, tweezers, and more bandages on a tray. She poured something into a shallow dish and put the needles and tweezers in to soak. She paused to inspect Tansy's cut again then met her eyes with a cheery, unworried smile. "It must be the weather."

"The weather?"

"Yes, first hint of spring and everyone pours outdoors. Working garden plots, repairing little things around the place, stretching and bending and using muscles that haven't been used since first snowfall. A good time for accidents. Animals are frisky, too. Unpredictable." The woman chattered on in a friendly manner, giving her opinion on everything from food for stomach ailments to burnt flour powder for diaper rash.

Her nonspecific prattle eased Tansy's nerves. She could also hear an occasional word or sentence from the waiting room and the low hum of conversation between Dr. Ellis and a patient.

Emmaline escorted Aunt Ophelia in as soon as she arrived. Tansy introduced the two older women then listened to Aunty O's dismay over her injury and Mrs. Ellis's reassurance that everything would be just fine. Tansy's attention wandered until she heard Art Blake's name.

"I haven't met him," declared her aunt, "but I must seek him out and thank him for his quick action."

"Aunty O, let me." The thought of her aunt elaborating on their gratitude and quite possibly inviting the man to share a meal as soon as they found a house horrified Tansy. She knew her aunt could be pushy—in the nicest possible way, of course. Tansy cringed, thinking of all her childhood stories tripping lightly off her aunt's tongue and into Mr. Blake's uninterested ears.

"Oh, no!" Aunty O dithered beside her. "Mrs. Ellis, her color has risen. What's wrong? Is it fever? Palpitations? Are you in much pain, dear? A drink of water, maybe? Should we call the doctor in?"

Mrs. Ellis checked her pulse and held the back of her hand to Tansy's forehead, apparently checking her temperature. Dr. Ellis came in, took one look at his patient, and repeated his wife's observations with the addition of listening to her heart and lungs.

Reaching to the very top shelf, the doctor secured a tall brown bottle. He poured an inch of amber liquid into a glass and offered it to Tansy.

She took the glass and wrinkled her nose at the odor.

"Dr. Ellis!" Aunt Ophelia dropped her helpless demeanor and became a posturing mother cat. "Surely you aren't giving my niece spirits."

"It's just a drop, woman. She needs something to sustain her while we close this cut in her arm. Drink it all at once, Tansy. No, don't sniff. It's easier to swallow if you don't. You can even hold your nose. Just pour it down."

Between the doctor's fingers, the label identified the contents of the bottle, eighty proof whiskey. Curiosity warred with deep dread as she lifted the glass. Her gaze darted between the doctor and her aunt. Her aunt's head jerked back and forth in a tight movement of disapproval. The doctor nodded encouragement.

Tansy did as she was told, pouring it to the back of her throat and gulping it down much as she did the spring tonic her aunt administered once a year.

Every muscle above her chest squeezed in rejection of the drink. Her throat constricted, her teeth clenched, and her eyelids compressed as if to keep her eyeballs from popping from their sockets.

Another wave of heat swept over Tansy's torso, face, and even the back of her neck. She sputtered and blew, choked and gasped. The doctor pounded her back with an open hand. Mrs. Ellis vigorously rubbed her uninjured arm. A spasm gripped her injured arm, and tears flowed down her cheeks. She finally managed a couple of lung-expanding, unaffected breaths.

This whole thing was so embarrassing. She'd frightened Aunty O. She'd been carried through the streets by a giant. She'd choked and nearly hurled that nasty drink all over the doctor.

That man didn't have a sympathetic nerve in his whole body. At least, she hadn't touched it. Her arm throbbed. Couldn't she go back to the boardinghouse and hide for the next decade?

Dr. Ellis looked deep into her eyes then nodded as if satisfied with what he saw.

"Mae, let's take care of this little lady so she can get home to her own bed and rest." He tilted the scotch over her arm, not wasting the precious liquor, but clearly rinsing the wound one last time.

With her good side, Tansy gripped the examining table as the room tilted. She pressed her back against the hard surface in an attempt to keep herself from slipping. A boat. The whole building must be dipping and swaying. She was in a cabin on a ship way out on the sea. Ridiculous. She was in Pierre, South Dakota, in the middle of the prairie. All of this was quite silly.

Tansy had to grin as Aunt Ophelia left her side to stare out the window.

Trembling, Aunt Ophelia held her handkerchief to her lips and took deep breaths. "I'm sorry, Tansy. I never could watch things like that. If any of the animals got hurt, Wayne had to find one of the farm hands or a neighbor to come hold them down."

"I don't need to be held down, Aunty O."

Dr. Ellis stood in the way, preparing his needle and thread. To see her aunt better, Tansy shifted on the examining table.

The doctor nudged her back, away from the edge. "Here now. Don't fall off like one of my drunken patients on Saturday night."

Tansy giggled.

Dr. Ellis scowled. "My wife will hold your hand, Tansy. This is going to hurt a bit."

Her aunt scooted back to her side, squeezed her hand, and bolted for the door. She paused as she pulled it open. "I'll be right outside, Tansy. Perhaps I'll step out on the porch. I feel the need for some fresh air."

Tansy giggled again. "Don't faint out there on your own, Aunty O. Perhaps you should take Emmaline with you."

Dr. Ellis jabbed the thread through the eye of the needle. "Emmaline knows to keep an evaluating surveillance of the waiting room and the porch. She's invaluable as the triage nurse."

He examined the wound. "This looks good." He reached for the jar.

Anticipating his need, Mrs. Ellis screwed off the top and held the medicine up. "This should feel cold, then numb the area."

Tansy didn't recognize the cream. She turned her head away rather than witness what would be coming next. When Dr. and Mrs. Ellis changed places, she glanced back in surprise.

Mrs. Ellis grinned and patted her arm. Her other hand held the needle. "My stitches are so much more sophisticated than Mark's. He stitches up the cowboys and farmhands who don't care how ugly their scars turn out. I take care of the delicate patients such as yourself. You will hardly see the line running down your arm."

"Thank you," Tansy whispered and turned away again.

Mrs. Ellis took her time to close the long gash. Each stitch pricked. The thread pulled steadily through her skin, followed by another jab. Tansy glanced over once to see the fancy needlework Mae Ellis performed. She found watching the needle enter her flesh made her a bit woozy. At times darkness obscured the activity around her. She preferred these moments of reprieve.

Finally, Dr. Ellis applied a salve over the stitches to combat infection.

"I'll call your aunt in now." Mrs. Ellis bustled out of the room, while the doctor wrapped gauze around the wound.

He also gave her instructions as to the care of the injury. "I want you to come in the day after tomorrow. If you see increasing redness, any swelling, or any leaking from the wound, however, you're to come back immediately. Immediately. Understand." He didn't give her a chance to respond but helped her to sit on the edge of the table.

Grateful, Tansy leaned toward him as the room swayed, then stilled.

He held her other arm until she was steady. "Are you feeling faint at all?"

She carefully shook her head. "No, I'm fine."

When Art abruptly left the doctor's home, he immediately tried to get the young woman's image out of his head. First he'd delivered a kitchen table to a family on the west side of town. He'd picked up a special order of teak wood from the railroad station.

And he'd stopped to help Jim Hart move a heavy trunk and several crates from the loading dock of the station warehouse onto Jim's wagon. Jim said the owner of the massive traveling chest had already gone with his wife to their home. A scurrilous grandmother-in-law had come to visit, and Jim seemed reluctant to hurry his business along in order to head home.

"I've got older relatives back East," admitted Art. "I hope they never come to visit. I was raised by uncles and a grandfather. They are a mean bunch, but I have to say they taught me all I know about wood, building, furniture, and string instruments."

"Since she didn't raise me, I don't have much to honor Barbara's grandmother for." Jim sighed and slapped his hat on his head. "But my wife remembers dusting her grandmother's hundreds of knickknacks. Evidently that gave my Barbara great pleasure." Jim laughed. "So, I honor her in deference to my wife and her love of useless figurines. I calculate that for the two months Grandmother's here, I'll get four months' worth of work done. Her voice alone drives me out of the house. Since I don't drink and don't play cards, I end up at the shop, working for all the hours that woman is awake. I can slip home in the afternoon when she takes a nap. I better get going."

"Sounds pretty miserable." Art walked the few feet to where his team and buckboard waited for him.

Jim swung up into his own rig. "It's harder on my wife. She can't get away for even an hour's reprieve."

"What? I thought your wife liked having her grandmother here."

"She does. But two women in one house is always a problem."

"It is?" Arthur had never lived with women. But come to think of it, Tansy and her aunt didn't seem to be adjusting to a household with just two women. Maybe he'd put too much emphasis on the aunt's pushy manner.

Arthur picked up his reins.

"One more thing, Art."

He'd been about to move his horses into action but paused.

"If I get mean and cantankerous in twenty years or so, would you push me over a cliff or something to save my family from the grief of a crabby, tetchy old man?"

Art laughed. "And who's going to perform the same service for my family?"

"We could make a pact to jump off the cliff together. But Art, you don't have to make arrangements for a convenient end to your sorry old self. You don't have any family to torment."

Art urged his horses into motion and raised his voice over the jingle of their harness. "That's right. But no one knows the future. I might get married tomorrow and have a passel of children one right after the other. Fifteen in all. You may mature to be a wise old man with a silver beard and a heart full of kindness."

Both men chuckled and waved as they parted ways. Art couldn't get their light-hearted conversation out of his thoughts. He realized his childhood experiences had not been the same as most people's. Jim griped about housing his wife's relative for several months. A shudder ran through Art at the thought of spotting any of his four living relatives on the streets of Pierre. Three uncles and a grandfather.

Mean. Cruel. Vindictive. Brutal. Vicious. And the worst—unpredictable.

Art shook the feeling of something evil crawling over his skin, took deep breaths of South Dakota's sun-soaked air, and concentrated on the beautiful wood in the back of his wagon. He pictured the wardrobe he would make and designed curlicues, acorns, and leaves to rim the tall piece of furniture. In ten minutes, he drew up behind his shop and unloaded the wood with care. He then headed his horses to the livery on the edge of town, where he boarded the fine animals.

His journey crossed the street where Dr. Ellis had his home and office. Somehow the horses turned the corner. Stopping in front of the two-storied house didn't seem to be so out of the ordinary. The young woman with the honey hair should be ready to go home. Perhaps she'd need a ride.

Moments later, he opened the exam door, his figure filling the frame. The young woman jerked in apparent surprise.

One word hissed through her lips before she tilted toward the floor.

"Shenanigans!"

Chapter 3

Art jumped toward the table and assisted Dr. Ellis in catching the girl. With a high-pitched exclamation, her aunt scurried in like a tiny, determined tornado. She pushed between the men so she could see her niece. Dr. Ellis let go and stepped back, leaving Art alone to hold Tansy, his arm around her back.

"It must have been a stab of pain." Her aunt Ophelia clenched her fists around the small reticule she held. "She hardly ever swears."

"Swears?" Art exchanged glances with the doctor.

"She said *shenanigans*, Mrs. Terrell. At least, that's what I heard." Dr. Ellis guided his patient out of her sitting position until he and Art successfully had her lying again on the exam table. "Mae, hand that bolster to Mr. Blake."

Art took the large, cylinder-shaped pillow. "That's what I heard as well. *Shenanigans.*"

Mrs. Ellis busied herself with restoring order to the tray and shelves.

Ophelia Terrell worried the faded purse she held, her fingers either clutching and releasing the top or pulling on the fringe at the bottom. "But *shenanigans* is her swear word. When she came to us from that awful family, she used many improper words. Wayne and I worked to improve her language and made tremendous progress in that first year. She was eight at the time. But after she abandoned the most common expletives, she came up with *shenanigans*. We tried to convince her that if the word substituted for an unacceptable term, it was as unacceptable as the original."

The woman tsked her disapproval, but a muscle at the corner of her mouth betrayed a lurking smile. She firmed her lips into a straight line. "Stubborn. She wouldn't give up her one-of-a-kind cuss word."

From Tansy's head, the doctor directed her aunt. "Mrs. Terrell, lift her feet so Mr. Blake can slip the bolster under. Scoot it higher to support her knees. I'm not letting Tansy go home until I figure out why she keeps fainting."

"Oh, I know what's behind that." Mrs. Terrell moved to follow the doctor's orders. "She probably didn't drink the water I sent with her. I packed her a basket of snacks. Probably untouched. She gets too focused on what she's doing. And I know she didn't come to the boardinghouse for lunch."

"Ah." Dr. Ellis patted Tansy's shoulder, even though she appeared to be still unconscious. "You're too engrossed in this shop, missy. Perhaps too stubborn to let go of one task to do another. Mae, would you get this young woman a sandwich and lemonade?"

Mrs. Ellis slipped out of the room with her good-natured agreement trailing behind.

"I have other patients to see," said the doctor. "Keep her in this position until my wife brings her some nourishment." The door closed behind the doctor, leaving the room in an awkward silence. Mrs. Terrell stood beside her niece, occasionally letting go of her reticule long enough to pat Tansy's hand.

"Tansy, pass Mr. Blake the sandwiches." Mrs. Ellis nudged her arm and nodded toward the serving plate on the table. Somehow, the doctor's order of lemonade and a sandwich for the patient had turned into a late lunch for the Ellis household, minus the doctor and Emmaline, but including three guests.

Tansy passed the plate but avoided looking directly at Mr. Blake. She heard his pleasant thank you and nodded a stiff response.

"Thank you, Mrs. Ellis." His rumbling voice stirred her attention. The man was hard to ignore. "I've missed having lunch with you."

The doctor's wife smiled with a great deal of warmth. Her effusive response reminded Tansy of a proud mother or aunt. The middle-aged, married mother of seven beamed her pleasure over his acceptance of her invitation. She turned to Aunt Ophelia. "Mr. Blake added two patient rooms at the back of the house and two bedrooms above. We have so much more room now for the children, and occasionally we have patients who need twenty-four-hour observation. We used to pluck the children out of their beds and double them up in another room. The addition took over a month to build, so Mr. Blake ate with us quite often. He also taught the boys, and even Emmaline, how to do some simple carpentry."

The carpenter took two halves of a sandwich and put the platter down on the table. "I miss your chocolate cake, Mrs. Ellis."

"Dessert is berry cobbler today, sir."

"Now that's a more-than-acceptable substitute. I hope you aren't saving that for supper."

"As long as we save some for Doc, we can serve it up now."

Tansy listened to the banter of her aunt, the children, Mrs. Ellis, and her rescuer. Arthur Blake spoke with ease to the doctor's wife and children. His words were more formal to her aunt. And since Tansy couldn't bring herself to join in, he didn't speak at all to her.

"Are you all right?" Aunty O's brow wrinkled as she leaned toward Tansy.

"Yes. . .no. Can we go home?"

Mrs. Ellis sprang to her feet and scurried around the table to examine her young guest. "What is it, dear?"

"I'm feeling a bit sick to my stomach." Tears welled up in her eyes. "I'm very tired."

"Perhaps you should spend the night with us. Charlie, go get your father."

One of the children darted out.

"No, really. I just want to go home." An image of the farmhouse surrounded by a white fence, the barn off to one side, and a plow, a wagon, and a one-row corn binder sitting before the home field momentarily blinded her to the doctor's comfortable kitchen.

Tansy wanted to go back to the farm, not to Bea's Boardinghouse. She clamped down hard on the ache bubbling in her chest. Embarrassment added to the emotional upheaval. Shame for her display of weakness forced her eyes shut. She refused to look at her dear aunt's worried face, the children's avid curiosity, the handsome stranger's bewilderment.

Mrs. Ellis patted her shoulder. "You've had a shock, dear. Your reaction is not unusual. We'll tuck you in bed, and you can sleep until your body tells you it's time to wake up."

"Aunty O?"

"She'll leave now and come back tomorrow to take you home."

Mr. Blake loomed over her and, without any warning, scooped her into his arms. He knew the way to the patient rooms and strode off as if he carried a burden no heavier than a big dog.

Tansy giggled.

"Laughing and crying at the same time." Mr. Blake gave her a little squeeze before hefting her higher in his arms. "You're going to be an interesting neighbor. On the other side of my shop is a Chinese laundry. Lo and Chen are very nice. You'll like them. The next shop over builds and sells bicycles. Two brothers operate that establishment. And the last shop on the corner is not occupied yet. There was talk of a milliner, but the lady went back East."

Tansy forced herself to ask the question on her mind. "Why are you telling me all this?"

"Just talk to be talking."

"I don't think I'll remember any of it. My head is so fuzzy."

"It doesn't matter. I'll tell you again." He took a few steps in silence. They'd gone back through the main part of the house, through a dining room and a sitting room, and had entered a hall that divided the home from the office.

Tansy peered over Mr. Blake's shoulder and saw the parade following. Aunt Ophelia, Mrs. Ellis, three girls of various heights, Charlie, and Dr. Ellis. She almost waved at the man at the end of the line. Instead, she giggled again.

"What's so funny?" Mr. Blake's voice rumbled above her ear.

"I'm not sure. First I felt like a puppy being taken outside for misbehavior. Now I feel like I'm at the head of a parade."

"For a parade, we should have a marching band. We'll have to be more organized next time."

"Heaven forbid there should be a next time."

"Miss Terrell, I am enjoying the commotion you've stirred up in the middle of my boring day."

Exhaustion poured over Tansy. Her heavy head rested on Mr. Blake's shoulder. Her arms and legs felt limp as noodles. A sigh escaped her lungs, and whatever witty response she had briefly considered fluttered away with all conscious thought.

The last thing she heard was Arthur Blake's deep voice. "The first or second room, Mrs. Ellis?"

Chapter 4

N ever sick."

Tansy stirred at the sound of Aunty O's voice. Even through a closed door, her opinion rang loud and clear.

"Not sick one day of her life. And now she has something important to do, something just for herself, her own future, her life! *Now* she swoons and casts up her accounts at the drop of a hat. Why, Doctor, why?"

Tansy heard deep mutterings from Dr. Ellis, her aunt's indignant, "Very well," and the clear shoe tapping of that lady's retreat.

The doorknob turned. Dr. Ellis peeked through the small opening. "Ah, good. You're awake. I have several things to discuss with you, young lady."

He came into the room, shut the door, then pulled a chair close to the head of the bed. Before sitting, he did a brief examination, checking her heart and her lungs, looking in her eyes, and feeling her pulse. This was the second round of this business today. He'd done the same when he changed her bandage first thing that morning. This time, he palpated her stomach and used his stethoscope to listen to her inner workings. That seemed appropriate to Tansy. She had thrown up the oatmeal Emmaline had served her for breakfast.

Now he sat in the chair at ease, as if he were just visiting with a friend. He talked a little about the children being at home for a few days because broken pipes had flooded their school building. He mentioned a couple of landscaping projects he would oversee for his wife that summer.

"I don't really have time to dig flower beds, but the boys are getting old enough to do it. Spring is a busy time. It's a different kind of busy on a farm, isn't it?"

"Yes, it is." Tansy thought of all the hours Uncle Wayne had devoted to newborn animals and seeds going into newly freshened soil. She remembered the joy that wrapped the farmer when he burst out of the house in the morning. A different joy settled in on him during the day. No matter how frustrating the running of the farm became, Uncle Wayne always returned with a mantle of contentment in the evening. If he hadn't gotten everything done, he'd at least accomplished something. He counted each small task as progress. Despair never tackled him and wrestled him to the ground.

Dr. Ellis leaned forward, his elbows resting on his knees. "I've got two theories as to why you're sick, Tansy."

She raised her eyebrows and waited.

"The first I don't believe is really a possibility, but I have to ask certain questions to rule out that theory."

She nodded but didn't feel up to asking her own questions to hurry him along with the diagnosis.

"Tansy, have you been courted by a young man since your uncle died?"

That query did not make one bit of sense. She answered quietly. "No."

"Before?"

She still didn't understand what that had to do with anything. She always kept to herself. Busy on the farm and shy at church. "No."

Dr. Ellis scrunched up his face. To Tansy, he didn't seem to want to pursue this line of interrogation. Oddly, his demeanor just barely hung on to the friendly, fatherly doctor. Did anger lurk under the verbal examination? Tansy had no explanation for this interview.

"Has a man bothered you?"

Well, Arthur Blake bothered her. She couldn't seem to act normally around him. She couldn't talk, breathe, think straight, or even eat. Yesterday at the dinner table, she thought she would choke on every bite. But she couldn't explain how he bothered her. He just did. "No."

He patted her knee through the blanket covering and leaned back. "Good, good. My other theory is more likely to be the cause of your ailments."

"I'm not really sick, am I? It was just the wound, the stitches, the liquor. . . ." She almost added the presence of Arthur Blake and his reappearance just when she thought he'd gone.

"You were strongly affected by your injury, but I think you were already run down. You've had a lot of responsibility thrust on you. Your uncle expected you to take care of your aunt. She's sold your home, moved you into a boardinghouse, and tasked you with turning a shell of a store into a presentable shop with no help as far as I can see."

"Aunty O isn't very strong, and the shop was Uncle Wayne's way of taking care of us."

"But *you* packed up the farmhouse, supervised the moving and storage, dove into cleaning and organizing the shop. During all this, you've not taken proper care of yourself." He stood and tucked his hands in his pockets. "My prescription for you is this: you are to work only eight to ten hours a day *with* breaks. You are to hire someone to do heavy lifting. You are to learn to tell your aunt no or at least 'not yet.'"

Arthur Blake had no idea why he was headed to the doc's house again. He'd picked up a bit of information at the hardware store, and it seemed imperative that Mrs. Terrell and her niece should be informed. But that wasn't enough reason to interrupt his working day.

Through the front window, he saw a few patients in the waiting room. He bypassed the office, followed the wraparound porch to the side, and knocked on the kitchen door.

A small hand shifted the curtain. One of the girls peeked through the window then opened the door.

"Hi, Mr. Blake. Are you going to fix the step on the back stairs? How'd you know the boys' roughhousing broke it this morning? I'm Annabelle."

"How'd you know I didn't know who you are?"

"You always get Merrybelle and me mixed up." She grinned at him, showing off a gap in her front teeth. She turned with a flourish, her skirts twirling. "Ma! Mr. Blake's here to fix the step."

Mae Ellis bustled into the room, untying and removing her work apron as she came. "However did you know? Did one of the boys come tell you?"

Three of the younger girls traipsed around the kitchen, blocking her progress and keeping Arthur at the door. The youngest, Milly Mae, glanced away from the table where she iced cookies. "Want a daisy or a tulip? I think I do daisies better than tulips, but tulips are purple and pink. Daisies are only white with a yellow candy in the middle."

"I'd like a daisy, Milly Mae. I like to suck on the candy after the cookie is gone."

"Me, too." She grabbed a cookie, hopped down from her stool, and carried it to him.

Arthur took a bite, made appreciative grunts, and edged into the room, aiming to reach the lady of the house. He licked the crumbs off his lips. "Are the Terrell ladies still here?"

"They're about to walk out the front door. You can catch them if you hurry."

"Thanks, Mrs. Ellis. Thanks for the cookie, girls. I'll be back with my tools to fix the step." He barreled down the hall, intent on catching the women before they left.

"I have news of a house for sale or rent." The words rushed out as soon as he came up behind them.

Tansy turned with a start. "Mr. Blake! Where did you come from?"

Aunt Ophelia rolled her eyes. "The kitchen, Tansy. He still has a part of a daisy in his hand." She turned to Arthur. "What's this about a house?"

"On Peabody Street."

"I know where that is, but there weren't any houses available over there. I looked."

"The Grants are moving to Colorado to be near their children. They just made the decision. It's a two-bedroom home with very small rooms, but it's comfortable and well built. The exterior trim and porch provides a lot of charm. A few years ago, I put in two closets."

Aunt Ophelia put a hand on Tansy's arm. "Let's get you settled at Miss Bea's, and I'll go look at the house and stop in at the bank."

The need to protect Tansy loosened Art's tongue. "Let me walk you home."

Mrs. Terrell looked at him skeptically, and he thought for a moment that she was going to decline his offer. In spite of his being helpful after Tansy's accident and delivering good news about a house, he had the impression that she didn't approve of his being there.

Protective of Tansy? Probably. But the young lady was old enough to fly from the nest.

Arthur reined in his own dislike. Old people were hard to please. Either they wanted you to slave away at the things important to their comfort, or they wanted you out from underfoot, clearly sending a message. Often the lecture implied you were lazy, disrespectful, a burden, and a pain in the most tender part of their anatomy. His uncles and grandpa had been particularly good at demeaning him while getting every ounce of energy out of his body to their advantage.

Normally he stayed clear of developing a relationship with anyone over a certain age. "A mile and a half past gracious" was his term for the elderly. He realized he was guilty of being ornery, contrary, and stubborn. But when he shook the dust of his relatives from his boots and walked away, he decided to be just as stubborn about developing the exact opposite attributes of his role models. He did pretty well unless he had to deal with an old coot for more than a day or two. By God's mercy, he worked mostly for himself and by himself.

He presented an arm to Mrs. Terrell as manners dictated. Then with a smile, he offered Tansy the other. She smiled back at him, and he knew why he'd interrupted his workday to deliver information to the ladies.

His heart warmed. Perhaps he had finally found a gal who captured his interest. The frown on her aunt's face dampened his fire, then reignited the blaze. Tansy Terrell might just be a damsel in distress, in need of a knight in shining armor to rescue her from a life of servitude.

Chapter 5

Aunt Ophelia burst through the door of their shared room at the boardinghouse. "I bought the house, Tansy. We can move in at the end of the week. The Grants are leaving a few bits and pieces of their furniture. You'll have to figure out what we can use of theirs and what we should get of ours in storage."

Tansy sat up in bed. "How long have I been asleep?"

"It's almost five o'clock."

Tansy gasped. "It's only been a couple of hours since Mr. Blake told us about the house. How did you manage so quickly?" She pushed the covers aside, thinking there was too much to do to be lying about.

"No, no, no." Aunty O pulled off her gloves and worked to loosen the hatpin securing the cute little straw bucket. "You stay in bed for the remainder of today. The doctor said you are to rest. Mrs. Bea is going to bring your dinner up here."

"Aunt Ophelia, we need to talk. You have a new hat, new gloves, and I've seen several new dresses lately. You buy a store and then a house. Where is all the money coming from?"

"Why, from the sale of the farm, of course. Mr. Wright at the bank says we're making wonderful investments. It's much better to own a home than to rent a room. 'Better not to spend money on rent. That's money lost,' he said. 'Better to buy a house.'"

"But Aunty O, shouldn't we keep some money in the bank for later?"

"Later we'll have money from the shop. And I want you to get some new clothes, as well. Shop owners wear a different style of clothing than women from the farms." Aunt Ophelia sat on the edge of her bed and folded her hands in her lap.

She'd always been very ladylike, and Tansy was aware that the ladies in the church held her in high regard, but she *was* a farmer's wife. And Tansy *was* a farmer's daughter, or at least, a farmer's niece. Could Aunty O possibly hold ambitions to rise to the top of high society? Society as it was in Pierre, South Dakota? Being the capitol, people of importance lived, dined, and socialized among the more ordinary citizens.

Her aunt picked up her purse, a new purse, and searched for something inside. "Of course, after our establishment is a success, we'll probably move into a larger home."

What was Tansy supposed to say? *Uncle Wayne, we need you. Aunty O is losing her mind.*

Tansy decided to try to guide her aunt back to some sensible plans. "Aunt Ophelia, have you been talking to your friends about supplying the canned goods?"

Her aunt stopped delving into the handbag. "No, actually. . .no. I haven't gotten to that particular."

"If we're going to call the shop Candy, Candles, and Canned Goods, we need someone to help us fill the shelves."

"Perhaps we could drop the canned goods. Candy and Candles sounds respectable. Canned goods are too closely connected to country living. The city dwellers might turn up their noses at something so commonplace."

"Aunty O, what has happened to you? Just a year ago, you were the queen of the county fair, raking in prizes for your beautiful candles, homemade candy, *and* your canned fruits and vegetables."

"Those prizes should have gone to you, dear. You've done the bulk of the work as I keep getting older and older."

Her expression stilled, and Tansy glimpsed a brief display of despair.

Aunty O stood abruptly. "I think you need some more rest, Tansy. Let's talk about this another time when your head isn't so full of worries."

"I think—"The door closed behind Aunty O. The opportunity to discuss the worries that were gathering in Tansy's head had passed. She flopped back on the pillow and groaned. "Father in heaven, I think I need some help."

Arthur Blake worked late into the night, finishing a chifforobe requested by the mayor's wife. The woman liked fancy, and Arthur had outdone himself. Three drawers ran across the bottom, each one carved with fancy flowers, the knob being at the center of large petals. The doors pulled out and pushed in with ease as if they glided on butter. The door on the left hid shelves. The door on the right hid a space for hanging clothes. Both doors flaunted fielded panels. A mirror stood between the two sides. Split spindles decorated the frame, and gadrooning ornamented both the top and bottom edges.

Arthur applied the last coat of a special oil he used on most of his furniture. He mixed olive oil, vinegar, and lemon oil in just the right proportions. As he rubbed it in, the piece glowed in the shop lights. He'd deliver it in the morning, do some odd jobs in homes that had been waiting for him this week, and then return to the project that was keeping him from making money.

Tansy Terrell. Her aunt was going to kindly and with great enthusiasm wear the girl out and put her in an early grave. She'd had three days to recover from the slash in her arm. Then her aunt got her dressed and out to take a quick peek at the house before the Grants had even finished packing their belongings to ship on the railroad to Longmont, Colorado.

Since aunt and niece accomplished little there, they took a detour to open the storage shed behind a friend's house so Tansy could refresh her mind as to what was available. Satisfied that her niece would sort details and bring things together neatly and in a timely manner, Aunt Ophelia dragged her to the dressmakers. There she purchased three dresses for Tansy, one for church and two to wear as owner of the shop.

Miss Bea had felt moved to intervene and see that the child rested. She told Arthur the poor girl used the handrail to haul herself up the stairs and then fell into bed. The landlady then persuaded the aunt to make an inventory of what she wanted to do instead of ordering the girl back on her feet. Aunt Ophelia's list of things to complete changed with her whims. For the rest of the day, the plump old woman blocked the stairs every time the skinnier old woman wanted to "discuss" things with her niece.

When the two Terrell ladies moved into the Grants' home, Arthur had stepped in to be another buffer between the demanding aunt and the biddable niece.

He carried wooden crates from his wagon to the back door of the house. Aunt Ophelia held the door open and patted his shoulder as he passed. "We're so grateful for your help."

Arthur cringed at the touch. "I'm pleased to be of service."

"When we're settled, you'll have to come back for supper. It will take a few weeks, but we won't forget you just because we don't see you every day."

That wording made it sound like he wasn't welcome during the time in between.

Art put a simple fact forth to test her reaction. "With our shops next to each other, I'm sure we'll visit more often."

"Oh, that wouldn't be a good idea." Aunt Ophelia let the door close and turned, placing her hands on her hips and casting a stern look at Arthur. "You're a businessman and don't have time to socialize during business hours."

Arthur mentally raised his eyebrows and kept his verbal response locked behind closed lips. This *was* business hours. He *wasn't* pursuing business interests at the moment. He'd left his shop and several profitable projects to haul this woman's belongings across town. In truth, he'd done it for Tansy.

In the last week, the romantic notions, the zing in his heart when he saw her, and the constant dwelling of her pert smile in his thoughts had convinced him he'd finally found the woman of his dreams. Literally! Last night in his sleep, she had sashayed into his workshop bringing him a sandwich and pie. She'd sat on his workbench and played one of his box guitars. Her smiles were just for him, and she sang bits and pieces of his favorite songs.

Waking up had doused his heart with reality. She wasn't his. Her aunt disliked him. He had some serious courting to do to win her.

Arthur carried the triple stack of crates into the kitchen where Tansy unpacked dishes. He set his burden on the table then proceeded to open them. The tops were nailed on and the wood splintery. He had protective gloves, but Tansy did not.

"These are the last marked kitchen."

"Thank you." Tansy opened a cabinet with high shelves.

"You shouldn't be stretching that arm. I'll do that." Arthur took the stack of dinner plates and put them on the first shelf. She handed him a pile of smaller plates. "This is a fine conglomeration of patterns."

Tansy laughed. "I like them. But don't let Aunty O hear you say that. She'll be off to buy a matching set. Fine china, no doubt." A heavy sigh escaped Tansy's lips. "Funny thing is a month ago, she would have told you fond stories of where the different designs came from and how they came to be in our kitchen."

She held up a mug with a chip on the rim and the handle missing. "This came to us by twister. Delivered right to our doorstep. It once belonged to Judge Rhyman and sat on his court bench at the county seat. Not our county, mind you, but a county twenty miles away. That happened before I came to live with Uncle Wayne and Aunt Ophelia."

He took the mug and placed it on the shelf. "I've been puzzled by something."

Tansy passed him two more cups. "I'll help if I can."

"Why is your last name the same as your aunt's? I would think your mother would have a married name which would be yours as well."

Arthur caught sight of a flash of a dimple when a smile flickered at the corner of her mouth.

"Franskotunshnieler. It's hard to spell."

"I should think so."

"Uncle Wayne tried twice and started calling me Tansy Terrell."

Arthur laughed out loud. "Is that true?"

"He said it was."

"I think I would have liked your uncle."

"You would have liked Aunty O, too."

Arthur gave her a quizzical look, and their glances caught. She looked so sad.

"Uncle Wayne told me to take care of her, but I don't think he expected this."

"What?"

Tansy sank into the kitchen-table chair. "She misses him. Everything she does makes me think she's trying to erase the life she was accustomed to so she won't be expecting him to be part of the shop and this house and living in Pierre." She turned the mug around in her hands and finally placed it in the cupboard. "Why would she expect Uncle Wayne to be in the middle of this absurdity? He'd be back on the farm, solid, unchanging, and making one day as predictable as the day before. I wouldn't be surprised if all this city life, shop owning, new clothes, and social climbing is just a disguise for how alone she feels."

"She has you."

Tansy looked at him seriously for a moment. He wondered if she was going to say what was on her mind. She surprised him. "But she doesn't have God."

"What makes you think that?"

"I've been praying more and more since Uncle Wayne died. I keep remembering his strength in prayer, his Bible reading, his guiding our talks into having our ideas agree with scripture. Aunty O always agreed, but I can't remember her ever leading. She'd say Uncle Wayne was head of the family, so he was supposed to steer our spiritual thinking. But I think a woman should have her own faith as well as her husband to lean on."

Arthur felt his eyes open wide. "Are you a suffragette?"

"I don't think so. But from what little I've read, I think I could be." She grinned at him, and her eyes twinkled. "If I weren't so busy." Her head tilted to one side. "Yes, I would like to vote."

Chapter 6

Ten days had passed since Tansy had worked in the shop. She turned her key in the lock and paused. As much as she'd prayed over this endeavor, it still draped a heavy shroud of dread across her shoulders. Rationally, she could persuade herself that this was a good future Uncle Wayne had left her. Emotionally, she wanted to be back on the farm, peeling potatoes.

Was she that opposed to change?

No, she was afraid. Fear pounded through her veins at unlikely moments. This morning when Aunty O said she had business to conduct and couldn't join her at the shop, Tansy's pulse had raced and her breathing rushed to outpace the beat of her heart.

This shop and living in the city would be a challenge, but not impossible. Moving to Pierre was not the change that had unbalanced her world. The change in Aunty O claimed that honor. If her aunt had remained steady and sensible, Tansy would feel secure. Tansy feared what tomorrow would bring. She feared the "business" her aunt would "conduct" today.

She leaned her head against the doorframe, her hand still on the key. "Lord, I must rely on You for wisdom. Thank You for sending Arthur. I know I'm supposed to rest in Your hands, and not put my faith in man. But it's nice to have him taking an interest in our well-being. Sometimes he seems to be a man not unlike Uncle Wayne. He follows You. Did You send him?"

Her new friend always talked about his shop, his customers, and his projects. His enthusiasm for his work also reminded her of her uncle. She coveted Art's attitude toward his chosen occupation. She quietly chuckled. After listening to her aunt's grand and vacillating plans, it was nice to engage in conversation that did not include visiting with the governor.

During the time Art had helped at the house, she knew his desire was to be back at the store. Part of that might be laid at Aunty O's feet. She hurried him out the door every chance she had. Why her aunt had decided to be unfriendly to this man who went out of his way to help them, she couldn't fathom.

Tansy pushed open the door. Two steps in, she stopped and looked around, her mouth hanging open. Arthur Blake had been here. Old shelves had been scrubbed of soot and repainted. The unit that had collapsed and injured her arm was either gone or rebuilt and painted. New shelves and a counter had been built. The counter was missing a glass top and front, but sliding wood doors opened and shut across the back. She supposed they had to order the glass. The floors were swept clean, and somehow, the lingering odor of smoke had vanished. How had he done that?

Amos Downside's building stretched the length of the block. The structure was subdivided into eight stores. Each front differed from its neighbors, so the impression was a row of individual shops scrunched together. He had had no luck finding a buyer for the entire assemblage. Somehow, he'd received permission to sell each section. That probably proved how influential the rich man was at city hall.

In Downside's effort to make his property marketable, he'd hired a cleaning crew to scrub the walls, ceilings, and floors of the smoke-damaged rooms. The most severely damaged areas were gutted and rebuilt. Thick walls of brick withstood the blazes. In the storefronts to the east of Art's shop, none of the rafters had collapsed. Arthur had told her the fire itself had not even reached this half of the block. Their damage was all secondary. Mr. Downside had replaced the large broken windows at the front and painted the outside.

Once the shell looked decent, Mr. Downside had left any remaining improvements to the new owners. Aunty O had not seen the unfinished status as an obstacle. Tansy smiled and glanced at the wall that separated her shop from Arthur's. No wonder the man had been fatigued the last few days. He worked his own business, helped her at the house, and secretly refurbished this shop. And he had scolded her!

She was doing too much. Ha!

True, Dr. Ellis had told her to pace herself. One day, she and her aunt had been putting clothes in closets and drawers. Tansy lifted a stack of linens out of a box and stood too quickly. She fainted and hit her head on a table. Aunty O had fussed. Dr. Ellis had lectured. Mae Ellis fed her. And Arthur. . . Art had brought her flowers.

Tansy sighed. She really liked him.

She'd allowed Arthur to do all the heavy stuff. She welcomed him each time he showed up. And she tried to keep her aunt's unreasonable disapproval at an acceptable level of behavior.

With a second glance at the dividing wall, Tansy closed the front door and did a survey of the room to decide what to do first.

A list of items still needing to be purchased? Too upsetting. Just how much money did Aunty O have available? How much had already slipped through her fingers?

She should look for small tables to use for display. Again, spending money that might not be available.

Names of women who would love to sell their canned goods to have some extra cash. That project might even be enjoyable. And if she presented Aunty O with the list, perhaps her aunt would be stirred to actually get commitments from the ladies.

"This is the last of these." Arthur put a wooden box on the table he'd made and centered in Tansy's shop. "You might want to keep some of these crates and the straw to pack customer's purchases."

He removed the bandana tied around his neck and wiped the sweat from his face. Looking around the room, he decided their two days of work—his done in snatched moments from his own jobs—had not moved them much closer to an opening date.

"That's a good idea." Tansy continued to empty the box she already had opened. She placed two lavender-scented, pastel purple candles on a shelf. Two dozen candles of different sizes and shapes only half filled the space. "We're going to need many more candles. Unless we find another box of them in storage, Aunty O is going to have to start making batches like she used to."

Art surveyed the bare shelving. "I suggest you look into buying candlesticks and sconces, candelabras and lanterns, and maybe even candle snuffers. It will help fill the shelves and attract customers."

Tansy appreciated Art's ideas, but sometimes what seemed simple to him just added to her sense of being overwhelmed. "Where do I find merchandise like that?"

"Order them from back East."

"I don't know if Aunty O has money for that kind of investment. And I don't know how to order things from back East. You make it sound easy, but I don't even know where to begin."

"Ask some of the other shop owners in town if they have contacts or catalogues. I have a few, but they are all focused on furniture."

The thought of approaching successful businessmen she didn't know and asking questions that revealed her ignorance made her uncomfortable. These consultations would be ten times worse than instigating a conversation at church.

Arthur should know by now how unfit she was to run a business. She assumed Dr. Ellis understood, as well. Aunty O didn't have a clue. She'd rather the rest of the commercial community remained unaware. She would just need to figure this out on her own. Besides, she was a smart girl. Uncle Wayne always told her so. Now was the time to prove him right. She could figure this out. Couldn't she?

Perhaps it would be better to change the subject with Art. "What do you think of our making candy here in the shop instead of at home?"

Arthur quit prying off the lid of yet another box. "Honestly, I think it's a bad idea."

Tansy was surprised but not offended by his response. Curiosity rose above any other feelings. Arthur explained everything so well and never embarrassed her. "Why?"

"What would you do if you were at a critical point of your candy making that demanded undivided attention, and a customer walked in?"

Tansy pictured the scenario in her mind. Before the calamity she envisioned played out, Arthur intruded on her thoughts. "There's also the possibility of an accident. You or one of your customers could be injured."

How much could Arthur know about kitchen work? A glimmer of indignation rose in her breast. "We've made candy for years. We know what we're doing."

"You're saying *we*, and it will most likely be just you. And in the years you've been making candy, has there ever been an accident, even just a little one?"

Tansy nodded and pulled her hand closer to her waist. "I burned my hand once pulling taffy. And I cut two fingers another time, chopping licorice."

Arthur didn't reply. Instead, he patted the top box in another stack. "Have you decided if you're going to put out your jellies and jams?"

Tansy glanced around the room at all the barren shelves. "I think it's something we're going to have to do. At least the farm wives can help supply the goods. Someone else to depend on other than Aunty O and me. That will be good."

"Tansy, is this a joint effort with your aunt, or are you all on your own?"

Again, she could have resented his tone of voice, but his concern was obviously for her welfare. He'd helped so much. He deserved her honesty. "At first, I thought it was us, but she seems to have lost interest."

"Is opening the store something you want to do?"

"Of course, it is. This is Uncle Wayne's plan to provide for us since the farm was too much for two women. I think he knew Aunty O would be overwhelmed by the volume of work."

"But did he intend the shop to be your project? Are you supposed to be the owner, supplier, shop clerk, and janitor?"

The anger rising in her chest must not be directed at Arthur. If she could deal patiently with her aunt, she could be courteous to her neighbor. "I'm supposed to take care of my aunt." Despite her effort, her words sounded hard and forced.

When he didn't respond, Tansy deliberately focused on her friend's face. She couldn't read his expression. She desperately needed to explain. Art shouldn't have hard feelings toward her uncle and her aunt. "This is the plan Uncle Wayne laid out for us. I don't have an alternative. I know Uncle Wayne wouldn't object if I had something else in mind." She shrugged. "I've thought about it. I've prayed about it. Nothing else has come to light."

Still Art said nothing.

"It really isn't so bad. Once we get the shop started, the details will fall into place." A doubt kept protruding, trying to poke holes in the fabric of her reasoning. "I have always enjoyed working in the kitchen with Aunty O, canning and making candy. I've helped her for years making candles. She's creative and thinks of ways to decorate plain old candles."

She held up a pair of the ornamental tapers. The lights were made of various shades of green wax. "She says with gas lights, and now Mr. Edison's electricity, people don't really need candles. They have gone from necessity to luxury, and they need to look special."

Arthur nodded. "She has a point, and I have to admit, I'm impressed with her craft. But if you're the one who does all the work, this shop will always be undersupplied."

"You manage to do all of your projects."

Art sat on the edge of the counter and ran his fingers through his hair. "I don't work in volume, and I am not trying to deliver three very different products."

Tansy agreed. She nodded. "And you have a head for business."

He stood abruptly. "Don't sell yourself short, Tansy."

She raised one eyebrow, questioning his view of her abilities.

Art walked over to where she stood beside the display. He placed his hands on her shoulders. "You are amazing. You've made numerous decisions with very limited back-ground. All of them have been good."

She started to protest, but he put a finger on her lips.

"You ask intelligent questions, and although you listen to me, I've noticed that you make up your own mind. When you've chosen a different path from the one I thought you'd take, you have sound reasons."

"But—"

He tapped the finger on her mouth. "And you use good judgment in handling your affairs. Your aunt wanted you to keep the storage space in your friends' outbuilding. But you realized the inconvenience to them and decided to utilize the back room here. If we could get your aunt to turn over the purse strings, I have no doubt, you'd handle that responsibility as well."

Tansy's heart warmed at his words, but the feel of his touch soon suppressed the pleasure of his verbal reassurance. She wanted to concentrate on what he said, but the physical effect of his finger on her lips seized her entire being.

He removed his fingertip, and she almost sighed, but his thumb returned to rub gently across her lower lip. She ducked her head, away from the intimate gesture. A quiver of shyness inched her away from the pleasure of having him so near. A button on his shirt caught her attention. A piece had broken off so that it was no longer round. The thread still looped through two holes and kept it from falling off. Someone, a woman, should replace it for him.

Her eyes left the focal spot of a damaged button and moved to meet his gaze. She became suspended in the warmth of his scrutiny. Did he feel the emotion?

"Tansy." Her name came from him on a breath.

His hand moved to the side of her face, cupping her chin, tilting her head so that her lips were ready to meet his.

"So!" Aunt Ophelia's voice rang with fury. "Mr. Blake, you are taking advantage of my niece's inexperience. I suggest you leave."

To Tansy's horror, Art stroked her cheek with his fingertips, turned, and nodded to her aunt. He moved away.

He'll speak. He'll tell her nothing wrong happened. He'll be able to make her see...

He picked up his hat, placed it on his head, and left through the back door.

Somehow it was worse that he chose the back door. He chose not to walk around her aunt standing at the front of the shop. He did not confront her. He'd left Tansy to face Aunty O's wrath alone.

Chapter 7

Arthur strode down Main Street, nodding to the people he knew, but not stopping for conversation. He glanced into the large windows of various shops, but gave none of the merchandise a second thought. His every idea had been captured by one image, the disappointment in Tansy's face, the last expression he'd seen before marching out.

He turned into the little café that served pastries and coffee in between breakfast and lunch, lunch and supper. The bird in the cuckoo clock popped out through his tiny gate once. Art noted the time, a quarter after two. He slid onto a chair at a small table next to the window. He could watch the passersby.

"What can I bring you, Mr. Blake?" The waitress wore a uniform, a dark skirt covered with an apron and a blue calico blouse with loose sleeves and a diminutive round collar.

Arthur had often thought her plump and motherly form and friendly expression were just right for the woman she was. Art knew from encounters at church that she had three children and a husband who worked as hard as she did. He considered the family to be within his small circle of friends.

"Just coffee, Esther."

With the mug, a carafe of coffee for refills, a small silver creamer, and a glass sugar dispenser before him, he could wait out the whole afternoon. He labeled the people he saw along the street as they walked by with places to go and things to do.

Mr. Anderson, a rolltop desk.

Gladys Myers, a side table for her son's bedroom.

Anna Orrison, a kitchen table.

Mr. and Mrs. Ralph Prescott III, dining room table, chairs, and sideboard.

Grant Dunham, bookcases and cabinets for his law office.

He knew all these people and many more, but he had few friends. Pastor Credence, Jim Hart, Greg Davis, and a few other men from church. He poured himself a second cup of coffee and doctored it with cream and sugar. Black coffee reminded him of his childhood home, where sweets and small niceties were frowned upon.

Esther placed a small plate in front of him. A disheveled piece of pie spread over the white dish. "It fell apart when I cut it at lunch. George won't let us serve mangled pie, but I can *give* you the piece rather than throw it away."

"Thanks, Esther." He managed a smile.

"You doing some heavy thinking?"

He nodded. "Had a problem. Handled it wrong. Now I've got a bigger problem."

She looked as if she would have joined him if she had a chance. With a glance from the empty chair at his table to the kitchen door, she sighed and started off. "Call me if your coffee grows cold."

Art's mouth watered. He picked up a fork and enjoyed the distraction of the lumps of apple and crust.

Jim Hart barreled down the sidewalk, passed Art in the window, stopped, and came back. He entered the café and bee-lined to Arthur's table, calling, "Coffee for me, too, Esther."

"I saw the pretty little shop owner in church Sunday." He accepted the coffee from Esther.

"Kids okay?" Art asked.

"Right as rain."

"Good to hear."

Esther walked away.

Jim gathered the sugar and cream closer. "So, Tansy Terrell's shop is right next to yours. That looks like opportunity, my good man."

Art scraped his fork across the remnants of his pie and lifted the last bits of crust and filling to his mouth. He said nothing.

"You *are* interested, aren't you?"

Art nodded.

Jim stirred his coffee, took a sip, then looked Art in the eye. "What? You don't want to talk about your marital status? We've talked about it when there weren't any young ladies to contemplate."

"Miss Terrell comes with a major disadvantage."

Jim twisted in his chair and signaled the waitress. "Esther, I'll have a piece of that pie."

Esther grinned and winked at Art. She'd sold a piece of pie by giving him the free slice.

Jim ate half his dessert before resuming his questioning. "What's the disadvantage?"

"She comes with an old relative. I don't particularly like old relatives. I've told you my uncles and grandfather just got crankier as they grew older." He'd been careful not to elaborate on his childhood. To him it sounded like whining. He'd made it through his past in one piece and created a present life that he enjoyed. As far as he could see, he'd made a future in Pierre, South Dakota, that would never be plagued by ranting old despots and geezers with heavy fists.

With his fork held high for emphasis, Jim changed the subject. "That reminds me. Barbara wants a special case built to display some of her mother's figurines. Part of the weight of the trunk you helped me manhandle was more treasures she's sharing from her collection."

"A curio cabinet?"

"Yes, that's right. Although Barbara's mother had another name for it, too. Something fancier."

"An *étagère*. I'll go by the house and talk to her."

"You amaze me. How do you know the name of a fancy piece of furniture? No one in Pierre could keep up with you. No wonder your business is thriving."

"You'd be surprised what fashions and decorator trends the governor's wife and her associates mine from letters and magazines. If someone buys it in New York City on Monday, our fine ladies have put it on their wish lists by Friday."

Jim looked a bit dazed. "You're exaggerating."

Arthur chuckled. "Yeah, maybe a little. But communication is not as slow as it used to be."

Jim nodded and stirred. "Back to the Terrells. You object to Ophelia Terrell? I knew her husband, Wayne, a hard worker, a kind neighbor. He really knew his Bible. He's going to be missed."

"I've been helping get the shop ready. Tansy is a wonderful young woman." Art struggled with how to word the account of their almost kiss. "Her aunt walked in when we were taking a break from unpacking. We were talking." He concentrated on his empty plate for a moment, sighed, then looked up at his friend. "I was standing very close to her."

For a moment, Art had to fight the urge to wipe a grin off Jim's face. Clenching his fists under the table, he returned to his story. "Mrs. Terrell accused me of taking advantage of Tansy. She ordered me out, and I left."

Jim put his fork down. "You didn't say anything to her?"

Art shook his head.

"You didn't say anything to Tansy?"

He answered under his breath. "No."

"Phew! That was a mistake. What were you thinking?"

"Walk away. The only way to win an argument with my family was to shut up and leave." He pumped the fingers of his clenched fists.

"You should have stayed. Protecting Tansy from the onslaught of her aunt's outrage would have been the noble thing to do. Both ladies would have been impressed."

"Neither of them were impressed. I can say that for sure."

"Well, it looks like a coward's escape rather than a strategic retreat."

"I know that."

"You have to explain."

"I know that."

"Well?"

Arthur brought his hands up from his lap and laid them palms down on either side of his empty cup and dirty plate. Again, he avoided looking Jim in the eye. "I don't know what to say."

Jim put his fork on the empty plate and pushed it away. "I don't think I can help you. I know what I'd say to Barbara if I'd really been a jerk. What Miss Terrell expects to hear—what she *needs* to hear—I have no idea."

Leaning back in the chair, Art let out a huff. "It doesn't matter. This is probably for the best. I can't court a woman who has promised to take care of her elderly aunt. Engaging her interest would be deceitful since I would have no intention of marrying her."

"Remember the list we made of desirable qualities in a bride?"

"Sure, but that was just in fun."

Several people came into the café, and Esther guided them away from where Art and Jim sat.

Nevertheless, Jim lowered his voice. "I remember putting the list together with Pastor Credence and several other men in Bible study."

"We were looking at the last chapter in Proverbs. Proverbs 31:10. 'Who can find a virtuous woman? For her price is far above rubies.'"

"Right, and we all contributed to a list of what we thought the words implied in modern times. I remember some like *thrifty, hard-working, kind, wise*, and lots more."

Arthur took offense at the wagging finger Jim pointed at him. The man was opinionated. Sometimes he liked that about his friend. Right now, he didn't. Jim's reasoning depended on generalities, not the state of affairs crushing Art's relationship with the girl next door. He'd try one more time to explain his reckoning. "I don't know if Tansy possesses even half of that list."

"The point is that nowhere on the list did we put 'no relatives.' Or more precisely, 'no old, cantankerous, hard-to-get-along-with relatives who might disapprove of you.'"

"Somehow, I don't think your interpretation applies to this situation." Art stuck two fingers into his front pocket, fishing for coins to pay for his coffee. The time had come to cut short this useless conversation and get back to work. A dozen projects awaited him.

Jim forcefully tapped his pointer finger on the table. "You just don't want it to. It's easier to shut up and leave."

Art stood. "Maybe so, but I promised myself never to be put in the place where older, useless relatives could make me feel obligated to do their bidding. Not drunken bullies and not seemingly sweet little old ladies."

Jim's words were a blur as Art left the café. He heard *mistake* and *stubborn*. Right now, he didn't want to be rational or patient. He needed to do something physical. Dig a ditch, climb a mountain, wrestle pigs, stomp a pile of snakes into submission. Or maybe go back to Nashville and break noses.

He stomped down the sidewalk, not caring how many astonished faces turned to watch him as he ignored pleasant greetings and friendly smiles. He should have been a blacksmith. He could fire up the forge and beat a glowing rod into the shape of a long blade.

An obstacle on the back step of his shop brought him to an abrupt halt. Of all places for Tansy to be, of all the things she could be doing, she'd planted herself in his way. With a hoop in one hand and a needle in the other, the woman who twisted his emotions combining joy and agony waited for him. Tansy Terrell calmly embroidered flowers on white cloth with sunny yellow thread.

Chapter 8

Tansy saw Arthur out of the corner of her eye. She concentrated on making another yellow petal on the scrap of linen that would be a pocket on her work apron. Her heart had jumped at the sight of him and now raced. Could she sit here calmly and engage in a composed conversation? Her Uncle Wayne's voice had echoed through her mind all afternoon. *"You don't butcher the cow for stepping in the milk bucket."*

Cows shouldn't be blamed for acting like cows. Sometimes people were wrongly accused of misdeeds, when honestly, they were just blundering. She needed to understand first, then forgive.

Uncle Wayne's wise counsel had guided and comforted her through the years. Now his sayings came back to help her deal with life. The cow line had kept her tongue in check while dealing with Aunty O. She had to giggle when she thought of how Uncle Wayne would say his wife was acting like a cow with a hind leg firmly stuck in the milk bucket.

It would seem she might have to rely on the same saying in her dealings with Art. When things were more serious, Uncle Wayne quoted from scripture. Proverbs 16:24 came to mind: "Pleasant words are as an honeycomb, sweet to the soul, and health to the bones." She needed to use healing words. Tansy's problem was discerning how serious the happenings of the day were. Was the scene with Art and Aunty O an inflated fiasco comparable to spilled milk? Or a colossal abyss revealing a fundamental difference in their basic views of life?

Colossal? Abyss? Surely inflated fiasco were better descriptive words.

Unsure of what exactly had occurred, Tansy decided to follow her uncle's example of handling problems rather than join her aunt in tirades and hysterics.

Tansy's head understood the sequence of events, but her heart was muddled over feelings. Arthur conjured up some strange physical reactions, most of them pleasant. . . though confusing. And feelings! Some were totally unfamiliar to her. She wanted to cling to Arthur's chest for security or pound that same chest with frustration.

She'd been sure he was going to kiss her. She was sure she would have liked that kiss.

When he abruptly left, a knife had sliced open her heart, but another of Uncle Wayne's sayings pulled her out of distress. "A wound to the heart responds to the first treatment you give. Bind it with misinformation, and it will never heal."

So here she sat, waiting for Arthur and hoping for an explanation that would be salve to her hurting heart. Another one of those unfamiliar feelings assailed her. Run?

Stand and confront? Melt away into the wooden step and avoid him altogether?

"Hi."

She looked up. He'd taken off his hat.

"May I sit with you?"

She nodded and scooted over.

He sat and rotated the brim of his hat through his fingers. "I'm sorry. I should have stayed and helped you deal with your aunt."

She giggled. That was the last thing she'd expected him to say.

"Are you going to cry and giggle at the same time? Like you did at Dr. Ellis's house?"

She giggled again. "No liquor. And I'm not weak." She darted a glance to his face then refocused on her needle and thread. "But I am nervous."

"Nervous?"

"About talking to you."

"You're brave. I walked away because I wasn't brave enough to face a conflict."

"My aunt has made a habit of overreacting since Uncle Wayne died."

"Did she tear into you?"

Tansy giggled again. She didn't *want* to laugh. This important conversation should be treated seriously. Another giggle bubbled in her throat. She swallowed to keep it down. "No, she tore into you. Your leaving was a good thing. She blustered for a while, but with no one to hurl the words at, she soon lost steam."

Tansy frowned. The next part had not been pleasant. Not that the first rant had been enjoyable. Tansy rested her hands in her lap, giving up on the scattering of yellow blooms. "Then as we walked home, she tore into me. Muttering all the way. I can't imagine what people thought as we passed them in the street. Once safe inside, I gave her a cup of tea and some molasses cookies then urged her to take a nap."

"You are good to your Aunty O, Tansy. I could never be so patient."

"You *are* patient. You've been very patient with me, explaining business things."

"You aren't old!"

Tansy inspected his face. Was he joshing her? "What does that have to do with it?"

He passed his hat through his fingers, rotating it all the way around twice before speaking. "My mother died when I was five. I know nothing of my father—he was never mentioned. My mother's father and brothers took me in. I stayed until I was sixteen and then took off."

His face told her so much more than his words. "They weren't good to you."

Art grunted deep in his throat. To Tansy, the noise sounded like the snort of an angry bull.

"I spent most of the first year cowering under the stairs."

Tansy reached out to take his hand. He let go of the hat and allowed her to weave her fingers through his.

Tansy took comfort in his touch. "Right after my parents died, a family took me in. They were a rough lot and yelled. A few times the mother hit me, but mostly it was just constant nagging and scolding in loud, furious voices. Aunty O and Uncle Wayne saved me from that."

A bitter laugh crossed Art's lips. "My grandfather couldn't catch me, but when my uncles did, my grandfather would use whatever was at hand to 'teach me respect.' He even picked up a crowbar once. I was so scared, I jerked and twisted, and slipped from my uncles' hands like a greased pig. Squealed like one, too."

A genuine smile claimed Art's face, and a soft laugh punctuated his next words. "It backfired on them. All that struggling and running and doing extra chores made me strong as an ox. Then they couldn't get the better of me even when it was three to one. There were three uncles."

She nodded. "Three. And the grandpa."

"Grandfather. Not Grandpa."

"It sounds awful, Art."

"It was, but it's over. And they taught me how to treat other people."

Tansy frowned. His story didn't sound like the source of his kind, mellow spirit.

He leaned back against the doorframe to his workroom. "When deciding how I should react in a situation, I consider what my relatives would have done. . .and then do the opposite."

She laughed and squeezed his hand. "So, you handled Aunty O by leaving."

"With my grandfather and uncles, you could not win a verbal fight. If I stayed, we'd fight physically. I learned to say nothing and get out. Finally, I got out permanently and came to Pierre."

"When did you start going to church?"

"At the harvest festival. There was a potluck and some fiddling music. I'm fond of fiddling music, and I'm very fond of food."

"I saw instruments hanging on the wall in your shop. Do you play those?"

Arthur nodded, pride lighting his eyes. "I play them, but I also make them. Banjos, regular guitars, and those primitive box guitars. Those are fun, and almost anyone can afford to buy one. To give my relatives credit, they did teach me to make the instruments and how to play. But they didn't appreciate when I got better than them and was paid to play at gatherings."

"I'd like to hear you play."

"I'll ask Pastor Credence if I can play along with the hymns on Sunday."

"Art?"

He put his hat on his head and covered both their hands with his. "What, sweet thing?"

"I think I should ask someone to talk to Aunty O. Sometimes I think I should ask Doc Ellis. Other times, I think Pastor Credence would be more help."

Art dropped her hand and stood. "Tansy, your aunt is getting old. In my experience, old people take pleasure in being unreasonable. They don't get better. They get meaner."

Tansy stood and put her hands on her hips, dropping her embroidery in the dirt. "Arthur Blake, my aunt is sweet, kindhearted, loving, compassionate, generous, thoughtful, and understanding. Something is wrong with her. She doesn't act like herself. I should help her."

Art bent to retrieve her hoop. He handed it to her and tilted his upper half in a slight bow. As he turned to leave, she grabbed his arm. "Don't you dare."

Was he really going to stop and talk to her? Nothing good would come of it. He needed to back away from Tansy and her aunt. With his nose firmly plucked from their business, he could apply it to the grindstone of his own business.

That presented a problem. Tansy Terrell stood between him and his work. He shouldn't be walking away from his own back door.

He could lecture himself and promise he'd start acting sensibly, but the memory of her sweet smile chucked all reason from his head. That was the whole crux of the problem, wasn't it? He heaved a mighty sigh, trying to knock the weight of being in love from his shoulders.

He looked down at that small, delicate hand on his sleeve. His gaze shifted to the elegant features of her face. This woman walked in grace and tantalized him with her gentle words. If only she wasn't encumbered with an overbearing aunt.

"Tansy, I agree."

"To what?"

"You said you wanted someone to speak to your aunt."

"Oh!" She shook his arm and let go. "Before your face turned to stone and you turned away from me like you never wanted to speak to me again? I didn't jump back to that point in our conversation, Art. A whole lot happened in between."

"Nothing happened. You dropped your sewing thing. I gave it back. You grabbed my arm. I stopped. That took all of half a minute."

"I'm not going to argue with you about that." She flounced her skirts and sat back down on the step.

He wondered if she would return to whatever it was she was doing with the cloth and thread. She looked adorable in the shade of his back stoop. He stepped out of the sun and returned to his seat. "If we aren't going to argue about that, what are we going to argue about?"

She punched the needle through the cloth, squealed, and stuck her finger in her mouth.

Art tried to keep his lips from betraying the smile that played at the corner of his mouth. "You hurt yourself?"

She nodded, fingertip still hidden behind her teeth. Her eyes twinkled when she looked up at him. Laugh lines deepened, and she began to giggle. He loved the sound. He pulled her finger out of her mouth and kissed the end of it.

"You missed." She pointed to the side of the finger. "This is where the needle stabbed me."

He kissed that spot.

She shook her head. "I'm thinking it might have been over here."

Enjoying the game, he obliged with a kiss to the other side of her finger. His real aim was to capture her lips.

The rattle of harness captured his attention. Moe Mobley led his mule down the alley, pulling a two-wheeled cart full of junk.

"Got some prize pickings for you, Arthur."

Art stood and peered over the scrappy, mismatched boards that made up the side of the wagon. "I'll take the two small doors and that broken chair. How much do you want?"

"I'd have to have sixty cents for all that. Did you see the mirror?"

"The mirror's cracked, Moe."

"Just one crack. You could still see your whole face on either side of it."

"Then I suggest you take it home and hang it where you could use it. Comb your hair. Maybe shave."

"I don't look in any mirrors if I can help it. 'Specially one that's already cracked. I was nigh on seven years old when a mirror shattered just 'cause I gave it a glance."

Arthur laughed as he dug change out of his pocket. "That was probably one of your ornery brothers playing a trick on you."

The men pulled Art's purchases out of the wagon and leaned them against the building.

"How about you, ma'am? Do you need a mirror to use in fixing yourself up beautiful?"

"That's two halves of a mirror that are currently snugged up against each other." Art studied the inside of the wagon. "I don't know that it would stay together if we lifted it."

"It stayed together when I put it in there. It's got a good frame. But I'm afraid if I haul it home, it'll break on the rough road to my cabin. Then I wouldn't have made my money out of my work I did today."

Tansy surprised Art by coming over to the wagon. "How much do you want for it?"

Moe rubbed his beard. "I've been toting it around all day. Protecting it. I guess I'd have to ask a whole dime."

Tansy shot back, "Nickel."

Moe rubbed the back of his neck, disturbing the long growth of shaggy hair. He rubbed his beard again. "Eight cents."

"Six and you have a deal."

He thought about it, eying her as if he could squeeze out another penny. "All right. Six cents."

Tansy started for her own back door. "Bring it in here."

She charged ahead, leaving Art and Moe to carefully lift the damaged mirror out of the cart.

"Isn't that the gal from the Terrell farm?"

"Yes."

"I didn't figure her to be such a mean haggler."

"Just because she's pretty doesn't make her a pushover, Moe."

"Pretty gals shouldn't pinch pennies like that."

As soon as they came in the door, Tansy pointed to a spot in her back room. Once the mirror leaned against the wall, she handed Moe a nickel and a penny.

She also handed him a paper package. "A piece of pie and a sandwich. I didn't remember to eat lunch. Do you mind taking it?"

"Not at all. I'll take it. Enjoy your mirror. Thanks." He held up his dinner. "Thanks again."

Chapter 9

A rt watched Moe leave. Finally. Now he might get that kiss he'd been waiting for. Since the first miss, the one interrupted by Aunty O, his mind had circled around to just what delights awaited him. Of course, the possibility existed that the actual kiss might fall short of expectations. But he didn't think so. Arthur smiled. He anticipated the connection to be more powerful than any other kiss he'd experienced. Not that he'd kissed many young women. But Tansy certainly had his attention unlike any young woman before her.

He watched as Tansy carefully wound a length of wire through the top of the mirror's frame and made a loop. Her fingers moved gracefully. A lock of hair fell forward and covered one eye and her cheek. She tossed her head to get it out of the way. Then she gripped the sides of the mirror.

"Here." Art sprang forward. "Let me do that."

She smiled at him, and jumping Jehosophat, his toes tingled.

"Thank you. There's a nail on this wall. See?" She pointed, and he almost forgot to watch, he was so interested in the way her lips moved when she spoke.

He hung the mirror, confident that the wire frame would keep the two pieces together unless someone jarred it. Tansy's improvised hanger was properly secured, so the mirror shouldn't fall. He stepped back expecting her to be close, close enough to surprise a kiss. She'd moved across the room.

"From here, I hardly notice the crack. I'll just use it to check my hair when I take my hat off, before I start dealing with customers."

She came to peer in the left side of the glass. The crack divided the mirror unevenly, one side wider than the other. She tucked the wayward strand behind her ear.

Art had wanted to be the one to do that. "Tansy."

"Hmm?"

He placed his hands on her shoulders and gently guided her into just the right position in front of him. "We really need to talk."

Merriment lit her face. "Talk?"

He growled, or was it a moan, deep in his throat. He was beyond understanding his own reactions to Tansy. He tilted his head forward.

Heavy fists pounded on wood. Someone assaulted Art's back door. "Arthur Truehouse Blake, are you in there?"

"Truehouse?" Tansy's voice squeaked.

Arthur's hands dropped from her shoulders and made fists at his sides. "Later."

300

He dashed to the door, but paused before exiting.

The man at his back door wore a black suit with the coat cut long. His bronze silk vest contrasted to the white shirt with stand-up collar. A thin tie circled his neck, clearly visible and knotted neatly in the front. A dapper black hat topped his nicely trimmed hair. Without dirt, sweat, grime, ratty clothes, and cussing, Arthur almost didn't recognize his uncle.

"I'm here." Art stepped out of the door and down Tansy's two steps into the alley.

Larry Blake turned, making a show of great delight at encountering his nephew. "My boy!" He rushed to embrace Art's stiff form and pounded his back with enthusiasm. "Father died two years ago, and the three of us came to miss you. We decided to find you and bring you home."

"This is my home." Art tried to keep the horror out of his voice. What did his uncle want? This wasn't a friendly visit. There had never been "friendly" in the relationships with his grandfather and uncles.

Larry clamped him in a side hold as restricting as any fighter's grip and guided him toward his shop. "I'm anxious to see what business you've developed here. This town has been good to you, hasn't it? I always believed in you, boy. Show your old uncle your property." He shoved Art ahead. "Then let's go get a meal. Do you have a place in Pierre that serves a good steak?"

Arthur mounted the step, avoiding the junk he'd purchased from Moe. He unlocked the back door. Before stepping in, he looked to the right. Tansy stood on her top step, watching. Eyes big and mouth hanging open, she obviously found boisterous Uncle Larry a surprise.

Tansy put both fists against her hips. Who had just ambushed Art in the alley? The man had a loud voice, but what he said wasn't unpleasant. His words indicated he was Art's uncle and proud of him, even missed him. From Art's descriptions of his childhood, she'd pictured an entirely different sort of person.

She shook her head and walked back into her shop, closing the door behind her. Life since leaving the farm had become complicated. And confusing. And stressful. She decided now was a good time to visit Pastor Credence.

Through the wood portion of the wall, she could hear Art's visitor's exclamations. She couldn't make out the words, but the man must be impressed with the furniture and instruments displayed in the front portion of the shop. Art had a small showroom in the front and, behind a partition, a large workshop. She and Art had set her space up in an opposite proportion. She had more room than she needed to exhibit her limited merchandise, and a cubbyhole room in the back where she planned to hide. And a large, narrow storage room where nothing was stored.

Checking to see that the front door remained locked, she glanced around the room and saw nothing amiss. Leaving early to give herself a moment with the pastor would not hinder the progress toward opening Tansy's Candy, Candles, and Canned Goods. The main obstacle to success was her own mind-set. Her prayers had not resulted in a shift of attitude. A daily battle against self brought her unwillingly to the shop.

As she walked through the downtown streets, townspeople greeted her. When she'd lived on the farm, her acquaintances in Pierre had been limited to a few folks she knew from church. Now she knew many by name and took pleasure in returning the greetings. She definitely wasn't as shy as she had been. That was a plus she hadn't anticipated. She liked having more assurance.

Art helped her there. He gave her confidence. She believed dealing with Aunty O also gave her a boost in self-esteem. The fact that Tansy hadn't locked her aunt in a closet or torn her own hair from her head said she had more gumption than she had assumed.

At the parsonage, Mrs. Credence invited her in and called her husband from his study.

"Hello, Miss Terrell, let's settle in the parlor. Edna will bring in some tea, and we can talk comfortably once she joins us."

With a gesture to a door off the entryway, Pastor Credence directed her to a cozy room with two small sofas and three stuffed chairs. A coffee table centered the room. Blues, greens, and golds blended to make a comfortable tone in the room. Nervous energy had hurried Tansy's steps. Now the tension eased and left her relaxed and hopeful.

Uncle Wayne had liked Pastor Credence and spoke highly of his wisdom. Perhaps he and his wife would have the discernment to guide her. She considered sharing her troubled feelings about Arthur Blake. Maybe. . .if the talk about Aunty O went well.

Mrs. Credence must have had a kettle of hot water on her stove. She bustled into the room with a tray in her hands only moments after Tansy and the preacher had settled.

Pastor Credence jumped up and took the tray to place on the coffee table. "She's brought cookies. She won't let me eat any, but you must try all three kinds. I recommend the dark squares. They're made with molasses."

Tansy smiled, feeling a little overwhelmed by the social pleasantries. She hoped she didn't spill the tea or leave cookie crumbs across the front of her blouse. Although she congratulated herself on making friends, so far she had not been required to entertain or be entertained in her house or theirs.

Complicated.

Life had become so very complicated since Uncle Wayne's passing. She felt tears forming and squinted to keep them from spilling. She managed to make appropriate responses as Mrs. Credence directed the conversation.

"Shall we pray?" Pastor Credence put his empty cup on the tray.

Where had that come from? Surely one prayed before consuming food, not after. That was how Uncle Wayne prayed, unless it was one of those spontaneous prayers he threw out when the need arose. Did Pastor Credence see her turmoil so easily?

Tansy glanced at Mrs. Credence. That warmhearted individual smiled encouragement and nodded. Tansy bent her head, ready for whatever benediction the pastor felt the need to invoke.

"Father in heaven, thank You for bringing us together. Our Tansy Terrell is heavy of heart. You know all and are prepared to give us good, not evil, when we ask. Help us to discern problems as they really are, not as Satan presents them cloaked with chaos and confusion. Guide us to Your answers where our answers are bound in human frailty. Amen."

Tansy had to fight down a sob caught in her throat.

Mrs. Credence reached over and patted Tansy's wrist. "We don't have to tackle it all at one time. Let's just look at one bit of the puzzle. What word is on the tip of your tongue right now?"

Tansy gulped and squeezed out one word. "Tansy."

Pastor Credence leaned forward, his elbows resting on his knees. "Your name?"

"Our problem starts and finishes with Tansy or Tansy's Candy, Candles, and Canned Goods." Wait. She was here to talk about Aunty O, to get help for Aunty O. This was about Aunty O, not her. "Why do they have to call it Tansy's? Why did my mother name me after a weed?"

A whispered sigh escaped Mrs. Credence. "A weed? I've never thought of Tansy as a weed."

"It is!" The words came out stronger than Tansy expected. She took a deep breath before continuing. "Tansy is a bug repellant. It's used in coffins."

"Yes, I did know that." Mrs. Credence offered the plate of cookies to Tansy, but she refused. Pastor Credence had been right. His wife did not offer him the treat. Mrs. Credence selected a light-colored round cookie. "This is my medicinal wafer. I change the ingredients according to the need. This batch contains anise, rose, and chamomile. It's for calming the nerves."

She offered the plate to Tansy once more. Tansy took the recommended cookie and nibbled along one edge.

She tried to smile. "It's nice. Not too sweet. I can't taste the rose, mostly the anise."

"I put that in to mask the chamomile. Howard doesn't like chamomile."

The pastor reached for the plate, and his wife shook her head. "After dinner, dear."

Pastor Credence sat back. "Do you ever bake with tansy, Edna?"

"No, I never have, although I've rubbed the leaves into lamb. It tastes a little bit like rosemary."

The pastor smacked his lips together. "I remember that. We had it for Easter, didn't we?"

"Yes." She patted Tansy's arm. "And as for it being a weed, don't you know, Tansy, it's always better to gather your herbs from the wild? The garden varieties are rarely as potent, in fragrance or in medicinal properties."

Pastor leaned forward, again resting his elbows on his knees. "Now just where did you get such a negative impression of your name? I'm sure Wayne and Ophelia would think Tansy to be a beautiful name."

Tansy perched her anise wafer on the edge of her saucer and sipped the cooling tea. When she nestled the cup back on the delicate plate, she sighed. "I don't know. Maybe the people I lived with before Uncle Wayne found me. I don't remember many words they spoke, but I do remember the harsh anger." She popped the rest of the wafer into her mouth and chewed thoroughly. Then she sipped her tea, grateful that the Credences allowed her time. They didn't press her with questions. They sat in companionable silence. Finally, she felt settled enough to continue. "I came to talk about Aunty O. I think she needs Uncle Wayne."

"That's what we see from our worldly perspective." Pastor Credence didn't seem surprised by the change of subject.

"You've seen it, too?" asked Tansy. "The way she's changed. Her clothes. The way she talks. And she doesn't like Ar—Mr. Blake."

Mrs. Credence's sweet face scrunched in a frown. "Yes, we've noticed, and we've prayed about it. Perhaps this is the opportunity we've been waiting for." She cocked her head at her husband.

"I believe this could be a start. Tansy, why don't you invite your aunt to come to our house for dinner. I'll go round up Arthur."

"He has a visitor." Tansy put her cup and saucer on the tray as she stood.

"A visitor?" Pastor Credence also stood.

"It was his uncle."

Mr. and Mrs. Credence spoke in unison. "His uncle?"

"Well, now, I may not bring Arthur back for dinner, Edna. You go ahead and entertain our guest. I'll see if our friend needs a hand. Where did you see them, Tansy?"

"At Art's shop, but the uncle said they would go find a steak dinner."

"I don't like the sound of this, Howard."

"Neither do I. I'll come back as soon as possible. Pray, dear." He kissed his wife's cheek and did not linger for a formal farewell to Tansy.

"What happened? Why is he in a rush?"

"We'll talk about it later. Your aunt is at home, I would think. Go fetch her and we women will have a cozy chat."

"About Arthur?"

"Of course not, dear, that would be gossip."

"But I want to know why Pastor Credence rushed off as if he had to rescue Art from his uncle."

"It's surprising that any of them would visit, that's all." Mrs. Credence gently pushed Tansy toward the door, but she dug in her heels.

"That's not all."

"That's all you're going to get out of me."

"Mrs. Credence, please!"

"Go get your aunt. By the time you get back, my husband and your young man might be back already."

Tansy didn't protest the part about her young man. More than anything, she wanted Arthur Truehouse Blake to be her young man. She scurried down the steps on a mission to bring back her aunt and find out what was going on.

Chapter 10

Arthur walked with his uncle to the hotel, planning to part ways as soon as possible. Larry's effusive flow of random talk had grown old before they even left the shop. Even though this relative kept up a jovial front, Art detected a frantic energy.

He didn't know what drove his uncle to exhibit this staged demeanor. He did recognize that the underlying fervor indicated desperation. The pressure of desperation heralded catastrophe. Arthur knew his uncles would react in some unpredictable way. He could foresee calamity even if he couldn't ascertain how it would unfold.

Arthur didn't offer a recommendation of a place to eat, so his uncle took the lead. At the hotel, Larry insisted Art come in for dinner, a steak, baked potato, great yeasty rolls, and a mound of buttery corn. Arthur didn't see the meal as reason enough to remain in his uncle's company, but neither did he want to make a scene on the main street of Pierre. He followed Larry into the hotel and directly to the dining area.

Art had never been in the busy hotel. His uncle moved so quickly, he only glimpsed the extravagant lobby before passing through the doors to the hotel restaurant. Scattered rectangular wooden tables packed the room. Most seated four, but several could accommodate twice as many. White linen cloths covered each, and polished cherrywood chairs looked comfortable and stylish. Cherrywood also trimmed the room's mantels and sideboards.

From a far corner, a man stood and waved.

Larry waved back. "Your uncle Matt's here as well. We're eager to bring you back into the fold."

"Fold? As in sheep?" Art's muttered words did not reach Larry, who now tugged him through the maze of tables and chairs. If Larry hadn't said his name, Art would never have recognized the man at the table was Matt. Again it was the clean, neat appearance that disguised his relative.

Matt stood and enfolded him in a painful hug. His excessive greeting didn't match the display Larry had put on, but it still made Art uncomfortable. Was it his imagination, or was that embrace meant to hurt and remind him of who was boss?

"Sit, sit. Have a drink." The big man pushed him into a chair.

"Still don't drink much, Matt." Art glanced at the nearly empty glass at his uncle's place.

A flash of anger lit the man's eyes. The hand on Arthur's shoulder bit into his flesh with a formidable squeeze. "What's with this Matt business? Have you forgotten we're related? It's Uncle Matt. Always will be."

Larry passed behind his brother and clasped his shoulders, successfully disconnecting the fierce hold Matt had on their nephew. "Easy, easy. Give the boy a break, Matt. He hasn't seen us in years. He doesn't know the changes we've managed since Pa died." He patted Matt's shoulders and nudged him toward his chair. Larry sat down in the one left between Art and Matt.

Larry's unrestrained grin beamed on Art. "Turned our lives around. Upstanding citizens. Trustworthy businessmen. Even go to church."

Matt continued to show a disgruntled attitude, and Art remembered how his uncle had always put great store in being treated with respect. He liked making his nephew display proper deference. Arthur doubted his uncles had actually changed much.

Larry poked Matt. "Tell our nephew how our business is booming. We've made a place for him."

Matt's attitude improved dramatically. He straightened in his chair and gave his attention to Art. It was a useless ploy on Art. Matt's convenient donning of a pleasant camaraderie didn't gain him any ground.

"We've put aside the construction business. No more adding rooms, enlarging kitchens, or creating built-in shelves. And we don't make much furniture anymore, either."

"That sounds like you're doing less, not more." Art studied Matt's face, expecting to see a flash of annoyance. His exasperation was brief, but clearly displayed in squinted eyes and furrowed brow.

"Instruments." Matt cleared his throat and forced a light tone. "Eighty percent of our sales are in instruments. We could use you. You make quality guitars, and those wooden flutes you used to make had a great tone." Matt cleared his throat again and looked around the room as if he hated being there. But he returned to Art with the false pleasantry. "Then there's your playing. When you play the instruments, people buy them thinking they can sound as good as you do. You remember the old days, don't you? You could mesmerize a crowd."

"That was probably the wrong thing to say, Uncle. I *do* remember the old days."

Larry shook Art's arm, dragging his attention away from his brother. "No, Matt, you forget how Sid explained it. Remember it isn't that we could *use* him? It's he *needs* us. He can be a proud owner in Blake's Finest Instruments. His prosperity is back in Nashville, not out here on an endless prairie, where there's no one but hayseeds to appreciate his talent."

"We have the Grand Opera House, you know." Not that Art had performed there. He'd only been to see one. Maybe he could take Tansy there. She'd enjoy that.

His uncles continued to talk. Art wanted to leave. Larry had said they were eager to bring him back in the fold, but instead, this reunion sounded like a fishing trip—and he was the fish. The bait was a lucrative partnership in their new business. The hook would snag his pride and ambition and pull him back. Once out of his pond and into their boiler pot, he'd be used and abused just as before.

They wanted his skills, and they figured he would be cheap labor. They figured wrong.

"Where is Uncle Sid?"

"Back home." Larry was still oozing enthusiasm. "I'm telling you, Arthur, this business is hopping. We can't leave it alone. Someone must mind the store."

Matt frowned. "We have to get back soon. You're coming with us."

"I'm staying here." Art scanned around the room. He knew a few people dining in the spacious restaurant.

Out of the corner of his eye, he caught the look that passed between the brothers. No way was he going with them. Their expressions shifted from sly to amiable. How could he get out of here?

"If the business is so taxing, why did two of you come to get me?"

Matt growled. "We thought it might take two of us to—"

"Persuade you how much we've changed and how much we appreciate you and how much we'd like the opportunity to reconcile and be a real family." That oily smile broadened across Larry's coarse features. "A family with a family business."

Matt chortled. "Blake's Finest Instruments."

Art put both hands on the table, palms flat against the white linen. The contrast of his rough, work-worn hands against the luxurious cloth made him relax. He knew where he belonged and where he was comfortable.

He glanced over at his uncles' hands. They didn't seem to be quite as scruffy as his. But making a guitar didn't mess up your hands as much as laying shingles on a roof. How much real work did they do?

He pushed back from the table.

"No, no, no," Larry protested. "You can't leave until we've fed you. The meals here are first class."

"I thought you wanted me to recommend a place." Could these men be truthful about anything?

"You're the native." Matt's voice was well greased by snake oil. At least, that possibility crossed Art's mind before his uncle continued. "We would have conceded to your superior knowledge of the eating establishments in your town."

Art surveyed the room, planning his escape route.

Pastor Credence appeared in the door between the lobby and the restaurant. He scanned the room and focused on their table. Arthur raised his arm and waved him over.

"Who's that?" Matt's curt inquiry jabbed at Art's nerves.

"The preacher from my church."

"What does he want?"

"Want? I don't think he wants anything."

Pastor Credence made his way through the room. "There you are, Arthur. Tansy and her aunt are already at the house. Edna is holding dinner for you." Pastor Credence turned to the men seated across from Art. "I'm Howard Credence, pastor of the Christian Prairie Church at the corner of Pine and Maple."

Art stood. "My uncles, Matt and Larry Blake, visiting from Nashville."

"Nice to meet you." Pastor shook hands with both men. "If you're still here on Sunday, you're welcome to join us."

"They won't be here." Art pushed in his chair. "They have a business that demands they return."

"We'll speak with you tomorrow, Art." Larry's smile stiffly sat on his face.

Matt didn't bother to smile.

As Art and his pastor passed through the outer doors into the crisp, cooling air of dusk, Credence leaned toward his companion. "Well, did I rescue you or ruin a fancy steak dinner?"

"Rescued. I think anything eaten at a table with those two would have tasted like skunk."

Tansy could not believe her eyes or ears. Aunty O had reverted to the woman who had raised her. She and Edna Credence bustled around the kitchen, doing the last-minute necessities to get the meal on the table. The two women chatted easily about which vegetables had grown well the summer before, the young wives at church who were expecting, the church picnic in May, and the need for a larger school building before next fall.

The task given Tansy required no thinking, so she eavesdropped on the older women. Setting the kitchen table for five people, she marveled as her aunt laughed over Mrs. Credence's description of a failed cake that tasted fine but looked like bread pudding. Aunty O never mentioned her desire to eat with Pierre's high society nor her interest in committees that had only the elite as members. As they chatted, Aunty O ignored fashion, the growing number of restaurants in Pierre, and the performances lined up at the Grand Opera House. Tansy was tickled. She felt a familiar giggle playing with her composure.

Pastor Credence came back with Art in plenty of time to bless the food and enjoy the company. Tansy relaxed. Finally, Art was seeing her aunt as she truly was, a loving, generous, and fun person.

Cake and coffee were served last. Pastor Credence beamed at his wife when she presented him with a full slice.

Aunty O didn't cut into her cake. "Arthur, Tansy doesn't know much about your uncles."

The people at the table stilled. Tansy pulled in a sharp breath. She had no idea where her aunt would go with this. She'd never said anything to her about Art's relatives. She'd never even said he had any.

Arthur turned toward Ophelia. "I don't talk about them much. We've never been much of a family."

Her aunt nodded. "Yes, that can happen. We had cousins we didn't visit with. Tansy's mother and I used to hide in the chicken coop if they came by. The first time we hid in the barn, but they found us. Then we learned Hiram was scared of chickens, and since he was the oldest, that kept the rest of them occupied elsewhere."

"He wouldn't admit he was afraid?" Pastor Credence asked.

"Right. He ordered the others around, but never around the coop." Aunty O looked at her lap. "I think we all have memories of childhood bullies."

Art had gone back to his cake, pointedly ignoring the conversation.

Aunty O picked up her fork. "And they all had an Achilles' heel. The trick was to find it."

Later, Art walked Tansy and her aunt home. Obviously, Aunty O was not going into the house to allow them to say goodnight, so Tansy smiled and bid her young man a good evening. His eyes held warm affection. Surely it wasn't just the glow of the gaslights. She held the unspoken promise of regard close to her heart as she prepared for bed.

Tansy had just tied her apron around her waist the next morning when Aunty O came into the kitchen, dressed to go out.

Tansy was befuddled. More peculiar behavior. "Where are you going?"

Her aunt fiddled with her hatpin, sticking it at just the right angle. "I'm going to breakfast with some lady friends."

"Breakfast? You're eating out for breakfast? What women? Who eats breakfast at a restaurant?"

"Café. One does not eat breakfast at a hotel. Women of a certain style eat out with their connections. It's a city custom, Tansy." She headed for the door.

"When will you be back?"

"So many questions, Tansy. I don't know how long these things last. I would assume I will be back before dinner."

Tansy's mouth fell open. Gone was the well-known and wonderful aunt who had appeared last night at the Credences' home. The unfamiliar and caustic aunt had returned.

Eggs and toast no longer sounded tempting. Tansy changed to go to the shop, but decided against it. She couldn't help worrying about Aunty O. She would wait for her and then perhaps persuade her to visit Edna Credence to thank her for the hospitality the night before. It would be a social call. A social call should appeal to her aunt.

Just over an hour later, the front door banged open. "Tansy, Tansy, you weren't at the store."

Tansy answered the excited call while running to the front of the house. "I'm here, Aunty. I decided to do some laundry."

Her aunt flapped her hands and motioned her toward the settee. "Never mind that. Sit, sit. Those uncles of your dear Arthur are up to no good."

Art had become her dear? Which aunt was this? The bossy aunt or the encouraging aunt?

She sat down slowly, not quite sure what was happening.

Aunty O sat in the overstuffed chair and folded her hands in her lap.

"I've been spying." A tiny smile lifted the corners of her mouth.

"What?"

"Don't sound so shocked. I remained perfectly respectable and circumspect, as well." She reached up and pulled the hatpin out, then placed her small brim hat on the arm of the chair.

Tansy was flummoxed. "Where have you been, and what have you been doing?"

"I didn't like the little I heard last night about your Arthur's uncles."

Why would Aunty O care? "You don't like Arthur."

"I like his uncles less."

"But—"

"Shush now and let me tell you what I found out."

Oh shenanigans! Where is this headed? Tansy managed to keep quiet.

"I went to the hotel."

"How did you know what hotel?"

Aunty O tsked. "You really aren't keeping up with things. Howard told Edna where he'd been."

"But—"

"Shush!"

Shenanigans!

"I sat close to the table where the uncles sat."

"How did you know who they were?"

"I asked the waiter."

"But—"

"The waiter was Billy Porter from church."

"All right. But—"

"Shush! I listened to the uncles talk. They intend to take Arthur back to Nashville whether he wants to go or not. And they intend to take over his store here."

"Why?"

"Because Art is the better craftsman and the better salesman. The uncles aren't popular in their own town."

"Why take over his store?"

"The profits will be higher in Nashville, but they recognize Arthur's business here is something that 'should not be tossed away.' That's what they said. 'Tossed away.' And so, one of them will stay here to mind the store."

"Arthur won't go."

"They're going to give him one more chance to come willingly."

"Then what?" Tansy gasped. "Are they going to hurt him? Are they going to knock him out, tie him up, and haul him away?"

"What an imagination! No, they are going to arrest him."

Chapter 11

D awn had pulled Art out of bed that morning. He couldn't stop smiling. With restless anticipation, thoughts of Tansy remained at the front of his mind. He believed he had the go-ahead to court her. Ophelia Terrell had actually been pleasant to him last night, even sympathetic.

Lying in bed had been impossible. He needed to do something. He needed to make something beautiful. He had a mind to create a piece of furniture women would sigh over. One woman in particular. Too bad he didn't have a crib on order. Women got all teary-eyed happy over baby beds. No crib, but he did have a fancy set of dining room chairs and a table that was ready for the last polish before delivery. He'd gone to his workroom to apply some elbow grease and his special furniture polish to the already magnificent wood.

The front and back doors stood open, propped by chunks of stone he'd found while out fishing. The chill of early morning kept him from sweating. He wanted to deliver the pieces later and didn't want to return home for a bath.

A double set of footsteps sounded as someone came through the front room. Larry appeared in the doorway between the showroom and his work area. His presence put a damper on Art's good mood.

Larry's forced cheerfulness had slipped this morning. He looked a bit hung over. But his clothing was still neat and respectable. Matt pushed him on into the workroom and stomped over the threshold. Matt's presence successfully doused his good mood altogether.

"You're up early," Matt growled. "Shouldn't leave your door open. Someone might come in and rob you."

Larry lowered himself to sit on a barrel. He seemed stiff, sore—perhaps he'd been in a bar fight. But that was the behavior of his uncles before this reformation. Surely, his discomfort could be blamed on arthritis. Art snorted.

Larry wiped the back of his hand under his nose. "Up early is good. You can get a lot of work done before the world gets busy."

Matt ran his fingertips along the smooth wood of Art's well-crafted project. He came to the same end of the table as his nephew and stood too close. Art refused to take a step back. He was four inches taller than Larry but only two inches taller than Matt. Matt's chest swelled as if to make himself bigger, and he pushed his face to within an inch of Art's.

"We can't spend days mollycoddling your 'independent spirit.' You can just get off your high horse and come back to your family. You're needed. Pa coulda turned you out on the street, but he didn't. He fed you, clothed you, and learned you a trade. It's time you returned that charity."

"I thought you said Grandfather was dead. I can't repay anything to a dead man. And there wouldn't have been a thing to repay except beatings and deprivation."

Matt ignored most of Art's words. "It doesn't matter that he's dead. It was family that took you in, family that gave you what you needed. We're family, and it's us you owe gratitude to."

Art stood taller. It felt good to look down on the meaner of the two men. He straightened his shoulders and allowed the full power of his contempt to come out in a sneer. "I don't owe *you* anything. *And* I'm not going with you."

Matt grabbed the front of Art's shirt with a chunky fist. He pushed the material upward as if he could lift Art as he had when he was a young boy.

Arthur grunted. He pressed one hand to the bully's chin. With a long arm, he reached around Matt and grabbed the center of his collar. A jerk backward with one hand and a mighty shove with the other forced the parasite let go of his hold on Art's shirt. A button popped off Art's shirt and hit the wall, but he didn't care. He twirled the culprit around and marched him to the back door. With a shove, his uncle flew over the two-step stoop and hit the dirt.

Art turned on Larry. "You too. Get out of my shop."

Larry sidled past him. He stumbled on the first step.

Art was disappointed he hadn't fallen. He moved to watch the men's hasty retreat. "Don't come back."

A couple of deep breaths helped to release the rest of his tension. He needed a normal day and some prayer to rid himself of the outrage he felt toward his old relations. They might dress better, but they still carried the stench of greed and malice in their hearts.

Art whistled a cheerful tune as he passed the last houses in town. He'd had enough time to himself, rubbing the oil into his chairs and praying. As he thought about Tansy and the miracle of her aunt's more tolerant view, he thanked God for His care.

His delivery was to the Parker house two miles into the country. Flowers carpeted the green hills. The birds seemed to be having a competition as to who could sing the prettiest. The morning sun was warm enough to toast his head and shoulders. The breeze cooled his skin and brought the fresh smell of sprouting corn to his nose.

He clucked his tongue and jiggled the reins, giving his horse permission to pick up his feet and prance a little. His horse seemed to have the inspiration of spring running through his veins, as well. He answered with a whinny and a bound forward.

Art grinned.

Last night, he'd left Tansy at her front door, and even though she hadn't said anything in particular, he knew he'd be welcome back. He was going to court her. Aunty O had been cordial all evening.

And his uncles. He'd told those shifty old men he wanted nothing to do with them, and he believed this time they got the message.

He heard a shout and looked over his shoulder. A lone horseman followed him. The badge on Benjamin Sloane's chest caught the rays of sun and flashed at Art. He pulled in the reins and his horse obediently stopped.

"What's up, Sheriff? Can I help you?"

"I've got to ask you to come back to town. Judge Ferguson wants to see you."

"I'm expected out at Parkers' this morning. Can I come by after the delivery?"

Sheriff Sloane shook his head. "There's a bit of trouble. Two men, who claim to be your uncles, are trying to put a lien on your property. That would include what's in your wagon."

"What? I don't owe them anything."

"That's what the judge thinks, but he wants to talk to you and your uncles. He must think they're scalawags. He's going to a lot of trouble to determine whether they have any legal ground to stand on. He sent a couple of my deputies out to bring in some of your first customers."

"Where are my uncles?"

"Cooling their heels at the saloon. I'm supposed to bring them back to the judge's office when we have all the key players in place."

"Key players?"

"You, those customers, Pastor Credence, and the mayor."

Art shook his head in bewilderment as he clucked his tongue and began the maneuver that would turn his horse and wagon back toward town. He raised his voice over the rattle of the harness and the creaking of the wagon. "Why the mayor?"

"Won't hurt to have a town official as a character witness. You've sung bass next to him in the church choir. How many years?"

"Eight."

"We should be there." Aunty O placed her hat back on her head and stood.

"Be where?" Tansy had trouble keeping up with her aunt's news, her personality changes, and her willingness to run here and there. Life in the city was far more adventurous than life on the farm had been. What she wouldn't give for prayer time as she milked the cows.

"Change your dress into something more fashionable. The yellow one with the vine pattern. The one we bought at Joan's Dress Display. And put your hair up. You'll look older and more sophisticated."

"Where am I going?"

"To stand by Arthur. To support him in his hour of need."

Tansy doubted she had the right to stand by Art "in his hour of need," but she was more than curious to find out what was going on. She was apprehensive. She didn't want him hurt in any way. "It'll take a few minutes to change. Aunty O, please move the kettle off the heat. I won't be washing clothes."

The clerk at the courthouse told them Arthur's name did not appear anywhere on the docket for today's proceedings. "Try at the offices of the judges."

The woman at the desk stopped them as they went out. "Wait. I can save you a lot of walking around. I'll telephone."

Aunty O's eyes lit up. She had wanted a telephone in the house and in the store. She quirked an eyebrow at her niece. "See? They're very useful."

Tansy ignored her and listened to the helpful woman speak to the operator. She hung the little black horn she'd held to her ear on the horseshoe shaped lever. "Ernestine says Judge Ferguson dragged some ruckus-makers into his chambers then shoved them out again. But he's going to meet with the principals at eleven-thirty in his office."

Aunty O pulled on Tansy's sleeve. "Do you think that's about Arthur?"

"I don't know."

The desk lady said, "I'll ask." She picked up the receiver again and waited a second before asking, "Ernestine, was Arthur Blake one of those the judge came down on?" She listened for a moment then shook her head at Tansy and her aunt. But the next second, she held up a finger. "Thanks, Ernestine. I'll tell you later. Got to get back to work."

She hung up. Her eyes were big and her grin mischievous. "Mr. Blake was not among those corralled by the judge. But he was the subject of the dispute. *And* his lawyer was there."

Aunty O squeezed Tansy's arm hard enough to make her wince. "Arthur has a lawyer?"

Tansy shrugged. She didn't know Arthur well enough to know if he had a lawyer. Why would he need a lawyer? What had he done? Or rather, what had those uncles done?

Aunty O jerked on Tansy's sleeve again and pointed to the large clock on the wall. "It's 11:10. Where's Judge Ferguson's office, miss?"

"Across the street and two buildings east. His name is listed on the front window."

"Thank you," Tansy called over her shoulder. Her aunt had already run for the door. Once outside, her aunt turned to the west.

Tansy scurried to catch up with her. "Wrong way, Aunty!"

"We're going to get my banker friend."

"Mr. Wright?"

"Right." Aunty's hat bobbed as she hustled down the street.

"Why?"

"He always says if I need any help at all, to call on him."

Tansy dragged her heels, slowing her aunt down. "But you don't need help. Arthur does."

"My niece loves Arthur Blake. You will probably marry him. That makes him family. My family."

Tansy grabbed her aunt's arm and stopped, actually digging in her heels to halt their progress. She successfully stopped her tiny, determined aunt. "What happened? Why are you acting like this?"

"Aren't I acting as I should?"

Tansy hesitated. Her aunt was behaving much more like she did before Uncle Wayne's passing. "Yes."

"Well then, where's the problem?"

"You haven't been acting as you should, and now you are. I'm confused. I *like* that you're more like you, but what happened?"

Aunty O looked around at the passing people and stepped closer. "Edna Credence asked me last night if Wayne asked me to take care of you. Well, he did."

Her aunty looked around again and leaned even closer. "Then she asked me if I was . . .taking care of you. I had to think. And you know what I saw when I started thinking about that question?"

Tansy slowly shook her head.

"I saw *you*, dear. . . ." Tears formed in the older woman's eyes. "And I saw I haven't been taking care of you."

In spite of being on the sidewalk of downtown Pierre, Tansy gathered her little aunt in her arms. "Aw, Aunty O. It's all right. We're going to be just fine."

Chapter 12

The reception area of Judge Ferguson's office overflowed with people. Art cordially pushed through the crowd, trying to reach the judge's secretary. Most of the people had a word of encouragement as he edged by.

"Don't worry. No one believes your uncles."

"They can't cause you trouble here. We know you too well."

"Chin up, Art. We won't let you go."

Harvey Coolidge sidled up to him. "I'm your lawyer, Art."

Art knew Harvey from church but had never had any legal dealings with him. "You are? How's that? Appreciate it, but I don't understand what's going on."

"I overheard those yahoo uncles of yours trying to put a lien on your property at the courthouse. They hadn't even served notice to you. We got into a rather heated discussion, and Judge Ferguson hauled us into his chambers to find out why we were disturbing the peace."

Art noticed the room had gone silent, and everyone listened intently to Harvey's account. There wasn't much privacy in a small town. But these were people he counted on, his customers and friends. He gladly accepted their support.

Harvey continued, "When the judge heard their story, he said he'd listen to both sides and determine whether they had enough evidence to go to court."

"Evidence of what?"

"Stealing."

"Stealing what?"

"They claim that when you left their employment, you took valuable tools with you."

"I took a banjo I'd made and my clothes."

"Not according to them."

A stir at the door caused Art to turn his head. Tansy, Mrs. Terrell, and Mr. Wright came in. The crowd shifted to give them room. His eyes met Tansy's and held. He was embarrassed for her to see all this fuss, but his heart warmed at the sight of her. She smiled. All his worries about the unnecessary turmoil his uncles had caused fled.

Art turned back to Harvey. "Why are all these people here?"

Harvey rubbed the back of his neck. "I'm not sure. I know the judge sent deputies to find some of your first clients. I think the rest are just here because they like you."

Art surveyed the crowd, smiling and nodding as he made eye contact with them. Tansy and her two companions managed to squeeze through to his side. He boldly put his arm around Tansy's shoulders and pulled her closer. The packed room allowed little movement. He didn't want her crushed or dragged away from him.

He saw her aunt inspecting the position of his arm. "Good morning, Mrs. Terrell, Mr. Wright. Thank you for coming. I don't know why the judge has called us here."

Mrs. Terrell patted his arm in a friendly gesture. Odd, since it was the arm around Tansy.

People shifted, and the tiny woman swayed. Mr. Wright immediately encircled her with his arm. Art raised an eyebrow and looked down at Tansy. With a nod of his head, he drew attention to the banker and her aunt. Tansy's eyes widened.

Harvey spoke up. "It's my guess that he doesn't want the court to waste its time on a frivolous lawsuit. He can do a summary and throw it out for lack of evidence. Here come your uncles."

The door had opened a bit. A shove from outside made the people rearrange themselves to accommodate it swinging open.

"Leave it open," said someone in the crowd. "It's getting stuffy."

"Yeah," another voice piped up, "and the atmosphere just went rancid with the addition of two more bodies."

"Hush now," a cultured lady spoke. "Mind where you are."

Art surveyed the room. He and Tansy were the only young people present. Most were older than his uncles. All represented at least one generation before his. Each one of them had taken time out of their busy day to make sure he didn't get cheated by his own relations. Shame crept into his heart. He'd shunned friendship with these people because of their age. He did their work. He was polite. But he kept them at a distance, because he believed their core was selfish, wicked, and greedy.

He'd been wrong.

The door to the inner office opened. Judge Ferguson stepped out and registered shock at the hubbub in his waiting room.

"What's going on here?" he demanded.

Answers flew across the room. Matt Blake raised his voice. "Judge! You made an appointment with us. I don't know why all these people are here, but we should be seen first. You said eleven-thirty, so eleven-thirty is our time."

Harvey Coolidge stepped around the receptionist desk, closer to the judge. "They're all here to witness for Art, sir."

"Is this your doing?"

"No sir. Word of mouth. They all just came. We have the three you called for, though."

"Step into my office with the principals."

"No, Judge," one of the men called out. "We want to hear what's what. These men have come against one of our upstanding citizens. The townspeople want to be in on what's going on. Art Blake is one of our own."

"My office doesn't have room for all of you."

"Then do it here," said the same man.

A voice called from the hall. "And talk loud enough so we can hear out here."

The judge laughed and waved his hands at those in front. "Move back. Give me some room." He sat on the front of the receptionist's desk.

"First, I want to hear"—he referred to his page of notes—"from Matt and Larry Blake."

"Here, sir." Larry spoke, standing tall and holding his hat in front of his chest. The brothers had pushed through the room and stood beside Art's lawyer.

"What is your relation to Arthur Blake?"

"Uncles," barked Matt.

"We raised the boy." Larry's entreating tone raked Art's nerves. "We took him in when he was a scrap of a lad of four."

"Six," Art corrected.

"You'll have your chance to speak, Mr. Blake. For now, just listen."

Larry forged on. "We fed him, clothed him, educated him, taught him our trade, and treated him like family."

"And then he left the family in the lurch," said Matt. "Stole our best equipment and took off in the middle of the night."

The judge tapped his finger on the side of the paper several times. "What kind of equipment?"

"Woodworking. Not just hammers and saws, but carving tools. All high quality, expensive stuff."

"And did he steal a wagon and horse?"

The brothers looked at each other then answered simultaneously. Matt said, "Yes," and Larry said, "No."

The judge turned away without displaying any attitude. Art wondered what he was thinking.

"Mr. Arthur Blake."

"Yes, sir?"

The uncles blustered for more say. The judge silenced them with a stern look.

"Sheriff, would you stand closer." Even informally seated on the desk, the judge exuded authority. "We may need your interference." He tapped the one sheet of notes against his knee. "Mr. Blake, did your uncles raise you?"

"For ten years."

"Did they provide for you?"

"In a manner of fashion."

Judge Ferguson studied Art for a moment before going to his next question. "Did you leave their care?"

"I left their household, sir."

Again, there was a reflective moment.

"Mr. Blake, did you steal from your uncles?"

"No, sir."

Matt jerked forward. "I can make a list. I remember each and every piece we had to buy again, because this ungrateful rascal pocketed our tools."

"Surely, he didn't carry saws away in his pockets."

Matt's face reddened, and he growled. Sheriff Sloane cleared his throat. Matt glanced over his shoulder and stepped back.

"One more thing, Mr. Blake. How many years has it been since you left Nashville?"

"Ten."

The judge peered at his notes. "I'd like to speak to Patrick Donahue next."

A man worked his way from the back to stand in front of the judge.

"That would be me, Judge. Do I need to swear on a Bible?"

"No, this is an informal inquiry."

"Right."

"It says here that you were the very first person in Pierre to give work to Mr. Blake."

"I reckon that could be true. He was new to town, I know."

"What did he do for you?"

"He took out an old window that was rotted in its frame. Replaced the wood and reset the glass. Then he put it back in the wall. He did a good job."

"Did he use his own tools?"

"No, sir, he didn't have any. Made me think he wasn't telling me the truth about him being a carpenter, but I took a chance, lent him my tools, and he did a good job. Better than I could have done. Better than ole Mike Breezer, who used to do all my repairs. But Mike passed away, so of course he couldn't fix my window. And I don't mean that Art fixed the window better than Mike 'cause Mike was dead, but better than Mike would have done had he still been alive."

Someone in the crowd hollered, "Dead carpenters don't hammer no nails."

Everyone laughed. The judge yelled, "Quiet! Or Sheriff Sloane will escort you all out."

A man close to the door raised his hand. "We're here to tell you our stories about Art. We can back up what he says. He had no tools at first and gathered them one by one as he had money."

"I don't have time to listen to thirty people tell me the same thing. Besides, all this is common knowledge to the community. Let me ask you this. Did anyone come here today to tell me a negative account of Art's dealings?"

Larry and Matt shot their hands into the air.

The judge cast them an impatient look. The sheriff whispered, "Put your hands down. He didn't mean you."

Judge Ferguson pulled out a large white handkerchief and wiped his brow. "I'm throwing this case out. These men don't have enough substantial evidence to hold up in court. Too much time has passed to prosecute the defendant. Statute of Limitations."

He looked Matt in the eye and then Larry. "You two are encouraged to leave our community and not come back. Your complaint is based on ignorance of the law. The falsehoods underpinning your arguments could land you in jail. Get out."

He stood. "That goes for the rest of you. Out of my office, not out of town. Thank you for being upstanding citizens, willing to go to court for the righteous. Now out, out, out."

Tansy hung on to Art's arm as they walked through town to their shops. The morning had been exciting, but that didn't explain her racing heartbeat. The cause of her symptoms patted the hand she had at his elbow.

Art's rumbling bass interrupted her revel in the thrill of being with him. "I have to deliver a table and chairs to the Parkers. Would you like to come with me?"

"Yes." Anything to spend more time with him.

"I took my wagon to the livery. Do you mind walking that far?"

"Not at all."

"But it's past lunchtime. I'm hungry. What about you?"

"I am."

"A picnic?"

"Yes."

They passed the alley between the hardware store and the bakery. Art stopped, abruptly turned, and led her between the cool, brick buildings.

"Is this a shortcut?" Tansy scrambled to keep up.

"This might be a long-cut."

"Then why are we going this way?" This was one of the times she wondered if understanding Art was difficult or if it was just understanding men that was the problem. Where was he taking her?

Halfway to the next block, Art stopped and turned Tansy to look in her eyes. His hands rested on her shoulders. "Tansy?"

"Yes." All right. She might learn something here if he was willing to explain.

"I don't want to talk about delivery to the Parkers, walking, picnics, none of that."

"You don't?" Could he have made this little detour to be alone with her?

"No."

"What do you want to talk about?" She thought she knew what his answer would be. There was warmth in his eyes that sent tingles across her skin.

"I don't want to talk."

Bubbly giggles edged up her throat. He'd better kiss her before they exploded.

"Tansy?"

She was going to kick him. "What?"

"May I court you?"

Surely the smile on her face obliterated the need for a word, but she went along with the game. "Yes."

"May I kiss you?"

With a huff of impatience, Tansy had lost the shyness she'd brought with her from the farm. She launched herself upward, wrapped her arms around his neck, and planted her lips on his. Almost. It might not have been the most efficient of kisses, because she missed by a good half inch. But Art made the necessary correction, and the kiss turned into the most perfect thing Tansy had experienced. He pulled back. "I take that as a yes."

"Was there a question?" She smiled at him, realizing in her heart that all of their questions had been answered.

Donita Kathleen Paul has given up on retiring. Each time she retires, she finds a new career. This time she married an author from New Mexico and is resurrecting skills as a wife and homemaker. She's delved into romance, fantasy, history, and is toying with time travel. Writing will always be a part of her life. "The more I take time off to allow my body to relax, the more active my brain gets. I'm having way too much fun to stop."

A Prickly Affair

by Donna Schlachter

Dedication

Dedicated first and foremost to God, the Creator of all.
Without Him, no story is worth telling.

To my husband, Patrick, who is the evidence of God's love for me.

And to my agent, Terrie Wolf, who believed in me.

It is of the LORD's mercies that we are not consumed,
because his compassions fail not.
They are new every morning: great is thy faithfulness.
LAMENTATIONS 3:22–23

Chapter 1

Double D Ranch, Near Cave Creek, Arizona Territory
1885

Sally Jo sank to the ground beneath the pain of her wrenched ankle. "Drat. I simply cannot walk one more step in these infernal boots."

Thomas Peabody, broad of shoulders and narrow of waist, knelt beside her, cupping her aching foot in hands more accustomed to roping steers or shooting the eye out of a gnat at a hundred yards. "Miss Sally, allow me to assist you."

Sally Jo stared into his eyes. Why hadn't she ever noticed they perfectly matched the color of the summer sky? "Why, Mr. Peabody, you're most gallant."

He straightened, reached a hand toward her, and pulled her to her feet. When she tried to put weight on her aching foot, a jab of pain like a hot poker shot through her, and she collapsed into his arms.

Right where she wanted to be.

He pulled her near, and she closed her eyes, offering her mouth to him. Greedily, as though drawing his very life essence from her, he covered her lips with his own. When she thought she would suffocate, she opened her eyes, and saw mirrored what her racing heart telegraphed to her own mind: this was love.

Lily Duncan surveyed the words written on the page as she chewed the end of her fountain pen. Ink blotches on her fingers attested to her hard work this morning. A clicking sound like a metronome tickled at the periphery of her hearing while she considered whether she needed to change the word *telegraphed* to something more ooshy-gooshy romantic.

Tsick-tsick-tssiicckk.

She tipped her head to listen. What was that sound?

Lily tossed her pen on the desk and glanced at the silver clock resting on the leather-topped surface. Time was running out. She had less than two hours to finish this story and get it on the last mail stage of the day. That snooty editor, Mr. Hogan, in New York, was waiting for it.

Not that she knew for certain he was snooty. Truth was, she didn't know anything about him. She'd only met him through correspondence, so he could be any age, any degree of pretentiousness, any color for that matter.

But that didn't stop her creating an image in her mind: middle-aged, a monocle, oiled hair parted down the middle and slicked back, muttonchop sideburns, and a beard, of course. A house on Fifth Avenue, society wife, private carriage, servants, and twelve children. At least.

She sighed. Thinking about all the reasons why she didn't like the man responsible for buying her stories to publish in his fancy Eastern magazine wasn't going to get the story written. Or mailed.

Tsick–tsick–tssiicckk.

She pushed back from the desk. What she'd written would have to do. She couldn't work with such a racket. She stepped to the window and listened. Not coming from the front. Must be out back. She crossed the bedroom-turned-office to the window facing the rear of the house.

This view was much more utilitarian than the rolling desert and giant saguaros surrounding the house on the other three sides. A small barn for her three horses, a hen house, corral, and privy filled her line of vision.

Tsick–tsick–tssiicckk.

Yes, this is where the sound came from.

And she knew its exact origin.

Lily hefted the Colt .38 on her hip. She'd take care of that she-rattler right now. She strode to the back door and stepped into the late afternoon heat of the desert.

The musky smell of mesquite, heated by the sun, filled her nose as she paused on the doorstep. How she loved the desert. She couldn't imagine living anywhere else.

Certainly not a place like New York City. No way. Give her cactus and rocks, cattle and dipping tanks, horses and leather any day. Unlike her heroines, she wouldn't darken the doorway of a town bigger than Cave Creek. And she sure wouldn't fall for the first man who looked at her twice.

Not that many men looked at her even once. She wasn't ugly. At least, not ugly like a javelina, with its short bristly hide and snarling tusks. And not ugly like a turkey vulture, with its naked head and red eyes.

She preferred men's dungarees to skirts. She wasn't much practiced at cooking and cleaning. But she could outshoot, outride, and outsmart most men she knew.

Which was probably why most men didn't take a second look at her.

Lily neared the woodpile. She'd been meaning to clean that mess up, sweep out the old tinder from the previous year. Even prop the wood up on a couple of timbers to discourage snakes and other varmints wanting to find a warm place to spend the night. But her best range cow had a difficult birth, and her horses needed shoeing, and the hole in the roof. . .

Too much work for one person. Not enough hours in the day to get everything done. What had she been thinking when she started writing?

An escape, that's what. Something to while away the long evenings.

Tsick–tsick–tssiicckk.

She pulled on a pair of leather gloves and tipped her head to one side. If she didn't get that low-down, no-good rattler out soon, there'd be a passel of little ones slithering around.

She glanced toward the horizon. The sun dropped like a lead sinker as though intent on ensuring she missed her deadline to get that story mailed today.

And she sure didn't need Mr. Persnickety Hogan upset that her latest installment of

Love in the Wild, Wild West wasn't on time.

She turned her attention back to the woodpile, and within a couple of minutes had the creature in view. The snake lay curled up against the house. Its rattle waggled ominously, that all-too-familiar sound warning her off. She drew her gun, stepped back a couple of feet, and aimed. When the puff of smoke cleared, the snake lay limp in the dust.

She picked up the snake, behind the jaw, and headed for the chopping block. After severing the charred meat around the wound with her axe, she nailed the body to the side of the house and skinned it. A rattlesnake skin as big as this one would fetch a couple of dollars in town, and the meat would go in her dinner pot.

Lily took the snake meat inside and prepared it, then popped the pieces into the cast-iron pot. She threw in a carrot that needed cooking, along with an onion and the last two potatoes in her larder, water, and salt and pepper, then plopped on the lid and tossed another stick of wood into the stove. Dinner would cook while she went to town.

A burlap sack held the skin. She grabbed the pages she'd written, then she and her trusty roan headed toward Cave Creek.

The spring rains had washed out a few bridges and swelled the washes to over-flowing, but had also nourished the desert and brought on a spurt of growth unlike any she'd seen for many years. Mesquite thrived, its needle-like leaves a bright shade of green. The cactus bloomed, bringing birds and bugs, coyotes and quail, roadrunners and red foxes.

The desert teemed with life.

Daisy Duncan, her pen name for the romances she wrote, lived an exciting life too. At least in Lil's head, she did. And the characters in her stories were always in love or falling in love. No heartbreak for them. No lonely nights in front of the fire. No missed dances or unfulfilled dreams.

No, Lily was much too realistic for that. The only child of now-deceased practical parents, raised in a harsh land following the war that nearly tore the country apart, she knew better than to get caught up in what-ifs and why-nots. She loved the desert. She loved not having to answer to anybody.

That was enough for her.

And whenever she felt the need for adventure or romance, well, she could write that.

Peter Golding grabbed the edge of the stage window to brace himself against the sudden wrenching turn. The driver seemed intent on putting them off the road—if the winding, rutted surface on which they rode could be called such.

The older woman in the wilted traveling outfit pressed against him with the force. The curtains, closed to keep out the dust and flies—both of which managed to penetrate the cabin of the coach—blocked his view. Which was probably just as well.

If he was going to die today, he didn't want to see how or when.

He wished he'd never left New York City, that he'd not listened to the pleadings of his uncle—and employer—to track down this writing wonder Miss Daisy Duncan and bring her back to the City. But wishing wouldn't change the facts.

He was to return with her, or not return at all.

So much for being part of the family business.

His only value lay in his ability to convince Miss Daisy Duncan to live and write in New York. Because the American public wanted to read every word she wrote, and if she wrote more, they'd want to read more. Which meant they'd buy more magazines and, ultimately, books.

That was the goal of this trip: to relay to Miss Daisy Duncan his firm's offer of a book contract.

And what author wouldn't want to hear those words?

He didn't anticipate that his offer to Miss Duncan would be completely unwanted. Judging by the topic and the imagery in her writing, this woman knew love and beauty. Why this queen of romance chose to live in such a dreadful place was beyond him. Perhaps she had an ailing mother who could not be moved. Perhaps she'd followed her true love to these parts and then he'd died, and she visited his grave every day and couldn't think of leaving him. Perhaps she hid from a recent broken heart, seeking solitude in the desert.

Whatever reason, he could only hope—and pray—she was ready to leave.

Not that he had much push with the Man Upstairs. No, he and God hadn't been much on speaking terms lately. God was for old women and children.

He had no need—and no room in his life—for God.

He peeked through a crack in the curtain and sighed. Why would anybody want to live and work in this hellish place? Scraggly bushes for trees. No green grass. No lakes, few rivers. Nothing but miles and miles of dusty desert, dotted with a few prickly cactus here and there. Completely unlike the rest of the country he'd travelled through to get here. He was certainly looking forward to the return trip. Perhaps he would take Miss Duncan on the stage to Phoenix then take the train east. Yes, that was the ticket.

He smiled to himself. Sometimes he surprised himself with his witticisms.

The stage righted itself and his fellow passengers settled back into their former upright positions. Would this trip never end? When first offered the opportunity to travel to Cave Creek, Arizona Territory, to fetch Miss Duncan, he was excited at the chance to see some different country.

But two train rides and a week later, he already longed for civilization. He was a city boy, and unashamed of the fact. He didn't like seedy hotels in small towns. He didn't care for unrecognizable food on his plate. He didn't like the smell emanating from him and the others in the stage after three days of travel without benefit of a hot bath each night.

He didn't like dust.

He swatted at a patch of dirt on his knee. He'd not packed enough clothes. This was his sixth day in these pants and his third in this shirt. He wasn't certain he'd ever get the dirt out of the collars and cuffs. Perhaps Cave Creek boasted a laundry. He would pay whatever it took to get his shirts clean.

Peter ran a finger around the neck of his last starched collar. Sweat, heat, and dust were not a good combination, and his skin chafed in the most awkward places from its ill treatment. But tonight he would rest in a comfortable bed in the best hotel in town.

Another hole in the road sent a shockwave up his spine. The fellow across from him let loose a foul-smelling cloud of gas. The woman beside Peter covered her nose with a handkerchief. Peter smiled as she tsk-tsked at the man, who shrugged his apology.

Peter leaned forward and stuck his nose past the curtain to breathe deep.

Even dust and heat from the outside was better than the stench inside.

To his surprise and pleasure, a whitewashed house drew into view.

At least, he thought it was a house.

A rickety picket fence surrounded the ramshackle structure, and smoke spewed from a chimney that hung at a precarious angle. Sheets draped the railing on the veranda, and a couple of children played in the dirt near the front step.

About half a block of empty space, then more buildings, these connected by a boardwalk and a covering indicated signs of human population. The driver shouted at the horses to "whoa-up" or something to that effect, and Peter once again braced against the window as the stage slowed.

When the stagecoach drew to a complete stop in front of the combination stage office, general store, and post office, he waited until the driver opened the door and pulled down the step before assisting the lone woman out. Brushing off his jacket and straightening his cravat, he stepped into the hot late afternoon sun of his destination.

Whether from extreme exhaustion or because he'd lost his land legs to the infernal rocking and rolling of the stage, he wasn't certain, but he hooked his heel on the lip of the coach. Flailing to catch his balance, he missed the next two steps. He landed unceremoniously in a heap in the dust and horse apples littering the street, the wind knocked out of him.

When he opened his eyes, he found himself staring at the worn boots of a cowboy, one who hadn't polished his footwear in a very long time. If ever.

And the hems of the man's dungarees were turned up several times, creating pockets which captured some of the desert floor, a coarse sand that looked as inviting as a beach at first glance but which was, in reality, sharp stones mixed with cactus needles.

A leather-covered hand reached down into his field of vision, and he grasped the offer of help. So humiliating to make his appearance in this way, but with any luck, he'd be gone within a couple of days.

He'd never see any of these yahoos again.

The person behind the hand yanked him to his feet as though he weighed only half of his hundred and sixty pounds, and he teetered on unsteady legs for a couple of heartbeats, brushing the dirt from his clothing, before raising his gaze to offer his thanks.

A pair of dark-brown eyes stared back at him beneath a wide-brimmed hat. Freckles dotted the nose and ebbed into a smattering of color across the cheeks. An intelligent brow and sharp chin framed the mouth that currently drew into a lopsided smile.

Or a sneer.

And long, brown hair cascaded over her shoulders.

He blinked. Dehydration—or dust, or hunger, or bad food—made him see things that weren't there.

A couple of more blinks to clear his vision.

No. He was definitely a she.

Chapter 2

How humiliating.

    Peter glanced around. A couple of townswomen tittered as they passed what was likely the most excitement they'd see in this burg today. Two boys chasing a dog slowed long enough to snicker in his direction before dashing down an alleyway.

How humiliating indeed.

He turned back to the woman. Despite her obvious leanings to wearing men's clothing, there was no disguising her femininity. High cheekbones, skin appearing so soft his fingers itched to touch tender flesh that looked as delicate as a Georgia peach. A rosebud mouth simply begging to be kissed—

He jerked his thoughts back. No woman in her right mind would kiss him after he'd made such a fool of himself in the middle of the main street of this Podunk town.

She stared at him, her eyes the color of hot chocolate, appraising him from head to foot, and surely finding him wanting.

Yet that sweet mouth didn't sneer or snarl. In fact, her gaze indicated she found the spectacle of him interesting.

Curiosity, yes. Disgust or disdain, no.

He bowed slightly and dipped his head in her direction. "Ma'am, thank you for your help."

Her eyes traveled his dusty and rumpled form once more before returning to his face, where she focused on his chin.

This time he offered his hand. "Peter Golding."

Rather than slipping her fingers into his grip to allow him the opportunity to show his respect by kissing the back of her hand, she gripped his in as firm a handshake as any he'd exchanged with a man. Her leather gloves were rough against his skin.

Her hand felt as natural in his own as though created to be there.

And the jolt of electricity that traveled the length of his arm and back down to tingle the tips of his fingers surprised him.

He shook off the feeling. He was here to find Miss Daisy Duncan and convince her to return to New York City with him, sealing his career in the publishing industry, and, in particular, with his uncle.

A mite opportunistic, perhaps, but necessary.

Despite being an editor of romance novels, he held no misconceptions about love.

That might be for other people.

But not for him.

Lily headed back to her spread, the sun at her back. She'd arrived in town right before the jangle of harness, the driver's coarse words, and the thunder of horses' hooves on the dusty street indicated the arrival of the stage.

And then that strange man fell at her feet. She giggled to herself. Those biddies in the general store sure enjoyed the spectacle, and even right now were likely gossiping about her.

Well, let them talk.

Chores awaited her attention at home. Stock needed watering. Cows needed tending. Not to mention the scraggly flowers and vegetables in her kitchen garden begging for water and weeding. She'd sorely neglected them the past few days while struggling to finish her story.

Flowers. A waste of time, her father would say.

But not her normally over-practical mother.

Mama loved daisies. Said the white petals surrounding the yellow center reminded her of angels, which reminded her of God. So she'd always managed to coax a few plants each season, and when the blooms were full, brought them into the house and put them in an empty canning jar of water.

Well, Lily didn't know about angels and God.

But daisies reminded her of Mama. Which was why she chose that as her pen name. And the two names beginning with the same letter sounded much more romantic than Lily.

Plain. Simple. Not romantic like Rose or Iris or Daisy.

She sighed. Maybe they had chosen the right name for her. Plain. Simple. Unromantic.

She chucked the reins, urging her mount into a lope. Time to get home and eat her rattler stew. This had been a busy day already. First, she'd finished the next installment in her story. Then she shot the snake.

Then she made a fool of herself—and likely of the poor man, too, if truth be told—by offering her hand to him.

Once again, she wished she were more like the heroines in her stories.

Peter waited until the two groups of ladies were waited on and left the store, giggling and whispering behind their hands, slying their eyes toward him. This town needed some livening up, if his fall into the street was the main topic of conversation today.

Once they left, he stepped up to the counter marked POST OFFICE. If Miss Daisy Duncan lived here, they would know. "I am looking for Miss Daisy Duncan. Can you tell me where she lives?"

The older woman, gray streaking her dark hair and wrinkles decorating the corners of her eyes, peered at him through her spectacles. "Friend of hers?"

"No ma'am."

The woman harrumphed. "Thought so. Because if you knew her, you'd know where she lived, wouldn't you?"

"Yes ma'am." Peter had heard stories of small towns, how everybody knew everybody and their business. The thought gave him nightmares. "Can you tell me where she lives?"

"What do you want with her?"

He sighed. "Ma'am, I'm sure Miss Duncan will tell you once we've had the opportunity to discuss the matter. But it is a private matter. I have come all the way from New York City to see her."

The woman's eyes widened and her mouth formed a tiny *O*, reminding Peter of a goldfish he'd once seen in a tank. "New York? Where she gets mail from?"

"Yes ma'am." One benefit—perhaps the only—of small town living was the postmistress knew every piece of mail each person received. "Can you tell me how to get to her house?"

"Sorry, son, I don't know."

Peter's heart thudded to the toes of his boots like a rock in a barrel. "But you talked like you knew her."

"I don't rightly know her. Don't know anything about Daisy Duncan 'ceptin' for three things."

"And what are those?"

"She sends tons of packages to New York City. And she gets lots of envelopes back."

"That's two things. What's the third?"

"Cactus Lil brings and picks up all that mail."

"Cactus Lil?"

"Yep. You met her. The one who picked you up out of the dirt."

Peter's ears burned at her words. Would he ever live this day down?

Not to mention he'd had the source of information in his hands—so to speak—and let her go.

Chapter 3

Peter spent a restless night and evening in the only hotel in town—which wasn't the high-quality establishment the stage driver promised—and rose the next morning to find there was no hot water for a bath.

He sat at a table in a corner by himself while all around him happy families and cheerful travelers abounded. What they were so enthusiastic about, he couldn't fathom. Already his uncle had sent two telegrams asking about his progress, even though he'd been here barely twelve hours.

So far, the only good thing was the coffee. Strong but not bitter, laced with plenty of sugar, hotter than love—as his mother used to say—and silky with the rich cream served in a cow-shaped jug.

If the coffee was any indication of how the rest of his day would go, he could bear it.

Despite having no eggs or biscuits, he managed to fill up with homemade bread, butter, and jam, along with a steak almost as big as the plate it was served on.

Sitting back, he patted his stomach. No doubt about it, that was the best meal he'd eaten since leaving New York.

He dropped a quarter on the table to pay for the meal, along with a nickel for the server, and pushed his chair back. Time to get to the real focus of his day: finding Miss Daisy Duncan.

And if that meant groveling at the feet of Cactus Lil—what kind of a name was that for a woman, anyway?—then so be it. He would do just about anything to achieve his goal and get back to civilization. He wouldn't spend one more day here than necessary.

He exited the hotel and paused, squinting in the morning sun. Just after eight, and already the temperature had to be in the eighties. What was it with this country? Was it closer to hell? Is that why everything looked so burnt up? So much heat. So little water.

On the boardwalk just outside the door stood a man wrapped in a long apron to protect his clothes, a broom in one hand. He nodded in Peter's direction. "Good morning, sir."

"Morning. Where is the livery?"

The man nodded, turned, and pointed down the street. "Over yonder. See the barn and corral? All them horses? That's where we keep the livery."

Ears burning, Peter tipped his hat in acknowledgment. "Thank you."

"Going riding, are you?" The man swiped at a speck of dust on the wood, sending it careening into Peter's shoe tips. "Nice day for a ride. Watch out for the rattlers, though."

Peter nodded, biting his tongue to keep his sarcasm in check. His sense of humor—finely tuned as it was—would likely be lost in this backwater community. "Good chatting with you."

"And you too."

The man resumed his sweeping as Peter turned in the direction of the livery. The *scritch-scratch* of the broom followed him the hundred feet or so to his destination: Walker's Livery.

He smiled at the irony of the name. Pure genius. He stepped into the darkened barn. A large black horse in the first stall shook its head in his direction as though warning him off. From a dark corner just inside the door, a nondescript mongrel with a black swath of hair over one eye like a pirate's patch, rose and stepped toward him, its curled tail slowly beating the air.

Peter stepped back. Another step and he was outside the barn once more, the sun beating on the back of his head.

"Kin I help ya?"

He jumped at the voice and whirled around, hands balling into fists as he assumed the classic pugilist form: left hand forward, right hand beneath the chin. While he had never actually fought outside the boxing ring before, he was prepared.

The stranger before him, dressed in worn but clean overalls, plaid shirt, and mud-caked boots, raised his hands in surrender. "Okay. Ya got me. I give up." The piece of straw between his teeth bobbed in time with his words. He held out a hand as large as a ham. "Name's Jed." He quirked his chin over Peter's shoulder. "And that there is my barn."

A soft growl sounded from behind Peter, and a shiver ran up his back. He moved a couple of steps from its source.

"And that there is my dog too. He guards the barn. And me." Jed tossed Peter a quick smile. "Likely if you lower your hands and lessen the bristle on the back of your neck, he'll back off."

Peter relaxed his shoulders and shook the man's hand, his own disappearing as though into a sack. "Peter Golding. I'm new in town."

Jed pushed his hat back on his head and pulled the stick of straw from his mouth. "You don't say."

"Yes." Peter caught the man's smile and the wrinkles in the corners of his eyes. "I see. You were—what do you call it here? Joshing me?"

"Right." Jed released his hand and replaced the straw. "What kin I do for ya?"

"I need to rent a horse and carriage."

"No carriages. Not much call for them. In fact, the doc is the only person in town who owns a carriage. And he's out on calls."

"A buggy, perhaps? Even an open phaeton would do."

"No buggy. No whatever that other thing is. Got a stock wagon for hauling hay and goods, but that's rented out for the month."

Peter's heart landed with a thunk right on top of his breakfast. "What can you rent me? I need to ride out to Miss Daisy Duncan's home. I understand it's several miles from town."

Jed removed his hat and scratched his head. "Well, I don't know any Daisy Duncan, Miss or otherwise. Know Cactus Lil Duncan. Lily Duncan. But she lives by herself."

Any expectation that this day would go more smoothly than the past several weeks evaporated like a snowflake. "Perhaps she is acquainted with Miss Daisy Duncan because she brings in and retrieves mail for her."

"That's as may be." Jed replaced his hat. "Come along. I have horses." He peered at Peter. "You know how to ride, doncha?"

Peter straightened and pushed his shoulders back. "I do. Academy trained. I also know dressage and have finaled in puissance several times."

Jed whistled, a long, drawn-out note. "Imagine that. Can't say I know what all that is, but I guess if you say you can ride, that'll suit."

Peter wasn't certain who his riding abilities would suit—Jed or the horse—but keeping his question to himself seemed the most expeditious at the moment. He followed Jed into the barn where the livery owner walked the length of the building, pausing to pat a nose here or tug a forelock there. Not seeming to find what he wanted, he turned and walked back toward Peter, finally stopping outside a stall holding a rusty-brown horse with a black mane.

"Old Sam should do. Not too lively. Not lazy, though. No siree, not lazy." He opened the door and led the beast out, tied him to a hitching ring in the walkway, then proceeded to put on the halter and saddle blanket, talking quietly to the gelding all the while. He looked over his shoulder. "Only thing to remember about Sam is he doesn't like rabbits."

Peter nodded. "That's a great name you have on your business."

Jed cocked his head. "Huh?"

"You know. Walker's Livery. For a business that rents horses and conveyances so you don't have to walk."

Another shake of the man's head.

Peter groaned.

He'd walked right into a mess of manure again, figuratively speaking.

He rolled his eyes at his ineptness. "Let me guess. Your last name is Walker. Right?"

"Right." Jed turned, a western saddle in his hands. "Wait until the boys at the general store hear that one. Just shows how dumb they all are. None of them ever said anything half so smart as that before." He slung the saddle over the horse's back and bent to pull the cinch rope tight. "This here should fit you fine."

"You wouldn't have an English saddle, would you?"

"English?"

Peter's breakfast dropped another inch. "Yes. No horn, more flat in the seat?"

"Nah, we ain't got no English saddle. No French and no Spanish ones, either." He tugged the stirrups loose then cupped his hands together. "Come on over here. We'll get you up, and I'll adjust the stirrups for you."

Peter complied rather than insist on mounting by himself. In minutes, Jed had him situated then untied the horse and handed the reins up over its head.

"You just go south out of town about three miles, take the road near the pile of big rocks, and ride until you get to Lil's house. Can't miss it. Less'n you like to ride with your eyes closed. Which I wouldn't recommend."

"Why do you call her Cactus Lil?"

"'Cuz she's just about as bristly as one. Not a tender bone in her body." He led the way out of the barn. "Course, we don't nobody call her that to her face. She might shoot us."

Peter swallowed hard. If this woman was related to Miss Daisy Duncan, he hoped she was a distant relation.

Because surely his Miss Daisy Duncan was nothing like this Cactus Lil.

Lily wheeled her quarter horse to the right and headed off a recalcitrant steer, sending it skittering back into the herd.

She tugged her bandana up over her nose. "Dumbest beasts on God's green earth."

Why the Good Lord felt it necessary to leave out the brains when He made these creatures, she couldn't say.

Probably just another reason why she couldn't buy into the whole God thing.

She reined in her horse and surveyed the cattle milling around. Quiet. At least for now. Time to fix the hole in the fence.

She urged the buckskin toward the supply wagon pressed up near the fence line. A pole, rotted near the ground, leaned haphazardly like a drunk on a binge in town. It needed to be replaced, or she'd spend all her time chasing cattle off the open range and back onto her property.

Beasts off private land had a life expectancy of about eight seconds. If the coyotes didn't get them first, roving bands of rustlers and low-life thieves would.

She dismounted and tied her horse under a mesquite tree then went to work. Her shovel chipped away at the hard-packed soil like a spoon on granite, a frustrating teaspoon at a time. She paused a couple of times to straighten her back and swipe the sweat from her forehead.

No matter how hard the work, Lily had no desire to live anywhere else. Even going into Cave Creek was like traveling to a foreign country for her. Even the cactus, prickly and unwieldy, soothed her soul.

Lily grabbed the exposed bottom of the fence post and tugged. Still pretty sturdy. She returned to her horse and mounted, then tossed her lariat loop over the top of the post and tied the other end of the rope to the saddle horn. Lining her horse up, she urged it forward until the rope went taut.

Within a few minutes, the post wiggled then sagged in her direction, until finally the force pulled the old wood from the ground.

She dismounted and went back to check the results. The only thing worse than a broken post in a hole was a broken tooth—her father said this to her after a failed attempt to pull a bad molar.

The post had come out intact.

She went back to the buckskin and untied the lariat. "Good work, Tom."

After returning the beast to its place beneath the tree, she continued her work. She dug the hole another foot deeper, planted the new post, filled in the hole, restrung the barbed wire, then stepped back to survey her work. Looked fine.

Next job was dipping the cattle. She'd noticed several shaking their heads and rubbing up against the fence posts. A quick check of a nearby heifer confirmed her initial suspicion: mites. Not her favorite task, and certainly not theirs either.

The sun beat down, hot on the back of her neck at barely nine. She'd been up for three hours and had another eight ahead before she could call it a day. Several doves cooed in the mesquite, and a cactus wren called from the top of a saguaro. She breathed in deep and exhaled slowly.

She and this country were perfectly suited for each other.

Sure, she knew what the townspeople called her behind her back. *Cactus Lil.* No doubt they had words like *prickly*, *tough*, and *uncomely* to describe her.

But she didn't care.

She was right where she was supposed to be.

She mounted and headed the cattle toward the gate on the other side of the pasture. The dipping tanks were in the next pasture, and she had a good hour's work just to get them there.

Best to get on with it.

No point delaying the inevitable.

Sweat trickled down Peter's back, pooling just above where his belt cinched off his pants. Pants now damp and dusty.

Although Jed Walker said he couldn't miss the Duncan ranch, apparently he had. His one-hour ride had multiplied into a two-hour roam through the most inhospitable countryside he'd ever encountered. His backside was sore already from the saddle, and despite Jed's assurance that the only thing this horse didn't like was rabbits, the beast spooked at every rock and every bird.

His legs were as tired as though he'd run a marathon from the effort of gripping the sides of the animal. And his hands, sweaty from the heat and the tension within him, ached from holding the reins.

He studied the surrounding landscape, looking for some evidence of life apart from himself and his mount. Nothing.

At least, nothing he could see squinting through tired eyes. He'd never known the sun to shine so bright, reflecting off the sand and rocks. He'd seen snow, of course, in New York City, and wished for some now. But even the whiteness of a snowbank in the middle of the day couldn't compare to this.

Wishing he'd worn a proper hat—not this narrow-brimmed fedora that was all the style in the City—he twisted in the saddle to survey in all directions. If he didn't find something—or somebody—soon, he'd have to turn back.

His tongue stuck to the roof of his mouth, and he wished for yet another thing he'd neglected to bring along with him—water. Peter pulled a handkerchief from his pocket and mopped his face and neck. His pale skin was not made for this kind of climate.

He reined the horse to a halt, and the creature dropped its head and nibbled at something it deemed worthy of eating. Peter could see nothing from his vantage point, but then again, he didn't know what was safe to eat and what wasn't. He'd heard stories of spiders as big as teacups and scorpions as big as lobsters. Plants that could kill you just by touching them. Animals that would eat you alive.

The breeze carried on it the smell of something green—mesquite, perhaps?—and manure. Or something very like it. He checked over the rear end of the horse—nothing there.

So the odor wasn't coming from his mount.

The road nestled down in a hollow between two slight rises. He listened again. A low moan met his ears. He cocked his head to determine the direction. His horse raised its head and twitched its ears to the right. Peter yanked on the reins and urged the beast in that direction. He would trust his mount's hearing over his own.

A couple of minutes later, he came to a fence line that brought him to a halt. A hundred yards inside the pasture stood a large tank, about twenty feet across, with a ramp that led down into it and another ramp leading out. The down ramp had a barrier on both sides shaped like a funnel which narrowed so that only one animal could go into the tank at a time.

He'd heard of these contraptions—a dipping tank.

Beyond, a cloud of dust indicated cattle on the move.

Which meant people.

Even just one person would be fine. So long as it was somebody who could tell him how to find Miss Daisy Duncan.

And then he could be out of here.

Lily's horse knew the man was there before she did, and she made a mental note not to allow the cattle or the work to distract so completely in the future. To survive in this land, she needed to stay on high alert, ready for the unexpected.

Her hand went to the grip of her trusty revolver, and a glance at her rifle ensured it also was at the ready. Until she knew if this was friend or foe—and she had no friends, so the latter was more likely—she would be on guard.

The rider—a man—waved in her direction and jabbed at his horse's sides, flapping the reins like a child on a stick horse. Whoever he was, he wasn't from around here. Nobody in their right mind would ride that way.

The man's horse trudged toward her, never increasing its gait no matter how much the man persisted in his scarecrow-like posturing.

Must be a rental horse.

The stranger from yesterday flashed into her mind. She probably shouldn't have offered to help him up. Likely embarrassed him. Might even have made him mad.

She unsnapped her holster.

She kept her horse moving, pushing the cattle to the tank. Once she got them going, most would follow. But she kept her eyes on the stranger, ignoring his hails and waves. She stiffened her shoulders and sat straighter in the saddle, glad for the bandana covering her face. The barbed wire fence suddenly seemed like a poor barrier between them.

Maybe he'd simply keep on riding if she looked tough enough.

And if not, she wouldn't go down without a fight.

Chapter 4

Peter stared at the rider before him. Downright unfriendly. Intimidating in his posture.

And all around, cattle milled and bawled and jostled for position.

"Do you know where Miss Daisy Duncan lives?"

Above the handkerchief covering his face, the man on horseback shook his head.

Peter persisted. "Do you know her?"

The man's eyes widened then squinted at him. No response.

Peter tried another tack. Perhaps if he feigned interest in the man's endeavors, he might get further. He sidled his horse toward the gate. For once the stubborn beast obeyed, and he was able to hook the latch with his toe.

The gate swung toward him, complaining on rusty hinges. He aimed the horse through the opening then leaned over to hook his toe in the top rail and pull the gate shut.

Peter studied the other man, who rode his horse as though born in the saddle. The individual cattle bawled and balked as they trotted up the short ramp, pushed on by the ones following close on their heels. The rider kept the line moving through the funnel. Most of the beasts hesitated as they came to the end of the ramp, but they ultimately leapt into the tank, disappeared beneath the surface, and then came up snorting and bellowing and scrambling for the ramp up and out.

Peter swallowed back another dry, dust-flavored mouthful of saliva, thankful he'd had the presence of mind to bring a handkerchief today. Although not accustomed to carrying such a thing—considering them more suited to old men with wheezy coughs and old women with rheumy eyes—he'd made certain to procure several in town.

Uncertain what to do with himself—for surely the stranger purposely ignored him—he edged nearer the tank to watch where the real action was taking place. A corrugated metal edging surrounded the hole in the ground, disappearing below the surface. The tank, wide enough for one animal to swim its length, long enough for up to three beasts at the same time, was a marvel of simplicity.

The same breeze which carried off the dust also brought to his nostrils the odors of the process before him—wet cowhide—not unlike that of a wet dog. Manure—not from the tank, he was certain, but rather from the enclosed areas surrounding him. And something else—slightly tarry.

He dismounted and tied the horse to the fence. The indifferent beast immediately lowered its head and snatched at mouthfuls of golden-brown grass before regarding him balefully. He hitched one foot over the bottom rail of the enclosure as he'd seen cowboys in town do. Perhaps a casual appearance would convince the stranger he was worth speaking to.

A large cow-creature leapt wide as if hoping to avoid the tank altogether, and splashed into the end of the container closest to him. Water splayed out in all directions, but most of it drowned his best boots in the smelly concoction.

"Hey, watch it!"

As soon as the words were out of his mouth, Peter wished he could snatch them back. The stranger reined in his horse and, although the kerchief still covered his face, Peter was certain his eyes crinkled at the corners.

He was laughing at this greenhorn. No doubt about it.

Well, Peter would show that man that he hadn't been born yesterday. He perched on the top rail of the fence, swung one leg over, then the other, until he was facing the tank. Sitting ramrod straight, he hooked his heels over the second rung. Satisfied with his stance, he turned to stare at the animal wading through the tank, refusing to give the stranger any more attention.

That would teach him to be so rude.

A number of cattle continued the dipping process, each one a close imitation of the one before. Several beasts—no doubt aware of what was going on, as they looked larger and more ornery than some of the less-experienced creatures—huddled in some sort of cattle solidarity. The stranger occasionally strove to separate one from its comrades, but then abandoned them and returned to the more compliant cattle.

The sun kissed the horizon as the final of the more willing animals leapt into the tank. Now the number of cattle on Peter's side of the corral outnumbered the remaining mini-herd on the stranger's side. To his amusement, the rider and horse, working as a team, darted and lunged in their attempts to cut one overly large bull from the stubborn bunch.

But the beast was in no mood to admit defeat. It lowered its head and splayed its front feet then pawed at the dusty ground. Peter smiled. This was going to be interesting. He'd read accounts and heard stories of bulls in this classic fighting stance.

The stranger and his mount stood their ground.

The bull stared at his opposition, its eyes glowing red in the waning sunlight.

Inch by agonizingly slow inch, the stranger shook out the lariat in his hand. Where just moments before he'd used this length of rope as a noise-maker—slapping his own thigh to get the cattle's attention—now the loop snaked toward the ground.

The bull's gaze followed the rope as though frozen, one foot lifted off the ground, its ears pitched sharply forward.

Peter held his breath, not wanting to break the mesmerizing spell the rider cast upon the creature, much as a snake charmer does a cobra. He stared at the gloved hand holding the rope, the narrow shoulders and narrower waist of the rider, the strong thighs gripping his mount, and the unusually small boots peeking through the stirrups.

If he didn't know better. . .

He shook off his foolishness. A small man could never be confused with a woman. And while this rider may be small in stature—more like a teen than a man—he had demonstrated his prowess in his control of these cattle and his horsemanship.

Then again, he'd been fooled the previous day. . .

The lariat snapped the air and rose like a cloud over the rider, spinning effortlessly. A rope typhoon threatened to engulf horse and all, and a soft moan that reminded him of the printing presses starting up on a cold morning carried on the breeze. Peter's gaze fixed on the loop which defied gravity and the laws of physics, hanging between earth and sky as though on invisible marionette strings.

A quick flick of the stranger's wrist, and the loop sailed through the air toward the bull. Mesmerized, Peter followed its action.

But the bull was not there.

Instead, the horse snorted and reared as the beast charged past it.

Straight toward him.

Frozen in time and place, nothing moved but the four-legged monster closing distance faster than Peter thought possible. Snorting and bellowing like a medieval fire-breathing dragon from a children's book. Shaking the earth like a wooly mammoth from pre-historic times.

Peter glanced around. His horse, startled by the commotion, now stood some fifty feet away.

No help there.

The instigator of this situation, the stranger who clearly didn't have a single hospitable bone in his body, sat frozen in place.

Peter looked back. Twenty feet. He had to make a choice. Jump off the fence? He doubted whether the creature would consider the wooden posts and rails a worthy adversary, and would likely crash through them, leaving nothing between him and the beast. His horse, a bigger coward than its rider, would not stick around.

He glanced at the bull again.

Ten feet.

Well, since the creature didn't want to go into the tank, perhaps that was the best place. Embarrassing, yes. But at least he'd be alive.

To paraphrase an old saying his uncle loved to quote, "He who dunks and runs away, lives to fight another day."

No, no, no!

Lily begged the charging bull to stop.

Panic and fear paralyzed as never before. Sure, she'd had a few close calls in the past. But not like this.

The greenhorn from town perched on top of the fence like a chicken waiting to get snatched by a low-circling hawk.

If anything happened to him, it would be her fault.

She jabbed her spurs into her frightened horse's sides. "Git, I say!"

Her mount dug in its hind legs, lowered its head, and took off after the bull like a thoroughbred out of the starting gate. They covered the twenty or so feet in not much more than a second or two. Her lariat sliced the air over her head like a bolt of lightning. She leaned forward, releasing the rope. The loop hung over the bull's horns for an agonizing additional second before settling.

Her horse jabbed its forelegs into the dust and sat back on its haunches as she tied the rope to the saddle horn. The bull's front legs came off the ground at the increased tension on the rope, and Lily uncoiled her back-up lariat.

Keeping her eyes on the enraged beast, she plied the rope overhead and, as her horse kept the first taut, timed her next throw to match its bucking and kicking, and scooped the bull's back legs neatly into the second lariat. This move worked better with a second horse and rider, but she'd managed it on her own in the past.

She tied the back-up rope to the horn and yanked on the slack. The loop closed and snagged the beast's legs together, pulling it off-balance. Another yank and the enraged creature was on its back, her horse pulling away, one step at a time, to keep it in that position. So long as it couldn't get its legs beneath it, the bull would be forced to remain on its side.

Assured her mount had the situation under control, she did a running dismount and headed for the fence.

The man was not there.

She glanced around. His mount stood some fifty feet away, chewing a mouthful of prairie grass.

Her cattle crowded the corral beyond the dipping tank, tails swishing. The remainder of the holdouts, three in total, stood with their backs to the far fence.

A shout and splashes from her left caught her attention.

Oh, no.

Sure, she'd wished him gone.

Well, gone he was.

Swimming.

In her dipping tank.

Full of mesquite creosote water, dead ticks, cow hair, and who knew what else.

She strode across the muddy ground and stood over the tank, hands on hips, looking down at the stranger. Peter something, didn't he say? Not that knowing his name made a bit of difference. She'd send him on his way just as quick whether his name was Peter-something or Davy Crockett.

The man's head bobbed to the surface, a hand reaching for her. "Help me, please. I cannot swim."

Couldn't swim? What kind of a fool purposely launched himself into a pool of water, knowing he couldn't swim? She grabbed his outstretched hand. Pulling this man out of bad situations was becoming a habit.

She found herself staring into his face. His eyes pleaded with her not to release him. Those blue-green eyes, deep as turquoise and about as pretty, beckoned to her, imbuing her with a strength she didn't know she had. Her heart flip-flopped like a flapjack in a frying pan.

She extracted him from the water's grip and yanked him out into the mud, where he flopped and heaved like the twenty-inch Gila trout she'd landed last year.

A trophy catch, to be sure.

The fish, not him.

Peter-something turned onto his back, his eyes still closed for a long minute, before fixing that dangerous-to-her-heart stare on her. "Thanks, Daisy."

"You are welcome."

His eyes widened, and a slow smile covered his face.

Realizing her mistake at once, she coughed and stuttered to cover herself. "Only the name's not Daisy. It's Lily. Don't know any Daisy Duncan."

"I didn't say Duncan. I said Daisy."

Trapped. Like a rat in a corner. With no way out.

Peter raised himself up on an elbow. From down here, Miss Daisy Duncan presented a picture of contrasts. The steamy romance writer dressed like a man. Rode like a native. Was as strong as most men he'd met in the city.

He struggled to his feet, swishing his wet hair back from his face. "Don't worry. I won't tell anybody who you are."

She squinted at him, her mouth a straight line. "You better not."

He held out his hands, palms facing her, in surrender. "Must be hard living on your own in this part of the country."

"Got nothing to do with it. Folks just don't need to know, that's all."

"Right." He dusted off his pants, although all he really accomplished was to swipe dust and dirt in streaks down his thighs. "Understood."

"Don't care if you understand. Just do as I say."

Peter sighed. This woman was going to be a tough nut to crack. "Do you treat every man who comes to visit you like this?"

She folded her arms across her chest and frowned. "Don't know. Never had a man visit me. Not unless he was selling something or trying to steal from me." Her fingers rested on the wooden grip of the very dangerous-looking gun hanging from her hip. "Are you selling or stealing?"

"Neither. In fact, I've come with a proposition for you."

She took a step back, the frown replaced with a different kind of downturned brow—one of puzzlement.

And something else.

Curiosity, perhaps?

"Proposition?"

"My name is Peter Golding."

"You told me that yesterday."

"And I'm from New York City."

"Figured as much." With that, she turned away and headed for her horse, which stood at the ready with the bull still down on its side. "Excuse me, but I need to finish dipping these animals before I lose the sun completely."

"Please, just a few minutes."

She backed the horse away from him, dragging the still-struggling bull, until she had the animal near the funnel to the dipping tank. She dismounted, untied the beast, and slapped it on the rump. The bull got to its feet, rear-first, and trotted down the ramp, into the tank, and up the other side as though it had fully intended to comply all along.

Daisy—or Lily, as she called herself—turned her mount toward the other three, and slapped her rope in their direction. They hesitated a couple of heartbeats before following the leader.

Peter released a pent-up breath, glad the ordeal was over, while Lily rounded the corral and opened the gate of the holding pen to the pasture. The cattle trotted into the open land. Although he didn't know much about bovines, he judged them pleased to get back to what they did best—eating.

He waited until she returned, reining in her mount a few feet from him. "As I was saying—"

She held up one hand to stop him. "As I said, not interested."

He looked around at the barren landscape all around him. Not a living thing moved—except the cattle. And snakes. And spiders. A shiver ran down his spine. He couldn't decide which was worse—being eaten alive by some monster of the desert, or returning to New York empty-handed.

No. Returning without Daisy wasn't an option.

And if he knew one thing, this woman was Daisy.

He studied the ground at his feet. Drab, dry, barren. Nothing grew here. Hardly any people lived here. The offer to move to New York City was an attractive package, since he could see no reason why anybody would choose to stay here if they didn't have to.

So the big question—the one that would determine his future—was: how to convince her?

He swiped at a rivulet of water running down his cheek. Certainly, his Miss Daisy Duncan wasn't a cowgirl. She never wore pants. Wouldn't even think of such a thing. She certainly didn't shoot or rope. Didn't straddle a horse like a man. Her skin wasn't browned by the sun or dried by the desert heat. Her hair was—

He brought himself up short. What was he thinking? Somehow he'd managed to create the perfect woman based on her writing. He'd envisioned her as a tender belle of the South because of her words, her obvious experience with love, and—wait a minute. Maybe she was spurning him because she was already pledged to another.

He gritted his teeth, ruing the fact he'd waited so long to put his brilliant idea into motion. Another had come along and stolen her heart.

His shoulders slumped. He'd come all this way for nothing. How could he return to the City with the news that Miss Daisy Duncan was an engaged or married woman? His uncle had allowed no room for failure for any reason.

He met her steady gaze. Her eyes, dark as a well and about as deep, stared back at him as though defying him to contradict her. To press his point. To insist on being heard.

Feeling as though he were dropping down into that well, Peter commanded his frozen brain to respond to her challenge.

But once again, he was back in boarding school, the victim of the latest bully. Afraid of his own shadow. Wanting so much to please and never measuring up.

Why he ever thought he could accomplish this seemingly simple task now struck him full force. Here he was, thirty years of age, unmarried, a junior editor to the senior editor, barely a half-step above the guy who emptied the trash cans in the office. Trying to work his way up the corporate staircase to the corner office his uncle and employer occupied.

What had he been thinking?

Her words pulled him back to the here and now, and he batted at an insect that buzzed around his ear.

"I'll leave you to find your way off my property." She quirked her kerchief-concealed chin in the direction of town. "The road is that way."

"But—"

"I'm not interested in what you are selling."

"As I said, I'm not—"

"Leave. Now." Her hand dropped to her gun. "Before I have to make my point more clear."

Of all the—he'd never met a woman—or a man—so downright cantankerous as this woman. She had her nerve.

He mounted his horse, grimacing as his wet backside hit the leather. The ride back to town was going to be uncomfortable. He'd probably get a blister. Or two. Peter gathered the reins and nudged his horse to move on. When the beast ignored him, he yanked on the reins and dug in his heels.

His mount turned to stare at him from one baleful eye, as though challenging him to try that move again. Well, he'd had enough of being pushed around today. He shortened the reins, forcing the horse's head up and, using the ends of the leather, slapped the animal's rump. "Git up, you stupid animal!"

The horse lowered its head and lunged forward, moving from a walk to a lope to a gallop before Peter could completely gain his seat. Flopping up and down, he struggled to get his rhythm as they charged down the road. Peter pulled back on the reins to slow the beast, but once again, it ignored his command.

Peter sighed and hunched low over the animal's shoulders.

The ride back to town would be shorter than the ride out here.

That was one consolation.

Chapter 5

Unable to face Daisy Duncan—or whatever she wanted to call herself—on an empty stomach, Peter lazed about his hotel room until nearing nine the next morning. In the restaurant, a petite woman—more a girl, really—took his order and returned just minutes later with a repeat of yesterday's fare—steak and bread.

After working his way through the food, he lingered over coffee, playing and replaying the humiliating events of the day before. He must look a complete fool to this woman.

He buried his face in his hands. How could he ever convince Daisy to return with him?

At this rate, his only hope was that Lily Duncan would fall off her horse laughing at him, and would then admit she needed his help. Maybe then she'd listen to him.

Because without a doubt, the woman he'd met yesterday needed nobody.

The bells on the town church pealed the hour, and he counted the chimes while his mind still worked on his predicament. Nine. Ten. Eleven.

Eleven!

He pushed his chair back and stood. He'd managed to while away the morning worrying about how to convince Miss Daisy Duncan to talk to him, but he was no closer to the answer to that conundrum than before. He tossed a couple of coins on the table to pay for his meal, adding another nickel for the server then headed for the door.

As he passed the front desk, the clerk called to him. "Mr. Golding. A telegram for you, sir."

Peter altered course and held out his hand, the food in his stomach tying itself into a knot the size of a large cabbage. The only person who would send a telegram would be his uncle, inquiring about the status of the mission.

His shaking fingers fumbled with the folded paper. He sighed. Should he take it to his room and read it? Perhaps his uncle was merely asking for an update.

He turned to the clerk. "If I need to send a response, where is the telegraph office?"

The man pointed. "Over there in the same storefront as the stage station and the general store and post office."

Wonderful. Now he could return to the scene of another humiliation. Would he ever be able to walk down the street of this town with his head held high?

His uncle's—his mother's brother—words came to mind: *"You are like a jackass in a rabbit's body. You never know whether to hop or run or stand your ground. And whichever you do, it's never the right choice."*

The man had pronounced many other choice proverbs over him, most having to do with never amounting to anything, never making the right choice, and never fitting in. *Square peg in a round hole* was another favorite.

Which was one reason he'd offered to come to this God-forsaken place and fetch back this woman author—to prove his uncle wrong for once.

Because the last words the man said to him at the train station was to make certain he returned with her.

Peter turned his attention back to the paper in his hand. Even if his uncle terminated his services, he would complete the task he'd set out to do. Pay for their return trip out of his own pocket. Present her to his uncle much like Captain John Smith presented Pocahontas to the King of England.

And then he, Peter Golding, would simply sink into obscurity. Forever known as the boss's nephew who completed his assignment despite all the circumstances stacked against him.

The words on the paper swam before his eyes: REQUIRE STATUS REPORT. STOP. RETURN CRITICAL. STOP. PROMOTION CAMPAIGN BEGUN. STOP. PHILLIP HOGAN.

Promotion campaign begun?

But they'd agreed they wouldn't mention Miss Duncan's appearance in New York City until Peter had her agreement to return with him. His uncle understood she might turn down their offer.

What was the man thinking? He wasn't, that's what. He just wanted to have his own way. He'd planned this all along.

As realization that his uncle was setting himself up as hero if Peter succeeded—and Peter as scapegoat if he failed—swept over him, he understood the true purpose of his mission: his uncle's elevation among his peers. This assignment had nothing to do with Peter proving his mettle, or his receiving a promotion to regular editor, or being moved out of the cubbyhole in the basement he called an office.

This wasn't about him at all.

Or really about Miss Daisy Duncan.

Well, he'd show his uncle who was the better man here.

He'd return with Miss Daisy Duncan on his arm.

And not just as an author for their publishing house.

No, he'd bring her back as his wife.

By noon, Lily's stomach rumbled. Time to stop for a bite to eat. Already she'd spent four hours riding the fence line, mending a couple of broken posts and restringing some wire. She'd pulled a mired calf from a watering hole. She studied the sky. Although the spring rains had watered the dry land, no more had come since. She might have to haul water to the pastures, or drive her cattle closer to the Agua Fria River running through her property.

Either choice was a lot of work. Keeping all her herds in the same four pastures meant the potential of overgrazing, and she'd have to bring in hay earlier than planned.

But hauling water was time consuming, and she'd have to put off other chores to do it.

She sighed as she turned her buckskin toward a clump of mesquite trees. Sometimes she felt stuck between the devil and the deep blue sea.

She smiled at the thought of the sea. Hard to imagine an expanse of water so wide she couldn't see the end of it, and so deep a body couldn't see the bottom. Few lakes around Cave Creek qualified for either of those descriptions.

Someday, she'd take a trip to see the ocean. Someday, when she didn't have cattle and stock depending on her. Someday—she reined in short, and her horse shook its head and stamped a foot in response.

She patted the quarter horse's neck. "Sorry, Tom. Just thinking, is all." She nudged his sides with her heels. "Walk on."

Someday wasn't likely to come for her. Her mother had talked plenty about going back to St. Louis to visit family. Her father wanted to see a big city like Chicago or New York.

But instead they'd stayed and ranched the land, because they knew someday she would take over from them.

Except their someday came much too soon.

And it looked like her someday might never come at all.

She dismounted and tied her mount to a mesquite tree, pulling her canvas lunch sack from behind her saddle and her canteen from the saddle horn. Slumping against the tree, she slid down the length of the trunk until her backside settled on the ground. She crossed her feet at the ankles and leaned her head back a moment. Blue sky peeked through the fully leafed branches, and nearby, a female cactus wren poked at the tender flesh of a saguaro while its brighter colored mate perched on the flowered crown, searching for insects.

She took a swig from the canteen, carefully capping the container before setting it beside her. She'd learned early in life not to waste the precious contents. A sip could mean the difference between life and death in this harsh land.

Lily gnawed on the beef sandwich she'd prepared in the wee hours of the morning, before the sun was even up. As she chewed, she thought about the stranger, Peter Golding.

She swallowed and drew another draft of water. He said he came from New York City. Although why he thought she'd be impressed with that was beyond her. What was he really doing here?

She sat up straight. Oh, no. Her editor was in New York City. Her mind cast back to mail she'd received from them. Most were checks addressed to Daisy, payment for stories she'd written. But one included a letter telling her an editor would be contacting her with a proposal.

She'd laughed when she read the words. Only Daisy Duncan, a character as fictitious as the heroines and heroes of her love stories, would receive a proposal by mail.

Could that be?

She frowned. Well, if he thought she was going to jump for joy at the notion of moving east, he had another thing coming. Her parents were buried on this land.

All the family she had was here.

Should she ride after him? Find out what this proposal was?

She shrugged. Didn't matter to her. She wasn't leaving her ranch.

She polished off the rest of her sandwich and most of a handful of dried apples. An extravagance, to be sure, but she'd not been thinking about cost when she bought them last month in town. She'd envisioned a dried apple pie, maybe some apple dumplings, not to mention a few jars of apple butter, and maybe a snack or two in the middle of the winter when apples were scarcer than hen's teeth. She returned the canteen and lunch sack to their places before mounting, then reined her mount around. "Come on, Tom. Time to get back to work."

As she headed for the next pasture to check the fences, she surveyed her surroundings with a new appreciation for the beauty around her. The mountains in the far background. Rolling desert mixed with greener pasture near the river and watering holes. A stand of cottonwoods over there. A forest of mesquite to the south. Saguaros standing tall and proud, the sentries of the desert. Everything reaching toward the heavens like a massive choir singing the praises of God.

She pulled Tom to a halt.

And where had that come from?

Sure, she believed in God. Believed He had made all she could see, and a lot of stuff she couldn't see. But praising Him?

She shook her head. Nah, leave that to preachers and choirs and angels and such.

She had no need to praise God.

And judging by His ignoring her prayers, He had no need of her praise.

Still, something niggled at her, deep down. And as though she had no control, she raised her hands in the air, mimicking the cactus and the trees, and sang the few words of the only hymn she could remember. One her mother used to sing and hum all the time.

Great is Thy faithfulness, great is Thy faithfulness,
Morning by morning new mercies I see.
All I have needed, Thy hand hath provided.
Great is Thy faithfulness, Lord, unto me.

Faithfulness, indeed. If God was faithful to her, He needed a new definition.

Peter watched the sight before him, spellbound at the simple yet intimate scene. If somebody had bet him ten dollars, he'd have said there wasn't a tender bone in Cactus Lil's body. But he'd have lost. For the sweet voice and the emotion-packed words told him otherwise.

Not wanting to break the beauty of the spell-binding moment before him, he waited until Lily's words drifted off on the air and she lowered her hands before urging his horse—a less-stubborn beast than the mount he'd been cursed with the day before—to close the distance between them. Today's horse, in fact, had eaten too many oats, since it was eager to run at the slightest urging. Peter kept a tight hold of the reins to deter the creature from running away with him, as it had already done on the ride from town. Whereas yesterday's trip took three hours, today the one-hour trip took less than forty minutes.

Up until this point, he'd experienced only the harshness of the desert, its unrelenting drive to destroy every bit of life that intruded into its hell-like boundaries. But seeing and hearing Lily singing praises to God had given him new eyes for the brown and gray landscape.

As he neared where she sat on her horse atop a small rise, he looked around more carefully. That tall cactus wore a crown of yellow flowers as beautiful as any golden headgear worn by the richest of kings. That stand of trees near the water stood straight and tall, their leaves a verdant green against the brown backdrop. A yellow-throated bird—a warbler, perhaps?—atop a fencepost reminded him of buttercups. And over there, a spotted brown rabbit moved from its camouflaged rock cluster into the open, its ears and nose twitching.

No doubt about it, beauty was there if he knew where to look.

Perhaps God hadn't forsaken this place.

Or him.

His mount shook its head against the tight rein, jangling the leathers, and Lily Duncan turned to face him. He raised his hat in greeting—he'd remembered to come prepared today, and in addition to the brand-spanking-new hat, he also sported a proper pair of riding boots—and two kerchiefs. Just in case.

She nodded. "You came back."

Not exactly the greeting he hoped for.

"I did." He groaned inwardly. What an inane reply. Why did this woman tongue-tie him? He tried again. "I don't think we got off on the right foot yesterday."

A smile tickled her lips, easing the crinkles in her forehead and around her eyes. Her leather-clad hands rested easily on the saddle horn, and when her mount shifted, she paid it no mind at all, but kept her coffee-colored eyes fixed on him. "You're right."

"Can we try again?"

"Haven't got time to sit around burning up daylight."

Ah, this was more like the Lily Duncan he'd met yesterday. "I heard you singing."

Her shoulders stiffened and the crinkles returned. "That was private."

"I didn't mean to intrude."

"You didn't intrude. You waited over there under that tree."

"You knew I was there?"

Another smile, only this one didn't just tickle her mouth. One side actually lifted in a true half-smile. "Sure. Can't take any chances in this country. Got to be on your guard all the time."

He glanced around. Nothing menacing poked its ugly head up. At least, none that he could see. "What's out there?"

"Rattlers. Coyotes. Dust storms. Stampeding cattle." Another smile. "Dipping tanks. Heels that hook on steps."

She had a point.

"Understood. Not every danger is immediately evident." Peter scratched his chin, images of ants crawling over him invading his thoughts. "You know your way around here."

She met his gaze. "Have to."

"What other tidbits of wisdom can you share with me?"

She quirked her chin at him. "You writing a book?"

He chuckled. "Not me. Just wondering what else I should keep an eye out for."

She shrugged. "Planning on getting lost?"

"Don't think so. If I did, what should I know?"

"Stay put. The more you wander, the more lost you'll get. If you don't know where you are, how can you know where you're going?"

"Good point. So I shouldn't follow a riverbed or look for water?"

"Most of the riverbeds are dried up. And if you ride down one, and it rains up in the mountains, you could get washed out. No, the best source of water around here is cactus."

He wrinkled his nose. "Seriously?"

She nodded. "The flat-leaved ones are best. So a prickly pear, a beaver tail. Cut off a leaf, peel back the skin, and suck out the middle. Not too much, but it'll get you out of a jam."

"Anything else?"

She edged her mount around to a clump of leaves shaped like sword blades. "This is an aloe plant. Sometimes they're real small, sometimes they're big like this one. In the middle is a thick gel that heals cuts and infections."

He stared at the plant whose ragged greenery looked razor-sharp. "Inside that?"

She laughed, her eyes crinkling at the corners. "Just don't hurt yourself. They are like a well-honed knife if you aren't careful." She squinted at him. "You do carry a knife, don't you?"

"Nope. And no gun, either."

She slapped her thigh, raising a cloud of dust from the front of her dungarees. "You are asking for trouble, city slicker."

He held out one hand and folded a finger as he checked off each item. "Lost, stay put. Cut, use aloe. Thirsty, drink cactus juice." He glanced at her. "That's three things. What else?"

"Don't go out unarmed."

He folded another digit.

"And don't get lost."

Peter tossed Lily an informal salute. This woman had a side he'd not noticed before. She could banter with the best of them. So why keep that part of her personality buried so deep? What happened in her past to wound her so she didn't trust folks? He swallowed past the lump growing in his chest.

Should he take a chance and ask for answers to these questions?

She studied him, silent and still. Even her horse seemed frozen in place.

He decided to take a chance. "How come you're so willing to talk to me today?"

"What do you mean? I talked to you yesterday when you fell in the dipping tank."

His cheeks burned at the memory. "Well, yes, you did. But today you seem more open to actual conversation."

She froze, and a look passed over her face, erasing the soft lines so her skin resembled cream-tinted marble—as hard and unyielding to the touch, as cold and unwelcoming as the stone itself.

An uneasiness deep within told him he'd stepped over the line when it came to this example of the female species.

After several long seconds, she blinked. "Why are you here?"

"Why were you singing?"

She shrugged. "Don't know. Saw the mountains and trees all raising up to heaven. And I remembered a song Mama used to sing. Couldn't help myself."

"Well, I want to thank you."

She tipped her head in question. "Why? I haven't done anything. Except help you up when you fall."

"And send me on my way." He tossed her a quick smile. "But it wasn't for that. Your singing made me look at my surroundings differently. To be honest, this desert perfectly mirrored my feelings. Dead. Dry. Abandoned. But your words made me look around. And I saw life, color, and movement."

"You should be a writer. Or a philosopher."

"What do you see?"

She glanced out over the landscape. "Everywhere I look, I see something today I didn't see yesterday. A flower in bloom. A nest of baby chicks. Signs of a coyote den with pups. Even a rattler nest. Spider webs." Her shoulders relaxed, and she turned to him. "So what is it you want? The letter said you had a proposal."

"First, tell me about yourself."

She shrugged, her dark hair cascading over her shoulders. "Not much to tell. Just me and my horses watching over the cattle out here."

"You live by yourself?"

"Do now."

"Married?"

"No."

"So it was just you and your parents?"

She nodded, her eyes glistening with a wetness. "Until they passed a few years back." She straightened, her hand resting on her pistol. "But don't you get any ideas. I can take care of myself and my ranch."

He held his hands in surrender, the bond they'd created vanishing like a vapor on the wind. "No ideas. Don't worry. You've seen how inept I am."

She relaxed again. "Not inept. A mite clumsy. But that's to be expected. You're new here. I expect if I went to New York City and tried to tip-toe around in heels and a dress, I'd be tripping over every crack in the sidewalk."

He smiled at the picture she presented. "Oh, if I managed to convince you to go to the City, I'd make certain you were comfortable."

She peered at him. "You would, would you? You mean it would be acceptable for me to wear these dungarees and boots?"

He glanced at the scuffed, manure-crusted footwear she wore. "Well, maybe I'd buy you some new boots."

She sniffed. "Got me better boots at the ranch. These are just work boots. I'm not ignorant, you know."

No, she wasn't ignorant. And she wasn't stupid, either. He would be careful with his words in the future.

"Could I visit with you again tomorrow?"

Her brow drew down. "Not going to tell me what you want?"

"I'd like to know more about you and your life here, first."

"Meet me at the ranch house around seven." She quirked her chin toward his mount. "Get this one again if you can. It's got more stamina and better manners than the one you had yesterday."

Peter's arms ached from the pressure of holding this horse back, and he couldn't imagine how he was going to make it through an entire day. "Fine. Seven it is."

Lily jerked her horse in the opposite direction. "Pack a lunch."

She jabbed at her mount with her spurs, and the pair raced down over the rise and out of sight.

He headed for town. Maybe tomorrow he could break through her crusty exterior.

Because despite the fine show she put on, Lily, a.k.a. Daisy Duncan, had a soft side.

Chapter 6

Lily sighed as Peter rode into the yard. They'd spent the last two days together, riding the range, as she pointed out various landmarks to him, naming the mountains and gullies, dipping their feet into the river as it bubbled over a small waterfall. She'd shown him where the turkey vultures nested, how to identify scorpion nests, and how to ride without wearing out his backside.

In return, he'd shared with her about New York City, how the ocean came right up to the docks there. How ships sailed in and out of the harbor every day carrying exotic goods from other lands, and taking American cotton, Jamaican rum, and Canadian salted fish to Europe and points beyond.

Sometimes, when he talked about the City, as he called it with great reverence, his eyes glazed over, and he was no longer sitting on her ranch. Instead, he was walking the streets of his beloved City, smelling the aromas of something called pretzels, feeling the cobblestones—whatever they were—under his feet, riding the cable cars across the Brooklyn Bridge.

Maybe it would be nice to take a trip out East and see some of those sights—especially the ocean. But when she lay in bed late at night, the images he painted filling her mind's eye, the dark enveloping her, she knew that would never happen. There were too many dangers.

Not that she was afraid of anybody or any animal. With a gun on one hip and a rope in her hand, she could handle any man, woman, or wild beast.

No, if she went there, she might not want to come back. Because despite her love for this land she called her own, something about Peter Golding called to her spirit.

Imagining her life without him was getting more difficult.

But if she went with him, what would that do to her?

She'd be a nobody in a sea of nobodies.

At least here, she knew who she was. Lily Duncan, rancher woman. Best roper and shooter in the territory.

Still, his stories of buildings so tall they blotted out the sun were intriguing, even though when she pressed him, he admitted five stories was the most he'd seen yet—but architects promised that buildings would soon be ten floors high and more. She looked overhead, trying to imagine how tall a structure would have to be to create a world where the sun never shone. The tallest building in Cave Creek was the hotel, and that was only three stories.

Still, visions of strolling the streets, her arm linked through his, was enticing. Not to be alone anymore. That would be nice. Comforting, even.

She rode to join him. "Morning."

He peered at her. "Sleep well?"

She hadn't, but if she admitted such, he'd want to know why. And she sure wasn't going to admit that thoughts of New York City and of him had kept her awake for the second night in a row.

She shook her head. "Stubborn calving."

Not exactly true. Not these last two nights. But there had been times she'd been up for three days straight during birthing season.

He nodded as though he understood. Which, of course, he couldn't. He'd never attended a calving, difficult or otherwise. Never worried he'd lose both cow and calf. Never wondered if he was leaving it too late to call in the horse doctor—if one was in the area. They tended to be itinerant and never where needed, it seemed.

No, he didn't understand her life, her worries, her thoughts. He might pretend to be interested. He might think he knew her.

But he didn't.

She headed her horse out of the yard. "Let's get going."

He shifted in the saddle. "We're a-burning sunlight."

She gritted her teeth. He had an irritating habit of adopting her manner of speech. Was he laughing at her? She drew a couple of long breaths then faced him. "You going to tell me about this proposal, or are we going to spend another day beating around the bush?"

"I am hoping to convince you to return with me to New York City. As the letter mentioned, I have a proposition for you. I wish to expand our relationship."

What was wrong with this man that he couldn't simply come out and say what he meant? All these high fallutin' words.

And Lily wasn't interested in any proposals he might make to her.

Because he wasn't interested in her.

He was only interested in her alter ego, Daisy Duncan.

She squared her shoulders and tightened her grip on the reins. "I'm not interested."

"You haven't heard me out."

He leaned over and gripped her mount's bridle, forcing her to halt. "Folks want to read more of Miss Daisy Duncan's stories. So we want to help you write more stories, maybe even a book. And that would be just the start."

Ah, the real reason he kept coming around. Not for her company. For the writing. "And you thought I'd want to move to New York?"

His face lit up, and he nodded with vigor, his chinstrap wobbling as he stood in the stirrups. "Yes. It's a beautiful city. So many things to offer. The symphony. The opera. Theater. Shopping. Culture."

"Why should I? What's in it for me?"

He sank into the saddle. "In it for you? Why, you'd become a famous author. People would clamor for your stories."

Every word he spoke was like another nail in the coffin surrounding her heart. "Is that all?"

"All? Do you know what an opportunity I'm offering you? To help grow your writing career. And if you're agreeable, to marry you."

Marriage.

A secret hope long abandoned as the years sped past. She was on the wrong side of twenty-five now. Beyond marriage. Beyond children, surely.

And yet that simple word raised a longing that gnawed at her heart and her gut.

She swallowed the lump in her throat threatening to choke her. "You make that sound as if it's part of the package. You get Daisy, and I get an arranged marriage."

"You don't sound very grateful."

Grateful. Maybe that was enough. Marriages had been built on less. Perhaps gratitude could grow into love. Or at least a tender emotional attachment. Not what she'd hoped for. Not like the love her parents experienced. But perhaps enough. "And what's in it for you?"

He stared slack-jawed at her several long moments. His horse shifted beneath him, and his Adam's apple worked up and down. "I was hoping to prove myself."

"Not very romantic."

He lifted one shoulder in a shrug. "Thought maybe you'd have enough romance for both of us. I'm the more practical type."

"You think because I write about love and romance that I'm just oozing it?"

He glanced around. "Well, I will admit, when I first figured out who you were, I was concerned. You aren't exactly the image of a steamy romance."

She straightened. "And why not?"

"Because—because Miss Daisy Duncan is—"

"I know. Tender. Genteel. Cultivated. A lady. All the things I'm not." She drew her pistol and pointed it in his general direction. "Go. You know your way back to town. And don't come back. Forget about Daisy Duncan. She doesn't really exist, as you so eloquently pointed out."

With spurs jangling, she galloped away from the most irritating man in the world, riding as though the devil was on her tail. When flecks of foam appeared on her horse's shoulders, she slowed to a lope, silently apologizing to the poor beast. She shouldn't take her frustration out on Old Tom.

And she couldn't take them out on the city slicker.

Because if she saw him again, it would likely be at the business end of her gun.

The muscles in Peter's arms burned with the strain of keeping his mount to a walk, but he persisted. He needed time to think. This morning hadn't gone as he'd hoped. The past few days were pleasant, and he thought Lily had begun to let down her guard. He'd thought his proposal would please her.

But this morning, something had changed. He went back through their conversation. His head snapped up. How stupid he'd been. To imply she was the woman he sought but not the woman he wanted—that his infatuation lay with someone who wasn't real—had sliced her to the bone as surely as if he'd plunged a knife into her heart.

To insinuate that Miss Daisy Duncan was something more in his mind than she was in reality was an insult.

He groaned. His ineptness had once again gotten him into trouble.

And her warning to stay away was certain to build tall walls around her that he might not be able to penetrate any time soon.

Except soon it must be, or he would have to send a telegram to his uncle and resign.

If he wasn't already fired.

This morning had brought yet another telegram. He hadn't responded to the first, having nothing at that point to say, and so his uncle had sent another to confirm the first was received.

And the wording of the second brooked no argument or further delay. He had to send a response when he returned to town. When he left the hotel this morning, he'd already been wording the reply in his mind: SUCCESS. STOP. RETURNING FORTHWITH. STOP.

But now his world had crashed in around him. What words would he use?

What words could he use?

And not only to convince his uncle to extend grace to complete his assignment. Yes, retaining his position was important. But not nearly as important as his true mission.

Because one thing was true—he'd lost his heart to this woman.

He must convince Miss Daisy Duncan—no, Miss Lily Duncan—to change her mind.

To remove Lily from the desert would be equivalent to destroying her very essence. And while who she was grated on his sensibilities and irritated him to no end, it was that very uniqueness that he'd fallen in love with.

He could not take this woman to New York City.

But he could not leave her here, either.

Lily stormed into her ranch house and slammed the door. Her mother's plates rattled on the shelves in the kitchen, and she half-expected them to crash down around her ears as surely as her life had done mere moments before.

She slumped into the rocking chair set before the bare hearth. What was she thinking? Were her thoughts any less mercenary than his? Marrying for gratitude went contrary to her beliefs, no matter how easy the man was on the eyes.

Lily rocked back and forth, seeking the soothing calm the old chair usually offered. Whenever she had a problem to worry through or an ache or a pain that kept her from sleep, this rocker reminded her of her mother. But today there was no peace.

Instead, her mind whirled in a dozen different directions. A dozen different whatifs. A dozen different if onlys. And none of them came with a clear answer.

She stared at the oak mantel, hewn from a length of tree her parents had hauled back here on one of their rare trips eastward before she was even born. The bare wood, framed on three sides by the original bark, glowed golden in the late afternoon sun peeking through the curtain. The rings she'd lovingly traced with her finger as a child at the ends of the log bespoke the mighty age of the tree. She'd counted almost a hundred at one time.

The bark showed scars from the cutting, from the journey here, from the time the mantel fell onto the stone hearth. Her father refused to patch or smooth out the rough spots, calling the damage character rather than blemish.

Her glance fell on the family Bible at one end of the mantel, and her mind cast back to cuddling in her mother's arms in this chair while her mother read. Ma's favorite book was Proverbs, filled with wisdom and pithy sayings.

Lily glanced around the room, seeing her parents in everything. Her father sitting at the small desk, going over the accounts, setting aside the coins to pay the feed bills and the grocery account. The curtains her mother sewed by lamplight. The rug she'd hooked, many of the lines crooked. On the walls, covers from old magazines mingled with needlework her mother had done. And over there, the table and chairs her father built.

Everything was old, faded. Papers curled. One of the chairs wobbled. A drawer stuck in the desk so much that she couldn't even pull it open now. Another project he'd meant to get to but never had the time or inclination. And she'd put it off, not having the heart to change anything he'd set his hand to.

Old, faded, curled, stuck.

Just like her.

Too old for any man with a drop of common sense to look at once, let alone twice. Faded over the years from too much sun and not enough pampering. Curled in her mind, dead set on doing things her way. Stuck in a life she loved, in a place she couldn't leave.

And here was a man offering her marriage. Sort of. Not her, of course, but Daisy Duncan. Well, would that be asking too much to be who he wanted? Could she change to suit him? She could doll herself up in a dress and heels, put balm on her hands so they weren't so rough. Learn how to put her hair up like the fancy girls in town.

She stood and paced the room, her mucky boots leaving tracks and bits of dirt and manure on the scarred wooden floors.

No, she wouldn't change to become what he obviously wanted—a wife at his beck and call. Probably expected her to live in the City and keep writing love stories on demand. Might expect her to support them both.

Didn't he realize that if she left this place, she wouldn't have any life left in her? That her love of this land fed her stories?

Still, there was something compelling about him she couldn't explain. The way he looked at her. As though he saw something in her. Something special. Something different.

She turned and retraced her steps. An emptiness welled in her heart at the thought of his eyes the color of the ocean, blue-green, like she'd read about in books. His reddish hair, the sun glinting off the golden strands, lighting him up as if he wore a halo.

But he was anything but an angel, and if she got herself connected to him, her heart wouldn't want to let him go. No, it was simply better to stay away. If she got used to him being around, that would make it so much harder when he left.

Because surely he would leave.

Everybody she'd ever loved had.

She paused. That realization left her as breathless as if she'd run all the way home from town without once stopping for breath. Which she'd done once. In primary school. When the boy she adored chose another girl at the local barn dance.

At the time, she believed she'd never recover from that betrayal.

But she had. And now when she saw the two—grown and married—in town, their six children in tow, she didn't wish her life any different than what she had.

No, her best bet was to keep her distance from Peter City Slicker. If he dared show up again, she'd teach him a lesson he wouldn't soon forget. She had to keep that wall between her heart and her head.

Because her head knew better.

She wouldn't get involved in a prickly affair that would stick and gouge, leaving her wounded and scarred.

Unlike the old oak mantel, those blemishes wouldn't give her character.

They'd give her a broken heart.

Chapter 7

Peter's head snapped up. He'd drifted off—yet again.

He looked around. The setting sun cast long shadows against the desert floor. The saguaros surrounded him like guards in a prison, black in the dim light. His mount, its head bent to eat—yet again—refused to budge when he yanked on the reins. "Come on, you stupid beast. If you were really any kind of horse, you'd have found your way back home by now."

The only response was the twitching of one ear.

Or was the creature merely flicking away a horsefly?

He gripped the leather straps in both hands and jabbed his heels into the horse's sides. This time, the animal raised its head and turned to look at him with one eye, the white showing against the dark-brown center as it munched its mouthful.

Peter glanced back the way he'd come, from the north. Or was it the south? He studied where the sun sank below the horizon, casting an orange glow all around the fiery orb that balanced on the edge of the earth. What was that saying? Ah yes. The sun rises in the east and sets in the west. That meant the mountains were east. And south. Much more confusing than finding his way in the City. A dust devil stirred up the desert soil and sand, whipping the grains into a frenzy as it crossed the dried-up river bottom, heading in his direction.

He tugged his hat down over his eyes, hunched his shoulders, and gripped his horse with his knees. The mini-tornado blew over them, blasting him with the shot-like granules.

His horse snorted, raised its head, and pulled the reins from Peter's hands. Unlike the gentle creatures he typically rode through Central Park, this mount, although stronger and larger physically, had no other positive characteristics.

And apparently, it had no love for sandstorms.

Before Peter could hunker down into the saddle, the beast reared, its front hooves flailing, and Peter rolled over its withers.

As if for good measure, his mount lashed out with a hind foot and planted a blow squarely into his right hip. Peter grunted and curled into a ball of pain. Lights flashed at the periphery of his vision, and waves of nausea threatened to overwhelm him.

He closed his eyes and wrapped his hands and arms around his head, uncertain where the next strike might come from. Afraid to move, afraid to breathe, he waited several long seconds as his heart beat a staccato in his ears.

Finally, he opened his eyes. All he could see from this vantage point was the ground.

Shifting onto his left hip, taking care not to move his right leg, he looked for his horse. Perhaps if he could pull himself up by the stirrups, he could manage to lie across the saddle and trust the stupid creature to take him back to the livery.

Nothing.

No, that wasn't completely true.

Through vision blurred by pain and tears, he was able to make out one thing.

A large brown horse, stirrups flying, racing away.

Leaving nothing behind but a cloud of dust.

Lily ran down a long corridor, her nightdress flapping at her feet, threatening to trip her. The candle in her hand refused to stay lit, and she stopped in front of a closed door to strike another match.

But the box was empty.

She needed to move—quickly—but she had no light.

She couldn't see which way to turn. The inky blackness threatened to overwhelm her, drown her in its depths.

She—

Lily sat up in bed, breathing heavily. A dream. Nothing more than a dream. She tucked loose tendrils that had come undone from the awkward braid she did up at night then sipped from the glass resting on the upended crate beside her bed.

Just another stupid dream.

Still, it might make a good scene in one of her stories.

She turned up the wick and lit the kerosene lamp on the crate. The flame, although feeble, instantly cast light into the dark shadows of the room. She picked up a notebook and pencil she kept handy for random ideas and snippets of dialogue, and soon filled out two pages of description about her dream.

Lily studied the words, trying to make sense of the dream. Wherever had those ideas come from? Certainly not from any personal experience. At least, none she could recall.

She tossed the writing tools on the crate table and extinguished the wick then settled into her bed again. Time to get back to sleep.

She closed her eyes, hoping the nightmare was ended, but instead sank into the same dream again. This time, she determined to follow it to its outcome, if only to use the complete scene in a story.

She turned a corner and faced a closed door, one she didn't recognize. There were a number of padlocks and latches, some with knobs, some requiring keys. She slipped all the locks and bolts she could until one remained.

She stared at the door, wondering what was on the other side.

Bang!

She jumped back, startled by the sudden noise.

But she had to know what—or who—was out there.

Bang!

She stepped closer to the door. "I'm locked in. I can't get out."
Bang! Bang!
Now it was her turn to slap the door. "Let me out. Help!"
She listened.
Nothing.
Then a voice. "You have what you need to unlock the door."
She had what she needed? What sense did that make?
She had nothing but a candle that wouldn't stay lit, an empty box of matches,
and—she patted her nightgown. A pocket. Something in there.
She stuck in tentative fingers and pulled out a key.
Lily tried the first padlock. It fit, turning easily.
She opened the door and stepped through the doorway and—
"Lily. Open up!"

Lily sat up in bed, blinking in the dark. Was the voice part of the dream? Or was it real?

More pounding on the door.

She grabbed her wrapper and shoved clumsy hands through shrunken armholes as she headed for the door where her rifle stood at the ready. Finally decently attired, she chambered a round then took a deep breath. "Who is it?"

"Walker from the livery in Cave Creek."

While not friends—she had no friends—Walker was an acquaintance she'd done business with a time or two. He'd sold her the roan, and he repaired tack and shoed her horses. Wedging her left foot behind the door and holding her rifle down at her side, she inched the door open. "What do you want?"

"Did you see Peter Golding today?" The man's hat hung from a chin string down his back, and his eyes, bloodshot and watery, bespoke a long day's work in the hay and dust. "You know who I'm talking about?"

Her heart raced at the mention of his name.

Take a breath. He means nothing to you.

She exhaled. "Sure. The city slicker from out East."

"Right. He hired a horse from me today."

She eased the door open and looked beyond the liveryman. "Why do you want to know about him?"

"His horse came back, but he didn't."

A raw, sore, weighty feeling came over her. She'd warned him, hadn't she? Told him not to get lost. To carry water. To head for town before something got him.

But she hadn't really thought something would.

Concern for this man who seemed intent on interfering with her life as much as he could grew in her. "'Spect you looked for him along the road as you came here?"

Walker nodded. "No sign of him."

She stepped back. "If you'll give me a couple of minutes, I'll help you look for him."

"Appreciate that, Miss Lily. Sure didn't want to disturb you, but didn't seem right to do nothing. He probably doesn't even have a gun."

"Nope. And if you're right, he's out there without water too. Any blood on the horse?"

Walker shook his head. "Nope. Horse is fine. Wouldn't surprise me if old Haymaker simply got tired of the slicker's city ways and dumped him."

She chuckled, despite the potentially dire circumstances. "Thought he was safer on that one than on Old Sam."

"Should have been."

She smiled. "Let me get dressed. I'll just be a minute."

Walker nodded. "I'll saddle your horse. Which one do you want?"

"Tom should be rested by now."

Lily closed the door and returned to her sleeping room, where she set her rifle on the bed and slipped into yesterday's dungarees and shirt. She sat on the edge of the bed and shoved her feet into her boots, but not until she'd upended them to check for scorpions.

None tonight, but a body couldn't get lazy.

Which is probably what happened to Peter Golding. He'd let down his guard and then along came calamity.

She strode to the door, rifle in hand, shrugged into her woolen blanket coat, and topped her head with her hat. A canteen and rain slicker hung inside the door, always ready for the next trip into the desert.

Walker came out of the barn, leading the roan. She mounted, and together they rode out to the road leading to town.

A full moon lit the night sky, and the stars twinkled afar off like candles in a windstorm. She was glad for the light, and the two loped for about a half a mile before she pulled to a halt, and Walker followed suit.

He tipped his head in question. "Did you hear something?"

"Nope." She scanned the desert surrounding them, hoping to see Peter Golding limping along, nothing more hurt than his feelings. But she saw no movement at all. "But I wonder if that stupid horse might have wandered off the path and dumped him somewhere out of sight."

"Not likely. Golding seemed a good rider. Knew enough about the horse to keep it under control."

"Unless it spooked and carried him off, then dumped him."

"Maybe. If that's the case, we could look for a week and not find him. That horse can run."

"What if he fell asleep? What would Haymaker do then?"

Walker grinned. "That's easy. He'd follow his nose to the greenest grass, the coolest water, and the best shade. And stay there as long as he could."

Lily clucked her reins and left the main road. "I only know one place where all three of those are found."

As they rode in the direction of her southwest pasture—the one near the oxbow in the Agua Fria River—she could think of nothing besides Peter Golding. Sure, he was prone to finding himself in the most ridiculous situations. He asked the craziest questions. Seemed intent on tearing her away from her beloved ranch and taking her to New York City, the last place on earth she wanted to be found. Why, she bet there weren't any horses there fit to ride. Not a steer in sight except on the dinner plate.

She simply couldn't imagine living in a place where she couldn't see the horizon. Couldn't smell the fresh ground. Couldn't plant a kitchen garden and grow her own tomatoes and beans. Couldn't walk into her house without worrying about tracking in mud. Couldn't—

She nudged her mount up over a small incline and headed for the grove of cottonwoods ahead. The temperature dropped a degree or two as she neared the water. In this particular place, low-lying ground meant the river was more prone to flood its bank in the rainy season. The desert floor lay bare of vegetation for several hundred feet on either side of the now much-diminished watershed ahead.

No sign of horse prints, though. Or boot prints, either.

Her mind cast back to her conversations with Peter. He'd seemed genuinely interested in her love for the desert.

But not her, apparently.

He was only interested in Miss Daisy Duncan. Who really only existed in his mind. She was none of the things he found admirable or mysterious. She grunted. A confounded conundrum was how one fellow had described her. As she was showing him the way to town with the business end of her Spencer rifle.

Not exactly the best way to strike up a close relationship.

But Peter, he was different, even though he didn't want her. He wanted his idea of Daisy. In that way, he wasn't any different than other men she'd come into contact with. Never satisfied with her as she truly was.

Still, she didn't wish him any ill, that was for certain. And although he wasn't her ideal man, she hoped they found him before the coyotes or rattlers did.

Lily glanced at the sky over the trees. No turkey vultures hovering on unseen currents. That was a good sign. Meant he wasn't dead. Yet.

She closed her eyes a moment and tossed up a quick prayer. "God, if You're listening—which I suspect You aren't—but if You could listen just this once, please keep that stupid city slicker safe. And help us find him quick. Amen."

Walker glanced in her direction, a half-smile on his face. She squared her shoulders and looked ahead.

Judging by his look, he thought she was loco.

Maybe she was.

Loco for a missing city slicker.

Chapter 8

Peter pressed his back into the cleft in the rocks near the bank of the river. Tired, sore, lost, and just a little afraid, it was the best he could find on short notice. Not knowing how long he was going to be out here, he felt a whole lot better knowing nothing could jump him from behind.

Not a huge consolation, to be certain, but some small comfort.

The leaves of the giant trees beside him—cottonwoods, perhaps?—whispered, as though telling the world of his hiding place. He wanted to shout at them to be quiet, to leave him be until the sun rose, and then he'd be on his way.

Although he hadn't strictly followed Lily's advice about staying put, the fifty or so feet he'd managed to travel between where that stupid horse dumped him head-over-keister, and the river, didn't seem a big deal. Except his hopes of getting something to drink were dashed when he looked down about ten feet from the top of the bank.

He rested his head on the rock behind him, weariness invading every cell of his body. Since coming to Cave Creek, he'd had more than his share of adventures. And misadventures. Had he been in Cave Creek only a few days? Seemed like a lifetime.

And if he wasn't found soon, the end of his lifetime.

Within arm's length of where he huddled grew a cactus, its needles sticking out dangerously in every direction. He tried to remember what Lily had told him. Something about getting water and nourishment from the local plants.

His tongue stuck to the roof of his mouth, and thoughts about the dinner he'd missed invaded his thoughts. But rather than satisfying him, his stomach rumbled all the more as he wondered whether today would have been fried chicken or ham steak.

Peter inched over to the plant, taking care not to jostle his aching hip, and threaded his hand through the barbarous needles. If he could break off one of the arms, he could get water.

If what Lily said was true.

He chuckled. The man at the mercantile had called her Cactus Lil. If that was a true moniker for her, she should know her desert plants.

And if it wasn't—well, he wouldn't dwell on that right now.

His fingers moved closer, closer to the trunk, and he took his attention off the needles and focused on his goal: to simply reach in there and pinch off the arm, exposing its inner core and enabling him to drink its precious nectar.

"Ouch!" He snatched his hand back, catching his shirt on other barbs. A dot of blood appeared on the finger he'd stabbed into a needle. "That hurt."

He looked around. Taking his eyes off the danger and focusing on the finish line wasn't the way to survive in this harsh country. The flesh of the cactus was too tough to simply snap or twist off an arm. He needed a cutting tool.

But he didn't have one. Despite his circumstances, he smiled as he recalled the expression on Lily's face when he told her he wasn't armed except with good intentions and a cocky idea that Daisy would fall into his arms at first sight.

No, he hadn't actually said that to her, but that's what he'd thought. After all, here he was, a knight in shining armor, so to speak, ready to rescue the damsel in distress from a life of hardship and seclusion.

He was offering his name, his household, his position in society—although that obviously wasn't a prime detail yet—and the opportunity to live with him happily ever after in his beloved city.

What he hadn't reckoned on was that Daisy—Lily—wouldn't see any value in what he held so dear. The idea that she wouldn't want to live his life hadn't dawned on him.

Peter found a broken piece of granite, sharp as a flint knife on one side. He hefted the rock in his hand. He scooted back to the cactus and, keeping his eye on the needles, got his hand close enough to hack and saw through the pale-green flesh until the arm sagged and tipped over.

Using his shirttail like oven mitts, Peter pulled the dismembered branch closer. He brushed the sand from the wound where once this arm connected to the main plant then wedged the entire thing in the rocks to hold the plant in place.

He bent over the stem and touched his tongue to the liquid oozing out. Cool. Wet. Slightly bitter. He pursed his lips around the end and sucked the fluid. Heeding her words to limit his consumption, he repeated the process twice more, by which time, the sun tickled the eastern horizon, reminding him that a new day would soon begin. He rested against the rock again. Once the sun came up, he would move to the shade beneath the trees and await his rescue.

For the first time since he was a child, he knew without a doubt help was on its way. And he knew that he wasn't as inept as he'd once believed. He'd managed to survive a night in the desert by himself. Unarmed. Alone.

And the other thing he now knew was that he wasn't as alone as he'd once thought. That maybe—just maybe—the God that Lily sang about was faithful. Even to someone as unfaithful as he'd been.

He raised his face to the sky, still dotted with stars, then closed his eyes. "God, thank You for keeping me safe. I know You are here to help me. Please send someone to find me. Amen."

He thought back to his childhood, to stories his mother told him. How God answered the prayers of the heroes of the faith. He'd listened with rapt attention then, marveling at how God would be so good to those men and women, but knowing that God would never do such great things in his life. He didn't deserve it. He didn't slay lions or giants. He didn't win wars. He didn't have that kind of faith.

Yet here he was today, thanking God for what He'd done. Perhaps all these years God *had* been doing those mighty things in his own life, and he simply hadn't seen them. Maybe God called the Davids and the Abrahams mighty because they allowed God to do the great things.

He sat up straight. He did believe in God. He simply didn't believe that God wanted anything to do with him, not on a personal level, anyway. Everything he'd read in the Bible said if he wanted God to pay attention to him, he needed to be brave. Bold. Courageous. Adventurous. He needed to hear God speak to him.

He shook his head. He'd never heard God's voice once in all his life. At least, not in any audible way.

Peter opened his eyes. The sun was up another few degrees. The saguaro in the distance stood tall and cast long shadows in his direction, as if pointing at him. Like an actor caught in the spotlight on a stage. The center of attention at a party.

He glanced around. Some party. Not exactly his idea of a celebration, but then, he'd made it to this new day, and that was enough to make him happy for now.

Lily's horse picked its way down the embankment leading to the river, and she released the reins to let it draw in great drafts of water, its ears flickering back and forth. Walker's mount followed suit, and the two sat in a comfortable silence.

Walker pushed his hat back on his head then uncapped his canteen and took a long drink before wiping his mouth with his sleeve. He offered the container to her, but she shook her head.

He nodded. Thankfully, he was a man of few words, and they'd ridden most of the evening on about twenty syllables in total. She liked that about him.

Not at all like the city slicker they searched for. He seemed uncomfortable in the quiet. Probably because he lived in the midst of the hustle and bustle of a big city. A body wouldn't have a minute's peace there.

No, siree. Give her the Double D Ranch anytime. Give her miles of open desert and grazing land, her closest neighbor four miles down the road.

She didn't need anybody, and sure as anything, nobody needed her.

Walker urged his horse along the shallow river bottom. "Don't see him here."

"You know his horse better than I do. Where would Haymaker dump him?"

Walker indicated a section of the grove where a number of ancient cottonwoods clustered together. "Over there. Best shade. Close to the water."

"And a patch of grass."

They covered the fifty or so yards and paused. Lily scanned the area. Sure enough, recent signs of a horse dotted the ground.

Walker studied the ground then pointed. "That's Haymaker's prints, all right. I recognize the chip in the left hind shoe. Been meaning to replace it."

"Good you didn't, or we might not have known the beast was here."

Walker twisted in his saddle. "Just because the horse was here doesn't mean he got this far with the rider, though. Haymaker could have toppled him ten miles from here."

"True. But we got to start somewhere." Her hopes of finding Peter alive and well diminished with the rising sun, now fully exposed at the far horizon. If they didn't find him soon, he'd die in the heat of the day. "Let's separate here. You work your way downstream, and I'll go upstream. Couple of miles, no more."

Walker nodded. "Sounds good. Meet back here in about an hour?"

"Yep. If we haven't found him by then, we'll have to come up with another plan."

She turned her horse back toward the river and headed north. The going would be easier than on dry land, and it was cooler down here. The smooth river pebbles were easy on the feet, and besides, she just felt better down here.

A light breeze picked up, encouraged by the difference in temperatures, and cactus wrens called as she rode past. Off to her left, a couple of coyotes watched her from a small rise, their yellow eyes fixed on her. The hair on the back of her neck bristled, and she stared at them until they rose and loped down the other side and out of sight.

She shrugged her back and shoulders, forcing the knots and stitches to flee. She'd be happy to turn around now and head back to her ranch, maybe grab a few hours of shut-eye before climbing back into the saddle and getting on with her life.

But she couldn't do that.

Thinking about Peter not getting on with his life was enough of a deterrent for her.

Oh, what would Sally Jo do? Not that her heroine was the smartest chick in the henhouse, but surely her sweet, compassionate nature would dictate her actions.

Lily allowed her horse to pick its way along as she considered her dilemma. Sally Jo, pretty, feminine, and much admired by the men in her small town, would persevere. She wouldn't give up, because she would believe she could make a difference.

She straightened. Maybe Sally Jo's story was more autobiographical than she realized. Sure, she never batted her lashes at anybody, man nor beast. And she'd never sprained her ankle or worn high-heeled boots.

But she'd helped her parents in their last days, and taken over running the ranch because she thought she could make a go of it. She believed she could turn the Double D into a profitable working proposition.

And she was always willing to lend a hand. Particularly to dumb city slickers who fell at her feet. Repeatedly.

So what was it about this particular city slicker that captured her attention and her thoughts? She wasn't out here for her health. Or even particularly for his. Walker could have brought along a couple of more men, and she'd have stayed at home, completely unaware of the predicament Peter Golding found himself in.

Lily reined in her mount as they turned a bend in the river. A grouping of about ten boulders, the size of a privy, marred the otherwise smooth desert floor ahead, marking a boundary of sorts between the river and the trees. Reddish-brown, about five feet tall, they'd somehow managed to survive countless centuries of the river overflowing its banks and washing over them, then months and even years of sitting in the blistering heat, waiting for the next rainy season.

And up there, in the damp sand near the riverbank, horse's hoof prints.

She kneed her mount closer. Yep, there was the notch in that left hind shoe.

Haymaker had been here.

Which meant Peter Golding may have been here.

She led her horse toward the cottonwoods to check for signs of grazing. As she crossed from the sand to the soil, she noted an indentation leading toward the rocks as though something had been dragged. Recently.

Lily's heart raced. He was near. She felt it deep in her soul. And whether she found him dead or alive—alive, hopefully—at least she would know.

She tied Tom to a low branch, leaving him enough lead to graze, then grabbed her canteen and trotted the twenty feet or so. "Peter. Peter Golding."

No sign of him.

"Oh, God, please help me find him."

She continued toward the river then rounded the rocks and slid to a stop.

A body lay on the ground before her, a hat pulled down over its face.

Her knees shook, and her breath came in ragged gasps. "No–o–o."

It couldn't be.

She was too late.

And then one booted foot moved. Twitched. And a hand raised up and shoved the hat aside.

She dropped to her knees, much as her character Sally Jo had done when she sprained her ankle. Except she didn't groan with pain or bat her lashes at her rescuer. Instead, she grabbed his arm and shook him. "Peter. Wake up."

He groaned. "Go 'way."

She peered into his face. His lips, dry and cracked, beckoned to her, but first things first. She opened the canteen and pressed the neck to his mouth. "Drink."

He sucked back the water until she pulled it away.

"Not too much. You'll be sick."

He grabbed for the canteen, but she replaced the cap and set it outside his reach.

Lily hooked an arm under his. "Come on. Let's get you up on my horse."

He shook his head, groggy and mumbling like the town drunk. "Stupid horse dumped me."

"Not your horse. Mine."

He opened his eyes for the first time and stared at her, mouth open, for several seconds before blinking and smiling. "You."

"Who else did you expect?" Really, this man could be so exasperating. "Get up."

"Thought I was dreaming."

"If your dream included sleeping out in the desert overnight, it must have been a nightmare."

He nodded. "I asked God to send help. And He sent you."

He pulled her into his embrace, an awkward hug that somehow pleased her. He hadn't had a lot of practice at hugging women, it seemed.

When he released her, he held her at arm's length and stared into her eyes. "I prayed. God heard me. I didn't think it was possible. Or likely."

His words echoed her thoughts exactly. She'd prayed, not really believing God would hear her. He hadn't seemed all that interested over the years. But this time was different. She had nowhere else to turn. Nobody else to help.

And He'd answered. Not just listened.

Truly responded.

He limped toward her horse, leaning heavily on her shoulder. "It seems you spend most of your time rescuing me."

His arm, stretched across her shoulder, was warm and intimate, sending a shock like electricity down her back. His hip butted against hers every other step like an awkward three-legged dance.

She smiled. "I don't mind, so long as you don't make it a habit. Can't always be there, you know. Got a spread to run."

The joy drained from his face and the muscles in his jaws worked hard a moment or two before relaxing. Seemed her words didn't please him much. Which part of her statement, she wasn't certain. But the thought that he wanted to be around her more warmed a fire in her belly.

She helped him get one foot into the stirrup and hoisted him onto her horse. He groaned and wobbled a couple of times, and she thought she might have to pick him up from the ground, but he found strength in his legs enough to hold himself upright.

She looked up into those eyes that mirrored the pictures of tropical seas she'd seen on postcards in the drugstore in town. Blue-green, cool as an ocean breeze, with little flecks of gold on the edges.

Not like her brown eyes, boring as all day and about as pretty as a cow pie.

He gave a curt nod, and she untied her horse and led the way downriver—using the sandy bank this time rather than her slogging through the cool water. As they made their way back to the rendezvous point with Walker, two questions nagged her.

Why would God choose to answer her prayers now?

And why wasn't Peter Golding happy when she said she wouldn't always be around to rescue him?

Chapter 9

Lily rode into town several hours later wearing her newer boots and fresh dunga-rees. She also wore a scarlet-red shirt her mother had given her many years ago at Christmas, one she'd sewn by hand and embellished with her own version of black-and-white daisies.

But Lily wasn't wearing that shirt for sentimental reasons.

She had a liaison.

With Peter Golding. Over breakfast at the hotel.

Feeling giddy as a schoolgirl, she'd tied her hair back with a black ribbon and donned best hat, grimacing at the slight sweat ring around the base of the crown. She wished she'd thought to clean it the previous night.

She dismounted in front of the hotel and hitched her horse to the rail, then loosened the saddle girth. The roan dipped its muzzle into the trough and drank greedily even though they'd been riding less than an hour and the sun was barely over the horizon.

Lily patted her mount on the withers and headed inside.

A man behind the counter nodded in her direction. "Can I help you?"

She couldn't think of one thing she needed right now except perhaps a place to wash her hands and make sure there was no dust on her cheeks before she sat to eat. But how to ask a perfect stranger such a private question?

She cleared her throat. "I just rode in and was wondering—"

He pointed down the hallway that cut through the building like a knife through butter. "Privy is out back. Wash bowl is inside the door."

Thankful she didn't have to spell out her needs, she followed his directions and strode down the hall, her heels echoing on the shining wooden floors. They looked clean, well-cared for. Maybe she'd ask him how he got them that way. She might like that at her own place.

After a quick trip out the back door, she returned and washed her hands in the lukewarm water. A glance in the wavy mirror on the wall revealed a patch of dust on one shoulder and a piece of a leaf caught in her hair, which she soon addressed.

She returned to the entryway, intent on asking the clerk about the floors, but he wasn't there, so she turned right and headed into the restaurant. Maybe she'd have a few minutes to herself to quiet the butterflies in her stomach. Although why the creatures should have invaded her gut was beyond her. This wasn't anything special. As Peter said, he simply wanted to thank her for rescuing him.

Lily thought the gesture unnecessary, since he'd already voiced—several times—his gratitude. But he insisted on her dining with him—his words, not hers. If she'd had her way, she'd have eaten standing over the sink at home like she always did.

But the truth was, since he looked so unhappy when she tried to deny his request, she demurred and accepted.

She stepped into the restaurant. Water glasses and flatware gleamed on the crisp, white tablecloths from the sunlight streaming in through windows on three sides of the room. Coffee cups and saucers waited to be filled at each setting.

And best of all, nobody else in the room.

At least, nobody she recognized. Three men sat at a table in a corner, chowing down on something that looked and smelled good. Ham and potatoes, eggs, and toast. And coffee.

Her stomach rumbled. It had been a long time since dinner, and she'd been up half the night.

She tugged on the sleeve of her shirt, conscious of the color and how it made her stand out in this sea of white. Still, the shade went well with her hair, and, she thought, brightened her complexion.

Lily waited as the serving girl approached. "Table for one?"

"Yes. No. Two, I mean."

The girl tipped her head to one side.

"Two. In a corner, please." If Peter was going to fawn all over her and thank her yet again for saving his sorry behind, she didn't want anybody else overhearing their conversation. Once thanked was enough, as her father used to say. Twice thanked was one time too many. "Mr. Peter Golding is meeting me."

The girl nodded and led the way to the corner opposite where the three men sat. "Will this suit?"

"Yes, thank you."

"Mr. Golding usually comes down about now." The girl set a sheet of paper on the table. "These here are the specials for breakfast. I'll bring coffee right away."

Lily scanned the list. "You mean we get to choose what we want?"

"Yes." She peered at her. "You were here a few days ago. Didn't you see a menu then?"

Lily shook her head. "Nope. I always order the steak."

The girl sniffed in a way that said her reply was less than desirable. In fact, she sounded just like Lily's Aunt Bella—nose in the air like she smelled something disgusting on Lily's boots—which sometimes there was.

Can't please some people. She sure couldn't ever please Aunt Bella.

She was sipping her coffee when Peter appeared in the doorway. He scanned the room, and when his eyes landed on her, his face lit up like a firecracker on the Fourth of July. She set her cup on the saucer, taking care not to spill the beverage, which wasn't easy because her hands shook. She clutched them in her lap, wringing her fingers into knots, wishing she'd thought to include a handkerchief to wipe the perspiration from her palms. Instead, she swiped them on the front of her dungarees.

Beaming, Peter limped across the room and dropped into a chair at her right hand instead of the seat across the table where she expected him to sit. "Good morning. I'm glad you came."

"Said I would. Don't usually say one thing and do another."

"No, I wouldn't expect that of you."

The girl came to the table and poured coffee into his cup. "Are you ready to order?"

He glanced at the menu. "I've enjoyed the steak. Are there eggs this morning?"

"Yes sir."

"Good. Steak and eggs." He looked at Lily. "And you?"

Lily nodded. "Fine with me."

They sat in companionable silence and sipped their coffee. A couple of times he set his cup down and cleared his throat as though about to speak. But after a hard swallow or two, he picked up the cup again. Or busied his hands rearranging the salt shaker.

After about the fourth time of watching this, she set her own cup down and tossed him a quick smile. "Seems there's something you want to say."

"Right."

"Well, you thanked me last night for finding you, and you're thanking me again this morning with a fine breakfast."

"That's not what I needed to talk to you about."

"Are we waiting for Walker?"

His brow drew down. "Walker?"

"Right. He brought you back into town."

"Right. Oh, Walker. Yes. Nice man."

"So he's not joining us?"

"No. Did I give that impression?"

He reached across the table, but her sweating hands were still in her lap, for which she was thankful. She didn't know what she'd have done if he held her hand. Likely slapped his face.

"No." She pursed her lips. "So just spit it out."

"Okay." He drew a deep breath. "Well, it's like this—"

At that moment, the girl appeared and set their meals on the table. "Anything else you want?"

Peter looked up. "No, thank you."

Lily stared at her plate. She'd have liked some *salsa roja* to liven up her food, and maybe a glass of water, but he seemed intent on speaking his piece. Although why he was struggling with what he had to say was beyond her.

It wasn't like he was going to ask her to marry him or something.

He was going to ask her to marry him. Here, now, in the restaurant of this low-grade hotel in a backwater town in the Arizona Territory. Because if he didn't ask her now, he would lose his nerve.

And his job. And his career.

Not that the latter two were important right now.

All he could focus on was hearing her say yes.

No doubt about it. This woman was a keeper.

Sure, she was rough around the edges. No matter how many bright red shirts she wore, or fancy new boots, or ribbons in her hair, she wouldn't be comfortable anywhere except riding the range and writing her sweet stories.

The contradiction of those two occupations still baffled him, but he didn't care.

He was in love with this woman, no matter how much he tried to tell himself otherwise, and he couldn't imagine returning to New York without her.

Or with her, to be honest.

Which created a conflict within him. If he couldn't live with her and couldn't live without her, then what was he to do?

His throat, parched with panic, begged for liquid. He drained his cup and set it down, hands shaking like a drunk coming off a two-week binge.

He'd lain awake ever since returning to town, mulling the problem over in his head. A double problem, as it turned out. Another telegram from his uncle awaited him when he arrived saddle sore, exhausted, and limping. Bring her back or else. Not in those exact words, but that precise meaning.

He wanted to bring her back with him. He wanted to keep his job. He wanted to move up in the company, perhaps become managing editor one day.

But he would not destroy this delicate desert rose—uh, lily.

When he'd risen that morning, his eye had fallen on the Bible sitting on the bedside table. He sat back on the bed and thumbed through, landing in a book he hadn't even known existed—Lamentations—where the words of Lily's song from chapter 3 jumped off the page at him: "They are new every morning: great is thy faithfulness" (v. 23).

As he dressed to come down and meet her, all his carefully rehearsed words fell to the ground like dust. In fact, the more he tried to come up with what to say, the more jumbled became his thoughts.

If he opened his mouth now, she'd see the mangled mess his tongue had become, for surely it was tied into knots so convoluted they'd never be unworked.

"Better eat your food before it gets cold."

Her words brought him back to reality. She cut into her steak, swished the meat into the yolks of her eggs then used a slice of toast to catch the drips as she forked in the mouthful.

Yes, his food was getting cold.

But his heart was warm with affection for this woman.

It was now or never.

He cleared his throat and she stopped chewing, watching him, those deep pools like dark chocolate truffles fresh from Paris assessing his every movement. His every word. "Well, what I wanted to say was—"

Yet again, the serving girl appeared at his elbow. He sighed. "Yes?"

"The clerk says there's a telegram for you marked urgent. Do you want me to bring it here?"

Peter's heart thundered. He pushed away from the table and dropped his napkin next to his plate. "No. I'll go to him. Thank you."

He twisted away from the table and caught his foot in the leg of his chair. The table teetered and he caught himself before both he and the table went to the floor. "Be right back."

Humiliated at his clumsiness once again, he hurried to the counter.

What must she think of him?

Lily polished off her coffee and signaled to the girl to refill her cup. While she waited, she glanced around the room. The three men in the corner were gone, and a businessman looking a little green around the gills wandered in. He caught her eye, but when his gaze drifted to the second table setting, his smile dropped and he chose a table set in a darkened corner.

Feeling a burp coming on, Lily searched in her lap for her napkin, but it wasn't there. She must have dropped it. She lifted the tablecloth and peered underneath. The square of cloth rested just left of her feet. She leaned down to pick it up and spied a folded piece of paper nearby, which she picked up.

The burp passed unnoticed, and she set the paper on the table and her napkin in her lap. Several minutes later, bored, she opened the note and spread it on the table.

A telegram.

Guilt tickled at her conscience as she read words intended for Peter.

PLANS FOR SHORT STORY COLLECTION IN PLACE. STOP. BRING HER BACK OR DO NOT RETURN. STOP. BIG PROMOTION PLANS READY. STOP. DO NOT DISAP-POINT ME. STOP. PHILLIP HOGAN.

The editor that published the magazine she wrote for regularly. Who signed her checks. Who wrote such glowing and complimentary letters to her about the popularity of her stories. Mr. Persnickety.

Lily's hand froze on the paper as the implication of the words sank in.

Peter wasn't interested in her.

He just needed a warm body to take back.

She tossed her napkin on the table.

Well, if that's all he wanted, let him take his horse.

Peter turned from the counter, the telegram crumpled in his hand. His uncle wasn't happy.

Well, fine. He'd made his choice.

He headed for the restaurant, determined to tell Miss Lily Duncan exactly how he felt.

There she was, striding toward him. All the better.

Except her hands were clenched into fists at her side.

This didn't look good.

She sidestepped him and brushed past, leaving behind a current of cold air that almost froze his resolve.

But he wouldn't—couldn't—let her leave like this.

He followed her outside to her horse. "Please wait."

She turned and thrust a piece of paper toward him. "I was a fool to think you were interested in me."

"I am."

"Sure. As some freakish anomaly who lives in the desert and eats snakes and writes about love when she's never actually been in love and never even been kissed and—" Lily stopped and slumped against her horse. "Now you know."

"Know what?"

"The truth. I'm a fraud. Nobody wants to read stories about love and romance from somebody who doesn't know what it feels like."

He opened the paper and read his uncle's words. "I'm sorry you had to see this."

"Sorry I found out what you really wanted?" Her eyes blazed. "Well, I'm not. I'm just glad I figured you out before I really made a fool of myself."

"Well, that would be a pleasant change."

Her brow drew down. "What would?"

"For someone else to look dumb for a change."

He held his breath as she processed his words, hoping now wasn't the time she'd draw her pistol and shoot him dead.

After several long seconds, her shoulders relaxed and she smiled. "I can see how that would be something different for you."

"You didn't see my response."

"Wasn't under the table."

"I told my employer—who is also my uncle, by the way—I was ready and willing to give up my job rather than trick you into a situation where you'll be miserable."

She peered at him. "You'd do that? For me?"

He pulled another piece of paper from his pocket. "Here."

"What is it?"

"Read it."

She studied the words. "It's a ticket back East." She looked up. "Were you just going to leave?"

"No. I was going back to put in my formal resignation, pack up my things, and find another job."

"Where?"

"I don't know. If you aren't with me, nothing else matters."

Chapter 10

Later that day, Lily set another length of wood on the chopping stump and swung her ax high over her head before letting the tool drop heavily, splitting the piece neatly in half. She tossed the two sections closer to the woodpile at the rear of the ranch house then turned to the next piece.

There was nothing like mindless hard work to take a body's mind off their troubles. And she had plenty of troubles.

After Peter's revelation this morning, she'd stood speechless for several heartbeats. He wanted to say more, but he couldn't seem to find the words.

So instead of messing things up—again—she mounted and rode out of town, leaving him standing there. She'd hazarded a single glance over her shoulder, and he lifted his hand and waved. She'd nodded so he'd know she saw him.

Riding out of town probably wasn't the response he'd hoped for. But until she knew the question, she couldn't know her answer.

She set another chunk of mesquite on the block, aimed high, and chopped. Eighteen. Nineteen. Twenty. Enough for one day. She swiped at a rivulet of sweat threatening to blind her then pushed her hat further back on her head. Going to be another hot one.

She studied the road from town. Nothing. Not that she expected him to come chasing after her. Maybe he accepted her riding away as her answer. Likely he'd crawl back to New York City and beg for his job.

It was the sensible thing to do.

She jammed the ax into the chopping stump and crossed the yard to the bench outside the back door. The shade cooled the air by a couple of degrees, and the rest was welcome.

She leaned her head back and closed her eyes, inhaling the warm scents of manure, mesquite, and sand. She loved this place. Not just her ranch—although the land was precious to her—but Cave Creek and Arizona Territory too. She opened her eyes and studied the patch of beavertail cactus near the corral, watched her buckskin flick flies off its legs with its long tail, listened to a cricket near the house singing for a mate.

She didn't want to leave here.

But now that she'd met Peter, he'd managed to carve a place in her heart she hadn't known existed.

She closed her eyes again. "God, You and me have just kind of renewed our friendship, and I don't have any right to ask You for anything else. Not after You saved Peter.

That was pure miracle, for sure. But God, if You could, would You tell me what to do next?"

She opened her eyes and whispered a soft "amen" which the midmorning breeze carried off. She thought of her parents. After her father died, her mother told her she didn't want to be anywhere he wasn't. They'd been married for so many years, she said, they were like one person now. And within just a couple of weeks, she was gone, too, leaving Lily all alone for the first time in her life.

As she recalled her mother's words, she understood them for the first time. While before Lily had fought tooth and nail to be her own person, to be the best at whatever she did, now she saw how being connected to another human being could be a good thing.

What if God had brought Peter into her life to show her how to love? The Bible said God is love, so He should know what He's talking about and what He's doing when it came to that particular topic.

She stood, her mind made up.

She would go wherever Peter went. And if that meant New York City, so be it. If God was behind it, she didn't want to miss it.

Peter rode into Lily's yard, uncertain of his welcome—a smile or her Spenser. He'd noted the rifle slung in the scabbard of her saddle and expected she was every bit as adept with that weapon as she was at everything else—completely unlike him.

In fact, this single thought had detained him and occupied his thoughts for the hour following Lily's abrupt and silent departure. How could he expect her to want to be with him when they had little in common?

But with God, all things were possible. That was another verse he'd read last night.

He stopped his hired horse near her front door, dismounted, and tied it to the hitching post. After a light tap on the door, he waited, swallowing hard, trying to work up enough spit to speak his piece.

He doubted he'd get another chance.

When she didn't answer, he walked to the rear of the house. The whole place looked well cared for, flowers decorating a sunny corner and a sturdy chicken house reminding him of the breakfast they'd shared just a few hours before.

A small barn, a corral, a chopping block, and a woodpile, and there, the woman who'd occupied his thoughts in recent days. Admittedly, at first, his selfish thoughts. And then perhaps once or twice his lustful thoughts.

But most recently, his romantic thoughts.

She stood as he neared, and he bit the inside of his cheek to hold back grunts of pain that would prove he wasn't man enough for her. She fussed with stray tendrils of that delightful hair crowning her head, a wondrous blend of Klimt gold and Van Gogh mocha.

She nodded in his direction then gave up on her hair, letting her hands fall to her sides. "You rented another of Walker's beasts."

He nodded. "I prefer a carriage, but I've given up hope of finding one around here."

"Do you give up so easily on everything?"

Her question bit, stinging him. The question was honest, and truth be told, he didn't like the answer he might have given before today. But things were different now. "Not anymore. And one thing I'm not giving up on is us."

"There *is* no us."

"Maybe not yet, but there will be."

She put her weight on one leg, leaning into her hip, creating a delicious curviness to her body he hadn't noticed before. "And just what is your proposal, city slicker?"

The word, which he'd bandied about so thoughtlessly before, took on an entirely different meaning. "I know you don't want to live in the city."

"And I know you don't want to live anywhere else."

His heart sank. He'd had this very same argument with himself already today. "Please hear me out."

"I'm listening." She sat on the bench and stuck her feet in front of her. "Sit down and take a load off. It's cooler here in the shade."

"I'll stand, thank you."

She smiled up at him. "Don't worry. I don't bite."

"That's not what they say in town."

A soft chuckle bubbled out. "'Spect I'm one of the major sources of gossip and discussion amongst that crowd."

He remained standing. Just in case. "Most of what they say is true."

She tossed her hair. "I bet. Such as I'm ornery. Did they share their little moniker they call me behind my back?"

"That name isn't everything you are. Your real name is a better description of who you are."

She snorted softly. "Lily. Boring. Pale. Delicate. Liable to wilt in the heat."

"No, not at all. Lilies grow in many places and survive under extreme conditions. Just think of water lilies that come in all shades of white, yellow, pink, and red. In some countries, water lilies are highly treasured. And wild lilies are rare." He paused, out of breath. Heat raced up his cheeks. "Just like you."

She stared at him a long moment. "Is that what you think of me?"

He hesitated. "I think you are the rarest of all. A precious flower. And my hope and prayer is that you will agree to be mine."

"But what about our differences?"

"I think we can come to an agreement where we can both be happy. After we marry—"

She stood and faced him. "Whoa there, pardner. Who said anything about getting married?"

"Well, I—uh—I—"

"Hadn't we best get that question resolved before we move on to the next part of the plan?"

She was right, and once again, he felt the idiot. He knelt before her on one knee and grasped her hand in his. "Miss Lily Duncan, will you marry me?"

"For better or for worse?"

He gazed into her eyes. "Till death us do part?"

One side of her mouth lifted. "Till death us do part."

He stood but kept hold of her hand. He didn't want to take a chance on her changing her mind before he got the rest of his words out. "You love this place. You write here, so I want to live here with you."

"And what about the city?"

"As the world-famous author you're going to become, you'll need to go there once in a while to sign a contract, meet your adoring fans, things like that. And while we're there, I'll show you some of the sights, such as Broadway plays, ballet, and the symphony."

She pulled her hands from his grip and clamped them to the sides of her head. "Stop. It isn't every day a girl accepts a marriage proposal and agrees to visit the city."

He stared at her. Had she accepted and agreed? "Is that a yes?"

"To both of your proposals."

He gathered her in his arms, and she melted into his embrace as if she'd been made just for him.

Which she had.

And he for her.

He closed his eyes and bent to kiss her, but she pushed him away. He opened his eyes, afraid to look at her.

She hooked a forefinger beneath his chin gently. "Maybe we can visit the city sooner rather than later."

"When?"

"As soon as the book is published. We can wrap our honeymoon into a book tour. I've heard that publishers put their authors up in fancy hotels and pay all their expenses. We deserve it."

He pulled her closer. "You deserve so much more than that."

"And it wouldn't have happened if you hadn't persevered past my prickly exterior."

Their lips touched, tentative at first, then with more fervor, until he was breathless. When at last they parted, a bright spot of red decorated each of her cheeks, and he expected his entire face was like a beet. He hugged her close then released her. "You know something, Lily, you aren't half as prickly as the townfolk say."

"And you aren't half as dumb as they say."

He chuckled. "So you do listen to what they say. Anything else you need to say before I kiss you again?"

She planted an index finger on her chin and stared past his shoulder. "Well, now that you mention it—"

His heart thudded into his boots. Would she change her mind? Had he ridden on the clouds only to be dashed back to reality?

She grasped his hands in hers. "Now that you mention it, I need to be here at least twice a year."

He exhaled. "Whatever you want, we shall do it."

"Okay. So long as we are here for the spring and fall, we could spend the rest of the year in the City."

"Why so important to be here during those months?"

"The daisies bloom in the spring. They were my mother's favorite."

"No problem. And the fall?"

"That's when the dipping happens. And we've got to teach you how to dip cattle without dunking yourself."

He smiled. She was making a joke. She wasn't changing her mind after all. He looped his arm in hers. "We need to ride to town to plan the wedding."

She nodded. "What a miracle this is. Who would have thought either of us could find love in the desert?"

"You're right. Thank goodness the Lord didn't give up on us. We both had prickly outsides, but God knew our hearts."

Donna Schlachter lives in Colorado, where the Wild West still lives. She travels extensively for research, choosing her locations based on local stories told by local people. She is a member of American Christian Fiction Writers and Sisters in Crime, and facilitates a local critique group. One of her favorite activities is planning her next road trip with hubby Patrick along as chauffeur and photographer. Donna has published twelve books under her own name and that of her alter ego, Leeann Betts, and she has ghost-written five books. You can follow her at www.HiStoryThruTheAges.wordpress.com and on Facebook at www.fb.me/DonnaSchlachterAuthor or Twitter at www.Twitter.com /DonnaSchlachter.

In Sheep's Clothing

by Pegg Thomas

Dedication

This story is dedicated to Jeff Thomas who spent countless hours with me in the sheep barn over the years, lending a hand in everything from doctoring to shearing to feeding the orphan lambs. Those were some of the best times of my life. I love you.

It is also dedicated to Gretchen Diffin and Laurie Kilgore,
my fellow shepherds and spinners. You gals crack me up!

The 1599 Geneva Bible, the translation common to early Colonial America, is used for the scripture quoted.

Chapter 1

Milford, Connecticut
April 10, 1702

With a final snip, another layer of guilt fell into Yarrow Fenn's lap. It landed amid the soft folds of wool from her loom. This cloth was quite possibly the best she'd ever made. She ran her fingers over the loosely woven threads. Once finished at the fulling mill, it would make a splendid gown. But not for her. The guilt pressed against her chest, tightening her shoulders. The traveling peddler would buy this bolt of cloth when he arrived in a few weeks. He'd sell it in Boston—in direct conflict with the king's law.

She cast a glance out the window, the sun already well above the horizon. Pushing aside the guilt, she folded her cloth into a flat bolt. After several futile attempts to tame her wayward hair under its linen cap, she pinned her straw hat over the top and slipped on her shawl before gathering the newly woven cloth into her arms.

Her room on the back of the saltbox-style house had its own entrance. She nudged the door shut behind her with her foot then hurried around the front of the house. She was neither quick nor quiet enough.

"Where are you going?" Pennyroyal, Yarrow's younger sister, stood in the front doorway with her hands on her eighteen-year-old hips, her belly straining against the pleats of her apron.

"'Tis the opening day of Tucker's Fulling Mill." That Penny could forget the main topic of conversation after church yesterday, the opening of the mill and the impending arrival of the new journeyman fuller, testified to her preoccupation with the coming babe.

"I had quite forgotten." Penny pressed the back of her wrist to her forehead. "Hurry back. I feel poorly again today. You shall need to start supper." She shut the door.

Pray the babe would come soon. Penny, ever the spoiled youngest of the three sisters, had bordered on tyrannical these past few weeks. But one must make allowances at a time like this. Yarrow shrugged and walked on.

Their house rested on the northern edge of Milford. Yarrow followed the road toward town. When she turned onto the main road, the steeply pitched roof of the new fulling mill on Beaver Creek was just visible. Excitement bubbled and eclipsed, for the moment, her guilt.

When King William III had signed the Wool Act of 1699, the result had been a financial blow to the citizens of Milford. The act's restrictions on selling any wool or wool product outside of their colony had put the old fulling mill out of business. That left the weavers of Milford the difficult task of hand-fulling their own cloth to achieve the necessary tightening and brushing of a finished fabric.

Yarrow was relieved to have that back-breaking chore off her shoulders. The line queued outside Tucker's Fulling Mill said she wasn't alone, and that boded well for the business. She took her place behind a knot of young women and caught part of their conversation.

"Ginny's mama saw him come off the boat last evening. She said she fairly swooned when he removed his hat and bowed to Mrs. Tucker."

"Is it true he does not wear a wig but grows out his own hair?"

"I heard 'tis the color of spun gold."

"Mr. Tucker told my papa that Mr. Maltby was the youngest journeyman fuller in all of Massachusetts Colony."

"They say he is not but two and twenty."

"He must be ever so talented."

"And tall, they say."

"And single."

The cluster heaved a collective sigh. One of them gave Yarrow a polite smile before turning back to her group. Yarrow pushed down a prick of irritation. She knew the exclusion wasn't intended to slight her. It would never occur to them to include her in their excited chatter about the new journeyman fuller. At the advanced age of four and twenty, all of Milford recognized her as a spinster. Likely all of Connecticut Colony.

Movement near its door signaled that Tucker's Fulling Mill was open for business. A tall man with golden hair stepped to a trestle table erected outside the door. He must be Mr. Peter Maltby, whose name had dominated the conversation after church. A ripple of excitement slid down the line. Any newcomer to the area drew attention, but a tradesman who eschewed the customary wig was something to set the town's tongues wagging. Being young and single, he set them on fire.

Tamping down any interest in the man himself, she watched as those in front of her presented their bolts of cloth for finishing. Yarrow was recognized as one of the best spinners and weavers in the colony. As a lad back in England, Papa had been apprenticed to a weaver, and she'd learned at her papa's knee. Yet it wasn't vanity, at least not entirely, that caused her to stroke the fabric in her hands. If she could sell three full bolts to the peddler when he came to town twice a year, instead of the usual single bolt left over after meeting the needs of her sisters' growing families, she might put aside enough to one day purchase a small cabin of her own, scandalous as that may be for an unmarried woman.

The guilt tweaked again. The penalty for breaking the king's law was severe, perhaps even death. Yarrow didn't actually sell her fabric outside of the colony. She sold it to Enos Watkins, the traveling peddler. He was free to sell it in the next town down the road. Except she knew he didn't. Quality cloth such as hers fetched a much higher price in Boston. Knowing he was selling her cloth across the colony's border made her uneasy, but Enos would never betray her as the source. He owed her for far worse. She knew what the church would say if they were caught.

The line crept along. Mr. Maltby took his time with each person, asking questions and jotting notes on slips of paper he tagged on the bolts. He was either very thorough or enjoying the batted eyes, practiced smiles, and soft laughter muffled behind dainty fingers. Most men doubtless enjoyed such attention.

Yarrow looked away, some of the sparkle erased from her morning. Most days she was happy enough with her life. Glancing back at those golden locks bent over another bolt of cloth, she sighed. Today was not one of those days.

Peter placed another lumpy bolt of woven fabric on the pile. He was supposed to miraculously turn it into a usable household textile. Mr. Tucker had warned him that the cloth-making skills of Milford might not be up to the standard he was accustomed to in Boston, but he hadn't thought they'd be this poor. It was one thing to tighten and brush a loosely woven bolt into an evenly stretched length of cloth. It was another to make a silk purse from a sow's ear, as Granny used to say.

He turned to the fulling mill's next customer, a simpering lass of no more than sixteen who flickered her eyelids so much he feared she had a sty. At least her bolt showed more promise than the last. He recorded her name and what the cloth was to be used for.

The next customer placed her bolt of cloth onto the table. The fabric glided over his fingers and draped across his palms. Wool finely spun and woven into a silken fabric. Mouth open, he savored the sensation a moment before looking up. And up. At the tallest woman he'd ever seen, her eyes almost level with his own when he straightened.

Light-brown hair framed her face beneath a wide-brimmed straw hat. Hazel eyes that matched her hair assessed him from under arched brows.

He shut his mouth and cleared his throat. "This cloth is outstanding."

"Thank you, sir."

"I have not seen the like in, well, maybe I have never seen the like."

She lowered her head, but not fast enough to hide the blush. Not a beautiful woman, but handsome enough with that pink on her cheeks.

"The weave is distinctive, and the fibers so finely spun."

"My papa taught me the weave pattern, his own creation. The wool comes from the town's flock of sheep."

"You spun the wool yourself?"

"I did."

Both spinner and weaver, was there no end to this woman's talent? An older woman behind her coughed. He was staring. He grabbed an order slip and dipped quill to ink. "For what purpose do you wish the cloth prepared?"

She paused a moment. "My sisters are in need of new gowns. I pray there shall be two dress lengths."

"Quite possibly." But why not a gown for herself? The dress she wore was plain, a work dress covered by a starched linen apron. Well made, but not the quality of the fabric in front of him. "Your name?"

"Miss Yarrow Fenn."

Yarrow? What an exotic name. He scratched it on the order.

"As you can see, we are taking in many orders today. I cannot say exactly when yours will be ready, but check back in about ten days."

"I will, sir, and thank you." She turned and walked away, a study in graceful movement. The long fringe of her shawl swayed with each step.

Another cough from the elderly lady next in line. He blinked. She gave him a toothless grin and plopped her misshapen bolt on the table.

Yarrow hurried past the front door of the house and around back to her sanctuary. She entered and inhaled the mellow scent of lavender. A smile played across her lips as her fingers caressed the wooden beam of the loom. This was her domain. Her spinning wheel, brought over from Wales by her mama's mama, sat in one corner near a window. Yarrow's narrow bed stood against the opposite wall, another window over it. An oaken chest, built by her papa's papa, held her few personal belongings under the third window. The luxury of glass windows, three of them no less, gave her natural light by which to create the fabrics that kept her sisters' families clothed.

She had plenty of linen spun to dress the loom but needed to spin more wool to weave through the linen warp. This next cloth would be sturdy stuff to make breeches for both brothers-in-law. With the sheep shearing finished last week, her fingers itched to begin spinning.

A knock rattled the door connecting her refuge to the main house. "Yarrow, have you returned?" Penny asked.

"I have." Yarrow straightened her apron and braced herself for whatever might come before she opened the door.

"What took so long at the fulling mill? You had only to drop off your bolt and return."

"The line was long before I arrived and plenty more behind me. The mill will do a good business."

"'Tis all well and good, but I need you to start supper." Penny sighed as though auditioning for a traveling thespian troupe. "Once 'tis started, run and fetch Marigold."

"Is there something I can—?"

"You know nothing about having babies. Tend to supper and then fetch our sister."

Yarrow bit her tongue. Their mama had passed away while Penny was barely walking, leaving the two older sisters to raise her. And spoil her. Pregnancy made some women bloom while others. . . Hopefully, Penny's disposition would sweeten once the babe arrived.

Yarrow entered the main house and crossed to the hearth. Built of native rock, it encompassed the entire west wall of the main room. She busied herself putting together a simple stew with a bit of leftover venison. She wrinkled her nose at the equally wrinkled potatoes, thankful they'd been able to plant the early crops in the garden last week. She pushed the stew near the fire where it would cook while she fetched Marigold.

A brisk walk through the settlement confirmed that spring was well underway. Dandelions dotted the meadow where the sheep grazed, watched over by the boys hired to tend them. Each spring the sheep were forced into the river for a short swim to wash the worst of the dirt from their fleeces. Once dry, they were sheared and the wool sold, which kept the settlement taxes low.

Since King William III had signed the Wool Act, however, they could only sell the wool within Connecticut Colony or to England herself. Sales to other colonies or any other ports were prohibited. Not only the wool but anything made of it. Taxes collected at both the port in Connecticut and again at the port in England destroyed any profit. Now they kept only enough sheep to supply buyers within the colony.

Including Yarrow.

With the weather so fine, she loved to sit outside and card the wool in preparation for spinning. Maybe this year she'd teach Marigold's oldest daughter to help her. With her niece's help, she could spin more yarn and weave more cloth to be taken to the fulling mill. A flush warmed her neck. She was interested in producing more cloth to sell and work toward her independence, not as an excuse to visit the fulling mill. Or to see the admiration in the piercing blue eyes of one Mr. Peter Maltby.

Chapter 2

The third time he dropped his garter, Peter growled and kicked it across the room. Not that it took much of a kick. If he stood in the center of the room, he could almost touch the walls on either side. He rose from the cot and fetched the garter from where it landed under the tiny table that rocked when he leaned on it. Pulling his stocking over his knee one more time, he got the leather strap buckled in place and buttoned the knee cuffs of his breeches.

Why was he all thumbs this morning? Church would be no different than church back home. Except that Deacon Williams wouldn't be there and that, if anything, should put a smile on Peter's face.

He grimaced. It might, if not for the hordes of fawning females who would no doubt assail him after services to inquire about their fabrics. Most of those fabrics were barely tolerable, quite a few downright awful. There was that one shining star. Truly a pearl among the pebbles. If only the mill's clientele contained two score of Miss Yarrow Fenns. With an array of cloth that fine to work with, he'd reach the level of master fuller in short order.

With a few carefully worded questions, because the last thing he needed was anyone thinking he had an interest in a woman right now, he'd learned from Mr. Tucker that Miss Fenn wasn't married because Enos Watkins, some local lad, had walked out on her, and what a shame that had been. A shame for her, but perhaps helpful to Peter. With no family of her own to care for, she might be persuaded to give spinning and weaving lessons to the other ladies of the town.

The front door of the mill banged against the wall.

"Are you ready, lad?" His boss bellowed up the stairs.

"I shall be there directly." Peter tucked in his shirt. He slid into his waistcoat then grabbed his neckcloth, tying it on the way down.

"You shall have the maidens in a swoon before the service starts," Mr. Tucker said.

"I pray not. Messy business reviving them all." And besides, he'd learned a hard lesson about manipulative females.

Sam Tucker chuckled.

Mr. Tucker's wife and three young children waited for them by the road. The walk to the clapboard-sided church wasn't long, but with the unabashed stares of the young ladies and the hawkish glares of their mamas, it held all the charm of running the gauntlet.

Peter slid onto the hard bench at the back of the church with the rest of the unmarried men. Across the room, the unmarried ladies settled onto matching wooden benches to be equally uncomfortable for the next three hours. But he shouldn't think that way. The worship and teaching should be the high point of his week. Hadn't Granny always told him so? She'd also told him to keep his face forward and not ogle the maids across the aisle. Not that he had. Well, not exactly.

With the slightest twist of his neck, his gaze raked across the occupants of the other side of the room. Several were staring his way, but his attention stopped on the tallest among them. While other tall women he'd known had displayed a tendency to slouch, Miss Fenn sat straight, her face tilted upward, her eyes closed.

Was she praying already? Before the service started?

A rustle brought Peter's attention back to the front where a portly man in a powdered wig approached the pulpit. He climbed the steep stairs and took his place on the half-circle platform fenced in with an ornately carved banister that reached almost to his armpits. He requested them to bow their heads for the opening prayer.

Very little of what followed penetrated Peter's thoughts. Uncomfortable both inside and out, he made a conscious effort not to fidget. He straightened his shoulders and puckered his brow in what he hoped was a thoughtful pose. His mind was then free to race back down the slope of his own imaginings.

He'd achieved the rank of journeyman before leaving Boston. Mr. Tucker had been most complimentary regarding Peter's work this first week. With any luck, he'd make master fuller by year's end. Once he had that status, he'd be free to move anywhere he liked among the colonies. A master fuller could write his own destiny.

Even a master fuller with a tarnished past.

Yarrow readied herself for the trip to the fulling mill to fetch her finished bolt of cloth. If she took an extra moment to straighten her hat and smooth the wrinkles from her apron, surely that originated from nerves concerning the condition of her cloth and not her appearance. She tucked the few coins extracted from her sisters into her pocket. They hadn't been happy to pay the fulling mill's fee. After all, they'd never paid Yarrow to full the cloth herself. *Or to card the wool, spin the yarn, or weave the cloth.* She pushed aside the grumbling thoughts and left the house.

Since her last walk to the fulling mill, many apple blossoms had fallen, littering parts of the road like snowy shadows under the trees. Treading on them released their innocent sweetness.

A dog raced down the road toward her, followed by a barefooted boy holding onto his straw hat. She smiled as the pair veered into the woods opposite the creek. If she and Enos had married, such a lad might have been hers.

She wrapped her arms around her middle and marched on. Dwelling on broken promises was a waste of time. Dreaming about how to achieve a level of independence would profit her more.

The rhythmic pounding of the mill, its wooden mallets driven by the great water wheel, greeted her as she drew near. The noise level increased when she opened the front door. The strong odors of lye soap and wet wool assailed her. Mallets of smooth wood hammered against wet fabric on one side of the mill, while the other held two huge, steaming vats. Mr. Maltby thrust a long paddle into one vat and lifted a soggy mass of fabric before lowering it back into the bath.

He glanced up and smiled. "Miss Fenn." He wiped his hands on his work apron. "You have come to fetch your cloth, I'll wager."

"Indeed, I have." She averted her eyes from his forearms, left bare beneath his rolled sleeves.

He pulled a bolt from a rack near the door, her name visible on the tag. "'Tis done. And I must say, 'twas a pure joy to work with."

Heat washed her cheeks. "How kind of you."

"Nothing of the sort." He placed the bolt on the counter and leaned against it, his blue eyes twinkling. "I would have a word with you, if you have the time."

She glanced around the mill. Sam Tucker tinkered with a spare mallet, in clear sight of the counter that separated her from Mr. Maltby. "I can spare a moment."

A confident grin exposed a shallow dimple on his left cheek. The only thing marring his good looks was a thin scar along his temple. "Have you ever considered teaching?"

"I am not a scholar, sir." She squashed a flicker of irritation. Why did everyone assume that an unmarried woman must run a dame school?

"My pardon, I failed to make myself clear." He tapped her bolt of cloth on the counter between them. "Have you ever considered teaching others to spin and weave?"

"Who am I to teach such a thing?"

"Who better to teach than an expert?" All humor gone, brown brows several shades darker than his hair drew into a serious line.

He thought her work that good?

"The considerable increase in the cost of textiles from England has forced many here in the colonies to relearn the arts of spinning and weaving. Sadly, few have had much instruction to do it well. Your work is excellent." He tapped the cloth again. "The uniformity of the yarn, the intricacy of the weave—" He shook his head. "The ladies of Milford need someone such as yourself to show them how to improve their cloth."

If she wasn't careful, Mr. Peter Maltby would turn her head.

"I do not know—"

"I can think of only one example of cloth I have seen any finer than this that was made here in the colonies. I handled it in Boston last year. I did not full it, it was finished by someone else, but the workmanship. . ." He stopped and looked at the bolt again, leaning forward until his nose was mere inches away. "If memory serves, it may have been woven in the same pattern."

Her spine turned to ice. Had he seen a bolt of hers that Enos had sold?

"I must be going." With trembling fingers, Yarrow pulled the coins from her pocket and dropped them on the counter before snatching her cloth to her chest. "Thank you, sir."

"About teaching. . .Miss Fenn?"

Yarrow hurried out the door, her heart thudding against her ribs. She pressed the palm of her hand to her forehead as she walked, trying to remember. Had she told him that the weave was her papa's original design when she dropped the bolt off? Perspiration dampened her brow, but she didn't lessen her pace. He'd recognized the weave of her cloth as the same weave he'd seen in Boston. What if he reported her to the authorities? He might even be an agent of the king. Why else would a journeyman everyone acknowledged was full of promise agree to come to a remote town in a different colony?

She needed to get away—and stay far away—from Mr. Peter Maltby.

Women were difficult to understand on the best of days, but Peter had no clue what had sent Miss Fenn out the door as if her skirt had caught fire. He'd complimented her on her talent. He'd compared her cloth to the finest he'd ever seen. Surely these were not the type of comments to offend. He scratched his head, fingering the scar near his temple.

"Do not try to figure them out, lad." His boss joined him at the counter. "'Tis more than her uncommon height that has kept the men of Milford away from that one. She would be a handful for any man. Very self-sufficient."

Peter nodded. He rather liked Miss Fenn's ability to look him in the eye. There was nothing of simper or coy about her. Besides, a woman needed to be self-sufficient if she were to instruct others. He must find a different way to approach her on that subject.

"I merely asked if she would be willing to give lessons on spinning and weaving. I have no idea why she took offense."

Mr. Tucker shrugged. "'Tis hard to figure. But you have a good idea there. Some of this cloth—" He gestured to the vats.

"Indeed. If she could impart even a fraction of her talent, the town would benefit greatly." And so would he. Salvaging poor cloth wouldn't raise him to the level of master fuller. He needed cloth like Miss Fenn produced.

Peter resumed his work at the vats, scouring all remains of the sheep's natural grease from the cloth before it would be beaten and tightened under the mallets. Then came the arduous task of stretching and shaping the cloth onto frames outside to dry before it was brushed and cropped to a fine finish. Or what should be a fine finish, if the original offering was worthy to be called cloth.

He lifted the soggy mess in the vat once more and snorted in disgust. This cloth would be barely adequate for a dress despite his best efforts. It certainly wouldn't showcase his talent.

He must find a way to enlist Miss Fenn's cooperation.

Chapter 3

O uch!" Eight-year-old Clara dropped the wool cards into her apron-covered lap and popped her finger into her mouth.

Yarrow set aside the wool she'd been hand-teasing. "Not like that, dearest." She wrapped her arm around Marigold's oldest child and picked up the wooden paddles, which had sharp metal teeth used to brush and prepare the teased wool for spinning.

"Keep your fingers on the handles, away from the teeth, then brush the wool between the cards, like so." She demonstrated the process for at least the tenth time that morning.

If she couldn't teach a child the simple task of carding, didn't that prove she had no business teaching anyone else to spin or weave?

And yet, Mr. Maltby's idea had taken root.

"Aunt Yarrow, may I be finished now?" Lashes the color of a downy chick flittered over baby-blue eyes, while adorable pink cheeks framed Clara's perfect Cupid's bow mouth.

"Indeed. Go straight into the house and let your mama know."

The little girl wiggled off the wooden bench and skipped to the house. Yarrow leaned against the rough bark of the maple tree, her foot swinging idly from the curved bench her papa had built around its trunk. It was the perfect place to sit on a spring day and prepare wool for spinning. Proper teasing and carding were necessary to produce the finest results. Even the best of weavers couldn't produce quality cloth from inferior yarn.

Yarrow had learned to tease and card wool when she was no older than Clara. Back then, most people still purchased their cloth ready-made from England, but Papa had been a forward-thinking man and perhaps a bit of a rebel. He insisted his family be able to support themselves, including making their own clothes. When the town of Milford started keeping a flock of sheep, he had moved his young family here. It was his middle daughter he'd schooled in the textile arts.

Had he sensed, somehow, that she would never marry?

She shook her head. Such a fanciful thought. Nobody but God knew what tomorrow would bring. They'd all been so sure she and Enos. . . But there was no sense looking back at what might have been. Enos Watkins was the traveling peddler now and nothing more. Yarrow sold him an extra bolt of cloth when she could and hoped they wouldn't get caught. A shiver tingled at the thought, despite the warmth of the day.

Giving lessons was a viable alternative to earn money. She grabbed another handful of wool from the large basket at her side and teased out the bits of grass and burrs stuck within. Her attempt with Clara aside, the idea of teaching was growing on Yarrow.

Perhaps she could earn enough that she wouldn't need to sell any fabric. That would be a worry—and guilt—off her shoulders. She shouldn't covet money as much as she did, but her desire wasn't for the money exactly, it was what the money represented. Independence. Living in the back room Papa had added to the family home was comfortable, but she was dependent on Penny and Archie, Penny's husband, who had inherited the house when Papa died.

If she weren't skirting the law, she wouldn't need to fear Mr. Maltby, even if he were an agent of the king. It would be nice to have someone with whom to discuss fine textiles. Someone who appreciated them as much as she did.

Someone far too handsome for her to be thinking about at her age.

"Miss Stanton, if I may offer my opinion?" Peter leaned against the counter—as if anyone could overhear him with the thud and slap of the fulling mallets doing their work across the mill. "Your cloth is nice, but I have a notion that Miss Fenn could be persuaded to give advanced instruction on spinning and weaving to the ladies of Milford." He looked both ways, knowing full well his boss had not yet arrived, and nobody else had entered the mill. "'Tis said that her father was the finest weaver in Connecticut Colony and that he passed on his knowledge to his daughter before he left this earth."

Miss Stanton's eyes widened and she, in turn, leaned into the counter. "'Tis true, I have heard the same. Have you finished a bolt of her cloth?"

He straightened and hooked his thumbs in the arm openings of his sleeveless waistcoat. "Indeed I have. I must admit, I have never handled the like." He raised his hand as if giving an oath. "Not even in Boston."

"Oh, my." Miss Stanton pressed her fingers to her chin. "You say she is willing to impart these skills to others?"

"I spoke to her about it myself just the other day, but unfortunately our discussion was interrupted."

"Ah." A knowing gleam darkened her brown eyes. "Perhaps I could pay her a visit on the morrow."

"It might be prudent to take a couple of ladies with you. Having more than one pupil would be a better use of her time."

"Indeed, I can see that."

Peter stepped from behind the counter and all but ushered Miss Stanton from the mill. When she turned to offer a final wave, he smiled and nodded. Whistling the jaunty tune to a song of which no preacher would approve, he returned to the counter and added Miss Stanton's coins to the tin box Mr. Tucker kept there.

His employer stepped through the door and cocked an eyebrow at him. "You are in a jovial mood this morning."

"'Tis a fine morning."

"Was that Miss Stanton walking away?" Mr. Tucker hung his hat on a peg beside the door and grabbed his apron.

"Indeed."

"Was she satisfied with her cloth?" He wrapped the long apron strings around his back and tied them in front under the modest swell of his belly.

"She seemed to be."

"But?" The eyebrow rose again.

"I might have suggested that a few lessons administered under the right person would improve the quality of her cloth." Peter offered a smile he hoped appeared sincere.

Sam Tucker chuckled and rubbed his jaw. "As I recall, the lady in question fled rather abruptly after your suggestion last week."

"Indeed. It occurred to me that I was not the proper person to approach Miss Fenn regarding this endeavor."

"You could be right."

Peter wiped a trickle of sweat from his brow. If he could get the proper cloth to work with before winter set in, all the better. With any luck, the seeds planted with Miss Stanton would sprout and produce good fruit.

A trio of women approached Yarrow where she sat on her bench carding wool. She knew all three but wasn't particularly close with any of them.

"I hope you do not think us impertinent," Amelia Stanton said. She was a couple of years younger than Yarrow, and they'd grown up together in Milford. "Yesterday when I fetched my cloth from the fulling mill, Mr. Maltby mentioned that you might be agreeable to teaching."

"He did?" Why would he? She'd given him no encouragement on that account. Quite the opposite, in fact.

"We all know your father's work." Betsy Clark nodded toward the other two ladies. "And we see the fine garments your sisters wear from the cloth you make."

Rebecca Harpin took a step closer. "My Robert would appreciate any help you could give me." She shrugged. "We bought our cloth from England until the law changed. I have had to learn as I go."

"Of course we will pay for your time." Color tinged Amelia's cheeks. "The banns have not been posted yet, but Mr. Wheeler and I have come to an understanding. He needs a wife who can clothe his family."

As well he should with four children from his first wife, God rest her soul. Had he approached Yarrow with thoughts of matrimony, she'd have run in the other direction. But Amelia fairly preened at her announcement.

The other two ladies nodded. Both were married and must be struggling to produce enough cloth for their families.

Yarrow's heart squeezed. Why hadn't she realized that others were struggling to do what she'd learned at her papa's knee? How could she have been so blind?

"I shall be happy to instruct you as best I can."

Amelia clasped her hands and all but bounced on her toes. "Thank you. We shall be the best of pupils. I promise."

Yarrow told them what they needed to bring, and they agreed to meet in the forenoons of Mondays, Wednesdays, and Fridays. Watching them leave, a smile teased her lips. How odd that Mr. Maltby had seen this need, and he so new to the town. A need she'd failed to see these past three years, since the passage of the Wool Act. Shortly after that news had reached their town, Papa had died. And then Enos had left. Blinded by her grief for a time, she'd grown used to being alone.

Penny stormed across the grass toward her. Well, almost alone. Her younger sister pulled to a stop with her arms crossed above her belly. "What is this all about?"

"Pardon?"

"I stopped Amelia and the others just now. They claim you have agreed to tutor them in cloth making. Is that true?"

"Indeed."

"Well, we shall just see about that." Penny turned on her heel and marched off. Doubtless straight to Marigold's house down the road.

That baby couldn't come soon enough. Her little sister was fast becoming a termagant. With a sigh, Yarrow settled back on her bench and waited for Marigold to appear.

Penny must have made good time, because Marigold came charging past the corner of the house before Yarrow's wool basket was half-full of carded fibers.

"How can you be so selfish?" Her eldest sister was drawn up like a she-bear guarding her cubs.

Yarrow stood. "How can you?"

That brought Marigold up short. She opened her mouth and then it shut again with a click. She crossed her arms and glared at Yarrow, the intimidating stance somewhat diminished, as the top of her head barely reached Yarrow's nose.

"These women have requested my help. They cannot afford to purchase cloth from England any more than we can. They did not have Papa to teach them how to spin and weave." Yarrow tilted her head. "Neither do they have a sister to create their cloth for them."

Marigold's stance wilted, and she cast a glance at the house where doubtless Penny watched from a window. "I had not thought of it that way."

"Nor I, or I would have offered my services much earlier."

"Indeed." Marigold squeezed Yarrow's arm. "You have a willing heart and able hands. You always did. Pray forgive me for—"

"Listening to our little sister?" Yarrow chuckled. "She cannot see past her own protruding middle right now, but I expect 'twill change once the babe arrives."

"I pray so, for all our sakes." Marigold sighed. "Will you still have time to teach Clara?"

"Of course, and happily so."

Marigold nodded and strode to the house.

Yarrow sat on her bench and picked up a handful of wool. The earthy scents of lanolin and sunshine brought comfort. Earning extra coins without selling cloth to Enos was a relief, but it was knowing she was helping her neighbors that lifted her spirits.

She had Peter Maltby to thank. He couldn't be an agent for the Crown. If he were, he'd be trying to trap her in a crime, not trying to help the other ladies of the town clothe their families. Wouldn't he?

Peter stood at the end of the second sermon and stretched. He nodded to several men he'd met, whose names he couldn't remember, then glanced across at the women's side of the church. Miss Fenn remained seated, speaking to the little blond-haired girl at her side. Such a quaint picture they presented, framed by the light from the window behind them. If only Miss Fenn had worn a gown made of her exceptional cloth, but even from where he stood, he could tell she hadn't. It perplexed him to think of her creating such lovely work exclusively for someone else.

"'Tis a sight to get a man's attention." Sam Tucker chuckled as he moved past Peter toward the door.

Peter slapped his hat against his thigh and followed his boss outside.

"Mr. Maltby." Miss Stanton approached as soon as he'd cleared the doorway. "I cannot thank you enough. Miss Fenn has agreed to instruct me, Mrs. Clark, and Mrs. Harpin." Her eyes sparkled. "We shall soon be wearing gowns as fine as anyone in this town."

"I'm happy to hear it." Happier than she could imagine. Even considering that the lessons would take weeks and the finished product wouldn't arrive in his hands until midsummer at the earliest, it still gave him hope for a return to Boston before the snow fell. He tapped his hat onto his head and touched the brim with his finger before excusing himself and striding after Mr. Tucker's family.

"You needn't be in such a hurry to join us after services." Mrs. Tucker glanced back at the church. "I'm happy to keep a plate warm for you. Although you might get a supper invitation elsewhere."

Peter loosened the cloth around his neck. "I never leave a gracious hostess waiting, ma'am. My granny taught me better manners."

She smiled. "I'm sure she did, but all the same, know that you are free to socialize as a young man ought. A man cannot find a wife if he does not look about."

Mr. Tucker tossed him a sympathetic grin. What was it about women that they all saw a single man as an object to be hustled to the altar?

"I expect I shall have plenty of time for looking once I have become a master fuller."

"I appreciate a man who has his priorities in order." Mr. Tucker clamped a hand on Peter's shoulder. "From what I have seen of your work so far, it shan't take you long."

That's all Peter wanted. And yet, a lovely woman speaking with a blond-haired little girl came to mind.

Chapter 4

The rhythmic click and whirl of the spinning wheel lulled Yarrow into a peaceful state. On a Thursday morning with nobody to give a lesson to, she sat on her bench and worked the smooth treadle of the spinning wheel with her bare foot. A slight breeze, not strong enough to blow the wool from her basket, brought cool refreshment to her spot under the tree. Sunshine filtered through the leaves above her. Dew-drenched earth released its loamy fragrance. Soft fibers slipped between her fingers and gathered into a fine thread before winding onto the spinning wheel's bobbin. The pattern repeated itself over and over, soothing her spirit like nothing else.

Lessons had gone well these past two weeks. They worked outside on fine days and inside when it rained or was too windy. The first lesson had convinced her that she needed to start with the very basics. One couldn't spin an even thread from wool that wasn't properly prepared. After the days of teasing and carding, she was proud to see much improvement in her pupils' progress. They'd start spinning on their own wheels next week. They'd be weaving a couple of weeks after that. And it wouldn't end there. At church last Sunday three more women had approached and asked to be in her second class. Imagine.

A butterfly swooped between Yarrow and the spinning wheel. She paused the wheel to watch it dip and soar. Such a delicate creature. A marvel of God's creation. She followed its path until it startled and darted away from the thicket behind the stable. Something moved in the dense brush at the forest's edge. A bear would make much more noise, so she remained still, hoping she might see a doe and fawn.

Instead, a fuzzy white face pushed its way through the thicket and into the yard. The sheep stuck its tongue out and issued a low-pitched *baa*. Another step, and the animal broke free of the thicket, followed closely by one, two, and then a third little lamb. Triplets. While the flock usually had a number of twins every year, triplets were rare.

The last one to come through the brush was tiny, only half the size of its siblings. It wobbled a bit on legs no thicker than Yarrow's thumb.

"You poor dear."

The mother sheep stopped at the sound of Yarrow's voice. The two larger lambs scurried into place, one on each side, and began to nurse, their tails wiggling. The littlest lamb joined them, but there was no room for it. The mother sheep lowered her head and butted the little lamb away.

"Now, see here." Yarrow rose, indignant that the mother would treat her lamb that way. The sheep baaed and trotted away, doubtless to find the flock she'd wandered from.

Her babies gamboled after her, the two larger lambs kicking up their heels. When they were almost to the road in front of the house, the littlest one fell. It bleated and struggled, but the mother and siblings never looked back.

Yarrow hurried over and lifted the lamb. Both its spindly front legs had slipped into a gopher's hole. It fought against her for a moment but soon gave up. It weighed less than a five-pound sack of tea. Its tummy was tucked up and pinched, nothing like the rounded bellies of its siblings.

"What am I to do with you?"

The front door of the house banged shut. "What is that?" Archie asked.

"A tiny lamb."

"Where did it come from?"

Yarrow pointed at the thicket. "The mother ewe came through with triplets, but she has rejected this one." She rubbed the little animal's nose. It nuzzled her fingers.

"They often reject a runt. Best knock it in the head. 'Twill only starve a slow death if you do not."

Yarrow hugged the wooly mite tighter. "I could never."

He grimaced and reached for the lamb. "Let me, then."

She took a step back. "No. I think I shall speak with Mr. Wade. He is very knowledgeable about sheep."

Archie grunted and shook his head before walking away.

"As if I would let him do such a thing." With the animal tucked securely under her arm, Yarrow strode down the road to the Wade's farm, first place past the fulling mill on the outskirts of town. She would find a way to save the lamb.

Peter dropped the rag he'd wiped his hands on and arched his back. Several bones popped and snapped along his spine.

"You are too young to sound like that." Mr. Tucker grinned from the other side of the cloth they'd finished stretching onto the frame. It joined two other filled frames in the sunny field beside the fulling mill. They'd been busy all morning.

"Wrestling that last bolt of cloth was enough to wear me out. Did she weave it of wool yarn or hemp rope?"

"Not the easiest piece to work with, to be sure." He cut a sly glance at Peter. "How goes your quest to improve the quality of the cloth we get?"

Peter smoothed the front of his work apron. "My quest?"

"Involving a certain Miss Fenn, if I recollect."

"'Twasn't a quest at all, I merely suggested—"

His boss laughed. "I'm teasing you, lad. 'Twas a right fine idea, and I'm glad you took the initiative to work it out with Miss Fenn. You could do worse than finding favor with her."

Heat crept along Peter's collar. The man wasn't any more subtle than his wife. Surely it wasn't a crime for a man to remain single in this town. "Since we are finished with this lot, I shall fetch more paper from the mercantile. We are almost out."

At Mr. Tucker's nod, Peter peeled off his apron and entered the mill. He hung the garment on its peg behind the door then straightened his neckcloth and hat as best he could without a looking glass. He stepped out and let the door bang shut, muffling the gears and mallets behind its stout wood.

Scurrying toward him in a sky-blue dress covered with a tan apron, wisps of light-brown hair escaping her linen cap upon which perched a plain straw hat, Miss Fenn gave every appearance of a lady on a mission. What was that she held? Peter stopped on the road and waited for her to reach him.

A tiny lamb nestled in her arms.

"How come you to have a lamb?" he asked.

Her cheeks, already rosy from her haste, darkened. "You shall think me silly, as does my brother-in-law."

"I'm sure that cannot be true."

"'Tis an orphan lamb, a triplet rejected by its mother."

Perhaps her brother-in-law had a point. Likely she'd no idea what she was getting herself into. He did. It brought back memories of the farm where he was raised. And his father. He worked up as much of a smile as he could. "Where are you off to in such a hurry?"

"The Wades' farm, just up the road. Mr. Wade is knowledgeable in all things concerning livestock."

"He is also out of town for a few days. I saw him yesterday at the beginning of his journey."

Her shoulders slumped, and she ran her fingers over the tiny animal's head.

His gut clenched. He could help her, but doing so would stir up memories he'd worked years to bury. Memories of a father he'd tried to forget. Then her clouded hazel eyes met his. No simpering, no coyness, nothing but sorrow. He possessed the knowledge to ease it. Peter rubbed the back of his neck.

"We shall need an old glove, kid leather is best, a narrow-necked bottle, twine, and the milk from a goat."

"You are familiar with raising sheep?" Hope brightened her eyes and added a sweet lilt to her voice.

"I have done my share." And hated every minute of it. Not because of the sheep, but because of what they represented—and who had owned them.

"I have an old glove at home and plenty of twine. Betsy Clark has several milking goats."

"I'm sure there is a bottle that will work in the mill. Give the lamb to me." He took the frail creature. It didn't protest the move, which wasn't a good sign. The earthy scent of newborn lamb stirred more painful memories. A box beside the kitchen stove, his mother hunched over her loom, his father's voice, the crash. . . Peter pulled in a quick breath. "Fetch the rest and meet me back here."

With a nod and a flash of a smile, she headed back toward town.

"Wait a moment."

She turned, the smile wavering.

"Get the milk from whichever goat gave birth most recently. First milk is best."

"I shall." Yarrow hurried away.

The baby lamb shivered against Peter's side despite the warm spring day. It would need to eat soon to survive.

"In for a penny, in for a pound." The lamb raised its head and looked at him. Did he know Peter was his best hope for survival? He lifted the lamb and grunted. Not he. She. A little ewe lamb. He sighed. The paper would have to wait. The rest of his morning would be spent playing nursemaid to an orphan lamb, all to ease the sorrow of Miss Yarrow Fenn.

Why did he care? Because Miss Fenn was critical to his plans for improved cloth with which to demonstrate his mastery of the fulling craft. Because as a master fuller he would be a respected man. A noble aspiration. The lamb snuggled against his side. Because the hazel of Miss Fenn's eyes should never be clouded in sorrow.

Careful not to slosh the goat's milk in her pot, Yarrow pushed open the door to the fulling mill with her hip. Steamy air fragrant with the familiar odors of wool and soap greeted her. Mr. Maltby finished whatever he was doing by the mallets and joined her.

"I have fetched what you asked for." Her breathlessness must be due to her haste to return with the lamb's supplies. She handed him the pot, glove, and twine.

"I found a bottle that will work." He pointed to a box on the floor by the counter. "The lamb is there."

Her heart nearly broke at the wee bundle of white curls huddled into a ball with its head flat on the bed of straw. "Is he going to be all right?"

"She."

"Pardon?"

"'Tis a she, not a he." Mr. Maltby didn't look up from the counter where he assembled the supplies. "Did you think to bring a spoon?"

"Nay, I did not." Should she have? Of course. How else would he get the goat's milk into the bottle? "I can fetch one now."

"No time. I shall make a funnel." He twisted a sheet of paper into a cone and poured the rich milk through it into the bottle.

"Betsy had a goat give birth this morning. She agreed its milk would be best for the lamb, and she had plenty to share."

He grunted, then snipped a finger from her glove, fitted it over the neck of the bottle, and tied it on with twine. Another quick snip and he'd cut a small slit in the end of the finger.

"That should do the trick." He knelt beside the counter and motioned for her to hand him the lamb. The poor creature sagged in his hand as if it had no more will to live.

Yarrow's heart twisted. Had she returned too late? Who knew how long it had been following its mother and siblings before she rescued it from the gopher's hole?

With infinite gentleness, Mr. Maltby eased the lamb across his knee, raised its head with one hand, and guided the nursing bottle with the other. But the lamb refused to open its mouth.

Yarrow was too late. She stifled a sob that threatened the back of her throat.

Mr. Maltby pushed his little finger into the lamb's mouth. Nothing happened. Then he wiggled it once, twice, and finally, the lamb responded by suckling on it. Shooting Yarrow a triumphant grin, he then slid the glove's finger into the lamb's mouth. It took a few tries to get it right, but the lamb latched onto the leather, and its tail wiggled from side to side, just as any nursing lamb's tail should.

"You have done it." Gratitude swelled in her chest.

"'Tis only the start. She shall need feeding every few hours for several days."

"I can do it." And be glad to. It was silly that the little lamb's life had come to mean so much to her in such a short period of time, but it had.

"You shall need to wash the glove and bottle between feedings to prevent spoilage. Cut the other fingers as I have this one, and you shall have plenty until the lamb is old enough to nibble grass."

"How can I thank you?"

"'Tis nothing I have not done before. Now you take over. Steady the lamb with your hand here, and hold the bottle like this. Keep your hand under her jaw."

Their hands met, and Yarrow almost dropped the bottle. Heads close above the lamb, she glanced into his blue eyes. Her heart skipped a beat or two and then thundered until he surely must have heard it.

"I think I have the way of it now." Was that husky sound her own voice?

"I dare say you do."

Why was his just as husky?

Sleepy lamb tucked against her body, the rest of her paraphernalia in a sack Mr. Maltby had loaned her, Yarrow walked home.

"You are a sweet thing. I know Archie will object, but I'm going to keep you." The lamb licked its lips and nestled against Yarrow's shoulder. What a perfectly wonderful feeling, to have saved a life.

With Mr. Maltby's assistance, of course. She would bake him something special when she returned the sack. Perhaps a plate of her molasses cookies. Those had been Papa's favorite treat.

The lamb shifted and sighed, its breath stirring the hair that had escaped Yarrow's cap.

"You shall need a name. Something as sweet as you. Let me think." Yarrow's mama had named her daughters after the plants that grew around their home. Useful plants with pretty flowers. Yarrow scanned the flora along the road until she saw a distinctive tall plant.

"Meadowsweet." How perfect. "Your name is Meadowsweet."

The lamb slept through her christening. A contented sleep brought on by a full belly, thanks to Mr. Maltby. Why had he helped? He had more important things to do than revive a fragile lamb. She'd no doubt interrupted his plans, as he had been on the road to town when they'd met. That he would stop and make time to help her attested to his good character. Could such a man also be an agent of the Crown? Surely not.

That he made her heart hammer at an alarming rate she was sure had nothing to do with her conclusion.

"Was that Miss Fenn walking away with a lamb in her arms?" Mr. Tucker dropped an armload of firewood on the stack.

"Indeed." Not that Peter wanted to talk about it.

"Whyever would she bring it here?"

His boss had a mind like a badger trap. Once he got hold of something, he didn't let go.

"She was on her way to find Martin Wade when we met along the road. As I knew he was out of town, I offered my assistance." That should be the end of it.

"You know sheep?"

But it wasn't. "Enough to get by in a pinch."

Mr. Tucker rubbed his jaw. "A man who knows sheep is a valuable man to have in Milford. Good to know."

Peter pulled off his apron. "It delayed my trip to town. I shall leave now." He slipped out the door before his boss could reply.

Of all the complications he didn't need, getting involved with the town's sheep flock was chief among them. He'd had a bellyful of that work growing up. All he needed was fine cloth to earn his status as master fuller. Then he'd set himself up back in Boston as a man of means. He'd find a wife, perhaps one as talented as Miss Fenn. They'd have a half-dozen children or so, give generously to the church, and be respected in the community. He'd prove he wasn't like his father.

First, he needed good cloth. Why hadn't he asked Miss Fenn about her teaching? Warmth crept up his neck at the thought of her hazel eyes, full of admiration when he'd rigged that simple nursing bottle for the lamb. Her gratitude had been so genuine, without a hint of artifice. So unlike. . .

He tugged at the collar of his shirt. Perhaps in a day or so he might seek her out to inquire after the lamb. If nothing else, the animal gave him the perfect opportunity to stop by and speak with her. As he entered the mercantile, it occurred to him that it was this thought, and not the ones of Boston, that had put a spring in his step.

Chapter 5

Meadowsweet startled and raced across the grass to Yarrow's side, kicking and bouncing the way any healthy lamb would. What a difference a few days made. Cleaned up and sporting a pink ribbon around her neck, she'd become the darling of Yarrow's pupils last Friday.

The clatter of a horse and wagon announced today's arrival of her pupils. Rebecca pulled back on the reins, and the horse stopped.

Amelia jumped from the wagon. "Look at her. She grew over the weekend."

"All young things grow like weeds. Here, take your wheel." Betsy handed Amelia a small spinning wheel, the style Mr. Newberry had been making for the ladies of Milford since he set up his woodworking shop in town two years ago.

Once all three wheels were unloaded, Rebecca moved the wagon and tied her horse to the hitching post out front.

"Meadowsweet, come here." Amelia knelt and held out her hand.

The little lamb eyed her from behind Yarrow's skirt but didn't budge.

"Perhaps she shall warm up as our lesson goes on," Yarrow said.

After two weeks of learning proper preparation, they had plenty of wool ready to spin. Yarrow's fingers fairly itched to get going. She'd never imagined that teaching would excite her creativity the way it had. She'd always enjoyed her work, but working with other women, their camaraderie, spurred her on to want to do more. The ladies got started, and she moved between them and their wheels, answering questions and demonstrating technique as needed.

"Mr. Maltby," Amelia said.

Yarrow looked up. He stood several feet away, his hat in his hands, golden hair gleaming in the midmorning light.

"Forgive me. I did not mean to intrude."

"Nonsense. Come and see what we have learned." Amelia's plump cheeks dimpled. "After all, 'twas your idea."

"Indeed, and we are grateful to you. Just see how much my spinning has improved already." Betsy patted the bobbin on her spinning wheel. "My Donald will thank you when he sees the shirt I shall make from this."

When he glanced at her, Yarrow swallowed and gestured toward the wheels. "Please, do join us."

He smiled, the corners of his eyes crinkling, the dimple on his cheek deepening.

As he bent over Betsy's wheel and exclaimed about her fine spinning, Meadowsweet emerged from under the bench.

"Ah, and here is the reason for my visit." Peter knelt, and the lamb took two steps toward him, stopping just out of his reach. "She looks well."

"Thanks to you." Yarrow knitted her fingers together at her waist. "I cannot tell you how grateful—"

He held up his hand. "Think nothing of it."

She'd thought of little else these past four days.

"I trust the lamb has not caused too much inconvenience?" Peter knew it had. Raising an orphan lamb was a huge undertaking. Once he had enjoyed it, before his brother's death.

"She is no trouble at all." The merriment in Yarrow's eyes put falsehood to her words. "Archie still thinks me daft for saving her, and Penny is not most pleased to have a lamb in the house. Although Meadowsweet is confined to my room."

"I have told Yarrow that my children would be more than happy to tend the little lamb," Mrs. Harpin said. "But she turned me down. I think she enjoys having something young to care for."

Yarrow's cheeks pinked in a most delightful fashion.

Peter cleared his throat. "Well, the lamb is prospering under her care."

He stepped away from Yarrow and leaned over Mrs. Clark's shoulder as she continued to spin. "You all seem to be prospering under her care."

He cast a quick glance at Yarrow. Was that gratitude in her eyes? For the praise of her teaching, or changing the subject away from her care of the lamb? She should have more than a lamb to care for. She should have children of her own. He shifted his attention back to the ladies and their spinning. This was the real reason for his visit, to assess how well the lessons were progressing. Not to contemplate the unmarried state of Miss Yarrow Fenn.

Yet the entire stroll back to the mill was filled with thoughts of her. Her tender expression while holding the lamb. Her smile when she caught him staring like a schoolboy. That enticing flush of pink that leaped readily to her cheeks. If he hadn't already decided his future—

But he had.

Teaching might be putting coins in Yarrow's pocket, but it was also slowing down her own fabric production, a point Penny had made to her at breakfast. That babe couldn't come soon enough. Even Archie had raised his brows at his wife's acidic words.

Yarrow snipped the final thread and gathered the linsey-woolsey cloth into her lap. The sturdy combination of linen and wool, woven into a tight twill, would wear well as breeches for her brothers-in-law.

A tickle of excitement stirred her stomach. She pressed her hand against it. It was time to take the cloth to the fulling mill. She chided herself for feeling this way and chalked it up to the lack of guilt this bolt produced, since she'd not sell it to Enos. She folded it carefully and set it aside while she pinned her hat in place and straightened her apron.

Meadowsweet stretched and yawned in her box. She licked her lips a few times, then stood on her back feet, front hooves on the top of the box's side.

"You shall outgrow that soon, and then what shall I do with you?"

While she was pleased that the lamb not only grew but thrived under her care, watching it also brought a pang of sorrow. Soon Meadowsweet would be weaned and would need to find her place among the flock. Having a little one of her own, albeit with four feet instead of two, had brought a special kind of fulfillment into Yarrow's life. Her room would be empty without Meadowsweet. And so, Yarrow feared, would her heart.

"But not today. Today we have a trip to the fulling mill." She lifted the lamb from its box and retrieved the folded cloth. "Mr. Maltby will be surprised at how much you have grown these past two weeks."

Two weeks where she'd only glimpsed him from across the aisle at church. Several times their eyes had met, but she'd always looked away. He'd shown her kindness, not interest, yet against all her best intentions, she couldn't help the flutter in her chest whenever he came to mind, which was far from infrequently. The teasing of her pupils didn't help. Since his one and only visit, they'd continued to make comments about him. Pointed comments kindly meant that nevertheless unsettled her.

"But enough of that." She pushed open the door. Meadowsweet trotted at her heels down the road.

When they arrived, Yarrow leaned down and petted the lamb.

"You stay here in the sunshine. I shall be out presently."

Despite her best effort to enter the mill while blocking the lamb, Meadowsweet darted between her feet and charged inside, hooves pattering across the plank floor.

"What is this?" Sam Tucker straightened behind the counter where he'd been writing in a ledger.

"My apologies, Mr. Tucker. I tried to prevent her from entering."

"Not to worry. 'Tisn't the first sheepy thing to enter my mill." He laughed and bent down to coax the lamb to him.

Yarrow cast a glance around the mill. Mr. Maltby wasn't there. Disappointment pinched, but she kept her smile in place.

Mr. Tucker stood and pulled a watch from his waistcoat. "Would you look at the time? I'm late for an appointment."

Yarrow lifted the cloth in her arms. Surely he had time to take her order.

"Not to fear, Miss Fenn, I shall make sure Peter is with you directly."

With a nod and wink, the mill owner slipped out the back door, leaving Yarrow alone with the steaming vats and slapping mallets. What an odd way for Mr. Tucker to behave.

Peter wiped his hands on a rag and watched his boss beat a hasty retreat toward town. What appointment could he possibly have in the middle of the day? And why hadn't he mentioned this before now? Puzzling. At least Peter had finished greasing the wheel's axle and gears.

He entered the back of the mill and tossed the rag onto a pile near the door. A high-pitched *baa* pulled him up short. A lamb wearing a pink ribbon hopped across the floor in a playful sideways motion. What was Meadowsweet doing in the mill?

He pivoted to face the counter. Miss Fenn held an armful of cloth and watched him. Why hadn't Mr. Tucker—ah. His boss had missed his calling. He should have been a matchmaker, not a fuller.

"I'm sorry." She took a step toward him. "Meadowsweet slipped in before I could stop her, and Mr. Tucker did not seem to mind."

"Nor should he." Peter pushed his hair back from his forehead. He must look a sight after crawling around the wheel with a pot of grease. "There is nothing in here that a little lamb will bother, after all."

Her answering smile lit up the room.

His traitorous heart flopped between his ribs.

"I have brought some linsey-woolsey."

"Excellent." He stepped forward then looked at his hands. "But give me a moment to remove any grease before I take it from you."

He dipped a bucket into the closest vat and plunged his hands into the soapy water. Breath hissed out between his teeth. It wasn't quite hot enough to scald a chicken, but it was close. He glanced at Miss Fenn as he dried his hands. Her smile had a mischievous tilt to it.

"There, now let me see your latest masterpiece."

She handed him the bolt. Nothing at all like the first bolt she'd given him, this was a material suitable for working clothes. But with her artistry, for he could think of no other way to describe it, this cloth was anything but simple.

"Stunning."

"'Tis only for everyday breeches for my brothers-in-law."

"Then they are blessed. I dare say a Grand Duke couldn't ask for better."

"Such flattery, when we both know a Grand Duke would wear only satins and silks."

"If he saw your linsey-woolsey, he would change his mind."

She cocked her head, brows raised, that rosy hue he hoped only he brought to her cheeks adding to her appeal.

"Would I say so if it were not the truth?"

She chuckled and shook her head. "I fear the truth might be a stretchy thing with you, Mr. Maltby."

"Peter."

She froze for a moment, and then glanced at Meadowsweet, who was poking her nose around the bottom of the door. She raised her eyes to his again. "Peter. Then you should call me Yarrow."

He released a breath he hadn't realized he'd been holding. "When first you told me, I remember thinking it quite an exotic name."

She twirled her finger in a lock of hair which had escaped her cap. "My mother named us after useful flowers. She said my hair was the color of wool dyed with yarrow."

"It was a favorite of my mother's to dye with."

"Did your family run a fulling mill then?"

Her words settled over him like a wet blanket over flames. His family. No. That was a topic he couldn't discuss.

"They did not." The abrupt chill of his voice changed the atmosphere. He placed the cloth on the counter. "For breeches, you said?"

At her bewildered nod, he scribbled her name and the purpose of the cloth on a piece of paper. "I must get back to work. We shall have this ready for you next week."

"Thank you." She left his name unsaid. "I shall return then." She scooped up the lamb and slipped out the door.

He was an unmitigated fool.

Flustered from her encounter with Peter, the walk home did little to clear Yarrow's head. He had given her permission to use his name, sending her pulse skittering. How could he then dismiss their conversation so abruptly? Perhaps she'd never understand men. For certain, they were changeable creatures at best. She'd learned that from Enos.

Maybe it was something more. She replayed their conversation in her mind. His demeanor had shifted right after she'd asked about his family. Why? There was more to Mr. Peter Maltby than met the eye. Had her first suspicion that he might be the king's agent been correct? She crossed her arms over her middle and hurried home.

A cry greeted her as she entered her room. Yarrow jerked open the connecting door. "Penny?"

"Fetch Marigold. Now!"

Her little sister stood in a puddle, one hand pressed to her back, the other grasping the mantel above the fireplace.

"Let me help you into a clean shift first."

"No. Fetch Marigold." Panic filled Penny's voice.

"Dearest, this is your first babe. It will take time. We shall get you comfortable, and then I shall run all the way to Marigold's. I promise." Yarrow clasped her sister's hands and gave them a squeeze.

With just a bit of coaxing, she got Penny into a clean shift and settled on the bed, a stack of pillows at her back. Then she kept her word and ran down the road to Marigold's.

Their older sister must have seen her coming, because she met Yarrow at the door, a basket in her hand.

"'Tis her time?"

"Indeed. She is asking for you."

"Stay with the children while I attend to her. They love playing with your lamb. I shall fetch the midwife."

Yarrow glanced down. Meadowsweet nibbled on the edge of her apron. She hadn't even noticed the lamb following her. Between the children, the lamb, and excitement over the impending birth, at least she'd be able to push thoughts of Mr. Peter Maltby aside for the day.

After the children had tired of playing with Meadowsweet, Yarrow fixed a pot of stew and then read to them until David, Marigold's husband, returned from his work at the docks. Meadowsweet bleated pitifully all the way home, her feeding time long past due. Yarrow fed the greedy little lamb as soon as they arrived. Then she tucked Meadowsweet in her box before opening the connecting door.

Marigold sat beside Penny while Mrs. Todd, the town's midwife, talked to Penny from the foot of the bed. Yarrow hurried to Penny's other side and grasped her sister's hand. Sweat matted Penny's hair, but she gritted her teeth and followed the midwife's instructions. Gone was the petulant little sister. In her place was a young woman of determination. Admiration caught Yarrow unaware. She glanced at Marigold and received an answering nod.

As so many first births, it was a lengthy process, but Penny's son arrived hale and hearty in the wee hours of the next morning. His first cry brought an answering one from the women around him. Mrs. Todd handed the babe to Yarrow. She had the cloths and water ready but was unprepared for the surge of emotion that threatened to overwhelm her when the babe lay in her arms, his red face wrinkled and wet and indefinably precious.

"'Tis something, is it not?" Mrs. Todd's smile radiated understanding. "I never tire of the miracle."

Miracle was exactly the right word. Yarrow whispered a prayer over the boy as she bathed him for the first time. Then she swaddled him in a fresh wrap and held him close, breathing in the unique scent of a newborn.

"She is ready for him." Marigold waved Yarrow over to the bed.

Penny pushed herself higher on the pillows and reached for her babe, a light in her eyes that Yarrow had never seen before. She handed the bundle to her sister and then stepped back. The bond between mother and child was a physical presence in the room, so powerfully did Yarrow feel it. Along with the love for her family came a sharp stab of reality.

It had been within her grasp once, until Enos had packed up and taken to the road. But that memory didn't bring the pain it used to. She looked at her empty arms and envisioned a babe there. One with hair like spun gold and eyes as blue as. . .no. She looked at her beaming sister. Yarrow was unlikely to ever have this moment for herself.

Chapter 6

If Peter visited during one of the lessons, under the guise of checking the progress of her pupils, Yarrow wouldn't toss him out on his ear. Which he deserved. He admitted that—at least to himself.

He'd mumbled some vague excuse for going to town before leaving a grinning Sam Tucker at the mill. Peter tugged at the stiffened neckcloth he normally only wore on Sunday. It wasn't like he'd wanted to notice her hazel eyes, or the depth of compassion that led her to rescue an orphan lamb, or the scent of lavender that clung to her, or the way her hair escaped its cap and feathered around her face. No. He'd had his future all planned out. He'd earn his rank of master fuller here, where journeymen were few and masters scarce. Then he'd make a hasty return to Boston before the winter set in. Once there, he'd become a model citizen. He'd prove to everyone that he wasn't like his father. It had been a good plan.

He kicked at a stone on the road and then glanced around to see if anyone had noticed. He was two and twenty, for heaven's sake. With a jerk, he straightened his shoulders and raised his chin. Soon he would be a man of means, not a journeyman living under the rafters of a smelly fulling mill. With a discreet movement, he sniffed at the shoulder of his coat. Definitely not under the rafters.

Too soon, he arrived at Miss Fenn's, but there were no spinners seated in the shade under the tree. He stopped for a moment. The unmistakable thump of a loom in motion caught his ear. He walked to the back of the house. A door stood open. Inside sat Miss Fenn before her loom, with her pupils gathered behind. He remained still and listened to her instruction.

Meadowsweet poked her head around the doorframe and baaed. The ladies turned to look. Heat gathered at the base of Peter's neck. He stepped forward.

"Have I arrived at an inconvenient time?"

"Not at all, Mr. Maltby. Come see what we are learning today." Miss Stanton waved him into the room.

Miss Fenn glanced his way then back at her weaving.

"Is this not the most beautiful pattern?" Mrs. Harpin ran her fingers over the cloth on the loom. "'Tis like nothing I have owned before, much less made myself. I cannot wait to try it on my own loom."

"Exquisite." He wasn't trying to flatter Miss Fenn. The weaving truly was exquisite. Unique, deceptively delicate, just like—he'd seen this pattern before she'd brought her first bolt to the mill.

In Boston.

He leaned closer to examine the texture. The master fuller he'd apprenticed to had bought a bolt like this last year. It was identical. This hadn't been fulled yet, but he knew what it would look like once it was finished.

"This is the same pattern as the first cloth you brought to the mill, but I have seen it somewhere else before."

He raised his eyes until they met Miss Fenn's.

What expression flashed through those depths of her eyes before she slid off the weaving bench? She stood and wiped her hands down the sides of her apron. The other women continued chatting about their weaving, but she stood silent. The hand she raised to tuck back her hair trembled.

Why was she afraid?

How Yarrow got through the rest of her class, she couldn't remember. Mr. Maltby hadn't lingered following his recognition of her weaving. At least he hadn't exposed her in front of her pupils. Yarrow closed her door behind Amelia, the last to leave.

"Yarrow," Penny called. Four days since the babe's birth, and she still wasn't regaining her strength.

"Coming." Yarrow pushed aside her concerns and smiled as she opened the connecting door.

Her sister jiggled a fussy Jonathan in her arms. "He will not settle for me. I have fed and changed him, but he will not settle." Tears dampened her face, highlighting the dark circles under her eyes.

"I shall take him." Yarrow reached for the babe. "You should rest."

"I believe I shall."

With the babe in her arms, Yarrow walked through her room and outside into the fresh air. Jonathan fussed and kicked, his little eyes squinched shut, until they were walking under the trees behind the house. Yarrow hummed an old lullaby. The same one she used to hum to Penny. Jonathan opened his eyes, and his little feet stilled. She transferred him to her shoulder and rubbed his back. Soon his little body relaxed into slumber.

If only she could find such comfort.

Would Mr. Maltby talk to her first? Or would he report her to the authorities? While she had technically not broken the law, because she'd sold her cloth here in Connecticut Colony, she knew that Enos had.

Jonathan sighed against her shoulder.

A sweet pain settled on her heart.

If she and Enos had married, she might be holding her own little one now. The day he'd turned his back and walked away, her dreams had shattered. Dreams of a home of her own. Dreams of babies. Dreams of sitting outside on a warm summer's night beside her husband looking up at the stars and contemplating what God would do in their lives together. All those dreams were gone.

It had taken a few months to adjust after the crushing disappointment, but she didn't hate Enos. She didn't wish him arrested. He'd surely be tried and found guilty. He'd at least face time in prison. For such an offense, he may even hang.

She shivered despite the warmth of the day.

Meadowsweet tugged at Yarrow's skirt, demanding her attention.

"Jealous are you, my sweet?" The lamb tilted her head up at a comical angle. Yarrow sank to the ground, her sleeping nephew on her shoulder, her lamb at her side. Her life was far from empty. The girlish dreams were gone, that was true, but she was not alone and not unloved.

Perhaps if she spoke with Mr. Maltby and explained the situation. If she owned up to what she had done. She'd sold her fabric—knowingly—to a peddler who'd sold it across the colony's border. In strict violation of the Wool Act.

Why?

Because she wanted a bit of independence. She wanted some money of her own. She wanted. . .and she hadn't waited for the Lord to provide. She hadn't trusted Him. In that moment, the crushing burden of the sin she carried became clear.

How had Yarrow Fenn's cloth found its way to Boston? There might have been any number of answers to Peter's question. Might have been, that is, if he didn't know better. One might argue that she had given it as a gift, but the bolt had been purchased by his master. Or that she'd taught that weave to someone else, but he knew that teaching was new to her. Or even that a bolt had been stolen and sold without her approval, but he'd seen the fear in her eyes. He raked his fingers through his hair.

The Wool Act forbid any buying or selling of wool or wool products between the colonies or to any entity other than England herself. Forbid. It was against the law.

But it didn't make sense that Miss Fenn should take her cloth to Boston. How would she travel, a woman alone? Who would purchase it from her if she did? None of it made sense.

He dropped to his narrow bunk and pulled off his neckcloth. The evening breeze that carried the scent of pines through his window cooled the back of his neck and made the flame of his candle dance. He stared into its light as the rustling of night creatures replaced the day's birdsong.

He must ask Miss Fenn. The thought both thrilled and spooked him. Such a conversation would doubtless lead to a deeper involvement with her. That would change his plans. To get involved would surely tie him to this town. To this fulling mill. To forever be the partner and not his own boss. He knew Sam Tucker expected him to stay. Peter may have even led him to believe that, without actually agreeing to anything. He groaned, pulled off his shoes, then flopped onto the bunk, one arm dangling down to the rough floor boards.

He'd never expected to meet Miss Fenn—Yarrow—and her expressive hazel eyes. The fear in them today tore at something deep inside him. He turned onto his back.

He must speak with her.

After church, Yarrow headed home to lay out their cold supper. She'd barely cleared the churchyard when footsteps hurried behind her. She turned and stifled a small gasp.

"Miss Fenn." Peter hailed her as he drew to her side. "I wondered if we might walk a bit."

Her heart kicked against her ribs. Mouth as dry as cold toast, she nodded. At least he'd chosen to speak with her first rather than going straight to the authorities.

They headed down the road, but not before Yarrow saw the stares, glimpsed the whispering lips behind hastily raised fingers. Shame burned at her core. Those women would gossip about her walking with Mr. Maltby for now, but soon they'd know it didn't stem from any regard he held for her. Soon they'd know of her crime—if not of her sin.

"Are you well?" His question took her by surprise.

"Well enough, thank you." As well as anyone could feel that had hardly slept the past two nights, preparing for what she'd done this morning.

"Splendid." He cleared this throat. "I suppose the best thing is to get right to the heart of the matter."

She closed her eyes and drew a deep breath. "Indeed." Her prayers this morning took on new meaning as a strength—not her own—settled over her.

"The cloth that you weave is very distinctive."

"A pattern my papa taught me."

"Indeed, I remember you mentioning that when first we met."

Her own words, pridefully spoken, returned to expose her.

"Miss Fenn." He halted and turned toward her. They had reached the edge of town opposite the mill where houses were few and branches canopied the road. "Yarrow."

She flicked her gaze to his eyes, less than a handspan higher than her own, and found no censure there. She swallowed.

He cleared his throat again. "I should like to think that there is a simple explanation for seeing your work in Boston."

There was. She had broken the law. "I sold it."

His jaw dropped, but he snapped it shut again. "I see. How did you manage?"

"I sold it to the traveling peddler."

Relief spread over his face, the dimple appearing in his cheek. "Of course. That makes perfect sense. I had quite forgotten about traveling peddlers."

"I knew he would sell it in Boston. Cloth brings a better price there."

His jaw dropped again, but he recovered just as quickly as the first time. "Even so, you have done nothing wrong."

She straightened her shoulders and looked him squarely in the eye. "I have, Mr. Maltby. I have trusted in my own hands and not in the providence of God."

He blinked.

"That is my sin, you see. I have skirted the king's law, I know it, and that is my guilt. But my sin is far greater. I have only this morning repented of it to the Lord."

"You have?"

"Indeed. If I had not, I could not have told you this. He has forgiven me, and I pray that you will too." She'd done it. With God's strength, she'd come clean. "I trust you shall do what you feel is right under the circumstances."

For maybe the first time in his life, Peter was speechless. And humbled. This impressive woman standing before him was someone he wanted in his life. She'd made his heart pound with her grace and her charm, but at this moment, he was captivated by her humility and strength. Oh, to win the love of such a creature. All his future plans paled in comparison.

First, he'd have to stop gawking at her like a stripling youth.

"Miss Fenn." He shook his head, stared back at the town for a moment, and then met her eyes again. "Yarrow. I am undone by your honesty. No, by your integrity."

"Mr. Maltby—"

"Peter."

That lovely blush crept over her cheeks again. "Peter, I have just admitted my guilt to you, my absolute lack of honesty and integrity."

"But that is the beauty of it. You needn't have done so. Oh, I may have figured out the selling of your cloth to the peddler, but 'tis a trifling matter. You have shared with me something much more profound, and I am honored." He removed his hat and sketched his finest bow before her.

"I confess that this is not the reception I had anticipated to my admission." Her hands fluttered at her sides in the most charming display of confusion. In fact, everything about her was charming. The sunlight dappling her straw hat, the breeze teasing her wayward wisps of hair, and the way she nibbled at her bottom lip. Yes, the very enticing way she nibbled on her bottom lip.

Yarrow cleared her throat. He jerked his stare from her mouth.

"Indeed." His mind jelled at her tentative smile, robbing him of anything else to say.

"With my admission, I have also given you knowledge about the peddler." Her brows drew together. "It grieves me that I have put him in a position to be exposed to the authorities. I want to assure you that I have no intention of selling any more cloth to him in the future."

What did he care about some traveling peddler? "Do not worry yourself on that account. I see no reason for this conversation to be repeated again, even between the two of us." He smiled and took her hand. "But I hope there will be many other conversations between us."

She blinked, and then her chin trembled. "Our last private conversation—"

"Entirely my fault. I owe you an apology for my behavior." He rubbed the back of her hand with his thumb. "'Tis not easy for me to speak of my family. There are things I would rather not remember."

"Are they still in Boston?"

He shook his head. "They have all passed away."

Hazel pools of sympathy accompanied the merest squeeze of her fingers. "I'm sorry."

He drew in a quick breath. "Let us turn to happier thoughts. Who in your family should I approach regarding courtship?"

The strength of his hand closed over hers was all that kept her from collapsing in the road at his feet. *Courtship.* A word she'd never thought to hear presented to her again. She opened her mouth, but no sound emerged. Rather than gape at him like a fish, she snapped it shut and pressed the fingers of her free hand to her forehead. With Papa gone and no brothers or close uncles, it seemed that Marigold's husband David would be the proper person to give his consent.

"Do you know how old I am?" Why had that slipped out of her mouth? She peeked up at him.

He chuckled. "As it happens, I have been informed. But did you know that in Boston it is not uncommon for women to wait until they are three and twenty, or even five and twenty before they marry?"

Could this be true? He must have read the question in her eyes.

"Indeed, 'tis quite common, I assure you. And unless I miss my guess, my age, height, weight, and likely the color of the buttons on my waistcoat were common knowledge before I set foot in Milford."

She giggled. Giggled! Something light and wonderful swirled in her middle, similar to what she'd experienced with Enos, but not entirely. This was deeper, richer.

"David Law, my eldest sister's husband."

"I shall make a point to acquaint myself with the gentleman soon."

She took a step back, gently removing her hand from his. "'Tis time I returned home. Meadowsweet will need her bottle, and I should assist Penny with her babe."

"Then allow me to see you home." He crooked his elbow with a small flourish, and she placed her fingers on his arm. Never in her wildest imaginings did she think today would bring joy in such abundance. First her cleansing confession during silent prayer at church, and now to be escorted home by a suitor, even if not an official one yet.

Chapter 7

The next few days passed in a blur for Yarrow. Her step was lighter, the sun shone brighter, and the birds sang sweeter. The buoyancy in her spirit came from her confession and forgiveness, made all the more freeing because she was done with that sin in her life for good. As Christ had instructed so many others, Yarrow would go and sin no more.

But the giddiness? That was due entirely to Peter. Her foot stilled on the treadle of her spinning wheel, the wool in her fingers forgotten. Peter. It was all so unexpected, so new. But until he approached David, she wouldn't breathe a word of their understanding.

Uncertainty pecked at her for a moment. She'd had an understanding with Enos, but that hadn't resulted in marriage. A courtship usually did, but not always. It was a time for couples to make the final decision. Enos had decided against her three years ago.

Comparing the two men was pointless. Her foot moved, and fibers slipped between her fingers, twisting into the finest yarn. Peter was well established, a journeyman already, and he'd promote to master fuller.

Enos hadn't been cut out for farming, like his father. He'd been itchy for something else, something grander than turning up dirt, he'd said. She should have noticed the signs of his wanderlust from the start, but she'd been a young woman in love.

Or had she?

The feelings evoked by Peter when he touched her hand or flashed his dimple her way were different from what she remembered with Enos. Certainly different from her relationship with him since he'd walked away. When he came to the house to purchase her cloth twice a year, they were cordial but stiff with each other. A couple of times he'd mentioned returning and opening a store here, but he'd not given any inclination that he'd like to resume their courtship if he did. Nothing to give her any hope.

Meadowsweet stirred from the sunny spot where she'd been napping. She stood and stretched before starting a shake that began with her head and ran down the length of her body, ending with a jaunty flick of her tail. She trotted to Yarrow and pushed against her leg.

"Hungry are you?" Yarrow stopped her wheel. "I could use a break myself."

The lamb followed her to her room. There was just enough milk for one more feeding. She picked up the bottle, which was Meadowsweet's signal to starting baaing. How could one little lamb make so much noise? Yarrow's fingers flew as she assembled the bottle before the noise woke baby Jonathan. Silence fell when she presented the bottle, broken only by the gulping and gurgling of Meadowsweet.

"Such a sweet little thing." Yarrow steadied the bottle in both hands. Her lamb was growing rapidly and gaining strength. If she wasn't careful, Meadowsweet would pull the bottle from her grasp.

A knock sounded on the door. Yarrow jumped.

"Forgive me. I did not mean to startle you." Peter filled the open doorway but didn't enter.

"It takes all my attention to assure she drinks her milk and we do not wear it."

He chuckled. "She has doubled her weight and more."

Yarrow nodded. "I had to tie a longer piece of ribbon around her neck this morning. The other had grown too tight." That the lamb thrived under her care pleased her more every day.

Meadowsweet had finished her bottle and was sniffing around looking for more. Yarrow picked up the milk crock and stepped outside. "I cannot thank you enough for all you have done to help with the lamb." She shrugged and looked up at him. "'Tis such a kindness."

"'Tis nothing if it brings a smile to your face."

She ducked her head as the telltale warmth of her blush washed her cheeks. How did a woman answer something like that? "I need to visit Betsy for more milk. Would you like to walk with me?"

His blue eyes sparkled. "I can think of no better way to spend a Thursday afternoon, but I must stop by the chandler's on the way back. Last night I nearly broke my toe for want of a fresh candle."

"Then, by all means, we must stop there."

They walked side by side down the road, little Meadowsweet dancing at their heels. Was ever a day so perfect?

"We are caught up at the mill," Peter said. "First time since we opened."

"I wondered how you came to be visiting on a Thursday afternoon." Her smile could coax bees from a field of clover.

"I would have come sooner if I could." He'd thought of nothing else since Sunday.

"You are always welcome."

"Am I?" He stopped and guided her to the side of the road as a freight wagon rumbled past. Meadowsweet followed them. "You are sure?"

"I am."

His heart did a double thump. He looked down the road at Milford. Its dirt street was not exactly bustling this far from the docks, but it was growing. Hammers rang and saws rasped in the distance. Three new homes and one new business were under construction. Someday it may rival Boston. A man could do worse than to start over here. With a lovely, talented woman by his side.

"Then if it pleases you, I will speak to David Law on Sunday after service." He held his breath until she nodded, half fearing she'd changed her mind.

She stepped onto the road again, continuing toward the Clarks' place. "I would like to know more about you and where you come from." She glanced up, her brow furrowed. "You have said your family is not easy to discuss, but tell me what you can about Boston. I was born near Cambridge, but we moved here when I was very young. I remember nothing of it."

Of course she would be curious. Women always were about these things. At least, he assumed they were. He swept his hand toward the forest. "It looks much like this, only with the forest farther removed from the town. More farms than here, where they can turn the ground between its rocks. The farm land I have seen here has better soil."

"You know a lot about farming."

"I grew up on a farm a mile southwest of Boston."

"Is that where you learned about sheep?"

"Indeed. My father owned a flock. Tending it was my responsibility from the time I was seven or eight."

"So young?"

He cleared his throat. "That is when my brother died." Clearing his throat didn't help much. Memories threatened to press it shut again. He glanced at Yarrow. She slipped her fingers around his sleeve. The pressure in his throat eased. Maybe he could talk to her about that time. Someday.

"How horrible for you."

He nodded.

"Let us talk about something else." She offered him an encouraging smile. "How did you come to be apprenticed to a fuller?"

No prying, no prodding. Did her compassion know no bounds? It might if she ever learned his whole past. Yet why would she, if they stayed here in Milford?

"I already knew sheep and wool, so it was no big step to go into the fuller's and ask for an apprenticeship."

"Your father did not arrange it?"

"No." And please don't ask why.

"You were an enterprising young man, then."

He'd been a desperate young man. "My mother was a weaver, did I mention that?"

She stopped so suddenly that Meadowsweet ran into the back of her legs. Yarrow laughed and made sure the lamb wasn't harmed before turning her smile to him. "You never did. No wonder the fulling mill was your choice."

"She did not create intricate patterns like yours, just sturdy twills and plain sacking. She sold them to other farmers' wives who needed hard-wearing cloth."

They continued chatting about wool and weaving until they reached the Clarks' place. Yarrow paid for her crock of fresh goat's milk, and he carried it back to her house, where she stowed Meadowsweet in the box. Then they went into town for his candles. He'd never spent a more relaxing afternoon in his life. Sunday couldn't come soon enough. Then he'd find Mr. Law and gain permission to officially court Yarrow.

It made no sense, even to her, but Yarrow still took the extra time to fuss with her hair and wipe the tiny smudge from her best dress. She wished she'd made herself at least one dress from her finest cloth. She'd been too greedy for the money that selling it brought. She closed her eyes and drew in a deep breath. She was forgiven. If God would remember her sin no more, then she needed to release it as well.

"Are you ready?" Penny's voice reached through the connecting door.

"Coming." With a final pin to secure her rebellious hair, she donned her cap and joined Penny and Archie for the walk to church.

The morning air was damp and warm with a heaviness that hinted of a storm later, but Yarrow paid it scant attention. Rain or sun, it didn't matter. Peter would speak with David after services. Bubbles of happiness threatened to burst from her chest.

Penny shot her a look, brows drawn together. "You are happy this morning."

"I'm happy every morning." Which was mostly true.

"I have noticed an extra spring to your step this past week," Archie said.

Was she that transparent? "I love this time of year. Everything is fresh and green. The flowers are blooming. There are so many reasons to be happy."

Penny shook her head but didn't argue. That alone was an improvement in her temperament. Yarrow was pleased that her sister had recovered enough to come to church. Little Jonathan nestled in his mother's arms. The more Penny relaxed and calmed, the more the babe did as well. Precisely as Marigold had predicted.

They neared the church, nodding to and speaking with friends and acquaintances along the way. Yarrow enjoyed this part of Sunday morning. It pleased her that they lived close enough to the church to walk. Aside from the welcome exercise before several hours of sitting on a hard bench, she took the time to catch up with a few friends.

"Yarrow." Rebecca Harpin left her husband and hurried to Yarrow's side. "Robert told me last evening that Enos is back."

"He is early then. He does not generally arrive until late June."

"'Tis more than that. Robert says he's come home to stay. To open a store here in Milford." Rebecca squeezed her arm and flashed a grin before rejoining her husband.

Enos moving back? Surely not. Mr. Harpin must have been mistaken. But as they turned onto the street where the church stood, there was Enos. She couldn't mistake him even from a distance. He stood a full head taller than the tallest man in Milford, topping even Peter by a couple of inches.

Yarrow's steps slowed, and she fell farther behind Penny and Archie. Perhaps Enos would enter the church before she arrived and spare her having to greet him.

He turned and spotted her. One corner of his mouth lifted in his lopsided grin. The one that used to send her heart fluttering. The one that now sent it to her heels. He stepped away from the church and approached her.

Penny stopped, but Archie leaned close and whispered as he took his wife's elbow and ushered her on toward the church. Yarrow could have kissed her brother-in-law.

"Yarrow." Enos had always said her name that way, in the butter-soft bass voice she'd loved. He stopped in front of her, so she had no choice but to stop as well. He pulled his hat from his raven-dark locks, and eyes the color of a rich plowed field met hers. His face was newly shaved, its dark stubble subdued for the moment, but the memory of its roughness against her fingertips surged through her.

"Enos." His name almost stuck in her throat.

He twisted the hat in his hands. "I'm moving back to Milford."

She swallowed. "I have just been told."

Black eyebrows rose, and he blinked. "Already? News travels fast." He shrugged. "I hope you are pleased."

Pleased that he was seeking her out on the very morning Peter would speak with David? But of course Enos couldn't know that. She pasted on a smile. "I'm very happy for you."

"I'm not moving back to my father's farm." He waved a hand toward the town's business district. "I'm planning to open a store."

"I'm sure your business will do well. The town has grown. It needs another store." She took a step to move around him.

He touched her elbow and stopped her.

"I would like to speak with you after services." He lowered his voice. "'Tis time to put things right between us."

No. No-no-no. The word echoed in her mind. This couldn't be happening. Not now.

Chapter 8

Peter fidgeted on the hard bench. He'd arrived earlier than usual, having informed Mr. Tucker the day before that he'd not wait to walk to church with them this morning. The knowing gleam in his boss's eye had started a warring faction within him. On the one hand, it needled him that his personal business wasn't private. On the other hand, pride that a woman such as Yarrow would consent to his suit had threatened the top buttons of his waistcoat.

Where was she? Her sister and brother-in-law were already seated. Peter fought the urge to go looking for her. When she finally walked into the church, she was followed far too closely by a tall man. A familiar-looking man. Indeed, someone that tall would be hard to forget. Where had Peter seen him before? The man turned and looked straight at him and it clicked.

Boston.

The church.

The day Peter had been brought before the elders.

The tall stranger who had given witness of Peter's alleged misconduct. . .with Deacon Williams's daughter.

Recognition stiffened the other man's shoulders as their eyes locked from across the room.

This couldn't be happening. Not now. Not yet. Not while he was still a journeyman. A master fuller might be listened to, might be believed, but not a journeyman. Not against someone who claimed to be a witness to the misdeed.

The tall man leaned down and whispered into Yarrow's ear, his hand momentarily on her back. She glanced up at him, and then across the room at Peter. He wished he were closer and could read her expression. Was it fear? Had that man already exposed him?

Blood pounded against Peter's eardrums. The urge to do something sang in his veins, but whether to punch the tall man for handling Yarrow or to run from the church before she heard of his disgrace he wasn't sure. So he remained conflicted, in his seat.

He couldn't remember the tall man's name. He had witnessed the scene between Esther and Peter, that part was true, but he'd completely misunderstood the moment. That the church had taken the word of a traveling peddler—

Traveling peddler. With Yarrow. His heart plummeted.

The tall man stopped beside him and lowered himself onto the bench beside Peter.

"What are you doing here?" the man asked in a low voice meant for Peter's ears only.

"Preparing to worship."

The man's mouth twisted. "That is not what I meant, and you know it. How come you to be here, in my hometown?"

"'Tis my home now. I work for Mr. Tucker at the fulling mill. Not that 'tis any concern of yours."

"You know it is. But it won't be after I have a word with the elders."

"Perhaps I should have a word with the elders as well."

Black brows drew into a flat line as the tall man turned to face him. "What do you mean?"

"Selling wool or anything made of wool across the colony's border is against the king's law."

The color drained from the man's well-tanned face.

The pastor climbed the steps to the pulpit, ceasing the low murmurs of conversation in the room. Peter didn't need words to comprehend the waves of fear and rage seeping from the man next to him.

But he'd give a month's pay to know what thoughts washed the color from Yarrow's face, hastily averted on the other side of the room.

Both sermons might as well have been spoken in German for all Yarrow understood them. The words garbled in her ears where they met the doubts that assailed her from within. Enos was back. He planned to speak with her after services. But Peter planned to speak with David. And why were they sitting next to each other? That Peter had said something to upset Enos was obvious. She's never seen Enos so pale and tight-lipped. Could Peter know that Enos was the traveling peddler who sold her cloth in Boston? Surely not.

Her stomach in knots, she twisted the narrow tie of her cap until it ripped in her hand. She stared at the ragged piece. Was her life about to be ripped in half as well?

The closing prayer finally ended, but Yarrow stayed where she was as the other single women filed out around her. She didn't need to stand to see the two tallest men in the room leave the building together.

Clara appeared at her side and hopped onto the bench.

"Mama said I can come to your class tomorrow and card more wool."

"That is fine." Yarrow patted her niece's knee while trying to catch a glimpse of the men through the window.

"Mama said I better learn quick because Mr. Watkins is back to town to stay."

"Yes, of course." Then Clara's words sank in. "Your mama knows Mr. Watkins is moving back?"

"Everyone does." Clara giggled. "He is so tall, nobody could not see him."

Indeed. Yarrow cast a glance around the room. Several of the women returned her gaze with a smile and a nod. Her face burned as she rose.

"Excuse me, Clara. I must hurry home and set supper out."

Yarrow slipped out the door, resisting the urge to lift her skirts and run for the safety and privacy of her room.

Neither man spoke until they'd cleared the churchyard and walked well past those who would have stopped them to speak. Peter stretched his legs to match the long strides of the peddler until the man turned into a patch of woods. Peter hesitated only a moment, then followed. Better to have their talk in total privacy.

The peddler stopped at a fallen tree, planted one foot on it, and leaned against his raised knee. "Despite what you think you know about me, I have no doubt what I saw concerning you and a certain deacon's daughter in Boston."

Peter stopped out of reach of the peddler and took a couple of deep breaths.

"You think you understood what you saw."

"Your hands were all over the woman."

"I was doing my level best to push her away."

"Indeed. And that provoked her tears, and her plea to me for assistance."

Peter growled low in his throat. "The woman missed her calling. She should have been on the stage."

The peddler straightened. "You would further besmirch the lady in question by likening her to a harlot from the stage?" Indignation colored his tone.

"I would." Peter took a step closer, anger adding flames to his voice. "For a full year before that day, I had done my best to avoid her. She was none too subtle in her regard for me, and while flattered—"

"Oh, I bet you were."

Peter unclenched his fists to prevent burying one in the peddler's nose.

"I can understand that you have never had a woman throw herself at you." He eyed the peddler up and down. "Indeed. This I can well understand."

The peddler took a step closer. A scant handspan separated the two men. Then the peddler turned and took two steps away before pivoting back. "I assume that you intend to demand my silence with the threat of exposing my sales practices."

Peter folded his arms across his chest. "Your crimes, I believe you mean."

The peddler's fists balled into knots, but before he could strike, a woolly-faced lamb with a pink ribbon around its neck broke through the brush behind him and ran toward Peter.

She should have stayed in her room, but Meadowsweet needed some exercise after her bottle, and Yarrow's hot room had been too confining for both of them. Despite the impending storm, they'd headed out for a walk.

"Meadowsweet." The lamb had never run off like this before. "Meadowsweet!"

Yarrow pushed aside a thick screen of branches and stepped past them, almost bumping into Enos.

She took his offered arm to steady herself. "What are you—?"

Movement caught her eye. Across the small clearing, Meadowsweet at his feet, stood Peter.

"Peter? Enos?"

A frown marred Peter's brow.

Yarrow stepped away from Enos, looking back and forth between the two men. What was happening here?

Peter pointed at the other man. "The Enos who walked out on you?"

"I did not walk out, exactly."

"Then, exactly, what did you do?" The tilt of Peter's head, his raised brow, the way he stood with his arms crossed, made it clear that he was baiting Enos.

But Yarrow also wanted to know the answer to his question.

Enos flushed red enough to be seen beneath his dark tan. "I had to make a name for myself before I could settle down. Become a man of business."

"Shady business, you mean," Peter said.

"I have moved back to Milford now. This is my home." Enos's emphasis on the last word was unmistakable.

Yarrow's head swam with all that had—and hadn't—happened this morning. "I do not understand." She pressed her fingers to her forehead. "What are you two doing here together?"

"I saw him in Boston this past winter." Enos tipped his chin to indicate Peter. "I gave testimony against him before the church."

"Testimony? What type of testimony?" None of this made sense.

"Inaccurate testimony, as it happens." Peter lowered his arms to his sides. "He witnessed something he misinterpreted."

Enos snorted. "So he says. But I know what I saw, and considering his father—"

Peter moved so quickly, neither she nor Enos saw the blow coming. Enos landed on his backside on the mossy ground, hand to his nose, blood seeping between his fingers.

"Enos!" Yarrow knelt by his side and glared up at Peter, who stood rubbing his knuckles and staring at his shoes.

Enos moved as if to stand, but Yarrow pressed her hand against his chest. She stood and faced Peter.

"I think you should go." The last thing she wanted was a fight between these men.

Thunder rumbled in the distance.

Peter nodded, turned, and took a piece of her heart with him.

There wasn't much to pack, just his spare clothes and his shaving kit. Peter turned around in his little room above the mill, almost deafened by the roar of rain pouring on the roof. He grabbed his extra shoe buckles off the wobbly table and stuffed them into his leather satchel. That was everything. With any luck, a boat would be leaving for Boston tonight.

He stomped down the stairs. Each step should have released another layer of frustration. Instead, they only added to it. He might have lived with the knowledge that the peddler knew of his disgrace at the church. He might have stayed and fought for Yarrow's hand. Surely he had claim against the man who walked out on her. But the peddler knew about Peter's father, and that was a shame he could not counter. He stopped at the bottom of the steps and sat. He couldn't counter it in Boston either. At least, not without the social layer of protection the status of master fuller would have given him.

Where could he start over?

Mr. Tucker burst through the door and slammed it shut again, water sluicing off his long coat and pooling at his feet.

"Ah, there you are. When you did not come back for supper, the missus..." Furrows creased his boss's forehead. "What is this?" He gestured to the leather satchel where Peter had dropped it when he'd sat.

"I'm leaving."

Mr. Tucker scratched at his collar, cast his gaze around the mill, and then looked back at Peter. "Does this have anything to do with Enos Watkin's return?"

"Indeed." But he didn't want to talk about it.

"Now, lad. Do not be hasty. The girl might not want him back."

Since the only option to not talking was to shove past his boss—his former boss—and run out into the rain, Peter sighed and said, "'Tis not just about Miss Fenn."

Mr. Tucker pulled the chair away from the wall and plunked it down in front of the steps where Peter sat. "Tell me."

He'd rather cut his tongue out with a pair of dull shears, but the kindly expression—the sort he'd always wanted to see on his father's face—loosened his tongue instead. "There was a situation in Boston."

"The girl who claimed you molested her?"

Shock bolted Peter to the wooden step. "You know?"

Mr. Tucker nodded. "Something like that is hard to keep secret."

"The others here? In Milford?"

"Nay. I made inquiries when your former boss suggested you needed employment elsewhere. He never believed the charge against you, you know."

His old master had stood behind him through the whole ordeal. "There is more." He swallowed, his throat as dry as chalk. "My father." He closed his eyes and shook his head, hunching over until his elbows rested on his knees.

Mr. Tucker's hand grasped Peter's shoulder. The squeeze was firm enough to be comforting.

"I know about that as well."

Peter jerked upright. "You cannot."

"Your master thought I should know the whole truth before I took you on."

"He knew?" He'd never said a word. Never even hinted that he knew. Never treated Peter with anything but kindness, even while he demanded strict obedience and dedication to the task at hand.

"Then you know why I must leave."

"I do not know any such thing. You are doing well here. You shall be a master fuller by the end of the year. My partner by the end of next year. And there is a young lady who will not care to see you leave."

"She does not know."

"Then tell her. . .before someone else does."

He'd left Yarrow and Watkins in the forest together. Was it already too late?

Chapter 9

Once she'd made sure that a bloodied nose was the extent of Enos's injury, Yarrow had called Meadowsweet and left Enos sitting on the forest floor. He'd tried to tell her something about Peter, but she wouldn't listen. If there was something she needed to know, then Peter was the person to tell her. She wouldn't listen to gossip, not even from Enos. Especially not from Enos.

After cleaning up from supper, she sank onto her bench under the tree. The downpour done, the tree protected her from the lingering drizzle. Only a few determined raindrops made it through its leaves. Thunder rumbled with the storm moving off. The gray skies and heavy clouds reflected her mood.

Peter hadn't spoken with David at all. Instead, he'd met with Enos in the woods.

Enos hadn't spoken with her after church. Instead, he'd gotten his nose bloodied.

Yarrow should be thankful. She was well rid of both of them. She wanted a man who would keep his word. Was that too much to ask?

Perhaps it was. She slouched back against the rough bark of the tree.

Meadowsweet raised her head from where she nibbled the grass at Yarrow's feet. Yarrow looked up to see what had caught the lamb's attention.

Peter.

He stood near the house, his hat in his hand, his golden hair plastered to his head.

Her heart ached. She blinked back the tears that threatened.

He advanced, his gaze unwavering, until he stood within an arm's reach of her.

"Yarrow."

"Peter." She wouldn't be impolite, but neither would she encourage him. If he wanted to tell her what Enos had hinted at, he would. And if he didn't. . .?

He twisted his poor hat. "There is something I should have told you."

"I gathered as much."

His brows drew together in a flat line. "Watkins did, then."

"He would have, but I stopped him."

"Why?" Hope colored his tone as water dripped off his nose.

"I do not listen to gossip. Not about you or anyone else."

"Of course you don't. I did not mean to imply. . ." He smashed the hat against his leg.

She stood. It was better than having to look up at him. "Shall we walk?"

"In the rain?"

"Unless you know a way to stop it."

He shrugged and put his hat on. They were almost out of the settlement, where the road became little more than a track through the woods before he spoke.

"I was accused of accosting a woman in Boston."

She stopped. Maybe she didn't want to hear this after all.

"Peter—"

"I should have told you before saying I would speak to your brother-in-law." He stepped in front of her as the rain picked up, shielding her.

"It does not matter—"

He took her shoulders in a feather-light hold, the heat of his palms branding her beneath the wet cloth. "It does. The worst part is not that she lied, not now, anyway. The worst part is that it was Watkins who witnessed what happened. He shall poison you against me."

She steeled herself to hear the answer she needed. "What happened?"

"Esther Williams is the daughter of one of our church deacons, a well-respected man. But she is nothing like her father." He wiped the water from his face. "I did not encourage her, but she continually sought me out. She is a beautiful girl, make no mistake, but far too forward."

Yarrow waited and prayed in her heart for wisdom. It would be so easy to trust this man who had already captured her heart. But was that wise?

"On that day when Enos saw us, I had been to the smithy to pick up a repaired gear. Esther knew I would be there. She had been nearby at church the day before when the blacksmith told me to pick it up." Pain, at the memories perhaps, creased his face for a moment before he continued. "The smithy is on the outskirts of town. She was waiting for me just out of sight of the buildings. I stopped and she. . ." Color crept up from his collar and over his cheeks. "She put her arms around me. Tried to kiss me. Nay. She did kiss me. I did not resist at first. As I said, she is a beautiful girl. By the time I had come to my senses and tried to push her away, a man was riding toward us."

"Enos."

"Indeed. You can see how it must have looked to him. Even more so when Esther saw him and called for help. She accused me of. . ." He shrugged. "She hoped to trap me into marriage, since her father would not have allowed it otherwise."

Yarrow closed her eyes and nodded. "I can see how it would have looked to Enos. But why would the church not hear your side? Not believe you?"

He stepped away from her, and the lash of the rain fell on her face.

"Because of my father."

Memories flooded Peter. Scorching memories. His mother's gasp. The crash. Granny's stricken face. He planted his hands on his hips to keep them from shaking.

"When my older brother Rodney died, Father blamed me. It was my job to feed the mules, you see. One day, Rodney knew that I wanted to go fishing, and he offered to feed them. Old Badger was a cranky mule, we all knew that. I never went into their corral, just forked their hay over the rail. Rodney went inside, I guess. Father found him. His head was kicked in."

"I'm so sorry."

He glanced at Yarrow, her cheeks wet with the combination of tears and rain. It tore at something deep within him. He should spare her hearing anymore. He turned his face from her and closed his eyes.

She slipped her fingers around his forearm and squeezed. "Go on. Tell me."

He shook his head. It was best if he walked away now, found a new town to start over. Virginia or even Carolina.

"Tell me."

He cast a quick glance her way, but once their eyes met, he couldn't look away. She'd blinked the tears back. Her hazel depths were calm, even comforting. He swallowed.

"Father changed after that. He started drinking. He did not come home some nights, and those were the good nights." He looked away and pulled in a long breath. "On the nights he came home, he was often violent." He fingered the scar that lined his temple. "With the farm left to a boy to run, it was failing. Granny spun wool and Mother wove simple cloth to sell to the neighbors. That was the only steady income we had. Income that Father used to buy more rum. One night, when the money jar above the fireplace was empty, he became enraged. At me for not keeping the farm profitable. At Mother for not making enough cloth. Even at Granny, his own mother."

Yarrow's grip on his arm tightened. He leaned toward her, pulled from her quiet strength.

"He grabbed the kettle from the hearth and hurled it at me. I dodged the worst of the strike, but stumbled over the lamb box and lost my balance. I fell against Mother's loom. It crashed, pinning her against the wall. It was not until he stormed out that Granny saw the blood."

"Your mother?"

He nodded. "One of the loom's support bars had snapped and pierced through her." He bit his lip and raised his eyes to the dripping branches above, letting the rain wash his tears. "It took her three days to die."

"Oh, Peter."

He couldn't look at Yarrow again. "I was twelve years old. Granny sent me to the fulling mill. To keep me safe. She died a month or so later, of shame or a broken heart, I'm not sure which."

"And your father?"

His harsh laugh hurt. "The church condemned him of my mother's death, but the law said it was an accident. After all, it was me he had meant to harm, not her. But the whole town knew him to be a cruel, violent man."

"So they believed the girl's word against you, thinking you were just like him."

Peter nodded. His deepest struggle was now laid bare before the woman he loved. Would she accept him in spite of what she'd learned? Or would she decide the risk that he might follow in his father's footsteps was too great? Especially after witnessing his confrontation with Watkins.

"I shall walk you home."

She started to object, but he raised his hand.

"You deserved to know the truth, but I kept it from you. Now you need time to decide what to believe and whether or not you can trust me."

She nodded. He walked her home, their silence broken only by the splash of their feet on the muddy road. His past was laid bare. He'd done the right thing. Why didn't he feel any relief?

Monday morning's sun struggled to break through a curtain of gray that hung over the land. The damp dreariness matched Yarrow's mood after an almost sleepless night. She smothered a yawn behind her hand before filling a bowl with porridge. She slid the bowl in front of Penny, who sat at the table with little Jonathan in her arms. Archie entered the room, and Yarrow hurried to fill two more bowls. She took her seat. They bowed their heads for the blessing.

"Amen." Archie picked up his spoon and looked at Yarrow. "Fancy that, Enos Watkins moving back to town and setting up a shop. Who would have thought?"

She swallowed the spoonful of porridge that had turned to ash in her mouth. "Indeed. Who would have?"

"He gave you no warning?" Penny asked.

"None."

"Odd, do you not think so?" Archie raised a brow, looking at his wife.

"Very odd, indeed," Penny answered.

"I wish him the best of luck. The way Milford is growing, we shall need another store to keep up with demand." Yarrow pushed a spoonful of porridge around the edge of her bowl. "Perhaps he shall be interested in buying some of my cloth."

"You would sell cloth we need to clothe our families?" Penny set her spoon down with a huff.

Yarrow had never told her sisters about the bolts of cloth sold to Enos. It was better that they thought she'd set them aside in her hope chest.

"With the fulling mill to do the finishing work, I shall be able to produce more than we need."

Archie nodded. "I expect that's so."

Penny glared at him.

Yarrow swallowed one last mouthful of the porridge and rose. "My pupils will be here shortly. With the drizzle outside, I need to clear space in my room to be ready for them."

She ignored her sister's pointed stare at the dishes on the table. It wouldn't harm Penny to wash up this morning. Yarrow had no more than closed the connecting door when someone tapped on the outside door. It was too early for her pupils to arrive.

Enos stood on her doorstep, hat in hand, the misty drizzle collecting on his black hair.

She stepped back but left the door open. "Come in."

"I have to talk to you."

She nodded, unsure if she wanted to encourage this talk.

"We left things unfinished between us—"

"We? We left things unfinished?" She straightened to her full height, hands on her hips. "You left. If things were unfinished, it was not me who left them undone."

He raised one hand, palm toward her. "I know. It was my fault. But I have returned now."

"So you have."

The pleading in his dark eyes was hard to ignore, but she wasn't going to make this easy for him. Why should she?

"'Twould please me to resume our relationship," he said, in that deep tone that used to warm her to her bones.

"Once you have your store open, I shall be happy to sell you fabric when I have extra to spare."

He groaned and rubbed the back of his neck. "That is not what I meant."

"What did you mean?" If her back got any stiffer, she feared she'd snap in two.

"Yarrow, I know I let you down. I let myself down." He opened his arms to his sides, lifting his shoulders in a shrug. "If you will have me back, I shall spend the rest of my life making it up to you."

Chapter 10

The drama of the past two days, coupled with two nights of almost no sleep, had caught up with Yarrow. She lay on her bed, a damp cloth over her eyes to block out the sunlight and ease her pounding head. Laughter from Marigold's children drifted in through the door, left open to allow whatever breeze there was to cool her room. The pungent odors of lye and tallow came with it.

Remorse at leaving her sisters to the task of soap making was eclipsed by wanting to curl into a ball and pretend the past two days had never happened. To go back to the woman she'd been last Saturday, the one poised to accept the suitor who sought permission from David to court her.

"Aunt Yarrow?"

Yarrow slid the cloth from her eyes. Clara stood on her toes and kept outside the room to fulfill her mother's admonition not to enter.

"Yes?"

"May we take Meadowsweet for a walk on the forest path?"

A wonderful idea, one that would bring more quiet to the yard. Yarrow nodded, trying not to grimace at the pain that caused. Clara smothered a squeal of delight behind her fingers before tiptoeing away in an exaggerated fashion.

Yarrow replaced the damp cloth. She should refresh it, but the thought of moving was too much for her. The children's laughter faded and soon she heard only the birds.

The front door of the house banged shut. That would be Penny, who had been inside nursing Jonathan.

"Did I tell you what she said to us at breakfast yesterday?" Penny asked.

Yarrow snapped out of her semi-doze.

"Not that I recall," Marigold said.

"She plans to sell her cloth to Enos for his new store."

"Not all of it, surely."

"That she would take any away from our family is ungracious of her."

"I suspect she just wants to earn a bit of coin. 'Tis not like we pay her for the cloth she makes us."

"That is all well and good, but it shan't clothe our husbands and children." The petulance in Penny's tone made Yarrow's teeth hurt. "And she is handsomely compensated for her work. Does not Archie provide her with her roof and meals?"

Archie? It was Papa who had built this house and this room. The nerve of her little sister, making Yarrow sound like a charity case.

"Most of the women in town are not blessed with a sister like ours. You should be thankful. We both should be." Marigold paused. "With Enos back in Milford, I would not be surprised if they resumed their relationship."

"He was here yesterday but did not stay long."

Had Penny been eavesdropping? Guilt nudged Yarrow. Wasn't that what she was doing now?

"I think she is more interested in that man from the fulling mill. She has walked out with him several times. Perhaps 'tis for the best if she picks one and marries him. Archie and I could use the room at the back of the house as our family grows."

Yarrow sat up, the cloth falling from her eyes. Indignation flooded her, souring her stomach and adding to the thumping in her temples. She rose and marched out the door.

"Perhaps 'tis for the best if I pack up and leave now."

Her sisters faced her, Marigold with cheeks the color of a ripe tomato, Penny with her sullen frown.

"Yarrow." Marigold raised her hand, palm up.

"I told you she was ungrateful."

"If you do not hush this minute, Penny, I vow I'll take you into the house and wash your mouth out just like I did when you were little." Marigold glared at their younger sister, whose bottom lip trembled as her chin lowered to her chest. Marigold turned back to Yarrow. "Please, forgive us for meddling where we should not. I just want you to be happy."

The sincerity in her sister's voice eased the ache in Yarrow's head, as did seeing the repentant tears on Penny's face.

To be happy. Was that possible with either man who'd asked for her heart? Could she trust Enos to stay? Could she trust Peter at all?

Almost a week without a word. Peter brushed the stray wool fibers from his Sunday best breeches. It was only Saturday, but he wanted to look his best for Yarrow. The weight that had ridden his chest all week refused to move. He needed to know if she could learn to trust him, knowing his past and knowing he'd kept it from her. He'd hoped she would come to the mill and pick up her finished cloth, but he wasn't surprised when she didn't.

She probably didn't want to see him at all, but he needed to see her.

He tugged on his waistcoat and stepped into his shoes, fitted with his best buckles. He combed his hair back into its queue, wishing once again that he had a looking glass in his tiny room. But this would have to do.

The walk to Yarrow's house was both too short and too long. His heart stammered, his legs alternated between long and short strides, and if he sweated any more he'd look like he'd been for a swim before he arrived.

He turned the last corner before her house. Another man walked toward him at a distance. A very tall man. Peter's heart dropped to his shoes. Watkins. Peter lengthened his stride and reached Yarrow's house first. She might turn him away, but at least he'd have his answer. Ignoring the pounding footsteps behind him, he strode to her back door and banged on it.

She opened the door. Her hair feathered around her face; her eyes were shadowed by darkness.

"Peter."

If only he could interpret the expression she wore. Before he could answer her, the hulking shadow of his adversary covered him.

Yarrow blinked, looked back and forth between the two men on her doorstep, then shut the door in their faces.

"Now see what you have done," Peter said, turning to glare at Watkins.

"What I have done?" Enos drew himself up to his full height.

Peter resisted the urge to poke him in the nose again. He disliked having to look up at someone. He wasn't used to it, and he definitely didn't like looking up to this man. Before he could unclench his fists, the door behind him flew open.

Yarrow stepped outside, skirted past them, and sat on her bench.

Peter followed, getting the jump on Watkins. "Yarrow."

"She is Miss Fenn to you." The gangly ape towered over Peter again.

Peter turned, his elbow cocked just enough to catch Watkins in the side. He feigned what he hoped would pass for an apologetic tilt of his head. "Beg your pardon, but the lady and I are on more intimate terms than that."

Watkins's dark skin flushed to the color of brick.

"Stop it, both of you," Yarrow said.

Watkins cleared his throat. "Yarrow—"

"Aunt Yarrow, help!" Whatever Watkins had been going to say was cut off by Yarrow's niece, who raced around the front of the house.

Yarrow shot to her feet. "What is it?"

"We took Meadowsweet for another walk today." The little girl's lips trembled.

Yarrow knelt before the child. "What has happened?"

"We walked her to the flock, thinking she would like to see the other sheep. Then a bear came over the hill. One of the shepherd boys shot at the bear, and it ran away. But the sheep all ran into the woods." She wiped at the tears spilling from her eyes. "Meadowsweet ran with them!"

Yarrow hugged the little girl close. "I shall find her. You hurry back to your mama." She waited for an answering nod before standing.

"The flock will have scattered. We best help round them up." Watkins took Yarrow's elbow.

She pulled free of his hold.

"The boy may have wounded the bear. Fetch your gun first." She looked at Peter. "You can take my father's. I shall get it." She hurried into the house.

Watkins hesitated.

"Better hurry." Peter grinned up at the taller man.

"I shall be back."

"I bet you will," Peter muttered.

Yarrow burst out of her back door, gun in one hand, powder horn and shot bag in the other.

Peter took the gun, an ancient musket. "Is it loaded?" She shook her head and handed him the powder and shot. He loaded it, thankful the shot bag held wadding too.

"Hurry." She inched toward the forest that pressed against the back of the stable.

He pulled the ramrod out and secured it below the barrel. "All set."

He had to trot to catch up with her, swatting branches out of his way. "Do you know where we are going?"

"Yes. If the bear came over a hill, I know which pasture they were in. The sheep would have scattered into the woods opposite the hill. This trail will take us there." She brushed through more branches that snapped back toward him.

Trail? He caught the next branch before it decapitated him. If this was a trail, nothing traveled it but deer. Except for maybe little girls and sheep. Something snagged his hat. He lost a minute finding it and jamming it back on his head.

"Wait a moment."

"Hurry."

Easier said than done. He dodged another hat-stealing limb. Watkins would have a worse time of it. That thought produced a smile.

"What are you grinning about?" Yarrow waited in a small clearing, hands on her hips.

He shrugged. "At the pleasure of chasing you through the forest."

She didn't have time to banter words or stare at his dimple, but she did anyway. "I suppose you find this amusing."

"Not amusing, because we have not found your lamb. Yet I cannot complain about the company or the view."

How could she possibly flush any warmer after chasing through the woods on a humid day? Yet, flush she did, heat burning from her neck upward. His frank appraisal was doing something inside her. She was pretty sure she'd have to repent about that later, after they found Meadowsweet. The way his gaze kept lingering on her lips, it might have to be after he kissed her as well. Then she'd have even more to repent of.

What about Enos?

She turned on her heel and set off down the trail. *Lord, I need Your help.* To find her lamb, and to sort out her emotions concerning not one, but two men. Two months ago she'd been content, mostly, with her life as the spinster sister. Now Enos was back proposing that they resume their relationship, and Peter tagged along at her heels. Her body was acutely aware of him in a way she'd never been of Enos.

She batted away a leafy branch in her path and glimpsed a patch of white and a pink ribbon to her left.

"Meadowsweet!"

The answering *baa* brought tears to her eyes. Yarrow took two steps toward the lamb and stopped when something else thrashed in the underbrush. Another glimpse of white.

"'Tis a sheep." Peter's breath was so close it tickled her ear.

More thrashing and a pitiful bleat followed. Peter moved past Yarrow, stepping slowly and carefully.

"She is injured. Looks like a broken leg," Peter said.

Yarrow knelt. Meadowsweet bounded into her arms. "What can we do?"

Peter lifted the musket and slung it across his back by its strap. "I shall carry her out as soon as I get her free. She has caught her leg in the fork of a fallen tree." He stooped behind the tree. A grunt, another bleat, and then he was standing. His hat missing, hair mussed from twigs and branches, a sheep draped across his shoulders, and dirt smudged on his face. He'd never looked more appealing.

Yarrow picked up his hat and handed it to him. "We had best hurry back and tend to that leg."

"Lead the way. I fear I would get us lost."

She picked up Meadowsweet and turned back down the trail, hiding her smile from him. They'd entered the same small clearing when movement caught her eye. She stopped, and Peter knocked into her from behind.

"Look." She pointed to a spot across the clearing. A black bear cub rolled in the grass, its four paws paddling in the air, a series of grunts expressing its pleasure of the moment.

Peter squeezed her shoulder. "Back away as quietly as you can." His voice stirred the air past her ear, more breathed than spoken.

She did as he said.

They had backed only a couple of steps when the injured sheep protested with a long *baa*. The cub rolled onto its haunches and squalled a cry, not unlike that of a startled infant.

"Do not move," Peter whispered against her ear. "We do not know where its mother is, but I suspect she may have been the one the shepherd boys saw. If we are still, perhaps the cub will move off on its own."

No such luck.

A woofing sound came from their right. Peter dropped his grip on her shoulder as the wounded sheep thrashed across his back. The mother bear lumbered into the far side of the clearing and rose onto her hind legs, her nose in the air searching for their scent. She woofed again, and the cub raced to her side.

The sheep on Peter's shoulders panicked.

"Get behind me." No longer a whisper, Peter's shout rang out above the sheep's bleating. The terrified animal kicked, entangling itself in the branches that brushed Peter's shoulders.

Yarrow glanced back at the clearing in time to see the mother bear drop to all fours.

"Go. Now." Peter pushed himself in front of Yarrow, unable to disentangle himself from the sheep and the branches, his musket useless across his back. He braced himself before her. "Run!"

Time stopped. Yarrow's blood froze in her veins. The lumbering creature charged across the clearing, a bellow issuing from its open mouth. She couldn't leave Peter. She tucked Meadowsweet between her feet and clawed at the musket on Peter's back.

A shot rang out.

She gasped, her heart beating against her ribs until she feared one might break under the pressure.

The bear crumpled to the ground then lurched upward again, one front leg dripping blood. She let loose a long moan, clicked her teeth, and staggered out of the clearing with her cub behind her.

"Who shot?" Yarrow asked, her hands trembling almost as much as her voice.

Peter got the wounded sheep untangled just as Enos stepped into the clearing, his musket raised and ready if the bear returned.

"Enos." She'd never been happier to see him in her life.

Chapter 11

Peter's heart sank to his heels and stayed there. Could any man look more the hero in a woman's eyes? Enos Watkins deserved Yarrow's brilliant smile. Even Meadowsweet pranced around the man's feet.

By comparison, Peter was covered in dirt, blood, and whatever else the injured sheep had let loose down his back that was even now soaking through his waistcoat and into his shirt.

He heaved a sigh and adjusted the now-docile animal across his shoulders to a more secure hold. If only he hadn't been encumbered with the silly beast. But Yarrow was safe.

No thanks to him.

"We need to get this sheep back to the shepherds. Its leg is broken." Yarrow's voice cut through Peter's inner turmoil.

"I shall accompany you," Watkins said.

Of course he would.

"In case the bear circles back again."

"You do not think it will, do you?" Yarrow asked in a breathless voice.

No. The bear was injured. It would either flee and hide or turn and fight. It had already run off. Watkins didn't need to be scaring Yarrow that way. But who was Peter to say anything? She'd listen to the hero, not him. He stomped along after them, silently fuming, while they strolled along ahead.

"Peter?"

He jerked and looked at Yarrow. Had he missed something said to him? "Yes?"

"I asked if you are tired. Do you need to rest? That sheep must be heavy."

It was, but he'd walk clear across the expanse of Connecticut Colony before he'd admit it in front of Watkins. "I'm fine."

The smirk on Watkins's face made Peter wish he could poke the man in the nose again. Which was nothing more than sour grapes on his part, and he knew it. A man knew when he'd been bested, and Peter Maltby had most certainly been bested.

They arrived at the pasture, and two shepherd boys broke off from circling the flock to join them. Peter sent them for a couple of flat sticks and soft moss. Yarrow turned her back while she ripped a strip of cloth from her petticoat. Watkins hung around for no reason whatsoever.

With the materials collected and the boys to hold the sheep down, Peter set the broken leg, wrapped it in moss, and supported it with the sticks. He secured the whole thing with the strips of petticoat. Within moments, the sheep limped away to join the flock, baaing until a lamb broke away from the group and joined her. Mother and lamb reunited.

"How precious." Yarrow held Meadowsweet in her arms.

"Back where she belongs." Watkins nodded. "And now, I shall be happy to walk you home."

"But. . ." She looked toward Peter.

"You go on. I shall watch the sheep for a while, make sure I did not bandage that leg too tightly." He spread his arms and looked down his front. "Then I need a bath and a change of clothing."

She smiled, her eyes full of warmth and promise. But not for him. Watkins took her by the elbow and they left. Peter sank to the ground, stretched out under the warm sun, and let his heartache soak into the damp grass beneath him.

Yarrow half-listened to Enos as they walked along the road. The trembling in her hands had stopped, her heart no longer pounded, and she could draw in a full breath again. Never had she been so afraid. Even in that fear, she'd known she couldn't abandon Peter. He'd been helpless, tangled with the sheep and the branches, but he'd shielded her with his own body. He would have died for her.

> *Greater love than this hath no man, when any man bestoweth his life for his friends (John 15: 13).*

The scripture quote from the book of John was one Yarrow had heard many times, one of Papa's favorite verses. To see it played out before her in such a dramatic moment—

"Are you listening to me?" Enos stopped in the road and half-turned toward her.

"Pardon?" Oh, dear. She hadn't been. Not at all.

"You have been through a shock. I shall see you home for now, but we shall talk more on the morrow. Make plans. Inform your family."

"Inform them? Of what?"

He blew out a breath before his lips curved into a patient smile. "About us. About our plans for the future."

"We have no plans for the future." She pulled her elbow from his grip and took a step away.

"The shock you have suffered—"

"Is over and done. I shall always be grateful to you for coming at just the right time and shooting that bear. But that does not change things between us."

He took a step closer, and she backed away.

"Yarrow."

She held up her hand. He stopped.

"I may have loved you once, but I'm not even sure of that now."

He glanced back down the road, toward where they'd left the sheep. Where they'd left Peter. "I suppose 'tis him."

She straightened, her hands grasping the folds of her skirt. "I suppose it is."

His dark eyes clouded. Was it regret? A tiny part of her hoped so, but she shook her head and pushed such small thoughts aside. She didn't love Enos.

She loved Peter.

And even if he'd never said it, his actions had.

"Thank you, but I shall find my own way home. I have something else I must do first." She turned, lifted her skirts, and flew down the road with Meadowsweet galloping at her heels. Gasping for air by the time she reached the pasture where she'd left Peter, she stopped and pressed a hand to her side. The flock had moved to the top of the hill, the shepherd boys forming a loose ring around them, but there was no sign of Peter. Where was he?

Meadowsweet bounded ahead into the tall grass. A grunt followed by, "What are you doing here?" brought a smile to Yarrow's face. She hurried toward the voice.

Peter lay on his back in the deep grass with Meadowsweet standing over him, her front hooves planted on his chest, her nose almost pressed on his.

"She likes you," Yarrow said.

His blue eyes widened when he looked up at her. "What are *you* doing here?"

Yarrow bit the corner of her lip then shrugged her shoulders. "I like you, too."

He pushed the lamb aside and rose, his eyes never leaving hers. "You do?"

She tucked the ever-wayward strands of hair behind her ear. She nodded, wishing she could read what was going on behind the dazzling blue of his eyes.

He reached out and tucked another wayward strand behind her other ear. "What about Watkins?"

"I'm glad he showed up when he did."

He looked away. "He protected you."

She touched the side of his face and turned it back toward her. "You protected me."

He shook his head.

"You put yourself between me and that bear, risked your life to keep me safe. Why?"

"Because I love you." Sparkles of silver danced in his eyes.

Matching sparkles danced in her middle in a pleasant and enticing way. "Then you shall still speak to David?"

He cupped her face, hands branding her skin with their warmth and the lingering scent of sheep. A scent she didn't mind in the least. "Are you certain?"

"Very. The man who put himself between me and an angry mother bear 'tisn't the kind of man who would accost an innocent woman on the road in Boston."

His hand trembled against her cheek. He lowered his head by inches, giving her all the time she needed to pull away.

Her lips parted slightly of their own accord. Her breath hitched. She leaned into his chest. One hand left her cheek and slid behind her back, pressing her into his embrace. She gasped, and then his lips met hers, warm and solid and full of promise.

Historical Note

King William III signed the Wool Act of 1699 (also known as the Restraining Act) in an attempt to secure England's monopoly on textiles, which Parliament felt was threatened by wool production in the colonies. While it created a hardship for colonists in America, it also served to fuel the early fires of rebellion. The town of Milford, Connecticut, really did own its own flock of sheep. It also had working fulling mills, although Tucker's Fulling Mill is strictly fictional.

Pegg Thomas lives on a hobby farm in Northern Michigan with Michael, her husband of *mumble* years. A life-long history geek, she writes "history with a touch of humor." An avid reader and writer, she enjoys fiction stories threaded through historical events and around historical figures. Civil War and Colonial are her favorite eras. Pegg is a regular blogger at ColonialQuills.com. When not working on her latest novel, Pegg can be found in her garden, in her kitchen, at her spinning wheel, tending her sheep, or on her trusty old horse, Trooper. See more at PeggThomas.com.

If You Liked This Book, You'll Also Like...

Of Rags and Riches Romance Collection
Nine couples meet during the transforming era of America's Gilded Age and work to build a future together through fighting for social reform, celebrating new opportunities for leisure activities, taking advantage of economic growth and new inventions, and more. Soon romances develop and legacies of faith and love are formed.
Paperback / 978-1-68322-263-7 / $14.99

The Calico and Cowboys Romance Collection
In the American Old West from Texas across the Plains to Montana, love is sneaking into the lives of eight couples who begin their relationships on the wrong foot. Faced with the challenges of taming the land, enduring harsh weather, and outsmarting outlaws, these couples' faith and love will be tested in exciting ways.
Paperback / 978-1-68322-402-0 / $14.99

Seven Brides for Seven Mail-Order Husbands Romance Collection
A small Kansas town is dying after the War Between the States took its best men. Seven single women are determined to see their town revived, so they devise a plan to advertise for husbands. But how can each make the best practical choice when her heart cries out to be loved?
Paperback / 978-1-68322-132-6 / $14.99

For 7 Bachelors, This Bouquet of Brides Means a Happily Ever After

A Bouquet of BRIDES COLLECTION

Mary Davis, Kathleen E. Kovach,
Paula Moldenhauer, Suzanne Norquist, Donita Kathleen Paul,
Donna Schlachter, Pegg Thomas

BARBOUR BOOKS
An Imprint of Barbour Publishing, Inc.

Print ISBN 978-1-68322-381-8

eBook Editions:
Adobe Digital Edition (.epub) 978-1-68322-383-2
Kindle and MobiPocket Edition (.prc) 978-1-68322-382-5

Published by Barbour Books, an imprint of Barbour Publishing, Inc., 1810 Barbour
Drive, Uhrichsville, Ohio 44683, www.barbourbooks.com

Our mission is to inspire the world with the life-changing message of the Bible.

Member of the
Evangelical Christian
Publishers Association

Printed in Canada.